The Honourable Schoolboy

'Not a page of this book is without intelligence and grace'
The New York Times

'The ultimate espionage novel . . . It is hard to see how even le Carré could surpass himself after this'
Publishers Weekly

'Compassionate, distinguished, terrifying . . . incomparably his finest book'
Cosmopolitan

'John le Carré is the premier spy novelist of his time. Perhaps of all time . . . all the good things are there: the Balkan complexities of plot; the Dickensian profusion of idiosyncratic characters; and above all le Carré's glistening social observation'
Time

'There are searing evocations of the battle-scarred Asian landscapes to match Graham Greene at his finest . . . It is le Carré's most ambitious, romantic and despairing work to date'
Newsweek

Also by the same author, and available from Coronet:

A PERFECT SPY

About the author

John le Carré was born in 1931. He received a public school education and attended the universities of Bern and Oxford. Later he taught at Eton and spent five years in the British Foreign Service. THE SPY WHO CAME IN FROM THE COLD, his third book, secured him a wide reputation and was followed by THE LOOKING-GLASS WAR, A SMALL TOWN IN GERMANY, THE NAIVE AND SENTIMENTAL LOVER, and his three Smiley novels, TINKER TAILOR SOLDIER SPY, THE HONOURABLE SCHOOLBOY and SMILEY'S PEOPLE, which are also available as an omnibus, THE QUEST FOR KARLA. He has also written THE LITTLE DRUMMER GIRL and A PERFECT SPY which was made into a hugely successful BBC TV serial. Though he divides his time between England and the continent, he is most at home in Cornwall.

JOHN le CARRÉ

The Honourable Schoolboy

CORONET BOOKS
Hodder and Stoughton

The extract from '1st September 1939' from *Collected Shorter Poems 1939–44* by W. H. Auden is reproduced by permission of Faber & Faber Ltd

First published in Great Britain in 1977 by Hodder and Stoughton Ltd

First published in paperback in 1978 by Pan Books Ltd

Coronet edition 1989
Fifth impression 1992

British Library C.I.P.

Le Carré, John *1931–*
The honourable schoolboy.
Rn: David John Moore Cornwell
I. Title
823'.914[F]

ISBN 0-340-49490-5

Printed and bound in Great Britain for Hodder and Stoughton Paperbacks, a division of Hodder and Stoughton Ltd, Mill Road, Dunton Green, Sevenoaks, Kent TN13 2YA (Editorial Office: 47 Bedford Square, London WC1B 3DP) by Clays Ltd, St Ives plc

For Jane, who bore the brunt,
put up with my presence and absence alike,
and made it all possible

Foreword

I offer my warm thanks to the many generous and hospitable people who found time to help me with my research for this novel.

In Singapore, Alwyne (Bob) Taylor, the *Daily Mail* correspondent; Max Vanzi of UPI; and Bruce Wilson of the *Melbourne Herald*.

In Hong Kong, Sydney Liu of *Newsweek;* Bing Wong of *Time;* H. D. S. Greenway of the *Washington Post;* Anthony Lawrence of the BBC; Richard Hughes, then of the *Sunday Times;* Donald A. Davis and Vic Vanzi of UPI; and Derek Davies and his staff at the *Far Eastern Economic Review*, notably Leo Goodstadt. I must also acknowledge with gratitude the exceptional co-operation of Major-General Penfold and his team at the Royal Hong Kong Jockey Club, who gave me the run of Happy Valley Racecourse and showed me much kindness without once seeking to know my purpose. I wish I could also name the several officials of the Hong Kong Government, and members of the Royal Hong Kong Police, who opened doors for me at some risk of embarrassment to themselves.

In Phnom Penh my genial host Baron Walther von Marschall took marvellous care of me, and I could never have managed without the wisdom of Kurt Furrer and Madame Yvette Pierpaoli, both of Suisindo Shipping and Trading Co, and presently in Bangkok.

But my special thanks must be reserved for the person who put up with me the longest, my friend David Greenway of the *Washington Post*, who allowed me to follow in his distinguished shadow through Laos, north-east Thailand and Phnom Penh. To David, to Bing Wong, and to certain Hong Kong Chinese friends who I believe will prefer to remain anonymous, I owe a great debt.

Last there is the great Dick Hughes, whose outward character and mannerisms I have shamelessly exaggerated for the part of old Craw. Some people, once met, simply elbow their way into a novel and sit there till the writer finds them a place. Dick is one. I am only sorry I could not obey his urgent exhortation to libel him to the hilt. My cruellest efforts could not prevail against the affectionate nature of the original.

And since none of these good people had any more notion than I did, in those days, of how the book would turn out, I must be quick to absolve them from my misdemeanours.

Terry Mayers, a veteran of the British Karate Team, advised me on certain alarming skills. For Miss Nellie Adams, for her stupendous bouts of typing, no praise is enough.

Cornwall,
20 February 1977

CONTENTS

Part 1 WINDING THE CLOCK

Part 2 SHAKING THE TREE

I and the public know
What all schoolchildren learn,
Those to whom evil is done
Do evil in return.

W. H. Auden

Part One

Winding The Clock

Chapter 1

How The Circus Left Town

Afterwards, in the dusty little corners where London's secret servants drink together, there was argument about where the Dolphin case history should really begin. One crowd, led by a blimpish fellow in charge of microphone transcription, went so far as to claim that the fitting date was sixty years ago when 'that arch-cad Bill Haydon' was born into the world under a treacherous star. Haydon's very name struck a chill into them. It does so even today. For it was this same Haydon who, while still at Oxford, was recruited by Karla the Russian as a 'mole', or 'sleeper', or in English, agent of penetration, to work against them. And who with Karla's guidance entered their ranks and spied on them for thirty years or more. And whose eventual discovery – thus the line of reasoning – brought the British so low that they were forced into a fatal dependence upon their American sister service, whom they called in their own strange jargon 'the Cousins'. The Cousins changed the game entirely, said the blimpish fellow: much as he might have deplored power tennis or bodyline bowling. And ruined it too, said his seconds.

To less flowery minds, the true genesis was Haydon's unmasking by George Smiley and Smiley's consequent appointment as a caretaker chief of the betrayed service, which occurred in the late November of 1973. Once George had got Karla under his skin, they said, there was no stopping him. The rest was inevitable, they said. Poor old George: but what a mind under all that burden!

One scholarly soul, a researcher of some sort, in the

jargon a 'burrower', even insisted, in his cups, upon January 26th 1841 as the natural date, when a certain Captain Elliot of the Royal Navy took a landing party to a fog-laden rock called Hong Kong at the mouth of the Pearl River and a few days later proclaimed it a British colony. With Elliot's arrival, said the scholar, Hong Kong became the headquarters of Britain's opium trade to China and in consequence one of the pillars of the imperial economy. If the British had not invented the opium market – he said, not entirely serious – then there would have been no case, no ploy, no dividend: and therefore no renaissance of the Circus following Bill Haydon's traitorous depredations.

Whereas the hard men – the grounded fieldmen, the trainers and the case officers who made their own murmured caucus always – they saw the question solely in operational terms. They pointed to Smiley's deft footwork in tracking down Karla's paymaster in Vientiane; to Smiley's handling of the girl's parents; and to his wheeling and dealing with the reluctant barons of Whitehall, who held the operational purse strings, and dealt out rights and permissions in the secret world. Above all, to the wonderful moment when he turned the operation round on its own axis. For these pros, the Dolphin case was a victory of technique. Nothing more. They saw the shotgun marriage with the Cousins as just another skilful bit of tradecraft in a long and delicate poker game. As to the final outcome: to hell. The king is dead, so long live the next one.

The debate continues wherever old comrades meet, though the name of Jerry Westerby, understandably, is seldom mentioned. Occasionally, it is true, somebody does, out of foolhardiness or sentiment or plain forgetfulness, dredge it up, and there is atmosphere for a moment; but it passes. Only the other day a young probationer just out of the Circus's refurbished training school at Sarratt – in the jargon again, 'the Nursery' – piped it out in the under-thirties bar, for instance. A watered-down version of the Dolphin case had recently been introduced at Sarratt as material for syndicate discussion, even play-lets, and the poor boy, still very green, was fairly brim-ming with excitement to discover he was in the know: 'But my *God*,' he protested, enjoying the kind of fool's freedom sometimes granted to naval midshipmen in the wardroom, 'my *God*, why does nobody seem to recognise Westerby's part in the affair? If *anybody* carried the load, it was Jerry Westerby. He was the spearhead. Well, wasn't he? Frankly?' Except, of course, he did not utter the name 'Westerby', nor 'Jerry' either, not least because he did not know them; but used instead the cryptonym allocated to Jerry for the duration of the case.

Peter Guillam fielded this loose ball. Guillam is tall and tough and graceful, and probationers awaiting first posting tend to look up to him as some sort of Greek god.

'Westerby was the stick that poked the fire,' he declared curtly, ending the silence. 'Any fieldman would have done as well, some a damn sight better.'

When the boy still did not take the hint, Guillam rose and went over to him and, very pale, snapped into his ear that he should fetch himself another drink, if he could hold it, and thereafter guard his tongue for several days or weeks. Whereupon, the conversation returned once more to the topic of dear old George Smiley, surely the last of the *true* greats, and what was he doing with himself these days, back in retirement? So many lives he had led; so much to recollect in tranquillity, they agreed.

'George went five times round the moon to our one,' someone declared loyally, a woman.

Ten times, they agreed. Twenty! *Fifty!* With hyperbole, Westerby's shadow mercifully receded. As in a sense, so did George Smiley's. Well, George had a marvellous innings, they would say. At *his* age what could you expect?

Perhaps a more realistic point of departure is a certain typhoon Saturday in mid–1974, three o'clock in the after-noon, when Hong Kong lay battened down waiting for the next onslaught. In the bar of the Foreign Correspon-dents' Club, a score of journalists, mainly from former

British colonies – Australian, Canadian, American – fooled and drank in a mood of violent idleness, a chorus without a hero. Thirteen floors below them, the old trams and double deckers were caked in the mud-brown sweat of building dust and smuts from the chimney-stacks in Kowloon. The tiny ponds outside the highrise hotels prickled with slow, subversive rain. And in the men's room, which provided the Club's best view of the harbour, young Luke the Californian was ducking his face into the handbasin, washing the blood from his mouth.

Luke was a wayward, gangling tennis player, an old man of twenty-seven who until the American pullout had been the star turn in his magazine's Saigon stable of war reporters. When you knew he played tennis it was hard to think of him doing anything else, even drinking. You imagined him at the net, uncoiling and smashing everything to kingdom come; or serving aces between double faults. His mind, as he sucked and spat, was fragmented by drink and mild concussion – Luke would probably have used the war-word 'fragged' – into several lucid parts. One part was occupied with a Wanchai bar girl called Ella for whose sake he had punched the pig policeman on the jaw and suffered the inevitable consequences: with the minimum necessary force, the said Superintendent Rockhurst, known otherwise as the Rocker, who was this minute relaxing in a corner of the bar after his exertions, had knocked him cold and kicked him smartly in the ribs. Another part of his mind was on something his Chinese landlord had said to him this morning when he called to complain of the noise of Luke's gramophone, and had stayed to drink a beer.

A scoop of some sort definitely. But what sort?

He retched again, then peered out of the window. The junks were lashed behind the barriers and the Star Ferry had stopped running. A veteran British frigate lay at anchor and Club rumours said Whitehall was selling it.

'Should be putting to sea,' he muttered confusedly, recalling some bit of naval lore he had picked up in his travels. 'Frigates put to sea in typhoons. Yes, *sir.*'

The hills were slate under the stacks of black cloudbank. Six months ago the sight would have had him cooing with pleasure. The harbour, the din, even the skyscraper shanties that clambered from the sea's edge upward to the Peak: after Saigon, Luke had ravenously embraced the whole scene. But all he saw today was a smug, rich British rock run by a bunch of plum-throated traders whose horizons went no further than their belly-lines. The Colony had therefore become for him exactly what it was already for the rest of the journalists: an airfield, a telephone, a laundry, a bed. Occasionally – but never for long – a woman. Where even experience had to be imported. As to the wars which for so long had been his addiction: they were as remote from Hong Kong as they were from London or New York. Only the Stock Exchange showed a token sensibility, and on Saturdays it was closed anyway.

'Think you're going to live, ace?' asked the shaggy Canadian cowboy, coming to the stall beside him. The two men had shared the pleasures of the Tet offensive.

'Thank you, dear, I feel perfectly topping,' Luke replied, in his most exalted English accent.

Luke decided it really was important for him to remember what Jake Chiu had said to him over the beer this morning, and suddenly like a gift from Heaven it came to him.

'I remember!' he shouted. 'Jesus, cowboy, I remember! Luke, you remember! My brain! It works! Folks, give ear to Luke!'

'Forget it,' the cowboy advised. 'That's badland out there today, ace. Whatever it is, forget it.'

But Luke kicked open the door and charged into the bar, arms flung wide.

'Hey! Hey! *Folks!*'

Not a head turned. Luke cupped his hands to his mouth.

'Listen you drunken bums, I got *news*. This is fantastic. Two bottles of Scotch a day and a brain like a razor. Someone give me a bell.'

Finding none, he grabbed a tankard and hammered it on

the bar rail, spilling the beer. Even then, only the dwarf paid him the slightest notice.

'So what's happened, Lukie?' whined the dwarf, in his queeny Greenwich Village drawl. 'Has Big Moo gotten hiccups again? I can't bear it.'

Big Moo was Club jargon for the Governor and the dwarf was Luke's chief of bureau. He was a pouchy, sullen creature with disordered hair that swept in black strands over his face, and a silent way of popping up beside you. A year back, two Frenchmen, otherwise rarely seen here, had nearly killed him for a chance remark he had made on the origins of the mess in Vietnam. They took him to the lift, broke his jaw and several of his ribs, then dumped him in a heap on the ground floor and came back to finish their drinks. Soon afterwards the Australians did a similar job on him when he made a silly accusation about their token military involvement in the war. He suggested that Canberra had done a deal with President Johnson to keep the Australian boys in Vung Tau which was a picnic, while the Americans did the real fighting elsewhere. Unlike the French, the Australians didn't even bother to use the lift. They just beat the hell out of the dwarf where he stood, and when he fell they added a little more of the same. After that, he learned when to keep clear of certain people in Hong Kong. In times of persistent fog for instance. Or when the water was cut to four hours a day. Or on a typhoon Saturday.

Otherwise the Club was pretty much empty. For reasons of prestige, the top correspondents steered clear of the place anyway. A few businessmen, who came for the flavour pressmen give, a few girls, who came for the men. A couple of television war tourists in fake battle-drill. And in his customary corner, the awesome Rocker, Superintendent of Police, ex-Palestine, ex-Kenya, ex-Malaya, ex-Fiji, an implacable warhorse with a beer, one set of slightly reddened knuckles, and a weekend copy of the *South China Morning Post*. The Rocker, people said, came for the class. And at the big table at the centre, which on weekdays was the preserve of United Press International, lounged the

Shanghai Junior Baptist Conservative Bowling Club, presided over by mottled old Craw the Australian, enjoying its usual Saturday tournament. The aim of the contest was to pitch a screwed-up napkin across the room, and lodge it in the wine rack. Every time you succeeded, your competitors bought you the bottle, and helped you drink it. Old Craw growled the orders to fire and an elderly Shanghainese waiter, Craw's favourite, wearily manned the butts and served the prizes. The game was not a zestful one that day, and some members were not bothering to throw. Nevertheless this was the group Luke selected for his audience.

'Big Moo's *wife's* got hiccups!' the dwarf insisted. 'Big Moo's wife's *horse* has got hiccups! Big Moo's wife's horse's *groom's* got hiccups! Big Moo's wife's horse's – '

Striding to the table Luke leapt straight on to it with a crash, breaking several glasses and cracking his head on the ceiling in the process. Framed up there against the south window in a half crouch he was out of scale to everyone: the dark mist, the dark shadow of the Peak behind it, and this giant filling the whole foreground. But they went on pitching and drinking as if they hadn't seen him. Only the Rocker glanced in Luke's direction, once, before licking a huge thumb and turning to the cartoon page.

'Round three,' Craw ordered, in his rich Australian accent. 'Brother Canada, prepare to fire. *Wait*, you slob. Fire.'

A screwed-up napkin floated toward the rack, taking a high trajectory. Finding a cranny it hung a moment, then flopped to the ground. Egged on by the dwarf, Luke began stamping on the table and more glasses fell. Finally he wore his audience down.

'Your Graces,' said old Craw with a sigh. 'Pray silence for my son. I fear he would have parley with us. Brother Luke, you have committed several acts of war today and one more will meet with our severe disfavour. Speak clearly and concisely, omitting no detail, however slight, and thereafter hold your water, sir.'

In their tireless pursuit of legends about one another, old Craw was their Ancient Mariner. Craw had shaken more sand out of his shorts, they told each other, than most of them would ever walk over; and they were right. In Shanghai, where his career had started, he had been teaboy and city editor to the only English-speaking journal in the port. Since then, he had covered the Communists against Chiang Kai-shek and Chiang against the Japanese and the Americans against practically everyone. Craw gave them a sense of history in this rootless place. His style of speech, which at typhoon times even the hardiest might pardonably find irksome, was a genuine hangover from the Thirties, when Australia provided the bulk of journalists in the Orient; and the Vatican, for some reason, the jargon of their companionship.

So Luke, thanks to old Craw, finally got it out.

'Gentlemen! – Dwarf, you damn Polack, leave go my foot! – Gentlemen.' He paused to dab his mouth with a handkerchief. 'The house known as High Haven is for sale and his Grace Tufty Thesinger has flown the coop.'

Nothing happened but he didn't expect much anyway. Journalists are not given to cries of amazement nor even incredulity.

'High Haven,' Luke repeated sonorously, 'is up for grabs. Mr Jake Chiu, the well-known and popular real estate entrepreneur, more familiar to you as my personal irate landlord, has been charged by Her Majesty's majestic government to *dispose* of High Haven. To wit, peddle. Let me go, you Polish bastard, I'll kill you!'

The dwarf had toppled him. Only a flailing, agile leap saved him from injury. From the floor, Luke hurled more abuse at his assailant. Meanwhile, Craw's large head had turned to Luke, and his moist eyes fixed on him a baleful stare that seemed to go on for ever. Luke began to wonder which of Craw's many laws he might have sinned against. Beneath his various disguises, Craw was a complex and solitary figure, as everyone round the table knew. Under the willed roughness of his manner lay a love of the East which seemed sometimes to string him tighter than he could stand, so that there were months when he would disappear from sight altogether, and like a sulky elephant go off on his private paths until he was once more fit to live with.

'Don't burble, your Grace, do you mind?' said Craw at last, and tilted back his big head imperiously. 'Refrain from spewing low-grade bilge into highly salubrious water, will you, Squire? High Haven's the spookhouse. Been the spookhouse for years. Lair of the lynx-eyed Major Tufty Thesinger formerly of Her Majesty's Rifles, presently Hong Kong's Lestrade of the Yard. Tufty wouldn't fly the coop. He's a hood, not a tit. Give my son a drink, Monsignor,' – this to the Shanghainese barman – 'he's wandering.'

Craw intoned another fire order and the Club returned to its intellectual pursuits. The truth was, there was little new to these great spy-scoops by Luke. He had a long reputation as a failed spook-watcher, and his leads were invariably disproved. Since Vietnam, the stupid lad saw spies under every carpet. He believed the world was run by them, and much of his spare time, when he was sober, was spent hanging round the Colony's numberless battalion of thinly-disguised China-watchers and worse, who infested the enormous American Consulate up the hill. So if it hadn't been such a listless day, the matter would probably have rested there. As it was, the dwarf saw an opening to amuse, and seized it:

'Tell us, Lukie,' he suggested, with a queer upward twisting of the hands, 'are they selling High Haven with *contents* or *as found*?'

The question won him a round of applause. Was High Haven worth more with its secrets or without?

'Do they sell it with *Major Thesinger*?' the South African photographer pursued, in his humourless sing-song, and there was more laughter still, though it was no more affectionate. The photographer was a disturbing figure, crewcut and starved, and his complexion was pitted like the battlefields he loved to haunt. He came from Cape Town, but they called him Deathwish the Hun. The saying was, he would bury all of them, for he stalked them like a mute.

For several diverting minutes now, Luke's point was lost entirely under a spate of Major Thesinger stories and Major Thesinger imitations in which all but Craw joined. It was recalled that the Major had made his first appearance on the Colony as an importer, with some fatuous cover down among the Docks; only to transfer, six months later, quite improbably, to the Services' list and, complete with his staff of pallid clerks and doughy, well-bred secretaries, decamp to the said spookhouse as somebody's replacement. In particular his *tête-à-tête* luncheons were described, to which, as it now turned out, practically every journalist listening had at one time or another been invited. And which ended with laborious proposals over brandy, including such wonderful phrases as: 'Now look here old man if you should ever bump into an interesting Chow from over the river, you know – one with *access*, follow me? – just you remember High Haven!' Then the magic telephone number, the one that 'rings spot on my desk, no middlemen, tape recorders, nothing, right?' – which a good half dozen of them seemed to have in their diaries: 'Here, pencil this one on your cuff, pretend it's a date or a girlfriend or something. Ready for it? Hong Kongside five-zero-two-four . . .'

Having chanted the digits in unison, they fell quiet. Somewhere a clock chimed for three fifteen. Luke slowly stood up and brushed the dust from his jeans. The old Shanghainese waiter gave up his post by the racks and reached for the menu in the hope that someone might eat. For a moment, uncertainty overcame them. The day was forfeit. It had been so since the first gin. In the background a low growl sounded as the Rocker ordered himself a generous luncheon:

'And bring me a cold beer, *cold*, you hear, boy? Muchee coldee. Chop chop.' The Superintendent had his way with natives and said this every time. The quiet returned.

'Well, there you are, Lukie,' the dwarf called, moving

away. 'That's how you win your Pulitzer, I guess. Congratulations, darling. Scoop of the year.'

'Ah, go impale yourselves, the bunch of you,' said Luke carelessly and started to make his way down the bar to where two sallow girls sat, army daughters on the prowl. 'Jake Chiu showed me the damn letter of instruction, didn't he? On Her Majesty's damn Service, wasn't it? Damn crest on the top, lion screwing a goat. Hi sweethearts, remember me? I'm the kind man who bought you the lollipops at the fair.'

'Thesinger don't answer,' Deathwish the Hun sang mournfully from the telephone. 'Nobody don't answer. Not Thesinger, not his duty man. They disconnected the line.' In the excitement, or the monotony, no one had noticed Deathwish slip away.

Till now, old Craw the Australian had lain dead as a dodo. Now, he looked up sharply.

'Dial it again, you fool,' he ordered, tart as a drill sergeant.

With a shrug, Deathwish dialled Thesinger's number a second time, and a couple of them went to watch him do it. Craw stayed put, watching from where he sat. There were two instruments. Deathwish tried the second, but with no better result.

'Ring the operator,' Craw ordered, across the room to them. 'Don't stand there like a pregnant banshee. Ring the operator, you African ape!'

Number disconnected, said the operator.

'Since when, man?' Deathwish demanded, into the mouthpiece.

No information available, said the operator.

'Maybe they got a new number, then, right, man?' Deathwish howled into the mouthpiece, still at the luckless operator. No one had ever seen him so involved. Life for Deathwish was what happened at the end of a viewfinder: such passion was only attributable to the typhoon.

No information available, said the operator.

'Ring Shallow Throat,' Craw ordered, now quite furious. 'Ring every damned striped-pants in the Colony!'

Deathwish shook his long head uncertainly. Shallow Throat was the official government spokesman, a hate-object to them all. To approach him for anything was bad face.

'Here, give him to me,' said Craw and rising to his feet shoved them aside to get to the phone and embark on the lugubrious courtship of Shallow Throat. 'Your devoted Craw, sir, at your service. How's your Eminence in mind and health? Charmed, sir, charmed. And the wife and veg, sir? All eating well, I trust? No scurvy or typhus? Good. Well now, perhaps you'll have the benison to advise me why the hell Tufty Thesinger's flown the coop?'

They watched him, but his face had set like a rock, and there was nothing more to read there.

'And the same to you, sir!' he snorted finally and slammed the phone back on its cradle so hard the whole table bounced. Then he turned to the old Shanghainese waiter. 'Monsignor Goh, sir, order me a petrol donkey and oblige! Your Graces, get off your arses, the pack of you!'

'What the hell for?' said the dwarf, hoping to be included in the command.

'For a story, you snotty little Cardinal, for a story your lecherous, alcoholic Eminences. For wealth, fame, women and longevity!'

His black mood was indecipherable to any of them.

'But what did Shallow Throat say that was so damn bad?' the shaggy Canadian cowboy asked, mystified.

The dwarf echoed him. 'Yeah, so what did he say, Brother Craw?'

'He said *no comment*,' Craw replied with fine dignity, as if the words were the vilest slur upon his professional honour.

So up the Peak they went, leaving only the silent majority of drinkers to their peace: restive Deathwish the Hun, long Luke, then the shaggy Canadian cowboy, very striking in his Mexican revolutionary moustache, the dwarf, attaching as ever, and finally old Craw and the two army girls: a plenary session of the Shanghai Junior Baptist Conservative Bowling Club, therefore, with ladies added – though the Club was sworn to celibacy. Amazingly, the jolly Cantonese driver took them all, a triumph of exuberance over physics. He even consented to give three receipts for the full fare, one for each of the journals represented, a thing no Hong Kong taxi-driver had been known to do before or since. It was a day to break all precedents. Craw sat in the front wearing his famous soft straw hat with Eton colours on the ribbon, bequeathed to him by an old comrade in his will. The dwarf was squeezed over the gear lever, the other three men sat in the back, and the two girls sat on Luke's lap, which made it hard for him to dab his mouth. The Rocker did not see fit to join them. He had tucked his napkin into his collar in preparation for the Club's roast lamb and mint sauce and a lot of potatoes.

'And another beer! But *cold* this time, hear that, boy? *Muchee coldee*, and bring it *chop chop*.'

But once the coast was clear, the Rocker also made use of the telephone, and spoke to Someone in Authority, just to be on the safe side, though they agreed there was nothing to be done.

The taxi was a red Mercedes, quite new, but nowhere kills a car faster than the Peak, climbing at no speed forever, air-conditioners at full blast. The weather continued awful. As they sobbed slowly up the concrete cliffs they were engulfed by a fog thick enough to choke on. When they got out it was even worse. A hot, unbudgeable curtain had spread itself across the summit, reeking of petrol and crammed with the din of the valley. The moisture floated in hot fine swarms. On a clear day they would have had a view both ways, one of the loveliest on earth: northward to Kowloon and the blue mountains of the New Territories which hid from sight the eight hundred million Chinese who lacked the privilege of British rule; southward to Repulse and Deep Water Bays and the open China Sea. High Haven after all had been built by the Royal

Navy in the Twenties in all the grand innocence of that service, to receive and impart a sense of power. But that afternoon, if the house had not been set among the trees, and in a hollow where the trees grew tall in their effort to reach the sky, and if the trees had not kept the fog out, they would have had nothing to look at but the two white concrete pillars with the bell-buttons marked 'day' and 'night' and the chained gates they supported. Thanks to the trees, however, they saw the house clearly, though it was set back fifty yards. They could pick out the drain-pipes, fire escapes and washing lines and they could admire the green dome which the Japanese army had added during their four years' tenancy.

Hurrying to the front in his desire to be accepted, the dwarf pressed the bell marked 'day'. A speaker was let into the pillar and they all stared at it, waiting for it to say something or, as Luke would have it, puff out pot-smoke. At the roadside, the Cantonese driver had switched on his radio full and it was playing a whining Chinese love song, on and on. The second pillar was blank except for a brass plate announcing the Inter Services Liaison Staff, Thesinger's threadbare cover. Deathwish the Hun had produced a camera and was photographing as methodically as if he were on one of his native battlefields.

'Maybe they don't work Saturdays,' Luke suggested, while they continued to wait, at which Craw told him not to be bloody silly: spooks worked seven days a week and round the clock, he said. Also they never ate, apart from Tufty.

'*Good* afternoon to you,' said the dwarf.

Pressing the night bell, he had put his twisted red lips to the vents of the speaker and affected an upper-class English accent, which to give him credit he managed surprisingly well.

'My name is Michael Hanbury-Steadly-Heamoor, and I'm personal bumboy to Big Moo. I should like, *pliss*, to speak to Major Thesinger on a matter of some urgency, *pliss*, there is a mushroom-shaped cloud the Major may not have noticed, it *appearce* to be forming over the *Pearl*

River and it's spoiling Big Moo's golf. *Thenk* you. Will you kindly open the gate?'

One of the blonde girls gave a titter.

'I didn't know he was a *Steadly*-Heamoor,' she said.

Abandoning Luke, they had tethered themselves to the shaggy Canadian's arm, and spent a lot of time whispering in his ear.

'He's Rasputin,' said one of the girls admiringly, stroking the back of his thigh., 'I've seen the film. He's the spitten image, aren't you, Canada?'

Now everybody had a drink from Luke's flask while they regrouped and wondered what to do. From the direction of the parked cab, the driver's Chinese love song continued dauntlessly, but the speakers on the pillars said nothing at all. The dwarf pressed both bells at once, and tried an Al Capone threat.

'Now see here, Thesinger, we know you're in there. You come out with your hands raised, uncloaked, throw down your dagger – *hey watch it, you stupid cow!*'

The imprecation was addressed neither to the Canadian, nor to old Craw – who was sidling towards the trees, apparently to meet a call of nature – but to Luke, who had decided to beat his way into the house. The gateway stood in a muddy service bay sheltered by dripping trees. On the far side was a pile of refuse, some new. Sauntering over to this in search of an illuminating clue, Luke had unearthed a piece of pig iron made in the shape of an S. Having carted it to the gate, though it must have weighed thirty pounds or more, he was holding it two-handed above his head and driving it against the staves, at which the gate tolled like a cracked bell.

Deathwish had sunk to one knee, his hollowed face clawed into a martyr's smile as he shot.

'Countıng five, Tufty,' Luke yelled, with another shattering heave. 'One . . .' He struck again. 'Two . . .'

Overhead an assorted flock of birds, some very large, lifted out of the trees and flew in slow spirals, but the thunder of the valley and the boom of the gate drowned their screams. Their taxi-driver was dancing about, clapping and laughing, his love song forgotten. Stranger still, in view of the menacing weather, an entire Chinese family appeared, pushing not one pram but two, and they began laughing also, even the smallest child, holding their hands across their mouths to conceal their teeth. Till suddenly the Canadian cowboy let out a cry, shook off the girls and pointed through the gates.

'For Lord's sakes what the heck's Craw doing? Old buzzard's jumped the wire.'

By now, whatever sense of normal scale there might have been had vanished. A collective madness had seized everyone. The drink, the black day, the claustrophobia, had gone to their heads entirely. The girls fondled the Canadian with abandon, Luke continued his hammering, the Chinese were hooting with laughter, until with divine timeliness the fog lifted, temples of blue-black cloud soared directly above them, and a torrent of rain crashed into the trees. A second longer and it hit them, drenching them in the first swoop. The girls, suddenly half naked, fled laughing and shrieking for the Mercedes, but the male ranks held firm – even the dwarf held firm – staring through the films of water at the unmistakable figure of Craw the Australian, in his old Etonian hat, standing in the shelter of the house under a rough porch that looked as if it were made for bicycles, though no one but a lunatic would bicycle up the Peak.

'Craw!' they screamed. 'Monsignor! The bastard's scooped us!'

The din of the rain was deafening, the branches seemed to be cracking under its force. Luke had thrown aside his mad hammer. The shaggy cowboy went first, and the dwarf followed, Deathwish with his smile and his camera brought up the tail, crouching and hobbling as he continued photographing blindly. The rain poured off them as it wanted, sloshing in red rivulets round their ankles as they followed Craw's trail up a slope where the screech of bullfrogs added to the row. They scaled a bracken ridge, slithered to a halt before a barbed wire fence, clambered through the parted strands and crossed a low ditch. By the time they reached him, Craw was gazing at the green cupola, while the rain despite the straw hat ran busily off his jaw, turning his trim fawn suit into a blackened, shapeless tunic. He stood as if mesmerised, staring upward. Luke, who loved him best, spoke first.

'Your Grace? Hey, wake up! It's me: Romeo. Jesus Christ, what the hell's eating him?'

Suddenly concerned, Luke gently touched his arm. But still Craw didn't speak.

'Maybe he died standing up,' the dwarf suggested, while grinning Deathwish photographed him on this happy off-chance.

Like an old prizefighter, Craw slowly rallied. 'Brother Luke, we owe you a handsome apology, sir,' he muttered.

'Get him back to the cab,' said Luke, and began clearing a way for him, but the old boy refused to move.

'Tufty Thesinger. A good scout. Not a flyer – not sly enough for flight – but a good scout.'

'Tufty Thesinger rest in peace,' said Luke impatiently. 'Let's go. Dwarf, move your ass.'

'He's stoned,' said the cowboy.

'Consider the clues, Watson,' Craw resumed, after another pause for meditation, while Luke tugged at his arm and the rain came on still faster. 'Remark first the empty cages over the window, whence airconditioners have been untimely ripped. Parsimony, my son, a commendable virtue, especially if I may say so, in a spook. Notice the dome, there? Study it carefully, sir. Scratch marks. Not, alas, the footprints of a gigantic hound, but the scratch marks of wireless aerials removed by the frantic, roundeye hand. Ever heard of a spookhouse without a wireless aerial? Might as well have a cathouse without a piano.'

The rainfall had reached a crescendo. Huge drops thumped around them like shot. Craw's face was a mix of things which Luke could only guess at. Deep in his heart it occurred to him that Craw really might be dying. Luke had seen little of natural death, and was very much on the alert for it.

'Maybe they just got rock-fever and split,' he said, trying again to coax him to the car.

'Very possibly, your Grace, very possibly indeed. It is certainly the season for rash, ungovernable acts.'

'Home,' said Luke, and pulled firmly at his arm. 'Make a path there, will you? Stretcher party.'

But the old man still lingered stubbornly for a last look at the English spookhouse flinching in the storm.

The Canadian cowboy filed first and his piece deserved a better fate. He wrote it that night, while the girls slept in his bed. He guessed the story would go best as a magazine piece rather than straight news, so he built it round the Peak in general and only used Thesinger as a peg. He explained how the Peak was traditionally Hong Kong's Olympus – 'the higher you lived on it, the higher you stood in society' – and how the rich British opium traders, Hong Kong's founding fathers, fled there to avoid the cholera and fever of the town; how even a couple of decades ago a person of Chinese race required a pass before he could set foot there. He described the history of High Haven, and lastly its reputation, fostered by the Chinese-language press, as a witches' kitchen of British Imperialist plots again Mao. Overnight the kitchen had closed and the cooks had vanished.

'Another conciliatory gesture?' he asked. 'Appeasement? All part of Britain's low-profile policy toward the Mainland? Or simply one more sign that in South East Asia, as everywhere else in the world, the British were having to come down from their mountain top?'

His mistake was to select a heavy English Sunday paper which occasionally ran his pieces. The D-Notice forbidding all reference to these events was there ahead of him. 'Regret your nice Havenstory unplaced,' the editor cabled, and shoved it straight on the spike. A few days later, returning to his room, the cowboy found it ransacked. Also, for several weeks his telephone developed a sort of laryngitis, so that he never used it without including an obscene reference to Big Moo and his retinue.

Luke went home full of ideas, bathed, drank a lot of black coffee and set to work. He telephoned airlines, government contacts, and a whole host of pale, over-brushed acquaintances in the US Consulate, who infuriated him with arch and Delphic answers. He pestered furniture removal firms which specialised in handling government contracts. By ten that night he had, in his own words to the dwarf, whom he also telephoned several times, 'proof-cooked-five-different-ways' that Thesinger, his wife, and all the staff of High Haven, had left Hong Kong by charter in the early hours of Thursday morning, bound for London. Thesinger's boxer dog, he learned by a happy chance, would follow by air cargo later in the week. Having made a few notes, Luke crossed the room, settled to his typewriter, bashed out a few lines, and dried up, as he knew he would. He began in a rush, fluently:

'Today a fresh cloud of scandal hangs over the embattled and non-elected government of Britain's one remaining Asian colony. Hot on the latest revelation of graft in the police and civil service comes word that the Island's most hush-hush establishment, High Haven, base for Britain's cloak-and-dagger ploys against Red China, has been summarily shut down.'

There, with a blasphemous sob of impotence, he stopped and pressed his face into his open hands. Nightmares: those he could stand. To wake, after so much war, shaking and sweating from unspeakable visions, with his nostrils filled with the stink of napalm on human flesh: in a way, it was a consolation to him to know that after all that pressing down, the floodgates of his feeling had burst. There had been times, experiencing those things, when he longed for the leisure to recover his power of disgust. If nightmares were necessary in order to restore him to the ranks of normal men and women, then he could embrace them with gratitude. But not in the worst of his nightmares had it occurred to him that having written the war, he might not be able to write the peace. For six night hours Luke fought with this awful deadness. Sometimes he thought of old Craw, standing there with the rain running off him, delivering his funeral oration: maybe *that* was the story? But whoever hung a story on the strange humour of a fellow hack?

Nor did the dwarf's own hashed-out version meet with much success, which made him very scratchy. On the face of it, the story had everything they asked for. It spoofed the British, it had *spy* written large, and for once it got away from the notion of America as the hangman of South East Asia. But all he had for a reply, after a five-day wait, was a terse instruction to stay on his rostrum and leave off trying to play the trumpet.

Which left old Craw. Though a mere sideshow by comparison with the thrust of the main action, the timing of what Craw did, and did not do, remains to this day impressive. He filed nothing for three weeks. There was small stuff he should have handled but he didn't bother. To Luke, who was seriously concerned for him, he seemed at first to continue his mysterious decline. He lost his bounce and his love of fellowship entirely. He became snappish and at times downright unkind, and he barked bad Cantonese at the waiters; even at his favourite, Goh. He treated the Shanghai Bowlers as if they were his worst enemies, and recalled alleged slights they had long forgotten. Sitting alone at his window seat, he was like an old boulevardier fallen on hard times, waspish, inward, slothful. Then one day he disappeared and when Luke called apprehensively at his apartment the old amah told him that 'Whisky Papa runrun London fastee'. She was a strange little creature and Luke was inclined to doubt her. A dull North German stringer for *der Spiegel* reported sighting Craw in Vientiane, carousing at the Constellation bar, but again Luke wondered. Craw-watching had always been something of an insider sport, and there was prestige in adding to the general fund.

Till a Monday came, and around midday the old boy

strolled into the Club wearing a new beige suit and a very fine buttonhole, all smiles and anecdotes once more, and went to work on the High Haven story. He spent money, more than his paper would normally have allowed him. He ate several jovial lunches with well-dressed Americans from vaguely titled United States agencies, some of them known to Luke. Wearing his famous straw hat, he took each separately to quiet, well-chosen restaurants. In the Club, he was reviled for diplomat-crawling, a grave crime, and this pleased him. Next, a China-watchers' conference summoned him to Tokyo, and with hindsight it is fair to assume he used that visit to check out other parts of the story that was shaping for him. Certainly he asked old friends at the conference to unearth bits of fact for him when they got home to Bangkok, or Singapore, or Taipei or wherever they came from, and they obliged because they knew he would have done the same for them. In an eerie way, he seemed to know what he was looking for before they found it.

The result appeared in its fullest version in a Sydney morning newspaper which was beyond the long arm of Anglo-American censorship. By common consent it recalled the master's vintage years. It ran to two thousand words. Typically, he did not lead with the High Haven story at all, but with the 'mysteriously empty wing' of the British Embassy in Bangkok, which till a month ago had housed a strange body called 'The Seato Co-ordination Unit', as well as a Visa Section boasting six second secretaries. Was it the pleasures of the Soho massage parlours, the old Australian enquired sweetly, which lured the Thais to Britain in such numbers that six second secretaries were needed to handle their visa applications? Strange, too, he mused, that since their departure, and the closure of that wing, long queues of aspirant travellers had *not* formed outside the Embassy. Gradually – he wrote at ease, but never carelessly – a surprising picture unfolded before his readers. He called British intelligence 'the Circus'. He said the name derived from the address of that organisation's secret headquarters, which overlooked a famous intersection of London streets. The Circus had not merely pulled out of High Haven, he said, but out of Bangkok, Singapore, Saigon, Tokyo, Manila, and Djakarta as well. And Seoul. Even solitary Taiwan was not immune, where an unsung British Resident was discovered to have shed three clerk-drivers and two secretarial assistants only a week before the article went to press.

'A hoods' Dunkirk,' Craw called it, 'in which Charter DC8s replaced the Kentish fishing fleets.'

What had prompted such an exodus? Craw offered several nimble theories. Were we witnessing yet one more cut in British government spending? The writer was sceptical. In times of travail, Britain's tendency was to rely more, not less, on spies. Her entire empire history urged her to do so. The thinner her trade routes, the more elaborate her clandestine efforts to protect them. The more feeble her colonial grip, the more desperate her subversion of those who sought to loosen it. No: Britain might be on the breadline, but the spies would be the last of her luxuries to go. Craw set up other possibilities and knocked them down. A gesture of *détente* toward Mainland China? he suggested, echoing the cowboy's point. Certainly Britain would do anything under the sun to keep Hong Kong clear of Mao's anti-colonial zeal – short of giving up her spies. Thus old Craw arrived at the theory he liked best:

'Right across the Far Eastern chequerboard,' he wrote, 'the Circus is performing what is known in the spy-trade as a duck-dive.'

But why?

The writer now quoted his 'senior American prebends of the intelligence church militant in Asia'. American intelligence agents generally, he said, and not just in Asia, were 'hopping mad about lax security in the British organisations'. They were hopping highest about the recent discovery of a top Russian spy – he threw in the correct tradename 'mole' – inside the Circus's London headquarters: a British traitor, whom they declined to name, but who in the words of the senior prebends had 'compromised every Anglo-American clandestine operation worth a dime for the last twenty years'. Where was the mole now? the writer had asked his sources. To which, with undiminished spleen, they had replied: 'Dead. In Russia. And hopefully both.'

Craw had never wanted for a wrap-up, but this one, to Luke's fond eye, had a real sense of ceremony about it. It was almost an assertion of life itself, if only of the secret life.

'*Is Kim the boy spy vanished for good, then, from the legends of the East?*' he asked. '*Shall the English pundit never again stain his skin, slip into native costume and silently take his place beside the village fires? Do not fear,*' he insisted. '*The British will be back! The time-honoured sport of spot-the-spook will be with us once again! The spy is not dead: he sleepeth.*'

The piece appeared. In the Club, it was fleetingly admired, envied, forgotten. A local English-language paper with strong American connections reprinted it in full, with the result that the mayfly after all enjoyed another day of life. The old boy's charity benefit, they said: a doffing of the cap before he passes from the stage. Then the overseas network of the BBC ran it, and finally the Colony's own torpid network ran a version of the BBC's version, and for a full day there was a debate about whether Big Moo had decided to take the muzzle off the local news services. Yet even with this protracted billing, nobody, not Luke, not even the dwarf, saw fit to wonder how the devil the old man had known the back way into High Haven.

Which merely proved, if proof were ever needed, that journalists are no quicker than anybody else at spotting what goes on under their noses. It was a typhoon Saturday after all.

Within the Circus itself, as Craw had correctly called the seat of British intelligence, reactions to Craw's piece varied according to how much was known by those who were doing the reacting. In Housekeeping Section, for instance, which was responsible for such tatters of cover as the

Circus could gather to itself these days, the old boy released a wave of pent-up fury which can only be understood by those who have tasted the atmosphere of a secret department under heavy siege. Even otherwise tolerant spirits became savagely retributive. Treachery! Breach of contract! Block his pension! Put him on the watch list! Prosecution the moment he returns to England! Down the market a little, those less rabid about their security took a kindlier view, though it was still uninformed. Well, well, they said a little ruefully, that was the way of it: name us a joe who didn't blow his top now and then, and specially one who'd been left in ignorance for as long as poor old Craw had. And after all, he'd disclosed nothing that wasn't generally available, now had he? Really those housekeeper people should show a *little* moderation. Look how they went for poor Molly Meakin the other night, sister to Mike and hardly out of ribbons, just because she left a bit of blank stationery in her waste basket!

Only those at the inmost point saw things differently. To them, old Craw's article was a discreet masterpiece of disinformation: George Smiley at his best, they said. Clearly, the story had to come out, and all were agreed that censorship at any time was objectionable. Much better, therefore, to let it come out in the manner of our choosing. The right timing, the right amount, the right tone: a lifetime's experience, they agreed, in every brushstroke. But that was not a view which passed outside their set.

Back in Hong Kong – clearly, said the Shanghai Bowlers, like the dying, the old boy had had a prophetic instinct of this – Craw's High Haven story turned out to be his swansong. A month after it appeared he had retired, not from the Colony but from his trade as a scribbler and from the Island too. Renting a cottage in the New Territories, he announced that he proposed to expire under a slanteye heaven. For the Bowlers he might as well have chosen Alaska. It was just too damn far, they said, to drive back when you were drunk. There was a rumour – untrue, since Craw's appetites did not run in that direction – that he had got himself a pretty Chinese boy as a companion. That was the dwarf's work: he did not like to be scooped by old men. Only Luke refused to put him out of mind. Luke drove out to see him one mid-morning after night-shift. For the hell of it, and because the old buzzard meant a lot to him. Craw was happy as a sandboy, he reported: quite his former vile self, but a bit dazed to be bearded by Luke without warning. He had a friend with him, not a Chinese boy, but a visiting fireman whom he introduced as George: a podgy, ill-sighted little body in very round spectacles who had apparently dropped in unexpectedly. Aside, Craw explained to Luke that this George was a backroom boy on a British newspaper syndicate he used to work for in the dark ages.

'Handles the geriatric side, your Grace. Taking a swing through Asia.'

Whoever he was, it was clear that Craw stood in awe of the podgy man, for he even called him 'your Holiness'. Luke had felt he was intruding and left without getting drunk.

So there it was. Thesinger's moonlight flit, old Craw's near death and resurrection; his swansong in defiance of so much hidden censorship; Luke's restless preoccupation with the secret world; the Circus's inspired exploitation of a necessary evil. Nothing planned but, as life would have it, a curtain-raiser to much that happened later. A typhoon Saturday; a ripple on the plunging, fetid, sterile, swarming pool which is Hong Kong; a bored chorus, still without a hero. And, curiously, a few months afterwards, it fell once more to Luke, in his rôle of Shakespearean messenger, to announce the hero's coming. The news came over the house wire while he was on stand-by and he published it to a bored audience with his customary fervour:

'Folks! Give ear! I have news! Jerry Westerby's back on the beat, men! Heading out East again, hear me, stringing for that same damn comic!'

'His *lordship*!' the dwarf cried at once in mock ecstasy. '*A dash of blue blood, I say*, to raise the vulgar tone! *Oorah for quality, I say*.' With a profane oath, he threw a napkin at the wine rack. 'Jesus,' he said, and emptied Luke's glass.

Chapter 2

THE GREAT CALL

On the afternoon the telegram arrived, Jerry Westerby was hacking at his typewriter on the shaded side of the balcony of his rundown farmhouse, the sack of old books dumped at his feet. The envelope was brought by the black-clad person of the postmistress, a craggy and ferocious peasant who with the ebbing of traditional forces had become the headman of the ragtag Tuscan hamlet. She was a wily creature but today the drama of the occasion had the better of her, and despite the heat she fairly scampered up the arid track. In her ledger the historic moment of delivery was later put at six past five, which was a lie but gave it force. The real time was five exactly. Indoors Westerby's scrawny girl, whom the village called the orphan, was hammering at a stubborn piece of goat's meat, vehemently, the way she attacked everything. The greedy eye of the postmistress spotted her, at the open window and from a good way off: elbows stuck out all ways and her top teeth jammed on to her lower lip: scowling, no doubt, as usual.

'Whore,' thought the postmistress passionately, 'now you have what you have been waiting for!'

The radio was blaring Verdi: the orphan would hear only classical music, as the whole village had learned from the scene she had made at the tavern the evening when the blacksmith tried to choose rock music on the juke box. She had thrown a pitcher at him. So what with the Verdi, and the typewriter and the goat, said the postmistress, the row was so deafening that even an Italian would have heard it.

Jerry sat like a locust on the wood floor, she recalled – maybe he had one cushion – and he was using the book-sack as a footstool. He sat splay-footed, typing between his knees. He had bits of flyblown manuscript spread round him, which were weighted with stones against the red-hot breezes which plagued his scalded hilltop, and a wicker flask of the local red at his elbow, no doubt for the moments, known even to the greatest artists, when natural inspiration failed him. He typed the eagle's way, she told them later amid admiring laughter: much circling before he swooped. And he wore what he always wore, whether he was loafing fruitlessly around his bit of paddock, tilling the dozen useless olive trees which the rogue Franco had palmed off on him, or paddling down to the village with the orphan to shop, or sitting in the tavern over a sharp one before embarking on the long climb home: buckskin boots which the orphan never brushed, and were consequently worn shiny at the toe, ankle socks which she never washed, a filthy shirt, once white, and grey shorts that looked as though they had been frayed by hostile dogs, and which an honest woman would long ago have mended. And he greeted her with that familiar burry rush of words, at once bashful and enthusiastic, which she did not understand in detail, but only generally, like a news broadcast, and could copy, through the black gaps of her decrepit teeth, with surprising flashes of fidelity.

'Mama Stefano, gosh, super, must be boiling. Here, sport, wet your whistle,' he exclaimed, while he slopped down the brick steps with a glass of wine for her, grinning like a schoolboy, which was his nickname in the village: the schoolboy, a telegram for the schoolboy, urgent from London! In nine months no more than a wad of paperback books and the weekly scrawl from his child, and now out of a blue sky this monument of a telegram, short like a demand, but fifty words prepaid for the reply! Imagine, fifty, the cost alone! Only natural that as many as possible should have tried their hand at reading it.

They had choked at first over *honourable*: 'The *honourable* Gerald Westerby.' Why? The baker, who had been a prisoner-of-war in Birmingham, produced a battered dictionary: *having honour, title of courtesy given to the son of a nobleman*. Of course. Signora Sanders, who lived across the valley had already declared the schoolboy to be of noble blood. The second son of a press baron, she had said, *Lord* Westerby a newspaper proprietor, dead. First the paper had died, then its owner – thus Signora Sanders, a wit, they had passed the joke round. Next *regret*, which was easy. So was *advise*. The postmistress was gratified to discover, against all expectation, how much good Latin the English had assimilated despite their decadence. The word *guardian* came harder for it led to *protector*, thence inevitably to unsavoury jokes among the menfolk, which the postmistress stamped on angrily. Till at last, step by step, the code was broken and the story out. The schoolboy had a guardian, meaning a substitute father. This *guardian* lay dangerously ill in hospital, demanding to see the schoolboy before he died. He wanted nobody else. Only honourable Westerby would do. Quickly they filled in the rest of the picture for themselves: the sobbing family gathered at the bedside, the wife prominent and inconsolable, refined priests administering the last sacraments, valuables being locked away, and all over the house, in corridors, back kitchens, the same whispered word: Westerby – where is honourable Westerby?

Lastly the telegram's signatories remained to be interpreted. There were three and they called themselves *solicitors*, a word which triggered one more swoop of dirty innuendo before *notary* was arrived at, and faces abruptly hardened. Holy Maria. If three notaries were involved, then so were large sums of money. And if all three had insisted upon signing, and prepaid that fifty word reply to boot, then not just large but mountainous sums! Acres! Wagon loads! No wonder the orphan had clung to him so, the whore! Suddenly everyone was clamouring to make the hill climb. Guido's Lambretta would take him as far as the water tank, Mario could run like a fox, Manuela the chandler's girl had a tender eye, the shadow of bereavement sat well on her. Repulsing all volunteers – and handing Mario a sharp cuff for the presumption – the postmistress locked the till and left her idiot son to mind the shop, though it meant twenty sweltering minutes and – if that cursed furnace of a wind was blowing up there – a mouthful of red dust for her toil.

They had not made enough of Jerry at first. She regretted this now, as she laboured through the olive groves, but the error had its reasons. First, he had arrived in winter when the cheap buyers come. He arrived alone, but wearing the furtive look of someone who has recently dumped a lot of human cargo, such as children, wives, mothers: the postmistress had known men in her time, and she had seen that wounded smile too often not to recognise it in Jerry: 'I am married but free,' it said, and neither claim was true. Second, the scented English major brought him, a known pig who ran a property agency for exploiting peasants: yet another reason to spurn the schoolboy. The scented major showed him several desirable farmhouses, including one in which the postmistress herself had an interest – also, by coincidence, the finest – but the schoolboy settled instead for the pederast Franco's hovel stuck on this forsaken hilltop she was now ascending: the devil's hill, they called it; the devil came up here when hell became too cool for him. Slick Franco of all people, who watered his milk and his wine and spent his Sundays simpering with popinjays in the town square! The inflated price was half a million lire of which the scented major tried to steal a third, merely because there was a contract.

'And everyone knows why the major favoured slick Franco,' she hissed through her frothing teeth, and her pack of supporters made knowing noises 'tch-tch' at each other, till she angrily ordered them to shut up.

Also, as a shrewd woman, she distrusted something in Jerry's make-up. A hardness buried in the lavishness. She had seen it with Englishmen before, but the schoolboy was in a class by himself, and she distrusted him; she held him dangerous through his restless charm. Today, of course, one could put down those early failings to the eccentricity of a noble English writer, but at the time, the postmistress had shown him no such indulgence. 'Wait till the summer,' she had warned her customers in a snarl, soon after his first shambling visit to her shop – pasta, bread, flykiller. 'In the summer he'll find out what he's bought, the cretin.' In the summer, slick Franco's mice would storm the bedroom, Franco's fleas would devour him alive, and Franco's pederastic hornets would chase him round the garden and the devil's red-hot wind would burn his parts to a frazzle. The water would run out, he would be forced to defecate in the fields like an animal. And when winter came round again the scented pig major could sell the house to another fool, at a loss to everyone but himself.

As to celebrity, in those first weeks the schoolboy showed not a shred of it. He never bargained, he had never heard of discounts, there was not even pleasure in robbing him. And when, in the shop, she drove him beyond his few miserable phrases of kitchen Italian, he did not raise his voice and bawl at her like the real English but shrugged happily and helped himself to whatever he wanted. A *writer*, they said: well, who was not? Very well, he bought quires of foolscap from her. She ordered more, he bought them. Bravo. He possessed books: a mildewed lot, by the look of them, which he carried in a grey jute sack like a poacher's and before the orphan came they would see him striding off into the middle of nowhere, the book-sack slung over his shoulder, for a reading session. Guido had happened on him in the Contessa's forest, perched on a log like a toad and leafing through them one after another, as if they were all one book and he had lost his place. He also possessed a typewriter of which the filthy cover was a patchwork of worn out luggage labels: bravo again. Just as any longhair who buys a paintpot calls himself an artist: *that* sort of writer. In the spring the orphan came and the postmistress hated her too.

A red-head, which was halfway to whoredom for a start. Not enough breast to nurse a rabbit, and worst of all a fierce eye for arithmetic. They said he found her in the town: whore again. From the first day, she had not let him out of her sight. Clung to him like a child. Ate with him, and sulked; drank with him, and sulked; shopped with him, picking up the language like a thief, till they became a minor local sight together, the English giant and his sulking wraith whore, trailing down the hill with their rush basket, the schoolboy in his tattered shorts grinning at everyone, the scowling orphan in her whore's sackcloth with nothing underneath, so that though she was plain as a scorpion the men stared after her to see her hard haunches rock through the fabric. She walked with all her fingers locked around his arm and her cheek against his shoulder, and she only let go of him to pay out meanly from the purse she now controlled. When they met a familiar face, he greeted it for both of them, flapping his vast free arm like a Fascist. And God help the man who, on the rare occasion when she went alone, ventured a fresh word or a wolf call: she would turn and spit like a gutter-cat, and her eyes burned like the devil's.

'And now we know why!' cried the postmistress, very loud, as, still climbing, she mounted a false crest. 'The orphan is after his inheritance. Why else would a whore be loyal?'

It was the visit of Signora Sanders to her shop which caused Mama Stefano's dramatic reappraisal of the schoolboy's worth, and of the orphan's motive. The Sanders was rich and bred horses further up the valley, where she lived with a lady friend known as the man-child who wore close-cut hair and chain belts. Their horses won prizes everywhere. The Sanders was sharp and intelligent and frugal in a way Italians liked, and she knew whomever was worth knowing of the few moth-eaten English scattered over the hills. She called ostensibly to buy a ham, a month ago it must have been, but her real quest was for the schoolboy. Was it true? she asked: 'Signor *Gerald*

Westerby, and living here in the village? A large man, pepper and salt hair, athletic, full of energy, an aristocrat, shy?' Her father the general had known the family in England, she said; they had been neighbours in the country for a spell, the schoolboy's father and her own. The Sanders was considering paying him a visit: what were the schoolboy's circumstances? The postmistress muttered something about the orphan, but the Sanders was unperturbed:

'Oh the Westerbys are *always* changing their women,' she said with a laugh, and turned toward the door.

Dumbfounded, the postmistress detained her, then showered her with questions.

But who was he? What had he done with his youth? A journalist, said the Sanders, and gave what she knew of the family background; the father a flamboyant figure, fair-haired like the son, kept racehorses, she had met him again not long before his death and he was still a man. Like the son he was never at peace: women and houses, changing them all the time; always roaring at someone, if not at his son then at someone across the street. The postmistress pressed harder. But in his own right: was the schoolboy distinguished in his own right? Well, he had certainly worked for some distinguished newspapers, put it that way, said the Sanders, her smile mysteriously broadening.

'It is not the English habit, as a rule, to accord distinction to journalists,' she explained, in her classic, Roman way of talking.

But the postmistress needed more, far more. His writing, his book, what was all *that* about? So long! So much thrown away! Basketsful, the rubbish carter had told her – for no one in his right mind would light a fire up there in summertime. Beth Sanders understood the intensity of isolated people, and knew that in barren places their intelligence must fix on tiny matters. So she tried, she really tried to oblige. Well, he certainly had *travelled* incessantly, she said, coming back to the counter and putting down her parcel. Today all journalists were travellers, of course, breakfast in London, lunch in Rome, dinner in Delhi, but Signor Westerby had been exceptional even by that standard. So perhaps it was a travel book, she ventured.

But *why* had he travelled? the postmistress insisted, for whom no journey was without a goal: *why*?

For the wars, the Sanders replied patiently: for wars, pestilence and famine. 'What else had a journalist to do these days, after all, but report life's miseries?' she asked.

The postmistress shook her head wisely, all her senses fixed upon the revelation: the son of a blond equestrian lord who bellowed, a mad traveller, a writer in distinguished newspapers! And was there a particular theatre? she asked – a corner of God's earth – in which he was a specialist? He was mostly in the East, the Sanders thought, after a moment's reflection. He had been everywhere, but there is a kind of Englishman for whom only the East is home. No doubt that was why he had come to Italy. Some men go dull without the sun.

And some women, too, the postmistress shrieked, and they had a good laugh.

Ah the East, said the postmistress, with a tragic slanting of the head – war upon war, why didn't the Pope stop it? As Mama Stefano ran on this way, the Sanders seemed to remember something. She smiled slightly at first, and her smile grew. An exile's smile, the postmistress reflected, watching her: she is like a sailor remembering the sea.

'He used to drag a sackful of books around,' she said. 'We used to say he stole them from the big houses.'

'He carries it now!' the postmistress cried, and told how Guido had stumbled on him in the Contessa's forest, the schoolboy reading on the log.

'He had notions of becoming a *novelist*, I believe,' the Sanders continued, in the same vein of private reminiscence: 'I remember his father telling us. He was *frightfully* angry. Roared all over the house.'

'The schoolboy? The *schoolboy* was angry?' Mama Stefano exclaimed, now quite incredulous.

'No, no. The father.' The Sanders laughed aloud. In the English social scale, she explained, novelists rated even worse than journalists. 'Does he also paint still?'

'Paint? He is a painter?'

He tried, said the Sanders, but the father forbade that also. Painters were the lowest of *all* creatures, she said, amid fresh laughter: only the successful ones were remotely tolerable.

Soon after this multiple bombshell the blacksmith – the same blacksmith who had been the target of the orphan's pitcher – reported having seen Jerry and the girl at the Sanders' stud, twice in one week, then three times, also eating there. And that the schoolboy had shown a great talent for horses, lunging and walking them with natural understanding, even the wildest. The orphan took no part, said the blacksmith. She sat in the shade with the man-child either reading from the book-sack or watching him with her jealous, unblinking eyes; waiting, as they all now knew, for the guardian to die. And today the telegram!

Jerry had seen Mama Stefano from a long way off. He had that instinct, there was a part of him that never ceased to watch: a black figure hobbling inexorably up the dust-path like a lame beetle in and out of the ruled shadows of the cedars, up the dry watercourse of slick Franco's olive groves, into their own bit of Italy as he called it, all two hundred square metres of it, but big enough to hit a tethered tennis-ball round a pole on cool evenings when they felt athletic. He had seen very early the blue envelope she was waving, and he had even heard the sound of her mewing carrying crookedly over the other sounds of the valley: the Lambrettas and the bandsaws. And his first gesture, without stopping his typing, was to steal a glance at the house to make sure the girl had closed the kitchen window to keep out the heat and the insects. Then, just as the postmistress later described, he went quickly down the steps to her, wine glass in hand, in order to head her off before she came too near.

He read the telegram slowly, once, bending over it to

get the writing into shadow, and his face as Mama Stefano watched it became gaunt, and private, and an extra huskiness entered his voice as he laid one huge, cushioned hand on her arm.

'*La sera*,' he managed, as he guided her back along the path. He would send his reply this evening, he meant. '*Molto grazie*, Mama. Super. Thanks very much. Terrific.'

As they parted she was still chatttering wildly, offering him every service under the sun, taxis, porters, phone calls to the airport, and Jerry was vaguely patting the pockets of his shorts for small or large change: he had momentarily forgotten, apparently, that the girl looked after the money.

The schoolboy had received the news with bearing, the postmistress reported to the village. Graciously, to the point of escorting her part of the way back; bravely, so that only a woman of the world – and one who knew the English – would have read the aching grief beneath; distractedly, so that he had neglected to tip her. Or was he already acquiring the extreme parsimony of the very rich?

But how did the *orphan* behave? they asked. Did she not sob and cry to the Virgin, pretending to share his distress?

'He has yet to tell her,' the postmistress whispered, recalling wistfully her one short glimpse of her, sideview, hammering at the meat: 'He has yet to consider her position.'

The village settled, waiting for the evening, and Jerry sat in the hornet field, gazing at the sea and winding the book-bag round and round, till it reached its limit, and unwound itself.

First there was the valley, and above it stood the five hills in a half ring, and above the hills ran the sea which at that time of day was no more than a flat brown stain in the sky. The hornet field where he sat was a long terrace shored by stones, with a ruined barn at one corner which had given them shelter to picnic and sunbathe unobserved until the hornets nested in the wall. She had seen them when she was hanging out washing, and run in to Jerry to tell him, and Jerry had unthinkingly grabbed a bucket of mortar from slick Franco's place and filled in all their entrances. Then called her down so that she could admire his handiwork: my man, how he protects me. In his memory he saw her exactly: shivering at his side, arms huddled across her body, staring at the new cement and listening to the crazed hornets inside and whispering, 'Jesus, Jesus,' too frightened to budge.

Maybe she'll wait for me, he thought.

He remembered the day he met her. He told himself that story often, because good luck was rare in Jerry's life, where women were concerned, and when it happened he liked to roll it around the tongue, as he would say. A Thursday. He'd taken his usual lift to town, in order to do a spot of shopping, or maybe to see a fresh set of faces and get away from the novel for a while; or maybe just to bolt from the screaming monotony of that empty landscape, which more often was like a prison to him, and a solitary one at that; or conceivably he might just hook himself a woman, which occasionally he brought off by hanging round the bar of the tourist hotel. So he was sitting reading in the trattoria in the town square – a carafe, plate of ham, olives – and suddenly he became aware of this skinny, rangy kid, red-head, sullen face and a brown dress like a monk's habit and a shoulder bag made out of carpet stuff.

'Looks naked without a guitar,' he'd thought.

Vaguely, she reminded him of his daughter Cat, short for Catherine, but only vaguely because he hadn't seen Cat for ten years, which was when his first marriage fell in. Quite why he hadn't seen her, he could even now not precisely say. In the first shock of separation, a confused sense of chivalry told him Cat did better to forget him. 'Best if she writes me off. Put her heart where her home is.' When her mother remarried, the case for self-denial seemed all the stronger. But sometimes he missed her very badly, and most likely that was why, having caught his interest, the girl held it. Did Cat go round like that, alone and spiked with tiredness? Had Cat got her freckles still, and a jaw like a pebble? Later, the girl told him she'd jumped the wall. She'd got herself a governess job with some rich family in Florence. Mother was too busy with the lovers to worry about the kids, but the husband had lots of time for the governess. She'd grabbed what cash she could find and bolted and here she was: no luggage, the police alerted, and using her last chewed banknote to buy herself one square meal before perdition.

There was not a lot of talent in the square that day – there never was – and by the time she sat down, that kid had got just about every able-bodied fellow in town giving her the treatment, from the waiters upward, purring 'beautiful missus' and much rougher stuff besides, of which Jerry missed the precise drift, but it had them all laughing at her expense. Then one of them tried to tweak her breast, at which Jerry got up and went over to her table. He was no great hero, quite the reverse in his secret view, but a lot of things were going around in his mind, and it might just as well have been Cat who was getting shoved into a corner. So yes: anger. He therefore clapped one hand on the shoulder of the small waiter who had made the dive for her, and one hand on the shoulder of the big one who had applauded such bravado, and he explained to them, in bad Italian, but in a fairly reasonable way, that they really must stop being pests, and let the beautiful missus eat her meal in peace. Otherwise he would break their greasy little necks. The atmosphere wasn't too good after that, and the little one seemed actually to be squaring for a fight, for his hand kept travelling toward a back pocket, and hitching at his jacket, till a final look at Jerry changed his mind for him. Jerry dumped some money on the table, picked up her bag for her, went back to collect his book-sack, and led her by the arm, all but lifting her off the ground, across the square to the Apollo.

'Are you English?' she asked on the way.

'Pips, core, the lot,' Jerry snorted furiously, which was the first time he saw her smile. It was a smile definitely worth working for: her bony little face lit up like a urchin's through the grime.

So, simmered down a bit, Jerry fed her, and with the advent of calm he began spinning the tale a bit, because after all those weeks without a focus it was natural he should make an effort to amuse. He explained that he was a newshound out to grass and now writing a novel, that it was his first shot, that he was scratching a long-standing itch, and that he had a dwindling pile of cash from a comic that had paid him redundancy – which was a giggle, he said, because he had been redundant all his life.

'Kind of golden handshake,' he said. He had put a bit down for the house, loafed a bit, and now there was precious little gold left over. That was the second time she smiled. Encouraged, he touched on the solitary nature of the creative life: 'But, Christ, you wouldn't believe the sweat of really, well *really* getting it all to come *out*, sort of thing . . .'

'Wives?' she asked, interrupting him. For a moment, he had assumed she was tuning to the novel. Then he saw her waiting, suspicious eyes, so he replied cautiously: 'None active,' as if wives were volcanoes, which in Jerry's world they had been. After lunch, as they drifted, somewhat plastered, across the empty square, with the sun pelting straight down on them, she made her one declaration of intent.

'Everything I own is in this bag, got it?' she asked. It was the shoulder bag, made out of carpet stuff. 'That's the way I'm going to keep it. So just don't anybody give me anything I can't carry. Got it?'

When they reached his bus stop she hung around, and when the bus came she climbed aboard after him and let Jerry buy her a ticket, and when she got out at the village she climbed the hill with him, Jerry with his book-sack, the girl with her shoulder bag, and that's how it was. Three nights and most of the days she slept and on the fourth night she came to him. He was so unprepared for her that he had actually left his bedroom door locked: he had a bit of a thing about doors and windows, specially at night. So that she had to hammer on the door and shout, 'I want to come into your bloody cot for Christ's sake!' before he opened up.

'Just never lie to me,' she warned, scrambling into his

bed as if they were sharing a dormitory feast. 'No words, no lies. Got it?'

As a lover, she was like a butterfly, he remembered: could have been Chinese. Weightless, never still, so unprotected he despaired of her. When the fireflies came out, the two of them knelt on the window-seat and watched them, and Jerry thought about the East. The cicadas shrieked and the frogs burped, and the lights of the fireflies ducked and parried round a central pool of blackness, and they would kneel there naked for an hour or more, watching and listening, while the hot moon drooped into the hill-crests. They never spoke on those occasions, nor reached any conclusions that he was aware of. But he gave up locking his door.

The music and the hammering had stopped, but a din of church bells had started, he supposed for evensong. The valley was never quiet, but the bells sounded heavier because of the dew. He sauntered over to the swingball, teasing the rope away from the metal pillar, then with his old buckskin boot kicked at the grass around the base, remembering her lithe little body flying from shot to shot and the monk's habit billowing.

'*Guardian* is the big one,' they had said to him. '*Guardian* means the road back,' they had said. For a moment longer Jerry hesitated, gazing downward again into the blüe plain where the very road, not figurative at all, led shimmering and straight as a canal toward the city and the airport.

Jerry was not what he would have called a thinking man. A childhood spent listening to his father's bellowing had taught him early the value of big ideas, and big words as well. Perhaps that was what had joined him to the girl in the first place, he thought. That's what she was on about: 'Don't give me anything I can't carry.'

Maybe. Maybe not. She'll find someone else. They always do.

It's time, he thought. Money gone, novel stillborn, girl too young: come on. It's *time*.

Time for what?

Time! Time she found herself a young bull instead of wearing out an old one. Time to let the wanderlust stir. Strike camp. Wake the camels. On your way. Lord knows, Jerry had done it before once or twice. Pitch the old tent, stay a little, move on; sorry, sport.

It's an order, he told himself. Ours not to reason. Whistle goes, the lads rally. End of argument. *Guardian.*

Rum how he'd had a feeling it was coming, all the same, he thought, still staring into the blurred plain. No great presentiment, any of that tripe: simply, yes, a sense of time. It was due. A sense of season. In place of a gay upsurge of activity, however, a sluggishness seized hold of his body. He suddenly felt too tired, too fat, too sleepy ever to move again. He could have lain down just here, where he stood. He could have slept on the harsh grass till she woke him or the darkness came.

Tripe, he told himself. Sheer tripe. Taking the telegram from his pocket, he strode vigorously into the house, calling her name:

'Hey, sport! Old thing! Where are you hiding? Spot of bad news.' He handed it to her. 'Doomsville,' he said, and went to the window rather than watch her read it.

He waited till he heard the flutter of the paper landing on the table. Then he turned round because there was nothing else for it. She hadn't said anything but she had wedged her hands under her armpits and sometimes her body-talk was deafening. He saw how the fingers waved blindly about, trying to lock on to something.

'Why not shove off to Beth's place for a bit?' he suggested. 'She'll have you like a shot, old Beth. Thinks the world of you. Have you long as you like, Beth would.'

She kept her arms folded till he went down the hill to send his telegram. By the time he came back, she had got his suit out, the blue one they had always laughed about – his prison gear, she called it – but she was trembling and her face had turned white and ill, the way it went when he dealt with the hornets. When he tried to kiss her, she was cold as marble, so he let her be. At night they slept together and it was worse than being alone.

* * *

Mama Stefano announced the news at lunchtime, breathlessly. The honourable schoolboy had left, she said. He wore his suit. He carried a grip, his typewriter and the book-sack. Franco had taken him to the airport in the van. The orphan had gone with them but only as far as the sliproad to the autostrada. When she got out she didn't say goodbye: just sat beside the road like the trash she was. For a while, after they dumped her, the schoolboy had remained very quiet and inward. He scarcely noticed Franco's ingenious and pointed questions, and he pulled at his tawny forelock a lot – the Sanders had called it pepper and salt. At the airport, with an hour to kill before the plane left, they had a flask together, also a game of dominoes, but when Franco tried to rob him for the fare, the schoolboy showed an unusual harshness, haggling at last like the true rich.

Franco had told her, she said: her bosom friend. Franco, maligned as a pederast. Had she not always defended him, Franco the elegant, Franco, the father of her idiot son? They had had their differences – who had not? – but let them only name for her, if they could, in the whole valley, a more upright, diligent, graceful, better dressed man than Franco, her friend and lover!

The schoolboy had gone back for his inheritance, she said.

Chapter 3

MR GEORGE SMILEY'S HORSE

Only George Smiley, said Roddy Martindale, a fleshy Foreign Office wit, could have got himself appointed captain of a wrecked ship. Only Smiley, he added, could have compounded the pains of that appointment by choosing the same moment to abandon his beautiful, if occasionally errant, wife.

At first or even second glance George Smiley was ill-suited to either part, as Martindale was quick to note. He was tubby and in small ways hopelessly unassertive. A natural shyness made him from time to time pompous, and to men of Martindale's flamboyance his unobtrusiveness acted as a standing reproach. He was also myopic, and to see him in those first days after the holocaust, in his round spectacles and his civil servant weeds, attended by his slender, tight-mouthed cupbearer Peter Guillam, discreetly padding the marshier by-paths of the Whitehall jungle; or stooped over a heap of papers at any hour of day or night in his scruffy throne-room on the fifth floor of the Edwardian mausoleum in Cambridge Circus which he now commanded, you would think it was he, and not the dead Haydon, the Russian spy, who deserved the tradename 'mole'. After such long hours of work in that cavernous and half-deserted building, the bags beneath his eyes turned to bruises, he smiled seldom, though he was by no means humourless, and there were times when the mere exertion of rising from his chair seemed to leave him winded. Reaching the upright position, he would pause, mouth slightly open, and give a little, fricative 'uh' before moving off. Another mannerism had him polishing his spectacles distractedly on the fat end of his tie, which left his face so disconcertingly naked that one very senior secretary – in the jargon, these ladies were known as 'mothers' – was on more than one occasion assailed by a barely containable urge, of which psychiatrists would have made all sorts of heavy weather, to start forward and shelter him from the impossible task he seemed determined to perform.

'George Smiley isn't just cleaning the stable,' the same Roddy Martindale remarked, from his luncheon table at the Garrick. 'He's carrying his horse up the hill as well. Haw haw.'

Other rumours, favoured mainly by departments which had entered bids for the charter of the foundered service, were less respectful of his travail.

'George is living on his reputation,' they said, after a few months of this. 'Catching Bill Haydon was a fluke.'

Anyway, they said, it had been an American tip-off, not George's *coup* at all: the Cousins should have had the credit, but they had waived it diplomatically. No, no, said others, it was the Dutch. The Dutch had broken Moscow Centre's code and passed the take through liaison: ask Roddy Martindale – Martindale, of course, being a professional trafficker in Circus misinformation. And so, back and forth, while Smiley, seemingly oblivious, kept his counsel and dismissed his wife.

They could hardly believe it.

They were stunned.

Martindale, who had never loved a woman in his life, was particularly affronted. He made a positive *thing* of it at the Garrick.

'The gall! Him a complete nobody and her half a Sawley! Pavlovian, that's what I call it. Sheer Pavlovian cruelty. After years of putting up with her perfectly healthy peccadilloes – driving her to them, you mark my words – what does the little man do? Turns round and with quite *Napoleonic* brutality kicks her in the teeth! It's a scandal. I shall tell everyone it's a scandal. I'm a tolerant man in my way, not unworldly I think, but Smiley has gone too far. Oh yes.'

For once, as occasionally occurred, Martindale had the picture straight. The evidence was there for all to read. With Haydon dead and the past buried, the Smileys had made up their differences and together, with some small ceremony, the reunited couple had moved back into their little Chelsea house in Bywater Street. They had even made a stab at being in society. They had gone out, they had entertained in the style befitting George's new appointment; the Cousins, the odd Parliamentary Minister, a variety of Whitehall barons all dined and went home full; they had even for a few weeks made a modestly exotic couple around the higher bureaucratic circuit. Till overnight, to his wife's unmistakable discomfort, George Smiley had removed himself from her sight, and set up camp in the meagre attics behind his throne-room in the Circus. Soon the gloom of the place seemed to work itself into the fabric of his face, like dust into the complexion of a prisoner. While in Chelsea, Ann Smiley pined, taking very hardly to her unaccustomed rôle of wife abandoned.

Dedication, said the knowing. Monkish abstinence. George is a saint. And at *his* age.

Balls, the Martindale faction retorted. Dedication to *what*? What was there left, in that dreary red-brick monster, that could possibly command such an act of self-immolation? What was there *anywhere*, in beastly Whitehall or, Lord help us, in beastly *England*, that could command it any more?

Work, said the knowing.

But *what* work? came the falsetto protests of these self-appointed Circus-watchers, handing round, like Gorgons, their little scraps of sight and hearing. What did he do up there, shorn of three-quarters of his staff, all but a few old biddies to brew his tea, his networks blown to smithereens? His foreign residencies, his reptile fund frozen solid by the Treasury – they meant his operational accounts – and not a friend in Whitehall or Washington to call his own? Unless you counted that loping prig Lacon at the

Cabinet Office to be his friend, always so determined to go down the line for him at every conceivable opportunity. And naturally *Lacon* would put up a fight for him: what else had he? The Circus was Lacon's power base. Without it, he was – well, what he was already, a capon. Naturally *Lacon* would sound the battle cry.

'It's a scandal,' Martindale announced huffily, as he cropped his smoked eel and steak-and-kidney and the club's own claret, up another twenty pence a crack. 'I shall tell everybody.'

Between the villagers of Whitehall and the villagers of Tuscany, there was sometimes surprisingly little to choose.

Time did not kill the rumours. To the contrary they multiplied, taking colour from his isolation and calling it obsession.

It was remembered that Bill Haydon had not merely been George Smiley's colleague, but Ann's cousin and something more besides. Smiley's fury against him, they said, had not stopped at Haydon's death: he was positively dancing on Bill's grave. For example, George had personally supervised the clearing of Haydon's fabled pepper-pot room overlooking the Charing Cross Road, and the destruction of every last sign of him, from his indifferent oil-paintings by his own hand to the leftover oddments in the drawers of his desk; even the desk itself, which he had ordered sawn up, and burned. And when *that* was done, they maintained, he had called in Circus workmen to tear down the partition walls. Oh yes, said Martindale.

Or, for another example, and frankly a most unnerving one, take the photograph which hung on the wall of Smiley's dingy throne-room, a passport photograph by the look of it, but blown up far beyond its natural size, so that it had a grainy and some said spectral look. One of the Treasury boys spotted it during an ad-hoc conference about scrapping the operational bank accounts.

'Is that Control's portrait by the by?' he had asked of Peter Guillam, purely as a bit of social chit chat. No sinister intent behind the question. Well, surely one was allowed to *ask*? Control, other names still unknown, was the legend of the place. He had been Smiley's guide and mentor for all of thirty years. Smiley had actually buried him, they said: for the very secret, like the very rich, have a tendency to die unmourned.

'No, it bloody well *isn't* Control,' Guillam the cupbearer had retorted, in that off-hand, supercilious way of his. 'It's Karla.'

And who was Karla when he was at home?

Karla, my dear, was the workname of the Soviet case officer who had recruited Bill Haydon in the first place, and had the running of him thereafter. 'A different sort of legend *entirely*, to say the least,' said Martindale, all a-quiver. 'It seems we've a real vendetta on our hands. How puerile can you get, I wonder?'

Even Lacon was a mite bothered by that picture.

'Now seriously, why do you hang him there, George?' he demanded, in his bold, head-prefect's voice, dropping in on Smiley one evening on his way home from the Cabinet Office. 'What does he mean to you, I wonder? Have you thought about that one? It isn't a little macabre, you don't think? The victorious enemy? I'd have thought he would get you down, gloating over you all up there?'

'Well, Bill's *dead*,' said Smiley, in that elliptical way he had sometimes of giving a clue to an argument, rather than the argument itself.

'And Karla's alive, you mean?' Lacon prompted. 'And you'd rather have a live enemy than a dead one? Is that what you mean?'

But questions of George Smiley at a certain point had a habit of passing him by; even, said his colleagues, of appearing to be in bad taste.

An incident which provided more substantial fare around the Whitehall bazaars concerned the 'ferrets', or electronic sweepers. A worse case of favouritism could not be remembered anywhere. My *God* those hoods had a nerve sometimes! Martindale, who had been waiting a year to have *his* room done, sent a complaint to his Under-Secretary. By hand. To be opened personally by. So did his Brother-in-Christ at Defence and so, nearly, did Hammer of Treasury, but Hammer either forgot to post his, or thought better of it at the last moment. It wasn't just a question of priorities, not at all. Not even of principle. *Money* was involved. *Public* money. Treasury had already had half the Circus rewired on George's insistence. His paranoia about eavesdropping knew no limits, apparently. Add to that, the ferrets were short-staffed, there had been industrial disputes about unsocial hours – oh, any number of angles! Dynamite, the whole subject.

Yet what had happened in the event? Martinale had the details at his manicured fingertips. George went to Lacon on a Thursday – the day of the freak heatwave, you remember, when everyone practically *expired*, even at the Garrick – and by the Saturday – a Saturday, *imagine* the overtime! – the brutes were swarming over the Circus, enraging the neighbours with their din, and tearing the place apart. A more *gross* case of blind preference had not been met with since – since, well, they allowed Smiley to have back that mangy old Russian researcher of his, Sachs, Connie Sachs, the don woman from Oxford, against all reason, calling her a mother when she wasn't.

Discreetly, or as discreetly as he could manage, Martindale went to quite some lengths to find out whether the ferrets had actually discovered anything, but met a blank wall. In the secret world, information is money, and by that standard at least, though he might not know it, Roddy Martindale was a pauper, for the inside to this inside-story was known only to the smallest few. It was true that Smiley called on Lacon in his panelled room overlooking St James's Park on the Thursday: and that the day was uncommonly hot for autumn. Rich shafts of sunlight poured on to the representational carpet, and the dust-specks played in them like tiny tropical fish. Lacon had even removed his jacket, though of course not his tie.

'Connie Sachs has been doing some arithmetic on Karla's handwriting in analogous cases,' Smiley announced.

'*Handwriting?*' Lacon echoed, as if handwriting were against the regulations.

'Tradecraft. Karla's habits of technique. It seems that where it was operable, he ran moles and sound-thieves in tandem.'

'Once more now in English, George, do you mind?'

Where circumstances allowed, said Smiley, Karla had liked to back up his agent operations with microphones. Though Smiley was satisfied that nothing had been said within the building which could compromise any 'present plans' as he called them, the implications were unsettling.

Lacon was getting to know Smiley's handwriting too.

'Any collateral for that rather academic theory?' he enquired, examining Smiley's expressionless features over the top of his pencil, which he held between his two index fingers, like a rule.

'We've been making an inventory of our own audio stores,' Smiley confessed with a puckering of his brow. 'There's a quantity of house equipment missing. A lot seems to have disappeared during the alterations of sixty-six.' Lacon waited, dragging it out of him. 'Haydon was on the building committee responsible for having the work carried out,' Smiley ended, as a final sop. 'He was the driving force, in fact. It's just – well, if the Cousins ever got to hear of it, I think it would be the last straw.'

Lacon was no fool, and the Cousins' wrath just when everyone was trying to smooth their feathers was a thing to be avoided at any cost. If he had had his way, he would have ordered the ferrets out the same day. Saturday was a compromise and without consulting anybody he despatched the entire team, all twelve of them, in two grey vans painted 'Pest Control'. It was true that they tore the place apart, hence the silly rumours about the destruction of the pepper-pot room. They were angry because it was the weekend, and perhaps therefore needlessly violent: the tax paid on overtime was frightful. But their mood changed fast enough when they bagged eight radio microphones in the first sweep, every one of them Circus standard-issue from audio stores. Haydon's distribution of them was classic, as Lacon agreed when he called to make his own inspection. One in a drawer of a disused desk, as if innocently left there and forgotten about, except that the desk happened to be in the coding room. One collecting dust on top of an old steel cupboard in the fifth-floor conference room – or, in the jargon, rumpus room. And one, with typical Haydon flair, wedged behind the cistern in the senior officers' lavatory next door. A second sweep, to include load-bearing walls, threw up three more embedded in the fabric during the building work. Probes, with plastic snorkel-straws to pipe the sound back to them. The ferrets laid them out like a game-line. Extinct, of course, as all the devices were, but put there by Haydon nevertheless, and tuned to frequencies the Circus did not use.

'Maintained at Treasury cost, too, I declare,' said Lacon, with the driest of smiles, fondling the leads which had once connected the probe microphones with the mains power supply. 'Or used to be, till George rewired the place. I must be sure to tell Brother Hammer. He'll be thrilled.'

Hammer, a Welshman, being Lacon's most persistent enemy.

On Lacon's advice Smiley now staged a modest piece of theatre. He ordered the ferrets to reactivate the radio-microphones in the conference room and to modify the receiver on one of the Circus's few remaining surveillance cars. Then he invited three of the least bending Whitehall desk-jockeys, including the Welsh Hammer, to drive in a half-mile radius round the building, while they listened to a pre-scripted discussion between two of Smiley's shadowy helpers sitting in the rumpus room. Word for word. Not a syllable out of place.

After which, Smiley himself swore them to absolute secrecy, and for good measure made them sign a declaration, drafted by the housekeepers expressly to inspire awe. Peter Guillam reckoned it would keep them quiet for about a month.

'Or less if it rains,' he added sourly.

Yet if Martindale and his colleagues in the Whitehall outfield lived in a state of primaeval innocence about the reality of Smiley's world, those closer to the throne felt equally removed from him. The circles around him grew smaller as they grew nearer, and precious few in the early days reached the centre. Entering the brown and dismal doorway of the Circus, with its temporary barriers manned by watchful janitors, Smiley shed none of his habitual privacy. For nights and days at a time, the door to his tiny office suite stayed closed and his only company was Peter Guillam, and a hovering dark-eyed factotum named Fawn, who had shared with Guillam the job of babysitting Smiley during the smoking-out of Haydon. Sometimes Smiley disappeared by the back door with no more than a nod, taking Fawn, a sleek, diminutive creature, with him and leaving Guillam to field the phone calls and get hold of him in emergency. The mothers likened his behaviour to the last days of Control, who had died in harness, thanks to Haydon, of a broken heart. By the organic processes of a closed society, a new word was added to the jargon. The unmasking of Haydon now became the *fall* and Circus history was divided into *before the fall* and *after* it. To Smiley's coming and goings, the physical *fall* of the building itself, three-quarters empty and, since the visit of the ferrets, in a wrecked condition, lent a sombre sense of ruin which at low moments became symbolic to those who had to live with it. What the ferrets destroy they do not put together: and the same, they felt perhaps, was true of Karla, whose dusty features, nailed there by their elusive chief, continued to watch over them from the shadows of his Spartan throne-room.

The little they did know was appalling. Such humdrum matters as personnel, for example, took on a horrific dimension. Smiley had blown staff to dismiss, and blown residencies to dismantle; poor Tufty Thesinger's in Hong

Kong for one, though being pretty far removed from the anti-Soviet scene, Hong Kong was one of the last to go. Round Whitehall, a terrain which like Smiley they deeply distrusted, they heard of him engaged in bizarre and rather terrible arguments over terms of severance and resettlement. There were cases, it seemed – poor Tufty Thesinger in Hong Kong once more supplied the readiest example – where Bill Haydon had deliberately encouraged the over-promotion of burnt-out officers who could be counted on not to mount private initiatives. Should they be paid off at their natural value, or at the inflated one which Haydon had mischievously set on them? There were others where Haydon for his own preservation had confected reasons for dismissal. Should they receive full pension? Had they a claim to reinstatement? Perplexed young Ministers, new to power since the elections, made brave and contradictory rulings. In consequence a sad stream of deluded Circus field officers, both men and women, passed through Smiley's hands, and the housekeepers were ordered to make sure that for reasons of security and perhaps aesthetics, none of these returnees from foreign residencies should set foot inside the main building. Nor would Smiley tolerate any contact between the damned and the reprieved. Accordingly, with grudging Treasury support from the Welsh Hammer, the housekeepers opened a temporary reception point in a rented house in Bloomsbury, under cover of a language school (Regret No Callers Without Appointment) and manned it with a quartet of pay-and-personnel officers. This body became inevitably the Bloomsbury Group, and it was known that sometimes for a spare hour or so Smiley made a point of slipping down there and, rather in the manner of a hospital visitor, offering his condolences to faces frequently unknown to him. At other times, depending on his mood, he would remain entirely silent, preferring to perch unexplained and Buddha-like in a corner of the dusty interviewing room.

What drove him? What was he looking for? If anger was the root, then it was an anger common to them all in those days. They could be sitting together in the raftered rumpus room after a long day's work, joking and gossiping; but if someone should let slip the names of Karla or his mole Haydon, a silence of angels would descend on them, and not even cunning old Connie Sachs, the Moscow-gazer, could break the spell.

Even more affecting in the eyes of his subordinates were Smiley's efforts to save something of the agent networks from the wreck. Within a day of Haydon's arrest, all nine of the Circus's Soviet and East European networks had gone cold. Radio links stopped dead, courier lines dried up and there was every reason to say that, if there had been any genuinely Circus-owned agents left among them, they had been rolled up overnight. But Smiley fiercely opposed that easy view, just as he refused to accept that Karla and Moscow Centre between them were invincibly efficient, or tidy, or logical. He pestered Lacon, he pestered the Cousins in their vast annexes in Grosvenor Square, he insisted that agent radio frequencies continue to be monitored, and despite bitter protest by the Foreign Office – Roddy Martindale as ever to the fore – he had open-language messages put out by the overseas services of the BBC ordering any live agent who should happen to hear them and know the codeword, to abandon ship immediately. And, little by little, to their amazement, came tiny flutterings of life, like garbled messages from another planet.

First, the Cousins, in the person of their suspiciously bluff local station chief Martello, reported from Grosvenor Square that an American escape line was passing two British agents, a man and a woman, to the old holiday resort of Sochi on the Black Sea, where a small boat was being fitted in readiness for what Martello's quiet men insisted on calling an 'exfiltration assignment'. By his description, he was referring to the Churayevs, linchpins of the *Contemplate* network which had covered Georgia and the Ukraine. Without waiting for Treasury sanction, Smiley resurrected from retirement one Roy Bland, a burly ex-Marxist dialectician and sometime field agent, who had been the network's case officer. To Bland, who had come down heavily in the fall, he entrusted the two Russian leash-dogs de Silsky and Kaspar, also in mothballs, also former Haydon protégés, to make up a standby reception party. They were still sitting in their RAF transport plane when word came through that the couple had been shot dead as they were leaving harbour. The exfiltration assignment had fallen through, said the Cousins. In sympathy, Martello personally telephoned Smiley with the news. He was a kindly man, by his own lights, and, like Smiley, old school. It was night-time, and raining furiously.

'Now don't go taking this too hardly, George,' he warned in his avuncular way. 'Hear me? There's fieldmen and there's deskmen and it's up to you and me to see that the distinction is preserved. Otherwise we all go crazy. Can't go down the line for every one of them. That's generalship. So you just remember that.'

Peter Guillam, who was at Smiley's shoulder when he took the call, swore later that Smiley showed no particular reaction: and Guillam knew him well. Nevertheless, ten minutes later, unobserved by anybody, he was gone, and his voluminous mackintosh was missing from its peg. He returned after dawn, drenched to the skin, still carrying the mackintosh over his arm. Having changed, he returned to his desk, but when Guillam, unbidden, tiptoed in to him with tea, he found his master, to his embarrassment, sitting rigidly before an old volume of German poetry, fists clenched either side of it, while he silently wept.

Bland, Kaspar and de Silsky begged for reinstatement. They pointed to little Toby Esterhase, the Hungarian, who had somehow gained readmittance, and demanded the same treatment, in vain. They were stood down and not spoken of again. To injustice belongs injustice. Though tarnished, they might have been useful, but Smiley would not hear their names; not then; not later; not ever. Of the immediate post-fall period, that was the lowest point. There were those who seriously believed –

inside the Circus as well as out – that they had heard the last beat of the secret English heart.

A few days after this catastrophe, as it happened, luck handed Smiley a small consolation. In Warsaw in broad daylight a Circus head agent on the run picked up the BBC signal and walked straight into the British Embassy. Thanks to ferocious lobbying by Lacon and Smiley between them he was flown home to London the same night disguised as a diplomatic courier, Martindale notwithstanding. Mistrusting his cover story Smiley turned the man over to the Circus inquisitors who, deprived of other meat, nearly killed him but afterwards declared him clean. He was resettled in Australia.

Next, still at the very genesis of his rule, Smiley was compelled to pass judgement on the Circus's blown domestic out-stations. His instinct was to shed everything: the safe houses, now totally unsafe; the Sarratt Nursery, where traditionally the briefing and training of agents and new entrants was conducted: the experimental audio laboratories in Harlow; the stinks-and-bangs school in Argyll; the water school in the Helford Estuary, where passé sailors practised the black arts of small-boat seacraft like the ritual of some lost religion; and the longarm radio transmission base at Canterbury. He would even have done away with the wranglers' headquarters in Bath where the code-breaking went on.

'Scrap the lot,' he told Lacon, calling on him in his rooms.

'And then what?' Lacon enquired, puzzled by his vehemence, which since the Sochi failure was more marked in him.

'Start again.'

'I see,' said Lacon, which meant, of course, that he didn't. Lacon had sheets of Treasury figures before him, and was studying them while he spoke.

'The Sarratt Nursery, for some reason which I fail to understand, is carried on the *military* budget,' he observed reflectively. 'Not on your reptile fund at all. The Foreign Office pays for Harlow – and I'm sure has long forgotten the fact – Argyll is under the wing of the Ministry of Defence, who most certainly won't know of its existence, the Post Office has Canterbury and the Navy has Helford. Bath, I'm pleased to say, is also supported from Foreign Office funds, over the particular signature of Martindale, appended six years ago and similarly faded from official memory. So they don't eat a thing. Do they?'

'They're dead wood,' Smiley insisted. 'And while they exist we shall never replace them. Sarratt went to the devil long ago, Helford is moribund, Argyll is farcical. As to the wranglers, for the last five years they've been working practically full time for Karla.'

'By Karla you mean Moscow Centre?'

'I mean the department responsible for Haydon and half a dozen – '

'I know what you mean. But I think it safer to stay with institutions if you don't mind. In that way we are spared the embarrassment of personalities. After all, that's what institutions are *for*, isn't it?' Lacon tapped his pencil rhythmically on his desk. Finally he looked up, and considered Smiley quizzically. 'Well, well, you *are* the root-and-bough man these days, George. I dread to think what would happen if you were ever to wield your axe round *my* side of the garden. Those outstations are gilt-edged stock. Do away with them now and you'll never get them back. Later, if you like, when you're on the road, you can cash them in and buy yourself something better. You mustn't sell when the market's low, you know. You must wait till you can take a profit.'

Reluctantly, Smiley bowed to his advice.

As if all these headaches were not enough, there came one bleak Monday morning when a Treasury audit pointed up serious discrepancies in the conduct of the Circus reptile fund over the period of five years before it was frozen by the fall. Smiley was forced to hold a kangaroo court, at which an elderly clerk in Finance Section, hauled from retirement, broke down and confessed to a shameful passion for a girl in Registry who had led him by the nose. In a ghastly fit of remorse, the old man went home and hanged himself. Against all Guillam's advice Smiley insisted on attending the funeral.

Yet it is a matter of record that from these quite dismal beginnings, and indeed from his very first weeks in office, George Smiley went over to the attack.

The base from which this attack was launched was in the first instance philosophical, in the second theoretical, and only in the last instance, thanks to the dramatic appearance of the egregious gambler Sam Collins, human.

The philosophy was simple. The task of an intelligence service, Smiley announced firmly, was not to play chase games but to deliver intelligence to its customers. If it failed to do this, those customers would resort to other, less scrupulous sellers or, worse, indulge in amateurish self-help. And the service itself would wither. Not to be seen in the Whitehall markets was not to be desired, he went on. Worse: unless the Circus produced, it would also have no wares to barter with the Cousins, nor with other sister services with whom reciprocal deals were traditional. Not to produce was not to trade, and not to trade was to die.

Amen, they said.

His theory – he called it his *premise* – on how intelligence could be produced with no resources, was the subject of an informal meeting held in the rumpus room not two months after his accession, between himself and the tiny inner circle which made up, to a point, his team of confidants. They were in all five: Smiley himself; Peter Guillam, his cupbearer; big, flowing Connie Sachs, the Moscow-gazer; Fawn, the dark-eyed factotum, who wore black gym-shoes and manned the Russian-style copper samovar and gave out biscuits; and lastly Doc di Salis, known as the Mad Jesuit, the Circus's head China-watcher. When God had finished making Connie Sachs, said the wags, He needed a rest, so He ran up Doc de Salis from the remnants. The Doc was a patchy, grubby little creature, more like Connie's monkey than her counterpart, and his features, it was true, from the spiky silver hair that strayed over his grimy collar, to the moist mis-shapen fingertips which picked like chicken beaks at everything around them, had an unquestionably ill-begotten look. If Beardsley had drawn him, he would have had him chained and hirsute, peeping round the corner of her enormous caftan. Yet di Salis was a notable orientalist, a scholar, and something of a hero too, for he had spent a part of the war in China, recruiting for God and the Circus, and another part in Changi jail, for the pleasure of the Japanese. That was the team: the Group of Five. In time it expanded, but to start with these five alone made up the famous cadre, and afterwards, to have been one of them, said di Salis, was 'like holding a Communist Party card with a single-figure membership number'.

First, Smiley reviewed the wreck, and that took some while, in the way that sacking a city takes some while, or liquidating great numbers of people. He simply drove through every back alley the Circus possessed, demonstrating quite ruthlessly how, by what method, and often exactly when, Haydon had laid bare its secrets to his Soviet masters. He had of course the advantage of his own interrogation of Haydon, and of the original researches which had led him to Haydon's discovery. He knew the track. Nevertheless, his peroration was a minor *tour de force* of destructive analysis.

'So no illusions,' he ended tersely. 'This service will never be the same again. It may be better, but it will be different.'

Amen again, they said, and took a doleful break to stretch their legs.

It was odd, Guillam recalled later, how the important scenes of those early months seemed all to play at night. The rumpus room was long and raftered, with high dormer windows which gave on to nothing but orange night sky and a coppice of rusted radio aerials, war relics which no one had seen fit to remove.

The *premise*, said Smiley when they had resettled, was that Haydon had done nothing against the Circus that was not directed, and that the direction came from one man personally: Karla.

His premise was, that in briefing Haydon, Karla was exposing the gaps in Moscow Centre's knowledge; that in ordering Haydon to suppress certain intelligence which came the Circus's way, in ordering him to downgrade or distort it, to deride it, or even to deny it circulation altogether, Karla was indicating the secrets he did not want revealed.

'So we can take the backbearings, can't we, darling?' murmured Connie Sachs, whose speed of uptake put her as usual a good length ahead of the rest of the field.

'That's right, Con. That's exactly what we can do,' said Smiley gravely. 'We can take the backbearings.' He resumed his lecture, leaving Guillam for one more mystified than before.

By minutely charting Haydon's path of destruction – his pugmarks as he called them – by exhaustively recording his selection of files; by reassembling, after aching weeks of research if necessary, the intelligence culled in good faith by Circus outstations, and balancing it, in every detail, against the intelligence distributed by Haydon to the Circus's customers in the Whitehall market place, it would be possible to take *backbearings* – as Connie so rightly called them – and establish Haydon's, and therefore Karla's, point of departure, said Smiley.

Once a correct backbearing had been taken, surprising doors of opportunity would open, and the Circus, against all outward likelihood, would be in a position to go over to the initiative – or, as Smiley put it – 'to *act*, and not merely to *react*.'

The premise, to use Connie Sachs's joyous description later, meant: 'Looking for another bloody Tutankhamun, with George Smiley holding the light and us poor Charlies doing the digging.'

At that time, of course, Jerry Westerby was not even a twinkle in their operational eye.

* * *

They went into battle next day, huge Connie to one corner, the crabbed little di Salis to his. As di Salis said, in a nasal, deprecating tone, which had a savage force: 'At least we do finally know why we're here.' Their families of pasty burrowers carved the archive in two. To Connie and 'my Bolshies' as she called them, went Russia and the Satellites. To di Salis and his 'yellow perils', China and the Third World. What fell between – source reports on the nation's theoretical Allies, for instance – was consigned to a special wait-bin for later evaluation. They worked, like Smiley himself, impossible hours. The canteen complained, the janitors threatened to walk out, but gradually the sheer energy of the burrowers infected even the ancillary staff and they shut up. A bantering rivalry developed. Under Connie's influence, backroom boys and girls who till now had scarcely been seen to smile, learned suddenly to chaff each other in the language of their great familiars in the world outside the Circus. Czarist imperialist running dogs drank tasteless coffee with divisive, deviationist chauvinist Stalinists and were proud of it. But the most impressive blossoming was unquestionably in di Salis, who interrupted his nocturnal labours with short but vigorous spells at the ping-pong table, where he would challenge all comers, leaping about like a lepidopterist after rare specimens. Soon the first fruits appeared, and gave them fresh impetus. Within a month, three reports had been nervously distributed, under extreme limitation, and even found favour with the sceptical Cousins. A month later a hardbound summary wordily entitled *Interim report on lacunae in Soviet intelligence regarding Nato sea to air strike capacity*, earned grudging applause from Martello's parent factory in Langley, Virginia, and an exuberant phone call from Martello himself.

'George, I *told* those guys!' he yelled, so loud that the telephone line seemed an unnecessary extravagance, 'I told them: "The Circus will deliver." Did they believe me. Did they hell!'

Meanwhile, sometimes with Guillam for company, sometimes with silent Fawn to babysit, Smiley himself conducted his own dark peregrinations and marched till he was half dead with tiredness. And still without reward, kept marching. By day, and often by night as well, he trailed the home counties and points beyond, questioning past officers of the Circus and former agents out to grass. In Chiswick, perched meekly in the office of a cut-price travel agent and talking in murmurs to a former Polish colonel of cavalry resettled as a clerk there, he thought he had glimpsed it; but like a mirage, the promise dissolved as he advanced on it. In a secondhand radio shop in Sevenoaks a Sudeten Czech held out the same hope to him, but when he and Guillam hurried back to confirm the story from Circus records, they found the actors dead and no one left to lead him further. At a private stud in Newmarket, to Fawn's near-violent fury, he suffered insult at the hand of a tweedy and opinionated Scot, a protégé of Smiley's predecessor Alleline, all in the same elusive cause. Back home, he called for the papers, only once more to see the light go out.

For this was the last and unspoken conviction of the premise which Smiley had outlined in the rumpus room: that the snare with which Haydon had trapped himself was not unique. That in the end-analysis, it was not Haydon's paperwork which had caused his downfall, not his meddling with reports, nor his 'losing' of inconvenient records. It was Haydon's panic. It was Haydon's spontaneous intervention in a field operation, where the threat to himself, or perhaps to another Karla agent, was suddenly so grave that his one hope was to suppress it despite the risk. This was the trick which Smiley longed to find repeated. And this was the question which, never directly, but by inference, Smiley and his helpers in the Bloomsbury reception centre canvassed:

'Can you remember any incident during your service in the field when in your opinion you were unreasonably restrained from following an operational lead?'

And it was dapper Sam Collins, in his dinner jacket, with his brown cigarette and his trim moustache and his Mississippi dandy's smile, summoned for a quiet chat one day, who breezed in to say: 'Come to think of it, yes, old boy, I can.'

But behind this question again, and Sam's crucial answer, stalked the formidable person of Miss Connie Sachs and her pursuit for Russian gold.

And behind Connie again, as ever, the permanently misted photograph of Karla.

'*Connie's got one, Peter,*' she whispered to Guillam over the internal telephone late one night. '*She's got one, sure as boots.*'

It was not her first find by any means, not her tenth, but her devious instinct told her straight away it was 'the genuine article, darling, mark old Connie's words'. So Guillam told Smiley and Smiley locked up his files and cleared his desk and said: 'All right, let her in.'

Connie was a huge, crippled, cunning woman, a don's daughter, a don's sister, herself some sort of academic, and known to the older hands as Mother Russia. The folklore said Control had recruited her over a rubber of bridge while she was still a débutante, on the night Neville Chamberlain promised 'peace in our time'. When Haydon came to power in the slipstream of his protector Alleline, one of his first and most prudent moves was to have Connie put out to grass. For Connie knew more about the byways of Moscow Centre than most of the wretched brutes, as she called them, who toiled there, and Karla's private army of moles and recruiters had always been her very special joy. Not a Soviet defector, in the old days, but his debriefing report had passed through Mother Russia's arthritic fingers; not a coat-trailer who had manoeuvred himself alongside an identified Karla talent-spotter, but Connie greedily rehearsed him in every detail of the quarry's choreography; not a scrap of hearsay over nearly forty years on the beat which had not been assumed into her pain-racked body, and lodged there among the junk of her compendious memory, to be turned up the moment she rummaged for it. Connie's mind, said Control once, in a kind of despair, was like the back of one enormous envelope. Dismissed, she went back to Oxford and the devil. At the time Smiley reclaimed her, her only recreation was *The Times* crossword and she was running at a comfortable two bottles a day. But that night, that modestly historic night, as she hauled her great frame along the fifth floor corridor toward George Smiley's inner room, she sported a clean grey caftan, she had daubed a pair of rosy lips not far from her own, and she had taken nothing stronger than a vile peppermint cordial all day long – of which the reek lingered in her wake – and a sense of occasion, they all decided afterwards, was stamped on her from the first. She carried a heavy plastic shopping bag, for she would countenance no leather. In her lair on a lower floor, her mongrel dog, christened Trot, and recruited on a wave of remorse for its late predecessor, whimpered disconsolately from beneath her desk, to the lively fury of her room-mate di Salis, who would often privily lash at the beast with his foot; or in more jovial moments content himself with reciting to Connie the many tasty ways in which the Chinese prepared their dogs for the pot. Outside the Edwardian dormers, as she passed them one by one, a racing late-summer rain was falling, ending a long drought, and she saw it – she told them all later – as symbolic, if not Biblical. The drops rattled like pellets on the slate roof, flattening the dead leaves which had settled there. In the anteroom the mothers continued stonily with their business, accustomed to Connie's pilgrimages, and not liking them the better for it.

'*Darlings,*' Connie murmured, waving her bloated hand to them like royalty. 'So loyal. So *very* loyal.'

There was one step downward into the throne-room – the uninitiated tended to stumble on it despite the faded warning notice – and Connie with her arthritis negotiated it as if it were a ladder while Guillam held her arm. Smiley watched her, plump hands linked on his desk, as she began solemnly unpacking her offerings from the carrier: not eye of newt, nor the finger of a birth-strangled babe – Guillam speaking once more – but files, a string of them, flagged and annotated, the booty of yet another of her impassioned skirmishes through the Moscow Centre archive, which until her return from the dead a few months before had, thanks to Haydon, lain mouldering for all of three long years. As she pulled them out, and smoothed the notes which she had pinned on them like markers in her paper-chase, she smiled that brimming smile of hers – Guillam again, for curiosity had obliged him to down tools and come and watch – and she was muttering 'there you little devil' and 'now where did *you* get to, you wretch?' not to Smiley or Guillam, of course, but to the documents themselves, for Connie had the affectation of assuming everything was alive and potentially recalcitrant, whether it was Trot her dog or a chair that obstructed her passage, or Moscow Centre, or finally Karla himself.

'A *guided tour*, darlings,' she announced, 'that's what Connie's been having. *Super* fun. Reminded me of Easter, when Mother hid painted eggs round the house and sent us gals off hunting for them.'

For perhaps three hours after that, interspersed with coffee and sandwiches and other unwanted treats which dark Fawn insisted on bringing to them, Guillam struggled to follow the twists and impulsions of Connie's extraordinary journey, to which her subsequent research had by now supplied the solid basis. She dealt Smiley papers as if they were playing cards, shoving them down and snatching them back with her crumpled hands almost before he had had a chance to read them. Over it all she was keeping up what Guillam called 'her fifth-rate conjurer's patter', the abracadabra of the obsessive burrower's trade. At the heart of her discovery, so far as Guillam could make out, lay what Connie called a Moscow Centre *goldseam*; a Soviet laundering operation to move clandestine funds into open-air channels. The charting of it was not complete. Israeli liaison had supplied one section, the Cousins another, Steve Mackelvore, head resident in Paris, now dead, a third. From Paris the trail turned East, by way of the Banque de l'Indochine. At this point also, the papers had been put up to Haydon's London Station, as the operational directorate was called, together with a recommendation from the Circus's depleted Soviet Research Section that the case be thrown open to full-scale enquiry in the field. London Station killed the suggestion stone dead.

'Potentially prejudicial to a highly delicate source,' wrote one of Haydon's minions, and that was that.

'File and forget,' Smiley muttered, distractedly turning pages. 'File and forget. We always have good reasons for doing nothing.'

Outside, the world was fast asleep.

'*Exactly*, dear,' said Connie very softly, as if she were afraid to wake him.

Files and folders were by then strewn all over the throne-room. The scene looked a lot more like a disaster than a triumph. For an hour longer, Guillam and Connie gazed silently into space or at Karla's photograph while Smiley conscientiously retraced her steps, his anxious face stooped to the reading lamp, its pudgy lines accentuated by the beam, his hands skipping over the papers, and occasionally lifting to his mouth so that he could lick his thumb. Once or twice he started to glance at her, or open his mouth to speak, but Connie had the answer ready before he put his question. In her mind, she was walking beside him along the path. When he had finished, he sat back, and took off his spectacles and polished them, not on the fat end of the tie for once, but on a new silk handkerchief in the top pocket of his black jacket, for he had spent most of the day cloistered with the Cousins on another fence-mending mission. While he did this, Connie beamed at Guillam and mouthed '*isn't he a love?*' – a favourite dictum when she was talking of her Chief, which drove Guillam nearly mad with rage.

Smiley's next utterance had the ring of mild objection.

'All the same, Con, a formal search request *did* go out from London Station to our residency in Vientiane.'

'Happened before Bill had time to get his hoof on it,' she replied.

Not seeming to hear, Smiley picked up an open file and held it to her across the desk.

'And Vientiane *did* send a lengthy reply. It's all marked up in the index. We don't seem to have that. Where is it?'

Connie had not bothered to receive the offered file.

'In the *shredder*, darling,' she said, and beamed contentedly at Guillam.

The morning had come. Guillam strolled round switching out the lights. The same afternoon, he dropped in at the quiet West End gaming club where, in the permanent night-time of his elected trade, Sam Collins endured the rigours of retirement. Expecting to find him overseeing his usual afternoon game of chemin-de-fer, Guillam was surprised at being shown to a sumptuous room marked 'management'. Sam was roosting behind a fine desk, smiling prosperously through the smoke of his habitual brown cigarette.

'What the hell have you done, Sam?' Guillam demanded in a stage whisper, affecting to look round nervously. 'Taken over the Mafia? Jesus!'

'Oh that wasn't necessary,' said Sam with the same raffish smile. Slipping a mackintosh over his dinner jacket, he led Guillam down a passage and through a fire door into the street, where the two men hopped into the back of Guillam's waiting cab, while Guillam still secretly marvelled at Sam's newfound eminence.

Fieldmen have different ways of showing no emotion and Sam's was to smile, smoke slower, and fill his eyes with a dark glow of particular indulgence, fixing them intently on his partner in discussion. Sam was an Asian hand, old Circus, with a lot of time behind him in the field: five years in Borneo, six in Burma, five more in Northern Thailand and latterly three in the Laotian capital of Vientiane, all under natural cover as a general trader. The Thais had sweated him twice but let him go, he'd had to leave Sarawak in his socks. When he was in the mood, he had stories to tell about his journeying among the northern hill tribes of Burma and the Shans, but he was seldom in the mood. Sam was a Haydon casualty. There had been a moment, five years back, when Sam's lazy brilliance had made him a serious contender for promotion to the fifth floor – even, said some, to the post of Chief itself, had not Haydon put his weight behind the preposterous Percy Alleline. So, in place of power, Sam was left to moulder in the field until Haydon contrived to recall him, and have him sacked for a trumped-up misdemeanour.

'Sam! How good of you! Take a pew,' said Smiley, all conviviality for once. 'Will you drink? Where are you in your day? Perhaps we should be offering you breakfast?'

At Cambridge, Sam had taken a dazzling First, thus confounding his tutors, who till then had dismissed him as a near idiot. He had done it, the dons afterwards told each other consolingly, entirely on memory. The more worldly tongues told a different tale, however. According to them, Sam had trailed a love affair with a plain girl at the Examination Schools, and obtained from her, among other favours, a preview of the papers.

Chapter 4

THE CASTLE WAKES

Now at first Smiley tested the water with Sam – and Sam, who liked a poker hand himself, tested the water with Smiley. Some fieldmen, and particularly the clever ones, take a perverse pride in not knowing the whole picture. Their art consists in the deft handling of loose ends, and stops there stubbornly. Sam was inclined that way. Having raked a little in his dossier, Smiley tried him out on several old cases which had no sinister look at all, but which gave a clue to Sam's present disposition and confirmed his ability to remember accurately. He received Sam alone because with other people present it would have been a different game: either more or less intense, but different. Later, when the story was out in the open and only follow-up questions remained, he did summon Connie and Doc di Salis from the nether regions, and let Guillam sit in too. But that was later, and for the time being Smiley plumbed Sam's mind alone, concealing from him entirely the fact that all casepapers had been destroyed, and that since Mackelvore was dead, Sam was at present the only witness to certain key events.

'Now Sam, do you remember at all,' Smiley asked, when he finally judged the moment right, 'a request that came in to you in Vientiane once, from here in London, concerning certain money drafts from Paris? Just a standard request it would have been, asking for "unattributable field enquiries, please, to confirm or deny" – that sort of thing. Ring a bell by any chance?'

He had a sheet of notes before him, so that this was just

one more question in a slow stream. As he spoke, he was actually marking something with his pencil, not looking at Sam at all. But in the same way that we hear better with our eyes closed, Smiley did sense Sam's attention harden: which is to say, Sam stretched out his legs a little, and crossed them and slowed his gestures almost to a halt.

'Monthly transfers to the Banque de l'Indochine,' said Sam, after a suitable pause. 'Hefty ones. Paid out of a Canadian overseas account with their Paris affiliate.' He gave the number of the account. 'Payment made on the last Friday of every month. Start date January seventy-three or thereabouts. It rings a bell, sure.'

Smiley detected immediately that Sam was settling to a long game. His memory was clear but his information meagre: more like an opening bid than a frank reply.

Still stooped over the papers, Smiley said: 'Now can we just wander over the course here a little, Sam. There's some discrepancy on the filing side, and I'd like to get your part of the record straight.'

'Sure,' said Sam again and drew comfortably on his brown cigarette. He was watching Smiley's hands, and occasionally, with studied idleness, his eyes – though never for too long. Whereas Smiley, for his part, fought only to keep his mind open to the devious options of a fieldman's life. Sam might easily be defending something quite irrelevant. He had fiddled a little bit on his expenses, for example, and was afraid he'd been caught out. He had fabricated his report rather than go out and risk his neck: Sam was of an age, after all, where a fieldman looks first to his own skin. Or it was the opposite situation: Sam had ranged a little wider in his enquiries than Head Office had sanctioned. Hard pressed, he had gone to the pedlars rather than file a nil return. He had fixed himself a side-deal with the local Cousins. Or the local security services had blackmailed him – in Sarratt jargon, the angels had put a burn on him – and he had played the case both ways in order to survive and smile and keep his Circus pension. To read Sam's moves, Smiley knew that he must stay alert to these and countless other options. A desk is a dangerous place from which to watch the world.

So, as Smiley proposed, they wandered. London's request for field enquiries, said Sam, reached him in standard form, much as Smiley had described. It was shown to him by old Mac who, until his Paris posting, was the Circus's linkman in the Vientiane Embassy. An evening session at their safe house. Routine, though the Russian aspect stuck out from the start, and Sam actually remembered saying to Mac that early: 'London must think it's Moscow Centre reptile money,' because he had spotted the cryptonym of the Circus's Soviet Research Section mixed in with the prelims on the signal. (Smiley noted that Mac had no business showing Sam the signal.) Sam also remembered Mac's reply to his observation: 'They should never have given old Connie Sachs the shove,' he had said. Sam had agreed whole-heartedly.

As it happened, said Sam, the request was pretty easy to meet. Sam already had a contact at the Indochine, a good one, call him Johnny.

'Filed here, Sam?' Smiley enquired politely.

Sam avoided answering that question directly and Smiley respected his reluctance. The fieldman who files all his contacts with Head Office, or even clears them, was not yet born. As illusionists cling to their mystique, so fieldmen for different reasons are congenitally secretive about their sources.

Johnny was reliable, said Sam emphatically. He had an excellent track record on several arms-dealing and narcotics cases, and Sam would swear by him anywhere.

'Oh, you handled those things too, did you, Sam?' Smiley asked respectfully.

So Sam had moonlighted for the local narcotics bureau on the side, Smiley noted. A lot of fieldmen did that, some even with Head Office consent: in their world, they likened it to selling off industrial waste. It was a perk. Nothing dramatic, therefore, but Smiley stored away the information all the same.

'Johnny was okay,' Sam repeated, with a warning in his voice.

'I'm sure he was,' said Smiley with the same courtesy.

Sam continued with his story. He had called on Johnny at the Indochine and sold him a cock-and-bull cover to keep him quiet, and a few days later, Johnny, who was just a humble counter-clerk, had checked the ledgers and unearthed the dockets and Sam had the first leg of the connection cut and dried. The routine went this way, said Sam:

'On the last Friday of each month a telexed money order arrived from Paris to the credit of a Monsieur Delassus presently staying at the Hotel Condor, Vientiane, payable on production of passport, number quoted.' Once again, Sam effortlessly recited the figures. 'The bank sent out the advice, Delassus called first thing on the Monday, drew the money in cash, stuffed it in a briefcase and walked out with it. End of connection,' said Sam.

'How much?'

'Started small and grew fast. Then went on growing, then grew a little more.'

'Ending where?'

'Twenty-five thousand US in big ones,' said Sam without a flicker.

Smiley's eyebrows lifted slightly. 'A month?' he said, in humorous surprise.

'The big table,' Sam agreed and lapsed into a leisurely silence. There is a particular intensity about clever men whose brains are under-used, and sometimes there is no way they can control their emanations. In that sense, they are a great deal more at risk, under the bright lights, than their more stupid colleagues. 'You checking me against the record, old boy?' Sam asked.

'I'm not checking you against anything, Sam. You know how it is at times like this. Clutching at straws, listening to the wind.'

'Sure,' said Sam sympathetically and, when they had exchanged further glances of mutual confidence, once more resumed his narrative.

So Sam checked at the Hotel Condor, he said. The porter there was a stock sub-source to the trade, everybody owned him. No Delassus staying there, but the front desk cheerfully admitted to receiving a little something for providing him with an accommodation address. The very next Monday – which happened to follow the last Friday of the month, said Sam – with the help of his contact Johnny, Sam duly hung around the bank 'cashing travellers' cheques and whatnot', and had a grandstand view of the said Monsieur Delassus marching in, handing over his French passport, counting the money into a briefcase and retreating with it to a waiting taxi.

Taxis, Sam explained, were rare beasts in Vientiane. Anyone who was anyone had a car and a driver, so the presumption was that Delassus didn't want to be anyone.

'So far so good,' Sam concluded, watching with interest while Smiley wrote.

'So far so *very* good,' Smiley corrected him. Like his predecessor Control, Smiley never used pads: just single sheets of paper, one at a time, and a glass top to press on, which Fawn polished twice a day.

'Do I fit the record or do I deviate?' asked Sam.

'I'd say you were right on course, Sam,' Smiley said. 'It's the *detail* I'm enjoying. You know how it is with records.'

The same evening, Sam said, hugger-mugger with his linkman Mac once more, he took a long cool look at the rogues' gallery of local Russians, and was able to identify the unlovely features of a Second Secretary (Commercial) at the Soviet Embassy, Vientiane, mid-fifties, military bearing, no previous convictions, full names given but unpronounceable and known therefore around the diplomatic bazaars as 'Commercial Boris'.

But Sam, of course, had the unpronounceable names ready in his head and spelt them out for Smiley slowly enough for him to write them down in block capitals.

'Got it?' he enquired helpfully.

'Thank you, yes.'

'Somebody left the card index on a bus, have they, old boy?' Sam asked.

'That's right,' Smiley agreed, with a laugh.

When the crucial Monday came round again a month later, Sam went on, he decided he would tread wary. So instead of gum-shoeing after Commercial Boris himself he stayed home and briefed a couple of locally based leash-dogs who specialised in pavement work.

'A lace curtain job,' said Sam. 'No shaking the tree, no branch lines, no nothing, Laotian boys.'

'Our own?'

'Three years at the mast,' said Sam. 'And *good*,' added the fieldman in him, for whom all his geese are swans.

The said leashdogs watched the briefcase on its next journey. The taxi, a different one from the month before, took Boris on a tour of the town and after half an hour dropped him back near the main square, not far from the Indochine. Commercial Boris walked a short distance, ducked into a second bank, a local one, and paid the entire sum straight across the counter to the credit of another account.

'So tra-la,' said Sam, and lit a fresh cigarette, not bothering to conceal his amused bewilderment that Smiley was rehearsing verbally a case so fully documented.

'Tra-la indeed,' Smiley murmured, writing hard.

After that, said Sam, they were home and dry. Sam lay low for a couple of weeks to let the dust settle, then put in his girl assistant to deliver the final blow.

'Name?'

Sam gave it. A home-based senior girl, Sarratt-trained, sharing his commercial cover. This senior girl waited ahead of Boris in the local bank, let him complete his paying-in forms, then raised a small scene.

'How did she do that, Sam?' Smiley enquired.

'Demanded to be served first,' said Sam with a grin. 'Brother Boris being a male chauvinist pig, thought he had equal rights and objected. Words passed.'

The paying-in slip lay on the counter, said Sam, and while the senior girl did her number she read it upside down: twenty-five thousand American dollars to the credit of the overseas account of a mickey-mouse aviation company called Indocharter Vientiane, SA: 'Assets, a handful of clapped-out DC3s, a tin hut, a stack of fancy letter paper, one dumb blonde for the front office and wildcat Mexican pilot known round town as Tiny Ricardo on account of his considerable height,' said Sam. He added: 'And the usual anonymous bunch of diligent Chinese in the back room, of course.'

Smiley's ears were so sharp at that moment that he could have heard a leaf fall; but what he heard, metaphorically, was the sound of barriers being erected, and he knew at once, from the cadence, from the tightening of the voice, from the tiny facial and physical things which made up an exaggerated show of throwaway, that he was closing on the heart of Sam's defences.

So in his mind he put in a marker, deciding to remain with the micky-mouse aviation company for a while.

'Ah,' he said lightly, 'you mean you knew the firm already?'

Sam tossed out a small card. 'Vientiane's not exactly your giant metropolis, old boy.'

'But you knew of it? That's the point.'

'Everybody in town knew Tiny Ricardo,' said Sam, grinning more broadly than ever, and Smiley knew at once that Sam was throwing sand in his eyes. But he played Sam along all the same.

'So tell me about Ricardo,' he suggested.

'One of the ex-Air America clowns. Vientiane was stiff with them. Fought the secret war in Laos.'

'And lost it,' Smiley said, writing again.

'Single-handed,' Sam agreed, watching Smiley put aside one sheet and take another from his drawer. 'Ricardo was local legend. Flew with Captain Rocky and that crowd. Credited with a couple of joyrides into Yunnan province for the Cousins. When the war ended he kicked around a bit then took up with the Chinese. We used to call those outfits Air Opium. By the time Bill hauled me home they were a flourishing industry.'

Still Smiley let Sam run. As long as Sam thought he was leading Smiley from the scent, he would talk the hindlegs off a donkey; whereas if Sam thought Smiley was getting too close, he would put up the shutters at once.

'Fine,' he said amiably, therefore, after yet more careful writing. 'Now let's go back to what Sam did next, may we? We have the money, we know whom it's paid to, we know who handles it. What's your next move, Sam?'

Well, if Sam remembered rightly he took stock for a day or two. There were *angles*, Sam explained, gathering confidence: there were little things that caught the eye. First, you might say, there was the Strange Case of Commercial Boris. Boris, as Sam had indicated, was held to be a bona fide Russian diplomat, if such a thing existed: no known connection with any other firm. Yet he rode around alone, had sole signing rights over a pot of money, and in Sam's limited experience, either one of these things spelt *hood* on one hand.

'Not just hood, a blasted supremo. A red-toothed four-square paymaster, colonel or upwards, right?'

'What other *angles*, Sam?' Smiley asked, keeping Sam on the same long rein; still making no effort to go for what Sam regarded as the centre of things.

'The money wasn't mainstream,' said Sam. 'It was oddball. Mac said so. I said so. We all said so.'

Smiley's head lifted even more slowly than before.

'Why?' he asked, looking very straight at Sam.

'The above-the-line Soviet residency in Vientiane ran three bank accounts round town. The Cousins had all three wired. They've had them wired for years. They knew every cent the residency drew and even, from the account number, whether it was for intelligence gathering or subversion. The residency had its own money-carriers, and a triple-signature system for any drawing over a thousand bucks. Christ, George, I mean it's all in the record, you know!'

'Sam, I want you to pretend that record doesn't exist,' said Smiley gravely, still writing. 'All will be revealed to you in due season. Till then, bear with us.'

'Whatever you say,' said Sam, breathing much more easily, Smiley noticed: he seemed to feel he was on firmer ground.

It was at this point that Smiley proposed they get old Connie to come and lend an ear, and perhaps Doc di Salis too, since South East Asia was, after all, Doc's patch. Tactically, he was content to bide his time with Sam's little secret; and strategically, the force of Sam's story was already of burning interest. So Guillam was sent to whip them in while Smiley called a break and the two men stretched their legs.

'How's trade?' Sam asked politely.

'Well, a *little* depressed,' Smiley admitted. 'Miss it?'

'That's Karla is it?' said Sam, studying the photograph.

Smiley's tone became at once donnish and vague.

'Who? Ah yes, yes it is. Not much of a likeness I'm afraid, but the best we can do as yet.'

They might have been admiring an early water colour.

'You've got some personal thing about him, haven't you?' said Sam ruminatively.

At this point Connie, di Salis and Guillam filed in, led by Guillam, with little Fawn needlessly holding open the door.

With the enigma temporarily set aside, therefore, the meeting became something of a war party: the hunt was up. First Smiley recapitulated for Sam, incidentally making it clear in the process that they were *pretending* there were no records – which was a veiled warning to the newcomers. Then Sam took up the tale where he had left off: about the *angles*, the little things that caught the eye; though really, he insisted, there was not a lot more to say. Once the trail led to Indocharter, Vientiane SA, it stopped dead.

'Indocharter was an overseas Chinese company,' said Sam with a glance at Doc di Salis. 'Mainly Swatownese.'

At the name 'Swatownese' di Salis gave a cry, part laughter, part lament. 'Oh they're the *very* worst,' he declared – meaning, the most difficult to crack.

'It was an overseas Chinese outfit,' Sam repeated for the rest of them, 'and the loony bins of South East Asia are jam-packed with honest fieldmen who have tried to unravel the life-style of hot money once it entered the maw of the overseas Chinese.' Particularly, he added, of the Swatownese or Chiu Chow, who were a people apart, and controlled the rice monopolies in Thailand, Laos, and several other spots as well. Of which league, said Sam, Indocharter, Vientiane SA, was classic. His trade cover had evidently allowed him to investigate it in some depth.

'First, the *société anonyme* was registered in Paris,' he said. 'Second, the *société*, on reliable information, was the property of a discreetly diversified overseas Shanghainese trading company based on Manila, which was itself owned by a Chiu Chow company registered in Bangkok, which in turn paid its dues to a totally amorphous outfit in Hong Kong called China Airsea, quoted on the local Stock Exchange, which owned everything from junk-fleets to cement factories to racehorses to restaurants. China Airsea was by Hong Kong standards a blue chip trading house, long-established and in good standing,' said Sam, 'and probably the only connection between Indocharter and China Airsea was that somebody's fifth elder brother had an aunt who was at school with one of the shareholders and owed him a favour.'

Di Salis gave another swift, approving nod, and linking his awkward hands, thrust them over one crooked knee and drew it to his chin.

Smiley had closed his eyes and seemed to have dozed off. But in reality he was hearing precisely what he had expected to hear: when it came to the full staffing of the firm of Indocharter, Sam Collins trod very lightly round a certain personality.

'But I think you mentioned there were also two *non*-Chinese in the firm, Sam,' Smiley reminded him. 'A dumb blonde, you said, and a pilot, Ricardo.'

Sam lightly brushed the objection aside.

'Ricardo was a madcap March hare,' he said. 'The Chinese wouldn't have trusted him with the stamp money.

The real work was all done in the back room. If cash came in, that's where it was handled, that's where it was lost. Whether it was Russian cash, opium cash or whatever.'

Di Salis, pulling frantically at one ear-lobe, was prompt to agree: 'Reappearing at will in Vancouver, Amsterdam or Hong Kong or wherever it suited somebody's very Chinese purpose,' he declared, and writhed in pleasure at his own perception.

Once again, thought Smiley, Sam had got himself off the hook. 'Well, well,' he said. 'And how did it go from there, Sam, in your authorised version?'

'London scrubbed the case.'

From the dead silence, Sam must have realised in a second that he had touched a considerable nerve. His sign language indicated as much: for he did not peer round at their faces, or register any curiosity at all. Instead, out of a sort of theatrical modesty, he studied his shiny evening shoes and his elegant dress socks, and drew thoughtfully on his brown cigarette.

'When did they do that then, Sam?' asked Smiley.

Sam gave the date.

'Go back a little. Still forgetting the record, right? How much did London know of your enquiries as you went along? Tell us that. Did you send progress reports from day to day? Did Mac?'

If the mothers next door had set a bomb off, said Guillam afterwards, nobody would have taken his eyes off Sam.

Well, said Sam easily, as if humouring Smiley's whim, he was an old dog. His principle in the field had always been to do it first and apologise afterwards. Mac's too. Operate the other way round and soon you have London refusing to let you cross the street without changing your nappies first, said Sam.

'So?' said Smiley patiently.

So the first word they sent to London on the case was, you might say, their last. Mac acknowledged the enquiry, reported the sum of Sam's findings and asked for instructions.

'And London? What did London do, Sam?'

'Sent Mac a top priority shriek pulling us both off the case and ordering him to cable back immediately confirming I had understood and obeyed the order. For good measure they threw in a rocket telling us not to fly solo again.'

Guillam was doodling on the sheet of paper before him: a flower, then petals, then rain falling on the flower. Connie was beaming at Sam as if it were his wedding day, and her baby eyes were brimming tears of excitement. Di Salis, as usual, was jiggling and fiddling like an old engine, but his gaze also, as much as he could fix it anywhere, was upon Sam.

'You must have been rather cross,' said Smiley.

'Not really.'

'Didn't you have any wish to see the case through? You'd made a considerable strike.'

'I was irked, sure.'

'But you went along with London's instructions?'

'I'm a soldier, George. We all are in the field.'

'Very laudable,' said Smiley, considering Sam once more, how he lounged smooth and charming in his dinner jacket.

'Orders is orders,' said Sam, with a smile.

'Indeed. And when you eventually got back to London, I wonder,' Smiley went on, in a controlled, speculative way, 'and you had your "welcome-home-well-done" session with Bill, did you happen to mention the matter, casually, at all, to Bill?'

'Asked him what the hell he thought he was up to,' Sam agreed, just as leisurely.

'And what did Bill have to answer there, Sam?'

'Blamed the Cousins. Said they had got in on the act ahead of us. Said it was their case and their parish.'

'Had you any reason to believe that?'

'Sure. Ricardo.'

'You guessed he was the Cousins' man?'

'He'd flown for them. He was on their books already.

He was a natural. All they had to do was keep him in play.'

'I thought we were agreed that a man like Ricardo would have no access to the real operations of the company?'

'Wouldn't stop them using him. Not the Cousins. Still be their case, even if Ricardo was a bummer. The hands-off pact would apply either way.'

'Let's go back to the moment when London pulled you off the case. You received the order, "Drop everything." You obeyed. But it was some while yet before you returned to London, wasn't it? Was there an aftermath of any kind?'

'Don't quite follow you, old boy.'

Once again, at the back of his mind, Smiley made a scrupulous record of Sam's evasion.

'For example your friendly contact at the Banque de l'Indochine. Johnny. You kept up with him, of course?'

'Sure,' said Sam.

'And did Johnny happen to mention to you, as a matter of history, what happened to the goldseam after you'd received your hands-off telegram? Did it continue to come in month by month, just as it had before?'

'Stopped dead. Paris turned the tap off. No Indocharter, no nothing.'

'And Commercial Boris, of no previous convictions? Does he live happily ever after?'

'Went home.'

'Was he due to?'

'Done three years.'

'They usually do more.'

'Specially the hoods,' Sam agreed, smiling.

'And Ricardo, the madcap Mexican flyer whom you suspect of being the Cousins' agent: what became of him?'

'Died,' said Sam, eyes on Smiley all the while. 'Crashed up on the Thai border. The boys put it down to an overload of heroin.'

Pressed, Sam had that date, too.

'Was there moaning at the bar about that, so to speak?'

'Not much. General feeling seemed to be that Vientiane would be a safer place without Ricardo emptying his pistol through the ceiling of the White Rose or Madame Lulu's.'

'Where was that feeling expressed, Sam?'

'Oh, at Maurice's place.'

'Maurice?'

'Constellation Hotel. Maurice is the proprietor.'

'I see. Thank you.'

Here there was a definite gap, but Smiley seemed disinclined to fill it. Watched by Sam and his three assistants and Fawn the factotum, Smiley plucked at his spectacles, tilted them, straightened them and returned his hands to the glass top desk. Then he took Sam all the way through the story again, rechecked dates and names and places, very laboriously in the way of trained interrogators the world over, listening by long habit for the tiny flaws and the chance discrepancies and the omissions and the changes of emphasis, and apparently not finding any. And Sam, in his sense of false security, let it all happen, watching with the same blank smile with which he watched cards slip across the baize, or the roulette wheel tease the white ball from one bay to another.

'Sam, I wonder whether you could possibly manage to stay the night with us?' Smiley said, when they were once more just the two of them. 'Fawn will do you a bed and so on. Do you think you could swing that with your club?'

'My dear fellow,' said Sam generously.

Then Smiley did a rather unnerving thing. Having handed Sam a bunch of magazines, he phoned for Sam's personal dossier, all volumes, and with Sam sitting there before him he read them in silence from cover to cover.

'I see you're a ladies' man,' he remarked at last, as the dusk gathered at the window.

'Here and there,' Sam agreed, still smiling. 'Here and there.' But the nervousness was quite apparent in his voice.

* * *

When night came, Smiley sent the mothers home and issued orders through Housekeeping Section to have archives cleared of all burrowers by eight at the latest. He gave no reason. He let them think what they wanted. Sam should lie up in the rumpus room to be on call, and Fawn should keep him company and not let him stray. Fawn took this instruction literally. Even when the hours dragged out and Sam appeared to doze, Fawn stayed folded like a cat across the threshold, but with his eyes always open.

Then the four of them cloistered themselves in Registry – Connie, di Salis, Smiley and Guillam – and began the long, cautious paperchase. They looked first for the operational casepapers which properly should have been housed in the South East Asian cut, under the dates Sam had given them. There was no card in the index and there were no casepapers either, but this was not yet significant. Haydon's London Station had been in the habit of waylaying operational files and confining them to its own restricted archive. So they plodded across the basement, feet clapping on the brown linoleum tiles, till they came to a barred alcove like an antechapel where the remains of what was formerly London Station's archive were laid to rest. Once again they found no card, and no papers.

'Look for the telegrams,' Smiley ordered, so they checked the signals ledgers, both incoming and outgoing, and for a moment Guillam at least was ready to suspect Sam of lying, till Connie pointed out that the relevant traffic sheets had been typed with a different typewriter: a machine, as it later turned out, which had not been acquired by housekeepers till six months after the date on the paper.

'Look for floats,' Smiley ordered.

Circus floats were duplicated copies of main serials which Registry ran off when casepapers threatened to be in constant action. They were banked in loose-leaf folders like back-numbers of magazines and indexed every six weeks. After much delving Connie Sachs unearthed the South East Asian folder covering the six-week period immediately following Collins's trace request. It contained no reference to a suspected Soviet goldseam and none to Indocharter, Vientiane SA.

'Try the PFs,' said Smiley, with a rare use of initials, which he otherwise detested. So they trailed to another corner of Registry and sorted through drawers of cards, looking first for personal files on Commercial Boris, then for Ricardo, then under aliases for Tiny, believed dead, whom Sam had apparently mentioned in his original ill-fated report to London Station. Now and then Guillam was sent upstairs to ask Sam some small point, and found him reading *Field* and sipping a large Scotch, watched unflinchingly by Fawn, who occasionally varied his routine – Guillam learned later – with press-ups, first on two knuckles of each hand, then on his fingertips. In the case of Ricardo they mapped out phonetic variations and ran them across the index also.

'Where are the organisations filed?' Smiley asked.

But of the *société anonyme* known as Indocharter, Vientiane, the organisations index contained no card either.

'Look up the liaison material.'

Dealings with the Cousins in Haydon's day were handled entirely through the London Station Liaison Secretariat, of which he himself for obvious reasons had personal command and which held its own file copies of all inter-service correspondence. Returning to the antechapel, they once more drew a blank. To Peter Guillam the night was taking on surreal dimensions. Smiley had become all but wordless. His plump face turned to rock. Connie, in her excitement, had forgotten her arthritic aches and pains and was hopping around the shelves like a teenager at the ball. Not by any means a born paper man Guillam scrambled after her pretending to keep up with the pack, and secretly grateful for his trips up to Sam.

'We've *got* him, George, darling,' Connie kept saying under her breath. 'Sure as boots we've *got* the beastly toad.'

Doc di Salis had danced away in search of Indocharter's Chinese directors – Sam, astonishingly, had the names of two still in his head – and was wrestling with these first in Chinese, then in Roman script, and finally in Chinese commercial code. Smiley sat in a chair reading the files on his knee like a man in a train, doughtily ignoring the passengers. Sometimes he lifted his head, but the sounds he heard were not from inside the room. Connie, on her own initiative, had launched a search for cross-references to files with which the casepapers should theoretically have been linked. There were subject files on mercenaries, and on freelance aviators. There were method files on Centre's techniques for laundering agent payments, and even a treatise, which she herself had written long ago, on the subject of below-the-line paymasters responsible for Karla's illegal networks functioning unbeknown to the mainstream residencies. Commercial Boris's unprounounceable last names had not been added to the appendix. There were background files on the Banque de l'Indochine and its links with the Moscow Narodny Bank, and statistical files on the growing scale of Centre's activities in South East Asia, and study files on the Vientiane residency itself. But the negatives only multiplied, and as they multiplied they proved the affirmative. Nowhere in their whole pursuit of Haydon had they come upon such a systematic and wholesale brushing-over of the traces. It was the backbearing of all time.

And it led inexorably east.

Only one clue that night pointed to the culprit. They came on it somewhere between dawn and morning while Guillam was dozing on his feet. Connie sniffed it out, Smiley laid it silently on the table, and three of them peered at it together under the reading light as if it were the clue to buried treasure: a clip of destruction certificates, a dozen in all, with the authorising cryptonym scribbled in black felt-tip along the middle line, giving a pleasing effect of charcoal. The condemned files related to 'top secret correspondence with H/Annexe' – that was to say, with the Cousins' Head of Station, then as now Smiley's Brother-in-Christ Martello. The reason for destruction was the same as that which Haydon had given to Sam

Collins for abandoning the field enquiries in Vientiane: '*Risk of compromising delicate American operation.*' The signature consigning the files to the incinerator was in Haydon's workname.

Returning upstairs, Smiley invited Sam once more to his room. Sam had removed his bow tie, and the stubble of his jaw against his open-necked white shirt made him a lot less smooth.

First, Smiley sent Fawn out for coffee. He let it arrive and he waited till Fawn had flitted away again before pouring two cups, black for both of them, sugar for Sam, a saccharine for Smiley on account of his weight problem. Then he settled in a soft chair at Sam's side rather than have a desk between them, in order to affiliate himself to Sam.

'Sam, I think I ought to hear a little about the girl,' he said, very softly, as if he were breaking sad news. 'Was it chivalry that made you miss her out?'

Sam seemed rather amused. 'Lost the files have you, old boy?' he enquired, with the same men's room intimacy.

Sometimes, in order to obtain a confidence, it is necessary to impart one.

'*Bill* lost them,' Smiley replied gently.

Elaborately, Sam lapsed into deep thought. Curling one card-player's hand he surveyed his fingertips, lamenting their grimy state.

'That club of mine practically runs itself these days', he reflected. 'I'm getting bored with it to be frank. Money, money. Time I had a change, made something of myself.'

Smiley understood, but he had to be firm.

'I've no resources, Sam. I can hardly feed the mouths I've hired already.'

Sam sipped his black coffee ruminatively, smiling through the steam.

'Who is she, Sam? What's it all about? No one minds how bad it is. It's water under the bridge, I promise you.'

Standing, Sam sank his hands in his pockets, shook his head, and rather as Jerry Westerby might have done, began meandering round the room, peering at the odd gloomy things that hung on the wall: group war photographs of dons in uniform; a framed and handwritten letter from a dead prime minister; Karla's portrait again, which this time he studied from very close, on and on.

'"Never throw your chips away,"' he remarked, so close to Karla that his breath dulled the glass. 'That's what my old mother used to tell me. "Never make a present of your assets. We get very few in life. Got to dole them out sparingly." Not as if there isn't a game going, is it?' he enquired. With his sleeve he wiped the glass clean. 'Very hungry mood prevails in this house of yours. Felt it the moment I walked in. The big table, I said to myself. Baby will eat tonight.'

Arriving at Smiley's desk, he sat himself in the chair as if testing it for comfort. The chair swivelled as well as rocked. Sam tried both movements. 'I need a search request,' he said.

'Top right,' said Smiley, and watched while Sam opened the drawer, pulled out a yellow flimsy and laid it on the glass to write.

For a couple of minutes, Sam composed in silence, pausing occasionally for artistic consideration, then writing again.

'Call me if she shows up,' he said and, with a facetious wave to Karla, made his exit.

When he had gone, Smiley took the form from the desk, sent for Guillam and handed it to him without a word. On the staircase Guillam paused to read the text.

'Worthington, Elizabeth alias Lizzie, alias Ricardo, Lizzie.' That was the top line. Then the details: 'Age about twenty-seven. Nationality British. Status, married, details of husband unknown, maiden name also unknown. 1972–3 common-law wife of Ricardo, Tiny, now dead. Last known place of residence Vientiane, Laos. Last known occupation: typist-receptionist with Indocharter Vientiane SA. Previous occupations: nightclub hostess, whisky saleswoman, high-class tart.'

Performing its usual dismal rôle these days Registry took about three minutes to regret 'no trace repeat no trace of subject'. Beyond this, the Queen Bee took issue with the term 'high-class'. She insisted that 'superior' was the proper way to describe that kind of tart.

Curiously enough, Smiley was not deterred by Sam's reticence. He seemed happy to accept it as part and parcel of the trade. Instead, he requested copies of all source reports which Sam had originated from Vientiane or elsewhere over the last ten years odd, and which had escaped Haydon's clever knife. And thereafter, in leisure hours, such as they were, he browsed through these, and allowed his questing imagination to form pictures of Sam's own murky world.

At this hanging moment in the affair, Smiley showed a quite lovely sense of tact, as all later agreed. A lesser man might have stormed round to the Cousins and asked as a matter of the highest urgency that Martello look out the American end of the destroyed correspondence and grant him a sight of it, but Smiley wanted nothing stirred, nothing signalled. So instead he chose his humblest emissary. Molly Meakin was a prim, pretty graduate, a little blue-stocking perhaps, a little inward, but already with a modest name as a capable desk officer, and Old Circus by virtue of both her brother and her father. At the time of the fall she was still a probationer, cutting her milk teeth in Registry. After it she was kept on as skeleton staff and promoted, if that is the word, to Vetting Section, whence no man, let alone woman, says the folklore, returns alive. But Molly possessed, perhaps by heredity, what the trade calls a natural eye. While those around her were still exchanging anecdotes about exactly where they were and what they were wearing when the news of Haydon's arrest was broken to them, Molly was setting up an unobtrusive and unofficial channel to her opposite number at the Annexe in Grosvenor Square, which by-passed the laborious procedures laid down by the Cousins since the fall. Her greatest ally was routine. Molly's visiting day was a Friday. Every Friday she drank coffee with Ed, who manned the computer; and talked classical music with

Marge, who doubled for Ed; and sometimes she stayed for old-tyme dancing or a game of shuffleboard or ten-pin bowling at the Twilight Club in the Annexe basement. Friday was also the day, quite incidentally, when she took along her little shopping-list of trace requests. Even if she had none outstanding, Molly was careful to invent some in order to keep the channel open, and on this particular Friday, at Smiley's behest, Molly Meakin included the name of Tiny Ricardo in her selection.

'But I don't want him sticking out in any way, Molly,' said Smiley anxiously.

'Of course not,' said Molly.

For smoke, as she called it, Molly chose a dozen other Rs and when she came to Ricardo she wrote down 'Richards query Rickard query Ricardo, profession teacher query aviation instructor,' so that the real Ricardo would only be thrown up as a possible identification. Nationality Mexican query Arab, she added: and she threw in the extra information that he might anyway be dead.

It was once more late in the evening before Molly returned to the Circus. Guillam was exhausted. Forty is a difficult age at which to stay awake, he decided. At twenty or at sixty the body knows what it's about, but forty is an adolescence where one sleeps to grow up or to stay young. Molly was twenty-three. She came straight to Smiley's room, sat down primly with her knees pressed tight together, and began unpacking her handbag, watched intently by Connie Sachs, and even more intently by Peter Guillam, though for different reasons. She was sorry she'd been so long, she said severely, but Ed had insisted on taking her to a re-run of *True Grit*, a great favourite in the Twilight Club, and afterwards she had had to fight him off, but hadn't wished to give offence, least of all tonight. She handed Smiley an envelope and he opened it, and drew out a long buff computer card. So did she fight him off or not? Guillam wanted to know.

'How did it play?' was Smiley's first question.

'Quite straightforward,' she replied.

'What an extraordinary-looking script,' Smiley exclaimed next. But as he went on reading his expression changed slowly to a rare and wolfish grin.

Connie was less restrained. By the time she had passed the card to Guillam, she was laughing outright.

'Oh *Bill*! Oh you wicked lovely man! Talk about pointing everybody in the wrong direction! Oh the devil!'

In order to silence the Cousins, Haydon had reversed his original lie. Deciphered, the lengthy computer printout told the following enchanting story.

Anxious lest the Cousins might have been duplicating the Circus's enquiries into the firm of Indocharter, Bill Haydon, in his capacity as Head of London Station, had sent to the Annexe a pro-forma hands-off notice, under the standing bilateral agreement between the services. This advised the Americans that Indocharter, Vientiane SA was presently under scrutiny by London and that the Circus had an agent in place. Accordingly, the Americans consented to drop any interest they might have in the case in exchange for a share of the eventual take. As an aid to the British operation, the Cousins did however mention that their link with the pilot Tiny Ricardo was extinct.

In short, as neat an example of playing both ends against the middle as anybody had met with.

'Thank you, Molly,' said Smiley politely, when everyone had had a chance to marvel. 'Thank you very much indeed.'

'Not at all,' said Molly, prim as a nursemaid. 'And Ricardo is definitely dead, Mr Smiley,' she ended, and she quoted the same date of death which Sam Collins had already supplied. With that, she snapped together the clasp of her handbag, pulled her skirt over her admirable knees, and walked delicately from the room, well observed once more by Peter Guillam.

A different pace, a different mood entirely, now overtook the Circus. The frantic search for a trail, any trail, was over. They could march to a purpose, rather than gallop in all directions. The amiable distinction between the two families largely fell away: the bolshies and the yellow perils became a single unit under the joint direction of Connie and the Doc, even if they kept their separate skills. Joy after that, for the burrowers, came in bits, like waterholes on a long and dusty trek, and sometimes they all but fell at the wayside. Connie took no more than a week to identify the Soviet paymaster in Vientiane who had supervised the transfer of funds to Indocharter, Vientiane SA – the Commercial Boris. He was the former soldier Zimin, a longstanding graduate of Karla's private training school outside Moscow. Under the previous alias of Smirnov, this Zimin was on record as having played paymaster to an East German *apparat* in Switzerland six years ago. Using the name Kursky, he had surfaced before that in Vienna. As a secondary skill he offered sound-stealing and entrapment, and some said he was the same Zimin who had sprung the successful honey-trap in West Berlin against a certain French senator who later sold half his country's secrets down the river. He had left Vientiane exactly a month after Sam's report had hit London.

After that small triumph, Connie set herself the apparently impossible task of defining what arrangements Karla, or his paymaster Zimin, might have made to replace the interrupted goldseam. Her touchstones were several. First, the known conservatism of enormous intelligence establishments, and their attachment to proven trade-routes. Second, Centre's presumed need, since large payments were involved, to replace the old system with a new one, fast. Third, Karla's complacency, both before the fall, when he had the Circus tethered, and since the fall, when it lay gasping and toothless at his feet. Lastly, quite simply, she relied upon her own encyclopaedic grasp of the subject. Gathering together the heaps of unprocessed raw material which had lain deliberately neglected during the years of her exile, Connie's team made huge arcs through the files, revised, conferred, drew charts and diagrams, pursued the individual handwriting of known operators, had migraines, argued, played ping-pong, and occasionally, with agonising caution, and Smiley's express consent, undertook timid investigations in the field. A friendly contact in the City was persuaded to visit an old acquaintance who specialised in off-shore Hong Kong companies. A Cheapside currency broker opened his books to Toby Esterhase, the sharp-eyed Hungarian survivor who was all that remained of the Circus's once glorious travelling army of couriers and pavement artists. So it went on, at a snail's pace: but at least the snail knew where it wanted to go. Doc di Salis, in his distant way, took the overseas Chinese path, working his passage through the arcane connections of Indocharter, Vientiane SA, and its elusive echelons of parent companies. His helpers were as uncommon as himself, either language students or elderly recycled China hands. With time they acquired a collective pallor, like inmates of the same dank seminary.

Meanwhile, Smiley himself advanced no less cautiously, if anything down yet more devious avenues, and through a greater number of doors.

Once more he sank from view. It was a time of waiting and he spent it in attending to the hundred other things that needed his urgent attention. His brief burst of teamwork over, he withdrew to the inner regions of his solitary world. Whitehall saw him; so did Bloomsbury still; so did the Cousins. At other times the throne-room door stayed closed for days at a time, and only dark Fawn the factotum was permitted to flit in and out in his gym-shoes, bearing steaming cups of coffee, plates of biscuits and occasional written memoranda, to or from his master. Smiley had always loathed the telephone, and now he would take no calls whatever, unless in Guillam's view they concerned matters of great urgency, and none did. The only instrument Smiley could not switch off controlled the direct line from Guillam's desk, but when he was in one of his moods he went so far as to put a teacosy over it in an effort to quell the ring. The invariable procedure was for Guillam to say that Smiley was out, or in conference, and would return the call in an hour's time. He then wrote out a message, handed it to Fawn, and eventually, with the initiative on his side, Smiley would ring back. He conferred with Connie, sometimes with di Salis, sometimes with both, but Guillam was not required. The Karla file was transferred from Connie's Research Section to Smiley's personal safe for good; all seven volumes. Guillam signed for them and took them in to him, and when Smiley lifted his eyes from the desk and saw them, the quiet of recognition came over him, and he reached forward as if to receive an old friend. The door closed again, and more days passed.

'Any word?' Smiley would ask occasionally of Guillam. He meant: 'Has Connie rung?'

The Hong Kong residency was evacuated around this time, and too late Smiley was advised of the housekeepers' elephantine efforts at repressing the High Haven story. He at once drew Craw's dossier, and again called Connie in for consultation. A few days later Craw himself appeared in London for a forty-eight-hour visit. Guillam had heard him lecture at Sarratt and detested him. A couple of weeks afterwards, the old man's celebrated article finally saw the light of day. Smiley read it intently, then passed it to Guillam, and for once he actually offered an explanation for his action: Karla would know very well what the Circus was up to, he said. Backbearings were a time-honoured pastime. However, Karla would not be human if he didn't sleep after such a big kill.

'I want him to hear from everyone just how dead we are,' Smiley explained.

Soon this broken-wing technique was extended to other spheres, and one of Guillam's more entertaining tasks was to make sure that Roddy Martindale was well supplied with woeful stories about the Circus's disarray.

And still the burrowers toiled. They called it afterwards the phoney peace. They had the map, Connie said later, and they had the directions, but there were still mountains to be moved in spoonfuls. Waiting, Guillam took Molly Meakin to long and costly dinners but they ended inconclusively. He played squash with her and admired her eye, he swam with her and admired her body, but she warded off closer contact with a mysterious and private smile, turning her head away and downward while she went on holding him.

Under the continued pressure of idleness Fawn the factotum took to acting strangely. When Smiley disappeared and left him behind, he literally pined for his master's return. Catching him by surprise in his little den one evening, Guillam was shocked to find him in a near foetal crouch, winding a handkerchief round and round his thumb like a ligature, in order to hurt himself.

'For God's sake, it's nothing personal, man!' Guillam cried. 'George doesn't need you for once, that's all. Take a few days' leave or something. Cool off.'

But Fawn referred to Smiley as the Chief, and looked askance at those who called him George.

It was toward the end of this barren phase that a new and wonderful gadget appeared on the fifth floor. It was brought in suitcases by two crewcut technicians and installed over three days: a green telephone destined, despite his prejudices, for Smiley's desk and connecting him directly with the Annexe. It was routed by way of Guillam's room, and linked to all manner of anonymous grey boxes which hummed without warning. Its presence only deepened the general mood of nervousness: what use was a machine, they asked each other, if they had nothing to put into it?

But they had something.

Suddenly the word was out. What Connie had found she wasn't saying, but news of the discovery ran like wildfire through the building: 'Connie's *home*! The burrowers are *home*! They've found the new goldseam! They've traced it all the way through!'

Through what? To whom? Where did it end? Connie and di Salis still kept mum. For a day and a night they trailed in and out of the throne-room laden with files, no doubt once more in order to show Smiley their workings.

Then Smiley disappeared for three days and Guillam only learned much later that 'in order to screw down every bolt' as he called it, he had visited both Hamburg and Amsterdam for discussions with certain eminent bankers of his acquaintance. These gentlemen spent a great while explaining to him that the war was over and they could not possibly offend against their code of ethics, and then they gave him the information he so badly needed: though it was only the final confirmation of all that the burrowers had deduced. Smiley returned, but Peter Guillam still remained shut out, and he might well have continued in this private limbo indefinitely, had it not been for dinner at the Lacons.

Guillam's inclusion was pure chance. So was the dinner. Smiley had asked Lacon for an afternoon appointment at the Cabinet Office, and spent several hours in cahoots with Connie and di Salis preparing for it. At the last moment Lacon was summoned by his parliamentary masters, and proposed pot-luck at his ugly mansion at Ascot instead. Smiley detested driving and there was no duty car. In the end, Guillam offered to chauffeur him in his draughty old Porsche, having first put a rug over him which he was keeping in case Molly Meakin consented to a picnic. On the drive, Smiley attempted small-talk, which came hard to him, but he was nervous. They arrived in rain and there was muddle on the doorstep about what to do with the unexpected underling. Smiley insisted that Guillam would make his own way and return at ten-thirty: the Lacons that he *must* stay, there was simply *masses* of food.

'It's up to you,' said Guillam to Smiley.

'Oh, of course. No I mean really, if it's all right with the Lacons, naturally,' said Smiley huffily and in they went.

So a fourth place was laid, and the overcooked steak was cut into bits till it looked like dry stew, and a daughter was despatched on her bicycle with a pound to fetch a second bottle of wine from the pub up the road. Mrs Lacon was doe-like and fair and blushing, a child bride who had become a child mother. The table was too long for four. She set Smiley and her husband one end and Guillam next to her. Having asked him whether he liked madrigals, she embarked on an endless account of a concert at her daughter's private school. She said it was absolutely *ruined* by the rich foreigners they were taking in to balance the books. Half of them couldn't sing in a Western way at all:

'I mean who wants one's child brought up with a lot of Persians when they all have six wives apiece?' she said.

Stringing her along, Guillam strove to catch the dialogue at the other end of the table. Lacon seemed to be bowling and batting at once.

'First, you petition *me*,' he boomed. 'You are doing that now, very properly. At this stage, you should give no more than a preliminary outline. Traditionally Ministers like nothing that cannot be written on a postcard. Preferably a *picture* postcard,' he said, and took a prim sip at the vile red wine.

Mrs Lacon, whose intolerance had a beatific innocence about it, began complaining about Jews.

'I mean they don't even eat the same *food* as we do,' she said. 'Penny says they get special herring things for lunch.'

Guillam again lost the thread till Lacon raised his voice in warning.

'Try to keep *Karla* out of this, George. I've asked you before. Learn to say *Moscow* instead, will you? They don't like personalities – however dispassionate your hatred of him. Nor do I.'

'Moscow then,' Smiley said.

'It's not that one *dislikes* them,' Mrs Lacon said. 'They're just different.'

Lacon picked up some earlier point. 'When you say a *large* sum, how large is large?'

'We are not yet in a position to say,' Smiley replied.

'Good. More enticing. Have you no panic factor?'

Smiley didn't follow that question any better than Guillam.

'What alarms you most about your discovery, George? What do you fear for, here, in your rôle of watchdog?'

'The security of a British Crown Colony?' Smiley suggested, after some thought.

'They're talking about Hong Kong,' Mrs Lacon

explained to Guillam. 'My uncle was Political Secretary. On Daddy's side,' she added. 'Mummy's brothers never did anything brainy at all.'

She said Hong Kong was nice but smelly.

Lacon had become a little pink and erratic. 'Colony – my God, hear that, Val?' he called down the table, taking time off to educate her. 'Richer than we are by half, I should think and, from where *I* sit, enviably more secure as well. A full twenty years their Treaty has to run, even if the Chinese enforce it. At this rate, they should see us out in comfort!'

'Oliver thinks we're *doomed*,' Mrs Lacon explained to Guillam excitedly, as if she were admitting him to a family secret, and shot her husband an angelic smile.

Lacon resumed his former confiding tone, but he continued to blurt and Guillam guessed he was showing off to his squaw.

'You would also make the point to me, wouldn't you – as background to the postcard as it were – that a major Soviet intelligence presence in Hong Kong would be appalling embarrassment to the Colonial government in her relations with Peking?'

'Before I went as far as that – '

'On whose magnanimity,' Lacon pursued, 'she depends from hour to hour for her survival, correct?'

'It's because of these very implications – ' Smiley said.

'Oh Penny, you're naked!' Mrs Lacon cried indulgently.

Providing Guillam with a glorious respite, she bounded off to calm an unruly small daughter who had appeared at the doorway. Lacon meanwhile had filled his lungs for an aria.

'We are therefore not only protecting Hong Kong from the *Russians* – which is bad enough, I grant you, but perhaps not *quite* bad enough for some of our higher-minded Ministers – we are protecting her from the wrath of Peking, which is universally held to be awful, right Guillam? *However* – ' said Lacon, and to emphasise the *volte face* went so far as to arrest Smiley's arm with his long hand so that he had to put down his glass – '*however*,' he warned, as his erratic voice swooped and rose again, 'whether our masters will swallow all that is quite another matter altogether.'

'I would not consider asking them to until I had obtained corroboration of our data,' Smiley said sharply.

'Ah, but you can't, can you?' Lacon objected, changing hats. 'You can't go beyond domestic research. You haven't the charter.'

'Without a reconnaissance of the information – '

'Ah, but what does that *mean*, George?'

'Putting in an agent.'

Lacon lifted his eyebrows and turned away his head, reminding Guillam irresistibly of Molly Meakin.

'Method is not my affair, nor are the details. Clearly you can do nothing to embarrass since you have no money and no resources.' He poured more wine, spilling some. 'Val!' he yelled. 'Cloth!'

'I do have *some* money.'

'But not for that purpose.' The wine had stained the tablecloth. Guillam poured salt on it while Lacon lifted the cloth and shoved his napkin ring under it to spare the polish.

A long silence followed, broken by the slow pat of wine falling on the parquet floor. Finally Lacon said: 'It is entirely up to you to define what is chargeable under your mandate.'

'May I have that in writing?'

'No, sir.'

'May I have your authority to take what steps are needed to corroborate the information?'

'No, sir.'

'But you won't block me?'

'Since I know nothing of method, and am not required to, it is hardly my province to dictate to you.'

'But since I make a formal approach – ' Smiley began.

Val, *do* bring a cloth! Once you make a formal approach I shall wash my hands of you entirely. It is the Intelligence Steering Group, not myself, who determines your scope of action. You will make your pitch. They will hear you out. From then on it's between you and them. I am just the midwife. Val, bring a cloth, it's everywhere!'

'Oh, it's my head on the block, not yours,' said Smiley, almost to himself. 'You're impartial. I know all about that.'

'*Oliver's* not impartial,' said Mrs Lacon gaily as she returned with the girl over her shoulder, brushed and wearing a nightdress. 'He's *terrifically* in favour of you, aren't you, Olly?' She handed Lacon a cloth and he began mopping. 'He's become a real *hawk* these days. Better than the Americans. Now say good night to everyone, Penny, come on.' She was offering the child to each of them in turn. 'Mr Smiley first . . . Mr Guillam, now Daddy . . . How's Ann, George, not off to the country again, I hope?'

'Oh very bonny, thank you.'

'Well, make Oliver give you what you want. He's getting *terribly* pompous, aren't you, Olly?'

She danced off, chanting her own rituals to the child.

'Hitty-pitty *without* the wall . . . hitty-pitty *within* the wall . . . and *bumps* goes Pottifer!'

Lacon proudly watched her go.

'Now, will you bring the Americans into it, George?' he demanded airily. 'That's a great catchpenny, you know. Wheel in the Cousins and you'd carry the committee without a shot fired. Foreign Office would eat out of your hand.'

'I would prefer to stay my hand on that.'

The green telephone, thought Guillam, might never have existed.

Lacon ruminated, twiddling his glass.

'Pity,' he pronounced finally. 'Pity. No Cousins, no panic factor . . .' He gazed at the dumpy, unimpressive figure before him. Smiley sat, hands linked, eyes closed, seemingly half asleep. 'And no credibility either,' Lacon went on, apparently as a direct comment upon Smiley's appearance. 'Defence won't lift a finger for you, I'll tell you that for a start. Nor will the Home Office. The Treasury's a toss-up, and the Foreign Office – depends who they send to the meeting and what they had for breakfast.' Again he reflected. 'George.'

'Yes?'

'Let me send you an advocate. Somebody who can ride point for you, draft your submission, carry it to the barricades.'

'Oh I think I can manage, thank you!'

'Make him rest more,' Lacon advised Guillam in a deafening whisper as they walked to the car. 'And try and get him to drop those black jackets and stuff. They went out with bustles. Goodbye, George! Ring me tomorrow if you change your mind and want help. Now drive carefully, Guillam. Remember you've been drinking.'

As they passed through the gates Guillam said something very rude indeed but Smiley was too deep inside the rug to hear.

'So it's Hong Kong then?' Guillam said, as they drove.

No answer, but no denial either.

'And who's the lucky fieldman?' Guillam asked, a little later, with no real hope of getting an answer. 'Or is that all part of foxing around with the Cousins?'

'We're not foxing around with them at all,' Smiley retorted, stung for once. 'If we cut them in, they'll swamp us. If we don't, we've no resources. It's simply a matter of balance.'

Smiley dived back into the rug.

But the very next day, lo and behold, they were ready.

At ten, Smiley convened an operational directorate. Smiley talked, Connie talked, di Salis fidgeted and scratched himself like a verminous court tutor in a Restoration comedy, till it was his own turn to speak out, in his cracked, clever voice. The same evening still, Smiley sent his telegram to Italy: a real one, not just a signal, codeword Guardian, copy to the fast growing file. Smiley wrote it out, Guillam gave it to Fawn, who whisked it off triumphantly to the all-night post office at Charing Cross. From the air of ceremony with which Fawn departed, one might have supposed that the little buff form was the highest point so far of his sheltered life. This was not so. Before the fall, Fawn had worked under Guillam as a scalp-hunter based in Brixton. By actual trade, though, he was a silent killer.

Chapter 5

A Walk In The Park

Throughout that whole sunny week Jerry Westerby's leave-taking had a bustling, festive air which never once let up. If London was holding its summer late, then so, one might have thought, was Jerry. Stepmothers, vaccinations, travel touts, literary agents and Fleet Street editors; Jerry, though he loathed London like the pest, took them all in his cheery pounding stride. He even had a London persona to go with the buckskin boots: his suit, not Savile Row exactly, but a suit undeniably. His prison gear, as the orphan called it, was a washable, blue-faded affair, the creation of a twenty-four-hour tailor named 'Pontschak Happy House of Bangkok', who guaranteed it *unwrinkable* in radiant silk letters on the tag. In the mild midday breezes it billowed as weightlessly as a frock on Brighton pier. His silk shirt from the same source had a yellowed, locker-room look recalling Wimbledon or Henley. His tan, though Tuscan, was as English as the famous cricketing tie which flew from him like a patriotic flag. Only his expression, to the very discerning, had that certain watchfulness, which also Mama Stefano the post-mistress had noticed, and which the instinct describes as 'professional', and leaves at that. Sometimes, if he anticipated waiting, he carted the book-sack with him, which gave him a bumpkin air: Dick Whittington had come to town.

He was based, if anywhere, in Thurloe Square where he lodged with his stepmother, the third Lady Westerby, in a tiny frilly flat crammed with huge antiques salvaged from abandoned houses. She was a painted, hen-like woman, snappish as old beauties sometimes are, and would often curse him for real or imagined crimes, such as smoking her last cigarette, or bringing in mud from his caged rambles in the park. Jerry took it all in good part. Sometimes, returning as late as three or four in the morning but still not sleepy, he would hammer on her door to wake her, though most often she was awake already; and when she had put on her make-up, he set her on his bed in her frou-frou dressing gown with a king-sized *crême de menthe frappée* in her little claw, while Jerry himself sprawled over the whole floor-space, among a magic mountain of junk, getting on with what he called his packing. The mountain was made of everything that was useless: old press cuttings, heaps of yellowed newspapers, legal deeds tied in green ribbon, and even a pair of custom-made riding boots, tree'd, but green with mildew. In theory Jerry was deciding what he would need of all this for his journey, but he seldom got much further than a keepsake of some kind, which set the two of them on a chain of memories. One night for example he unearthed an album of his earliest stories.

'Hey Pet, here's a good one! Westerby really rips the mask off this one! Make your heart beat faster does it, sport? Get the old blood stirring?'

'You should have gone into your uncle's business,' she retorted, turning the pages with great satisfaction. The uncle in question was a gravel king, whom Pet used freely to emphasise old Sambo's improvidence.

Another time they found a copy of the old man's will from years back – 'I, Samuel, also known as Sambo, Westerby' – jammed in with a bunch of bills and solicitors' correspondence addressed to Jerry in his function as executor, all stained with whisky, or quinine, and beginning 'We regret'.

'Bit of a turn-up, that one,' Jerry muttered uncomfortably, when it was too late to re-bury the envelope to the mountain. 'Reckon we could bung it down the old whatnot, don't you, sport?'

Her boot-button eyes glowed furiously.

'Aloud,' she ordered, in a booming, theatrical voice, and in no time they were wandering together through the insoluble complexities of trusts that endowed grandchildren, educated nephews and nieces, the income to this wife for her lifetime, the capital to so-and-so on death or marriage; codicils to reward favours, others to punish slights.

'Hey, know who that was? Dread cousin Aldred, the one who went to jug! Jesus, why'd he want to leave *him* money? Blow it in one night!'

And codicils to take care of the racehorses, who might otherwise come under the axe: 'My horse Rosalie in Maison Laffitte, together with two thousand pounds a year for stabling . . . my horse Intruder presently under training in Dublin, to my son Gerald for their respective lifetimes, on the understanding he will support them to their natural deaths . . .'

Old Sambo, like Jerry, dearly loved a horse.

Also for Jerry: stock. Only for Jerry: the company's stock in millions. A mantle, power, responsibility; a whole grand world to inherit and romp around in – a world offered, promised even, then withheld: 'My son to manage all the newspapers of the group according to the style and codes of practice established in my lifetime.' Even a bastard was owned to: a sum of twenty thousands, free of duty payable to Miss Mary Something of the Green, Chobham, the mother of my acknowledged son Adam. The only trouble was: the cupboard was bare. The figures on the account sheet wasted steadily away from the day the great man's empire tottered into liquidation. Then changed to red and grew again into long blood-sucking insects swelling by a nought a year.

'Ah well, Pet,' said Jerry, in the unearthly silence of early dawn, as he tossed the envelope back on the magic mountain. 'Shot of him now, aren't you, sport?' Rolling on to his side, he grabbed the pile of faded newspapers – last editions of his father's brainchildren – and, as only old pressmen can, fumbled his way through all of them at once. 'Can't go chasing the dolly birds where *he* is, can he, Pet?' – a huge rustle of paper – 'Wouldn't put it past him, mind. Wouldn't be for want of trying, I daresay.' And in a quieter voice, as he turned back to glance at the little doll on the edge of his bed, her feet barely reaching the carpet: 'You were always his *tai-tai*, sport, his number one. Always up stuck for you. Told me. "Most beautiful girl in the world, Pet is." Told me. Very words. Bellowed it at me across Fleet Street once. "Best wife I ever had."'

'Damn devil,' said his stepmother in a soft, sudden rush of pure North Country dialect, as the creases collected like a surgeon's pins round the red seam of her lips. 'Rotten devil, I hate every inch of him.' And for a while they stayed that way, neither of them speaking, Jerry lying pottering with his junk and yanking at his forelock, she sitting, joined in some kind of love for Jerry's father.

'You should have sold ballast for your Uncle Paul,' she sighed, with the insight of a much deceived woman.

On their last night Jerry took her out to dinner, and afterwards, back in Thurloe Square, she served him coffee in what was left of her Sèvres service. The gesture led to disaster. Wedging his broad forefinger unthinkingly into the handle of his cup, Jerry broke it off with a faint *putt* which mercifully escaped her notice. By dexterous palming, he contrived to conceal the damage from her until he was able to gain the kitchen and make a swap. God's wrath is inescapable, alas. When Jerry's plane staged in Tashkent – he had wangled himself a concession on the trans-Siberian route – he found to his surprise that the Russian authorities had opened a bar at one end of the waiting room: in Jerry's view amazing evidence of the country's liberalisation. Groping in his jacket pocket for hard currency to pay for a large vodka, he came instead on the pretty little porcelain question-mark with its snapped-off edges. He forswore the vodka.

In business matters he was equally amenable, equally compliant. His literary agent was an old cricketing acquaintance, a snob of uncertain origins called Mencken, known as Ming, one of those natural fools for whom English society and the publishing world in particular are ever ready to make a comfortable space. Mencken was bluff and gusty and sported a grizzled beard, perhaps in order to suggest he wrote the books he hawked. They lunched in Jerry's club, a grand, grubby place which owed its survival to amalgamation with humbler clubs, and repeated appeals through the post. Huddled in the half-empty dining room, under the marble eyes of empire builders, they lamented Lancashire's lack of fast bowlers. Jerry wished Kent would 'hit the damn ball, Ming, not peck at it'. Middlesex, they agreed, had some good young ones coming on: but 'Lord help us, *look* at the way they pick 'em,' said Ming, shaking his head and cutting his food all at once.

'Pity you ran out of steam,' Ming bawled, to Jerry and anyone else who cared to listen. 'Nobody's brought off the eastern novel recently, my view. Greene managed it, if you can take Greene, which I can't, too much popery. Malraux if you like philosophy, which I don't. Maugham you can *have*, and before that it's back to Conrad. Cheers. Mind my saying something?' Jerry filled Ming's glass. 'Go easy on the Hemingway stuff. All that grace under pressure, love with your balls shot off. They don't like it, my view. It's been *said*.'

Jerry saw Ming to his cab.

'Mind my saying something?' Mencken repeated. 'Longer sentences. Moment you journalist chappies turn your hand to novels, you write too short. Short paragraphs, short sentences, short chapters. You see the stuff in column inches, 'stead of across the page. Hemingway was just the same. Always trying to write novels on the back of a matchbox. Spread yourself, my view.'

'Cheerio, Ming. Thanks.'

'Cheerio, Westerby. Remember me to your old father, mind. Must be getting on now, I suppose. Still it comes to us all.'

Even with Stubbs, Jerry near enough preserved the same

sunny temper; though Stubbs, as Connie Sachs would have said, was a known toad.

Pressmen, like other travelling people, make the same mess everywhere and Stubbs, as the group's managing editor, was no exception. His desk was littered with tea-stained proofs and ink-stained cups and the remains of a ham sandwich that had died of old age. Stubbs himself sat scowling at Jerry from the middle of it all as if Jerry had come to take it away from him.

'Stubbsie. Pride of the profession,' Jerry murmured, shoving open the door, and leaned against the wall with his hands behind him, as if to keep them in check.

Stubbs bit something hard and nasty on the tip of his tongue before returning to the file he was studying at the top of the muck on his desk. Stubbs made all the weary jokes about editors come true. He was a resentful man with heavy grey jowls and heavy eyelids that looked as though they had been rubbed with soot. He would stay with the Daily until the ulcers got him, and then they would send him to the Sunday. Another year, he would be farmed out to the women's magazines to take orders from children till he had served his time. Meanwhile he was devious, and listened to incoming phone calls from correspondents without telling them he was on the line.

'Saigon,' Stubbs growled, and with a chewed ballpoint marked something in a margin. His London accent was complicated by a half-hearted twang left over from the days when Canadian was the Fleet Street sound. 'Christmas three years back. Ring a bell?'

'What bell's that, old boy?' Jerry asked, still pressed against the wall.

'A *festive* bell,' said Stubbs, with a hangman's smile. 'Fellowship and good cheer in the bureau, when the group was fool enough to maintain one out there. A Christmas party. You gave it.' He read from a file. '"To Christmas luncheon, Hotel Continental, Saigon." Then you list the guests, just the way we ask you to. Stringers, photographers, drivers, secretaries, messenger boys, hell do I know? Cool seventy pounds changed hands in the interest of public relations and festive cheer. Recall that?' He went straight on. 'Among the guests you have Smoothie Stallwood entered. He was *there*, was he? Stallwood? His usual act? Oiling up the ugliest girls, saying the right things?'

Waiting, Stubbs nibbled again at whatever it was he had on the tip of his tongue. But Jerry propped up the wall, ready to wait all day.

'We're a left-wing group,' said Stubbs, launching on a favourite dictum. 'That means we disapprove of fox-hunting and rely for our survival on the generosity of one illiterate millionaire. Records say Stallwood ate his Christmas lunch in Phnom Penh, lashing out hospitality on dignitaries of the Cambodian government, God help him. I've spoken to Stallwood, and he seems to think that's where he was. Phnom Penh.'

Jerry slouched over to the window and settled his rump against an old black radiator. Outside, not six feet from him, a grimy clock hung over the busy pavement, a present to Fleet Street from the founder. It was mid-morning but the hands were stuck at five to six. In a doorway across the street, two men stood reading a newspaper. They wore hats, and the newspaper obscured their faces, and Jerry reflected how lovely life would be if watchers only looked like that in reality.

'Everybody screws this comic, Stubbsie,' he said thoughtfully after another longish silence. 'You included. You're talking about three bloody years ago. Stuff it, sport. That's my advice. Pop it up the old back passage. Best place for that one.'

'It's not a comic, it's a rag. Comic's a colour supplement.'

'Comic to me, sport. Always was, always will be.'

'Welcome,' Stubbs intoned with a sigh. 'Welcome to the Chairman's choice.' He took up a printed form of contract. 'Name: Westerby, Clive Gerald,' he declaimed, pretending to read from it. 'Profession: aristocrat. Welcome to the son of old Sambo.' He tossed the contract on the desk. 'You take the both. The Sunday and the Daily. Seven day coverage, wars to tit-shows. No tenure or pension, expenses at the meanest possible level. Laundry in the field only and that doesn't mean the whole week's wash. You get a cable card but don't use it. Just air-freight your story and telex the number of the waybill and we'll put it on the spike for you when it arrives. Further payment by results. The BBC is also graciously pleased to take voice interviews from you at the usual derisory rates. Chairman says it's good for prestige, whatever the hell that means. For syndication – '

'Allelujah,' said Jerry in a long outward breath.

Ambling to the desk, he took up the chewed ballpoint, still wet from Stubbs's lick, and without a glance at its owner, or the wording of the contract, scrawled his signature in a slow zigzag along the bottom of the last page, grinning lavishly. At the same moment, as if summoned to interrupt this hallowed event, a girl in jeans unceremoniously kicked open the door and dumped a fresh sheaf of galleys on the desk. The phones rang – perhaps they had been ringing for some while – the girl departed, balancing absurdly on her enormous platform heels; an unfamiliar head poked round the door and yelled 'old man's prayer meeting, Stubbsie'; an underling appeared, and moments later Jerry was being marched down the chicken run: administration, foreign desk, editorial, pay, diary, sports, travel, the ghastly women's magazines. His guide was a twenty-year-old bearded graduate and Jerry called him 'Cedric' all the way through the ritual. On the pavement he paused, rocking slightly, heel to toe and back, as if he were drunk, or punchdrunk.

'*Super*,' he muttered, loud enough for a couple of girls to turn and stare at him as they passed. 'Excellent. Marvellous. Splendid. Perfect.' With that, he dived into the nearest watering-hole, where a bunch of old hands were propping up the bar, mainly the industrial and political caucus, boasting about how they nearly had a page-five lead.

'Westerby! It's the Earl himself! It's the *suit*! The same suit! And the Early-bird's inside it, for Christ's sake!'

Jerry stayed till 'time' was called. He drank frugally,

nevertheless, for he liked to keep a clear head for his walks in the park with George Smiley.

To every closed society there is an inside and an outside, and Jerry was on the outside. To walk in the park with George Smiley, in those days, or – free of the professional jargon, to make a clandestine rendezvous with him; or as Jerry himself might have expressed it, if he ever, which God forbid, put a name to the larger issues of his destiny, 'to take a dive into his other, better life' – required him to saunter from a given point of departure, usually some rather under-populated area like the recently extinguished Covent Garden, and arrive still on foot at a given destination at a little before six, by which time, he assumed, the Circus's depleted team of pavement-artists had taken a look at his back and declared it clean. On the first evening his destination was the embankment side of Charing Cross underground station, as it was still called that year, a busy, scrappy spot where something awkward always seems to be happening to the traffic. On the last evening it was a multiple bus stop on the southern pavement of Piccadilly where it borders Green Park. There were, in all, four occasions, two in London and two at the Nursery. The Sarratt stuff was operational – the obligatory re-bore in tradecraft, to which all fieldmen must periodically submit – and included much to be memorised, such as phone numbers, word codes and contact procedures; such as open-code phrases for insertion into plain language telex messages to the comic; such as fallbacks and emergency action in certain, it was hoped, remote contingencies. Like many sportsmen Jerry had a clear, easy memory for facts and when the inquisitors tested him they were pleased. Also they rehearsed him in the strong-arm stuff, with the result that his back bled from hitting the worn matting once too often.

The sessions in London consisted of one very simple briefing and one very short farewell.

The pickups were variously contrived. At Green Park, by way of a recognition signal, he carried a Fortnum &

Mason carrier-bag and managed, however long the bus queue became, by a series of grins and shuffles, to remain neatly at the back of it. Hovering at the embankment, on the other hand, he clutched an out-of-date copy of *Time* magazine, bearing by coincidence the nourished features of Chairman Mao on the cover, of which the red lettering and border on a white field stood out strongly in the slanting sunlight. Big Ben struck six and Jerry counted the chimes, but the ethic of such meetings requires they do not happen on the hour nor on the quarter, but in the vaguer spaces in-between, which are held to be less conspicuous. Six o'clock was the autumn witching hour, when the smells of every wet and leaf-blown country cricket field in England were wafted up-river with the damp shreds of dusk, and Jerry passed the time in a pleasurable half-trance, scenting them thoughtlessly and keeping his left eye, for some reason, wedged tight shut. The van, when it lumbered up to him, was a battered green Bedford with a ladder on the roof and 'Harris Builder' painted out, but still legible on the side: an old surveillance-horse put out to grass, with steel flaps over the windows. Seeing it pull up, Jerry started forward at the same moment as the driver, a sour boy with a hare lip, shoved his spiky head through the open window.

'Where's Wilf then?' the boy demanded rudely. 'They said you got Wilf with you.'

'You'll have to make do with me,' Jerry retorted with spirit. 'Wilf's on a job.' And opening the back door he clambered straight in and slammed it, for the passenger seat in the front cab was deliberately crammed with lengths of plywood so that there was no room for him to sit there.

That was the only conversation they had, ever.

In the old days, when the Circus had a natural non-commissioned class, Jerry would have counted on some amiable small talk. No longer. When he went to Sarratt, the procedure was little different except that they bounced along for fifteen miles or so, and if he was lucky, the boy remembered to throw in a cushion to prevent the total rupture of Jerry's backside. The driver's cab was blocked off from the belly of the van where Jerry crouched, and all he had to look through, as he slid up and down the wooden bench and clutched the grab handles, were the cracks at the edges of the steel window screens, which gave at best a perforated view of the world outside, though Jerry was quick enough to read the landmarks.

On the Sarratt run he passed depressing segments of out-of-date factories resembling poorly whitewashed cinemas in the twenties, and a brick road-house with 'wedding receptions catered for' in red neon. But his feelings were at their most intense on the first evening, and on the last, when he visited the Circus. On the first evening, as he approached the fabled and familiar turrets – the moment never failed him – a sort of muddled saintliness came over him: 'This is what service is all about.' A smear of red brick was followed by the blackened stems of plane trees, a salad of coloured lights came up, a gateway flung past him and the van thudded to a stop. The van doors were slammed open from outside, at the same time as he heard the gates close and a male, sergeant-major voice shout: 'Come on, man, *move* it for Christ's sake,' and that was Guillam, having a bit of fun.

'Hullo, Peter boy, how's trade? *Jesus*, it's cold!'

Not bothering to reply, Peter Guillam slapped Jerry on the shoulder briskly, as if starting him on a race, closed the door fast, locked it top and bottom, pocketed the keys and led him off at a trot down a corridor which the ferrets must have ripped apart in fury. Plaster was hacked away in clumps, exposing the lath beneath; doors had been torn from their hinges; joists and lintels were dangling; dust sheets, ladders, rubble lay everywhere.

'Had the Irish in, have you?' Jerry yelled. 'Or just an all-ranks dance?'

His questions were lost in the clatter. The two men climbed fast and competitively, Guillam bounding ahead and Jerry on his heels, laughing breathlessly, their feet thundering and scraping on the bare wood steps. A door delayed them and Jerry waited while Guillam fiddled with the locks. Then waited again the other side while he reset them.

'Welcome aboard,' said Guillam more quietly.

They had reached the fifth floor. They trod quietly now, no more romping, English subalterns called to order. The corridor turned left, then right again, then rose by a few narrow steps. A cracked fisheye mirror, steps again, two up, three down, till they came to a janitor's desk, unmanned. To their left lay the rumpus room, empty, with smoking chairs pulled into a rough ring and a good fire burning in the grate. Thus to a long, brown-carpeted room marked 'Secretariat' but in fact the anteroom, where three mothers in pearls and twinsets quietly typed by the glow of reading lamps. At the far end of this room, one more door, shut, unpainted and very grubby round the handle. No fingerplate, no escutcheon for the lock. Just the screwholes, he noticed, and the halo where one had been. Pushing it open without knocking, Guillam shoved his head through the gap and announced something quietly into the room. Then backed away and quickly ushered Jerry past him: Jerry Westerby, into the presence.

'Gosh, super, George, hullo.'

'And don't ask him about his wife,' Guillam warned in a fast, soft murmur that hummed in Jerry's ear for a good spell afterwards.

Father and son? That kind of relationship? Brawn to brain? More exact, perhaps, would be a son to his adopted father, which in the trade is to be held the strongest tie of all.

'Sport,' Jerry muttered, and gave a husky laugh.

English friends have no real way of greeting each other, least of all across a glum civil service office with nothing more lovely to inspire them than a deal desk. For a fraction of a second Jerry laid his cricketer's fist alongside Smiley's soft hesitant palm, then lumbered after him at a distance to the fireside, where two armchairs awaited them: old leather, cracked, and much sat in. Once again, in this erratic season, a fire burned in the Victorian grate, but very small by comparison with the fire in the rumpus room.

'And how was Lucca?' Smiley enquired, filling two glasses from a decanter.

'Lucca was great.'

'Oh dear. Then I expect it was a wrench to leave.'

'Gosh, no. Super. Cheers.'

'Cheers.'

They sat down.

'Now why *super*, Jerry?' Smiley enquired, as if *super* were not a word he was familiar with. There were no papers on the desk and the room was bare, more like a spare room than his own.

'I thought I was done for,' Jerry explained. 'On the shelf for good. Telegram took the wind right out of my sails. I thought, well, Bill's blown me sky high. Blew everyone else, so why not me?'

'Yes,' Smiley agreed, as if sharing Jerry's doubts, and peered at him a moment in frank speculation. 'Yes, yes, quite. However, on balance it seems he never got around to blowing the Occasionals. We've traced him to pretty well every other corner of the archive, but the Occasionals were filed under "friendly contacts" in the Territorials' cut, in a separate archive altogether, one to which he had no natural access. It's not that he didn't think you important enough,' he added hastily, 'it's simply that other claims on him took priority.'

'I can live with it,' said Jerry with a grin.

'I'm glad,' said Smiley, missing the joke. Rising he refilled their glasses, then went to the fire and, taking up a brass poker, began stabbing thoughtfully at the coals. 'Lucca. Yes. Ann and I went there. Oh, eleven, twelve years ago it must have been. It rained.' He gave a little laugh. In a cramped bay at the further end of the room, Jerry glimpsed a narrow, bony-looking camp bed with a row of telephones at the head. 'We visited the *bagno*, I remember,' Smiley went on. 'It was the fashionable cure. Lord alone knows what we were curing.' He attacked the fire again and this time the flames flew alive, daubing the rounded contours of his face with strokes of orange, and making gold pools of his thick spectacles. 'Did you know the poet Heine had a great adventure there? A romance? I rather think it must be why we went, come to think of it. We thought some of it would rub off.'

Jerry grunted something, not too certain, at that moment, who Heine was.

'He went to the *bagno*, he took the waters, and while doing so he met a lady whose name alone so impressed him that he made his wife use it from then on.' The flames held him for a moment longer. 'And you had an adventure there too, didn't you?'

'Just a flutter. Nothing to write home about.'

Beth Sanders, Jerry thought automatically, as his world rocked, then righted itself. A natural, Beth was. Father a retired General, High Sheriff of the County. Old Beth must have an aunt in every secret office in Whitehall.

Stooping again, Smiley propped the poker in a corner, laboriously, as if he were laying a wreath. 'We're not necessarily in competition with affection. We simply like to know where it lies.' Jerry said nothing. Over his shoulder, Smiley glanced at Jerry, and Jerry pulled a grin to please him. 'The name of Heine's lady-love, I may tell you, was *Irwin Mathilde*,' Smiley resumed and Jerry's grin became an awkward laugh. 'Yes, well it does sound better in German, I confess. And the novel, how will that fare? I'd hate to think we'd scared away your muse. I don't think I'd forgive myself, I'm sure.'

'No problem,' said Jerry.

'Finished?'

'Well, you know.'

For a moment there was no sound but the mothers' typing and the rumble of traffic from the street below.

'Then we shall make it up to you when this is over,' Smiley said, 'I insist. How did the Stubbs scene play?

'No problem,' said Jerry again.

'Nothing more we need do for you to smooth your path?'

'Don't think so.'

From beyond the anteroom they heard the shuffle of footsteps all in one direction. It's a war party, Jerry thought, a gathering of the clans.

'And you're game and so on?' Smiley asked. 'You're, well, *prepared*? You have the will?'

'No problem.' Why can't I say something different? he asked himself. Bloody needle's stuck.

'A lot of people haven't these days. The will. Specially in England. A lot of people see *doubt* as legitimate philosophical posture. They think of themselves in the middle, whereas of course really, they're nowhere. No battle was ever won by spectators, was it? We understand that in this service. We're lucky. Our present war began in 1917, with the Bolshevik Revolution. It hasn't changed yet.'

Smiley had taken up a new position, across the room from him, not far from the bed. Behind him, an old and grainy photograph glittered in the new firelight. Jerry had noticed it as he came in. Now, in the strain of the moment, he felt himself to be the object of a double scrutiny: by Smiley, and by the blurred eyes of the portrait dancing in the firelight behind the glass. The sounds of preparation multiplied. They heard voices and snatches of laughter, the squeak of chairs.

'I read somewhere,' Smiley said, 'an historian, I suppose he was – an American, anyway – he wrote of generations that are born into debtors' prisons and spend their lives buying their way to freedom. I think ours is such a generation. Don't you? I still feel strongly that I owe. Don't you? I've always been grateful to this service, that it gave me a chance to pay. Is that how *you* feel? I don't think we should be afraid of . . . devoting ourselves. Is that old-fashioned of me?'

Jerry's face clamped tight shut. He always forgot this part of Smiley when he was away from him, and remembered it too late when he was with him. There was a bit of the failed priest in old George, and the older he grew, the more prominent it became. He seemed to assume that the whole blasted western world shared his worries and had to be talked round to a proper way of thinking.

'In that sense, I think we may legitimately congratulate ourselves on being a trifle old-fashioned – '

Jerry had had enough.

'Sport,' he expostulated, with a clumsy laugh, as the colour rose to his face. 'For Heaven's sake. You point me and I'll march. Okay? You're the owl, not me. Tell me the shots, I'll play them. World's chock-a-block with milk-and-water intellectuals armed with fifteen conflicting arguments against blowing their blasted noses. We don't need another. Okay? I mean, Christ.'

A sharp knock at the door announced the reappearance of Guillam.

'Peace pipes all lit, Chief.'

To his surprise, over the clatter of this interruption, Jerry thought he caught the term 'ladies' man', but whether it was a reference to himself or the poet Heine he could not say, nor did he particularly care. Smiley hesitated, frowned, then seemed to wake again to his surroundings. He glanced at Guillam, then once more at Jerry, then his eyes settled on that middle distance which is the special preserve of English academics.

'Well, then, yes, let's start winding the clock,' he said in a withdrawn voice.

As they trooped out, Jerry paused to admire the photograph on the wall, hands in pockets, grinning at it, hoping Guillam would hang back too, which he did.

'Looks as though he's swallowed his last sixpence,' said Jerry. 'Who is he?'

'Karla,' said Guillam. 'Recruited Bill Haydon. Russian hood.'

'Sounds more like a girl's name. How you keeping?'

'It's the codename of his first network. There's a school of thought that says it's also the name of his one love.'

'Bully for him,' said Jerry carelessly and, still grinning, drifted beside him toward the rumpus room. Perhaps deliberately, Smiley had gone ahead, out of earshot of their conversation. 'Still with that loony girl, the flute-player, are you?' Jerry asked.

'She got less loony,' said Guillam. They took a few more paces.

'Bolted?' Jerry enquired sympathetically.

'Something like that.'

'And he's *all right*, is he?' Jerry asked dead casually, nodding at the solitary figure ahead of them. 'Eating well, good coat, all that stuff?'

'Never been better. Why?'

'Just asked,' said Jerry, very pleased.

From the airport Jerry rang his daughter, Cat, a thing he rarely did, but this time he had to. He knew it was a mistake before he put the money in, but he still persisted, and not even the terribly familiar voice of the early wife could put him off.

'Gosh, hullo! It's me actually. Super. Listen: how's Phillie?'

Phillie was her husband, a civil servant nearly eligible for a pension, though younger than Jerry by about thirty muddled lives.

'Perfectly well, thank you,' she retorted in the frosty tone with which old wives defend new mates. 'Is that why you rang?'

'Well I did just think I might chat up old Cat, actually. Going out East for a bit, back in harness,' he said. He felt he should apologise. 'It's just the comic needs a hack out there,' he said, and heard a clatter as the receiver hit the hall chest. Oak, he remembered. Barley-twist legs. Another of old Sambo's leftovers.

'Daddy?'

'Hi!' he yelled as if the line were bad, as if she had taken him by surprise. 'Cat? Hullo, hey listen, *sport*, did you get my postcards and stuff?' He knew she had. She had thanked him regularly in her weekly letters.

Hearing nothing but 'Daddy' repeated in a questioning voice, Jerry asked jovially: 'You do still collect stamps, don't you? Only I'm going that way, you see. East.'

Planes were called, others landed, whole worlds were

changing places but Jerry Westerby, speaking to his daughter, was motionless in the procession.

'You used to be a demon for stamps,' he reminded her.

'I'm seventeen.'

'Sure, sure, what do you collect now? Don't tell me. Boys!' With the brightest humour he kept it going while he danced from one buckskin boot to the other, making his own jokes and supplying his own laughter. 'Listen, I'm sending you some money. Blatt and Rodney are fixing it, sort of birthday and Christmas put together, better talk to Mummy before spending it. Or maybe Phillie, what? He's a sound sort of bloke, isn't he? Turn Phillie loose on it, kind of thing he likes to get his teeth into.' He opened the kiosk door to raise an artificial flurry. ''Fraid they're calling my flight there, Cat,' he bawled over the clatter. 'Look, mind how you go, d'you hear? Watch yourself. Don't give yourself too easy. Know what I mean?'

He queued for the bar a while but at the last moment the old eastern hand in him woke up and he moved across to the cafeteria. It might be some while before he got his next glass of fresh cow's milk. Standing in the queue, Jerry had a sensation of being watched. No trick to that: at an airport everyone watches everyone, so what the hell? He thought of the orphan and wished he'd had time to get himself a girl before he left, if only to take away the bad memory of their necessary parting.

Smiley walked, one round little man in a raincoat. Social journalists with more class than Jerry, shrewdly observing his progress through the purlieus of the Charing Cross Road, would have recognised the type at once: the mackintosh brigade personified, cannonfodder of the mixed sauna parlours and the naughty bookshops. These long tramps had become a habit for him. With his new-found energy he could cover half the length of London and not notice it. From Cambridge Circus, now that he knew the byways, he could take any of twenty routes and never cross the same path twice. Having selected a beginning, he would let luck and instinct guide him while his other mind plundered the remoter regions of his soul. But this evening his journey had a pull to it, drawing him south and westward, and Smiley yielded. The air was damp and cold, hung with a harsh fog that had never seen the sun. Walking, he took his own island with him, and it was crammed with images, not people. Like an extra mantle the white walls encased him in his thoughts. In a doorway, two murderers in leather coats were whispering; under a streetlamp a dark-haired boy angrily clutched a violin case. Outside a theatre, a waiting crowd burned in the blaze of lights from the awning overhead, and the fog curled round them like fire smoke. Never had Smiley gone into battle knowing so little and expecting so much. He felt lured, and he felt pursued. Yet when he tired, and drew back for a moment, and considered the logic of what he was about, it almost eluded him. He glanced back and saw the jaws of failure waiting for him. He peered forward and through his moist spectacles saw the phantoms of great hopes dancing in the mist. He blinked around him and knew there was nothing for him where he stood. Yet he advanced without the ultimate conviction. It was no answer to rehearse the steps that had brought him to this point – the Russian goldseam, the imprint of Karla's private army, the thoroughness of Haydon's efforts to extinguish knowledge of them. Beyond the limits of these external reasons, Smiley perceived in himself the existence of a darker motive, infinitely more obscure, one which his rational mind continued to reject. He called it Karla, and it was true that somewhere in him, like a left-over legend, there burned the embers of hatred toward the man who had set out to destroy the temples of his private faith, whatever remained of them: the service that he loved, his friends, his country, his concept of a reasonable balance in human affairs. It was true also that a lifetime or two ago, in a sweltering Indian jail, the two men had actually faced each other, Smiley and Karla, across an iron table: though Smiley had no reason at the time to know he was in the presence of his destiny. Karla's head was on the block in Moscow; Smiley had tried to woo him to the West, and

Karla had kept silent, preferring death or worse to an easy defection. And it was true that now and then the memory of that encounter, of Karla's unshaven face and watchful, inward eyes, came at him like an accusing spectre out of the murk of his little room, while he slept fitfully on his bunk.

But hatred was really not an emotion which he could sustain for any length of time, unless it was the obverse side of love.

He was approaching the King's Road in Chelsea. The fog was heavier because of the closeness of the river. Above him the globes of streetlights hung like Chinese lanterns in the bare branches of the trees. The traffic was sparse and cautious. Crossing the road he followed the pavement till he came to Bywater Street and turned into it, a cul-de-sac of neat flat-fronted terrace cottages. He trod discreetly now, keeping to the western side, and the shadow of the parked cars. It was the cocktail hour, and in other windows he saw talking heads and shrieking, silent mouths. Some he recognised, some she even had names for: Felix the cat, Lady Macbeth, the Puffer. He drew level with his own house. For their return, she had had the shutters painted blue and they were blue still. The curtains were open because she hated to be enclosed. She sat alone at her escritoire, and she might have composed the scene for him deliberately: the beautiful and conscientious wife, ending her day, attends to matters of administration. She was listening to music and he caught the echo of it carried on the fog. Sibelius. He wasn't good at music, but he knew all her records and he had several times praised the Sibelius out of politeness. He couldn't see the gramophone but he knew it lay on the floor, where it had lain for Bill Haydon when she was trailing her affair with him. He wondered whether the German dictionary lay beside it, and her anthology of German poetry. Several times, over the last decade or two, usually during reconciliations, she had made a show of learning German so that Smiley would be able to read aloud to her.

As he watched, she got up, crossed the room, paused in

front of the pretty gilt mirror to adjust her hair. The notes she wrote to herself were jammed into the frame. What was it this time? he wondered. *Blast garage. Cancel lunch Madeleine. Destroy butcher.* Sometimes, when things were tense, she had sent him messages that way: *force George to smile, apologise insincerely for lapse.* In very bad times, she wrote whole letters to him, and posted them there for his collection.

To his surprise she had put out the light. He heard the bolts slide on the front door. Drop the chain, he thought automatically. Double lock the Banhams. How many times do I have to tell you bolts are as weak as the screws that hold them in place? Odd all the same: he had somehow supposed she would leave the bolts open in case he might return. Then the bedroom light went on, and he saw her body framed in silhouette in the window as, angel-like, she stretched her arms to the curtains. She drew them almost to her, stopped, and momentarily he feared she had seen him, till he remembered her short-sightedness and her refusal to wear glasses. She's going out, he thought. She's going to doll herself up. He saw her head half turn as if she had been addressed. He saw her lips move, and break into a puckish smile as her arms lifted again, this time to the back of her neck, and she began to unfasten the top button of her housecoat. In the same moment, the gap between the curtains was abruptly closed by other, impatient hands.

Oh *no*, thought Smiley hopelessly. Please! Wait till I've gone!

For a minute, perhaps longer, standing on the pavement, he stared in disbelief at the blacked-out window, till anger, shame and finally self-disgust broke in him together like a physical anguish and he turned and hurried blindly back toward the King's Road. Who was it this time? Another beardless ballet dancer, performing some narcissistic ritual? Her vile cousin Miles, the career politician? Or a one-night Adonis spirited from the nearby pub?

* * *

When the outside telephone rang Peter Guillam was sitting alone in the rumpus room a little drunk, languishing equally for Molly Meakin's body and George Smiley's return. He lifted the receiver at once and heard Fawn, out of breath and furious.

'I've lost him!' he shouted. 'He's bilked me!'

'Then you're a bloody idiot,' Guillam retorted with satisfaction.

'Idiot nothing! He heads for home, right? Our usual ritual. I'm waiting for him, I stand off, he's coming back to the main road, looks at me. Like I'm dirt. Just *dirt*. Next thing I know I'm on my own. How does he do it? Where does he go? I'm his friend aren't I? Who the hell does he think he is? Fat little runt, I'll kill him!'

Guillam was still laughing as he rang off.

Chapter 6

The Burning Of Frost

In Hong Kong it was Saturday again but the typhoons were forgotten and the day burned hot and clear and breathless. In the Hong Kong club a serenely Christian clock struck eleven and the chimes tinkled in the panelled quiet like spoons dropped on a distant kitchen floor. The better chairs were already taken by readers of last Thursday's *Telegraph*, which gave a quite dismal picture of the moral and economic miseries of their homeland.

'Pound's in the soup again,' a crusted voice growled through a pipe. 'Electricians out. Railways out. Pilots out.'

'Who's *in*? More the question,' said another, just as crusted.

'If I was the Kremlin I'd say we were doing a first-class *job*,' said the first speaker, barking out the final word to give it a military indignation, and with a sigh ordered up a couple of dry martinis. Neither man was above twenty-five years old, but being an exiled patriot in search of a quick fortune can age you pretty fast.

The Foreign Correspondents' Club was having one of its churchy days when burghers far outnumbered news-men. Without old Craw to hold them together, the Shanghai Bowlers had dispersed and several had left the Colony altogether. The photographers had been lured to Phnom Penh by the promise of some great new fighting now the wet season was ended. The cowboy was in Bangkok for an expected revival of student riots, Luke was at the bureau and his boss the dwarf was slouched grumpily at the bar surrounded by sonorous British suburbanites in dark trousers and white shirts discussing the eleven hundred gearbox.

'But *cold* this time. Hear that? Muchee coldee and bring it *chop chop*!'

Even the Rocker was muted. He was attended this morning by his wife, a former Bible School teacher from Borneo, a dried-out shrew in bobbed hair and ankle socks who could spot a sin before it was committed.

And a couple of miles eastward on Cloudview road, a thirty-cent ride on the one-price city bus, in what is said to be the most populated corner of our planet, on North Point, just where the city swells toward the Peak, on the sixteenth floor of a highrise block called 7A, Jerry Westerby was lying on a mattress after a short but dreamless sleep, singing his own words to the tune of 'Miami Sunrise' and watching a beautiful girl undress. The mattress was seven feet long, intended to be used the other way on by an entire Chinese family, and for about the first time in his life his feet didn't hang over the end. It was longer than Pet's cot by a mile, longer even than the bed in Tuscany, though in Tuscany it hadn't mattered because he had a real girl to curl round and with a girl you don't lie so straight. Whereas the girl he was watching was framed in a window opposite his own, ten yards or miles out of reach, and on every one of the nine mornings he had woken here, she had stripped and washed herself this way, to his considerable enthusiasm, even applause. When he was lucky he followed the whole ceremony, from the moment when she tipped her head sideways to let her black hair fall to her waist, until she chastely wound a sheet about her and rejoined her ten-strong family in the next room where they all lived. He knew the family intimately. Their washing habits, their tastes in music, cooking and love-making, their celebrations, their flaring, dangerous rows. The only thing he wasn't sure of was whether she was two girls or one.

She vanished, but he kept on singing. He felt eager, which was how it took him every time, whether he was about to gumshoe down a back alley in Prague to swap little packages with a terror-stricken joe in a doorway or – his finest hour, and for an Occasional unprecedented – row three miles in a blackened dinghy to scrape a radio operator off a Caspian beach. As the clamps tightened, Jerry discovered the same surprising mastery of himself, the same jollity and the same alertness. And the same barking funk, not necessarily a contradiction. It's today, he thought. The kissing's over.

There were three tiny rooms and they were parquet floored all through. That was the first thing he noticed every morning because there was no furniture anywhere, except the mattress and the kitchen chair and the table where his typewriter sat, the one dinner plate, which did duty as an ashtray, and the girlie calendar, vintage 1960, of a red-head whose charms had long since lost their bloom. He knew the type exactly: green eyes, a temper, and a skin so sensitive it looked like a battlefield every time you laid a finger on it. Add one telephone, one ancient record player for seventy-eights only and two very real opium pipes suspended from business-like nails on the wall, and he had a complete inventory of the wealth and interests of Deathwish the Hun, now in Cambodia, from whom Jerry had rented the apartment. And the book-sack, his own, beside the mattress.

The gramophone had run down. He climbed happily to his feet, tightening the makeshift sarong around his stomach. As he did so, the telephone began ringing, so he sat again and, grabbing the flex, dragged the instrument toward him across the floor. It was Luke as usual, wanting to play.

'Sorry, sport. Doing a story. Try solo whist.'

Dialling the speaking clock, Jerry heard a Chinese squawk, then an English squawk and set his watch by the second. Then he went to the gramophone and put on 'Miami Sunrise' again, loud as it would go. It was his only record, but it drowned the gurgle of the useless airconditioner. Still humming, he pulled open the one wardrobe, and from an old leather grip on the floor picked out his father's yellowed tennis racket vintage nineteen thirty odd, with S.W. in marking ink on the pommel. Unscrewing the handle he fished from the recess four lozenges of subminiature film, a worm of grey wadding, and a battered subminiature camera with measuring chain, which the conservative in him preferred to the flashier models which the Sarratt smudges had tried to press on him. Loading a cassette into the camera, he set the film speed and took three sample light-readings of the red-head's bosom before slopping to the kitchen in his sandals, where he lowered himself devoutly to his knees before the fridge and loosened the Free Forresters tie which held the door in place. With a wild tearing noise, he passed his right thumbnail down the rotted rubber strips, took out three eggs and re-tied the tie. Waiting for them to boil, he lounged at the window, elbows on the sill, peering fondly through the burglar wire at his beloved rooftops which descended like giant stepping stones to the sea's edge.

The rooftops were a civilisation for themselves, a breath-taking theatre of survival against the raging of the city. Within their barbed-wire compounds, sweatshops turned out anoraks, religious services were held, mah-jong was played, and fortune tellers burned joss and consulted huge brown volumes. Ahead of him lay a formal garden made of smuggled earth. Below, three old women fattened Chow puppies for the pot. There were schools for dancing, reading, ballet, recreation and combat, there were schools in culture and the wonders of Mao, and this morning, while Jerry's eggs boiled, an old man completed his long rigmarole of callisthenics before opening the tiny folding chair where he performed his daily reading of the great man's Thoughts. The wealthier poor, if they had no roof, built themselves giddy crow's nests, two foot by eight, on home-made cantilevers driven into their drawing room floors. Deathwish maintained there were suicides all the time. That was what grabbed him about the place, he said. When he wasn't fornicating, he liked to hang out of the window with his Nikon, hoping to catch one, but he never did. Down to the right lay the graveyard, which

Deathwish said was bad luck and knocked a few dollars off the rent.

While he was eating, the phone rang again.

'What story?' said Luke.

'Wanchai whores have hijacked Big Moo,' Jerry said. 'Taken him to Stonecutters Island and are holding him to ransom.'

Other than Luke, it tended to be Deathwish's women who called, but they didn't want Jerry instead. The shower had no curtain so Jerry had to squat in a tiled corner, like a boxer, in order not to flood the bathroom. Returning to the bedroom, he put on his suit, grabbed a bread knife, and counted twelve wood blocks from the corner of the room. With the knife blade he dug up the thirteenth. In a hollowed recess cut into the tar-like undersurface lay one plastic bag containing a roll of American dollar bills of large and small denominations; one escape passport, driving licence and air travel card in the name of Worrell, contractor; and one small-arm, which, in defiance of every Circus regulation under the sun, Jerry had procured from Deathwish, who did not care to take it on his travels. From this treasure chest he extracted five one-hundred dollar bills and, leaving the rest untouched, replaced the wood block. He dropped the camera and two spare cassettes into his pockets then stepped on to the tiny landing, whistling. His front door was guarded by a white-painted grille which would have delayed a decent burglar for ninety seconds. Jerry had picked the lock when he had nothing better to do, and that was how long it took him. He pressed the button for the lift, and it arrived full of Chinese who all got out. It happened every time. Jerry was just too big for them, too ugly and too foreign.

From scenes like these, thought Jerry, with willed cheerfulness, as he plunged into the pitch darkness of the city-bound bus, Saint George's children go forth to save the empire.

'*Time spent in preparation is never time wasted*' runs the Nursery's laborious maxim on counter-surveillance.

Sometimes Jerry became Sarratt man and nothing else.

By the ordinary logic of things he could have gone to his destination directly: he had every right. By the ordinary logic of things there was no reason on earth, particularly after their revelries of last night, why Jerry should not have taken a cab to the front door, barged gaily in, bearded his new-found bosom friend and be done with it. But this was not the ordinary logic of things, and in the Sarratt folklore, Jerry was approaching the operational moment of truth: the moment when the back door closed on him with a bang, after which there was no way out but forward. The moment when every one of his twenty years of tradecraft rose in him and shouted 'caution'. If he was walking into a trap, this was where the trap was sprung. Even if they knew his route in advance, still the static posts would be staked out ahead of him, in cars and behind windows, and the surveillance teams locked on to him in case of fumble or branch lines. If there was ever a last opportunity to test the water before he jumped, it was now. Last night, around the haunts, he could have been watched by a hundred local angels and still not have known for certain he was their quarry. But here he could weave and count the shadows: here, in theory at least, he had a chance to know.

He glanced at his watch. Exactly twenty minutes to go and even at Chinese rather than European pace he needed seven. So he sauntered, but never idly. In other countries, in almost any place in the world outside Hong Kong, he would have given himself far longer. Behind the Curtain, Sarratt lore said, half a day, preferably more. He'd have posted himself a letter, just so that he could walk halfway down the street, stop dead at the postbox and double back, checking the feet that faltered, and the faces that ducked away; looking for the classic formations, a two this side, a three across the road, a front tail who floats ahead of you.

But paradoxically, though this morning he zealously went through the steps, another side of him knew he was wasting his time: knew that in the East a roundeye could live all his life in the same block and never have the smallest notion of the secret tic-tac on his doorstep. At every corner of each teeming street he entered, men waited, lounged and watched, strenuously employed in doing nothing. The beggar who suddenly stretched his arms and yawned, the crippled shoe-shine boy who dived for his escaping feet, and having missed them drove the backs of his brushes together in a whipcrack, the old hag selling bi-racial pornography who cupped her hand and shrieked one word into the bamboo scaffolding above her: though in his mind Jerry recorded them, they were as obscure to him today as they had been when he first came east – twenty? Lord help us, twenty-five years ago. Pimps? Numbers boys? Dope peddlars pushing the coloured twists of candy paper – 'yellow two dollar, blue five dollar? You chase dragon, like quickshot?' Or were they ordering up a bowl of rice from the food stalls across the way? In the East, sport, survival is knowing you don't know.

He was using the reflection in the marble cladding of the shops: shelves of amber, shelves of jade, credit card signs, electrical gadgets and pyramids of black luggage which nobody ever seemed to carry. At Cartier's a beautiful girl was laying pearls on a velvet tray, putting them to bed for the day. Sensing his presence she lifted her eyes to him; and in Jerry, despite his preoccupation, the old Adam briefly stirred. But one glance at his shambling grin and his scruffy suit and his buckskin boots told her all she needed to know: Jerry Westerby was not a potential customer. There was news of fresh battles, Jerry noticed, passing a news-stand. The Chinese-language press carried frontpage photographs of decimated children, screaming mothers and troops in American-style helmets. Whether Vietnam, or Cambodia, or Korea, or the Philippines, Jerry couldn't tell. The red characters of the headline had the effect of splashed blood. Maybe Deathwish was in luck.

Thirsty from last night's booze, Jerry cut through the Mandarin and plunged into the twilight of the Captain's Bar, but he only drank water in the Gents. Back in the lobby he bought a copy of *Time* but didn't like the way the plain-clothes crushers looked at him, and left. Joining the crowds again, he sauntered toward the post office, built 1911 and since pulled down, but in those days a rare and hideous antique made beautiful by the clumsy concrete of the buildings around it. Then he doubled through the arches into Pedder Street, passing under a green corrugated bridge where mailbags trailed like turkeys on the gibbet. Doubling yet again, he crossed to the Connaught Centre, using the footbridge to thin out the field.

In the glittering steel lobby a peasant woman was scrubbing out the teeth of a stationary escalator with a wire brush, and on the promenade a group of Chinese students gazed in respectful silence at Henry Moore's *Oval with Points*. Looking back, Jerry glimpsed the brown dome of the old law courts dwarfed by the Hilton's beehive walls: *Regina versus Westerby*, he thought, 'and the prisoner is charged with blackmail, corruption, pretended affection and a few others we shall dream up before the day is out'. The harbour was alive with shipping, most of it small. Beyond it, the New Territories, pocked with excavation, shoved vainly against muddy clouds of smog. At their feet, new godowns, and factory chimneys belching brown smoke.

Retracing his steps he passed the big Scottish business houses, Jardines, Swire, and noticed that their doors were barred. Must be a holiday, he thought. Ours or theirs? In Statue Square, a leisurely carnival was taking place with fountains, beach umbrellas, Coca-Cola sellers, and about half a million Chinese who stood in groups or shuffled past him like a barefoot army, darting glances at his size. Loudspeakers, building drills, wailing music. He crossed Jackson Road and the noise level fell a little. Ahead of him, on a patch of perfect English lawn, fifteen white-clad figures lounged. The all-day cricket match had just begun. At the receiving end, a lank, disdainful figure in an outdated cap was fiddling with his batting gloves. Pausing, Jerry watched, grinning in fond familiarity. The bowler bowled. Medium pace, bit of inswing, dead wicket. The batsman played a gracious stroke, missed and took a leg-bye in slow motion. Jerry foresaw a long dull innings to no applause. He wondered who was playing whom, and decided it was the usual Peak mafia playing itself. On the leg boundary, across the road, rose the Bank of China, a vast and fluted cenotaph festooned with crimson slogans loving Mao. At its base, granite lions looked on sightlessly while flocks of white-shirted Chinese photographed each other against their flanks.

But the bank which Jerry had his eye on stood directly behind the bowler's arm. A Union Jack was posted at its pinnacle, an armoured van more confidently at its base. The doors stood open and their burnished surfaces glittered like fool's gold. While Jerry continued his shambling arc toward it, a gang of helmeted guards, escorted by tall Indians with elephant guns emerged suddenly from the interior blackness and nursed three black money boxes down the wide steps as if they held the Host itself. The armoured van drove away and for a sickening moment Jerry had visions of the bank's doors closing after it.

Not logical visions. Not nervous visions either. Merely that for a moment Jerry expected fumble with the same trained pessimism with which a gardener foresees drought or an athlete a foolish sprain on the eve of a great match; or a fieldman with twenty years on the clock foresees just one more unpredictable frustration. But the doors stayed open, and Jerry veered away to the left. Give the guards time to relax, he thought. Shepherding the money will have made them nervous. They'll see too sharply, they'll remember things.

Turning, he began a slow, dreamy stroll toward the Hong Kong Club: Wedgwood porticoes, striped blinds and a smell of stale English food at the doorway. Cover is not a lie, they tell you. Cover is what you believe. Cover is who you are. *On Saturday morning Mr Gerald Westerby, the not very distinguished journalist, heads for a favourite watering-hole* . . . On the Club steps Jerry paused, patted his pockets, then turned full circle and struck out purposefully for his destination, making two long sides of the square, as he watched for the last time for the slurring feet and turned-down glances. *Mr Gerald Westerby, discovering he is short of weekend cash, decides on a quick visit to the bank.* Elephant guns slung carelessly at their shoulders, the Indian guards studied him without interest.

Except, Mr Gerald Westerby doesn't!

Cursing himself for being a damned fool, Jerry remembered that the time was after twelve o'clock, and that at twelve sharp the banking halls were closed. After twelve, it was upstairs only, and that was the way he had planned it.

Relax, he thought. You're thinking too much. Don't think: do. *In the beginning was the deed.* Who had said that to him once? Old George, for God's sake, quoting Goethe. Coming from him of all people!

As he began the run-in, a wave of dismay hit him, and he knew it was fear. He was hungry. He was tired. Why had George left him alone like this? Why did he have to do everything for himself? Before the fall, they'd have posted babysitters ahead of him – even someone inside the bank – just to watch for rain. They'd have had a reception team to skim the take almost before he left the building, and an escape car in case he had to slip away in his socks. And in London – he thought sweetly, talking himself down – they'd have had dear old Bill Haydon – wouldn't they? – passing it all to the Russians, bless him. Thinking this, Jerry willed upon himself an extraordinary hallucination, quick as the flash of a camera, and as slow to fade. God had answered his prayers, he thought. The old days were here again after all, and the street was alive with a grandslam supporting cast. Behind him a blue Peugeot had pulled up and two bullish roundeyes sat in it studying a Happy Valley racecard. Radio aerial, the works. From his left, American matrons sauntered by, laden with cameras and guidebooks, and a positive obligation to observe. And from the bank itself, as he advanced swiftly on its portals, a couple of solemn money-men emerged, wearing just that grim stare watchers sometimes use in order to discourage an enquiring eye.

Senility, Jerry told himself. You're over the hill, sport, no question. Dotage and funk have brought you to your knees. He bounded up the steps, jaunty as a cock-robin on a hot spring day.

The lobby was as big as a railway station, the canned music as martial. The banking area was barred and he saw no one lurking, not even a phantom stand-off man. The lift was a gold cage with a spittoon filled with sand for cigarettes, but by the ninth floor the largeness of downstairs had all gone. Space was money. A narrow cream corridor led to an empty reception desk. Jerry strolled easily, marking the emergency exit and the service lift which the bearleaders had already charted for him in case he had to do a duckdive. Queer how they knew so much, he thought, with so few resources; must have dug out an architect's drawing from somewhere. On the counter, one teak sign reading Trustee Department Enquiries. Beside it, one grimy paperback on fortune-telling by the stars, open and much annotated. But no receptionist because Saturdays are different. On Saturdays you get the best ride, they had said. He looked cheerfully round, nothing on his conscience. A second corridor ran the width of the building, office doors to the left, soggy vinyl-covered partitions to the right. From behind the partitions came the slow pat of an electric typewriter as someone typed a legal document, and the slow Saturday sing-song of Chinese secretaries without a lot to do except wait for lunch and the free afternoon. There were four glazed doors with penny-sized eyeholes for looking in or out. Jerry ambled down the corridor, glancing through each as if glancing were his recreation, hands in pockets, a slightly daft smile aloft. The fourth on the left, they had said, one door, one window. A clerk walked past him, then a secretary on dinky, clicking heels, but Jerry, though scruffy, was European and wore a suit and neither challenged him.

'Morning, gang,' he muttered, and they wished him 'Good day, sir,' in return.

There were iron bars at the end of the corridor and iron bars over the windows. A blue night-light was fixed to the ceiling, he supposed for security but he didn't know: fire, space protection, he didn't know, the bearleaders hadn't mentioned it, and stinks and bangs were not his thing. The first room was an office, unoccupied except for a few dusty sports trophies on the window-sill and an embroidered coat of arms of the bank athletics club on the pegboard wall. He passed a pile of apple boxes marked 'Trustee'. They seemed to be full of deeds and wills. The cheese-paring tradition of the old China trading houses died hard, apparently. A notice on the wall read 'Private' and another 'By Appointment Only'.

The second door gave on to a corridor and a small archive which was likewise empty. The third was a 'Directors Only' lavatory, the fourth had a staff notice-board mounted directly beside it and a red light bulb mounted on the jamb and an important nameplate in Letraset saying 'J. Frost, Deputy Chief Trustee, Appointments Only, do NOT enter when light is ON'. But the light was not ON, and the penny-sized eyehole showed one man at his desk alone, and the only company he had was a heap of files, and scrolls of costly paper bound in green silk on the English legal pattern, and two closed-circuit television sets for the stock exchange prices, dead, and the harbour view, mandatory to the higher executive image, sliced into pencil-grey lines by mandatory Venetian blinds. One shiny, podgy, prosperous little man in a sporty linen suit of Robin Hood green, working far too conscientiously for a Saturday. Moisture on his brow; black crescents beneath his arms, and – to Jerry's informed eye – the leaden immobility of a man recovering very slowly from debauch.

A corner room, thought Jerry. One door only, this one. One shove and you're away. He took a last glance up and down the empty corridor. Jerry Westerby on stage, he thought. If you can't talk, dance. The door gave immediately. He stepped gaily inside wearing his best shy smile.

'Gosh, Frostie, hullo, *super*. Am I early or late? Sport – I say – most *extraordinary* thing back there. In the corridor – nearly fell over them – lot of apple boxes full of legal bumph. "Who's Frostie's client?" I asked myself. "Cox's Orange Pippins? Or Beauty of Bath?" Beauty of Bath, knowing you. Thought it was rather a giggle, after last night's high jinks round the parlours.'

All of which, feeble though it might have sounded to the astonished Frost, got him into the room with the door closed, fast, while his broad back masked the only eyehole and his soul sent prayers of gratitude to Sarratt for a soft landing, and prayers of preservation to his Maker.

A moment of theatricality followed Jerry's entry. Frost lifted his head slowly, keeping his eyes half shut, as if the light were hurting them, which it probably was. Spotting Jerry, he winced and looked away, then looked at him again to confirm that he was flesh. Then he wiped his brow with his handkerchief.

'Christ,' he said. 'It's his nibs. What the hell are you doing here, you disgusting aristocrat?'

To which Jerry, still at the door, responded with another large grin, and a lifting of one hand in a Red Indian salute, while he marked down the worry points precisely: the two telephones, the grey box for inter-office speaking and the wardrobe safe with a keyhole but no combination lock.

'How did they let you in? I suppose you flashed your Honourable at them. What do you mean by it, barging in here?' Not half as displeased as his words suggested, Frost had left his desk and was waddling down the room. 'This isn't a cathouse you know. This is a respectable bank. More or less.'

Arriving at Jerry's considerable bulk, he stuck his hands on his hips and gazed at him, shaking his head in wonder. Then he patted Jerry's arm, then prodded him in the stomach, amid more shaking of the head.

'You alcoholic, dissolute, lecherous, libidinous . . .'

'Newshound,' Jerry prompted.

Frost was not above forty but nature had already printed on him the crueller marks of littleness, such as a floorwalker's fussiness about the cuffs and fingers, and a moistening of his lips and pursing of them all at once. What redeemed him was a transparent sense of fun, which leapt to his damp cheeks like sunlight.

'Here,' said Jerry. 'Poison yourself,' and offered him a cigarette.

'Christ,' said Frost again, and with a key from his chain opened an old-fashioned walnut cupboard, full of mirror and rows of cocktail sticks with artificial cherries, and trick tankards with pin-ups and pink elephants.

'Bloody Mary do you?'

'Bloody Mary would slip down grateful, sport,' Jerry assured him.

On the keychain, one brass Chubb key. The safe was also Chubb, a fine one, with a battered gold medallion fading into the old green paint.

'I'll say one thing for you blueblooded rakes,' Frost called while he poured and shook the ingredients like a chemist. 'You do know the haunts. Drop you blindfold in the middle of Salisbury Plain, I reckon you'd find a cathouse in thirty seconds flat. My virgin sensitive nature took yet another grave jolt last night. Rocked to its frail little bearings, it was – say when! – I'll take a few addresses off you sometime, when I'm healed. If I ever am, which I doubt.'

Sauntering over to Frost's desk, Jerry riffled idly through his correspondence, then began playing with the switches of the speaking box, patting them up and down one by one with his enormous index finger, but getting no answers. A separate button was marked 'engaged'. Pressing it, Jerry saw a rose gleam in the eyehole as the caution-light went on in the corridor.

'As to those girls,' Frost was saying, his back still turned to Jerry while he rattled the sauce bottle. 'Wicked they were. Shocking.' Laughing delightedly, Frost advanced across the room, holding the glasses wide. 'What were their names? Oh dear, oh dear!'

'Seven and twenty-four,' said Jerry distractedly.

He was stooping as he spoke, looking for the alarm button he knew would be somewhere on the desk.

'Seven and twenty-four!' Frost repeated, rapturously. 'What poetry! What a memory!'

At knee level, Jerry had found a grey box screwed to the drawer-pillar. The key was vertical, at the off position. He pulled it out and dropped it into his pocket.

'I said what a wonderful memory,' Frost repeated, rather puzzled.

'You know newshounds, sport,' said Jerry, straightening. 'Worse than wives, us newshounds are, when it comes to memories.'

'Here. Come off there. That's holy ground.'

Picking up Frost's large desk diary, Jerry was studying it for the day's engagements.

'Jesus,' he said. 'It's all go, isn't it? Who's N, sport? N, eight to twelve? Not your mother-in-law is she?'

Ducking his mouth to the glass Frost drank greedily, swallowed, then made a farce of choking, writhing and recovering. 'Keep her out of this, do you mind? You nearly gave me a heart attack. Bung-ho.'

'N for nuts? N for Napoleon? Who's N?'

'Natalie. My secretary. Very nice. Legs go right up to its bottom, so they tell me. Never been there myself, so I don't know. My one rule. Remind me to break it sometime. Bung-ho,' he said again.

'She in?'

'I think I heard her dulcet tread, yes. Want me to give her a buzz? I'm told she puts on a very nice turn for the upper classes.'

'No thanks,' said Jerry, and setting down the diary, looked at Frost four square, man to man, though the fight was uneven, for Jerry was a whole head taller than Frost, and a lot broader.

'Incredible,' Frost declared reverently, still beaming at Jerry. 'Incredible, that's what it was.' His manner was devoted, even possessive. 'Incredible girls, incredible company. I mean why should a bloke like me bother with a bloke like you? A mere Honourable at that? Dukes are my level. Dukes and tarts. Let's do it again tonight. Come on.'

Jerry laughed.

'I mean it. Scout's honour. Let's die of it before we're too old. On me this time, the whole treat.' In the corridor, heavy footsteps sounded, coming nearer. 'Know what *I'm* going to do? Try me. I'm going to go back to the Meteor with you, and I'm going to call Madame Whoosit, and I'm going to insist on a – what's eating you?' he said, catching Jerry's expression.

The footsteps slowed, then stopped. A black shadow filled the eyehole and stayed.

'Who is he?' said Jerry quietly.

'Milky.'

'Who's Milky?'

'Milky Way, my boss,' said Frost, as the footsteps moved away, and closing his eyes, crossed himself devoutly. 'Going home to his very lovely lady wife, the distinguished Mrs Way alias Moby Dick. Six foot eight and a cavalry moustache. Not him. Her.' Frost giggled.

'Why didn't he come in?'

'Thought I had a client, I suppose,' said Frost carelessly, again puzzled by Jerry's watchfulness, and by his quiet. 'Apart from the fact that Moby Dick would kick him to death if she caught him with the smell of alcohol on his evil lips at this hour of the day. Cheer up, you've got me to look after you. Have the other half. You look a bit pious today. Gives me the creeps.'

When you get in there, go, the bearleaders had said. *Don't feel his bones too long, don't let him get comfy with you.*

'Hey Frostie,' Jerry called, when the footsteps had quite faded. 'How's the missus?' Frost had his hand out for Jerry's glass. 'Your missus. How's she doing?'

'Still ailing nicely, thank you,' said Frost uncomfortably.

'Ring the hospital did you?'

'This morning? You're crazy. I wasn't coherent till eleven o'clock. If then. She'd have smelt my breath.'

'When are you next visiting?'

'Look. Shut up. Shut up about her. Do you mind?'

With Frost watching him, Jerry drifted to the safe. He

tried the big handle but it was locked. On the top, covered in dust, lay a heavy riot stick. Taking it in both hands he played a couple of distracted cricket shots, and put it back, while Frost's puzzled stare followed him alertly.

'I want to open an account, Frostie,' said Jerry, still at the safe.

'You?'

'Me.'

'From all you told me last night you haven't the resources to open a bloody piggy bank. Not unless your distinguished dad kept a bit in the mattress, which I somehow doubt.' Frost's world was slipping fast but he tried desperately to hold on to it. 'Look, get yourself a bloody drink and stop playing Boris Karloff on a wet Wednesday, will you? Let's go to the gee-gees. Happy Valley, here we come. I'll buy you lunch.'

'I didn't mean we'd open *my* account exactly, sport. I meant someone else's,' Jerry explained.

In a slow, sad comedy, the fun drained out of Frost's little face, and he muttered 'Oh *no*, oh Jerry,' under his breath, as if he were witnessing an accident in which Jerry, not Frost, were the victim. For the second time, footsteps approached down the corridor. A girl's, short and quick. Then a sharp knock. Then silence.

'Natalie?' said Jerry quietly. Frost nodded. 'If I was a client, would you introduce me?' Frost shook his head. 'Let her in.'

Frost's tongue, like a scared pink snake, peeked out from between his lips, looked quickly round, then vanished.

'Come!' he called, in a hoarse voice, and a tall Chinese girl with thick glasses collected some letters from his out-tray.

'Enjoy your weekend, Mr Frost,' she said.

'See you Monday,' said Frost.

The door closed again.

Coming across the room, Jerry put an arm around Frost's shoulders and guided him, unresisting, quickly to the window.

'A trust account, Frostie. Lodged in your incorruptible hands. Sharpish.'

In the square, the carnival continued. On the cricket field, somebody was out. The lank batsman in the outmoded cap had dropped into a crouch and was patiently repairing the pitch. The fieldsmen lay about and chatted.

'You set me up,' said Frost simply, trying to get used to the notion. 'I thought I had a friend at last and now you want to screw me. And you a lord.'

'Shouldn't mingle with newshounds, Frostie. Rough bunch. No sporting instinct. Shouldn't have shot your mouth off. Where do you keep the records?'

'Friends *do* shoot their mouths off,' Frost protested. 'That's what friends are for! To *tell* each other!'

'Then tell me.'

Frost shook his head. 'I'm a Christian,' he said stupidly. 'I go every Sunday, I never miss. I'm afraid it's quite out of the question. I'd rather lose my place in society than commit a breach of confidence. It's known of me, right? No go. Sorry about that.'

Jerry edged closer along the sill, till their arms were all but touching. The big window-pane was trembling from the traffic. The Venetian blinds were red with building smuts. Frost's face worked pitifully as he wrestled with the news of his bereavement.

'Here's the deal, sport,' said Jerry, very quietly. 'Listen carefully. Right? It's a stick and carrot job. If you don't play, the comic will blow the whistle on you. Front page mugshot, banner headlines, continued back page, col six, the works. "Would you buy a second-hand trust account from this man?" Hong Kong the cess-pit of corruption and Frostie the slavering monster. That line. We'd tell them how you play roundeye musical beds at the young bankers' club, just the way you told it to me, and how till recently you maintained a wicked love-nest over on Kowloonside, only it went sour on you because she wanted more bread. Before they did all that, of course, they'd check the story out with your Chairman and maybe with your missus too, if she's well enough.'

A rainstorm of sweat had broken on Frost's face without warning. One moment his sallow features had shown an oily moistness and that was all. The next they were drenched and the sweat was running unchecked off his plump chin and falling on his Robin Hood suit.

'It's the booze,' he said stupidly, trying to staunch it with his handkerchief. 'I always get this when I drink. Bloody climate, I shouldn't be exposed to it. No one should. Rotting out here. I hate it.'

'That's the *bad* news,' Jerry continued. They were still at the window, side by side, like two men loving the view. 'The good news is five hundred US into your hot little hand, compliments of Grub Street, no one any the wiser, and Frostie for Chairman. So why not sit back and enjoy it? See what I mean?'

'And may I *enquire*,' Frost said at last, with a disastrous shot at sarcasm, 'to what end or purpose you wish to peruse this file in the first place?'

'Crime and corruption, sport. The Hong Kong connection. Grub Street names the guilty men. Account number four four two. Do you keep it here?' Jerry asked, indicating the safe.

Frost made a 'No' with his lips, but no sound came out.

'Both the fours, then the two. Where is it?'

'Look,' Frost muttered. His face was a hopeless mess of fear and disappointment. 'Do me a favour, will you? Keep me out of it. Bribe one of my Chinese clerks, okay? That's the proper way. I mean I've got a position here.'

'You know the saying, Frostie. In Hong Kong even the daisies talk. I want *you*. You're here, and you're better qualified. Is it in the strong room?'

You have to keep it moving, they said, *you have to raise the threshold all the time. Lose the initiative once and you lose it for ever.*

As Frost dithered, Jerry affected to run out of patience. With one very large hand, he seized hold of Frost's shoulder and spun him round, and backed him till his little shoulders were flat against the safe.

'Is it in the strong room?'

'How should I know?'

'I'll tell you how,' Jerry promised, and nodded hard at Frost so that his forelock flopped up and down. 'I'll tell you, sport,' he repeated, tapping Frost's shoulder lightly with his free hand. 'Because otherwise, you're forty and on the road, with a sick wife, and bambinos to feed, and school fees, and the whole catastrophe. It's one thing or t'other, and the moment's now. Not five minutes on but now. I don't care how you do it but make it sound normal and keep Natalie out of it.'

Jerry guided him back into the middle of the room, where his desk stood, and the telephone. There are parts in life which are impossible to play with dignity. Frost's that day was one. Lifting the receiver, he dialled a single digit.

'Natalie? Oh, you haven't gone. Listen, I'll be staying on for an hour yet, I've just had a client on the phone. Tell Syd to leave the strong room on the key. I'll close up when I go, right?'

He slumped into his chair.

'Straighten your hair,' said Jerry, and returned to the window while they waited.

'Crime and corruption, my arse,' Frost muttered. 'All right, suppose he cuts a few corners. Name me a Chinese who doesn't. Name a Brit who doesn't. Do you think that brings the Island to its feet?'

'Chinese, is he?' said Jerry, very sharply.

Coming back to the desk, Jerry himself dialled Natalie's number. No answer. Lifting Frost gently to his feet, Jerry led him to the door.

'Now don't go locking up,' he warned. 'We'll need to put it back before you leave.'

Frost had returned. He sat glumly at the desk, three folders before him on the blotter. Jerry poured him a vodka. Standing at his shoulder while Frost drank it, Jerry explained how a collaboration of this sort worked. Frostie wouldn't feel a thing, he said. All he had to do was leave everything where it lay, then step into the corridor, closing the door carefully after him. Beside the door was a staff noticeboard: Frostie had no doubt observed it often. Frostie should place himself before this noticeboard and read the notices diligently, all of them, until he heard Jerry give two knocks from within, when he could return. While reading he should take care to keep his body at such an angle as to obscure the peephole, so that Jerry would know he was still there, and passers-by would not be able to see in. Frost could also console himself with the thought that he had betrayed no cofidences, Jerry explained. The worst that Higher Authority could ever say – or the client, for that matter – was that by abandoning his room when Jerry was inside it, he had committed a technical breach of the bank's security regulations.

'How many papers are there in the folders?'

'How should I know?' asked Frost, slightly emboldened by his unexpected innocence.

'Count 'em, will you, sport? Attaboy.'

There were fifty exactly, which was a great deal more than Jerry had bargained for. There remained the fallback against the eventuality that Jerry, despite these precautions, might be disturbed.

'I'll need application forms,' he said.

'What bloody application forms? I don't keep forms,' Frost retorted. 'I've got *girls* who bring me forms. No, I haven't. They've gone home.'

'To open my trust account with your distinguished house, Frostie. Spread here on the table, with your hospitality goldplated fountain pen – will you? You're taking a break while I fill them in. And that's the first instalment,' he said. Drawing a little wad of American dollar bills from his hip pocket, he tossed it on the table with a pleasing slap. Frost eyed the money but did not pick it up.

Alone, Jerry worked fast. He disentangled the papers from the clasp and laid them out in pairs, photographing them two pages to a shot, keeping his big elbows close to his body for stillness, and his big feet slightly apart for balance, like a slip-catch at cricket, and the measuring chain just brushing the papers for distance. When he was not satisfied he repeated a shot. Sometimes he bracketed the exposure. Often he turned his head and glanced at the circle of Robin Hood green in the eyehole to make sure Frost was at his post and not, even now, calling in the armoured guards. Once, Frost grew impatient and tapped on the glass and Jerry growled at him to shut up. Occasionally he heard footsteps approach and when that happened he left everything on the table with the money and the application forms, put the camera in his pocket and ambled to the window to gaze at the harbour and yank at his hair, like a man contemplating the great decisions of his life. And once, which is a fiddly game when you have big fingers and you're under stress, he changed the cassette, wishing the old camera's action a shade more quiet. By the time he called Frost back, the folders were once more on his desk, the money was beside the folders, and Jerry was feeling cold and just a little murderous.

'You're a bloody fool,' Frost announced, feeding the five hundred dollars into the buttondown pocket of his tunic.

'Sure,' he said. He was looking round, brushing over his traces.

'You're out of your dirty little mind,' Frost told him. His expression was oddly resolute. 'You think you can bust a man like him? You might as well try and take Fort Knox with a jemmy and a box of firecrackers as take the lid off that crowd.'

'Mister Big himself. I like that.'

'No you won't, you'll hate it.'

'Know him, do you?'

'We're like ham and eggs,' said Frost sourly. 'I'm in and out of his place every day. You know my passion for the high and mighty.'

'Who opened his account for him?

'My predecessor.'

'Been here, has he?'

'Not in my day.'

'Ever seen him?'

'Canidrome in Macao.'

'The *where*?'

'Macao dog races. Losing his shirt. Mixing with the common crowd. I was with my little Chinese bird, the one before last. She pointed him out to me. "Him?" I said. "Him? Oh yes, well he's a client of mine." Very impressed she was.' A flicker of his former self appeared in Frost's subdued features. 'I'll tell you one thing: *he* wasn't doing badly for himself. Very nice blonde party he had with him. Roundeye. Film star by the look of her. Swedish. Lot of conscientious work on the casting couch. Here – '

Frost managed a ghostly smile.

'Hurry, sport. What is it?'

'Let's make it up. Come on. We'll go on the town. Blow my five hundred bucks. You're not really like that, are you? It's just something you do for your living.'

Groping in his pocket, Jerry dug out the alarm key and dropped it into Frost's passive hand.

'You'll need this,' he said.

On the great steps as he left stood a slender, well-dressed young man in low-cut American slacks. He was reading a serious-looking book in the hard back edition, Jerry couldn't see what. He had not got very far into it, but he was reading it intently, like somebody determined upon improving his mind.

Sarratt man once more, the rest blanked out.

Heeltap, said the bearleaders. Never go there straight. If you can't cache the take, you must at least queer the scent. He took taxis, but always to somewhere specific. To the Queen's Pier, where he watched the out-island ferries loading, and the brown junks skimming between the liners. To Aberdeen, where he meandered with the sight-seers gawping at the boat people and the floating restaurants. To Stanley Village, and along the public beach, where pale-bodied Chinese bathers, a little stooped as if the city were still weighing on their shoulders, chastely paddled with their children. *Chinese never swim after the moon festival*, he reminded himself automatically, but he couldn't remember off-hand when the moon festival was.

He had thought of dropping the camera at the hat-check room at the Hilton Hotel. He had thought of night safes, and posting a parcel to himself; of special messengers under journalistic cover. None worked for him – more particularly none worked for the bearleaders. It's a solo, they had said; it's a do-it-yourself or nothing. So he bought something to carry: a plastic shopping bag and a couple of cotton shirts to flesh it out. When you're hot, said the doctrine, make sure you have a distraction. Even the oldest watchers fall for it. And if they flush you and you drop it, who knows? You may even hold off the dogs long enough to get out in your socks. He kept clear of people all the same. He had a living terror of the chance pickpocket. In the hire garage on Kowloonside, they had the car ready for him. He felt calm – he was coming down – but his vigilance never relaxed. He felt victorious and the rest of what he felt was of no account. Some jobs are grubby.

Driving, he watched particularly for Hondas, which in Hong Kong are the poor-bloody-infantry of the watching trade. Before leaving Kowloon he made a couple of passes through sidestreets. Nothing. At Junction Road he joined the picnic convoy and continued toward Clear Water Bay for another hour, grateful for the really bad traffic, for there is nothing harder than unobtrusively ringing the changes between a trio of Hondas caught in a fifteen-mile snarl-up. The rest was watching mirrors, driving, getting there, flying solo. The afternoon heat stayed fierce. He had the airconditioning full on but couldn't feel it. He passed acres of potted plants, Seiko signs, then quilts of paddies and plots of young trees growing for the new-year market. He came to a narrow sand lane to his left and turned sharply into it, watching his mirror. He pulled up, parked for a while with the rear lid up, pretending to let the engine cool. A pea-green Mercedes slid past him, smoked windows, one driver, one passenger up. It had been behind him for some while. But it stuck to the main road. He crossed the road to the café, dialled a number, let the phone ring four times and rang off. He dialled the number again; it rang six times and as the receiver was lifted he rang off again. He drove on, lumbering through remnants of fishing villages to a lakeside where the rushes were threaded far out into the water, and doubled by their own straight reflection. Bullfrogs bellowed and light pleasure yachts switched in and out of the heat haze. The sky was dead white and reached right into the water. He got out. As he did so, an old Citroën van hobbled down the road, several Chinese aboard: Coca-Cola hats, fishing tackle, kids; but two men, no women, and the men ignored him. He made for a row of clapboard balcony-houses, very rundown and fronted with concrete lattice walls like houses on an English sea-front, but the paint on them paler because of the sun. Their names were done in heavy poker work on bits of ship's timber: Driftwood, Susy May, Dun-romin. There was a Marina at the end of the track but it was closed down and the yachts now harboured somewhere else. Approaching the houses, Jerry glanced casually at the upper windows. In the second from the left stood a lurid vase of dried flowers, their stems wrapped in silver paper. All clear, it said. Come in. Pushing open the little gate, he pressed the bell. The Citroën had stopped at the lakeside. He heard the doors slam at the same time as he heard the misused electronics over the entryphone loudspeaker.

'What bastard's that?' a gravel voice demanded, its rich Australian tones thundering through the atmospherics, but the catch on the door was already buzzing and when he shoved it he saw the gross figure of old Craw in his kimono planted at the top of the staircase, hugely pleased, calling him 'Monsignor' and 'you thieving pommie dog', and exhorting him to haul his ugly upper-class backside up here and put a bloody drink under his belt.

The house reeked of burning joss. From the shadows of a ground floor doorway a toothless amah grinned at him, the same strange little creature whom Luke had questioned while Craw was absent in London. The drawing room was on the first floor, the grimy panelling strewn with curling photographs of Craw's old pals, journalists he'd worked with for all of fifty years of crazy oriental history. At the centre stood a table with a battered Remington where Craw was supposed to be composing his life's memoirs. The rest of the room was sparse. Craw, like Jerry, had kids and wives left over from half a dozen existences, and after meeting life's immediate needs there wasn't much money for furniture.

The bathroom had no window.

Beside the handbasin, a developing tank and brown bottles of fixer and developer. Also a small editor with a ground-glass screen for reading negatives. Craw switched off the light and for numberless years in space laboured in the total darkness, grunting and cursing and appealing to the Pope. Beside him Jerry sweated and tried to chart the old man's actions by his swearing. Now, he guessed, Craw was feeding the narrow ribbon from the cassette on to the spool. Jerry imagined him holding it too lightly for fear of marking the emulsion. In a moment he'll be doubting whether he's holding it at all, thought Jerry. He'll be having to will his fingertips into continuing the movement. He felt sick. In the darkness old Craw's cursing grew much louder, but not loud enough to drown the scream of water-birds from the lake. He's deft, thought Jerry, reassured. He can do it in his sleep. He heard the grinding of bakelite as Craw screwed down the lid, and a muttered 'Go to bed you little heathen bastard'. Then the strangely dry rattle as he cautiously shook the airbubbles out of the developer. Then the safety light went on with a snap as loud as a pistol shot, and there was old Craw himself once more, red as a parrot from the glow, stooped over the sealed tank, quickly pouring in the hypo, then confidently overturning the tank and setting it right again while he watched the old kitchen timer stammer through the seconds.

Half stifled with nerves and heat, Jerry returned alone to the drawing room, poured himself a beer and slumped into a cane chair, looking nowhere while he listened to the steady running of the tap. From the window came the bubbling of Chinese voices. At the lake's edge the two fishermen had set up their tackle. The children were watching them, sitting in the dust. From the bathroom came the scratching of the lid again, and Jerry leapt to his feet, but Craw must have heard him, for he growled 'wait' and closed the door.

Airline pilots, journalists, spies, the Sarratt doctrine warned. *It's the same drag. Bloody inertia interspersed with bouts of bloody frenzy.*

He's taking first look, thought Jerry: in case it's fumble. In the pecking order, it was Craw, not Jerry, who had to make his peace with London. Craw, who in the worst contingency, would order him to take a second bite of Frost.

'What are you doing in there, for Christ's sake?' Jerry yelled. 'What goes on?'

Perhaps he's having a pee, he thought absurdly.

Slowly the door opened. Craw's gravity was awesome.

'They haven't come out,' said Jerry.

He had the feeling of not reaching Craw at all. He was going to repeat himself in fact, loudly. He was going to dance about and made a damn scene. So that Craw's answer, when it finally came, came just in time.

'To the contrary, my son.' The old boy took a step forward and Jerry could see the films now, hanging behind him like black wet worms from Craw's little clothes line, pink pegs holding them in place. 'To the contrary, sir,' he said, 'every frame is a bold and disturbing masterpiece.'

Chapter 7

More About Horses

In the Circus the first scraps of news on Jerry's progress arrived in the early morning, in a deadly quiet, and thereafter set the weekend upside down. Knowing what to expect Guillam had taken himself to bed at ten and slumbered fitfully between bouts of anxiety for Jerry, and frankly lustful visions of Molly Meakin with and without her sedate swimming suit. Jerry was due to present himself to Frost just after four a.m. London time and by three-thirty Guillam was clattering in his old Porsche through the foggy streets toward Cambridge Circus. It could have been dawn or dusk. He arrived at the rumpus room to find Connie completing *The Times* crossword and Doc di Salis reading the meditations of Thomas Traherne, plucking his ear and jiggling his foot at the same time, like a one-man percussion band. Restless as ever, Fawn flitted between them, dusting and tidying, a headwaiter impatient for the next sitting. Now and then he sucked his teeth and let out a breathy 'tah' in barely controlled frustration. A pall of tobacco smoke hung like a raincloud across the room and there was the usual stink of rank tea from the samovar. Smiley's door was closed and Guillam saw no cause to disturb him. He opened a copy of *Country Life*. Like waiting at the bloody dentist, he thought, and sat staring mindlessly at photographs of great houses till Connie softly put down her crossword, sat bolt upright and said 'Listen'. Then he heard a quick snarl from the Cousins' green telephone before Smiley picked it up. Through the open doorway to his own room Guillam glanced at the row of electronic boxes. On one, a green caution light burned for as long as the conversation lasted. Then the pax rang in the rumpus room – pax being jargon for internal phone – and this time Guillam reached it before Fawn.

'He's entered the bank,' Smiley announced cryptically over the pax.

Guillam relayed the message to the gathering. 'He's gone into the bank,' he said, but he might have been talking to the dead. Nobody gave the slightest sign of hearing.

By five Jerry had come out of the bank. Nervously contemplating the options, Guillam felt physically sick. Burning was a dangerous game and like most pros Guillam hated it, though not for reasons of scruple. First there was the quarry or, worse, the local security angels. Second there was the burn itself, and not everybody responded logically to blackmail. You got heroes, you got liars, you got hysterical virgins who put their heads back and screamed blue murder even when they were enjoying it. But the real danger came now, when the burn was over and Jerry had to turn his back on the smoking bomb and run. Which way would Frost jump? Would he telephone the police? His mother? His boss? His wife? 'Darling, I'll confess all, save me and we'll turn over a new leaf.' Guillam did not even rule out the ghastly possibility that Frost might go directly to his client: 'Sir, I have come to purge myself of a gross breach of bank confidence.'

In the fusty eeriness of early morning, Guillam shuddered, and fixed his mind resolutely on Molly.

On the next occasion the green phone sounded, Guillam didn't hear it. George must have been sitting right over the thing. Suddenly the pinlight in Guillam's room was glowing and it continued glowing for fifteen minutes. It went out and they waited, all eyes fixed on Smiley's door, willing him from his seclusion. Fawn was frozen in mid-movement, holding a plate of brown marmalade sandwiches which nobody would ever eat. Then the handle tipped and Smiley appeared with a common-or-garden search request form in his hand, already completed in his own neat script and flagged 'stripe' which meant 'urgent for Chief' and was the top priority. He gave it to Guillam and asked him to take it straight to the Queen Bee in Registry and stand over her while she looked up the name. Receiving it, Guillam recalled an earlier moment when he had been presented with a similar form, made out in the name of Worthington, Elizabeth alias Lizzie, and ending 'high-class tart'. And as he departed, he heard Smiley quietly inviting Connie and di Salis to accompany him to the throne-room, while Fawn was packed off to the unclassified library in search of the current edition of *Who's Who in Hong Kong*.

The Queen Bee had been specially summoned for the dawn shift, and when Guillam walked in on her, her lair looked like a tableau of 'The Night London Burned', complete with an iron bunk and a small primus stove, though there was a coffee machine in the corridor. All she needs is a boiler suit and a portrait of Winston Churchill, he thought. The details on the trace read 'Ko forename Drake other names unknown, date of birth 1925 Shanghai, present address Seven Gates, Headland Road, Hong Kong, occupation Chairman and Managing Director of China Airsea Ltd, Hong Kong'. The Queen Bee launched herself on an impressive paperchase but all she finally came up with was the information that Ko had been appointed to the Order of the British Empire under the Hong Kong list in 1966 for 'social and charitable service to the Colony', and that the Circus had responded 'nothing recorded against', to a vetting enquiry from the Governor's office before the award was passed up for approval. Hurrying upstairs with his glad intelligence, Guillam was awake enough to remember that China Airsea Ltd, Hong Kong, had been described by Sam Collins as the ultimate owner of that mickey-mouse airline in Vientiane which had been the beneficiary of Commercial Boris's bounty. This struck Guillam as a most orderly connection. Pleased with himself, he returned to the throne-room to be greeted by dead silence. Strewn over the floor lay not just the current edition of *Who's Who* but several back-numbers as well: Fawn, as usual, had overreached himself. Smiley sat at his desk and he was staring at a sheet of notes in his own handwriting. Connie and di Salis were staring at Smiley, but Fawn was absent again, presumably on another errand. Guillam handed Smiley the trace form with the Queen Bee's findings written along the middle in her best Kensington copperplate. At the same moment the green phone crackled again. Lifting the receiver Smiley began jotting on the sheet before him.

'Yes. Thanks, I have that. Go on, please. Yes, I have that also.' And so on for ten minutes, till he said: 'Good. Till this evening then,' and rang off.

Outside in the street, an Irish milkman was enthusiastically proclaiming that he never would be the wild rover no more.

'Westerby's landed the complete file,' Smiley said finally – though like everyone else he referred to him by his cryptonym. 'All the figures.' He nodded as if agreeing with himself, still studying the paper. 'The film won't be here till tonight but the shape is already clear. Everything that was originally paid through Vientiane has found its way to the account in Hong Kong. Right from the very beginning Hong Kong was the final destination of the goldseam. All of it. Down to the last cent. No deductions, not even for bank commission. It was at first a humble figure, then rose steeply, why we may only guess. All as Collins described. Till it stopped at twenty-five thousand a month and stayed there. When the Vientiane arrangement ended, Centre didn't miss a single month. They switched to the alternative route immediately. You're right, Con. Karla never does anything without a fallback.'

'He's a professional, darling,' Connie Sachs murmured. 'Like you.'

'Not like me.' He continued studying his own jottings. 'It's a lockaway account,' he declared in the same matter-of-fact tone. 'Only one name is given and that's the founder of the trust. Ko. "Beneficiary unknown," they say. Perhaps we shall see why tonight. Not a penny has been drawn,' he said, singling out Connie Sachs. He repeated that: 'Since the payments started over two years ago, not a single penny has been drawn from the account. The balance stands in the order of half a million American dollars. With compound interest it's naturally rising fast.'

To Guillam, this last piece of intelligence was daylight madness. What the hell was the point to half a million dollar goldseam if the money was not even used when it reached the other end? To Connie Sachs and di Salis, on the other hand, it was patently of enormous significance. A crocodile smile spread slowly across Connie's face and her baby eyes fixed on Smiley in silent ecstasy.

'Oh *George*,' she breathed at last, as the revelation gathered in her. 'Darling. *Lockaway*! Well, that's quite a different kettle of fish. Well of course it had to be, didn't it! It had all the signs. From the very first *day*. And if fat, stupid Connie hadn't been so blinkered and old and doddery and idle, she'd have read them off *long* ago! You leave me alone, Peter Guillam, you lecherous young toad.' She was pulling herself to her feet, her crippled hands clamped over the chair arms. 'But who can be worth so much? Would it be a network? No, no, they'd never do it for a *network*. No precedent. Not a wholesale thing, that's unheard of. So who can it be? Whatever can he *deliver* that would be worth so much?' She was hobbling toward the door, tugging the shawl over her shoulders, slipping already from their world to her own. '*Karla* doesn't pay money out like that.' They heard her mutterings follow her. She passed the mothers' lane of covered typewriters, muffled sentinels in the gloom. '*Karla's* such a mean prig he thinks his agents should work for him for *nothing*! Course he does. *Pennies*, that's what he pays them. Pocket money. Inflation is all very well, but half a million dollars for one little mole. I never heard such a thing!'

In his quirkish way di Salis was no less impressed than Connie. He sat with the top part of his crabbed, uneven body tilted forward, and he was stirring feverishly in the bowl of his pipe with a silver knife as if it were a cookpot which had caught on the flame. His silver hair stood wry as a cockscomb over the dandruffed collar of his crumpled black jacket.

'Well, well, no wonder Karla wanted the bodies buried,' he blurted suddenly, as if the words had been jerked out of him. 'No wonder. Karla's a China hand too, you know. It is attested. I have it from Connie.' He clambered to his feet, holding too many things in his little hands: pipe, tobacco tin, his penknife and his Thomas Traherne. 'Not sophisticated naturally. Well one doesn't expect that. Karla's no scholar, he's a soldier. But not blind either, not by a long chalk, she tells me. *Ko.*' He repeated the name at several different levels. 'Ko. *Ko.* I must see the character. It depends entirely on the characters. *Height . . . Tree* even, yes, I can see tree . . . or can I? . . . oh and several other concepts. "Drake" is mission school of course. Shanghainese mission boy: Well, well. Shanghai was where it all started you know. First Party cell *ever* was in Shanghai. Why did I say that? *Drake Ko.* Wonder what his real names are. We shall find that all out very shortly no doubt. Yes, good. Well I think I might go back to my reading too. Smiley, do you think I might have a coal-scuttle in my room? Without the heating on, one simply freezes up. I've asked the housekeepers a dozen times and had nothing but impertinence for my pains. *Anno domini* I'm afraid, but the winter is almost upon us I suppose. You'll show us the raw material as soon as it arrives, I trust? One doesn't like to work too long on potted versions. I shall make a *curriculum vitae.* That will be my first thing. Ko. Ah, thank you, Guillam.'

He had dropped his Thomas Traherne. Accepting it he dropped his tobacco tin, so Guillam picked up that as well. 'Drake Ko. Shanghainese doesn't mean a thing of course. Shanghai was the real melting pot. Chiu Chow's the answer, judging by what we know. Still, mustn't jump the gun. Baptist. Well, the Chiu Chow Christians mostly are, aren't they? Swatownese: where did we have that? Yes, the intermediate company in Bangkok. Well, that figures well enough. Or Hakka. They're not mutually exclusive, not by any means.' He stalked after Connie into the corridor, leaving Guillam alone with Smiley, who rose and, going to an armchair, slumped into it staring sightlessly at the fire.

'Odd,' he remarked finally. 'One has no sense of shock. Why is that, Peter? You know me. Why is it?'

Guillam had the wisdom to keep quiet.

'A big fish. In Karla's pay. Lockaway accounts, the threat of Russian spies at the very centre of the Colony's life. So why no sense of shock?'

The green telephone was barking again. This time Guillam took the call. As he did so, he was surprised to see a fresh folder of Sam Collins's Far Eastern reports lying open on the desk.

That was the weekend. Connie and di Salis sank without trace; Smiley set to work preparing his submission; Guillam smoothed feathers, called in the mothers and arranged for typing in shifts. On the Monday, carefully briefed by Smiley, he telephoned Lacon's private secretary. He did it very well. 'No drumbeats,' Smiley had warned. 'Keep it very idle.' And Guillam did just that. There had been talk over dinner the other evening – he said – of convening the Intelligence Steering Group to consider certain *prima facie* evidence:

'The case has firmed up a little, so perhaps it would be sensible to fix a date. Give us the batting order and we'll circulate the document in advance.'

'A *batting order*? Firmed up? Where *ever* do you people learn your English?'

Lacon's private secretary was a fat voice called Pym. Guillam had never met him, but he loathed him quite unreasonably.

'I can only tell him,' Pym warned. 'I can tell him and I can see what he says and I can ring you back. His card is *very* heavily marked this month.'

'It's just one little waltz if he can manage it,' said Guillam and rang off in a fury.

You bloody well wait and see what hits you, he thought.

* * *

When London is having its baby, the folklore says, the fieldman can only pace the waiting room. Airline pilots, newshounds, spies: Jerry was back with the bloody inertia.

'We're in mothballs,' Craw announced. 'The word is well done and hold your water.'

They talked every two days at least, limbo calls between two third-party telephones, usually one hotel lobby to another. They disguised their language with a mix of Sarratt wordcode and journalistic mumbo-jumbo.

'Your story is being checked out on high,' Craw said. 'When our editors have wisdom, they will impart it in due season. Meanwhile, slap your hand over it and keep it there. That's an order.'

Jerry had no idea how Craw talked to London and he didn't care as long as it was safe. He assumed some co-opted official from the huge, untouchable, above-the-line intelligence fraternity was playing linkman: but he didn't care.

'Your job is to put in mileage for the comic and tuck some spare copy under your belt which you can wave at Brother Stubbs when the next crisis comes,' Craw said to him. 'Nothing else, hear me?'

Drawing on his jaunts with Frost, Jerry bashed out a piece on the effect of the American military pullout on the nightlife of Wanchai: 'What's happened to Susie Wong since war-weary GIs with bulging wallets have ceased to flock in for rest and recreation?' He fabricated – or, as journalists prefer it, *hyped* – a 'dawn interview' with a disconsolate and fictitious bar-girl who was reduced to accepting Japanese customers, air-freighted his piece and got Luke's bureau to telex the number of the waybill, all as Stubbs had ordered. Jerry was by no means a bad reporter, but just as pressure brought out the best in him, sloth brought out the worst. Astonished by Stubbs's prompt and even gracious acceptance – a 'herogram' Luke called it, phoning through the text from the bureau – he cast around for other heights to scale. A couple of sensational corruption trials were attracting good houses, starring the usual crop of misunderstood policemen, but after taking a look at them, Jerry concluded they hadn't the scale to travel. England had her own these days. A 'please-matcher' ordered him to chase a story floated by a rival comic about the alleged pregnancy of Miss Hong Kong but a libel suit got there ahead of him. He attended an arid government press briefing by Shallow Throat, himself a humourless reject from a Northern Irish daily, idled away a morning researching successful stories from the past that might stand re-heating; and on the strength of rumour about army economy cuts, spent an afternoon being trailed round the Gurkha garrison by a public relations major who looked about eighteen. And no the major *didn't* know, thank you, in reply to Jerry's cheerful enquiry, what his men would do for sex when their families were sent home to Nepal. They would be visiting their villages about once every three years, he thought; and he seemed to think that was quite enough for anyone. Stretching the facts till they read as if the Gurkhas were already a community of military grass widowers, 'Cold Showers in a Hot Climate for Britain's Mercenaries', Jerry triumphantly landed himself an inside lead. He banked a couple more stories for a rainy day, lounged away the evenings at the Club and inwardly gnawed his head off while he waited for the Circus to produce its baby.

'For Christ's sake,' he protested to Craw. 'The bloody man's practically public property.'

'All the same,' said Craw firmly.

So Jerry said 'Yes, sir,' and a couple of days later, out of sheer boredom, began his own entirely informal investigation into the life and loves of Mr Drake Ko, OBE, Steward of the Royal Hong Kong Jockey Club, millionaire and citizen above suspicion. Nothing dramatic; nothing, in Jerry's book, disobedient; for there is not a fieldman born who does not at one time or another stray across the borders of his brief. He began tentatively, like journeys to a forbidden biscuit box. As it happened, he had been considering proposing to Stubbs a three-part series on the Hong Kong super-rich. Browsing in the reference shelves of the Foreign Correspondents' Club before lunch one day, he unconsciously took a leaf from Smiley's book and turned up Ko, Drake, in the current edition of *Who's Who in Hong Kong*: married, one son, died 1968; sometime law student of Gray's Inn, London, but not a successful one, apparently, for there was no record of his having been called to the Bar. Then a rundown of his twenty-odd directorships. Hobbies: horseracing, cruising and jade. Well, whose aren't? Then the charities he supported, including a Baptist church, a Chiu Chow Spirit Temple and the Drake Ko Free Hospital for Children. Backed all the possibilities, Jerry reflected with amusement. The photograph showed the usual soft-eyed, twenty-year-old beautiful soul, rich in merit as well as goods, and was otherwise unrecognisable. The dead son's name was Nelson. Jerry noticed: Drake and Nelson, British admirals. He couldn't get it out of his mind that the father should be named after the first British sailor to enter the China Seas, and the son after the hero of Trafalgar.

Jerry had a lot less difficulty than Peter Guillam in making the connection between China Airsea in Hong Kong and Indocharter SA in Vientiane, and he was amused to read in the China Airsea company prospectus that its business was described as a 'wide spread of trading and transportation activities in the South East Asian theatre' – including rice, fish, electrical goods, teak, real estate and shipping.

Devilling at Luke's bureau, he took a bolder step: the sheerest accident shoved the name of Drake Ko under his nose. True, he had looked up Ko in the card index. Just as he had looked up a dozen or twenty other wealthy Chinese in the Colony; just as he had asked the Chinese clerk, in perfectly good faith who *she* thought were the most exotic Chinese millionaires for his purpose. And while Drake might not have been one of the absolute front runners, it took very little to draw the name from her, and consequently the papers. Indeed, as he had already protested to Craw, there was something flattening, not to say dreamlike, about pursuing by hole-and-corner methods a man so publicly evident. Soviet intelligence agents, in Jerry's limited experience of the breed, normally came in more modest versions. Ko seemed king-sized by comparison.

Reminds me of old Sambo, Jerry thought. It was the first time this intimation struck him.

The most detailed offering appeared in a glossy periodical called *Golden Orient*, now out of print. In one of its last editions, an eight-page illustrated feature titled 'The Red Knights of Nanyang' concerned itself with the growing number of overseas Chinese with profitable trade relations with Red China, commonly known as fat-cats. Nanyang, as Jerry knew, meant the realms south of China; and implied to the Chinese a kind of Eldorado of peace and wealth. To each chosen personality the feature devoted a page and a photograph, generally shot against a background of his possessions. The hero of the Hong Kong interview – there were pieces from Bangkok, Manila, and Singapore as well – was that 'much-loved sporting personality and Jockey Club Steward', Mr Drake Ko, President, Chairman, Managing Director and chief shareholder of China Airsea Ltd, and he was shown with his horse Lucky Nelson at the end of a successful season in Happy Valley. The horse's name momentarily arrested Jerry's Western eye. He found it macabre that a father should christen a horse after his dead son.

The accompanying photograph revealed rather more than the spineless mugshot in *Who's Who*. Ko looked jolly, even exuberant, and he appeared, despite his hat, to be hairless. The hat was at this stage the most interesting thing about Ko, for it was one which no Chinese, in Jerry's limited experience, had ever been seen to wear. It was a beret, worn sloping, and putting Ko somewhere between a British soldier and a French onion seller. But above all, it had for a Chinese the rarest quality of all: self mockery. He was apparently tall, he was wearing a Burberry, and his long hands stuck out of the sleeves like twigs. He seemed genuinely to like the horse, and one arm rested easily on its back. Asked why he still ran a junk fleet when these were commonly held to be unprofitable, he replied: 'My people are Hakka from Chiu Chow. We breathed the water, farmed the water, slept on the water. Boats are my element.' He was fond also of describing his journey from Shanghai to Hong Kong in 1951. At that time the border was still open and there were no effective restrictions on immigration. Nevertheless, Ko chose to make the trip by fishing junk, pirates, blockades and bad weather notwithstanding: which was held at the very least to be eccentric.

'I'm a very lazy fellow,' he was reported as saying. 'If the wind will blow me for nothing, why should I walk? Now I've got a sixty-foot cruiser but I still love the sea.'

Famous for his sense of humour, said the article.

A good agent must have entertainment value, say the Sarratt bearleaders: that was something Moscow Centre also understood.

There being no one watching, Jerry ambled over to the card index and a few minutes later had taken possession of a thick folder of presscuttings, the bulk of which concerned a share scandal in 1965, in which Ko and a group of Swatownese had played a shady part. The Stock Exchange enquiry, not surprisingly, proved inconclusive and was shelved. The following year Ko got his OBE. 'If you buy people,' old Sambo used to say, 'buy them thoroughly.'

In Luke's bureau they kept a bunch of Chinese researchers, among them a convivial Cantonese named Jimmy who often appeared at the Club and was paid at Chinese rates to be the oracle on Chinese matters. Jimmy said the Swatownese were a people apart, 'like Scots or Jews', hardy, clannish and notoriously thrifty, who lived near the sea so that they could run for it when they were persecuted or starving or in debt. He said their women were sought after, being beautiful, diligent, frugal and lecherous.

'Writing yourself another novel, your lordship?' the dwarf asked endearingly, coming out of his office to find out what Jerry was up to. Jerry had wanted to ask why a Swatownese should have been brought up in Shanghai, but he thought it wiser to bend course toward a less delicate topic.

Next day, Jerry borrowed Luke's battered car. Armed with a standard-size thirty-five millimetre camera he drove to Headland Road, a millionaire's ghetto between Repulse Bay and Stanley, where he made a show of rubbernecking at the outside of the villas there, as many idle tourists do. His cover story was still that feature for Stubbs on the Hong Kong super-rich: even now, even to himself, he would scarcely have admitted to going there on acount of Drake Ko.

'He's raising Cain in Taipei,' Craw had told him casually in one of their limbo calls. 'Won't be back till Thursday.' Once again, Jerry accepted without question Craw's lines of communication.

He did not photograph the house called Seven Gates, but he took several long, stupid gazes at it. He saw a low, pantiled villa set well back from the road, with a big verandah on the seaward side and a pergola of white-painted pillars cut against the blue horizon. Craw had told him that Drake must have chosen the name because of Shanghai, whose old city walls were pierced with seven gates: 'Sentiment, my son. Never underrate the power of sentiment upon a slanteye, and never count on it either. Amen.' He saw lawns, including to his amusement a croquet lawn. He saw a fine collection of azaleas and hibiscus. He saw a model junk about ten feet long set on a concrete sea, and he saw a garden bar, round like a bandstand, with a blue and white striped awning over it, and a ring of empty white chairs presided over by a boy in a white coat and trousers and white shoes. The Ko's were evidently expecting company. He saw other houseboys washing a tobacco-coloured Rolls-Royce Phantom saloon. The long garage was open, and he recorded a Chrysler station-wagon of some kind, and a Mercedes, black, with the licence plates removed, presumably as part of some repair. But he was meticulous about giving equal attention to the other houses in Headland Road and photographed three of them.

Continuing to Deep Water Bay he stood on the shore gazing at the small armada of stockbroker junks and launches which bobbed at anchor on the choppy sea, but was not able to pick out *Admiral Nelson*, Ko's celebrated ocean-going cruiser – the ubiquity of the name Nelson was becoming positively oppressive. About to give up, he heard a cry from below him, and walking down a rickety wooden causeway found an old woman in a sampan grinning up at him and pointing to herself with a yellow chicken's leg she had been sucking with her toothless gums. Clambering aboard he indicated the boats and she took him on a tour of them, laughing and chanting while she sculled, and keeping the chicken leg in her mouth. *Admiral Nelson* was sleek and low-lined. Three more boys in white ducks were diligently scouring the decks. Jerry tried to calculate Ko's monthly housekeeping bill, just for staff alone.

On the drive back, he paused to examine the Drake Ko Free Hospital for Children and established, for what it was worth, that that too was in excellent repair. Next morning early, Jerry placed himself in the lobby of a chintzy highrise office building in Central, and read the brass plates of the business companies housed there. China Airsea and its affiliates occupied the top three floors, but somewhat predictably there was no mention of Indocharter, Vientiane SA, the former recipient of twenty-five thousand US dollars on the last Friday of every month.

The cuttings folder in Luke's bureau had contained a cross-reference to US Consulate archives. Jerry called there next day, ostensibly to check out his story on the American troops in Wanchai. Under the eye of an unreasonably pretty girl, Jerry drifted, picked at a few things, then settled on some of the oldest stuff they had, which dated from the very early Fifties when Truman had put a trade embargo on China and North Korea. The Hong Kong Consulate had been ordered to report infringements, and this was the record of what they had unearthed. The favourite commodity, next to medicines and electrical goods, was oil, and 'the United States Agencies', as they were styled, had gone for it in a big way, setting traps, putting out gun boats, interrogating defectors and prisoners, and finally placing huge dossiers before Congressional and Senate Sub-Committees.

The year in question was 1951, two years after the Communist takeover in China and the year Ko sailed to Hong Kong from Shanghai without a cent to his name. The operation to which the bureau's reference directed him was Shanghainese, and to begin with, that was the only connection it had with Ko. Many Shanghainese immigrants in those days lived in a crowded, insanitary hotel on the Des Voeux Road. The introduction said that they were like one enormous family, welded together by shared suffering and squalor. Some had escaped together from the Japanese before escaping from the Communists.

'After enduring so much at Communist hands,' one culprit told his interrogators, 'the least we could do was make a little money out of them.'

Another was more aggressive. 'The Hong Kong fat-cats are making millions out of this war. Who sells the Reds their electronic equipment, their penicillin, their rice?'

In fifty-one there were two methods open to them, said the report. One was to bribe the frontier guards and truck the oil across the New Territories and over the border. The other was taking it by ship, which meant bribing the harbour authorities.

An informant again: 'Us Hakka know the sea. We find boat, three hundred tons, we rent. We fill with drums of oil, make false manifest and false destination. We reach international waters, run like hell for Amoy. Reds call us brother, profit one hundred per cent. After a few runs we buy boat.'

'Where did the original money come from?' the interrogator demanded.

'Ritz Ballroom,' was the disconcerting answer. The Ritz was a high-class pick-up spot right down the King's Road on the waterfront, said a footnote. Most of the girls were Shanghainese. The same footnote named members of the gang. Drake Ko was one.

'Drake Ko was very tough boy,' said a witness's statement given in fine print in the appendix. 'You don't tell no fairy story to Drake Ko. He don't like politician people one piece. Chiang Kai-shek. Mao. He say they all one person. He say he big supporter of Chiang Mao-shek. One day Mr Ko lead our gang.'

As to organised crime, the investigation turned up nothing. It was a matter of history that Shanghai, by the time it fell to Mao in forty-nine, had emptied three-quarters of its underworld into Hong Kong; that the Red Gang and the Green Gang had fought enough battles over the Hong Kong protection rackets to make Chicago in the twenties look like child's play. But not a witness could be found who admitted to knowing anything about Triads or any other criminal outfit.

Not surprisingly, by the time Saturday came round and Jerry was on his way to Happy Valley races, he possessed quite a detailed portrait of his quarry.

The taxi charged double because it was the races and Jerry paid because he knew it was the form. He had told Craw he was going and Craw had not objected. He had brought Luke along for the ride, knowing that sometimes two are less conspicuous than one. He was nervous of bumping into Frost, because roundeye Hong Kong is a very small city indeed. At the main entrance he telephoned the management to raise some influence, and in due course a Captain Grant appeared, a young official to whom Jerry explained that this was work: he was writing the place up for the comic. Grant was a witty, elegant man who smoked Turkish cigarettes through a holder, and everything Jerry said seemed to amuse him in a fond, if rather remote way.

'You're the son, then,' he said finally.

'Did you know him?' said Jerry, grinning.

'Only *of* him,' Captain Grant replied, but he seemed to like what he had heard.

He gave them badges, and offered them drinks later. The second race was just over. While they talked, they heard the roar of the crowd set-to and rise and die like an avalanche. Waiting for the lift Jerry checked the notice-board to see who had taken the private boxes. The hardy annuals were the Peak mafia: The Bank – as the Hong Kong and Shanghai Bank liked to call itself – Jardine Matheson, the Governor, the Commander, British Forces. Mr Drake Ko, OBE, though a Steward of the Club, was not among them.

'Westerby! Good *God*, man, who the hell ever let you in here? Listen, is it true your dad went bust before he died?'

Jerry hesitated, grinning, then belatedly drew the card from his memory: Clive Somebody, pigs-in-clover solicitor, house in Repulse Bay, overpowering Scot, all false affability and an open reputation for crookedness. Jerry had used him for background in a Macao-based gold swindle and concluded that Clive had had a slice of the cake.

'Gosh, Clive, super, marvellous.'

They exchanged banalities, still waiting for the lift.

'Here. Give us your card. Come on! I'll make your fortune yet.' *Porton*, thought Jerry: Clive Porton. Tearing the racecard from Jerry's hand, Porton licked his big thumb, turned to a centre page and ringed a horse's name in ballpoint. 'Number seven in the third, you can't go wrong,' he breathed. 'Put your shirt on it, okay? Not every day I give away money, I'll tell you.'

'What did the slob sell you?' Luke enquired, when they were clear of him.

'Thing called Open Space.'

Their ways divided. Luke went off to place bets and wangle his way into the American Club upstairs. Jerry on an impulse took a hundred dollars' worth of Lucky Nelson and set a hasty course for the Hong Kong Club's luncheon room. 'If I lose,' he thought drily, 'I'll chalk it up to George.' The double doors were open and he walked straight in. The atmosphere was of dowdy wealth: a Surrey golf club on a wet weekend, except that those brave enough to risk the pickpockets wore real jewels. A group of wives sat apart, like expensive unused equipment, scowling at the closed-circuit television and moaning about servants and muggings. There was a smell of cigar smoke and sweat and departed food. Seeing him shamble in – the awful suit, the buckskin boots, 'Press' written all over him – their scowls darkened. The trouble with being exclusive in Hong Kong, their faces said, was that not enough people are thrown out. A school of serious drinkers had gathered at the bar, mainly carpet-baggers from the London merchant banks with beer-bellies and fat necks before their time. With them, the Jardine Matheson second eleven, not yet grand enough for the firm's private box: groomed, unlovable innocents for whom Heaven was money and promotion. Apprehensively, he glanced round for Frostie, but either the gee-gees hadn't drawn him today, or he was with some other crowd. With one grin and one vague flap of the hand for all of them, Jerry winkled out the under-manager, saluted him like a lost friend, talked airily of Captain Grant, slipped him twenty bucks for himself, signed up for the day in defiance of every regulation, and stepped gratefully on to the balcony with still eighteen minutes before the off: sun, the stink of dung, the feral rumble of a Chinese crowd, and Jerry's own quickening heartbeat that whispered 'horses'.

For a moment, Jerry hung there, grinning, taking in the view, because every time he saw it was the first time.

The grass at Happy Valley racecourse must be the most valuable crop on earth. There was very little of it. A narrow ring ran round the edge of what looked like a London borough recreation ground which sun and feet have beaten into dirt. Eight scuffed football pitches, one rugger pitch, one hockey, gave an air of municipal neglect. But the thin green ribbon which surrounded this dingy package in that year alone was like to attract a cool hundred million sterling through legal betting, and the same amount again in the shade. The place was less a valley than a firebowl: glistening white stadium one side, brown hills the other, while ahead of Jerry and to his left lurked the other Hong Kong: a cardhouse Manhattan of grey sky-scraper slums crammed so tight they seemed to lean on one another in the heat. From each tiny balcony a bamboo pole stuck out like a pin put in to brace the structure. From each pole hung innumerable flags of black laundry, as if something huge had brushed against the building, leaving these tatters in its wake. It was from places like these, for all but the tiniest few that day, that Happy Valley offered the gambler's dream of instantaneous salvation.

Away to the right of Jerry shone newer, grander buildings. There, he remembered, the illegal bookies pitched their offices and by a dozen arcane methods – tic-tac, walkie-talkie, flashing lights – Sarratt would have been entranced by them – kept up their dialogue with legmen round the course. Higher again ran the spines of shaven hilltop slashed by quarries and littered with the ironmongery of electronic eavesdropping. Jerry had heard somewhere that the saucers had been put there for the Cousins, so that they could track the sponsored over-flights of Taiwanese U2s. Above the hills, dumplings of white cloud which no weather ever seemed to clear away. And above the cloud, that day, the bleached China sky aching in the sun, and one hawk slowly wheeling. All this, Jerry took in at a single, grateful draught.

For the crowd it was the aimless time. The focus of attention, if anywhere, was the four fat Chinese women in fringed Hakka hats and black pyjama suits who were marching down the track with rakes, prinking the precious grass where the galloping hoofs had mussed it. They moved with the dignity of total indifference: it was as if the whole of Chinese peasantry were depicted in their gestures. For a second, in the way crowds have, a tremor of collective affinity reached out to them, and was forgotten.

The betting put Clive Porton's Open Space third favourite. Drake Ko's Lucky Nelson was in with the field at forty to one, which meant nowhere. Edging his way past a bunch of festive Australians, Jerry reached the corner of the balcony and, craning, peered over the tiers of heads to the owners' box, cut off from the common people by a green iron gate and a security guard. Shading his eyes and wishing he had brought binoculars, he made out one fat, hard-looking man in a suit and dark glasses, accompanied by a young and very pretty girl. He looked half Chinese, half Latin, and Jerry put him down as Filipino. The girl was the best that money could buy.

Must be with his horse, thought Jerry, recalling old Sambo. Most likely in the paddock, briefing his trainer and the jockey.

Striding back through the luncheon room to the main lobby, he dropped into a wide back-stairway for two floors and crossed a hall to the viewing gallery, which was filled with a vast and thoughtful Chinese crowd, all men, staring downward in devotional silence into a covered sandpit filled with noisy sparrows and three horses, each led by his permanent male groom, the mafoo. The mafoos held their charges miserably, as if sick with nerves. The elegant Captain Grant was looking on, so was an old White Russian trainer called Sacha whom Jerry loved. Sacha sat on a tiny folding chair, leaning slightly forward as if he were fishing. Sacha had trained Mongolian ponies in the treaty days of Shanghai, and Jerry could listen to him all night: how Shanghai had had three racecourses, British, International and Chinese; how the British merchant princes kept sixty, even a hundred horses apiece and sailed them up and down the coast, competing like madmen with each other from port to port. Sacha was a gentle, philosophical fellow with faraway blue eyes and an all-in wrestler's jaw. He was also the trainer of Lucky Nelson. He sat alone, watching what Jerry took to be a doorway out of his own line of sight.

A sudden hubbub from the stands caused Jerry to turn sharply toward the sunlight. A roar sounded, then one high, strangled shriek as the crowd on one tier swayed and an axehead of grey and black uniforms tore into it. An instant later and a swarm of police was dragging some wretched pickpocket, bleeding and coughing, into the tunnel stairway for a voluntary statement. Dazzled, Jerry returned his gaze to the interior darkness of the sand-paddock, and took a moment to focus on the fogged outline of Mr Drake Ko.

The identification was nowhere near immediate. The first person Jerry noticed was not Ko at all, but the young Chinese jockey standing at old Sacha's side, tall boy, thin as wire where his silks were nipped into his breeches. He was slapping his whip against his boot as if he had seen the gesture in an English sporting print, and he was wearing Ko's colours ('sky blue and sea-grey quartered' said the article in *Golden Orient*) and like Sacha he was staring at something out of Jerry's sight. Next, from under the platform where Jerry stood, came a bay griffin, led by a giggly fat mafoo in filthy grey overalls. His number was hidden by a rug, but Jerry knew the horse already from its photograph, and he knew it even better now: he knew it really well, in fact. There are some horses that are simply superior to their class, and Lucky Nelson to Jerry's eye was one. Bit of quality, he thought, nice long rein, a bold eye. None of your jail-bait chestnut with a light mane and tail that take the women's vote in every race: given the local form, which is heavily restricted by the climate, Lucky Nelson was as sound as anything he'd seen here. Jerry was sure of it. For one bad moment he was anxious about the horse's condition: sweating, too much gloss on the flanks and quarters. Then he looked again at the bold eye, and the slightly unnatural sweatlines, and his heart rose again: cunning devil's had him hosed down to make him look poorly, he thought, in joyous memory of old Sambo.

It was only at that late point, therefore, that Jerry moved his eye from the horse to its owner.

Mr Drake Ko, OBE, the recipient to date of a cool half million of Moscow Centre's American dollars, the avowed supporter of Chiang Mao-shek, stood apart from everyone, in the shadow of a white concrete pillar ten feet in diameter: an ugly but inoffensive figure at first glance, tall, with a stoop that should have been occupational: a dentist, or a cobbler. He was dressed in an English way, in baggy grey flannels and a black double-breasted blazer too long in the waist, so that it emphasised the disjointedness of his legs and gave a crumpled look to his spare body. His face and neck were as polished as old leather and as hairless, and the many creases looked sharp as ironed pleats. His complexion was darker than Jerry had expected: he would almost have suspected Arab or Indian blood. He wore the same unsuitable hat of the photograph, a dark blue beret, and his ears stuck out from under it like pastry roses. His very narrow eyes were stretched still finer by its pressure. Brown Italian shoes, white shirt, open neck. No props, not even binoculars: but a marvellous half-million-dollar smile, ear to ear, partly gold, that seemed to relish everyone's good fortune as well as his own.

Except there was a hint – some men have it, it is like a tension: headwaiters, doormen, journalists can spot it at a glance; old Sambo *almost* had it – there was a hint of resources instantly available. If things were needed, hidden people would bring them at the double.

The picture sprang to life. Over the loudspeaker the clerk of the course ordered the jockeys to mount. The giggly mafoo pulled off the rug, and Jerry to his pleasure noticed that Ko had had the bay's coat back-brushed to emphasise his supposedly poor condition. The thin jockey made the long, awkward journey to the saddle, and with nervous friendliness called down to Ko on the other side of him. Ko, already moving away, swung round and snapped something back, one inaudible syllable, without looking where he spoke or who picked it up. A rebuke? An encouragement? An order to a servant? The smile had lost none of its exuberance, but the voice was hard as a whipcrack. Horse and rider took their leave. Ko took his, Jerry raced back up the stairs, through the lunch room to the balcony, waded to the corner, and looked down.

By then, Ko was no longer alone, but married.

Whether they arrived together on the stand, whether she followed him at a moment's distance, Jerry was never sure. She was so small. He spotted a glitter of black silk and a movement round it as men deferred – the stand was filling up – but at first he looked too high and missed her. Her head was at the level of their chests. He picked her up again at Ko's side, a tiny, immaculate Chinese wife, sovereign, elderly, pale, so groomed you could never imagine she had been any other age or worn any clothes but these Paris-tailored black silks, frogged and brocaded like a hussar's. *Wife's a handful*, Craw had said, extemporising as they sat bemused in front of the tiny projector. *Pinches from the big stores. Ko's people have to get in ahead of her and promise to pay for whatever she nicks.*

The article in *Golden Orient* referred to her as 'an early business partner'. Reading between the lines, Jerry guessed she'd been one of the girls at the Ritz Ballroom.

The crowd's roar had gathered throat.

'Did you do him, Westerby? Did you do him, man?' Scottish Clive Porton was bearing down on him, sweating heavily from drink. 'Open Space, for God's sake! Even at those odds you'll make a dollar or two! Go on man, it's a cert!'

The 'off' spared him a reply. The roar choked, lifted and swelled. All round him a pitter-patter of names and numbers fluttered in the stands, the horses sprang from their traps, drawn forward by the din. The lazy first furlong had begun. Wait: frenzy will follow the inertia. In the dawn light when they train, Jerry remembered, their hoofs are muffled in order to spare the residents their slumbers. Sometimes in the old days, drying out between war stories, Jerry would get up early and come down here just to watch them, and if he was lucky, and found an influential friend, go back with them to the airconditioned, multi-storey stables where they lived, to watch the grooming and the cosseting. Whereas by day the howl of traffic drowned their thunder entirely and the glittering cluster that advanced so slowly made no sound at all, but floated on the thin emerald river.

'Open Space all the way,' Clive Porton announced uncertainly, as he watched through his glasses. 'The favourite's done it. Splendid. Well done, Open Space, well done, lad.' They began the long turn before the final straight. '*Come* on Open Space, stretch for it man, *ride*! Use your whip, you cretin!' Porton screamed, for by now it was clear even to the naked eye that the sky blue and sea-grey colours of Lucky Nelson were heading for the front, and that his competitors were courteously making way for him. A second horse put up a show of challenging, then flagged, but Open Space was already three lengths behind while his jockey worked furiously with his whip on the air around his mount's quarters.

'Objection!' Porton was shouting. 'Where's the Stewards for God's sake? That horse was pulled! I never saw a horse so pulled in my life!'

As Lucky Nelson loped gracefully past the post, Jerry quickly turned his gaze to the right again, and down. Ko appeared unmoved. It was not oriental inscrutability: Jerry had never subscribed to that myth. Certainly it was not indifference. It was merely that he was observing the satisfactory unfolding of a ceremony: Mr Drake Ko watches a march-past of his troops. His little mad wife stood poker-backed beside him as if, after all the struggles of her life, they were finally playing her anthem. For a second Jerry was reminded of old Pet in her prime. Just the way Pet looked, thought Jerry, when Sambo's pride came in a good eighteenth. Just the way she stood, and coped with failure.

The presentation was a moment for dreams.

While the scene lacked a cake-stall, the sunshine was certainly far beyond the expectation of the most sanguine organiser of an English village fête; and the silver cups were a great deal more lavish than the scratched little beaker presented by the squire for excellence in the three-legged race. The sixty uniformed policemen were also perhaps a trifle ostentatious. But the gracious lady in a nineteen-thirties turban who presided over the long white table was as mawkish and arrogant as the most exacting patriot would have wished. She knew the form exactly. The Chairman of the Stewards handed her the cup and she quickly held it away from her as if it were too hot for her hands. Drake Ko and his wife, both grinning hugely, Ko still in his beret, emerged from a cluster of delighted supporters and grabbed the cup, but they tripped so fast and merrily back and forth across the roped-off patch of grass that the photographer was caught unprepared and had to ask the actors to re-stage the moment of consummation. This annoyed the gracious lady quite a lot, and Jerry caught the words 'bloody bore' drawled out over the chatter of the onlookers. The cup was finally Ko's, the gracious lady took sullen delivery of six hundred dollars' worth of gardenias, East and West returned gratefully to their separate cantonments.

'Do him?' Captain Grant enquired amiably. They were sauntering back toward the stands.

'Well *yes*, actually,' Jerry confessed with a grin. 'Bit of a turn-up, wasn't it?'

'Oh, it was Drake's race, all right,' said Grant drily. They walked a little. 'Clever of you to spot it. More than we did. Do you want to talk to him?'

'Talk to who?'

'Ko. While he's flushed with victory. Perhaps you'll get something out of him for once,' said Grant with that fond smile. 'Come, I'll introduce you.'

Jerry did not falter. As a reporter he had every reason to say 'yes'. As a spy – well, sometimes they say at Sarratt that nothing is insecure but thinking makes it so. They sauntered back to the group. The Ko party had formed a rough circle round the cup and the laughter was very loud. At the centre, closest to Ko, stood the fat Filipino with his beautiful girl, and Ko was clowning with the girl, kissing her on both cheeks, then kissing her again, while everyone laughed except Ko's wife, who withdrew deliberately to the edge and began talking to a Chinese woman her own age.

'That's Arpego,' said Grant in Jerry's ear and indicated the fat Filipino. 'He owns Manila and most of the out-islands.'

Arpego's paunch sat forward over his belt like a rock stuffed inside his shirt.

Grant did not make straight for Ko, but singled out a burly bland-faced Chinese of forty in an electric blue suit, who seemed to be some kind of aide. Jerry stood off, waiting. The plump Chinese came over to him, Grant at his side.

'This is Mr Tiu,' said Grant quietly. 'Mr Tiu, meet Mr Westerby, son of the famous one.'

'You wanna talk to Mr Ko, Mr Wessby?'

'If it's convenient.'

'Sure it's convenient,' said Tiu euphorically. His chubby hands floated restlessly in front of his stomach. He wore a gold watch on his right wrist. His fingers were curled, as if to scoop water. He was sleek and shiny and he could have been thirty or sixty. 'Mr Ko win a horse-race, everything's convenient. I bring him over. Stay here. What's your father's name?'

'Samuel,' said Jerry.

'*Lord* Samuel,' said Grant firmly, and inaccurately.

'Who is he?' Jerry asked aside, as plump Tiu returned to the noisy Chinese group.

'Ko's majordomo. Manager, chief bag carrier, bottle washer, fixer. Been with him since the start. They ran away from the Japanese together in the war.'

And his chief crusher too, Jerry thought, watching Tiu waddling back with his master.

Grant began again with the introductions.

'Sir,' he said, 'this is Westerby, whose famous father, the Lord, had a lot of very slow horses. He also bought several race-courses for the bookmakers.'

'What paper?' said Ko. His voice was harsh and powerful and deep, yet to Jerry's surprise he could have sworn he caught a trace of an English North Country accent, reminiscent of old Pet's.

Jerry told him.

'That the paper with the girls!' Ko yelled gaily. 'I used to read that paper when I was in London, during my residence there for the purpose of legal study at the famous

Gray's Inn of Court. Do you know why I read your paper, Mr Westerby? It is my sound opinion that the more papers which are printing pretty girls in preference to politics today, the more chance we get of a damn sight better world, Mr Westerby,' Ko declared, in a vigorous mixture of misused idiom and boardroom English. 'Kindly tell that to your paper from me, Mr Westerby. I give it to you as free advice.'

With a laugh, Jerry opened his notebook.

'I backed your horse, Mr Ko. How does it feel to win?'

'Better than losing, I think.'

'Doesn't wear off?'

'I like it better every time.'

'Does the same go for business?'

'Naturally.'

'Can I speak to Mrs Ko?'

'She's busy.'

Jotting, Jerry was disconcerted by a familiar smell. It was of a musky, very pungent French soap, a blend of almonds and rosewater favoured by an early wife: but also, apparently, by the shiny Tiu for his greater allure.

'What's your formula for winning, Mr Ko?'

'Hard work. No politics. Plenty sleep.'

'Are you a lot richer than you were ten minutes ago?'

'I was pretty rich ten minutes ago. You may tell your paper also I am a great admirer of the British way of life.'

'Even though we don't work hard? And make a lot of politics?'

'Just tell them,' Ko said, straight at him, and that was an order.

'What makes you so lucky, Mr Ko?'

Ko appeared not to hear this question, except that his smile slowly vanished. He was staring straight at Jerry, measuring him through his very narrow eyes, and his face had hardened remarkably.

'What makes you so lucky, sir?' Jerry repeated.

There was a long silence.

'No comment,' Ko said, still into Jerry's face.

The temptation to press the question had become irresistible. 'Play fair, Mr Ko,' Jerry urged, grinning largely. 'The world's full of people who dream of being as rich as you are. Give them a clue, won't you? What makes you so lucky?'

'Mind your own damn business,' Ko told him, and without the smallest ceremony turned his back on him and walked away. At the same moment, Tiu took a leisurely half pace forward, arresting Jerry's line of advance, with one soft hand on his upper arm.

'You going to win next time round, Mr Ko?' Jerry called over Tiu's shoulder at his departing back.

'You better ask the horse, Mr Wessby,' Tiu suggested with a chubby smile, hand still on Jerry's arm.

He might as well have done so, for Ko had already rejoined his friend Mr Arpego, the Filipino, and they were laughing and talking just as before. *Drake Ko was very tough boy*, Jerry remembered. *You don't tell no fairy story to Drake Ko*. Tiu doesn't do so badly either, he thought.

As they walked back toward the grandstand, Grant was laughing quietly to himself.

'Last time Ko won he wouldn't even lead the horse into the paddock after the race,' he recalled. 'Waved it away. Didn't want it.'

'Why the hell not?'

'Hadn't expected it to win, that's why. Hadn't told his Chiu Chow friends. Bad face. Maybe he felt the same when you asked him about his luck.'

'How did he get to be a Steward?'

'Oh, had Tiu buy the votes for him, no doubt. The usual thing. Cheers. Don't forget your winnings.'

Then it happened: Ace Westerby's unforeseen scoop.

The last race was over, Jerry was four thousand dollars to the good and Luke had disappeared. Jerry tried the American Club, Club Lusitano and a couple of others, but either they hadn't seen him or they'd thrown him out. From the enclosure there was only one gate, so Jerry joined the march. The traffic was chaotic. Rolls-Royces and Mercedes vied for kerb space and the crowds were shoving from behind. Deciding not to join the fight for taxis, Jerry started along the narrow pavement and saw to his surprise Drake Ko, alone, emerging from a gateway across the road, and for the first time since Jerry had set eyes on him he was not smiling. Reaching the roadside, he seemed undecided whether to cross, then settled for where he was, gazing at the on-coming traffic. He's waiting for the Rolls-Royce Phantom, thought Jerry, remembering the fleet in the garage at Headland Road. Or the Merc, or the Chrysler. Suddenly Jerry saw him whip off the beret and, clowning, hold it into the road, as if to draw rifle fire. The wrinkles flew up around his eyes and jaw, his gold teeth glittered in welcome and instead of a Rolls-Royce, or a Merc, or a Chrysler, a long red Jaguar E-type with a soft top folded back screeched to a stop beside him, oblivious of the other cars. Jerry couldn't have missed it if he'd wanted to. The noise of the tyres alone turned every head along the pavement. His eye read the number, his mind recorded it. Ko climbed aboard with all the excitement of someone who might never have ridden in an open car before, and he was already talking and laughing before they pulled away. But not before Jerry had seen the driver, her fluttering blue headscarf, dark glasses, long blonde hair, and enough of her body, as she leaned across Drake to lock his door, to know that she was a hell of a lot of woman. Drake's hand was resting on her bare back, fingers splayed, his spare hand was waving about while he no doubt gave her a blow-by-blow account of his victory, and as they set off together he planted a very un-Chinese kiss on her cheek, and then, for good measure, two more: but all, somehow, with a great deal more sincerity than he had brought to the business of kissing Mr Arpego's escort.

On the other side of the road stood the gateway Ko had just come out of, and the iron gate was still open. His mind spinning, Jerry dodged the traffic and walked through. He was in the old Colonial Cemetery, a lush place, scented with flowers and shaded by heavy overhanging trees. Jerry had never been here and he was shocked to enter such seclusion. It was built up an opposing slope round an old chapel that was gently falling into disuse. Its cracking walls glinted in the speckled evening light. Beside it, from a chickenwire kennel, an emaciated Alsatian dog howled at him in fury.

Jerry peered round, not knowing why he was here or what he was looking for. The graves were of all ages and races and sects. There were White Russian graves and their orthodox headstones were dark and scrolled with Czarist grandeur. Jerry imagined heavy snow on them and their shape still coming through. Another stone described a restless sojourn of a Russian princess and Jerry paused to read it: Tallin to Peking, with dates, Peking to Shanghai, dates again, to Hong Kong in forty-nine, to die. 'And estates in Sverdlovsk', the inscription ended defiantly. Was Shanghai the connection?

He rejoined the living: three old men in blue pyjama suits sat on a shaded bench, not talking. They had hung their cage-birds in the branches overhead, close enough to hear one another's song above the noise of traffic and cicadas. Two gravediggers in steel helmets were filling a new grave. No mourners watched. Still not knowing what he wanted, he reached the chapel steps. He peered through the door. Inside was pitch dark after the sunlight. An old woman glared at him. He drew back. The Alsatian dog howled at him still louder. It was very young. A sign said 'Verger' and he followed it. The shriek of the cicadas was deafening, even drowning the dog's barking. The scent of flowers was steamy and a little rotten. An idea had struck him, almost an intimation. He was determined to pursue it.

The verger was a kindly distant man and spoke no English. The ledgers were very old, the entries resembled ancient bank accounts. Jerry sat at a desk slowly turning the heavy pages, reading the names, the dates of birth, death, and burial; lastly the map reference: the zone, and the number. Having found what he was looking for, he stepped into the air again, and made his way along a different path, through a cloud of butterflies, up the hill toward the cliff-side. A bunch of schoolgirls watched him from a footbridge, giggling. He took off his jacket and trailed it over his shoulder. He passed between high shrubs and entered a slanted coppice of yellow grass where the headstones were very small, the mounds only a foot or two long. Jerry sidled past them, reading the numbers, till he found himself in front of a low iron gate marked seven two eight. The gate was part of a rectangular perimeter, and as Jerry lifted his eyes he found himself looking at the statue of a small boy in Victorian knickerbockers and an Eton jacket, life size, with tousled stone curls and rosebud stone lips, reading or singing from an open stone book while real butterflies dived giddily round his head. He was an entirely English child, and the inscription read *Nelson Ko in loving memory*. A lot of dates followed, and it took Jerry a second to understand their meaning: ten successive years with none left out and the last 1968. Then he realised they were the ten years the boy had lived, each one to be relished. On the bottom step of the plinth lay a large bunch of orchids, still in their paper.

Ko was thanking Nelson for his win. Now at least Jerry understood why he did not care to be invaded with questions about his luck.

There is a kind of fatigue, sometimes, which only fieldmen know: a temptation to gentleness which can be the kiss of death. Jerry lingered a moment longer, staring at the orchids and the stone boy, and setting them, in his mind, beside everything he had seen and learned of Ko till now. And he had an overwhelming feeling – only for a moment, but dangerous at any time – of completeness, as if he had met a family, only to discover it was his own. He had a feeling of arrival.

Here was a man, housed this way, married that way, striving and playing in ways Jerry effortlessly understood. A man of no particular persuasion, yet Jerry saw him in that moment more clearly than he had ever seen himself. A Chiu Chow poor-boy who becomes a Jockey Club Steward with an OBE, and hoses down his horse before a race. A Hakka water-gypsy who gives his child a Baptist burial and an English effigy. A capitalist who hates politics. A failed lawyer, a gangboss, a builder of hospitals who runs an opium airline, a supporter of spirit temples who plays croquet and rides about in a Rolls-Royce. An American bar in his Chinese garden, and Russian gold in his trust account. Such complex and conflicting insights did not, at that moment, alarm Jerry in the least; they presaged no foreboding or paradox. Rather, he saw them welded by Ko's own harsh endeavour into a single but many-sided man not too unlike old Sambo. Stronger still – for the few seconds that it lasted – he had an irresistible feeling of being in good company, a thing he had always liked. He returned to the gate in a mood of calm munificence, as if he, not Ko, had won the race. It was not till he reached the road that reality returned him to his senses.

The traffic had cleared and he found a taxi straight away. They had driven a hundred yards when he saw Luke performing lonely pirouettes along the kerb. Jerry coaxed him aboard and dumped him outside the Foreign Correspondents' Club. From the Furama Hotel he rang Craw's home number, let it ring twice, rang it again and heard Craw's voice demanding 'Who the bloody hell is that?' He asked for a Mr Savage, received a foul rebuke and the information that he was ringing the wrong number, allowed Craw half an hour to get to another phone, then walked over to the Hilton to field the return call.

Our friend had surfaced in person, Jerry told him. Been put on public view on account of a big win. When it was over a very nice blonde party gave him a lift in her sports car. Jerry recited the licence number. They were definitely friends, he said. Very demonstrative and un-Chinese. At *least* friends, he would say.

'Roundeye?'

'Of course she was bloody well roundeye! Who the hell ever heard of a – '

'Jesus,' said Craw softly, and rang off before Jerry even had a chance to tell him about little Nelson's shrine.

Chapter 8

The Barons Confer

The waiting room of the pretty Foreign Office conference house in Carlton Gardens was slowly filling up. People in twos and threes, ignoring each other, like mourners for a funeral. A printed notice hung on the wall saying 'Warning, no confidential matter to be discussed'. Smiley and Guillam perched disconsolately beneath it, on a bench of salmon velvet. The room was oval, the style Ministry of Works rococo. Across the painted ceiling, Bacchus pursued nymphs who were a lot more willing to be caught than Molly Meakin. Empty firebuckets stood against the wall and two government messengers guarded the door to the interior. Outside the curved sash windows, autumn sunlight filled the park, making each leaf crisp against the next. Saul Enderby strode in, leading the Foreign Office contingent. Guillam knew him only by name. He was a former Ambassador to Indonesia, now chief pundit on South East Asian affairs, and said to be a great supporter of the American hard line. In tow, one obedient Parliamentary Under-Secretary, a trade union appointment, and one flowery, overdressed figure who advanced on Smiley on tiptoe, hands held horizontal, as if he had caught him napping.

'Can it be?' he whispered exuberantly. 'Is it? It *is*! George Smiley, all in your feathers. My dear, you've lost simply pounds. Who's your nice boy? Don't tell me. Peter Guillam. I've heard all about him. *Quite* unspoilt by failure, I'm told.'

'Oh *no*!' Smiley cried involuntarily. 'Oh Lord. *Roddy*.'

'What do you mean? "Oh no. Oh Lord, Roddy,"' Martindale demanded, wholly undeterred in the same vibrant murmur. '"Oh *yes*" is what you mean! "Yes, Roddy. Divine to see you, Roddy!" Listen. Before the riff-raff come. How is the exquisite Ann? For my very own ears. Can I make a dinner for the two of you? You shall choose the guests. How's that? And yes I *am* on the list, if that's what's going through your ratlike little mind, young Peter Guillam, I've been translated, I'm a goodie, our new masters adore me. So they should, the fuss I've made of them.'

The interior doors opened with a bang. One of the messengers shouted 'Gentlemen!' and those who knew the form stood back to let the women file ahead. There were two. The men followed and Guillam brought up the tail. For a few yards it might have been the Circus: a makeshift bottleneck at which each face was checked by janitors, then a makeshift corridor leading to what resembled a builders' cabin parked at the centre of a gutted stairwell: except that it had no windows and was suspended from wires and held tight by guy-ropes. Guillam had lost sight of Smiley entirely, and as he climbed the hardboard steps and entered the safe room he saw only shadows hovering under a blue nightlight.

'Do *do* something, somebody,' Enderby growled in the tones of a bored diner complaining about the service. 'Lights, for God's sake. *Bloody* little men.'

The door slammed behind Guillam's back, a key turned in the lock, an electronic hum did the scale and whined out of earshot, three striplights stammered to life, drenching everyone in their sickly pallor.

'Hoorah,' said Enderby, and sat down. Later, Guillam wondered how he had been so sure it was Enderby calling in the darkness, but there are voices you can hear before they speak.

The conference table was covered in a ripped green baize like a billiards table in a youth club. The Foreign Office sat one end, the Colonial Office at the other. The separation was visceral rather than legal. For six years the two departments had been formally married under the grandiose awnings of the Diplomatic Service, but no one in his right mind took the union seriously. Guillam and Smiley sat at the centre, shoulder to shoulder, each with empty chairs to the other side of him. Examining the cast, Guillam was absurdly aware of costume. The Foreign Office had come sharply dressed in charcoal suits and the secret plumage of privilege: both Enderby and Martindale wore Old Etonian ties. The Colonialists had the homeweave look of country people come to town, and the best they could offer in the way of ties was one Royal Artilleryman: honest Wilbraham, their leader, a fit lean schoolmasterly figure with crimson veins on his weatherbeaten cheeks. A tranquil woman in church-organ brown supported him, and to the other side a freshly-minted boy with freckles and a shock of ginger hair. The rest of the committee sat across from Smiley and Guillam, and had the air of seconds in a duel they disapproved of and they had come in twos for protection: dark Pretorius of the Security Service with one nameless woman bag-carrier; two pale warriors from Defence; two Treasury bankers, one of them Welsh Hammer. Oliver Lacon was alone and had set himself apart from everyone, for all the world the person least engaged. Before each pair of hands lay Smiley's submission in a pink and red folder marked 'Top Secret Withhold', like a souvenir programme. The 'withhold' meant keep it away from the Cousins. Smiley had drafted it, the mothers had typed it, Guillam himself had watched the eighteen pages come off the duplicators and supervised the hand-stitching of the twenty-four copies. Now their handiwork lay tossed around this large table, among the water glasses and the ashtrays. Lifting a copy six inches above the table, Enderby let it fall with a slap.

'All read it?' he asked. All had.

'Then let's go,' said Enderby and peered round the table with bloodshot, arrogant eyes. 'Who'll start the bowling? Oliver? You got us here. You shoot first.'

It crossed Guillam's mind that Martindale, the great

scourge of the Circus and its works, was curiously subdued. His eyes were turned dutifully to Enderby, and his mouth sagged unhappily.

Lacon meanwhile was setting out his defences. 'Let me say first that I'm as much taken by surprise in this as anyone else,' he said. 'This is a real body-blow, George. It would have been helpful to have had a little preparation. It's a little uncomfortable for *me*, I have to tell you, to be the link to a service which has rather cut its links of late.'

Wilbraham said 'hear, hear'. Smiley preserved a Mandarin silence. Pretorius of the competition frowned in agreement.

'It also comes at an awkward time,' Lacon added portentously. 'I mean the thesis, your thesis *alone*, is – well, momentous. A lot to swallow. A lot to face up to, George.'

Having thus secured his back way out, Lacon made a show of pretending there might not be a bomb under the bed at all.

'Let me try to summarise the summary. May I do that? In bald terms, George. A prominent Hong Kong Chinese citizen is under suspicion of being a Russian spy. That's the nub?'

'He is known to receive very large Russian subventions,' Smiley corrected him, but talking to his hands.

'From a secret fund devoted to financing penetration agents?'

'Yes.'

'*Solely* for financing them? Or does this fund have other uses?'

'To the best of our knowledge it has no other use at all,' said Smiley in the same lapidary tone as before.

'Such as – propaganda – the informal promotion of trade – kickbacks, that kind of thing? No?'

'To the best of our knowledge: no,' Smiley repeated.

'Ah, but how good's their knowledge?' Wilbraham called from below the salt. 'Hasn't been too good in the past, has it?'

'You see what I'm getting at?' Lacon asked.

'We would want *far* more corroboration,' the Colonial lady in church brown said with a heartening smile.

'So would we,' Smiley agreed mildly. One or two heads lifted in surprise. 'It is in order to obtain corroboration that we are asking for rights and permissions.'

Lacon resumed the initiative.

'Accept your thesis for a moment. A secret intelligence fund, all much as you say.'

Smiley gave a remote nod.

'Is there any suggestion that he subverts the Colony?'

'No.'

Lacon glanced at his notes. It occurred to Guillam that he had done a lot of homework.

'He is not, for example, preaching the withdrawal of their sterling reserves from London? Which would put us a further nine hundred million pounds in the red?'

'To my knowledge: no.'

'He is not telling us to get off the Island. He is not whipping up riots or urging amalgamation with the Mainland, or waving the wretched treaty in our faces?'

'Not that we know.'

'He's not a leveller. He's not demanding effective trade unions, or a free vote, or a minimum wage, or compulsory education, or racial equality, or a separate parliament for the Chinese instead of their tame assemblies, whatever they're called?'

'Legco and Exco,' Wilbraham snapped. 'And they're not tame.'

'No, he isn't, said Smiley.

'Then what *is* he doing?' Wilbraham interrupted excitedly. 'Nothing. That's the answer. They've got it all wrong. It's a goose-chase.'

'For what it's worth,' Lacon proceeded, as if he hadn't heard, 'he probably does as much to enrich the Colony as any other wealthy and respected Chinese businessman. Or as little. He dines with the Governor, but he is not known to rifle the contents of his safe, I assume. In fact, to all outward purposes, he is something of a Hong Kong prototype: Steward of the Jockey Club, supports the charities, pillar of the integrated society, successful, benevolent, has the wealth of Croesus and the commercial morality of the whorehouse.'

'I say, that's a bit hard!' Wilbraham objected. 'Steady on, Oliver. Remember the new housing estates.'

Again Lacon ignored him:

'Short of the Victoria Cross, a war disability pension and a baronetcy, therefore, it is hard to see how he could be a less suitable subject for harassment by a British service, or recruitment by a Russian one.'

'In my world we call that good cover,' said Smiley.

'*Touché*, Oliver,' said Enderby with satisfaction.

'Oh everything's cover these days,' said Wilbraham mournfully, but it didn't get Lacon off the hook.

Round one to Smiley, thought Guillam in delight, recalling the dreadful Ascot dinner: *Hitty-pitty within the wall, and bumps goes Pottifer*, he chanted inwardly, with due acknowledgment to his hostess.

'Hammer?' said Enderby, and the Treasury had a brief fling in which Smiley was hauled over the coals for his financial accounts, but no one except the Treasury seemed to find Smiley's transgression relevant.

'This is not the purpose for which you were granted a secret float,' Hammer kept insisting in Welsh outrage. 'That was post mortem funds only – '

'Fine, fine, so Georgie's been a naughty boy,' Enderby interrupted in the end, closing him down. 'Has he thrown his money down the drain or has he made a cheap killing? That's the question. Chris, time the Empire had its shout.'

Thus bidden, Colonial Wilbraham formally took the floor, backed by his lady in church brown and his red-haired assistant, whose young face was already set bravely in protection of his headmaster.

Wilbraham was one of those men who are unconscious of how much time they take to think. 'Yes,' he began after an age. 'Yes. Yes, well I'd like to stay with the money, if I may, much as Lacon did, to begin with.' It was already clear that he regarded the submission as an assault upon his territory. 'Since the money is all we've got to go on,' he remarked pointedly, turning back a page in his folder. 'Yes.' And there followed another interminable hiatus. 'You say here the money first of all came from Paris through Vientiane.' Pause. 'Then the Russians switched systems, so to speak, and it was paid through a different channel altogether. A Hamburg–Vienna–Hong Kong tie-up. Endless complexities, subterfuges, all that – we'll take your word for it – right? Same amount, different hat, so to speak. Right. Now why d'you think they did that, so to speak?

So to speak, recorded Guillam, who was very susceptible to verbal tics.

'It is sensible practice to vary the routine from time to time,' Smiley replied, repeating the explanation he had already offered in the submission.

'*Tradecraft*, Chris,' Enderby put in, who liked his bit of jargon, and Martindale, still *piano*, shot him a glance of admiration.

Again Wilbraham slowly wound himself up.

'We've got to be guided by what Ko *does*,' Wilbraham declared, with puzzled fervour, and rattled his knuckles on the baize table. 'Not by what he *gets*. That's my argument. After all, I mean dash it, it's not Ko's own money is it? Legally it's nothing to do with him.' The point caused a moment's puzzled silence. 'Page two, top. Money's all in trust.' A general shuffle as everyone but Smiley and Guillam reached for their folders. 'I mean, not only is none of it being *spent*, which in itself is jolly odd – I'll come to that in a bit – it's *not Ko's money*. It's in trust, and when the claimant comes along, whoever he or she is, it will be the claimant's money. Till then it's the trust's money. So to speak. So, I mean, *what's Ko done wrong*? Opened a trust? No law against that. Done every day. Specially in Hong Kong. The *beneficiary* of the trust – oh, well, he could be anywhere! In Moscow, or Timbuctoo or . . .' He didn't seem to be able to think of a third place, so he dried up, to the discomfort of his ginger-headed assistant, who scowled straight at Guillam as if to challenge him. 'Point is: what's against *Ko*?'

Enderby was holding a matchstick to his mouth, and rolling it between his front teeth. Conscious, perhaps, that his adversary had made a good point badly – whereas his own speciality tended to be the reverse – he took it out and contemplated the wet end.

'Hell's all this balls about *thumbprints*, George?' he asked, perhaps in an effort to deflate Wilbraham's success. 'Like something out of Phillips Oppenheim.'

Belgravia Cockney, thought Guillam: the last stage of linguistic collapse.

Smiley's answers contained about as much emotion as a speaking clock.

'The use of thumbprints is old banking practice along the China coast. It dates from the days of widespread illiteracy. Many overseas Chinese prefer to use British banks rather than their own, and the structure of this account is by no means extraordinary. The beneficiary is not named, but identifies himself by a visual means, such as the torn half of a banknote, or in this case his left thumbprint on the assumption that it is less worn by labour than the right. The bank is unlikely to raise an eyebrow provided that whoever founded the trust has indemnified the trustees against charges of accidental or wrongful payment.'

'Thank you,' said Enderby, and did more delving with the matchstick. 'Could be Ko's *own* thumbprint I suppose,' he suggested. 'Nothing to stop him doing that, is there? *Then* it would be his money all right. If he's trustee and beneficiary all at once, of *course* it's his own damn money.'

To Guillam, the issue had already taken a quite ludicrous wrong turning.

'That's pure supposition,' Wilbraham said after the usual two-minute silence. 'Suppose Ko's doing a favour for a chum. Just suppose that for a moment. And this chum's on a fiddle, so to speak, or doing business with the Russians at several removes. Your Chinese *loves* a conspiracy. Get up to *all* the tricks, even the nicest of 'em. Ko's no different, I'll be bound.'

Speaking for the first time, the red-haired boy ventured direct support.

'The submission rests on a fallacy,' he declared bluntly, speaking at this stage more to Guillam than to Smiley. Sixth-form puritan, thought Guillam: thinks sex weakens you and spying is immoral. '*You* say Ko is on the Russian payroll. *We* say that's not demonstrated. We say the trust *may* contain Russian money, but that Ko and the trust are separate entities.' In his indignation he went on too long. 'You're talking about guilt. Whereas *we* say Ko's done nothing wrong under Hong Kong law and should enjoy the due rights of a Colonial subject.'

Several voices pounced at once. Lacon's won. 'No one is talking about guilt,' he retorted. 'Guilt doesn't enter into it in the least degree. We're talking about security. Solely. Security, and the desirability or otherwise of investigating an apparent threat.'

Welsh Hammer's Treasury colleague was a bleak Scot, as it turned out, with a style as bald as the sixth-former's.

'Nobody's sizing up to infringe Ko's Colonial rights either,' he snapped. 'He hasn't any. There's nothing in Hong Kong law *whatever* which says the Governor cannot steam open Mr Ko's mail, tap Mr Ko's telephone, suborn his maid or bug his house to kingdom come. Nothing whatever. There are a few other things the Governor can do too, if he feels like it.'

'Also speculative,' said Enderby, with a glance to Smiley. 'Circus has no local facilities for those high-jinks and anyway in the circumstances they'd be insecure.'

'They would be scandalous,' said the red-haired boy unwisely, and Enderby's gourmet eye, yellowed by a lifetime's luncheons, lifted to him, and marked him down for future treatment.

So that was the second, inconclusive skirmish. They hacked about in this way till coffee break, no victor and no corpses. Round two a draw, Guillam decided. He wondered despondently how many rounds there would be.

'What's it all about?' he asked Smiley under the buzz. 'They won't make it go away by talking.'

'They have to reduce it to their own size,' Smiley explained uncritically. Beyond that, he seemed bent on oriental self-effacement, and no prodding from Guillam was going to shake him out of it. Enderby demanded fresh ashtrays. The Parliamentary Under-Secretary said they should try to make progress.

'Think what it's costing the taxpayer, just having us sit here,' he urged proudly. Lunch was still two hours away.

Opening round three, Enderby moved the ticklish issue of whether to advise the Hong Kong Government of the intelligence regarding Ko. This was impish of him, in Guillam's view, since the position of the shadow Colonial Office (as Enderby referred to his homespun *confrères*) was still that there was no crisis, and consequently nothing for anyone to be advised of. But honest Wilbraham, failing to see the trap, walked into it and said:

'Of course we should advise Hong Kong! They're self-administering. We've no alternative.'

'Oliver?' said Enderby with the calm of a man who holds good cards. Lacon glanced up, clearly irritated at being drawn into the open. 'Oliver?' Enderby repeated.

'I'm *tempted* to reply that it's Smiley's case and Wilbraham's Colony and we should let them fight it out,' he said, remaining firmly on the fence.

Which left Smiley: 'Oh well, if it were the Governor and nobody else I could hardly object,' he said. 'That is, if you feel it's not too much for him,' he added dubiously, and Guillam saw the red-head stoke himself up again.

'Why the dickens should it be too much for the Governor?' Colonial Wilbraham demanded, genuinely perplexed. 'Experienced administrator, shrewd negotiator. Find his way through anything. Why's it too much?'

This time, it was Smiley who made the pause. 'He would have to encode and decode his own telegrams of course,' he mused, as if he were even now working his way obliviously through all the implications. 'We couldn't have him cutting his staff in on the secret, naturally. That's asking too much of anyone. Personal code books – well we can fix him up with those, no doubt. Brush up his coding if he needs it. There is also the problem, I suppose, of the Governor being forced into the position of *agent provocateur* if he continues to receive Ko socially – which he obviously must. We can't frighten the game at this stage. Would he mind that? Perhaps not. Some people take to it quite naturally.' He glanced at Enderby.

Wilbraham was already expostulating. 'But good heavens, man – if Ko's a Russian spy, which we say he isn't anyway – if the Governor has him to dinner, and perfectly naturally, in confidence, commits some minor indiscretion – well, it's damned unfair. It could ruin the man's career. Let alone what it could do to the Colony! He *must* be told!'

Smiley looked sleepier than ever.

'Well of course if he's given to being indiscreet,' he murmured meekly, 'I suppose one *might* argue that he's not a suitable person to be informed anyway.'

In the icy silence Enderby once more languidly took the matchstick from his mouth.

'Bloody odd it would be, wouldn't it, Chris,' he called cheerfully down the table to Wilbraham, 'if Peking woke up one morning to the glad news that the Governor of Hong Kong, Queen's representative and what have you, head of the troops and so forth, made a point of entertaining Moscow's ace spy at his dinner table once a month. *And* gave him a medal for his trouble. *What's* he got so far? Not a K is it?'

'An OBE,' said somebody *sotto voce*.

'Poor chap. Still, he's on his way, I suppose, He'll work his way up, same as we all do.'

Enderby, as it happened, had his knighthood already, whereas Wilbraham was stuck in the bulge, owing to the growing shortage of colonies.

'There is no case,' said Wilbraham stoutly, and laid a hairy hand flat over the lurid folder before him.

* * *

A free-for-all followed, to Guillam's ear an *intermezzo*, in which by tacit understanding the minor parts were allowed to chime in with irrelevant questions in order to get themselves a mention in the minutes. The Welsh Hammer wished to establish *here and now* what would happen to Moscow Centre's half million dollars of reptile money if by any chance they fell into British hands. There could be no question of their simply being recycled through the Circus, he warned. Treasury would have sole rights. Was that clear?

It was clear, Smiley said.

Guillam began to discern a gulf. There were those who assumed, even if reluctantly, that the investigation was a *fait accompli*; and those who continued to fight a rearguard action against its taking place. Hammer, he noticed to his surprise, seemed reconciled to an investigation.

A string of questions on 'legal' and 'illegal' residencies, though wearisome, served to entrench the fear of a red peril. Luff, the parliamentarian, wanted the difference spelt out to him. Smiley patiently obliged. A 'legal' or 'above-the-line' resident, he said, was an intelligence officer living under official or semi-official protection. Since the Hong Kong Government, out of deference to Peking's sensitivities about Russia, had seen fit to banish all forms of Soviet representation from the Colony – embassy, consular, Tass, Radio Moscow, Novosti, Aeroflot, Intourist and the other flags of convenience which legals traditionally sailed under – then by definition it followed that any Soviet activity on the Colony had to be carried out by an illegal or below-the-line apparatus.

It was this presumption which had directed the efforts of the Circus's researchers toward discovering the replacement money-route, he said, avoiding the jargon 'goldseam'.

'Ah well, then, we've forced the Russians into it,' said Luff with satisfaction. 'We've only ourselves to thank. We victimise the Russians, they bite back. Well, who's surprised by that? It's the *last* government's hash we're settling. Not ours at all. Go in for Russian-baiting, you get what you deserve. Natural. We're just reaping the whirlwind as usual.'

'What have the Russians got up to in Hong Kong *before* this?' asked a clever backroom-boy from the Home Office.

The Colonialists at once sprang to life. Wilbraham began feverishly leafing through a folder, but seeing his red-headed assistant straining at the leash he muttered:

'You'll do that one then, John, will you? Good,' and sat back looking ferocious. The brown-clad lady smiled wistfully at the torn baize cloth, as if she remembered it when it was whole. The sixth-former made his second disastrous sally:

'We consider the precedents here very enlightening indeed,' he began aggressively. 'Moscow Centre's previous attempts to gain a toehold on the Colony have been one and all, without exception, abortive and completely low grade.' He reeled off a bunch of boring instances.

Five years ago, he said, a bogus Russian Orthodox archimandrite flew in from Paris in an effort to make links with remnants of the White Russian community:

'This gentleman tried to press-gang an elderly restaurateur into Moscow Centre's service and was promptly arrested. More recently, we have had cases of ship's crew coming ashore from Russian freighters which have put in to Hong Kong for repair. They have made ham-fisted attempts to suborn longshoremen and dock workers whom they consider to be leftist oriented. They have been arrested, questioned, made complete fools of by the press, and duly confined to their ship for the rest of its stay.' He gave other equally milk-and-water examples and everyone grew sleepy, waiting for the last lap: 'Our policy has been *exactly* the same each time. As soon as they're caught, right away, culprits are put on public show. Press photographs? As many as you like, gentlemen. Television? Set up your cameras. Result? Peking hands us a nice pat on the back for containing Soviet imperialist expansionism.' Thoroughly over-excited, he found the nerve to address himself directly to Smiley. 'So you see, as to your networks of illegals, to be frank, we discount them. Legal, illegal, above-the-line, below it: our view is, the Circus is doing a bit of special pleading in order to get its nose back under the wire!'

Opening his mouth to deliver a suitable rebuke, Guillam felt a restraining touch on his elbow and closed it again.

There was a long silence, in which Wilbraham looked more embarrassed than anybody.

'Sounds more like *smoke* to me, Chris,' said Enderby drily.

'What's he driving at?' Wilbraham demanded nervously.

'Just answering the point your bully-boy made for you, Chris. Smoke. Deception. Russians are waving their sabres where you can watch 'em, and while your heads are all turned the wrong way, they get on with the dirty work t'other side of the Island. To wit, Brother Ko. Right, George?'

'Well, that is our view, yes,' Smiley conceded. 'And I suppose I *should* remind you – it's in the submission actually – that Haydon himself was always very keen to argue that the Russians had nothing going in Hong Kong.'

'Lunch,' Martindale announced without much optimism. They ate it upstairs, glumly, off plastic catering trays delivered by van. The partitions were too low, and Guillam's custard flowed into his meat.

Thus refreshed, Smiley availed himself of the after-luncheon torpor to raise what Lacon had called the panic factor. More accurately he sought to entrench in the meeting a sense of logic behind a Soviet presence in Hong Kong, even if, as he put it, Ko did not supply the example:

How Hong Kong, as Mainland China's largest port, handled forty per cent of her foreign trade.

How an estimated one out of every five Hong Kong residents travelled legally in and out of China every year: though many-time travellers doubtless raised the average.

How Red China maintained, in Hong Kong, *sub rosa*, but with the full connivance of the authorities, teams of first-class negotiators, economists and technicians to watch over Peking's interest in trade, shipping and development;

and how every man jack of them constituted a natural intelligence target for 'enticement, or other forms of secret persuasion', as he put it.

How Hong Kong's fishing and junk fleets enjoyed dual registration in Hong Kong and along the China coast, and passed freely in and out of China waters –

Interrupting, Enderby drawled a supporting question:

'And Ko owns a junk fleet. Didn't you say he's one of the last of the brave?'

'Yes, yes he does.'

'But he doesn't visit the Mainland himself?'

'No, never. His assistant goes, but not Ko, we gather.'

'Assistant?'

'He has a manager body named Tiu. They've been together for twenty years. Longer. They share the same background, Hakka, Shanghai and so forth. Tiu's his front man on several companies.'

'And Tiu goes to the Mainland regularly?'

'Once a year at least.'

'All over?'

'Canton, Peking, Shanghai are on record. But the record is not necessarily complete.'

'But Ko stays home. Queer.'

There being no further questions or comments on that score, Smiley resumed his Cook's tour of the charms of Hong Kong as a spy base. Hong Kong was unique, he stated simply. Nowhere on earth offered a tenth of the facilities for getting a toehold on China.

'*Facilities!*' Wilbraham echoed. 'Temptations more like.'

Smiley shrugged. 'If you like, temptations,' he agreed. 'The Soviet service is not famous for resisting them.' And amid some knowing laughter, he went on to recount what was known of Centre's attempts till now against the China target as a whole: a joint précis by Connie and di Salis. He described Centre's efforts to attack from the north, by means of the wholesale recruitment and infiltration of her own ethnic Chinese. Abortive, he said. He described a huge network of listening posts all along the four-and-a-half-thousand-mile Sino-Soviet land border: unproductive, he said, since the yield was military whereas the threat was political. He recounted the rumours of Soviet approaches to Taiwan, proposing common cause against the China threat through joint operations and profit-sharing: rejected, he said, and probably designed for mischief, to annoy Peking, rather than to be taken at face value. He gave instances of the Russian use of talent-spotters among overseas Chinese communities in London, Amsterdam, Vancouver, and San Francisco; and touched on Centre's veiled proposals to the Cousins some years ago for the establishment of an 'intelligence pool' available to China's common enemies. Fruitless, he said. The Cousins wouldn't play. Lastly he referred to Centre's long history of savage burning and bribery operations against Peking officials in overseas posts: product indeterminate, he said.

When he had done all this, he sat back, and restated the thesis which was causing all the trouble.

'Sooner or later,' he repeated, 'Moscow Centre has to come to Hong Kong.'

Which brought them to Ko once more, and to Roddy Martindale, who, under Enderby's eagle eye, made the next real passage of arms.

'Well what do *you* think the money's for, George? I mean we've heard all the things it *isn't* for, and we've heard it's not being spent. But we're no *forrarder*, are we, bless us? We don't seem to *know* anything. It's the same old question: how's the money being earned, how's it being spent, what should we *do*?'

'That's three questions,' said Enderby cruelly under his breath.

'It is *because* we don't know,' said Smiley woodenly, 'that we are asking permission to find out.'

Someone from the Treasury benches said: 'Is half a million a lot?'

'In my experience unprecedented,' said Smiley. 'Moscow Centre' – dutifully he avoided *Karla* – 'detests having to buy loyalty at any time. For them to buy it on this scale is unheard of.'

'But *whose* loyalty are they buying?' someone complained.

Martindale the gladiator, back to the charge: 'You're selling us short, George. I know you are. You have an inkling, of course you have. Now cut us in on it. Don't be so coy.'

'Yes, can't you kick a few ideas around for us?' said Lacon, equally plaintively.

'Surely you can go down the line a *little*,' Hammer pleaded.

Even under this three-pronged attack Smiley still did not waver. The panic factor was finally paying off. Smiley himself had triggered it. Like scared patients they were appealing to him for a diagnosis. And Smiley was declining to provide one, on the grounds that he lacked the data.

'Really, I cannot do more than give you the facts as they stand. For me to speculate aloud at this stage would not be useful.'

For the first time since the meeting had begun, the Colonial lady in brown opened her mouth and asked a question. Her voice was melodious and intelligent.

'On the matter of precedents, then, Mr Smiley?' – Smiley ducked his head in a quaint little bow – 'Are there precedents for secret Russian moneys being paid to a stake-holder? In other theatres, for instance?'

Smiley did not immediately answer. Seated only a few inches from him, Guillam swore he sensed a sudden tension, like a surge of energy, passing through his neighbour. But when he glanced at the impassive profile, he saw only a deepening somnolence in his master, and a slight lowering of the weary eyelids.

'There have been a few cases of what we call *alimony*,' he conceded finally.

'*Alimony*, Mr Smiley?' the Colonial lady echoed, while her red-haired companion scowled more terribly, as if divorce were something else he disapproved of.

Smiley picked his way with extreme care. 'Clearly there are agents, working in hostile countries – hostile from the Soviet point of view – who for reasons of cover cannot enjoy their pay while they are in the field.' The brown-clad lady delicately nodded her understanding. 'The normal practice in such cases is to bank the money in Moscow and make it available to the agent when he is free to spend it. Or to his dependants if – '

'If he gets the chop,' said Martindale with relish.

'But Hong Kong is not Moscow,' the Colonial lady reminded him with a smile.

Smiley had all but come to a halt. 'In rare cases where the incentive is money, and the agent perhaps has no stomach for eventual resettlement in Russia, Moscow Centre has been known, under duress, to make a comparable arrangement in, say, Switzerland.'

'But not in Hong Kong?' she persisted.

'No. Not. And it is unimaginable, on past showing, that Moscow would contemplate parting with alimony on such a scale. For one thing, it would be an inducement to the agent to retire from the field.'

There was laughter, but when it died, the brown-clad lady had her next question ready.

'But the payments began modestly,' she persisted pleasantly. 'The inducement is only of relatively recent date?'

'Correct,' said Smiley.

Too damn correct, thought Guillam, starting to get alarmed.

'Mr Smiley, if the dividend were of sufficient value to them, do you think the Russians *would* be prepared to swallow their objections and pay such a price? After all, in absolute terms the money is entirely trivial beside the value of a great intelligence advantage.'

Smiley had simply stopped. He made no particular gesture. He remained courteous, he even managed a small smile, but he was plainly finished with conjecture. It took Enderby, with his blasé drawl, to blow the question away.

'Look, children, we'll be doing the theoreticals all day if we're not careful,' he cried, looking at his watch. 'Chris, do we wheel the Americans in here? If we're not telling the Governor, where do we stand on telling the gallant allies?'

George saved by the bell, thought Guillam.

At the mention of the Cousins, Colonial Wilbraham came in like an angry bull. Guillam guessed he had sensed the issue looming, and determined to kill it immediately it showed its head.

'Vetoed, I'm afraid,' he snapped, without any of his customary delay. 'Absolutely. Whole host of grounds. Demarcation for one. Hong Kong's our patch. Americans have no fishing rights there. None. Ko's a British subject, for another, and entitled to some protection from us. I suppose that's old fashioned. Don't care too much, to be frank. Americans would go clean overboard. Seen it before. God knows where it would end. Three: small point of protocol.' He meant this ironically. He was appealing to the instincts of an ex-ambassador, trying to rouse his sympathy. 'Just a small point, Enderby. Telling the Americans and not telling the Governor – if *I* was the Governor, put in that position, I'd turn in my badge. That's all I can say. You would too. Know you would. You do, I do.'

'Assuming you found out,' Enderby corrected him.

'Don't worry. I'd find out. I'd have 'em ten deep crawling over his house with microphones for a start. One or two places in Africa where we let them in. Disaster. Total.' Plonking his forearms on the table, one over the other, he stared at them furiously.

A vehement chugging as if from an outboard motor announced a fault in one of the electronic bafflers. It choked, recovered and zoomed out of hearing again.

'Be a brave man who diddled you on that one, Chris,' Enderby murmured with a long admiring smile, into the strained silence.

'Endorsed,' Lacon blurted out of the blue.

They know, thought Guillam simply. George has squared them. They know he's done a deal with Martello and they know he won't say so because he's determined to lie dead. But Guillam saw nothing clearly that day. While the Treasury and Defence factions cautiously concurred on what seemed to be a straight issue – 'keep the Americans out of it' – Smiley himself appeared mysteriously unwilling to toe the line.

'But there does *remain* the headache of what to do with the raw intelligence,' he said. 'Should you decide that my service may not proceed, I mean,' he added doubtfully, to the general confusion.

Guillam was relieved to find Enderby equally bewildered:

'Hell's that mean?' he demanded, running with the hounds for a moment.

'Ko has financial interests all over South East Asia,' Smiley reminded them. 'Page one of my submission.' Business; clatter of papers. 'We have information, for example, that he controls through intermediaries and strawmen such oddities as a string of Saigon nightclubs, a Vientiane-based aviation company, a piece of a tanker fleet in Thailand . . . several of these enterprises could well be seen to have political overtones which are *far* within the American sphere of influence. I would have to have your written instruction, naturally, if I were to ignore our side of the existing bi-lateral agreements.'

'Keep talking,' Enderby ordered, and pulled a fresh match from the box in front of him.

'Oh, I think my point is made, thank you,' said Smiley politely. 'Really it's a very simple one. Assuming we don't proceed, which Lacon tells me is the balance of probability today, what am I to do? Throw the intelligence on the scrap-heap? Or pass it to our allies under the existing barter arrangements?'

'Allies,' Wilbraham exclaimed bitterly. 'Allies? You're putting a pistol at our heads, man!'

Smiley's iron reply was all the more startling for the passivity which had preceded it.

'I have a standing instruction from this committee to repair our American liaison. It is written into my charter, by yourselves, that I am to do everything possible to nurture the special relationship and revive the spirit of mutual confidence which existed before – Haydon. "To get us back to the top table," you said . . .' He was looking directly at Enderby.

'*Top table*,' someone echoed – a quite new voice. 'Sacrificial altar if you ask me. We already burned the Middle East and half Africa on it. All for the special relationship.'

But Smiley seemed not to hear. He had relapsed once more into his posture of mournful reluctance. Sometimes, his sad face said, the burdens of his office were simply too much for him to bear.

A fresh bout of post-luncheon sulkiness set in. Someone complained of the tobacco smoke. A messenger was summoned.

'Devil's happened to the extractors?' Enderby demanded crossly. 'We're stifling.'

'It's the parts,' the messenger said. 'We put in for them months ago, sir. Before Christmas it was, sir, nearly a year come to think of it. Still you can't blame delay, can you, sir?'

'Christ,' said Enderby.

Tea was sent for. It came in paper cups which leaked on to the baize. Guillam gave his thoughts to Molly Meakin's peerless figure.

It was almost four o'clock when Lacon rode disdainfully in front of the armies and invited Smiley to state 'just exactly what it is you're asking for in practical terms, George. Let's have it all on the table and try to hack out an answer.'

Enthusiasm would have been fatal. Smiley seemed to understand that.

'One, we need rights and permissions to operate in the South East Asian theatre – deniably. So that the Governor can wash his hands of us' – a glance at the Parliamentary Under-Secretary – 'and so can our own masters here. Two, to conduct certain domestic enquiries.'

Heads shot up. The Home Office at once grew fidgety. Why? Who? How? *What* enquiries? If it's domestic it should go to the competition. Pretorius of the Security Service was already in a ferment.

'Ko read law in London,' Smiley insisted. 'He has connections here, social and business. We should naturally have to investigate them.' He glanced at Pretorius. 'We would show the competition all our findings,' he promised. He resumed his bid.

'As regards money, my submission contains a full breakdown of what we need at once, as well as supplementary estimates for various contingencies. Finally we are asking permission, at local as well as Whitehall level, to reopen our Hong Kong residency as a forward base for the operation.'

A stunned silence greeted this last item, to which Guillam's own amazement contributed. Nowhere, in any of the preparatory discussions at the Circus, or with Lacon, had anybody, not even Smiley himself, to Guillam's knowledge, raised the slightest question of reopening High Haven or establishing its successor. A fresh clamour started.

'Failing that,' he ended, overriding the protests, 'if we cannot have our residency, we request, at the very least, blindeye approval to run our own below-the-line agents on the Colony. No local awareness, but approval and protection by London. Any existing sources to be retrospectively legitimised. In writing,' he ended, with a hard glance at Lacon, and stood up.

Glumly, Guillam and Smiley sat themselves once more in the waiting room on the same salmon bench where they had begun, side by side, like passengers travelling in the same direction.

'*Why?*'Guillam muttered once, but asking questions of George Smiley was not merely in bad taste that day: it was a pastime expressly forbidden by the cautionary notice which hung above them on the wall.

Of all the damn-fool ways of overplaying one's hand, thought Guillam dismally. You've thrown it, he thought. Poor old sod: finally past it. The one operation which could put us back in the game. Greed, that's what it was. The greed of an old spy in a hurry. I'll stick with him, thought Guillam. I'll go down with the ship. We'll open a chicken farm together. Molly can keep the accounts and Ann can have bucolic tangles with the labourers.

'How do you feel?' he asked.

'It's not a matter of feeling,' Smiley replied.

Thanks very much, thought Guillam.

The minutes turned to twenty. Smiley had not stirred. His chin had fallen on to his chest, his eyes had closed, he might have been at prayer.

'Perhaps you should take an evening off,' said Guillam.

Smiley only frowned.

A messenger appeared, inviting them to return. Lacon was now at the head of the table, and his manner was prefectorial. Enderby sat two away from him, conversing in murmurs with the Welsh Hammer. Pretorius glowered like a storm cloud, and his nameless lady pursed her lips in an unconscious kiss of disapproval. Lacon rustled his notes for silence and like a teasing judge began reading off the committee's detailed findings before he delivered the verdict. The Treasury had entered a serious protest, on the record, regarding the misuse of Smiley's management account. Smiley should also bear in mind that any requirement for domestic rights and permissions should be cleared with the Security Service in advance and not 'sprung on them like a rabbit out of a hat in the middle of a full-dress meeting of the committee'. There could be no earthly question of reopening the Hong Kong residency. Simply on the issue of time alone, such a step was impossible. It was really a quite shameful proposal, he implied. Principle was involved, consultation would have to be at the highest level, and since Smiley had already moved specifically against advising the Governor of his findings – Lacon's doff of the cap to Wilbraham here – it was going to be very hard to make a case for re-establishing a residency in the foreseeable future, particularly bearing in mind the unhappy publicity attaching to the evacuation of High Haven.

'I must accept that view with great reluctance,' said Smiley gravely.

Oh for God's sake, thought Guillam: let's at least go down fighting!

'Accept it how you like,' said Enderby – and Guillam could have sworn he saw in the eyes of both Enderby and the Welsh Hammer a gleam of victory.

Bastards, he thought simply. No free chickens for you. In his mind he was taking leave of the whole pack of them.

'Everything else,' said Lacon, putting down a sheet of paper and taking up another, 'with certain limiting conditions and safeguards regarding desirability, money and the duration of the licence, is granted.'

The park was empty. The lesser commuters had left the field to the professionals. A few lovers lay on the damp grass like soldiers after the battle. A few flamingoes dozed. At Guillam's side, as he sauntered euphorically in Smiley's wake, Roddy Martindale was singing Smiley's praises: 'I think George is simply marvellous. Indestructible. And *grip*. I adore grip. Grip is my favourite human quality. George has it in spades. One takes quite a different view of these things when one's translated. One grows to the scale of them, I admit. Your father was an Arabist, I recall?'

'Yes,' said Guillam, his mind yet again on Molly, wondering whether dinner was still possible.

'And frightfully *Almanach de Gotha*. Now was he an A.D. man or a B.C. man?'

About to give a thoroughly obscene reply, Guillam realised just in time that Martindale was enquiring after nothing more harmful than his father's scholarly preferences.

'Oh B.C.! – B.C. All the way,' he said. 'He'd have gone back to Eden if he could have done.'

'Come to dinner.'

'Thanks.'

'We'll fix a date. Who's *fun* for a change? Who do you like?'

Ahead of them, floating on the dewy air, they heard the drawling voice of Enderby applauding Smiley's victory.

'*Nice* little meeting. Lot achieved. Nothing given away. *Nicely* played hand. Land this one and you can just about build an extension, I should think. And the Cousins will play ball, will they?'he bellowed as if they were still inside the safe room. 'You've tested the water there? They'll carry your bags for you and not hog the match? Bit of a cliffhanger that one, I'd have thought, but I suppose you're up to it. You tell Martello to wear his crêpe soles, if he's got any, or we'll be in deep trouble with the Colonials in no time. Pity about old Wilbraham. He'd have run India rather well.'

Beyond them again, almost out of sight among the trees, the little Welsh Hammer was making energetic gestures to Lacon, who was stooping to catch his words.

Nice little conspiracy too, thought Guillam. He glanced back and was surprised to see Fawn the babysitter hurrying after them. He seemed at first a long way off. Shreds of mist obscured his legs entirely. Only the top of him reached above the sea. Then suddenly he was much closer, and Guillam heard his familiar plaintive bray calling 'Sir, sir,' trying to catch Smiley's attention. Quickly placing Martindale out of earshot, Guillam strode up to him.

'What the devil's the matter? Why are you bleating like that?'

'They've found a girl! Miss Sachs, sir, she sent me to tell him specially.' His eyes shone bright and slightly crazy. '"Tell the Chief they've found the girl." Her very words, personal for Chief.'

'Do you mean she *sent* you here?'

'Personal for Chief immediate,' Fawn replied evasively.

'I said: "did she send you here?"' Guillam was seething. 'Answer, "no, sir, she did not." You bloody little drama queen, racing round London in your plimsolls! You're out of your mind.' Snatching the crumpled note from Fawn's hand, he read it cursorily. 'It's not even the same name. Hysterical bloody nonsense. You go straight back to your hutch, do you hear? The Chief will give the matter his attention when he returns. Don't you dare stir things up like that again.'

'*Whoever* was he?' Martindale enquired, quite breathless with excitement, as Guillam returned. 'What a darling little creature! Are all spies as pretty as that? How positively Venetian. I shall volunteer at once.'

The same night a ragged conference was held in the rumpus room, and the quality was not improved by the euphoria – in Connie's case alcoholic – brought on by Smiley's triumph at the steering conference. After constraints and tensions of the last months Connie charged in all directions. The girl! The girl was the clue! Connie had shed all her intellectual bonds. Send Toby Esterhase to Hong Kong, house her, photograph her, trace her, search her room! Get Sam Collins in, *now*! Di Salis fidgeted, simpered, puffed at his pipe and jiggled his feet, but for that evening he was entirely under Connie's spell. He even spoke once of 'a natural line to the heart of things' – meaning, yet again, the mystery girl. No wonder little Fawn had been infected by their zeal. Guillam felt almost apologetic for his outburst in the park. Indeed, without Smiley and Guillam to put the dampers on, an act of collective folly could very easily have taken place that night and God knows where it might not have led. The secret world has plenty of precedents of sane people breaking out that way, but this was the first time Guillam had seen the disease in action.

So it was ten o'clock or more before a brief could be drafted for old Craw, and half past before Guillam blearily bumped into Molly Meakin on his way to the lift. In consequence of this happy coincidence – or had Molly planned it? he never knew – a beacon was lit in Peter Guillam's life which burned fiercely from then on. With her customary acquiescence, Molly consented to be driven home, though she lived in Highgate, miles out of his way, and when they reached her doorstep she as usual invited him in for a quick coffee. Anticipating the familiar frustrations – 'no-Peter-please-Peter-*dear*-I'm sorry' – Guillam was on the brink of declining, when something in her eye – a certain calm resolution as it seemed to him – caused him to change his mind. Once inside her flat, she closed the door and put it on the chain. Then she led him demurely to her bedroom, where she astonished him with a joyous and refined carnality.

Chapter 9

CRAW'S LITTLE SHIP

In Hong Kong it was forty-eight hours later and a Sunday evening. In the alley Craw walked carefully. Dusk had come early with the fog, but the houses were jammed too close to let it in, so it hung a few floors higher, with the washing and the cables, spitting hot polluted raindrops which raised smells of orange in the food stalls and ticked on the brim of Craw's straw hat. He was in China here, at sea level, the China he loved most, and China was waking for the festival of night: singing, honking, wailing, beating gongs, bargaining, cooking, playing tinny tunes through twenty different instruments: or watching motionless from doorways how delicately the fancy-looking Foreign Devil picked his way among them. Craw loved it all, but most tenderly he loved his *little ships*, as the Chinese called their secret whisperers, and of these Miss Phoebe Wayfarer, whom he was on his way to visit, was a classic, if modest, example.

He breathed in, savouring the familiar pleasures. The East had never failed him. 'We colonise them, your Graces, we corrupt them, we exploit them, we bomb them, sack their cities, ignore their culture and confound them with the infinite variety of our religious sects. We are hideous not only in their sight, Monsignors, but in their nostrils as well – the stink of the roundeye is abhorrent to them and we're too thick even to know it. Yet when we have done our worst, and more than our worst, my sons, we have barely scratched the surface of the Asian smile.'

Other roundeyes might not have come here so willingly alone. The Peak mafia would not have known it existed. The embattled British wives in their government housing ghettos in Happy Valley would have found here everything they hated most about their billet. It was not a bad part of town, but it was not Europe either: the Europe of Central and Pedder Street half a mile away, of electric doors that sighed for you as they admitted you to the airconditioning. Other roundeyes, in their apprehension, might have cast inadvertent glares, and that was dangerous. In Shanghai, Craw had known more than one man die of an accidental bad look. Whereas Craw's look was at all times kindly, he deferred, he was modest in his manner, and when he stopped to make a purchase, he offered respectful greetings to the stallholder in bad but robust Cantonese. And he paid without carping at the surcharge befitting his inferior race.

He bought orchids and lamb's liver. He bought them every Sunday, distributing his custom fairly between rival stalls and – when his Cantonese ran out – lapsing into his own ornate version of English.

He pressed the bell. Phoebe, like old Craw himself, had an entryphone. Head Office had decreed they should be standard issue. She had twisted a piece of heather into her mail box for good joss, and this was the safety signal.

'Hi,' a girl's voice said, over the speaker. It could have been American or it could have been Cantonese, offering an interrogative '*Yes?*'

'Larry calls me Pete,' Craw said.

'Come on up, I have Larry with me at this moment.'

The staircase was pitch dark and stank of vomit and Craw's heels clanked like tin on the stone treads. He pressed the time switch but no light went on so he had to grope his way for three floors. There had been a move to find her somewhere better but it had died with Thesinger's departure and now there was no hope and, in a way, no Phoebe either.

'Bill,' she murmured, closing the door after him, and kissed him on both mottled cheeks, the way pretty girls may kiss kind uncles, though she was not pretty. Craw gave her the orchids. His manner was gentle and solicitous.

'My dear,' he said. 'My *dear.*'

She was trembling. There was a bedsitting room with a cooker and a handbasin, there was a separate lavatory with a shower. That was all. He walked past her to the basin, unwrapped the liver and gave it to the cat.

'Oh you spoil her, Bill,' said Phoebe, smiling at the flowers. He had laid a brown envelope on the bed but neither of them mentioned it.

'How's *William*?' she said, playing with the sound of his name.

Craw had hung his hat and stick on the door and was pouring Scotch: neat for Phoebe, soda for himself.

'How's Pheeb? That's more to the point. How's it been out there, the cold long week? Eh Pheeb?'

She had ruffled the bed and laid a frilly nightdress on the floor because so far as the block was concerned Phoebe was the half-*kwailo* bastard who whored with the fat foreign devil. Over the crushed pillows hung her picture of Swiss Alps, the picture every Chinese girl seemed to have, and on the bedside locker the photograph of her English father, the only picture she had ever seen of him: a clerk from Dorking in Surrey, just after his arrival on the Island, rounded collars, moustache, and staring, slightly crazy eyes. Craw sometimes wondered whether it was taken after he was shot.

'It's all right *now*,' said Phoebe. 'It's fine *now*, Bill.'

She stood at his shoulder, filling the vase, and her hands were shaking badly, which they usually did on Sundays. She wore a grey tunic dress in honour of Peking, and the gold necklace given to her to commemorate her first decade of service to the Circus. In a ridiculous spurt of gallantry, Head Office had decided to have it made at Asprey's, then sent out by bag, with a personal letter to her signed by Percy Alleline, George Smiley's luckless predecessor, which she had been allowed to look at but not keep. Having filled the vase, she tried to carry it to the table but it slopped, so Craw took it.

'*Hey* now, take it easy, won't you?'

She stood for a moment, still smiling at him, then with a long slow sob of reaction slumped into a chair. Sometimes she wept, sometimes she sneezed, or was very loud and laughed too much, but always she saved the moment for his arrival, however it took her.

'Bill, I get so frightened sometimes.'

'I know, dear, I know.' He sat at her side, holding her hand.

'That new boy in features. He *stares* at me, Bill, he watches everything I do. I'm sure he works for someone. Bill, who does he work for?'

'Maybe he's a little amorous,' said Craw, in his softest tone, as he rhythmically patted her shoulder. 'You're an attractive woman, Phoebe. Don't you forget that, my dear. You can exert an influence without knowing it.' He affected a paternal sternness. 'Now have you been flirting with him? There's another thing. A woman like you can flirt without being conscious of the fact. A man of the world can spot these things, Phoebe. He can tell.'

Last week it was the janitor downstairs. She said he was writing down the hours she came and went. The week before, it was a car she kept seeing, an Opel, always the same one, green. The trick was to calm her fears without discouraging her vigilance: because one day – as Craw never allowed himself to forget – one day, she was going to be right. Producing a bunch of handwritten notes from the bedside, she began her own debriefing, but so suddenly that Craw was overrun. She had a pale, large face which missed being beautiful in either race. Her trunk was long, her legs were short, and her hands Saxon, ugly and strong. Sitting on the edge of the bed, she looked suddenly matronly. She had put on thick spectacles to read. Canton was sending a student commissar to address Tuesday's cadre, she said, so the Thursday meeting was closed and Ellen Tuo had once more lost her chance to be secretary for an evening —

'Hey, steady down now,' Craw cried, laughing. 'Where's the fire, for God's sake!'

Opening a notebook on his knee, he tried to catch up with her. But Phoebe would not be checked, not even by Bill Craw, though she had been told he was in fact a colonel, even higher. She wanted it behind her, the whole confession. One of her routine targets was a leftist intellectual group of university students and Communist journalists which had somewhat superficially accepted her. She had reported on it weekly without much progress. Now, for some reason, the group had flared into activity. Billy Chan had been called to Kuala Lumpur for a special conference, she said, and Johnny and Belinda Fong were being asked to find a safe store for a printing press. The evening was approaching fast. While she ran on, Craw discreetly rose and put on the lamp so that the electric light would not shock her once the day faded altogether.

There was talk of joining up with the Fukienese in North Point, she said, but the academic comrades were opposed as usual. 'They're opposed to *everything*,' said Phoebe savagely, 'the snobs. And anyway that stupid bitch Belinda is months behind on her dues and we may quite well chuck her out of the Party unless she stops gambling.'

'And quite right too, my dear,' said Craw sedately.

'Johnny Fong says Belinda's pregnant and it isn't his. Well I hope she is. It will shut her up . . .' said Phoebe, and Craw thought: we had that trouble a couple of times with *you* if I remember rightly, and it didn't shut you up, did it?

Craw wrote obediently, knowing that neither London nor anyone else would ever read a word of it. In the days of its wealth the Circus had penetrated dozens of such groups, hoping in time to break into what was idiotically referred to as the Peking–Hong Kong shuttle and so get a foot in the Mainland. The ploy had withered and the Circus had no brief to act as watchdog for the Colony's security, a rôle which Special Branch jealously guarded for itself. But little ships, as Craw knew very well, cannot change course as easily as the winds that drive them. Craw played her along, pitching in with the follow-up questions, checking sources and subsources. Was it hearsay, Pheeb? Well, where did Billy Lee get *that* one from, Pheeb? Was it possible Billy Lee was needling the story a bit – for face, Pheeb, giving it the old needle? He used the journalistic term because, like Jerry and Craw himself, Phoebe was in her other profession a journalist, a freelance gossip writer feeding Hong Kong's English-language press with titbits about lifestyles of the local Chinese aristocracy.

Listening, waiting, vamping as the actors call it, Craw told himself her story, just as he had told it on the refresher course at Sarratt five years ago, when he was back there getting a rebore in the black arts. The triumph of the fortnight, they had told him afterwards. They had made it a plenary session in anticipation. Even the directing staff had come to hear him. Those who were off duty had asked for a special van to bring them in early from their Watford housing estate. Just to hear old Craw, the eastern hand, sitting under the antlers in the converted library, sum up a lifetime in the Game. *Agents who recruit themselves*, ran the title. There was a lectern on the podium but he didn't use it. Instead, he sat on a plain chair, with his jacket off and his belly hanging out and his knees apart and shadows of sweat darkening his shirt, and he told it to them the way he would have told it to the Shanghai Bowlers, on a typhoon Saturday in Hong Kong, if only circumstance had allowed.

Agents who recruit themselves, your Graces.

No one knew the job better, they told him – and he believed them. If the East was Craw's home, the little ships were his family, and he lavished on them all the fondness for which the overt world had somehow never given him an outlet. He raised and trained them with a love that would have done credit to a father; and it was the hardest moment in an old man's life when Tufty Thesinger did his moonlight flit and left Craw unwarned, temporarily without a purpose or a life-line.

Some people are agents from birth, Monsignors – he told them – appointed to the work by the period of history, the place, and their own natural dispositions. In their cases, it was simply a question of who got to them first, your Eminences:

'Whether it's us; whether it's the opposition; or whether it's the bloody missionaries.'

Laughter.

Then the case histories with names and places changed, and among them none other than codename Susan, a little ship of the female gender, Monsignors, South East Asian theatre, born in the year of turmoil 1941, of mixed blood. He was referring to Phoebe Wayfarer.

'Father a penniless clerk from Dorking, your Graces. Came East to join one of the Scottish houses that plundered the coast six days a week and prayed to Calvin on the seventh. Too broke to get himself a European wife, lads, so he takes a forbidden Chinese girl and sets her up for a few pence, and codename Susan is the result. Same year the Japanese appear on the scene. Call it Singapore, Hong Kong, Malaya, the story's the same, Monsignors. They appear overnight. To stay. In the chaos, codename Susan's father does a very noble thing: "To hell with caution, your Eminences," he says. "This is the time for good men and true to stand up and be counted." So he marries the lady, your Graces, a course of action I would not normally counsel, but he does, and when he's married her he christens his daughter codename Susan and joins the Volunteers, which was a fine body of heroic fools who formed a local home guard against the Nipponese hordes. The next day, not being a natural man-at-arms, your Graces, he gets his arse shot off by the Japanese invader and promptly expires. Amen. May the clerk from Dorking rest in peace, your Graces.'

As old Craw crosses himself, gusts of laughter sweep the room. Craw does not laugh with them, but plays the straight man. There are fresh faces in the front two rows, uncut, unlined, television faces; Craw guesses they are new entrants whipped in to hear The Great One. Their presence sharpens his performance. Henceforth he has a special eye for the front rows.

'Codename Susan is still in rompers when her good father meets his *quietus*, lads, but all her life she's going to remember: when the chips are down, the British stand by their commitments. Every year that passes, she's going to love that dead hero a little more. After the war, her father's old trading house remembers her for a year or two, then conveniently forgets her. Never mind. At fifteen, she's ill from having to keep her sick mother and work the ballrooms to finance her own schooling. Never mind. A welfare worker takes up with her, fortunately a member of our distinguished brethren, your Reverends; and he guides her in our direction.' Craw mops his brow. 'Codename Susan's rise to wealth and godliness has begun, your Graces,' he declares. 'Under journalist cover we bring her into play, give her Chinese newspapers to translate, send her on little errands, involve her, complete her education and train her in nightwork. A little money, a little patronage, a little love, a little patience and it's not too long before our Susan has seven legal trips to Mainland China to her credit, including some very windy tradecraft. Skilfully performed, your Graces. She has played courier, and made one crash approach to an uncle in Peking, which paid off. All this, lads, despite the fact she's half a *kwailo* and not naturally trusted by the Chinese.

'And who did she think the Circus was, all that time?' Craw bellowed at his enthralled audience – 'who did she think we were, lads?' The old magician drops his voice, and lifts a fat forefinger. 'Her father,' he says, in the silence. 'We're that dead clerk from Dorking. Saint George, that's who we are. Cleansing the overseas Chinese communities of *harmful elements*, whatever the hell they are. Breaking the Triads and the rice cartels and the opium gangs and the child prostitution. She even saw us, when she had to, as the secret ally of Peking, because we, the Circus, had the interest of all *good* Chinese at heart.' Craw ran a ferocious eye over the rows of child faces longing to be stern.

'Do I see someone smiling, your Graces?' he demanded, in a voice of thunder. He didn't.

'Mind you, Squires,' Craw ended, 'there's a part of her knew damn well it was all baloney. That's where *you* come in. That's where your fieldman is ever at the ready. Oh yes! We're keepers of the faith, lads. When it shakes, we stiffen it. When it falls, we've got our arms out to catch it.' He had reached his zenith. In counterpoint, he let his voice fall to a mellow murmur. 'Be the faith ever so crackpot, your Graces, never despise it. We've precious little else to offer them these days. Amen.'

All his life, in his unashamedly emotional way, old Craw would remember the applause.

Her debriefing finished, Phoebe hunched forward, her forearms on her knees, the knuckles of her big hands backed loosely against each other like tired lovers. Craw rose solemnly, took her notes from the table and burnt them at the gas ring.

'Bravo, my dear,' he said quietly. 'A sterling week if I may say so. Anything else?'

She shook her head.

'I mean, to burn,' he said.

She shook her head again.

Craw studied her. 'Pheeb, my dear,' he declared at last, as if he had reached a momentous decision. 'Get off your hunkers. It's time I took you out to dinner.' She looked round at him, confused. The drink had raced to her head, as it always did. 'An amiable dinner between fellow scribblers, once in a while, is not inconsistent with cover, I venture to suggest. How about it?'

She made him look at the wall while she put on a pretty frock. She used to have a humming bird but it died. He bought her another but it died too so they agreed the flat was bad luck for humming birds and gave up on them.

'One day I'll take you skiing,' he said, as she locked the front door behind them. It was a joke between them, to do with her snow scene over the bed.

'Only for one day?' she replied. Which was also a joke, part of the same habitual repartee.

In that year of turmoil, as Craw would say, it was still

clever to eat in a sampan on Causeway Bay. The smart set had not discovered it, the food was cheap and unlike food elsewhere. Craw took a gamble and by the time they reached the waterfront the fog had lifted and the night sky was clear. He chose the sampan furthest out to sea, deep in among a cluster of small junks. The cook squatted at the charcoal brazier and his wife served, the hulls of the junks loomed over them, blotting out the stars, and the boat children scampered like crabs from one deck to another while their parents chanted slow funny catechisms across the black water. Craw and Phoebe crouched on wood stools under the furled canopy, two foot above the sea, eating mullet by lamplight. Beyond the typhoon shelters ships slid past them, lighted buildings on the march, and the junks hobbled in their wakes. Inland, the Island whined and clanged and throbbed, and the huge slums twinkled like jewel-boxes opened by the deceptive beauty of the night. Presiding over them, glimpsed between the dipping fingers of the masts, sat the black Peak, Victoria, her sodden face shrouded with moonlit skeins: the goddess, the freedom, the lure of all that wild striving in the valley.

They talked the arts. Phoebe was doing what Craw thought of as her cultural number. It was very boring. One day, she said drowsily, she would direct a film, perhaps two, on the *true*, the *real* China. Recently she had seen an historical romance made by Run Run Shaw, all about the palace intrigues. She considered it excellent but a little too – well – *heroic*. Theatre, now. Had Craw heard the good news that the Cambridge Players might be bringing a new revue to the Colony in December? At present it was only a rumour, but she hoped it would be confirmed next week.

'*That* should be fun, Pheeb,' said Craw heartily.

'It will *not* be fun at all,' Phoebe retorted sternly. 'The Players specialise in biting social satire.'

In the darkness Craw smiled and poured Phoebe more beer. You can always learn, he told himself: Monsignors, you can always learn.

Till, with no prompting that she could have been aware of, Phoebe began talking about her Chinese millionaires, which was what Craw had been waiting for all evening. In Phoebe's world, the Hong Kong rich were royalty. Their foibles and excesses were handed round as freely as in other places the lives of actresses or footballers. Phoebe knew them by heart.

'So who's pig of the week this time, Pheeb?' Craw asked genially.

Phoebe was unsure. 'Whom shall we elect?' she said, affecting coquettish indecision. There was the pig PK of course, his sixty-eighth birthday on Tuesday, a third wife half his age and how does PK celebrate? Out on the town with a twenty-year-old slut.

Disgusting, Craw agreed. 'PK,' he repeated. 'PK was the fellow with the gateposts, wasn't he?'

One hundred thousand Hong Kong, said Phoebe. Dragons nine foot high, cast in fibreglass and perspex so that they lit up from inside. Or it might be the pig YY she reflected judiciously, changing her mind. YY was certainly a candidate. YY had married one month ago exactly, that nice daughter of JJ Haw, of Haw and Chan, the tanker kings, a thousand lobsters at the wedding. Night before last, he turned up at a reception with a brand new mistress, bought with his wife's money, a nobody except that he had dressed her at Saint-Laurent and decked her out in a four-string choker of Mikimoto pearls, hired of course, not given. Despite herself, Phoebe's voice faltered and softened.

'Bill,' she breathed, 'that kid looked completely fantastic beside the old frog, you should have seen.'

Or maybe Harold Tan, she pondered dreamily. Harold had been specially nasty. Harold had flown his kids home from their Swiss finishing schools for the festival, first-class return from Geneva. At four in the morning they were all cavorting naked round the pool, the kids and their friends, drunk, pouring champagne into the water while Harold tried to photograph the action.

Craw waited, in his mind holding the door wide open

for her, but still she wouldn't pass through, and Craw was far too old a dog to push her. Chiu Chow were best, he said archly. 'Chiu Chow wouldn't get up to all that nonsense. Eh Pheeb? Very long pockets the Chiu Chow have, and very short arms,' he advised her. 'Make a Scotsman blush, your Chiu Chow would, eh Pheeb?'

Phoebe had no place for irony. 'Do not believe it,' she retorted demurely. 'Many Chiu Chow are both generous and high-minded.'

He was willing the man on her, like a conjurer willing a card, but still she hesitated, walked round it, reached for the alternatives. She mentioned this one, that one, lost the thread, wanted more beer, and when he had all but given up she remarked, quite dreamily:

'And as for Drake Ko, he is a complete *lamb*. Against Drake Ko, no bad words at *all* please.'

Now it was Craw's turn to walk away. What did Phoebe think of old Andrew Kwok's divorce, he asked. Christ, *that* must have been a costly one! They say she would have given him the push long ago, but she wanted to wait till he'd made his pile and was really worth divorcing. Any truth in that one, Pheeb? And so on, three, five names, before he allowed himself to take the bait.

'Have you ever heard of old Drake Ko keeping a roundeye mistress at any time? They were talking about it in the Hong Kong Club only the other day. Blonde party, said to be quite a dish.'

Phoebe liked to think of Craw in the Hong Kong Club. It satisfied her colonial yearnings.

'Oh *everyone* has heard,' she said wearily, as if Craw as usual were light years behind the hunt. 'There was a time when *all* the boys had them – didn't you know? PK had two, of course. Harold Tan had one, till Eustace Chow stole her, and Charlie Wu tried to take *his* to dinner at the Governor's but his *tai-tai* wouldn't let the chauffeur pick her up.'

'Where'd they get them from for Christ sakes?' Craw asked with a laugh. 'Lane Crawford?'

'From the airlines, where do you think?' Phoebe retorted

with heavy disapproval. 'Air-hostesses moonlighting on their stop-overs, five hundred US a night for a white-woman whore. *And* including the English lines, don't deceive yourself, the English were the worst by far. Then Harold Tan liked his so much he made an arrangement with her, and the next thing they were all moving into flats and walking round the stores like duchesses any time they came to Hong Kong for four days, enough to make you *sick*. Mind you, Liese is a different kettle of fish entirely. Liese has class. She is extremely aristocratic, her parents own fabulous estates in the South of France and also an out-island in the Bahamas and it is purely for reasons of moral independence that she refuses to accept their wealth. You only have to look at her bone structure.'

'*Liese*,' Craw repeated. '*Liese?* Kraut, eh? Don't hold with Krauts. No racial prejudices but don't care for Krauts, I'm afraid. Now what's a nice Chiu Chow boy like Drake doing with a hateful Hun for a concubine, I ask myself. Still, you should know Pheeb, you're the expert, it's your bailiwick, my dear, who am I to criticise?'

They had moved to the back of the sampan and were lying in the cushions side by side.

'Don't be utterly ridiculous,' Phoebe snapped. 'Liese is an aristocratic English girl.'

'Tra la la,' said Craw and for a while gazed at the stars.

'She has a most positive and refining influence on him.'

'Who does?' said Craw, as if he had lost the thread.

Phoebe spoke through gritted teeth. '*Liese* has a refining influence on *Drake Ko*. Bill, listen. Are you asleep? Bill, I think you should take me home. Take me home, please.'

Craw gave a low sigh. These lovers' tiffs between them were six-monthly events at least, and had a cleansing effect on their relationship.

'My dear. Phoebe. Give ear to me, will you? For one moment, right? No English girl, highborn, fine-boned or knock-kneed, can possibly be named *Liese* unless there is a Kraut at work somewhere. That's for openers. What's her other name?'

'Worth.'

'Worth what? All right, that was a joke. Forget it. Elizabeth, that's what she is. Contracted to Lizzie. Or Liza. Liza of Lambeth. You mis-heard. There's blood for you if you like: *Miss Elizabeth Worth*. I could see the bone structure there all right. Not Liese, dear. Lizzie.'

Phoebe became openly furious.

'Don't you tell me how to pronounce *anything*!' she flung at him. 'Her name is *Liese* pronounced *Leesa* and written L-I-E-S-E because I *asked* her and I wrote it *down* and I have printed that name in – oh Bill.' Her forehead fell on his shoulder. 'Oh Bill. Take me home.'

She began weeping. Craw cuddled her against him, gently patting her shoulder.

'Ah now cheer up, my dear, the fault was mine, not yours. I should have known that she was a friend of yours. A fine society woman like Liese, a woman of beauty and fortune, locked in romantic attachment to one of the Island's new nobility: how could a diligent newshound like Phoebe fail to befriend her? I was blind. Forgive me.' He allowed a decent interval. 'What happened?' he asked indulgently. 'You interviewed her, did you?'

For the second time that night, Phoebe dried her eyes with Craw's handkerchief.

'She begged me. She's not my friend. She is far too grand to be my friend. How could she be? She begged me not to print her name. She is here incognito. Her life depends upon it. If her parents know she is here, they will send for her at once. They are fantastically influential. They have private planes, everything. The minute they know she is living with a Chinese man, they would bring fantastic pressure to bear just to get her back. "Phoebe," she said. "Of all people in Hong Kong, you will understand best what it means to live under the shadow of intolerance." She appealed to me. I promised.'

'Quite right,' said Craw stoutly. 'Don't you ever break that promise, Pheeb. A promise is a bond.' He gave an admiring sigh. 'Life's byways, I always maintain, are even stranger than life's highways. If you put that in your paper, your editor would say you were soft in the head, I dare say. And yet it's true. A shining wonderful example of human integrity for its own sake.' Her eyes had closed, so he gave her a jolt in order to keep them open. 'Now where does a match like that have its genesis, I ask myself. What star, what happy chance, could bring together two such needful souls? In Hong Kong too, for God's sake.'

'It was fate. She was not even living here. She had withdrawn from the world altogether after an unhappy love affair and she had decided to spend the rest of her life making exquisite jewellery in order to give the world something beautiful among all its suffering. She flew in for a day or two, just to buy some gold, and quite by chance, at one of Sally Cale's fabulous receptions, she met Drake Ko and that was that.'

'And thereafter the course of true love ran sweet, eh?'

'Certainly not. She met him. She loved him. But she was determined not to get embroiled, and returned home.'

'*Home?*' Craw echoed, mystified. 'Where's home for a woman of her integrity?'

Phoebe laughed. 'Not to the South of France, silly. To Vientiane. To a city no one ever visits. A city without high life, or any of the luxuries to which she was accustomed from birth. That was her chosen place. Her island. She had friends there, she was interested in Buddhism and art and antiquity.'

'And where does she hang out now? Still in some humble croft, is she, clinging to her notions of abstinence? Or has Brother Ko converted her to less frugal paths?'

'Don't be sarcastic. Drake has given her a most beautiful apartment, naturally.'

That was Craw's limit: he knew it at once. He covered the card with others, he told her stories about old Shanghai. But he didn't take another step toward the elusive Liese Worth, though Phoebe might have saved him a lot of legwork.

'Behind every painter,' he liked to say, 'and behind every fieldman, lads, there should be a colleague standing with a mallet, ready to hit him over the head when he has gone far enough.'

In the taxi home she was calm again but shivering. He saw her right to the door in style. He had forgiven her entirely. On the doorstep he made to kiss her, but she held him back from her.

'Bill. Am I really any use? Tell me. When I'm no use, you must throw me out, I insist. Tonight was nothing. You are sweet, you pretend, I try. But it was still nothing. If there is other work for me I will take it. Otherwise, you must throw me aside. Ruthlessly.'

'There'll be other nights,' he assured her, and only then did she let him kiss her.

'Thank you, Bill,' she said.

'So there you are, your Graces,' Craw reflected happily, as he took the taxi on to the Hilton. 'Codename Susan toiled and span and she was worth a little less each day, because agents are only ever as good as the target they're pointed at, and that's the truth of them. And the one time she gave us gold, pure gold, Monsignors' – in his mind's eye, he held up that same fat forefinger, one message for the uncut boys spellbound in the forward rows – 'the *one time*, she didn't even know she'd done it – and she *never could*!'

The best jokes in Hong Kong, Craw had once written, are seldom laughed at because they are too serious. That year there was the Tudor pub in the unfinished highrise building, for instance, where genuine, sour-faced English wenches in period *décolleté* served genuine English beer at twenty degrees below its English temperature, while outside in the lobby, sweating coolies in yellow helmets toiled round the clock to finish off the elevators. Or you could visit the Italian *taverna* where a cast-iron spiral staircase pointed to Juliet's balcony but ended instead in a blank plaster ceiling; or the Scottish inn with kilted Chinese Scots who occasionally rioted in the heat, or when the fares rose on the Star Ferry. Craw had even attended an opium den with airconditioning and Muzak churning out Greensleeves. But the most bizarre, the most contrary for Craw's money, was this rooftop bar overlooking the harbour, with its four-piece Chinese band playing Noel Coward, and its straight-faced Chinese barmen in periwigs and frock coats looming out of the darkness and enquiring in good Americanese, 'what was his drinking pleasure?'

'A beer,' Craw's guest growled, helping himself to a handful of salted almonds. 'But *cold*. Hear that? *Muchee coldee*. And bring it *chop chop*.'

'Life smiles upon your Eminence?' Craw enquired.

'Drop all that, d'you mind? Gets on my wick.'

The Superintendent's embattled face had one expression only and that was of a bottomless cynicism. If man had a choice between good and evil, his baleful scowl said, he chose evil any time: and the world was cut down the middle, between those who knew this, and accepted it, and those long-haired pansies in Whitehall who believed in Father Christmas.

'Found her file yet?'

'No.'

'She calls herself Worth. She's had her syllables removed.'

'I know what she bloody calls herself. She can call herself bloody Mata Hari for all I care. There's still no file on her.'

'But there was?'

'Right cobber, there *was*,' the Rocker simpered furiously, mimicking Craw's accent. '"*There was*, and now there isn't." Do I make myself clear or shall I write it in invisible ink on a carrier pigeon's arse for you, you heathen bloody Aussie?'

Craw sat quiet a while, sipping his drink in steady, repetitive movements.

'Would Ko have done that?'

'Done what?' The Rocker was being wilfully obtuse.

'Had her file nicked?'

'Could have done.'

'The missing-record malady appears to be spreading,' Craw commented after further pause for refreshment. 'London sneezes and Hong Kong catches the cold. My professional sympathies, Monsignor. My fraternal commiserations.' He lowered his voice to a toneless murmur. 'Tell me, is the name Sally Cale music to your Grace's ear?'

'Never heard of her.'

'What's her racket?'

'Chichi Antiquities Limited, Kowloonside. Pillaged art treasures, quality fakes, images of the Lord Buddha.'

'Where from?'

'Real stuff comes from Burma, way of Vientiane. Fakes are home produce. Sixty-year-old dyke,' he added sourly, addressing himself cautiously to another beer. 'Keeps Alsatians and chimpanzees. Just up your street.'

'Any form?'

'You're joking.'

'I am advised that it was Cale who introduced the girl to Ko.'

'So what? Cale pimps the roundeye lay. The Chows like her for it and so do I. I asked her to fix me up once. Said she hadn't got anything small enough, cheeky sow.'

'Our frail beauty was here allegedly on a gold-buying kick. Does that figure?'

The Rocker looked at Craw with fresh loathing and Craw looked at the Rocker, and it was a collision of two immovable objects.

'Course it bloody figures,' said the Rocker contemptuously. 'Cale had the corner in bent gold from Macao, didn't she?'

'So where did Ko fit in the bed?'

'Ah, come off it, don't pussyfoot around. Cale was the front man. It was Ko's racket all along. That fat bulldog of his went in as partner with her.'

'Tiu?'

The Rocker had lapsed once more into beery melancholy, but Craw would not be deflected, and put his mottled head very close to the Rocker's battered ear.

'My Uncle George will be highly appreciative of all available intelligence on the said Cale. Right? He will reward merit richly. He is particularly interested in her as of the fatal moment when she introduced my little lady to her Chow protector, and up to the present day. Names, dates, track record, whatever you've got in the fridge. Hear me?'

'Well you tell your Uncle George he'll get me five bloody years in Stanley jail.'

'And you won't want for company there either, will you, Squire?' said Craw pointedly.

This was an unkind reference to recent sad events in the Rocker's world. Two of his senior colleagues had been sent down for several years apiece, and there were others dolefully waiting to join them.

'Corruption,' the Rocker muttered in fury. 'They'll be discovering bloody steam next. Bloody Boy Scouts, they make me retch.'

Craw had heard it all before, but he heard it again now, for he had the golden gift of listening, which at Sarratt they prize far higher than communication.

'Thirty thousand bloody Europeans and four million bloody slanteyes, a different bloody morality, some of the best-organised bloody crime syndicates in the bloody world. What do they expect me to do? We can't stop crime, so how do we control it? We dig out the big boys and we do a deal with them, of course we do: "Right, boys. No casual crime, no territorial infringements, everything clean and decent and my daughter can walk down the street any time of day or night. I want plenty of arrests to keep the judges happy and earn me my pathetic pension, and God help anybody who breaks the rules or is disrespectful to authority." All right they pay a little squeeze. Name me one person on this whole benighted Island who doesn't pay a little squeeze along the line. If there's people *paying* it, there's people *getting* it. Stands to reason. And if there's people getting it . . . Besides,' said the Rocker, suddenly bored with his own theme, 'your Uncle George knows it all already.'

Craw's lion's head lifted slowly, until his dreadful eye was fixed squarely on the Rocker's averted face.

'George knows *what*, may I enquire?'

'Sally bloody Cale. We turned her inside out for you people years ago. Planning to subvert the bloody pound sterling or some damn thing. Bullion dumping on the Zürich gold markets, I ask you. Load of old cobblers as usual, if you want my view.'

It was another half-hour before the old Australian climbed wearily to his feet, wishing the Rocker long life and felicity.

'And you keep your arse to the sunset,' the Rocker growled.

Craw did not go home that night. He had friends, a Yale lawyer and his wife, who owned one of Hong Kong's two hundred odd private houses, an elderly rambling place on Pollock's Path high up on the Peak, and they had given him a key. A consular car was parked in the driveway, but Craw's friends were known for their addiction to the diplomatic whirl. Entering his room Craw seemed not at all surprised to find a respectful young American seated in the wicker armchair reading a heavy novel: a blond, trim boy in a neat diplomatic-looking suit. Craw did not greet this person, or remark his presence in any way, but instead placed himself at the glass-topped writing desk and, on a single sheet of paper, in the best tradition of his Papal mentor Smiley, began blocking out a message in capital letters, personal for His Holiness, heretical hands keep off. Afterwards, on another sheet, he set out the key to match it. When he had finished, he handed both to the boy, who with great deference put them in his pocket and departed swiftly without a word. Left alone, Craw waited till he heard the growl of the limousine before opening and reading the signal which the boy had left for him. Then he burned it and washed the ash down the sink before stretching himself gratefully on the bed.

A Gideon's day, but I can surprise them yet, he thought. He was tired. Christ, he was tired. He saw the serried faces of the Sarratt children. But we progress, your Graces. Inexorably we progress. Albeit at the blind man's speed, as we tap-tap along in the dark. Time I smoked a little opium, he thought. Time I had a nice little girl to cheer me up. Christ, he was tired.

Smiley was equally tired, perhaps, but the text of Craw's message, when he received it an hour later, quickened him remarkably: the more so since the file on Miss Cale, Sally, last known address Hong Kong, art faker, illicit bullion dealer and occasional heroin trafficker, was for once alive and well and intact in the Circus archives. Not only that. The cryptonym of Sam Collins, in his capacity as the Circus's below-the-line resident in Vientiane, was blazoned all over it like the bunting of a long-awaited victory.

Chapter 10

TEA AND SYMPATHY

It has been laid at Smiley's door more than once since the curtain was rung down on the Dolphin case that now was the moment when George should have gone back to Sam Collins and hit him hard and straight just where it hurt. George could have cut a lot of corners that way, say the knowing; he could have saved vital time.

They are talking simplistic nonsense.

In the first place, time was of no account. The Russian goldseam, and the operation it financed, whatever that was, had been running for years, and undisturbed would presumably run for many more. The only people who were demanding action were the Whitehall barons, the Circus itself, and indirectly Jerry Westerby, who had to eat his head off with boredom for a couple more weeks while Smiley meticulously prepared his next move. Also, Christmas was approaching, which makes everyone impatient. Ko, and whatever operation he was controlling, showed no sign of development. 'Ko and his Russian money stood like a mountain before us,' Smiley wrote later, in his departing paper on Dolphin. 'We could visit the case whenever we wished, but we could not move it. The problem was going to be, not how to stir ourselves, but how to stir Ko to the point where we could read him.'

The lesson is clear: long before anyone else, except perhaps Connie Sachs, Smiley already saw the girl as a potential lever and, as such, the most important single character in the cast – far more important, for instance, than Jerry Westerby, who was at any time replaceable.

This was just one of many good reasons why Smiley made it his business to get as close to her as security considerations allowed. Another was that the whole nature of the link between Sam Collins and the girl still floated in uncertainty. It's so easy now to turn round and say 'obvious' but at that time the issue was anything but cut and dried. The Cale file gave an indication. Smiley's intuitive feeling for Sam's footwork helped fill in some blanks; hasty backbearings by Registry produced clues and the usual batch of analogous cases; the anthology of Sam's field reports was illuminating. The fact remains that the longer Smiley held Sam off, the closer he came to an independent understanding of the relationships between the girl and Ko, and between the girl and Sam: and the stronger his bargaining power when he and Sam next sat down together.

And who on earth could honestly say how Sam would have reacted under pressure? The inquisitors have had their successes, true, but also failures. Sam was a very hard nut.

One more consideration also weighed with Smiley, though in his paper he is too gentlemanly to mention it. A lot of ghosts walked in those post-fall days, and one of them was a fear that, buried somewhere in the Circus, lay Bill Haydon's chosen successor: that Bill had brought him on, recruited and educated him against the very day when he himself, one way or another, would fade from the scene. Sam was originally a Haydon nominee. His later victimisation by Haydon could easily have been a put-up job. Who was to say, in that very jumpy atmosphere, that Sam Collins, manoeuvring for readmission, was not the heir elect to Haydon's treachery?

For all these reasons George Smiley put on his raincoat and got himself out on the street. Willingly, no doubt – for at heart, he was still a case man. Even his detractors gave him that.

In the district of old Barnsbury, in the London borough of Islington, on the day that Smiley finally made his discreet appearance there, the rain was taking a mid-morning pause. On the slate rooftops of Victorian cottages, the dripping chimney pots huddled like bedraggled birds among the television aerials. Behind them, held up by scaffolding, rose the outline of a public housing estate abandoned for want of funds.

'Mr – ?'

'Standfast,' Smiley replied politely, from beneath his umbrella.

Honourable men recognise each other instinctively. Mr Peter Worthington had only to open his front door and run his eye over the plump, rainsoaked figure on the step – the black official briefcase, with EIIR embossed on the bulging plastic flap, the diffident and slightly shabby air – for an expression of friendly welcome to brighten his kindly face.

'That's it. Jolly decent of you to come. Foreign Office is in Downing Street these days, isn't it? What did you do? Tube from Charing Cross, I suppose? Come on in, have a cuppa.'

He was a public-school man who had gone into state education because it was more rewarding. His voice was moderate and consoling and loyal. Even his clothes, Smiley noticed, following him down the slim corridor, had a sort of faithfulness. Peter Worthington might be only thirty-four years old, but his heavy tweed suit would stay in fashion – or out of it – for as long as its owner needed. There was no garden. The study backed straight on to a concrete playground. A stout grille protected the window, and the playground was divided in two by a high wire fence. Beyond it stood the school itself, a scrolled Edwardian building not unlike the Circus, except that it was possible to see in. On the ground floor, Smiley noticed children's paintings hanging on the walls. Higher up, test-tubes in wooden racks. It was playtime and, in their own half, girls in gymslips were racing after a handball. But on the other side of the wire the boys stood in silent groups, like pickets at a factory gate, blacks and whites separate. The study was knee deep in exercise books. A pictorial guide to the kings and queens of

England hung on the chimney breast. Dark clouds filled the sky and made the school look rusty.

'Hope you don't mind the noise,' Peter Worthington called from the kitchen. 'I don't hear it any more, I'm afraid. Sugar?'

'No, no. No sugar, thank you,' said Smiley with a confessive grin.

'Watching the calories?'

'Well, a little, a little.' Smiley was acting himself, but more so, as they say at Sarratt. A mite homelier, a mite more careworn: the gentle, decent civil servant who had reached his ceiling by the age of forty, and stayed there ever since.

'There's lemon if you want it!' Peter Worthington called from the kitchen, clattering dishes inexpertly.

'Oh, no thank you! Just the milk.'

On the threadbare study floor lay evidence of yet another, smaller child: bricks, and a scribbling book with Ds and As scrawled endlessly. From the lamp hung a Christmas star in cardboard. On the drab walls, Magi and sleds and cotton wool. Peter Worthington returned carrying a tea tray. He was big and rugged, with wiry brown hair going early to grey. After all the clattering, the cups were still not very clean.

'Clever of you to choose my free period,' he said, with a nod at the exercise books. 'If you can call it free, with that lot to correct.'

'I do think you people are very underrated,' Smiley said, mildly shaking his head. 'I have friends in the profession myself. They sit up half the night, just correcting the work, so they assure me and I've no reason to doubt them.'

'They're the conscientious ones.'

'I trust I may include you in that category.'

Peter Worthington grinned, suddenly very pleased. 'Afraid so. If a thing's worth doing it's worth doing well,' he said, helping Smiley out of his raincoat.

'I could wish that view were a little more widely held, to be frank.'

'You should have been a teacher yourself,' said Peter Worthington and they both laughed.

'What do you do with your little boy?' said Smiley, sitting down.

'Ian? Oh he goes to his Gran's. My side, not hers,' he added, as he poured. He handed Smiley a cup. 'You married?' he asked.

'Yes, yes I am, and very happily so too, if I may say so.'

'Kids?'

Smiley shook his head, allowing himself a small frown of disappointment. 'Alas,' he said.

'That's where it hurts,' said Peter Worthington, entirely reasonably.

'I'm sure it does,' said Smiley. 'Still, we'd have liked the experience. You feel it more, at our age.'

'You said on the phone there was some news of Elizabeth,' said Peter Worthington. 'I'd be awfully grateful to hear it, I must say.'

'Well nothing to be excited about,' said Smiley cautiously.

'But hopeful. One must have hope.'

Smiley stooped to the official black plastic briefcase and unlocked the cheap clasp.

'Well now, I wonder whether you'll oblige me,' he said. 'It's not that I'm holding back on you, but we do like to be sure. I'm a belt and braces man myself and I don't mind admitting it. We do exactly the same with our foreign deceases. We never commit ourselves until we're *absolutely sure*. Forenames, surname, full address, date of birth if we can get it, we go to no end of trouble. Just to be safe. Not *cause*, of course, we don't do *cause*, that's up to the local authorities.'

'Shoot ahead,' said Peter Worthington heartily. Noticing the exaggeration in his tone, Smiley glanced up, but Peter Worthington's honest face was turned away and he seemed to be studying a pile of old music stands heaped in a corner.

Licking his thumb, Smiley laboriously opened a file on his lap and turned some pages. It was the Foreign Office file, marked 'Missing Person', and obtained by Lacon on a pretext to Enderby. 'Would it be asking too much if I went through the details with you from the beginning? Only the salient ones naturally, and only what you wish to tell me, I don't have to say that, do I? My headache is, you see, I'm actually not the normal person for this work. My colleague Wendover, whom you met, is sick, I'm afraid – and, well, we don't always like to put *everything* on paper do we? He's an admirable fellow but when it comes to report writing I do find him a little *terse*. Not sloppy, far from it, but sometimes a little wanting on the human picture side.'

'I've always been absolutely frank. Always,' said Peter Worthington rather impatiently to the music stands. 'I believe in that.'

'And for *our* part, I can assure you, we at the Office do respect a confidence.'

A sudden lull descended. It had not occurred to Smiley, till this moment, that the scream of children could be soothing; yet as it stopped, and the playground emptied, he had a sense of dislocation which took him a moment to get over.

'Break's over,' said Peter Worthington with a smile.

'I'm sorry?'

'Break. Milk and buns. What you pay your taxes for.'

'Now first of all there is no question here, according to my colleague Wendover's notes – nothing against him, I hasten to say – that Mrs Worthington left under any kind of constraint . . . Just a minute. Let me explain what I mean by that. Please. She left voluntarily. She left alone. She was not unduly prevailed upon, lured, or in any wise the victim of unnatural pressure. Pressure for instance which, let us say, might in due course be the subject of a legal court action by yourself or others against a third party not so far named?'

Longwindedness, as Smiley knew, creates in those who must put up with it an almost unbearable urge to speak. If they do not interrupt directly, they at least counter with pent-up energy: and as a schoolmaster, Peter Worthington was not by any means a natural listener.

'She left alone, absolutely alone, and my entire position is, was, and always has been, that she was free to do so. If she had *not* left alone, if there had been others involved, men, God knows we're all human, it would have made no difference. Does that satisfy your question? Children have a right to both parents,' he ended, stating a maxim.

Smiley was writing diligently but very slowly. Peter Worthington drummed his fingers on his knee, then cracked them, one after another, in quick impatient salvo.

'Now in the interim, Mr Worthington, can you please tell me whether a custody order has been applied for in respect of – '

'We always knew she'd wander. That was understood. I was her anchor. She called me "my anchor". Either that or "schoolmaster". I didn't mind. It wasn't badly meant. It was just, she couldn't bear to say *Peter*. She loved me as a *concept*. Not as a figure perhaps, a body, a mind, a person, not even as a partner. As a concept, a necessary adjunct to her personal, human completeness. She had an urge to please, I understand that. It was part of her insecurity, she longed to be admired. If she paid a compliment, it was because she wished for one in return.'

'I see,' said Smiley, and wrote again, as if physically subscribing to this view.

'I mean nobody could have a girl like Elizabeth as a wife and expect to have her all to himself. It wasn't natural. I've come to terms with that now. Even little Ian had to call her Elizabeth. Again I understand. She couldn't bear the chains of "Mummy". Child running after her calling "Mummy". Too much for her. That's all right, I understand that too. I can imagine it might be hard for you, as a childless man, to understand how a woman of any stamp, a mother, well cared for and loved and looked after, not even having to earn, can literally walk out on her own son and not even send him a postcard from that day to this. Probably that worries, even disgusts you. Well, I take a different view, I'm afraid. At the time, I grant you: yes, it was hard.' He glanced toward the wired playground. He spoke quietly with no hint at all of self-pity. He might have been talking to a pupil. 'We try to teach people freedom here. Freedom within citizenship. Let them develop their individuality. How could *I* tell *her* who *she* was? I wanted to be there, that's all. To be Elizabeth's friend. Her longstop: that was another of her words for me. "My longstop". The point is, she didn't *need* to go. She could have done it all here. At my side. Women need a prop, you know. Without one – '

'And you still have not received any direct word of her?' Smiley enquired meekly. 'Not a letter, not even that postcard to Ian, nothing?'

'Not a sausage.'

Smiley wrote. 'Mr Worthington, to your knowledge, has your wife ever used another name?' For some reason the question threatened to annoy Peter Worthington quite considerably. He flared, as if he were responding to impertinence in class, and his finger shot up to command silence. But Smiley hurried on. 'Her *maiden* name, for instance? Perhaps an abbreviation of her married one, which in a non-English speaking country *could* create difficulties with the natives – '

'Never. Never, *never*. You have to understand basic human behavioural psychology. She was a text-book case. She couldn't wait to get rid of her father's name. One very good reason why she married me was to have a *new* father and a *new* name. Once she'd got it, why should she give it up? It was the same with her romancing, her wild, *wild* story telling. She was trying to escape from her environment. Having done so, having succeeded, having found *me*, and the stability which I represent, she naturally no longer needed to *be* someone else. She *was* someone else. She was fulfilled. So *why* go?'

Again Smiley took his time. He looked at Peter Worthington as if in uncertainty, he looked at his file, he turned to the last entry, tipped his spectacles and read it, obviously not by any means for the first time.

'Mr Worthington, if our information is correct, and we

have good reason to believe it is – I'd say our estimate was a conservative eighty per cent sure, I'd go *that* far – your wife is at present using the surname *Worth*. And she is using a forename with a German spelling, curiously enough, L-I-E-S-E. Pronounced not Liza, I am told, but Leesa. I wondered whether you were in a position to confirm or deny this suggestion, also the suggestion that she is actively connected with a Far Eastern jewellery business with ramifications extending to Hong Kong and other major centres. She appears to be living in a style of affluence and good social appearance, moving in quite high circles.'

Peter Worthington absorbed very little of this, apparently. He had taken a position on the floor, but seemed unable to lower his knees. Cracking his fingers once more, he glared impatiently at the music stands crowded like skeletons into the corner of the room, and was already trying to speak before Smiley had ended.

'Look. This is what I want. That whoever approaches her should make the right kind of point. I don't want any passionate appeals, no appeals to conscience. All that's out. Just a straight statement of what's offered, and she's welcome. That's all.'

Smiley took refuge in the file.

'Well before we come to *that*, if we could just continue going through the facts, Mr Worthington – '

'There *aren't* facts,' said Peter Worthington, thoroughly irritated again. 'There are just two people. Well, three with Ian. There *aren't* facts in a thing like this. Not in *any* marriage. That's what life teaches us. Relationships are *entirely* subjective. I'm sitting on the floor. *That's* a fact. You're writing. *That's* a fact. Her mother was behind it. *That's* a fact. Follow me? Her father is a raving criminal lunatic. *That's* a fact. Elizabeth is *not* the daughter of the Queen of Sheba *or* the natural grandchild of Lloyd George. Whatever she may say. She has *not* got a degree in Sanskrit, which she chose to tell the headmistress who still believes it to this day. "When are we going to see your charming

Oriental wife again?" She knows no more about jewellery than I do. *That's* a fact.'

'Dates and places,' Smiley murmured to the file. 'If I could just check those for a start.'

'Absolutely,' said Peter Worthington handsomely, and from a green tin tea-pot refilled Smiley's cup. Blackboard chalk was worked into his large fingertips. It was like the grey in his hair.

'It was really the mother that messed her up, I'm afraid, though,' he went on, in the same entirely reasonable tone. 'All that urgency about putting her on the stage, then ballet, then trying to get her into television. Her mother just wanted Elizabeth to be admired. As a substitute for herself, of course. It's perfectly natural, psychologically. Read Berne. Read anyone. That's just *her* way of defining *her* individuality. Through her daughter. One must respect that those things happen. I understand all that, now. She's okay, I'm okay, the world's okay, Ian's okay, then suddenly she's off.'

'Do you happen to know whether she communicates with her mother, incidentally?'

Peter Worthington shook his head.

'Absolutely not, I'm afraid. She'd seen through her entirely by the time she left. Broken with her completely. The one hurdle I can safely say I helped her over. My one contribution to her happiness – '

'I don't think we have her mother's address here,' said Smiley, leafing doggedly through the pages of the file. 'You don't – '

Peter Worthington gave it to him rather loud, at dictation speed.

'And now the dates and places,' Smiley repeated. '*Please.*'

She had left him two years ago. Peter Worthington repeated not just the date but the hour. There had been no scene – Peter Worthington didn't hold with scenes – Elizabeth had had too many with her mother – they'd had a happy evening, as a matter of fact, *particularly* happy. For a diversion he'd taken her to the kebab house.

'Perhaps you spotted it as you came down the road? – The Knossos, it's called, next door to the Express Dairy?'

They'd had wine and a real blow-out, and Andrew Wiltshire, the new English master, had come along to make a three. Elizabeth had introduced this Andrew to Yoga only a few weeks before. They had gone to classes together at the Sobell Centre and become great buddies.

'She was really *into* Yoga,' he said with an approving nod of the grizzled head. 'It was a real *interest* for her. Andrew was just the sort of chap to bring her out. Extrovert, unreflective, physical . . . perfect for her,' he said determinedly.

The three of them had returned to the house at ten, because of the babysitter, he said: himself, Andrew and Elizabeth. He'd made coffee, they'd listened to music, and around eleven Elizabeth gave them both a kiss and said she was going over to her mother's to see how she was.

'I had understood she had broken with her mother,' Smiley objected mildly, but Peter Worthington chose not to hear.

'Of course, *kisses* mean nothing with her,' Peter Worthington explained, as a matter of information. 'She kisses everybody, the pupils, her girlfriends – she'd kiss the dustman, anyone. She's *very* outgoing. Once again, she can't leave anyone alone. I mean *every* relationship has to be a conquest. With her child, the waiter at the restaurant . . . then when she's won them, they bore her. Naturally. She went upstairs, looked at Ian and I've no doubt used the moment to collect her passport and the housekeeping money from the bedroom. She left a note saying "sorry" and I haven't seen her since. Nor's Ian,' said Peter Worthington.

'Er, has *Andrew* heard from her?' Smiley enquired, with another tilt of his spectacles.

'Why should he have done?'

'You said they were friends, Mr Worthington. Sometimes third parties become intermediaries in these affairs.'

On the word *affair*, he looked up and found himself staring directly into Peter Worthington's honest, abject eyes: and for a moment the two masks slipped simultaneously. Was Smiley observing? Or was he being observed? Perhaps it was only his embattled imagination – or did he sense, in himself and in this weak boy across the room, the stirring of an embarrassed kinship? 'There should be a *league* for deceived husbands who feel sorry for themselves. You've all got the same boring, awful charity!' Ann had once flung at him. You never knew your Elizabeth, Smiley thought, still staring at Peter Worthington: and I never knew my Ann.

'That's all I can remember really,' said Peter Worthington. 'After that, it's a blank.'

'Yes,' said Smiley, inadvertently taking refuge in Worthington's repeated assertion. 'Yes, I understand.'

He rose to leave. A little boy was standing in the doorway. He had a shrouded, hostile stare. A placid heavy woman stood behind him, holding him by both wrists above his head, so that he seemed to swing from her, though really he was standing by himself.

'Look, there's Daddy,' said the woman, gazing at Worthington with brown, attaching eyes.

'Jenny, hi. This is Mr Standfast from the Foreign Office.'

'How do you do?' said Smiley politely and after a few minutes' meaningless chatter, and a promise of further information in due course, should any become available, quietly took his leave.

'Oh and happy Christmas,' Peter Worthington called from the steps.

'Ah yes. Yes indeed. And to you too. To all of you. Happy indeed, and many more of them.'

In the transport café they put in sugar unless you asked them not to, and each time the Indian woman made a cup, the tiny kitchen filled with steam. In twos and threes, not talking, men ate breakfast, lunch or supper, depending on the point they had reached in their separate days. Here also Christmas was approaching. Six greasy coloured glass balls dangled over the counter for festive cheer, and a net stocking appealed for help for spastic kids. Smiley stared at an evening paper, not reading it. In a corner not twelve feet from him little Fawn had taken up the babysitter's classic position. His dark eyes smiled agreeably on the diners and on the doorway. He lifted his cup with his left hand, while his right idled close to his chest. Did Karla sit like this? Smiley wondered. Did Karla take refuge among the unsuspecting? Control had. Control had made a whole second, third or fourth life for himself in a two-roomed upstairs flat, beside the Western by-pass, under the plain name of Matthews, not filed with housekeepers as an alias. Well, 'whole' life was an exaggeration. But he had kept clothes there, and a woman, Mrs Matthews herself, even a cat. And taken golf lessons at an artisans' club on Thursday mornings early, while from his desk in the Circus he poured scorn on the great unwashed, and on golf, and on love, and on any other piffling human pursuit which secretly might tempt him. He had even rented a garden allotment, Smiley remembered, down by a railway siding. Mrs Matthews had insisted on driving Smiley to see it in her groomed Morris car on the day he broke the sad news to her. It was as big a mess as anyone else's allotment: standard roses, winter vegetables they hadn't used, a toolshed crammed with hosepipes and seedboxes.

Mrs Matthews was a widow, pliant but capable.

'All I want to know,' she had said, having read the figure on the cheque. 'All I want to be sure of, Mr Standfast: is he *really* dead, or has he gone back to his wife?'

'He is really dead,' Smiley assured her, and she believed him gratefully. He forbore from adding that Control's wife had gone to her grave eleven years ago, still believing her husband was something in the Coal Board.

Did Karla have to scheme in committees? Fight cabals, deceive the stupid, flatter the clever, look in distorting mirrors of the Peter Worthington variety, all in order to do the job?

He glanced at his watch, then at Fawn. The coinbox stood next to the lavatory. But when Smiley asked the proprietor for change, he refused it on the grounds that he was too busy.

'Hand it over, you awkward bastard!' shouted a long-distance driver all in leather. The proprietor briskly obliged.

'How did it go?' Guillam asked, taking the call on the direct line.

'Good background,' Smiley replied.

'Hooray,' said Guillam.

Another of the charges later levelled against Smiley was that he wasted time on menial matters, instead of delegating them to his subordinates.

There are blocks of flats near the Town and Country Golf Course on the northern fringes of London that are like the superstructure of permanently sinking ships. They lie at the end of long lawns where the flowers are never quite in flower, the husbands man the lifeboats all in a flurry at about eight-thirty in the morning and the women and children spend the day keeping afloat until their menfolk return too tired to sail anywhere. These buildings were built in the thirties and have stayed a grubby white ever since. Their oblong, steelframed windows look on to the lush billows of the links, where weekday women in eyeshades wander like lost souls. One such block is called Arcady Mansions, and the Pellings lived in number seven, with a cramped view of the ninth green which vanished when the beeches were in leaf. When Smiley rang the bell he heard nothing except the thin electric tinkle: no footsteps, no dog, no music. The door opened and a man's cracked voice said 'Yes?' from the darkness, but it belonged to a woman. She was tall and stooping. A cigarette hung from her hand.

'My name is *Oates*,' Smiley said, offering a big green card encased in cellophane. To a different cover belongs a different name.

'Oh it's you is it? Come in. Dine, see the show. You sounded younger on the telephone,' she boomed in a curdled voice striving for refinement. 'He's in here. He thinks you're a spy,' she said, squinting at the green card. 'You're not, are you?'

'No,' said Smiley. 'I'm afraid not. Just a snooper.'

The flat was all corridors. She led the way, leaving a vapour trail of gin. One leg slurred as she walked, and her right arm was stiff. Smiley guessed she had had a stroke. She dressed as if nobody had ever admired her height or sex. And as if she didn't care. She wore flat shoes and a mannish pullover with a belt that made her shoulders broad.

'He says he's never heard of you. He says he's looked you up in the telephone directory and you don't exist.'

'We like to be discreet,' Smiley said.

She pushed open a door. 'He exists,' she reported loudly, ahead of her into the room. 'And he's not a spy, he's a snooper.'

In a far chair, a man was reading the *Daily Telegraph*, holding it in front of his face so that Smiley only saw the bald head, and the dressing gown, and the short crossed legs ending in leather bedroom slippers; but somehow he knew at once that Mr Pelling was the kind of small man who would only ever marry tall women. The room carried everything he could need in order to survive alone. His television, his bed, his gas fire, a table to eat at and an easel for painting by numbers. On the wall hung an over-coloured portrait photograph of a very beautiful girl with an inscription scribbled diagonally across one corner, in the way that film stars wish love to the unglamorous. Smiley recognised it as Elizabeth Worthington. He had seen a lot of photographs already.

'Mr Oates, meet Nunc,' she said, and all but curtsied.

The *Daily Telegraph* came down with the slowness of a garrison flag, revealing an aggressive, glittering little face with thick brows and managerial spectacles.

'Yes. Well just who are you precisely?' said Mr Pelling. 'Are you Secret Service or aren't you? Don't shilly shally, out with it and be done. I don't hold with snooping you see. What's that?' he demanded.

'His *card*,' said Mrs Pelling, offering it. 'Green in hue.'

'Oh, we're exchanging notes are we? *I* need a card too, then, Cess, don't I? Better get some printed, my dear. Slip down to Smith's, will you?'

'Do you like *tea*?' Mrs Pelling asked, peering down at Smiley with her head on one side.

'What are you giving him tea for?' Mr Pelling demanded, watching her plug in the kettle. 'He doesn't need tea. He's not a guest. He's not even Intelligence. I didn't ask him. Stay the week,' he said to Smiley. 'Move in if you like. Have her bed. *Bullion Universal Security Advisers*, my Aunt Fanny.'

'He wants to talk about Lizzie, darling,' said Mrs Pelling, setting a tray for her husband. 'Now be a father for a change.'

'Fat lot of good her bed would do *you*, mind,' said Mr Pelling, taking up his *Telegraph* again.

'For those kind words,' said Mrs Pelling and gave a laugh. It consisted of two notes, like a birdcall, and was not meant to be funny. A disjointed silence followed.

Mrs Pelling handed Smiley a cup of tea. Accepting it, he addressed himself to the back of Mr Pelling's newspaper. 'Sir, your daughter Elizabeth is being considered for an important appointment with a major overseas corporation. My organisation has been asked in confidence – as a normal but very necessary formality these days – to approach friends and relations in this country and obtain character references.'

'That's *us*, dear,' Mrs Pelling explained, in case her husband hadn't understood.

The newspaper came down with a snap.

'Are you suggesting my daughter is of bad character? Is that what you're sitting here, drinking my tea, suggesting?'

'No, sir,' said Smiley.

'No, sir,' said Mrs Pelling, unhelpfully.

A long silence followed, which Smiley was at no great pains to end.

'Mr Pelling,' he said finally, in a firm and patient voice.

'I understand that you spent many years in the Post Office, and rose to a high position.'

'Many, *many* years,' Mrs Pelling agreed.

'I worked,' said Mr Pelling from behind his newspaper once more. 'There's too much talk in the world. Not enough work done.'

'Did you employ criminals in your department?'

The newspaper rattled, then held still.

'Or Communists?' said Smiley, equally gently.

'If we did we damn soon got rid of them,' said Mr Pelling, and this time the newspaper stayed down.

Mrs Pelling snapped her fingers. 'Like *that*,' she said.

'Mr Pelling,' Smiley continued, in the same bedside manner, 'the position for which your daughter is being considered is with one of the major eastern companies. She will be specialising in air transport and her work will give her advance knowledge of large gold shipments to and from this country, as well as the movement of diplomatic couriers and classified mails. It carries an extremely high remuneration. I don't think it unreasonable – and I don't think you do – that your daughter should be subject to the same procedures as any other candidate for such a responsible – and desirable – post.'

'Who employs *you*?' said Mr Pelling. 'That's what I'm getting at. Who says *you're* responsible?'

'Nunc,' Mrs Pelling pleaded. 'Who says anyone is?'

'Don't *Nunc* me! Give him some more tea. You're hostess, aren't you? Well act like one. It's high time Lizzie was rewarded and I'm frankly displeased that it hasn't occurred before now, seeing what they owe her.'

Mr Pelling resumed his reading of Smiley's impressive green card. '"Correspondents in Asia, USA and Middle East." Pen friends I suppose *they* are. Head Office in South Molton Street. Any enquiries telephone bla bla bla. Who do I get then? Your partner in crime, I suppose.'

'If it's South Molton Street he *must* be all right,' said Mrs Pelling.

'Authority without responsibility,' Mr Pelling said,

dialling the number. He spoke as if someone were holding his nostrils. 'I don't hold with it I'm afraid.'

'*With* responsibility,' Smiley corrected him. 'We, as a company, are pledged to indemnify our customers against any dishonesty on the part of staff we recommend. We are insured accordingly.'

The number rang five times before the Circus switchboard answered it, and Smiley hoped to God there wasn't going to be a muddle.

'Give me the Managing Director,' Mr Pelling ordered. '*I* don't care if he's in conference! Has he got a name? Well what is it? Well you tell Mr Andrew Forbes-Lisle that Mr Humphrey Pelling desires a personal word with him. Now.' Long wait. *Well done thought Smiley. Nice touch.* 'Pelling here. I've a man calling himself Oates sitting in front of me. Short, fat and worried. What do you want me to do with him?'

In the background, Smiley heard Peter Guillam's resonant, officer-like tones all but ordering Pelling to stand up when he addressed him. Mollified, Mr Pelling rang off.

'Does Lizzie know you're talking to us?' he asked.

'She'd laugh her head off if she did,' said his wife.

'She may not even know she is being considered for the post,' said Smiley. 'More and more, the tendency these days is to make the approach after clearance has been obtained.'

'It's for Lizzie, Nunc,' Mrs Pelling reminded him. 'You know you love her although we haven't heard of her for a year.'

'You don't write to her at all?' Smiley asked, sympathetically.

'She doesn't want it,' said Mrs Pelling with a glance at her husband.

The tiniest grunt escaped Smiley's lips. It could have been regret, but it was actually relief.

'Give him more tea,' her husband ordered. 'He's wolfed that lot already.'

He stared quizzically at Smiley yet again. 'I'm still not

sure he's not Secret Service, even now,' he said. 'He may not be glamour, but that could be deliberate.'

Smiley had brought forms. The Circus printer had run them up last night, on buff paper – which was fortunate, for in Mr Pelling's world, it turned out, forms were the legitimisation of everything, and buff was the respectable colour. So the men worked together like two friends solving a crossword, Smiley perched at his side and Mr Pelling doing the pencil work, while his wife sat smoking and staring through the grey net curtains, turning her wedding ring round and round. They did date and place of birth – 'Up the road at the Alexandra Nursing Home. Pulled it down, now, haven't they, Cess? Turned it into one of those ice-cream blocks.' They did education, and Mr Pelling gave his views on that subject.

'I never let one school have her too long, did I, Cess? Keep her mind alert. Don't let it get into a rut. A change is worth a holiday, I said. Didn't I, Cess?'

'He's read books on education,' said Mrs Pelling.

'We married late,' he said, as if explaining her presence.

'We wanted her on the stage,' she said. 'He wanted to be her manager, among other things.'

He gave other dates. There was a drama school and there was a secretarial course.

'Grooming,' Mr Pelling said. 'Preparation, not education, that's what I believe in. Throw a bit of everything at her. Make her worldly. Give her deportment.'

'Oh, she's got the deportment,' Mrs Pelling agreed, and with the click of her throat blew out a lot of cigarette smoke. '*And* the worldliness.'

'But she never *finished* secretarial college?' Smiley asked, pointing to the panel. 'Or the drama.'

'Didn't need to,' said Mr Pelling.

They came to previous employers. Mr Pelling listed half a dozen in the London area, all within eighteen months of one another.

'All bores,' said Mrs Pelling pleasantly.

'She was looking around,' said her husband airily. 'She was taking the pulse before committing herself. I made her, didn't I, Cess? They all wanted her but I wouldn't fall for it.' He flung out an arm at her. 'And don't say it didn't pay off in the end!' he yelled. 'Even if we aren't allowed to talk about it!'

'She liked the ballet best,' said Mrs Pelling. 'Teaching the children. She *adores* children. *Adores* them.'

This annoyed Mr Pelling very much. 'She's making a *career*, Cess,' he shouted, slamming the form on his knee. 'God Almighty, you cretinous woman, do you want her to go back to him?'

'Now what was she doing in the Middle East exactly?' Smiley asked.

'Taking courses. Business schools. Learning Arabic,' said Mr Pelling, acquiring a sudden largeness of view. To Smiley's surprise he even stood, and gesticulating imperiously, roamed the room. 'What got her there in the first place, I don't mind telling you, was an unfortunate marriage.'

'Jesus,' said Mrs Pelling.

Upright, he had a prehensile sturdiness which made him formidable. 'But we got her back. Oh yes. Her room's always ready when she wants it. Next door to mine. She can find me any time. Oh yes. We helped her over that hurdle, didn't we, Cess? Then one day I said to her – '

'She came with a darling English teacher with curly hair,' his wife interrupted. 'Andrew.'

'Scottish,' Mr Pelling corrected her automatically.

'Andrew was a *nice* boy but no match for Nunc, was he, darling?'

'He wasn't enough for her. All that Yogi-bear stuff. Swinging by your tail is what I call it. Then one day I said to her: "Lizzie: Arabs. That's where your future is."' He clicked his fingers, pointing at an imaginary daughter. '"Oil. Money. Power. Away you go. Pack. Get your ticket. Off."'

'A nightclub paid her fare,' said Mrs Pelling. 'It took her for one hell of a ride too.'

'It did no such thing!' Mr Pelling retorted, hunching his

broad shoulders to yell at her, but Mrs Pelling continued as if he weren't there.

'She answered this advertisement, you see. Some woman in Bradford with a soft line of talk. A bawd. "Hostesses needed, but not what you'd think," she said. They paid her air fare and the moment she landed in Bahrein they made her sign a contract giving over all her salary for the rent of her flat. From then on they'd got her, hadn't they? There was nowhere she could go, was there? The Embassy couldn't help her, no one could. She's beautiful, you see.'

'You stupid bloody hag. We're talking about a *career!* Don't you love her? Your own daughter? You unnatural mother! My God!'

'She's got her career,' said Mrs Pelling complacently. 'The best in the world.'

In desperation Mr Pelling turned to Smiley. 'Put down "reception work and picking up the language" and put down – '

'Perhaps you could tell me,' Smiley mildly interjected, as he licked his thumb and turned the page ' – this might be the way to do it – of any experience she has had in the transportation industry.'

'And put down' – Mr Pelling clenched his fists and stared first at his wife, then at Smiley, and he seemed in two minds as to whether to go on or not – 'Put down "working for the British Secret Service in a high capacity". Undercover. Go on! Put it down! There. It's out now.' He swung back at his wife. 'He's in security, he said so. He's got a right to know and she's got a right to have it known of her. No daughter of mine's going to be *an unsung heroine. Or* unpaid! She'll get the George Medal before she's done, you mark my words!'

'Oh balls,' said Mrs Pelling wearily. 'That was just one of her *stories*. You know that.'

'Could we *possibly* take things one by one?' Smiley asked, in a tone of gentle forbearance. 'We were talking, I think, of experience in the transportation industry.'

Sage-like, Mr Pelling put his thumb and forefinger to his chin.

'Her first *commercial* experience,' he began ruminatively. 'Running her own show entirely, you understand – when everything came together, and jelled, and really began to pay off – apart from the Intelligence side I'm referring to – employing staff and handling large quantities of cash and exercising the responsibility she's capable of – came in how do you pronounce it?'

'Vi-ent-iane,' his wife droned, with perfect Anglicisation.

'Capital of La-os,' said Mr Pelling, pronouncing the word to rhyme with chaos.

'And what was the name of the firm, please?' Smiley enquired, pencil poised over the appropriate panel.

'A distilling company,' said Mr Pelling grandly. 'My daughter Elizabeth owned and managed one of the major distilling concessions in that war-torn country.'

'And the name?'

'She was selling kegs of unbranded whisky to American layabouts,' said Mrs Pelling, to the window. 'On commission, twenty per cent. They bought their kegs and left them to mature in Scotland as an investment to be sold off later.'

'*They*, in this case, being . . .?' Smiley asked.

'Then her lover went and filched the money,' Mrs Pelling said. 'It was a racket. Rather a good one.'

'Sheer unadulterated balderdash!' Mr Pelling shouted. 'The woman's insane. Disregard her.'

'And what was her address at that time, please?' Smiley asked.

'Put down "representative",' said Mr Pelling, shaking his head as if things were quite out of hand. 'Distiller's representative and secret agent.'

'She was living with a pilot,' said Mrs Pelling. 'Tiny, she called him. If it hadn't been for Tiny, she'd have starved. He was gorgeous but the war had turned him inside out. Well, of *course* it would! Same with *our* boys, wasn't it? Missions night after night, day after day.' Putting back her head, she screamed very loud: '*Scramble!*'

'She's mad,' Mr Pelling explained.

'Nervous wrecks at eighteen, half of them. But they stuck it. They loved Churchill, you see. They loved his *guts*.'

'Blind mad,' Mr Pelling repeated. 'Barking. Mad as a newt.'

'I'm sorry,' said Smiley, writing busily. 'Tiny who? The pilot? What was his name?'

'Ricardo. Tiny Ricardo. A *lamb*. He died you know.' she said, straight at her husband. 'Lizzie was *heartbroken*, wasn't she, Nunc? Still, it was probably the best way.'

'She wasn't living with *anyone*, you anthropoid ape! It was a put-up, the whole thing. She was working for the British Secret Service!'

'Oh my Christ,' said Mrs Pelling hopelessly.

'*Not* your Christ. *My* Mellon. Take that down, Oates. Let me see you write it down. *Mellon*. The name of her commanding officer in the British Secret Service was M-E-L-L-O-N. Like the fruit but twice as many l's. Mellon. Pretending to be a plain simple trader. *And* making quite a decent thing of it. Naturally, an intelligent man, he would. But underneath' – Mr Pelling drove a fist into his open palm making an astonishingly loud noise – 'but underneath the bland and affable exterior of a British businessman, this same Mellon, two l's, was fighting a secret and lonely war against Her Majesty's enemies and my Lizzie was helping him do it. Drug dealers, Chinese, homosexuals, every single foreign element sworn to the subversion of our island nation, my gallant daughter Lizzie and her friend Colonel Mellon between them fought to check their insidious progress! And that's the honest truth.'

'*Now* ask me where she gets it from,' said Mrs Pelling, and leaving the door open, trailed away down the corridor grumbling to herself. Glancing after her, Smiley saw her pause and seem to tilt her head, beckoning to him from the gloom. They heard a distant door slam shut.

'It's true,' said Pelling stoutly, but more quietly. 'She

did, she did, she did. My daughter was a senior and respected operative of our British Intelligence.'

Smiley did not reply at first, he was too intent on writing. So for a while there was no sound but the slow scratch of his pen on paper, and the rustle as he turned the page.

'Good. Well then, I'll just take those details too, if I may. In confidence naturally. We come across quite a lot of it in our work, I don't mind telling you.'

'*Right*,' said Mr Pelling, and sitting himself vigorously on a plastic-covered dumpty, he pulled a single sheet of paper from his wallet and thrust it into Smiley's hand. It was a letter, hand-written, one and a half sides long. The scipt was at once grandiose and childish, with high, curled I's for the first person, while the other characters appeared more cautiously. It began 'My dearest darling Pops' and it ended 'Your One True Daughter Elizabeth', and the message between, the bulk of which Smiley committed to his memory, ran like this: 'I have arrived in Vientiane which is a flat town, a bit French and wild but don't worry, I have important news for you which I have to impart immediately. It is possible you may not hear from me for a bit but don't worry even if you hear bad things. I'm all right and cared for and doing it for a Good Cause you would be proud of. As soon as I arrived I contacted the British Trade Consul Mister Mackervoor a British and he sent me for a job to Mellon. I'm not allowed to tell you so you'll have to trust me but Mellon is his name and he's a well-off English trader here but that's only half the story. Mellon is Dispatching me on a mission to Hong Kong and I'm to investigate Bullion and Drugs, pretending otherwise, and he's got men everywhere to look after me and his real name isn't Mellon. Mackervoor is in on it only secretly. If anything happens to me it will be worth it anyway because you and I know the Country matters and what's one life among so many in Asia where life counts for naught anyway? This is good Work, Dad, the kind we dreamed of you and me and specially you when you were in the war fighting for your family and loved ones. Pray for me and look after Mum. I will always love you even in prison.'

Smiley handed back the letter. 'There's no date,' he objected flatly. 'Can you give me the date, Mr Pelling? Even approximately?'

Pelling gave it not approximately but exactly. Not for nothing had he spent his working life handling the Royal Mails.

'She's never written to me since,' said Mr Pelling proudly, folding the letter back into his wallet. 'Not a word, not a peep have I had out of her from that day to this. Totally unnecessary. We're one. It was said, I never alluded to it, neither did she. She'd tipped me the wink. I knew. She knew I knew. You'll never get finer understanding between daughter and father than that. Everything that followed: Ricardo, whatever his name was, alive, dead, who cares? Some Chinaman she's on about, forget him. Men friends, girl friends, business, disregard everything you hear. It's cover, the lot. They own her, they control her completely. She works for Mellon and she loves her father. Finish.'

'You've been very kind,' said Smiley, packing together his papers. 'Please don't worry, I'll see myself out.'

'See yourself how you like,' Mr Pelling said with a flash of his old wit.

As Smiley closed the door, he had resumed his armchair, and was ostentatiously looking for his place in the *Daily Telegraph.*

In the dark corridor the smell of drink was stronger. Smiley had counted nine paces before the door slammed, so it must have been the last door on the left, and the furthest from Mr Pelling. It might have been the lavatory, except the lavatory was marked with a sign saying 'Buckingham Palace Rear Entrance'. He called her name very softly and heard her yell 'Get out.' He stepped inside and found himself in her bedroom, and Mrs Pelling sprawled on the bed with a glass in her hand, riffling through a heap of picture postcards. The room itself, like her husband's, was fitted up for a separate existence, with a cooker and a sink and a pile of unwashed plates. Round the walls were snapshots of a tall and very pretty girl, some with boy friends, some alone, mainly against oriental backgrounds. The smell was of gin and cat.

'He won't leave her alone,' Mrs Pelling said. 'Nunc won't. Never could. He tried but he never could. She's beautiful, you see,' she explained for the second time, and rolled on to her back while she held a postcard above her head to read it.

'Will he come in here?'

'Not if you dragged him, darling.'

Smiley closed the door, sat in a chair, and once more took out his notebook.

'She's got a dear sweet Chinaman,' she said, still gazing at the postcard upside down. 'She went to him to save Ricardo and then she fell in love with him. He's a real father to her, the first she ever had. It's all come out right after all. All the bad things. They're over. He calls her *Liese*,' she said. 'He thinks it's prettier for her. Funny really. We don't like Germans. We're patriotic. And now he's fiddling her a lovely job, isn't he?'

'I understand she prefers the name Worth, rather than Worthington. Is there a reason for that, that you know of?'

'Cutting that boring schoolmaster down to size I should think.'

'When you say she did it to *save* Ricardo, you mean of course that – '

Mrs Pelling let out a stage groan of pain.

'*Oh* you men. When? Who? Why? How? In the bushes, dear. In a telephone box, dear. She bought Ricardo his life, darling, with the only currency she has. She did him proud then left him. What the hell, he was a slug.' She took up another postcard, and studied the picture of palm trees and an empty beach. 'My little Lizzie went behind the hedge with half of Asia before she found her Drake. But she found him.' As if hearing a noise, she sat up sharply and stared at Smiley most intently while she straightened her hair. 'I think you'd better go, dear,' she said, in the same low voice, while she turned herself toward the mirror. 'You give me the galloping creeps to be honest. I can't do with trustworthy faces round me. Sorry darling, know what I mean?'

At the Circus, Smiley took a couple of minutes to confirm what he already knew. Mellon, with two l's exactly as Mr Pelling had insisted, was the registered workname and alias of Sam Collins.

Chapter 11

SHANGHAI EXPRESS

In the scheme of things as they are now conveniently remembered, there is at this point a deceptive condensation of events. Somewhere around here in Jerry's life Christmas came and went in a succession of aimless drinking sessions at the Foreign Correspondents' Club, and a series of last-minute parcels to Cat clumsily wrapped in holly paper at all hours of the night. A revised trace request on Ricardo was submitted formally to the Cousins, and Smiley personally took it to the Annexe in order to explain himself more fully to Martello. But the request got snarled up in the Christmas rush – not to mention the impending collapse of Vietnam and Cambodia – and didn't complete its round of the American departments till well into the New Year, as the dates in the Dolphin file show. Indeed, the *crucial* meeting with Martello and his friends on the Drug Enforcement side did not take place till early February. The wear of this prolonged delay on Jerry's nerves was appreciated intellectually within the Circus, but not, in the continued mood of crisis, felt or acted on. For that, one may again blame Smiley, depending where one stands, but it is very hard to see what more he could have done, short of calling Jerry home: particularly since Craw continued to report in glowing terms on his general disposition. The fifth floor was working flat out all the time and Christmas was hardly noticed apart from a rather battered sherry party at midday on the twenty-fifth, and a break later while Connie and the mothers played the Queen's speech very loud in order to shame heretics like

Guillam and Molly Meakin, who found it hilarious and did bad imitations of it in the corridors.

The formal induction of Sam Collins to the Circus's meagre ranks took place on a really freezing day in mid-January and it had a light side and a dark side. The light side was his arrest. He arrived at ten exactly, on a Monday morning, not in a dinner jacket, but in a dapper grey overcoat with a rose in the buttonhole, looking miraculously youthful in the cold. But Smiley and Guillam were out, cloistered with the Cousins, and neither the janitors nor housekeepers had any brief to admit him, so they locked him in a basement for three hours where he shivered and fumed till Smiley returned to verify the appointment. There was more comedy about his room. Smiley had put him on the fourth floor next to Connie and di Salis, but Sam wouldn't wear that and wanted the fifth. He considered it more suitable to his acting rank of co-ordinator. The poor janitors humped furniture up and down stairs like coolies.

The dark side was harder to describe, though several tried. Connie said Sam was *frigid*, a disturbing choice of adjective. To Guillam he was *hungry*, to the mothers *shifty*, and to the burrowers *too smooth by half*. The strangest thing, to those who did not know the background, was his self-sufficiency. He drew no files, he made no bids for this or that responsibility, he scarcely used the telephone, except to place racing bets or oversee the running of his club. But his smile went with him everywhere. The typists declared that he slept in it, and hand-washed it at week-ends. Smiley's interviews with him took place behind closed doors, and bit by bit the product of them was communicated to the team.

Yes, the girl had fetched up in Vientiane with a couple of hippies who had overrun the Katmandu trail. Yes, when they dumped her she had asked Mackelvore to find her a job. And yes, Mackelvore had passed her on to Sam, thinking that on looks alone she must be exploitable: all, reading between the lines, much as the girl had described in her letter home. Sam had had a couple of lowgrade drug ploys mouldering on his books at the time and was otherwise, thanks to Haydon, becalmed, so he thought he might as well put her alongside the flying boys and see what came up. He didn't tell London because London at that point was killing everything. He just went ahead with her on trial and paid her out of his management fund. What came up was Ricardo. He also let her follow an old lead to the bullion racket in Hong Kong, but that was all before he realised she was a total disaster. It was a positive relief to Sam, he said, when Ricardo took her off his hands and got her a job with Indocharter.

'So what else does he know?' Guillam demanded indignantly. 'That's not much of a ticket, is it, for screwing up the pecking order, horning in on our meetings.'

'He knows *her*,' said Smiley patiently, and resumed his study of Jerry Westerby's file, which of late had become his principal reading. 'We are not above a little blackmail ourselves from time to time,' he added with maddening tolerance, 'and it is perfectly reasonable that we should have to submit to it occasionally.' Whereas Connie, with unwonted coarseness, startled everyone by quoting – apparently – President Johnson on the subject of J. Edgar Hoover: 'George would rather have Sam Collins inside the tent pissing out than outside the tent pissing in,' she declared, and gave a schoolgirl giggle at her own audacity.

And most particularly, it was not till mid-January, in the course of his continued excursions into the minutiae of the Ko background, that Doc di Salis unveiled his amazing discovery of the survival of a certain Mr Hibbert, a China missionary in the Baptist interest, whom Ko had mentioned as a referee when he applied to read law in London.

All much more spread out, therefore, than the contemporary memory conveniently allows: and the strain on Jerry accordingly all the greater.

'There's the possibility of a knighthood,' Connie Sachs said. They had said it already on the telephone.

It was a very sober scene. Connie had bobbed her hair. She wore a dark brown hat and a dark brown suit, and she carried a dark brown handbag to contain the radio microphone. Outside in the little drive, in a blue cab with the engine and the heater on, Toby Esterhase the Hungarian pavement artist, wearing a peaked cap, pretended to doze while he received and recorded the conversation on the instruments beneath his seat. Connie's extravagant shape had acquired a prim discipline. She held a Stationery Office notebook handy, and a Stationery Office ballpoint pen between her arthritic fingers. As to the remote di Salis, the art had been to modernise him a little. Under protest, he wore one of Guillam's striped shirts, with a dark tie to match. The result, somewhat surprisingly, was quite convincing.

'It's *extremely* confidential,' Connie said to Mr Hibbert, speaking loud and clear. She had said that on the telephone as well.

'Enormously,' di Salis muttered in confirmation, and flung his arms about till one elbow settled awkwardly on his knobbly knee, and a crabbed hand enclosed his chin, then scratched it.

The Governor had recommended one, she said, and now it was up to the Board to decide whether or not they would pass the recommendation on to the *Palace*. And on the word *Palace* she cast a restrained glance at di Salis, who at once smiled brightly but modestly, like a celebrity at a chat show. His strands of grey hair were slicked down with cream, and looked (said Connie later) as though they had been basted for the oven.

'So you *will* understand,' said Connie, in the precise accents of a female newsreader, 'that in order to *protect* our noblest institutions against embarrassment, a very thorough enquiry has to be made.'

'The *Palace*,' Mr Hibbert echoed, with a wink in di Salis's direction. 'Well I'm blowed. The Palace, hear that, Doris?' He was very old. The record said eighty-one, but his features had reached the age where they were once more unweathered. He wore a clerical dog-collar and a tan cardigan with leather patches on the elbows and a shawl around his shoulders. The background of the grey sea made a halo round his white hair. '*Sir Drake Ko*,' he said. 'That's one thing I'd not thought of, I will say.' His North Country accent was so pure that, like his snowy hair, it could have been put on. '*Sir Drake*,' he repeated. 'Well I'm blowed. Eh, Doris?'

A daughter sat with them, thirty to forty-odd, blonde, and she wore a yellow frock and powder but no lipstick. Since girlhood, nothing seemed to have happened to her face, beyond a steady fading of its hopes. When she spoke she blushed, but she rarely spoke. She had made pastries, and sandwiches as thin as handkerchiefs, and seed-cake on a doily. To strain the tea she used a piece of muslin with beads to weight it stitched round the border. From the ceiling hung a pronged parchment lampshade made in the shape of a star. An upright piano stood along one wall with the score of 'Lead Kindly Light' open on its stand. A sampler of Kipling's *If* hung over the empty fire grate, and the velvet curtains on either side of the sea window were so heavy they might have been there to screen off an unused part of life. There were no books, there was not even a Bible. There was a very big colour television set and there was a long line of Christmas cards hung laterally over string, wings downward, like shot birds halfway to hitting the ground. There was nothing to recall the China coast, unless it was the shadow of the winter sea. It was a day of no weather and no wind. In the garden, cacti and shrubs waited dully in the cold. Walkers went quickly on the promenade.

They would like to take notes, Connie added: for it is Circus folklore that when the sound is being stolen, notes should be taken, both as fallback and for cover.

'Oh, you write away,' Mr Hibbert said encouragingly. 'We're not all elephants, are we, Doris? Doris is, mind, wonderful her memory is, good as her mother's.'

'So what we'd like to do first,' said Connie – careful all the same to match the old man's pace – 'if we may, is what we do with all character witnesses, as we call them, we'd like to establish exactly how long you've known Mr Ko, and the circumstances of your relationship with him.'

Describe your access to Dolphin, she was saying, in a somewhat different language.

Talking of others, old men talk about themselves, studying their image in vanished mirrors.

'I was born to the calling,' Mr Hibbert said. 'My grandfather, he was called. My father, he had, oh a *big* parish in Macclesfield. My uncle died when he was twelve, but he still took the Pledge, didn't he, Doris? I was in missionary training-school at twenty. By twenty-four I'd set sail for Shanghai to join the Lord's Life Mission. The *Empire Queen* she was called. We'd more waiters than passengers the way I remember it. Oh dear.'

He aimed to spend a few years in Shanghai teaching and learning the language, he said, and then with luck transfer to the China Inland Mission and move to the interior.

'I'd have liked that. I'd have liked the challenge. I've always liked the Chinese. The Lord's Life wasn't posh, but it did a job. Now those *Roman* schools, well they were more like your monasteries, *and* with all that entails,' said Mr Hibbert.

Di Salis, the sometime Jesuit, gave a dim smile.

'Now we'd got *our* kids in from the streets,' he said. 'Shanghai was a rare old hotchpotch, I can tell you. We'd everything and everyone. Gangs, corruption, prostitution galore, we'd politics, money and greed and misery. All human life was there, wasn't it, Doris? She wouldn't remember, really. We went back after the war, didn't we, but they soon chucked us out again. She wasn't above eleven, even then, were you? There weren't the places left after that, well not like Shanghai, so we came back here. But we *like* it, don't we, Doris?' said Mr Hibbert, very conscious of speaking for both of them. 'We like the *air*. That's what we like.'

'Very much,' said Doris, and cleared her throat with a cough into her large fist.

'So we'd fill up with whatever we could get, that's what it came to,' he resumed. 'We had old Miss Fong. Remember Daisy Fong, Doris? Course you do – Daisy and her bell? Well she wouldn't really. My, how the time goes, though. A Pied Piper, that's what Daisy was, except it was a bell, and her not a man, and she was doing God's work even if she did fall later. Best convert I ever had, till the Japs came. She'd go down the streets, Daisy would, ringing the daylights out of that bell. Sometimes old Charlie Wan would go along with her, sometimes I'd go, we'd choose the docks or the nightclub areas – behind the Bund maybe – Blood Alley we called that street, remember, Doris? – she wouldn't really – and old Daisy would ring her bell, ring, ring!' He burst out laughing at the memory: he saw her before him quite clearly, for his hand was unconsciously making the vigorous movements of the bell. Di Salis and Connie politely joined in his laughter, but Doris only frowned. 'Rue de Jaffe, that was the worst spot. In the French concession not surprisingly, where the houses of sin were. Well they were everywhere really, Shanghai was jam-packed with them. Sin City they called it. And they were right. Then a few kids gathered and she'd ask them: 'Any of you lost your mothers?' And you'd get a couple. Not all at once, here one, there one. Some would try it on, like, for the rice supper, then get sent home with a cuff. But we'd always find a *few* real ones, didn't we, Doris, and bit by bit we had a school going, forty-four we had by the end, didn't we? Some boarders, not all. Bible Class, the three R's, a bit of geography and history. That's all we could manage.'

Restraining his impatience, di Salis had fixed his gaze on the grey sea and kept it there. But Connie had arranged her face in a steady smile of admiration, and her eyes never left the old man's face.

'That's how Daisy found the Ko's,' he went on, oblivious of his erratic sequence. 'Down in the docks, didn't she, Doris, looking for their mother. They'd come up from Swatow, the two of them. When was that? Nineteen thirty-six I suppose. Young Drake was ten or eleven, and his brother Nelson was eight, thin as wire they were; hadn't had a square meal for weeks. They became rice Christians overnight, I can tell you! Mind you, they hadn't names in those days, not English naturally. They were boat people, Chiu Chow. We never really found out about the mother, did we, Doris? "Killed by the guns," they said. "Killed by the guns." Could have been Japanese guns, could have been Kuomintang. We never got to the bottom of it, why should we? The Lord had her and that was that. Might as well stop all the questions and get on with it. Little Nelson had his arm all messed. Shocking really. Broken bone sticking through his sleeve, I suppose the guns did that as well. Drake, he was holding Nelson's good hand, and he wouldn't let it go for love nor money at first, not even for the lad to eat. We used to say they'd one good hand between them, remember, Doris? Drake would sit there at table clutching on to him, shovelling rice into him for all he was worth. We had the doctor in: *he* couldn't separate them. We just had to put up with it. "You'll be Drake," I said. "And you'll be Nelson, because you're both brave sailors, how's that?" It was your mother's idea, wasn't it, Doris? She'd always wanted boys.'

Doris looked at her father, started to say something, and changed her mind.

'They used to stroke her hair,' the old man said, in a slightly mystified voice. 'Stroke your mother's hair and ring old Daisy's bell, that's what they liked. They'd never seen blonde hair before. Here, Doris, how about a drop more *saw*? Mine's run cold so I'm sure theirs has. *Saw*'s Shanghainese for tea,' he explained. 'In Canton they call it *cha*. We've kept some of the old words, I don't know why.'

With an exasperated hiss, Doris bounded from the room, and Connie seized the opportunity to speak.

'Now, Mr Hibbert, we have no note of a *brother* till now,' she said, in a slightly reproachful tone. 'He was younger, you say. Two years younger? Three?'

'No note of *Nelson*?' The old man was amazed. 'Why, he loved him! Drake's whole life, Nelson was. Do anything for him. No note of *Nelson*, Doris?'

But Doris was in the kitchen, fetching *saw*.

Referring to her notes, Connie gave a strict smile.

'I'm afraid it's we who are to blame, Mr Hibbert, I see here that Government House has left a blank against *brothers and sisters.* There'll be one or two red faces in Hong Kong quite shortly, *I* can tell you. You don't happen to remember Nelson's date of birth, I suppose? Just to shortcut things?'

'No, my goodness! Daisy Fong would remember of course, but she's long gone. Gave them all birthdays, Daisy did, even when they didn't know them theirselves.'

Di Salis hauled on his ear lobe, pulling his head down. 'Or his Chinese forenames?' he blurted in his high voice. '*They* might be useful, if one's checking?'

Mr Hibbert was shaking his head. 'No note of Nelson! Bless my soul! You can't really think of Drake, not without little Nelson at his side. Went together like bread and cheese, we used to say. Being orphans, naturally.'

From the hall, they heard a telephone ringing and, to the secret surprise of both Connie and di Salis, a distinct 'Oh *hell*' from Doris in the kitchen as she dashed to answer it. They heard clippings of angry conversation against the mounting whimper of a tea-kettle. 'Well, *why* isn't it? Well if it's the bloody brakes, *why* say it's the clutch? No, we *don't* want a new car. We want the old one repaired for God's sake.' With a loud 'Christ' she rang off, and returned to the kitchen and the screaming kettle.

'Nelson's Chinese forenames,' Connie prompted gently, through her smile, but the old man shook his head.

'You'd have to ask old Daisy that,' he said. 'And she's long in Heaven, bless her.' Di Salis seemed about to contest the old man's claim to ignorance, but Connie shut him up with a look. *Let him run*, she was urging. *Force him and we'll lose the whole match.*

The old man's chair was on a swivel. Unconsciously, he had worked his way clockwise, and now he was talking to the sea.

'They were like chalk and cheese,' Mr Hibbert said. 'I never saw two brothers so different, nor so faithful, and that's a fact.'

'Different in what *way*?' Connie asked invitingly.

'Little Nelson now, he was frightened of the cockroaches. That was the first thing. We didn't have your modern sanitation, naturally. We'd to send them down to the hut and, oh dear, those cockroaches, they flew about that hut like bullets! Nelson wouldn't go near the place. His arm was mending well enough, he was eating like a fighting cock, but that lad would hold himself in for days on end rather than go inside the hut. Your mother promised him the moon if he'd go. Daisy Fong took a stick to him and I can see his eyes still, he'd look at you sometimes and clench his one good fist and you'd think he'd turn you to stone, that Nelson was a rebel from the day he was born. Then one day we looked out of the window and there they were. Drake with his arm round little Nelson's shoulder, leading him down the path to keep him company while he did his business. Notice how they walk different, the boat children?' he asked brightly, as if he saw them now. 'Bow-legged from the cramp.'

The door was barged open and Doris came in with a tray of fresh tea, making a clatter as she set it down.

'Singing was just the same,' he said and fell silent again, gazing at the sea.

'Singing *hymns*?' Connie prompted brightly, glancing at the polished piano with its empty candleholders.

'Drake, he'd belt anything out as long as your mother was at the piano. Carols. "There is a green hill". Cut his own throat for your mother, Drake would. But young Nelson, I never heard him sing one note.'

'You heard him later all right,' Doris reminded him harshly, but he preferred not to notice her.

'You'd take his lunch away, his supper, but he'd not even say his Amens. He'd a real quarrel with God from the start.' He laughed with sudden freshness. 'Well those are your real believers, I always say. The others are just polite. There's no true conversion, not without a quarrel.'

'Damn garage,' Doris muttered, still fuming after her telephone call, as she hacked at the seed-cake.

'Here! Is your driver all right?' Mr Hibbert cried. 'Shall Doris take out to him? He must be freezing to death out there! Bring him in, go on!' But before either of them could answer, Mr Hibbert had started talking about his war. Not Drake's war, nor Nelson's, but his own, in unjoined scraps of graphic memory. 'Funny thing was, there was a lot who thought the Japs were just the ticket. Teach those upstart Chinese Nationalists where to get off. Let alone the Communists, of course. Oh, it took quite a while for the scales to fall, I can tell you. Even after the bombardments started. European shops closed, Taipans evacuated their families, Country Club became a hospital. But there were still the ones who said "don't worry". Then one day, *bang*, they'd locked us up, hadn't they, Doris. *And* killed your mother into the bargain. She'd not the stamina, had she, not after her tuberculosis. Still, those Ko brothers were better off than most, for all that.'

'Oh. Why was that?' Connie enquired, all interest.

'They'd the knowledge of Jesus to guide and comfort them, hadn't they?'

'Of course,' said Connie.

'Naturally,' di Salis chimed, linking his fingers and hauling at them. '*Indeed* they had,' he said unctuously.

So with the Japs, as he called them, the mission closed and Daisy Fong with her handbell led the children to join the stream of refugees, who by cart, bus or train, but mostly on foot, were taking the trail to Shangjao and finally to Chungking where Chiang's Nationalists had set up their temporary capital.

'He can't go on too long,' Doris warned at one point, in an aside to Connie. 'He gets gaga.'

'Oh yes I can, dear,' Mr Hibbert corrected her with a fond smile. 'I've had my share of life now. I can do what I like.'

They drank the tea and talked about the garden, which had been a problem ever since they settled here.

'They tell us, get the ones with silver leaves, they stand the salt. I don't know, do we, Doris? They don't seem to take, do they?'

With his wife's death, Mr Hibbert somehow said, his

own life had ended too: he was marking time until he joined her. He had had a living in the north of England for a while. After that he'd done a bit of work in London, propagating the Bible.

'Then we came south, didn't we, Doris? I don't know why.'

'For the air,' she said.

'There'll be a party, will there, at the Palace?' Mr Hibbert asked. 'I suppose Drake might even put us down for invites. Think of that, Doris. You'd like that. A Royal Garden Party. Hats.'

'But you did return to Shanghai,' Connie reminded him eventually, shuffling her notes to call him back. 'The Japanese were defeated, Shanghai was reopened and back you went. Without your wife, of course, but you returned all the same.'

'Oh ay, we went.'

'So you saw the Ko's again. You all met up and you had a marvellous old natter, I'm sure. Is that what happened, Mr Hibbert?'

For a moment it seemed he hadn't taken in the question, but suddenly with a delayed action he laughed. 'By Jove and weren't they real little men by then, too. Fly as fly they were! *And* after the girls, saving your presence, Doris. I always say Drake would have married you, dear, if you'd given him any hope.'

'Oh *honestly*, Dad,' Doris muttered and scowled at the floor.

'And Nelson, oh *my* he was the firebrand!' He drank his tea with the spoon, carefully, as if he were feeding a bird. '"Where Missie?" His first question that was, Drake's. He wanted your mother. "Where Missie?" He'd forgotten all his English, so'd Nelson. I'd to give them lessons later. So I told him. He'd seen enough of death by then, *that* was for sure. Wasn't as if he didn't believe in it. "Missie dead," I said. Nothing else to say. "She's dead, Drake, and she's with God." I never saw him weep before or since, but he wept then and I loved him for it. "I lose two mothers," he says to me. "Mother dead, now Missie dead." We prayed for her, what else can you do? Little Nelson now, he didn't cry or pray. Not him. He never took to her the way Drake did. Nothing personal. She was enemy. We all were.'

'*We* being who precisely, Mr Hibbert?' di Salis asked coaxingly.

'Europeans, capitalists, missionaries: all of us carpet-baggers who were there for their souls, or their labour, or their silver. All of us,' Mr Hibbert repeated, without the least hint of rancour. 'Exploiters. That's how he saw us. Right, in a way, too.' The conversation hung awkwardly for a moment till Connie carefully retrieved it.

'So anyway, you reopened the mission, and you stayed till the Communist takeover of forty-nine, I assume, and for those four years at least you were able to keep a fatherly eye on Drake and Nelson. Is that how it went, Mr Hibbert?' she asked, pen poised.

'Oh, we hung the lamp on the door again, yes. In forty-five, we were jubilant, same as anyone else. The fighting had stopped, the Japs were beaten, the refugees could come home. Hugging in the street, there was, the usual. We'd money, reparation I suppose, a grant. Daisy Fong came back, but not for long. For the first year or two the surface held, but not really, even then. We were there as long as Chiang Kai-shek could govern – well, he was never much of a one for that, was he? By forty-seven we'd the Communism out on the streets – and by forty-nine it was there to stay. International Settlement long gone, of course, concessions too, and a good thing. The rest went slowly. You got the blind ones, as usual, who said the old Shanghai would go on for ever, same as you did with the Japs. Shanghai had corrupted the Manchus, they said; the warlords, the Kuomintang, the Japanese, the British. Now she'd corrupt the Communists. They were wrong of course. Doris and me – well, we didn't believe in corruption, did we, not as a solution to China's problems, nor did your mother. So we came home.'

'And the Ko's?' Connie reminded him, while Doris noisily hauled some knitting out of a brown paper bag.

The old man hesitated, and this time it was not senility, perhaps, which slowed his narrative, but doubt. 'Well, yes,' he conceded, after an awkward gap. 'Yes, rare adventures those two had, *I* can tell you.'

'*Adventures*,' Doris echoed angrily, as she clicked her knitting needles. 'Rampages more like.'

The light was clinging to the sea, but inside the room it was dying and the gas fire puttered like a distant motor.

Several times, escaping from Shanghai, Drake and Nelson were separated, the old man said. When they couldn't find each other they ate their hearts out till they did. Nelson, the young one, he got all the way to Chungking without a scratch, surviving starvation, exhaustion and hellish air bombardments which killed thousands of civilians. But Drake, being older, was drafted into Chiang's army, though Chiang did nothing but run away, hoping that the Communists and the Japanese would kill each other.

'Charged all over the shop, Drake did, trying to find the front and worrying himself to death about Nelson. And of course Nelson, well, he was twiddling his thumbs in Chungking wasn't he, boning up on his ideological reading. They'd even the *New China Daily* there, he told me afterwards, *and* published with Chiang's agreement. Fancy that! There was a few others of his mind around, and in Chungking they got their heads together rebuilding the world for when the war ended, and one day, thank God, it did.'

In nineteen forty-five, said Mr Hibbert simply, their separation was ended by a miracle: 'One chance in thousands, it was, millions. That road back littered with streams of lorries, carts, troops, guns, all pouring toward the coast, and there was Drake running up and down like a madman: "Have you seen my brother?"'

The drama of the instant suddenly touched the preacher in him, and his voice lifted.

'And one little dirty fellow put his arm on Drake's elbow. "Here. You. Ko." Like he's asking for a light. "Your brother's two trucks back, talking the hindlegs off a bunch of Hakka Communists." Next thing, they're in each other's arms and Drake won't let Nelson out of his sight till they're back in Shanghai and *then* not!'

'So they came to see you,' Connie suggested cosily.

'When Drake got back to Shanghai, he'd one thing in his mind and one only. Brother Nelson should have a formal education. Nothing else on God's good earth mattered to Drake except Nelson's schooling. *Nothing*. Nelson must go to school.' The old man's hand thudded on the chair arm. '*One* of the brothers at least would make the grade. Oh, he was adamant, Drake was! *And* he did it,' said the old man. 'Drake swung it. He would. He was a real fixer by then. Drake was nineteen years of age, odd, when he came back from the war. Nelson was going on seventeen, and worked night and day too – on his studies, of course. Same as Drake did, but Drake worked with his body.'

'He was a crook,' Doris said under her breath. 'He joined a gang and stole. When he wasn't pawing *me*.'

Whether Mr Hibbert heard her, or whether he was simply answering a standard objection in her was not clear.

'Now Doris, you must see those Triads in perspective,' he corrected her. 'Shanghai was a city state. It was run by a bunch of merchant princes, robber barons and worse. There were no unions, no law and order, life was cheap and hard and I doubt Hong Kong's that different today once you scratch the surface. Some of those so-called English gentlemen would have made your Lancashire mill-owner into a shining example of Christian charity by comparison.' The mild rebuke administered, he returned to Connie and his narrative. Connie was familiar to him: the archetypal lady in the front pew: big, attentive, in a hat, listening indulgently to the old man's every word.

'They'd come round to tea, see, five o'clock, the brothers. I'd to have everything ready, the food on the table, lemonade they liked, called it soda. Drake came in from the docks, Nelson from his books, and they'd eat not hardly talking, then back to work, wouldn't they,

Doris? They'd dug out some legendary hero, the scholar Che Yin. Che Yin was so poor he'd had to teach himself to read and write by the light of the fireflies. They'd go on about how Nelson was to emulate him. "Come on Che Yin," I'd say, "have another bun to keep your strength up." They'd laugh a bit and away they'd go again. "Bye bye, Che Yin, off you go." Now and then when his mouth wasn't too full, Nelson would have a go at me on the politics. *My*, he'd some ideas! Nothing *we* could have taught him, I can tell you, we didn't know enough. Money the root of all evil, well I'd never deny *that*! I'd been preaching it myself for years! Brotherly love, comradeship, religion the opiate of the masses, well I couldn't go along with that, but clericalism, high church baloney, popery, idolatry – well, he wasn't too far wrong there either, the way I saw it. He'd a few bad words against us British too, not but what we deserved them, I dare say.'

'Didn't stop him eating your food, did it?' Doris said in another low-toned aside. '*Or* renouncing his religious background. Or smashing the mission to pieces.'

But the old man only smiled patiently. 'Doris, my dear, I have told you before and I'll tell you again. The Lord reveals himself in many ways. So long as good men are prepared to go out and seek for truth and justice and brotherly love, He'll not be kept waiting too long outside the door.'

Colouring, Doris dug away at her knitting.

'She's right of course. Nelson *did* smash up the mission. Renounced his religion too.' A cloud of grief threatened his old face for a moment, till laughter suddenly triumphed. 'And my billy-oh didn't Drake make him smart for it! Didn't he give him a dressing down though! Oh dear, oh dear! "Politics," says Drake. "You can't eat them, you can't sell them and saving Doris's presence you can't sleep with them! All you can do with them is smash temples and kill the innocent!" I've never seen him so angry. *And* gave Nelson a hiding, he did! Drake had learned a thing or two down in the docks, *I* can tell you!'

'And you *must*,' di Salis hissed, snakelike in the gloom. 'You must tell us *everything*. It's your duty.'

'A student procession,' Mr Hibbert resumed. 'Torchlight, after the curfew, group of Communists out on the streets for a shindy. Early forty-nine, spring it would have been I suppose, things were just beginning to hot up.' In contrast to his earlier ramblings, Mr Hibbert's narrative style had become unexpectedly concise. 'We were sitting by the fire, weren't we, Doris? Fourteen, Doris was, or was it fifteen? We used to love a fire, even when there wasn't the need, took us home to Macclesfield. And we hear this clattering and chanting outside. Cymbals, whistles, gongs, bells, drums, oh, a shocking din. I'd a notion something like this might have been happening. Little Nelson, he was forever warning me in his English lessons. "You go home, Mr Hibbert. You're a good man," he used to say, bless him. "You're a good man but when the floodgates burst, the water will cover the good and the bad alike." He'd a lovely turn of phrase, Nelson, when he wanted. It went with his faith. Not invented. *Felt*. "Daisy," I said – Daisy Fong, that was, she was sitting with us, her as rang the bell – "Daisy, you and Doris go to the back courtyard, I think we're about to have company." Next thing I knew, *smash*, someone had tossed a stone through the window. We heard voices, of course, shouting, and I picked out young Nelson even then, just from his voice. He'd the Chiu Chow *and* the Shanghainese, of course, but he was using Shanghainese to the lads, naturally. "Condemn the imperialist running dogs!" he's yelling. "Down with the religious hyenas!" Oh, the slogans they dream up! They sound all right in Chinese but shove 'em into English and they're rubbish. Then the door goes and in they come.'

'They smashed the cross,' said Doris, pausing to glare at her pattern.

It was Hibbert this time, not his daughter, who startled his audience with his earthiness.

'They smashed a damn sight more than that, Doris!' Mr Hibbert rejoined cheerfully. 'They smashed the lot. Pews, the Table, the piano, chairs, lamps, hymn books, Bibles. Oh, they'd a real old go. *I* can tell you. Proper little pigs, they were. "Go on," I says. "Help yourselves. What man hath put together will perish, but you'll not destroy God's word, not if you chop the whole place up for matchwood." Nelson, he wouldn't look at me, poor lad. I could have wept for him. When they'd gone, I looked round and I saw old Daisy Fong standing there in the doorway and Doris behind her. She'd been watching, had Daisy. Enjoying it. I could see it in her eyes. She was one of them, at heart. Happy. "Daisy," I said. "Pack your things and go. In this life you can give yourself or withhold yourself as you please, my dear. But never lend yourself. That way you're worse than a spy."'

While Connie beamed her agreement, di Salis gave a squeaky, offended wheeze. But the old man was really enjoying himself.

'Well, so we sat down, me and Doris here, and we'd a bit of a cry together, I don't mind admitting, hadn't we, Doris? I'm not ashamed of tears, never have been. We missed your mother sorely. Knelt down, had a pray. Then we started clearing up. Difficult to know where to begin. Then in comes Drake!' He shook his head in wonder. '"Good evening, Mr Hibbert," he says, in that deep voice of his, plus a bit of my North Country that always made us laugh. And behind him, there's little Nelson standing with a brush and pan in his hand. He'd still that crooked arm, I suppose he has now, smashed in the bombs when he was little, but it didn't stop him brushing. I can tell you. That's when Drake went for him, oh cursing him like a navvy! I'd never heard him like it. Well, he *was* a navvy wasn't he, in a manner of speaking?' He smiled serenely at his daughter. 'Lucky he spoke the Chiu Chow, eh, Doris? I only understand the half of it myself, not that, but my *hat*! F-ing and blinding like I don't know what.'

He paused, and closed his eyes a moment, either in prayer or tiredness.

'It wasn't Nelson's fault, of course. Well we knew that already. He was a leader. Face was involved. They'd started marching, nowhere much in mind, then somebody calls to him: "Hey! Mission boy! Show us where your loyalties are now!" So he did. He had to. Didn't stop Drake lamming into him, all the same. They cleaned up, we went to bed, and the two lads slept on the chapel floor in case the mob came back. Came down in the morning, there were the hymn books all piled up neatly, those that had survived, same with the Bibles. They'd fixed a cross up, fashioned it theirselves. Even patched up the piano, though not to tune it, naturally.'

Winding himself into a fresh knot, di Salis put a question. Like Connie, he had a notebook open, but he had not yet written anything in it.

'What was Nelson's *discipline* at this time?' he demanded, in his nasal indignant way, and held his pen ready to write.

Mr Hibbert gave a puzzled frown.

'Why, the Communist Party, naturally.'

As Doris whispered 'Oh *Daddy*' into her knitting, Connie hastily translated.

'What was Nelson studying, Mr Hibbert, and where?'

'Ah *discipline*. *That* kind of discipline!' Mr Hibbert resumed his plainer style.

He knew the answer exactly. What else had he and Nelson to talk about in their English lessons – apart from the Communist gospel, he asked – but Nelson's own ambitions? Nelson's passion was engineering. Nelson believed that technology, not Bibles, would lead China out of feudalism.

'Shipbuilding, roads, railways, factories: that was Nelson. The Angel Gabriel with a slide-rule and a white collar and a degree. That's who *he* was, in his mind.'

Mr Hibbert did not stay in Shanghai long enough to see Nelson achieve this happy state, he said, because Nelson did not graduate till fifty-one –

Di Salis's pen scratched wildly on the notebook.

' – but Drake, who'd scraped and scrounged for him those six years,' said Mr Hibbert – over Doris's renewed references to the Triads – 'Drake stuck it out, and he had his reward, same as Nelson did. He saw that vital piece of paper go into Nelson's hand, and he knew his job was done and he could get out, just like he'd always planned.'

Di Salis in his excitement was growing positively avid. His ugly face had sprung fresh patches of colour and he was fidgeting desperately on his chair.

'And *after* graduating – what then?' he said urgently. 'What did he *do*? What became of him? Go on, please. *Please* go on.'

Amused by such enthusiasm, Mr Hibbert smiled. Well, according to Drake, he said, Nelson had first joined the shipyards as a draughtsman, working on blueprints and building projects, and learning like mad whatever he could from the Russian technicians who'd poured in since Mao's victory. Then in fifty-three, if Mr Hibbert's memory served him correctly, Nelson was privileged to be chosen for further training at the Leningrad University in Russia, and he stayed on there till, well, late fifties anyway.

'Oh, he was like a dog with two tails, Drake was, by the sound of him!' Mr Hibbert could not have looked more proud if it had been his own son he was talking of.

Di Salis leaned suddenly forward, even presuming, despite cautionary glances from Connie, to jab his pen in the old man's direction. 'So *after* Leningrad: what did they do with him *then*?'

'Why, he came back to Shanghai, naturally,' said Mr Hibbert with a laugh. '*And* promoted, he was, after the learning he'd acquired, and the standing: a shipbuilder, Russian taught, a technologist, an administrator! Oh, he loved those Russians! Specially after Korea. They'd machines, power, ideas, philosophy. His promised land, Russia was. He looked up to them like —' His voice, and his zeal, both died. 'Oh dear,' he muttered, and stopped, unsure of himself for the second time since they had listened to him. 'But that couldn't last for ever could it? Admiring Russia: how long was that fashionable in Mao's new wonderland? Doris dear, get me a shawl.'

'You're wearing it,' Doris said.

Tactlessly, stridently, di Salis still bore in on him. He

cared for nothing now except the answers: not even for the notebook open on his lap.

'He returned,' he piped. 'Very well. He rose in the hierarchy. He was Russian trained, Russia oriented. Very well. *What comes next?*'

Mr Hibbert looked at di Salis for a long time. There was no guile in his face, and none in his gaze. He looked at him as a clever child might, without the hindrance of sophistication. And it was suddenly clear that Mr Hibbert didn't trust di Salis any more and, indeed, that he didn't like him.

'He's dead, young man,' Mr Hibbert said finally, and swivelling his chair, stared at the sea view. In the room it was already half dark, and most of the light came from the gas fire. The grey beach was empty. On the wicket gate a single seagull perched black and vast against the last strands of evening sky.

'You said he still had his crooked arm,' di Salis snapped straight back. 'You said you supposed he still had. You said it about *now*! I heard it in your voice!'

'Well now, I think we have taxed Mr Hibbert quite enough,' said Connie brightly and, with a sharp glance at di Salis, stooped for her bag. But di Salis would have none of it.

'I don't believe him!' he cried in his shrill voice. 'How? When did Nelson die? Give us the dates!'

But the old man only drew his shawl more closely round him, and kept his eyes to the sea.

'We were in Durham,' Doris said, still looking at her knitting, though there was not the light to knit by. 'Drake drove up and saw us in his big chauffeur-driven car. He took his henchman with him, the one he calls Tiu. They were fellow crooks together in Shanghai. Wanted to show off. Brought me a platinum cigarette lighter, and a thousand pounds in cash for Dad's church and flashed his OBE at us in its case, took me into a corner and asked me to come to Hong Kong and be his mistress, right under Dad's nose. Bloody sauce! He wanted Dad's signature on something. A guarantee. Said he was going to read law at Gray's Inn. At his age, I ask you! Forty-two! Talk about mature student! He wasn't, of course. It was all just face and talk as usual. Dad said to him: "How's Nelson?" and – '

'Just one minute, please,' Di Salis had made yet another ill-judged interruption. 'The date? *When* did all this happen, please? I must have *dates*!'

'Sixty-seven. Dad was almost retired, weren't you, Dad?'

The old man did not stir.

'All right, sixty-seven. What month? Be precise, please!'

He all but said 'be precise, *woman*', and he was making Connie seriously anxious. But when she again tried to restrain him, he ignored her.

'April,' Doris said after some thought. 'We'd just had Dad's birthday. That's why he brought the thousand quid for the church. He knew Dad wouldn't take it for himself because Dad didn't like the way Drake made his money.'

'All right. Good. Well done. April. So Nelson died pre-April sixty-seven. What details did Drake supply of the circumstances? Do you remember that?'

'None. No details. I told you. Dad asked, and he just said "dead" as if Nelson was a dog. So much for brotherly love. Dad didn't know where to look. It nearly broke his heart and there was Drake not giving a hoot. "I have no brother. Nelson is dead." And Dad still praying for Nelson, weren't you, Dad?

This time the old man spoke. With the dusk, his voice had grown considerably in force.

'I prayed for Nelson and I pray for him still,' he said bluntly. 'When he was alive I prayed that one way or another he would do God's work in the world. I believed he had it in him to do great things. Drake, he'd manage anywhere. He's tough. But the light of the door at the Lord's Life Mission would not have burned in vain, I used to think, if Nelson Ko succeeded in helping to lay the foundation of a just society in China. Nelson might *call* it Communism. Call it what he likes. But for three long years your mother and I gave him our Christian love, and I won't have it said, Doris, not by you or anyone, that the light of God's love can be put out for ever. Not by politics, not by the sword.' He drew a long breath. 'And now he's dead, I pray for his soul, same as I do for your mother's,' he said, sounding strangely less convinced. 'If that's popery, I don't care.'

Connie had actually risen to go. She knew the limits, she had the eye, and she was scared of the way di Salis was hammering on. But di Salis on the scent knew no limits at all.

'So it was a *violent* death, was it? Politics and the sword, you said. *Which* politics? Did Drake tell you that? Actual *killings* were relatively rare, you know. I think you're holding out on us!'

Di Salis also was standing, but at Mr Hibbert's side, and he was yapping these questions downward at the old man's white head as if he were acting in a Sarratt playlet on interrogation.

'You've been so *very* kind,' said Connie gushingly to Doris. 'Really we've all we could possibly need *and* more. I'm sure it will all go through with the knighthood,' she said, in a voice pregnant with message for di Salis. 'Now away we go and thank you both *enormously*.'

But this time it was the old man himself who frustrated her.

'And the year after, he lost his other Nelson too, God help him, his little boy,' he said. 'He'll be a lonely man, will Drake. That was his last letter to us, wasn't it, Doris? "Pray for my little Nelson, Mr Hibbert," he wrote. And we did. Wanted me to fly over and conduct the funeral. I couldn't do it, I don't know why. I never much held with money spent on funerals, to be honest.'

At this, di Salis literally pounced: and with a truly terrible glee. He stooped right over the old man, and he was so animated that he grabbed a fistful of shawl in his feverish little hand.

'Ah! Ah *now*! But did he ever ask you to pray for Nelson *senior*? Answer me that.'

'No,' the old man said simply. 'No, he didn't.'

'Why not? Unless he wasn't really dead, of course! There are more ways than one of dying in China, aren't there, and not all of them are fatal! *Disgraced*: is that a better expression?'

His squeaky words flew about the firelit room like ugly spirits.

'They're to go, Doris,' the old man said calmly to the sea. 'See that driver right, won't you, dear? I'm sure we should have taken out to him, but never mind.'

They stood in the hall, making their goodbyes. The old man had stayed in his chair and Doris had closed the door on him. Sometimes, Connie's sixth sense was frightening.

'The name *Liese* doesn't mean anything to you, does it, Miss Hibbert?' she asked, buckling her enormous plastic coat. 'We have a reference to a *Liese* in Mr Ko's life.'

Doris's unpainted face made an angry scowl.

'That's Mum's name,' she said. 'She was German Lutheran. The swine stole that too, did he?'

With Toby Esterhase at the wheel, Connie Sachs and Doc di Salis hurried home to George with their amazing news. At first, on the way, they squabbled about di Salis's lack of restraint. Toby Esterhase particularly was shocked, and Connie seriously feared the old man might write to Ko. But soon the import of their discovery overwhelmed their apprehensions, and they arrived triumphant at the gates of their secret city.

Safely inside the walls, it was now di Salis's hour of glory. Summoning his family of yellow perils once more, he set in motion a whole variety of enquiries, which sent them scurrying all over London on one false pretext or another, and to Cambridge too. At heart di Salis was a loner. No one knew him, except Connie perhaps and, if Connie didn't care for him, then no one liked him either. Socially he was discordant and frequently absurd. But neither did anyone doubt his hunter's will.

He scoured old records of the Shanghai University of Communications, in Chinese the Chiao Tung – which had a reputation for student Communist militancy after the thirty-nine forty-five war – and concentrated his interest upon the Department of Marine Studies, which included both administration and ship-building in its curriculum. He drew lists of Party cadre members of both before and after forty-nine, and pored over the scant details of those entrusted with the takeover of big enterprises where technological knowhow was required: in particular the Kiangnan shipyard, a massive affair from which the Kuomintang elements had repeatedly to be purged. Having drawn up lists of several thousand names, he opened files on all those who were known to have continued their studies at Leningrad University and afterwards reappeared at the shipyard in improved positions. A course of shipbuilding at Leningrad took three years. By di Salis's computation, Nelson should have been there from fifty-three to fifty-six and afterwards formally assigned to the Shanghai municipal department in charge of marine engineering, which would then have returned him to Kiangnan. Accepting that Nelson possessed not only Chinese forenames which were still unknown, but quite possibly had chosen a new surname for himself into the bargain, di Salis warned his helpers that Nelson's biography might be split into two parts, each under a different name. They should watch for dovetailing. He cadged lists of graduates and lists of enrolled students both at Chiao Tung and at Leningrad and set them side by side. China-watchers are a fraternity apart, and their common interests transcend protocol and national differences. Di Salis had connections not only in Cambridge, and in every Oriental archive, but in Rome, Tokyo and Munich as well. He wrote to all of them, concealing his goal in a welter of other questions. Even the Cousins, it turned out later, had unwittingly opened their files to him. He made other enquiries even more arcane. He despatched burrowers to the Baptists, to delve among records of old pupils at the Mission Schools, on the off-chance that Nelson's Chinese names had, after all, been taken down and filed.

He tracked down any chance records of the deaths of mid-ranking Shanghai officials in the shipping industry.

That was the first leg of his labours. The second began with what Connie called the Great Beastly Cultural Revolution of the mid-Sixties and the names of such Shanghainese officials who, in consequence of criminal pro-Russian leanings, had been officially purged, humiliated, or sent to a May 7th school to rediscover the virtues of peasant labour. He also consulted lists of those sent to labour reform camps, but with no great success. He looked for any references, among the Red Guards' harangues, to the wicked influence of a Baptist upbringing upon this or that disgraced official, and he played complicated games with the name of *KO*. It was at the back of his mind that, in changing his name, Nelson might have hit upon a different character which retained an internal kinship with the original – either homophonic or symphonetic. But when he tried to explain this to Connie, he lost her.

Connie Sachs was pursuing a different line entirely. Her interest centred on the activities of known Karla-trained talent-spotters working among overseas students at the University of Leningrad in the fifties; and on rumours, never proven, that Karla, as a young Comintern agent, had been lent to the Shanghai Communist underground after the war, to help them rebuild their secret apparatus.

It was in the middle of all this fresh burrowing that a small bombshell was delivered from Grosvenor Square. Mr Hibbert's intelligence was still fresh from the presses, in fact, and the researchers of both families were still frantically at work, when Peter Guillam walked in on Smiley with an urgent message. He was as usual deep in his own reading, and as Guillam entered he slipped a file into a drawer and closed it.

'It's the Cousins,' Guillam said gently. 'About Brother Ricardo, your favourite pilot. They want to meet with you at the Annexe as soon as possible. I'm to ring back by yesterday.'

'They want *what*?'

'To meet you. But they use the preposition.'

'*Do* they? Do they *really*? Good Lord. I suppose it's the German influence. Or it is old English? Meet *with*. Well I must say.' And he lumbered off to his bathroom to shave.

Returning to his own room, Guillam found Sam Collins sitting in the soft chair, smoking one of his beastly brown cigarettes and smiling his washable smile.

'Something up?' Sam asked, very leisurely.

'Get the hell out of here,' Guillam snapped.

Sam was in general nosing around a lot too much for Guillam's liking, but that day he had a firm reason for distrusting him. Calling on Lacon at the Cabinet Office to deliver the Circus's monthly imprest account for his inspection, he had been astonished to see Sam emerging from his private office, joking easily with Lacon and Saul Enderby of the Foreign Office.

Chapter 12

The Resurrection Of Ricardo

Before the fall, studiously informal meetings of intelligence partners to the special relationship were held as often as monthly and followed by what Smiley's predecessor Alleline had liked to call 'a jar'. If it was the American turn to play host, then Alleline and his cohorts, among them the popular Bill Haydon, would be shepherded to a vast rooftop bar, known within the Circus as the planetarium, to be regaled with dry martinis and a view of West London they could not otherwise have afforded. If it was the British turn, then a trestle table was set up in the rumpus room, and a darned damask tablecloth spread over it, and the American delegates were invited to pay homage to the last bastion of clubland spying, and incidentally the birthplace of their own service, while they sipped South African sherry disguised by cut-glass decanters on the grounds that they wouldn't know the difference. For the discussions, there was no agenda and by tradition no notes were taken. Old friends had no need of such devices, particularly since hidden microphones stayed sober and did the job better.

Since the fall, these niceties had for a while stopped dead. Under orders from Martello's headquarters at Langley, Virginia, the 'British liaison', as they knew the Circus, was placed on the arm's-length list, equating it with Jugoslavia and the Lebanon, and for a while the two services in effect passed each other on opposite pavements, scarcely lifting their eyes. They were like an estranged couple in the middle of divorce proceedings. But by the time that grey winter's morning had come along when Smiley and Guillam, in some haste, presented themselves at the front doors of the Legal Advisor's Annexe in Grosvenor Square, a marked thaw was already discernible everywhere, even in the rigid faces of the two Marines who frisked them.

The doors, incidentally, were double, with black grilles over black iron, and gilded feathers on the grilles. The cost of them alone would have kept the entire Circus ticking over for a couple more days at least. Once inside them, they had the sensation of coming from a hamlet to a metropolis.

Martello's room was very large. There were no windows and it could have been midnight. Above an empty desk an American flag, unfurled as if by a breeze, occupied half the end wall. At the centre of the floor a ring of airline chairs was clustered round a rosewood table, and in one of these sat Martello himself, a burly, cheerful-looking Yale man in a country suit which seemed always out of season. Two quiet men flanked him each as sallow and sincere as the other.

'George, this is good of you,' said Martello heartily, in his warm, confiding voice, as he came quickly forward to receive them. 'I don't need to tell you. I *know* how busy you are. I *know*. Sol.' He turned to two strangers sitting across the room, so far unnoticed, the one young like Martello's quiet men, if less smooth; the other, squat and tough and much older, with a slashed complexion and a crewcut; a veteran of something. 'Sol,' Martello repeated. 'I want you to meet one of the true legends of our profession, Sol: Mr George Smiley. George, this is Sol Eckland, who's high in our fine Drug Enforcement Administration, formerly the Bureau of Narcotics and Dangerous Drugs, now rechristened, right Sol? Sol, say hullo to Pete Guillam.'

The elder of the two men put out a hand and Smiley and Guillam each shook it, and it felt like dried bark.

'Sure,' said Martello, looking on with the satisfaction of a matchmaker. 'George, ah, remember Ed Ristow, also in narcotics, George? Paid a courtesy call on you over there a few months back? Well, Sol has taken over from Ristow. He has the South East Asian sphere. Cy here is with him.'

Nobody remembers names like the Americans, thought Guillam.

Cy was the young one of the two. He had sideburns and a gold watch and he looked like a Mormon missionary: devout, but defensive. He smiled as if smiling had been part of his course, and Guillam smiled in return.

'What happened to Ristow?' Smiley asked, as they sat down.

'Coronary,' growled Sol the veteran, in a voice as dry as his hand. His hair was like wire wool crimped into small trenches. When he scratched it, which he did a lot, it rasped.

'I'm sorry,' said Smiley.

'Could be permanent,' said Sol, not looking at him, and drew on his cigarette.

Here, for the first time, it passed through Guillam's mind that something fairly momentous was in the air. He caught a hint of real tension between the two American camps. Unheralded replacements, in Guillam's experience of the American scene, were seldom caused by anything as banal as illness. He went so far as to wonder in what way Sol's predecessor might have blotted his copybook.

'Enforcement, ah, naturally has a strong interest in our little joint venture, ah, George,' Martello said, and with this unpromising fanfare, the Ricardo connection was indirectly announced, though Guillam detected there was still a mysterious urge, on the American side, to pretend their meeting was about something different – as witness Martello's vacuous opening comments:

'George, our people in Langley like to work very closely indeed with their good friends in narcotics,' he declared, with all the warmth of a diplomatic *note verbale*.

'Cuts both ways,' Sol the veteran growled in confirmation and expelled more cigarette smoke while he scratched his iron-grey hair. He seemed to Guillam at root a shy man, not comfortable here at all. Cy his young sidekick was a lot more at ease:

'It's parameters, Mr Smiley, sir. On a deal like this, you get some areas, they overlap entirely.' Cy's voice was a little too high for his size.

'Cy and Sol have hunted with us before, George,' Martello said, offering yet further reassurance. 'Cy and Sol are family, take my word for it. Langley cuts Enforcement in, Enforcement cuts Langley in. That's the way it goes. Right, Sol?'

'Right,' said Sol.

If they don't go to bed together soon, thought Guillam, they just *may* claw each other's eyes out instead. He glanced at Smiley and saw that he too was conscious of the strained atmosphere. He sat like his own effigy, a hand on each knee, eyes almost closed as usual, and he seemed to be willing himself into invisibility while the explanation was acted out for him.

'Maybe we should all just get ourselves up to date on the latest details, first,' Martello now suggested, as if he were inviting everyone to wash.

First before what? Guillam wondered.

One of the quiet men used the workname Murphy. Murphy was so fair he was nearly albino. Taking a folder from the rosewood table Murphy began reading from it aloud with great respect in his voice. He held each page singly between his clean fingers.

'Sir, Monday subject flew to Bangkok with Cathay Pacific Airlines, flight details given, and was picked up at the airport by Tan Lee, our reference given, in his personal limousine. They proceeded directly to the Airsea permanent suite at the Hotel Erawan.' He glanced at Sol. 'Tan is managing director of Asian Rice and General, sir, that's Airsea's Bangkok subsidiary, file references appended. They spent three hours in the suite and – '

'Ah, Murphy,' said Martello, interrupting.

'Sir?'

'All that "reference given", "reference appended". Leave

that out, will you? We all know we have files on these guys. Right?'

'Right, sir.'

'Ko alone?' Sol demanded.

'Sir, Ko took his manager Tiu along with him. Tiu goes with him most everywhere.'

Here chancing to look at Smiley again, Guillam intercepted an enquiring glance from him directed at Martello. Guillam had a notion he was thinking of the girl – had *she* gone too? – but Martello's indulgent smile didn't waver, and after a moment Smiley seemed to accept this, and resumed his attentive pose.

Sol meanwhile had turned to his assistant and the two of them had a brief private exchange:

'Why the hell doesn't somebody bug the damn hotel suite, Cy? What's holding everyone up?'

'We already suggested that to Bangkok, Sol, but they've got problems with the party walls, they got no proper cavities or something.'

'Those Bangkok clowns are drowsy with too much ass. That the same Tan we tried to nail last year for heroin?'

'Now, that was Tan *Ha*, Sol. This one's Tan *Lee*. They have a great lot of Tans out there. Tan Lee's just a front man. He plays link to Fatty Hong in Chiang Mai. It's Hong who has the connections to the growers and the big brokers.'

'Somebody ought to go out and shoot that bastard,' Sol said. Which bastard wasn't quite clear.

Martello nodded at pale Murphy to go on.

'Sir, the three men then drove down to Bangkok port – that's Ko and Tan Lee and Tiu, sir – and they looked at twenty or thirty small coasters tied up along the bank. Then they drove back to Bangkok airport and subject flew to Manila, Philippines, for a cement conference at the Hotel Eden and Bali.'

'Tiu didn't go to Manila?' Martello asked, buying time.

'No, sir. Flew home,' Murphy replied, and once more Smiley glanced at Martello.

'Cement my ass,' Sol exclaimed. 'Those the boats that do the run up to Hong Kong, Murphy?'

'Yes, sir.'

'We know those boats,' expostulated Sol. 'We been going for those boats for years. Right, Cy?'

'Right.'

Sol had rounded on Martello, as if he were personally to blame. 'They leave harbour clean. They don't take the stuff aboard till they're at sea. Nobody knows which boat will carry, not even the captain of the selected vessel, until the launch pulls alongside, gives them the dope. When they hit Hong Kong waters, they drop the dope overboard with markers and the junks scoop it in.' He spoke slowly, as if speaking hurt him, forcing each word out hoarsely. 'We been screaming at the Brits for years to shake those junks out, but the bastards are all on the take.'

'That's all we have, sir,' said Murphy, and put down his report.

They were back to the awkward pauses. A pretty girl, armed with a tray of coffee and biscuits, provided a temporary reprieve, but when she left the silence was worse.

'Why don't you just tell him?' Sol snapped finally. 'Otherwise maybe I will.'

Which was when, as Martello would have said, they finally got down to the nitty-gritty.

Martello's manner became both grave and confiding: a family solicitor reading a will to the heirs. 'George, ah, at our request Enforcement here took a kind of a second look at the background and the record of the missing pilot Ricardo, and as we half surmised, they've dug up a fair quantity of material which till now has not come to light as it should have done, owing to various factors. There's no profit, in my view, to pointing the finger at anyone and besides Ed Ristow is a sick man. Let's just agree that, however it happened, the Ricardo thing fell into a small gap between Enforcement and ourselves. That gap has since closed and we'd like to rectify the information for you.'

'Thank you, Marty,' said Smiley patiently.

'Seems Ricardo's alive after all,' Sol declared. 'Seems like it's a prime snafu.'

'A *what*?' Smiley asked sharply, perhaps before the full significance of Sol's statement had sunk in.

Martello was quick to translate. 'Error, George. Human error. Happens to all of us. *Snafu*. Even you, okay?'

Guillam was studying Cy's shoes, which had a rubbery gloss and thick welts. Smiley's eyes had lifted to the side wall, where the benevolent features of President Nixon gazed down encouragingly on the triangular union. Nixon had resigned a good six months ago, but Martello seemed rather touchingly determined to tend his lamp. Murphy and his mute companion sat still as confirmands in the presence of the bishop. Only Sol was for ever on the move, alternately scratching at his crimped scalp or sucking on his cigarette like an athletic version of di Salis. He never smiles, thought Guillam extraneously: he's forgotten how.

Martello continued. 'Ricardo's death is formally recorded in our files as on or round August twenty-one, George, correct?'

'Correct,' said Smiley.

Martello drew a breath and tilted his head the other way as he read his notes. 'However, on September, ah, two – couple of weeks after his death, right? – it, ah, seems Ricardo made personal contact with one of the narcotics bureaux in the Asian theatre, then known as BNDD but primarily the same house, okay? Sol would, ah, prefer not to mention *which* bureau, and I respect that.' The mannerism *ah*, Guillam decided, was Martello's way of keeping talking while he thought. 'Ricardo offered the bureau his services on a sell-and-tell basis regarding an, ah, opium mission he claimed to have received to fly right over the border into, ah, Red China.'

* * *

A cold hand seemed to seize hold of Guillam's stomach at this moment and stay there. His sense of occasion was all the greater following the slow lead-in through so much unrelated detail. He told Molly afterwards that it was as if 'all the threads of the case had suddenly wound themselves together in a single skein' for him. But that was hindsight and he was boasting a little. Nevertheless the shock – after all the tiptoeing and the speculation and the paperchases – the plain shock of being almost physically projected into the Chinese Mainland: that certainly was real, and required no exaggeration.

Martello was doing his worthy solicitor act again.

'George, I have to fill you in on, ah, a little more of the family background here. During the Laos thing, the Company used a few of the northern hilltribes for combat purposes, maybe you knew that. Right up there in Burma, know those parts, the Shans? Volunteers, follow me? Lot of those tribes were one-crop communities, ah, opium communities, and in the interests of the war there, the Company had to, ah, well turn a blind eye to what we couldn't change, follow me? These good people have to live and many knew no better and saw nothing wrong in, ah, growing that crop. Follow me?'

'Jesus Christ,' said Sol under his breath. 'Hear that, Cy?'

'I heard, Sol.'

Smiley said he followed.

'This policy, conducted, ah, by the Company, caused a very brief and very temporary rift between the Company on the one side and the, ah, Enforcement people here, formerly the Bureau of Narcotics. Because, well, while Sol's boys were out to, well, ah, suppress the abuse of drugs, and quite rightly, and, ah, ride down the shipments, which is their job, George, and their duty, it was in the Company's best interest – in the best interest of the war, that is – at this point in time, you follow, George – to, well, ah, turn a blind eye.'

'Company played godfather to the hilltribes,' Sol growled. 'Menfolk were all out fighting the war, Company people flew up to the villages, pushed their poppy crops, screwed their women and flew their dope.'

Martello was not so easily thrown. 'Well we think that's overstating things a little, Sol, but the, ah, rift was there and that's the point as far as our friend George is concerned. Ricardo, well he's a tough cookie. He flew a lot of missions for the Company in Laos, and when the war ended, the Company resettled him and kissed him off and pulled up the ladder. Nobody messes around with those boys when there's no war for them any more. So, ah, maybe at that, the, ah, gamekeeper Ricardo turned into the, ah, poacher Ricardo, if you follow me – '

'Well not *absolutely*,' Smiley confessed mildly.

Sol had no such scruples about unpalatable truths. 'Long as the war was on, Ricardo carried dope for the Company to keep the home fires burning up in the hill villages. War ended, he carried it for himself. He had the connects and he knew where the bodies were buried. He went independent, that's all.'

'Thank you,' said Smiley, and Sol went back to scratching his crewcut.

For the second time, Martello backed toward the story of Ricardo's embarrassing resurrection.

They must have done a deal between them, thought Guillam. Martello does the talking. 'Smiley's our contact,' Martello would have said. 'We play him our way.'

On the second of September seventy-three, said Martello, an *un-named narcotics agent in the South East Asian theatre*, as he insisted on describing him, 'a young man quite new to the field, George', received a nocturnal telephone call at his home from a self-styled Captain Tiny Ricardo, hitherto believed dead, formerly a Laos mercenary with Captain Rocky. Ricardo offered a sizeable quantity of raw opium at standard buy-in rates. In addition to the opium, however, he was offering hot information at what he called a bargain-basement price for a quick sale. That is to say fifty thousand US dollars in small notes, and a West German passport for a one-time journey out. The un-named narcotics agent met Ricardo later that night at a parking lot and they quickly agreed on the sale of the opium.

'You mean he *bought* it?' Smiley asked, most surprised.

'Sol tells me there is a, ah, fixed tariff for such deals, – right Sol? – known to everyone in the game, George, and, ah, based upon a percentage of the street value of the haul, right?' Sol growled an affirmative. 'The, ah, un-named agent had a standing authority to buy-in at that tariff and he exercised it. No problem. The agent also, ah, expressed himself willing, subject to higher consent, to supply Ricardo with quick-expiry documentation, George' – he meant, it turned out later, a West German passport with only a few days to run – 'in the event, George – an event not yet realised, you follow me – that Ricardo's information prove to be of reasonable value, since policy is to encourage informants at all costs. But he made it clear – the agent – that the whole deal – the passport and the payment for the information – was subject to ratification and authority – of Sol's people back at headquarters. So he bought the opium, but he held on the information. Right, Sol?'

'On the button,' Sol growled.

'Sol, ah, maybe you should handle this part,' Martello said.

When Sol spoke, he kept the rest of himself still for once. Just his mouth moved.

'Our agent asked Ricardo for a teaser so's the information could be evaluated back home. What we call taking it to first base. Ricardo comes up with the story he's been ordered to fly the dope over the border into Red China and bring back an unspecified load in payment. That's what he said. His teaser. He said he knew who was behind the deal, he said he knew the Mister Big of all the Mister Bigs, they all do. He said he knew all the story, but so do they all, once more. He said he embarked on his journey for the Mainland, chickened out and hedgehopped home over Laos ducking the radar screens. That's all he said. He didn't say where he set out from. He said he owed a favour to the people who sent him, and if they ever found him they'd kick his teeth right up his throat. That's what's in the protocol, word for word. His teeth up his throat.

So he was in a hurry, hence the favourable price of fifty grand. He didn't say who the people were, he did not produce one scrap of positive collateral apart from the opium, but he said he had the plane still, hidden, a Beechcraft, and he offered to show this plane to our agent at the next occasion of their meeting, subject to there being serious interest back at headquarters. That's all we have,' said Sol, and devoted himself to his cigarette. 'Opium was a couple of hundred kilos. Good stuff.'

Martello deftly took back the ball:

'So the un-named narcotics agent filed his story, George. And he did what we'd all do. He took down the teaser and he sent it back to headquarters and he told Ricardo to lie low till he heard back from his people. See you in ten days, maybe fourteen. Here's your opium-money, but for information-money you have to wait a little. There's regulations. Follow me?'

Smiley nodded sympathetically, and Martello nodded back at him while he went on talking.

'So here it is. Here's where you get your human error, right? It could be worse but not much. In our game there's two views of history: conspiracy and fuck-up. Here's where we get the fuck-up, no question at all. Sol's predecessor, Ed, now ill, evaluated the material and on the evidence – now you met him, George, Ed Ristow, a good sound guy – and on the evidence available to him, Ed decided, understandably but wrongly, not to proceed. Ricardo wanted fifty grand. Well, for a major haul I understand that's chickenfeed. But Ricardo, he wanted payment on the nail. A one-time, and out. And Ed – well Ed had responsibilities, and a lot of family trouble, and Ed just didn't see his way to investing that sum of public American money in a character like Ricardo, when no haul is guaranteed, who has all the passes, knows all the fast steps, and is maybe squaring up to take that field agent of Ed's, who is only a young guy, for one hell of a journey. So Ed killed it. No further action. File and forget. All squared away. Buy the opium, but not the rest.'

Maybe it was a real coronary after all, Guillam reflected,

marvelling. But with another part of him he knew it could have happened to himself and even had: the pedlar who has the big one, and you let it through your fingers.

Rather than waste time in recrimination, Smiley had quietly moved ahead to the remaining possibilities.

'Where is Ricardo now, Marty?' he asked.

'Not known.'

His next question was much longer in coming, and was scarcely a question so much as a piece of thinking aloud.

'To bring back an *unspecified load in payment*,' he repeated. 'Are there any theories as to what type of load that might have been?'

'We guessed gold. We don't have second vision, any more than you do,' Sol said harshly.

Here Smiley simply ceased to take part in the proceedings for a while. His face set, his expression became anxious and, to anyone who knew him, inward, and suddenly it was up to Guillam to keep the ball rolling. To do this, like Smiley, he addressed Martello.

'Ricardo did not give any hint of where he was to deliver his return load?'

'I told you. Pete. That's all we have.'

Smiley was still non-combatant. He sat staring mournfully at his folded hands. Guillam hunted for another question:

'And no hint of the anticipated *weight* of the return load, either?' he asked.

'Jesus Christ,' said Sol, and, misreading Smiley's attitude, slowly shook his head in wonder at the kind of deadbeat company he was obliged to keep.

'But you *are* satisfied it was Ricardo who approached your agent?' Guillam asked, still in there, throwing punches.

'One hundred per cent,' said Sol.

'Sol,' Martello suggested, leaning across to him. 'Sol, why don't you just give George a blind copy of that original field report? That way he has everything we have.'

Sol hesitated, glanced at his sidekick, shrugged, and

finally with some reluctance drew a flimsy sheet of India paper from a folder on the table beside him, from which he solemnly tore off the signature.

'Off the record,' he growled, and at this point Smiley abruptly revived, and, receiving the report from Sol's hand, studied both sides intently for a while in silence.

'And, where, please, is the un-named narcotics agent who wrote this document,' he enquired finally, looking first at Martello, then at Sol.

Sol scraped his scalp. Cy began shaking his head in disapproval. Whereas Martello's two quiet men showed no curiosity whatever. Pale Murphy continued reading among his notes, and his colleague gazed blankly at the ex-President.

'Shacked up in a hippy commune north of Katmandu,' Sol growled, through a gush of cigarette smoke. 'Bastard joined the opposition.'

Martello's bright endpiece was wonderfully irrelevant: 'So, ah, that's the reason, George, why *our* computer has Ricardo dead and buried, George, when the overall record – on reconsideration by our Enforcement friends – gives no grounds for that, ah, assumption.'

So far it had seemed to Guillam that the boot was all on Martello's foot. Sol's boys had made fools of themselves, he was saying, but the Cousins were nothing if not magnanimous and they were willing to kiss and make up. In the post-coital calm which followed Martello's revelations, this false impression prevailed a little longer.

'So, ah, George, I would say that henceforward, we may count – you, we, Sol here – on the fullest co-operation of all our agencies. I would say there was a very positive side to this. Right, George? Constructive.'

But Smiley in his renewed distraction only lifted his eyebrows and pursed his lips.

'Something on your mind, George?' Martello asked. 'I said, is there something on your mind?'

'Oh. Thank you. *Beechcraft*,' Smiley said. 'Is that a single-engined plane?'

'Jesus,' said Sol under his breath.

'Twin, George, twin,' said Martello. 'Kind of executive runabout kind of thing.'

'And the weight of the opium load was four hundred kilos, the report says.'

'Just short of half of one ton, George,' said Martello at his most solicitous. 'A *metric* ton,' he added doubtfully, to Smiley's shadowed face. 'Not your English ton, George, naturally. Metric.'

'And it would be carried *where* – the opium, I mean?'

'Cabin,' said Sol. 'Most likely unscrewed the spare seats. Beechcrafts come different shapes. We don't know which this was because we never got to see it.'

Smiley peered once more at the flimsy which he still clutched in his pudgy hand. 'Yes,' he muttered. 'Yes, I suppose they would have done.' And with a gold lead-pencil he wrote a small hieroglyphic in the margin before relapsing into his private reverie.

'Well,' said Martello brightly. 'Guess us worker-bees had better get back to our hives and see where that gets us, right, Pete?'

Guillam was halfway to his feet as Sol spoke. Sol had the rare and rather terrible gift of natural rudeness. Nothing had changed in him. He was in no way out of control. This was the way he talked, this was the way he did business, and other ways patently bored him:

'Jesus *Christ*, Martello, what kind of game are we playing round here? This is the big one, right? We have put our finger on maybe the most important single narcotics target in the entire South East Asian scene. Okay, so there's liaison. The Company has finally gone to bed with Enforcement because she had to buy us off on the hilltribe thing. Don't think that makes *me* horny. Okay, so we have a hands-off deal with the Brits on Hong Kong. But Thailand's ours, so's the Philippines, so's Taiwan, so's the whole damn theatre, so's the war, and the Brits are on their ass. Four months ago the Brits came in and made their pitch. Great, so we roll it to the Brits. What they been doing all the time? Rubbing soap into their pretty faces. So when do they get to shave, for God's sakes? We got money riding on this. We got a whole apparatus standing by, ready to shake out Ko's connections across the hemisphere. We been looking *years* for a guy like this. And we can nail him. We have enough legislation – boy do we have legislation! – to pin a ten-to-thirty on him and *then* some! We got drugs on him, we got arms, we got embargoed goods, we got the biggest damn load of Red gold we ever saw Moscow hand to one man in our *lives*, and we got the first proof ever, if this guy Ricardo is telling a correct story, of a Moscow-subsidised drug-subversion programme which is ready and willing to carry the battle into Red China in the hopes of doing the same for them as they're already doing for us.'

The outburst had woken Smiley like a douche of water. He was sitting forward on the edge of his chair, the narcotics agent's report crumpled in his hand, and he was staring appalled, first at Sol, finally at Martello.

'Marty,' he muttered. 'Oh my Lord. *No*.'

Guillam showed greater presence of mind. At least he threw in an objection:

'You'd have to spread half a ton awfully *thin*, wouldn't you, Sol, to hook eight hundred million Chinese?'

But Sol had no use for humour, or objections either, least of all from some pretty-faced Brit.

'And do we go for his jugular?' he demanded, keeping straight on course. 'Do we hell. We pussyfoot. We stand on the sidelines. "Play it delicate. It's a British ballgame. Their territory, their joe, their party." So we weave, we dance around. We float like a butterfly and sting like one. Jesus, if *we'd* been handling this thing, we'd have had that bastard trussed over a barrel months ago.' Slapping the table with his palm, he used the rhetorical trick of repeating his point in different language. 'For the first time ever we have gotten ourselves a sabre-toothed Soviet Communist corrupter in our sights, pushing dope and screwing up the area and taking Russian money and we can *prove* it!' It was all addressed to Martello. Smiley and Guillam might not have been there at all. 'And you just remember another thing,' he advised Martello in conclusion. 'We got big people wanting mileage out of this. Impatient people. Influential. People very angry with the dubious part your Company has indirectly played in the supply and merchandising of narcotics to our boys in Vietnam, which is why you cut us in on this in the first place. So maybe you better tell some of those limousine liberals back in Langley Virginia it's time for them to shit or get off the pot. Pot in *both senses*,' he ended in a humourless pun.

Smiley had turned so pale that Guillam was genuinely afraid for him. He wondered whether he had had a heart attack, or was going to faint. From where Guillam sat, his cheeks and complexion were suddenly an old man's and his eyes, as he too addressed Martello only, had an old man's fire:

'However, there is an agreement. And so long as it stands, I trust that you will stick to it. We have your general declaration that you will abstain from operations in British areas unless our permission has been granted. We have your particular promise that you will leave to us the entire development of this case, outside surveillance and communication, *regardless of where the development leads*. That was the contract. A complete hands-off in exchange for a complete sight of the product. I take that to mean this: *no* action by Langley and *no* action by any other American agency. I take that to be your absolute word. And I take your word to be still good, and I regard that understanding as irreducible.'

'Tell him,' said Sol, and walked out, followed by Cy, his sallow Mormon sidekick. At the door he turned, and jabbed a finger in Smiley's direction.

'You ride our wagon, we tell you where to get off and where to stay topsides,' he said.

The Mormon nodded: 'Sure do,' he said and smiled at Guillam as if in invitation. On Martello's nod, Murphy and his fellow quiet man followed them out of the room.

Martello was pouring drinks. In his office, the walls were also rosewood – a fake laminate, Guillam noticed, not the real thing – and when Martello pulled a handle he revealed an ice machine that vomited a steady flow of pellets in the shape of rugby balls. He poured three whiskies without asking the others what they wanted. Smiley looked all in. His plump hands were still cupped over the ends of his airline chair, but he was leaning back like a spent boxer between rounds, staring at the ceiling, which was perforated by twinkling lights. Martello set the glasses on the table.

'Thank you, sir,' Guillam said. Martello liked a 'sir'.

'You bet,' said Martello.

'Who else have your headquarters told?' Smiley said, to the stars. 'The Revenue Service? The Customs Service? The Mayor of Chicago? Their twelve best friends? Do you realise that not even my masters know we are in collaboration with you? God in heaven.'

'Ah, come on now, George. We have politics, same as you. We have promises to keep. Mouths to buy. Enforcement's out for our blood. That dope story's gotten a lot of airtime on the Hill. Senators, the House Subcommittees, the whole garbage. Kid comes back from the war a screaming junkie, first thing his Pa does is write to his Congressman. Company doesn't care for all those bad rumours. It likes to have its friends on its own side. That's showbiz, George.'

'Could I please just know what the deal is?' Smiley asked. 'Could I have it in plain words, at least?'

'Oh now, there's no *deal*, George. Langley can't deal with what she doesn't own, and this is *your* case, your property, your . . . We fish for him – you do, with a little help from us maybe – we do our best and then if, ah, we don't come up with anything, why, Enforcement will get in on the act a little and, on a very friendly and controllable basis, try their skill.'

'At which point it's open season,' Smiley said. 'My goodness, what a way to run a case.'

When it came to pacification, Martello was a very old hand indeed:

'George. *George.* Suppose they nail Ko. Suppose they

fall on him out of the trees next time he leaves the Colony. If Ko's going to languish in Sing-Sing on a ten-to-thirty rap, why, we can pick him clean at will. Is that so very terrible suddenly?'

Yes it bloody well is, thought Guillam. Till it suddenly dawned on him, with a quite malignant glee, that Martello himself was not *witting* on the subject of Brother Nelson, and that George had kept his best card to his chest.

Smiley was still sitting forward. The ice in his whisky had put a damp frost round the outside of the glass, and for a time he stared at it, watching the tears slide on to the rosewood table.

'So how long have we got on our own?' Smiley asked. 'What's our head start before the narcotics people come barging in?'

'It's not rigid, George. It's not *like* that! It's parameters, like Cy said.'

'Three months?'

'That's generous, a little generous.'

'Less than three months?'

'Three months, inside of three months, ten to twelve weeks – in that *area*, George. It's fluid. It's between friends. Three months outside. I would say.'

Smiley breathed out in a long slow sigh. 'Yesterday we had all the time in the world.'

Martello dropped the veil an inch or two. 'Sol is not that conscious, George,' he said, careful to use Circus jargon rather than his own. 'Ah, Sol has blank areas,' he said, half by way of admission. 'We don't just throw him the whole carcass, know what I mean?'

Martello paused, then said, 'Sol goes to first echelon. No further. Believe me.'

'And what does first echelon mean?'

'He knows Ko is in funds from Moscow. Knows he pushes opium. That's all.'

'Does he know of the girl?'

'Now she's a case in point, George. The girl. That girl went with him on the trip to Bangkok. Remember

Murphy describing the Bangkok trip? She stayed in the hotel suite with him. She flew on with him to Manila. I saw you read me there. I caught your eye. But we had Murphy delete that section of the report. Just for Sol's benefit.' Very slightly, Smiley seemed to revive. 'Deal stands, George,' Martello assured him munificently. 'Nothing's added, nothing's subtracted. You play the fish, we'll help you eat it. Any help along the way, you just have to pick up that green line and holler.' He went so far as to lay a consoling hand on Smiley's shoulder, but sensing that he disliked the gesture, abandoned it rather quickly. 'However, if you ever *do* want to pass us the oars, why, we would merely reverse that arrangement and – '

'Steal our thunder and get yourselves thrown off the Colony into the bargain,' said Smiley, completing the sentence for him. 'I want one more thing made clear. I want it written down. I want it to be the subject of an exchange of letters between us.'

'Your party, you choose the games,' said Martello expansively.

'My service will play the fish,' Smiley insisted, in the same direct tone. 'We will also land it, if that is the angling expression. I'm not a sportsman, I'm afraid.'

'Land it, beach it, hook it, sure.'

Martello's good will, to Guillam's suspicious eye, was tiring a little at the edges.

'I insist on it being *our* operation. Our man. I insist on first rights. To have him and to hold him, until we see fit to pass him on.'

'No problem, George, no problem at all. You take him aboard, he's yours. Soon as you want to share him, call us. It's as simple as that.'

'I'll send round a written confirmation in the morning.'

'Oh don't bother to do that, George. We have people. We'll have them collect it for you.'

'I'll send it round,' said Smiley.

Martello stood up. 'George, you just got yourself a deal.'

'I had a deal already,' Smiley said. 'Langley broke it.'
They shook hands.

The case history has no other moment like this. In the trade it goes under various smart phrases. 'The day George reversed the controls' is one – though it took him a good week, and brought Martello's deadline that much nearer. But to Guillam the process had something far more stately about it, far more beautiful than a mere technical re-tooling. As his understanding of Smiley's intention slowly grew, as he looked on fascinated while Smiley laid down each meticulous line, summoned this or that collaborator, put out a hook here, and took in a cleat there, Guillam had the sensation of watching the turn-round of some large ocean-going vessel as it is coaxed and nosed and gentled into facing back along its own course.

Which entailed – yes – turning the entire case upside down, or reversing the controls.

They arrived back at the Circus without a word spoken. Smiley took the last flight of stairs slowly enough to revive Guillam's fears for his health, so that as soon as he was able he rang the Circus doctor and gave him a rundown of the symptoms as he saw them, only to be told that Smiley had been round to see him a couple of days ago on an unrelated matter and showed every sign of being indestructible. The throne-room door closed, and Fawn the babysitter once more had his beloved chief to himself. Smiley's needs, where they filtered through, had the smack of alchemy. Beechcraft aeroplanes: he wished for plans and catalogues, and also – provided they could be obtained unattributably – any details of owners, sales and purchases in the South East Asian region. Toby Esterhase duly disappeared into the murky thickets of the aircraft sales industry, and soon afterwards Fawn handed to Molly Meakin a daunting heap of back-numbers of a journal called *Transport World* with handwritten instructions from Smiley in the traditional green ink of his office to mark down any advertisements for Beechcraft planes which might have caught the eye of a potential buyer during the six-month period before the pilot Ricardo's abortive opium mission into Red China.

Again on Smiley's written orders, Guillam discreetly visited several of di Salis's burrowers and, without the knowledge of their temperamental superior, established that they were still far from putting the finger on Nelson Ko. One old fellow went so far as to suggest that Drake Ko had spoken no less than the truth in his last meeting with old Hibbert, and that Brother Nelson was dead indeed. But when Guillam took this news to Smiley he shook his head impatiently, and handed him a signal for transmission to Craw, telling him to obtain from his local police source, preferably on a pretext, all recorded details of the travel movements of Ko's manager Tiu in and out of Mainland China.

Craw's long answer was on Smiley's desk forty-eight hours later, and it appeared to give him a rare moment of pleasure. He ordered out the duty driver, and had himself taken to Hampstead, where he walked alone over the Heath for an hour, through sunlit frost, and according to Fawn stood gawping at the ruddy squirrels before returning to the throne-room.

'But don't you *see*?' he protested to Guillam, in an equally rare fit of excitement that evening – 'Don't you *understand*, Peter?' – shoving Craw's dates under his nose, actually stubbing his finger on one entry – 'Tiu went to Shanghai six weeks before Ricardo's mission. How long did he stay there? Forty-eight hours. Oh you are a dunce!'

'I'm nothing of the kind,' Guillam retorted. 'I just don't happen to have a direct line to God, that's all.'

In the cellars, cloistered with Millie McCraig the head listener, Smiley replayed old Hibbert's monologues, scowling occasionally – said Millie – at di Salis's clumsy bullying. Otherwise, he read and prowled, and talked to Sam Collins in short, intensive bursts. These encounters, Guillam noticed, cost Smiley a lot of spirit, and his bouts of ill-temper – which Lord knows were few enough for a man with Smiley's burdens – always occurred after Sam's departure. And even when they had blown over, he looked more strained and lonely than ever, till he had taken one of his long night walks.

Then on about the fourth day, which in Guillam's life was a crisis day for some reason – probably the argument with Treasury, who resented paying Craw a bonus – Toby Esterhase somehow slipped through the net of both Fawn and Guillam, and gained the throne-room undetected, where he presented Smiley with a bunch of Xeroxed contracts of sale for one brand new four-seater Beechcraft to the Bangkok firm of Aerosuis and Co, registered in Zürich, details pending. Smiley was particularly jubilant about the fact that there were four seats. The two at the rear were removable, but the pilot's and co-pilot's were fixed. As to the actual sale of the plane, it had been completed on the twentieth of July: a scant month, therefore, before the crazy Ricardo set off to infringe Red China's airspace, and then changed his mind.

'Even Peter can make *that* connection,' Smiley declared, with heavy skittishness. 'Sequence, Peter, sequence, come on!'

'The plane was sold two weeks after Tiu returned from Shanghai,' Guillam replied, reluctantly.

'And so?' Smiley demanded. 'And so? What do we look at next?'

'We ask ourselves who owns the firm of Aerosuis,' Guillam snapped, really quite irritated.

'Precisely. Thank you,' said Smiley in mock relief. 'You restore my faith in you, Peter. Now then. Whom do we discover at the helm of Aerosuis, do you think? The Bangkok representative, no less.'

Guillam glanced at the notes on Smiley's desk, but Smiley was too quick and clapped his hands over them.

'Tiu,' Guillam said, actually blushing.

'Hoorah. Yes. Tiu. Well done.'

But by the time Smiley sent again for Sam Collins that evening, the shadows had returned to his pendulous face.

Still the lines were thrown out. After his success in the aircraft industry, Toby Esterhase was reassigned to the liquor trade and flew to the Western Isles of Scotland, under the guise of a Value Added Tax inspector, where he spent three days making a spot check of the books of a house of whisky distillers who specialised in the forward selling of unmatured kegs. He returned – to quote Connie – leering like a successful bigamist.

The multiple climax of all this activity was an extremely long signal to Craw, drafted after a full-dress meeting of the operational directorate – the Golden Oldies, to quote Connie yet again, with Sam Collins added. The meeting followed an extended ways and means session with the Cousins, at which Smiley refrained from all mention of the elusive Nelson Ko, but requested certain additional facilities of surveillance and communication in the field. To his collaborators, Smiley explained his plans this way.

Till now the operation had been limited to obtaining intelligence about Ko and the ramifications of the Soviet goldseam. Much care had been taken to prevent Ko from becoming aware of the Circus's interest in him.

He then summarised the intelligence they had so far collected: Nelson, Ricardo, Tiu, the Beechcraft, the dates, the inferences, the Swiss-registered aviation company – which as it now turned out possessed no premises and no other aircraft. He would prefer, he said, to wait for the positive identification of Nelson, but every operation was a compromise and time, partly thanks to the Cousins, was running out.

He made no mention at all of the girl, and he never once looked at Sam Collins while he delivered his address.

Then he came to what he modestly called the *next phase*.

'Our problem is to break the stalemate. There are operations which run better for not being resolved. There are others which are worthless until they *are* resolved and the Dolphin case is one of these.' He gave a studious frown, and blinked, then whipped off his spectacles and, to the secret delight of everyone, unconsciously subscribed to his own legend by polishing them on the fat end of his tie. 'I propose to do this by turning our tactic inside out.

In other words, by declaring to Ko our interest in his affairs.'

It was Connie, as ever, who put an end to the suitably dreadful silence. Her smile was also the fastest – and the most knowing.

'He's smoking him out,' she whispered to them all in ecstasy. 'Same as he did with Bill, the clever hound! Lighting a fire on his doorstep, aren't you, darling, and seeing which way he runs. Oh *George*, you lovely, lovely man, the best of all my boys, I do declare!'

Smiley's signal to Craw used a different metaphor to describe the plan, one which fieldmen favour. He referred to *shaking Ko's tree*, and it was clear from the remainder of the text that, despite the considerable dangers, he proposed to use the broad back of Jerry Westerby to do it.

As a footnote to all this, a couple of days later Sam Collins vanished. Everyone was very pleased. He ceased to come in and Smiley did not refer to him. His room, when Guillam sneaked in covertly to look it over, contained nothing personal to Sam at all except a couple of unbroken packs of playing cards and some garish book matches advertising a West End nightclub. When he sounded out the housekeepers, they were for once unusually forthcoming. His price was a kiss-off gratuity, they said, and a promise to have his pension rights reconsidered. He had not really had much to sell at all. A flash in the pan, they said, never to reappear. Good riddance.

All the same, Guillam could not rid himself of a certain unease about Sam, which he often conveyed to Molly Meakin over the next few weeks. It was not just about bumping into him at Lacon's office. He was bothered about the business of Smiley's exchange of letters with Martello confirming their verbal understanding. Rather than have the Cousins collect it, with the consequent parade of a limousine and even a motor-cycle outrider in Cambridge Circus, Smiley had ordered Guillam to run it round to Grosvenor Square himself with Fawn babysitting. But Guillam was snowed under with work, as it happened, and Sam as usual was spare. So when Sam volunteered to take it for him, Guillam let him, and wished to God he never had. He wished it still, devoutly.

Because instead of handing George's letter to Murphy or his faceless running-mate, said Fawn, Sam had insisted on going in to Martello personally. And had spent more than an hour with him alone.

Part Two

Shaking The Tree

Chapter 13

LIESE

Star Heights was the newest and tallest block in the Midlevels, built on the round, and by night jammed like a huge lighted pencil into the soft darkness of the Peak. A winding causeway led to it, but the only pavement was a line of kerbstone six inches wide between the causeway and the cliff. At Star Heights, pedestrians were in bad taste. It was early evening and the social rush hour was nearing its height. As Jerry edged his way along the kerb, the Mercedes and Rolls-Royces brushed against him in their haste to deliver and collect. He carried a bunch of orchids wrapped in tissue: larger than the bunch which Craw had presented to Phoebe Wayfarer, smaller than the one Drake Ko had given the dead boy Nelson. These orchids were for nobody. 'When you're my size, sport, you have to have a hell of a good reason for whatever you do.'

He felt tense but also relieved that the long, long wait was over.

A straight foot-in-the-door operation, your Grace, Craw had advised him at yesterday's protracted briefing. *Shove your way in there and start pitching and don't stop till you're out the other side.*

With one leg, thought Jerry.

A striped awning led to the entrance hall and a perfume of women hung in the air, like a foretaste of his errand. *And just remember Ko owns the building*, Craw had added sourly, as a parting gift. The interior decoration was not quite finished. Plates of marble were missing round the mail boxes. A fibreglass fish should have been spewing water into a terrazzo fountain, but the pipes had not yet been connected and bags of cement were heaped in the basin. He headed for the lifts. A glass booth was marked 'Reception' and the Chinese porter was watching him from inside it. Jerry only saw the blur of him. He had been reading when Jerry arrived, but now he was staring at Jerry, undecided whether to challenge him, but half reassured by the orchids. A couple of American matrons in full warpaint arrived, and took up a position near him.

'Great blooms,' they said, poking in the tissue.

'Super, aren't they. Here, have them. Present! Come on! Beautiful women. Naked without them!'

Laughter. The English are a race apart. The porter returned to his reading and Jerry was authenticated. A lift arrived. A herd of diplomats, businessmen and their squaws shuffled into the lobby, sullen and bejewelled. Jerry ushered the American matrons ahead of him. Cigar smoke mingled with the scent, slovenly canned music hummed forgotten melodies. The matrons pressed the button for twelve.

'You visiting with the Hammersteins too?' they asked, still looking at the orchids.

At the fifteenth, Jerry made for the fire stairs. They stank of cat, and rubbish from the shoot. Descending he met an amah carrying a nappy bucket. She scowled at him till he greeted her, then laughed uproariously. He kept going till he reached the eighth floor where he stepped back into the plush of the residents' landing. He was at the end of a corridor. A small rotunda gave on to two gold lift doors. There were four flats, each a quadrant of the circular building, and each with its own corridor. He took up a position in the B corridor with only the flowers to protect him. He was watching the rotunda, his attention on the mouth of the corridor marked C. The tissue round the orchids was damp where he'd been clutching it too tight.

'It's a firm weekly date,' Craw had assured him. 'Every

Monday, flower arrangement at the American Club. Regular as clockwork. She meets a girlfriend there, Nellie Tan, works for Airsea. They take in the flower arrangement and stay for dinner afterwards.'

'So where's Ko meanwhile?'

'In Bangkok. Trading.'

'Well let's bloody well hope he stays there.'

'Amen, sir. Amen.'

With a shriek of new hinges unoiled, the door at his ear was yanked open and a slim young American in a dinner-jacket stepped into the corridor, stopped dead, and stared at Jerry and the orchids. He had blue, steady eyes and he carried a briefcase.

'You looking for me with those things?' he enquired, with a Boston society drawl. He looked rich and assured. Jerry guessed diplomacy or Ivy League banking.

'Well I don't think so actually,' Jerry confessed, playing the English bloody fool. '*Cavendish*,' he said. Over the American's shoulder Jerry saw the door quietly close on a packed bookshelf. 'Friend of mine asked me to give these to a Miss *Cavendish* at 9D. Waltzed off to Manila, left me holding the orchids, sort of thing.'

'Wrong floor,' said the American strolling toward the lift. 'You want one up. Wrong corridor too. D's over the other side. Thattaway.'

Jerry stood beside him, pretending to wait for an *up* lift. The *down* lift came first, the young American stepped easily into it and Jerry resumed his post. The door marked C opened, he saw her come out, and turn to double-lock it. Her clothes were everyday. Her hair was long and ashblonde but she had tied it in a pony tail at the nape. She wore a plain halter-neck dress and sandals, and though he couldn't see her face he knew already she was beautiful. She walked to the lift, still not seeing him and Jerry had the illusion of looking in on her through a window from the street.

There were women in Jerry's world who carried their bodies as if they were citadels to be stormed only by the bravest, and Jerry had married several; or perhaps they grew that way under his influence. There were women who seemed determined to hate themselves, hunching their backs and locking up their hips. And there were women who had only to walk toward him to bring him a gift. They were the rare ones and for Jerry at that moment she led the pack. She had stopped at the gold doors and was watching the lighted numbers. He reached her side as the lift arrived and she still hadn't noticed him. It was jammed full, as he had hoped it would be. He entered crabwise, intent on the orchids, apologising, grinning and making a show of holding them high. She had her back to him, and he was standing at her shoulder. It was a strong shoulder, and bare either side of the halter, and Jerry could see small freckles and a down of tiny gold hairs disappearing down her spine. Her face was in profile below him. He peered down at it.

'Lizzie?' he said, uncertainly. 'Hey, *Lizzie*, it's me, Jerry.'

She turned sharply and stared up at him. He wished he could have backed away from her because he knew her first response would be physical fear of his size, and he was right. He saw it momentarily in her grey eyes, which flickered before holding him in their stare.

'Lizzie *Worthington*!' he declared more confidently. 'How's the whisky, remember me? One of your proud investors. Jerry. Chum of Tiny Ricardo's. One fifty-gallon keg with my name on the label. All paid and above board.'

He had kept it quiet on the assumption that he might be raking up a past she was keen to disown. He had kept it so quiet that their fellow passengers heard either 'Raindrops keep fallin' on my head' over the Muzak, or the grumbling of an elderly Greek who thought he was boxed in.

'Why of course,' she said, and gave a bright, air-hostess smile. 'Jerry! Her voice faded as she pretended to have it on the tip of her tongue. 'Jerry – er – ' She frowned and looked upward like a repertory actress doing Forgetfulness. The lift stopped at the sixth floor.

'Westerby,' he said promptly, getting her off the hook.

'Newshound. You put the bite on me in the Constellation bar. I wanted a spot of loving comfort and all I got was a keg of whisky.'

Somebody next to him laughed.

'Of *course*! Jerry *darling*! How could I possibly . . . So I mean what are you doing in Hong Kong? My *God*!'

'Usual beat. Fire and pestilence, famine. How about you? Retired I should think, with your sales methods. Never had my arm twisted so thoroughly in my life.'

She laughed delightedly. The doors had opened at the third floor. An old woman shuffled in on two walking sticks.

Lizzie Worthington sold in all a cool fifty-five kegs of the blushful Hippocrene, your Grace, old Craw had said. *Every one of them to a male buyer and a fair number of them, according to my advisers, with service thrown in. Gives a new meaning to the term 'good measure', I venture to suggest.*

They had reached the ground floor. She got out first and he walked beside her. Through the main doors he saw her red sports car with its roof up waiting in the bay, jammed among the glistening limousines. She must have phoned down and ordered them to have it ready, he thought: if Ko owns the building he'll make damn sure she gets the treatment. She was heading for the porter's window. As they crossed the hall she went on chattering, pivoting to talk to him, one arm held wide of her body, palm upward like a fashion model. He must have asked her how she liked Hong Kong, though he couldn't remember doing so:

'I adore it, Jerry, I simply *adore* it. Vientiane seems – oh, *centuries* away. You know Ric died?' She threw this in heroically, as if she and death weren't strangers to each other. 'After Ric, I thought I'd never care for anywhere again. I was completely wrong, Jerry. Hong Kong *has* to be the most fun city in the world. Lawrence darling, I'm sailing my red submarine. It's hen night at the club.'

Lawrence was the porter, and the key to her car dangled from a large silver horseshoe which reminded Jerry of Happy Valley races.

'Thank you, Lawrence,' she said sweetly and gave him a smile that would last him all night. 'The *people* here are so marvellous, Jerry,' she confided to him in a stage whisper as they moved toward the main entrance. 'To *think* what we used to say about the Chinese in Laos! Yet here, they're just the most marvellous and outgoing and inventive people ever.' She had slipped into a stateless foreign accent, he noticed. Must have picked it up from Ricardo and stuck to it for chic. 'People think to themselves: "Hong Kong – fabulous shopping – tax-free cameras – restaurants – " but honestly, Jerry, when you get under the surface, and meet the *true* Hong Kong, and the *people* – it's got everything you could possibly want from life. Don't you adore my new car?'

'So that's how you spend the whisky profits.'

He held out his open palm and she dropped the keys into it so that he could unlock the door for her. Still in dumb show he gave her the orchids to hold. Behind the black Peak a full moon, not yet risen, glowed like a forest fire. She climbed in, he handed her the keys and this time he felt the contact of her hand and remembered Happy Valley again, and Ko's kiss as they drove away.

'Mind if I ride on the back?' he asked.

She laughed and pushed open the passenger door for him. 'Where are you going with those gorgeous orchids anyway?'

She started the engine, but Jerry gently switched it off again. She stared at him in surprise.

'Sport,' he said quietly. 'I cannot tell a lie. I'm a viper in your nest, and before you drive me anywhere, you'd better fasten your seat belt and hear the grisly truth.'

He had chosen this moment carefully because he didn't want her to feel threatened. She was in the driving seat of her own car, under the lighted awning of her own apartment block, within sixty feet of Lawrence the porter, and he was playing the humble sinner in order to increase her sense of security.

'Our chance reunion was not entire chance. That's point one. Point two, not to put too fine an edge on it, my paper told me to run you to earth and besiege you with many searching questions regarding your late chum Ricardo.'

She was still watching him, still waiting. On the point of her chin she had two small parallel scars like claws, quite deep. He wondered who had made them, and what with.

'But Ricardo's dead,' she said, much too early.

'Sure,' said Jerry consolingly. 'No question. However the comic is in possession of what they're pleased to call a hot tip that he's alive after all and it's my job to humour them.'

'But that's absolutely absurd!'

'Agreed. Totally. They're out of their minds. The consolation prize is two dozen well-thumbed orchids and the best dinner in town.'

Turning away from him she gazed through the windscreen, her face in the full glare of the overhead lamp, and Jerry wondered what it must be like to inhabit such a beautiful body, living up to it twenty-four hours a day. Her grey eyes opened a little wider and he had a shrewd suspicion that he was supposed to notice the tears brimming and the way her hands grasped the steering wheel for support.

'Forgive me,' she murmured. 'It's just – when you love a man – give everything up for him – and he dies – then one evening, out of the blue – '

'Sure,' said Jerry. 'I'm sorry.'

She started the engine. 'Why should you be sorry? If he's alive, that's bonus. If he's dead, nothing's changed. We're on a pound to nothing.' She laughed. 'Ric always said he was indestructible.'

It's like stealing from a blind beggar, he thought. She shouldn't be let loose.

She drove well but stiffly and he guessed – because she inspired guesswork – that she had only recently passed her test and that the car was her prize for doing so. It was the calmest night in the world. As they sank into the city, the harbour lay like a perfect mirror at the centre of the jewel box. They talked places. Jerry suggested the Peninsula but she shook her head.

'Okay. Let's go get a drink first,' he said. 'Come on, let's blow the walls out!'

To his surprise she reached across and gave his hand a squeeze. Then he remembered Craw. She did that to everyone, he had said.

She was off the leash for a night: he had that overwhelming sensation. He remembered taking Cat, his daughter, out from school when she was young, and how they had to do lots of different things in order to make the afternoon longer. At a dark disco on Kowloonside they drank Rémy Martin with ice and soda. He guessed it was Ko's drink and she had picked up the habit to keep him company. It was early and there were maybe a dozen people, no more. The music was loud and they had to yell to hear each other, but she didn't mention Ricardo. She preferred the music and listening with her head back. Sometimes she held his hand, and once put her head on his shoulder, and once she blew him a distracted kiss and drifted on to the floor to perform a slow, solitary dance, eyes closed, slightly smiling. The men ignored their own girls and undressed her with their eyes, and the Chinese waiters brought fresh ashtrays every three minutes so that they could look down her dress. After two drinks and half an hour she announced a passion for the Duke and the big-band sound, so they raced back to the Island to a place Jerry knew where a live Filipino band gave a fair rendering of Ellington. Cat Anderson was the best thing since sliced bread, she said. Had he heard Armstrong and Ellington together. Weren't they just the greatest? More Rémy Martin while she sang 'Mood Indigo' to him.

'Did Ricardo dance?' Jerry asked.

'Did he dance?' she replied softly, as she tapped her foot and lightly clicked her fingers to the rhythm.

'Thought Ricardo had a limp,' Jerry objected.

'*That* never stopped him,' she said, still absorbed by the

music. 'I'll never go back to him, you understand. Never. That chapter's closed. And how.'

'How'd he pick it up?'

'Dancing?'

'The limp.'

With her finger curled round an imaginary trigger she fired a shot into the air.

'It was either the war or an angry husband,' she said. He made her repeat it, her lips close to his ear.

She knew a new Japanese restaurant where they served *fabulous* Kobe beef.

'Tell me how you got those scars,' he asked as they were driving there. He touched his own chin. 'The left and the right. What did it?'

'Oh hunting innocent foxes,' she said with a light smile. 'My dear papa was horse mad. He still is, I'm afraid.'

'Where does he live?'

'Daddy? Oh the usual tumble-down schloss in Shropshire. *Miles* too big but they won't move. No staff, no money, ice cold three-quarters of the year. Mummy can't even boil an egg.'

He was still reeling when she remembered a bar where they gave heavenly curry canapés, so they drove around until they found it and she kissed the barman. There was no music but for some reason he heard himself telling her all about the orphan, till he came to the reasons for their break-up, which he deliberately fogged over.

'Ah, but Jerry darling,' she said sagely. 'With twenty-five years between you and her, what else can you expect?'

And with nineteen years and a Chinese wife between you and Drake Ko what the hell can *you* expect? he thought, with some annoyance.

They left – more kisses for the barman – and Jerry was not so intoxicated by her company, nor by the brandy-sodas, to miss the point that she made a phone call, allegedly to cancel her date, that the call took a long time, and that when she returned from it she looked rather solemn. In the car again, he caught her eye and thought he read a shadow of mistrust.

'Jerry?'

'Yes?'

She shook her head, laughed, ran her palm along his face, then kissed him. 'It's fun,' she said.

He guessed she was wondering whether, if she had really sold him that keg of unbranded whisky, she would so thoroughly have forgotten him. He guessed she was also wondering whether, in order to sell him the keg, she had thrown in any fringe benefits of the sort Craw had so coarsely referred to. But that was her problem, he reckoned. Had been from the start.

In the Japanese restaurant they were given the corner table, thanks to Lizzie's smile and other attributes. She sat looking into the room, and he sat looking at Lizzie, which was fine by Jerry but would have given Sarratt the bends. By the candlelight he saw her face very clearly and was conscious for the first time of the signs of wear: not just the claw marks on her chin, but her lines of travel, and of strain, which to Jerry had a determined quality about them, like honourable scars from all the battles against her bad luck and her bad judgment. She wore a gold bracelet, new, and a bashed tin watch with a Walt Disney dial on it, and scratched gloved hand pointing to the numerals. Her loyalty to the old watch impressed him and he wanted to know who gave it to her.

'Daddy,' she said distractedly.

A mirror was let into the ceiling above them, and he could see her gold hair and the swell of her breasts among the scalps of other diners, and the gold dust of the hairs on her back. When he tried to hit her with Ricardo, she turned guarded: it should have occurred to Jerry, but it didn't, that her attitude had changed since she made the phone call.

'What guarantee do I have that you will keep my name out of your paper?' she asked.

'Just my promise.'

'But if your editor knows I was Ricardo's girl, what's to stop him putting it in for himself?'

'Ricardo had lots of girls. You know that. They came in all shapes and sizes and ran concurrently.'

'There was only one of *me*,' she said firmly, and he saw her glance toward the door. But then she had that habit anyway, wherever she was, of looking round the room all the time for someone who wasn't there. He let her keep the initiative.

'You said your paper had a hot tip,' she said. 'What do they mean by that?'

He had boned up his answer to this with Craw. It was one they had actually rehearsed. He delivered it therefore with force if not conviction.

'Ric's crash was eighteen months ago in the hills near Pailin on the Thai-Cambodian border. That's the official line. No one found a body, no one found wreckage and there's talk he was doing an opium run. The insurance company never paid up and Indocharter never sued them. Why not? Because Ricardo had an exclusive contract to fly for them. For that matter, why doesn't someone sue Indocharter? You for instance. You were his woman. Why not go for damages?'

'That is a *very* vulgar suggestion,' she said in her duchess voice.

'Beyond that, there's rumours he's been seen recently around the haunts a little. He's grown a beard but he can't cure the limp, they say, nor his habit of sinking a bottle of Scotch a day, nor, saving your presence, chasing after everything that wears a skirt within a five mile radius of wherever he happens to be standing.'

She was forming up to argue, but he gave her the rest while he was about it.

'Head porter at the Rincome Hotel, Chiang Mai, confirmed the identification from a photograph, beard notwithstanding. All right, us roundeyes all look the same to them. Nevertheless he was pretty sure. Then only last month a fifteen-year-old girl in Bangkok, particulars to hand, took her little bundle to the Mexican Consulate and named Ricardo as the lucky father. I don't believe in eighteen month pregnancies and I assume you don't. And don't look at *me* like that, sport. It's not my idea, is it?'

It's London's, he might have added, as neat a blend of fact and fiction as ever shook a tree. But she was actually looking past him, at the door again.

'Another thing I'm to ask you about is the whisky racket,' he said.

'It was *not* a racket, Jerry, it was a perfectly valid business enterprise!'

'Sport. *You* were straight as a die. No breath of scandal attaches. Etcetera. But if *Ric* cut a few too many corners, now, that *would* be a reason for doing the old disappearing act, wouldn't it?'

'That wasn't Ric's way,' she said finally, without any conviction at all. 'He liked to be the big man around town. It wasn't his way to run.'

He seriously regretted her discomfort. It ran quite contrary to the feelings he would have wished for her in other circumstances. He watched her and he knew that argument was something that she always lost; it planted a hopelessness in her; a resignation to defeat.

'For example,' Jerry continued – as her head fell forward in submission – 'were we to prove that your Ric, in flogging *his* kegs, had stuck to the cash and instead of passing it back to the distillery – pure hypothesis, no shred of evidence – then in that case – '

'By the time our partnership was wound up, *every* investor had a certificated contract with interest from the date of purchase. Every penny we borrowed was duly accounted for.'

Till now it had all been footwork. Now he saw his goal looming, and he made for it fast.

'Not *duly*, sport,' he corrected her, while she continued to stare downward at her uneaten food. 'Not duly at all. Those settlements were made six months *after* the due date. *Un*duly. That's a very eloquent point in my view. Question: who bailed Ric out? According to *our* information the whole world was going for him. The distillers, the creditors, the law, the local community. Every one of them had the knife sharpened for him. Till one day: *bingo!* Writs withdrawn, shades of the prison bars recede. How? Ric was on his knees. Who's the mystery angel? Who bought his debts?'

She had lifted her head while he was speaking and now, to his astonishment, a radiant smile suddenly lit her face and the next thing he knew, she was waving over his shoulder at someone he couldn't see till he looked into the ceiling mirror and caught the glitter of an electric blue suit, and a full head of black hair, well greased; and between the two, a foreshortened chubby Chinese face set on a pair of powerful shoulders, and two curled hands held out in a fighter's greeting, while Lizzie piped him aboard.

'Mr Tiu! What a marvellous coincidence. It's *Mr Tiu*! Come on over! Try the beef. It's *gorgeous*. Mr Tiu, this is Jerry from Fleet Street. Jerry, this is a very good friend of mine who helps look after me. He's interviewing me, Mr Tiu! Me! It's most exciting. All about Vientiane and a poor pilot I tried to help a hundred years ago. Jerry knows everything about me. He's a miracle!'

'We met,' said Jerry, with a broad grin.

'Sure,' said Tiu, equally happy, and as he spoke, Jerry once more caught the familiar smell of almonds and rosewater mixed, the one his early wife had so much liked. 'Sure,' Tiu repeated. 'You the horse-writer, okay?'

'Okay,' Jerry agreed, stretching his smile to breaking-point.

Then, of course, Jerry's vision of the world turned several somersaults, and he had a whole lot of business to worry about: such as appearing to be as tickled as everybody else by the amazing good luck of Tiu's appearance; such as shaking hands, which was like a mutual promise of future settlement; such as drawing up a chair and calling for drinks, beef and chopsticks and all the rest. But the thing that stuck in his mind even while he did all this – the memory that lodged there as permanently as later events allowed – had little to do with Tiu, or his hasty arrival. It was the expression on Lizzie's face as she first caught sight of him, for the fraction of a second before the lines of courage drew the gay smile out of her. It explained to him as nothing else could have done the paradoxes that comprised her: her prisoner's dreams, her borrowed personalities which were like disguises in which she could momentarily escape her destiny. Of course she had summoned Tiu. She had no choice. It amazed him that neither the Circus nor himself had predicted it. The Ricardo story, whatever the truth of it, was far too hot for her to handle by herself. But the expression in her grey eyes as Tiu entered the restaurant was not relief, but resignation: the doors had slammed on her again, the fun was over. 'We're like those bloody glow-worms,' the orphan had whispered to him once, raging about her childhood, 'carting the bloody fire round on our backs.'

Operationally, of course, as Jerry recognised immediately, Tiu's appearance was a gift from the gods. If information was to be fed back to Ko, then Tiu was an infinitely more impressive channel for it than Lizzie Worthington could ever hope to be.

She had finished kissing Tiu, so she handed him to Jerry.

'Mr Tiu, you're my witness,' she declared, making a great conspiracy of it. 'You must remember every word I say. Jerry, go straight on *just* as if he wasn't here. I mean, Mr Tiu's as silent as the *grave*, aren't you? *Darling*,' she said, and kissed him again. 'It's *so* exciting,' she repeated, and they all settled down for a friendly chat.

'So what you looking for, Mr Wessby?' Tiu enquired, perfectly affably, while he tucked into his beef. 'You a horse-writer, why you bother pretty girls, okay?'

'Good point, sport! Good point! Horses much safer, right?'

They all laughed richly, avoiding one another's eyes.

The waiter put a half bottle of Black Label Scotch in front of him. Tiu uncorked it and sniffed at it critically before pouring.

'He's looking for *Ricardo*, Mr Tiu. Don't you understand? He thinks Ricardo is *alive*. Isn't that wonderful? I mean, I have no vestige of feeling for Ric, now, naturally, but it would be lovely to have him back with us. Think of the party we could give!'

'Liese tell you that?' Tiu asked, pouring himself two inches of Scotch. 'She tell you Ricardo still around?'

'*Who*, old boy? Didn't get you. Didn't get the first name.'

Tiu jabbed a chopstick at Lizzie. 'She tell you he's alive? This pilot guy? This Ricardo? Liese tell you that?'

'I never reveal my sources, Mr Tiu,' said Jerry, just as affably. 'That's a journalist's way of saying he's made something up,' he explained.

'A horse-writer's way, okay?'

'That's it, that's it!'

Again Tiu laughed, and this time Lizzie laughed even louder. She was slipping out of control again. Maybe it's the drink, thought Jerry, or maybe she goes for the stronger stuff and the drink has stoked the fire. And if he calls me horse-writer again, maybe I'll take a defensive action.

Lizzie again, a party-piece:

'Oh Mr Tiu, Ricardo was so *lucky*! Think who he had. Indocharter – me – everyone. There I was, working for this little airline – some dear Chinese people Daddy knew – and Ricardo like all the pilots was a shocking businessman – got into the most *frightful* debt' – with a wave of her hand she brought Jerry into the act – 'my God, he even tried to involve *me* in one of his schemes, can you imagine! – selling whisky, if you please – and suddenly my lovely, dotty Chinese friends decided they needed another charter pilot. They settled his debts, put him on a salary, they gave him an old banger to fly – '

Jerry now took the first of several irrevocable steps.

'When Ricardo went missing he wasn't flying an old banger, sport. He was flying a brand-new Beechcraft,' he corrected her deliberately. 'Indocharter never had a Beechcraft to their names. They haven't now. My editor's checked it right through, don't ask me how. Indocharter never hired one, never leased one, never crashed one.'

Tiu gave another jolly whoop of laughter.

Tiu is a very cool bishop, your Eminence, Craw had warned. *Ran Monsignor Ko's San Francisco diocese with exemplary efficiency for five years and the worst the narcotics artists could hang on him was washing his Rolls-Royce on a saint's day.*

'Hey Mr Wessby, maybe Liese stole them one!' Tiu cried, in his half-American accent. 'Maybe she go out nights steal aircraft from other airlines!'

'Mr Tiu, that's very naughty of you!' Lizzie declared.

'How you like that, horse-writer? How you like?'

The merriment at their table was by now so loud for three people that several heads turned to peer at them. Jerry saw them in the mirrors, where he half expected to spot Ko himself, with his crooked boat-people's walk, swaying toward them through the wicker doorway. Lizzie plunged wildly on.

'Oh it was a complete fairy tale! One moment Ric can scarcely eat – *and* owed all of us money, Charlie's savings, my allowance from Daddy – Ric practically ruined us all. Of course, everyone's money just naturally belonged to him – and the next thing we knew, Ric had work, he was in the clear, life was a ball again. All those other poor pilots grounded, and Ric and Charlie flying all over the place like – '

'Like blue-arsed flies,' Jerry suggested, at which Tiu was so doubled with hilarity that he was obliged to hold on to Jerry's shoulder to keep himself afloat – while Jerry had the uncomfortable feeling of being physically measured for the knife.

'Hey, listen, that pretty good! Blue-arse fly! I like that! You pretty funny fellow, horse-writer!'

It was at this point, under the pressure of Tiu's cheerful insults, that Jerry used very good footwork indeed. Afterwards, Craw said the best. He ignored Tiu entirely, and picked up that other name which Lizzie had let slip.

'Yeah, whatever happened to old Charlie by the way,

Lizzie?' he said, not having the least idea who Charlie was. 'What became of him after Ric did his disappearing number? Don't tell me he went down with his ship as well?'

Once more she floated away on a fresh wave of narrative, and Tiu patently enjoyed everything he heard, chuckling and nodding while he ate.

He's here to find out the score, Jerry thought. He's much too sharp to put the brakes on Lizzie. It's me he's worried about, not her.

'Oh, Charlie's indestructible, *completely* immortal,' Lizzie declared, and once more selected Tiu as her foil: 'Charlie *Marshall*, Mr Tiu,' she explained. 'Oh you should meet him, a fantastic half-Chinese, all skin and bones and opium and a completely brilliant pilot. His father's old Kuomintang, a terrific brigand and lives up in the Shans. His mother was some poor Corsican girl – you know how the Corsicans *flocked* into Indo-China – but really he is an utterly fantastic character. Do you know why he calls himself Marshall? His father wouldn't give him his own name. So what does Charlie do? Gives himself the highest rank in the army instead. "My Dad's a general but I'm a marshal," he'd say. Isn't that cute? And *far* better than *admiral*, I mean.'

'Super,' Jerry agreed. 'Marvellous. Charlie's a prince.'

'Liese some pretty utterly fantastic character herself, Mr Wessby,' Tiu remarked handsomely, so on Jerry's insistence they drank to that – to her fantastic character.

'Hey what's all this *Liese* thing actually?' Jerry asked as he put down his glass. 'You're *Lizzie*. Who's this Liese? Mr Tiu, I don't know the lady. Why am I left out of the joke?'

Here Lizzie did definitely turn to Tiu for guidance, but Tiu had ordered himself some raw fish and was eating it rapidly and with total devotion.

'Some horse-writer ask pretty damn questions,' he remarked through a full mouth.

'New town, new leaf, new name,' Lizzie said finally, with an unconvincing smile. 'I wanted a change, so I chose a new name. Some girls get a new hair-do, I get a new name.'

'Got a new fellow to go with it?' Jerry asked.

She shook her head, eyes down, while Tiu let out a whoop of laughter.

'What's happened to this town, Mr Tiu?' Jerry demanded, instinctively covering for her. 'Chaps all gone blind or something? Crikey, I'd cross continents for her, wouldn't you? Whatever she calls herself, right?'

'Me I go from Kowloonside to Hong Kongside, no further!' said Tiu, hugely entertained by his own wit. 'Or maybe I stay Kowloonside and call her up, tell her come over see me one hour!'

At which Lizzie's eyes stayed down and Jerry thought it would be quite fun, on another occasion when they all had more time, to break Tiu's fat neck in several places.

Unfortunately, however, breaking Tiu's neck was not at present on Craw's shopping list.

The money, Craw had said. *When the moment's right, open up one end of the goldseam and that's your grand finale.*

So he started her off about Indocharter. Who were they, what was it like to work for them? She rose to it so fast he began to wonder whether she enjoyed this knife-edge existence more than he had realised.

'Oh it was a fabulous adventure, Jerry! You can't begin to imagine it, I assure you,' Ric's multi-national accent again: '*Airline*! Just the word is so absurd. I mean don't for a minute think of your bright new planes and your glamorous hostesses and champagne and caviar or anything like that *at all*. This was work. This was pioneering, which is what drew me in the first place. I could *perfectly* well have simply lived off Daddy, or my aunts, I mean mercifully I'm totally independent, but *who* can resist challenge? All we started out with was a couple of dreadful old DC3s *literally* stuck together with string and chewing gum. We even had to *buy* the safety certificate. Nobody would issue them. After that we flew literally anything. Hondas, vegetables, pigs – oh the boys had such a story about those poor pigs. They broke loose, Jerry. They came into the first class, even into the cabin, imagine!'

'Like passengers,' Tiu explained, with his mouth full. 'She fly first-class pigs, okay, Mr Wessby?'

'What routes?' Jerry asked when they had recovered from their laughter.

'You can see how he interrogates me, Mr Tiu? I never knew I was so glamorous! So mysterious! We flew everywhere, Jerry. Bangkok, Cambodia sometimes. Battambang, Phnom Penh, Kampong Cham when it was open. Everywhere. Awful places.'

'And who were your customers? Traders, taxi jobs – who were the regulars?'

'Absolutely anyone we could get. Anyone who could pay. Preferably in advance, naturally.'

Pausing from his Kobe beef, Tiu felt inspired to offer social chitchat.

'Your father some big lord, okay, Mr Wessby?'

'More or less,' said Jerry.

'Lords some pretty rich fellows. Why you gotta be a horse-writer, okay?'

Ignoring Tiu entirely, Jerry played his trump card and waited for the ceiling mirror to crash on to their table.

'There's a story that you people had some local Russian embassy link,' he said easily, straight at Lizzie. 'That ring a bell at all, sport? Any Reds under your bed at all, if I may ask?'

Tiu was taking care of his rice, holding the bowl under his chin and shovelling it nonstop. But this time, significantly, Lizzie didn't give him half a glance.

'*Russians*?' she repeated, puzzled. 'Why on earth should Russians come to *us*? They had regular Aeroflot flights in and out of Vientiane every week.'

He would have sworn, then and later, that she was telling the truth. But toward Lizzie herself he acted not quite satisfied. 'Not even *local* runs?' he insisted. 'Fetching and carrying, courier service or whatever?'

'Never. How could we? Besides, the Chinese simply *loathe* the Russians, don't they, Mr Tiu?'

'Russians pretty bad people, Mr Wessby,' Tiu agreed. 'They smell pretty bad.'

So do you, thought Jerry, catching that first-wife's scent again.

Jerry laughed at his own absurdity: 'I've got editors like other people have stomach ache,' he protested. 'He's *convinced* we can do a Red-under-the-bed job. "Ricardo's Soviet Paymasters" . . . "Did Ricardo take a dive for the Kremlin?"'

'*Paymaster*?' Lizzie repeated, utterly mystified. 'Ric never received a penny from the Russians. What *are* they talking about?'

Jerry again. 'But Indocharter did, didn't they? – Unless my lords and masters have been sold a total pup, which I suspect they have been, as usual. They drew money from the local Embassy and piped it down to Hong Kong in US dollars. That's *London's* story and they're sticking to it.'

'They're mad,' she said confidently. 'I've never heard such nonsense.'

To Jerry she seemed even relieved that the conversation had taken this improbable course. Ricardo alive – there, she was drifting through a minefield. Ko as her lover – that secret was Ko's or Tiu's to dispense, not hers. But Russian money – Jerry was as certain as he dared be that she knew nothing and feared nothing about it.

He offered to ride back with her to Star Heights, but Tiu lived that way, she said.

'See you again pretty soon, Mr Wessby,' Tiu promised.

'Look forward to it, sport,' said Jerry.

'You wanna stick to horse-writing, hear that? In my opinion, you get more money that way, Mr Wessby, okay?' There was no menace in his voice, nor in the friendly way he patted Jerry's upper arm. Tiu did not even speak as if he expected his advice to be taken as any more than a confidence between friends.

Then suddenly it was over. Lizzie kissed the headwaiter, but not Jerry. She sent Jerry, not Tiu, for her coat, so that she wouldn't be alone with him. She scarcely looked at him as she said goodbye.

Dealing with beautiful women, your Grace, Craw had warned, *is like dealing with known criminals, and the lady you are about to solicit undoubtedly falls within that category.* Wandering home through the moonlit streets – the long trek, beggars, eyes in doorways notwithstanding – Jerry subjected Craw's dictum to closer scrutiny. On *criminal* he really couldn't rule at all: *criminal* seemed a pretty variable sort of standard at the best of times, and neither the Circus nor its agents existed to uphold some parochial concept of the law. Craw had told him that in slump periods Ricardo had made her carry little parcels for him over frontiers. Big deal. Leave it to the owls. *Known* criminal however was quite a different matter. *Known* he would go along with absolutely. Remembering Elizabeth Worthington's caged stare at Tiu, he reckoned he had known that face, that look and that dependence, in one guise or another, for the bulk of his waking life.

It has been whispered once or twice by certain trivial critics of George Smiley that at this juncture he should somehow have seen which way the wind was blowing with Jerry, and hauled him out of the field. Effectively, Smiley was Jerry's case officer, after all. He alone kept Jerry's file, welfared and briefed him. Had he been in his prime, they say, instead of halfway down the other side, he would have read the warning signals between the lines of Craw's reports, and headed Jerry off in time. They might just as well have complained that he was a second-rate fortune-teller. The facts, as they came to Smiley, are these:

On the morning following Jerry's *pass* at Lizzie Worth or Worthington – the jargon has no sexual connotation – Craw debriefed him for more than three hours on a car pickup, and his report describes Jerry as being, quite reasonably, in a state of 'anti-climactic gloom'. He appeared, said Craw, to be afraid that Tiu, or even Ko, might blame the girl for her 'guilty knowledge' and even lay hands on her. Jerry referred more than once to Tiu's patent contempt for the girl – and for himself, and he suspected for all Europeans – and repeated his comment about travelling from Kowloonside to Hong Kongside for her and no further. Craw countered by pointing out that Tiu could at any time have shut her up; and that her knowledge, on Jerry's own testimony, did not extend even as far as the Russian goldseam, let alone to brother Nelson.

Jerry, in short, was producing the standard post-operational manifestations of a fieldman. A sense of guilt, coupled with foreboding, an involuntary movement of affiliation toward the target person: these are as predictable as a burst of tears in an athlete after the big race.

At their next contact – an extended limbo call on day two, at which, to buoy him up, Craw passed on Smiley's warm personal congratulations somewhat ahead of receiving them from the Circus – Jerry sounded in altogether better case, but he was worried about his daughter Cat. He had forgotten her birthday – he said it was tomorrow – and wished the Circus to send her at once a Japanese cassette player with a bunch of cassettes to start off her collection. Craw's telegram to Smiley names the cassettes, asks for immediate action by housekeepers, and requests that shoemaker section – the Circus forgers, in other words – run up an accompanying card in Jerry's handwriting, text given: 'Darling Cat. Asked a friend of mine to post this in London. Look after yourself, my dearest, love to you now and ever, Pa.' Smiley authorised the purchase, instructing housekeepers to dock the cost from Jerry's pay at source. He personally checked the parcel before it was sent, and approved the forged card. He also verified what he and Craw already suspected: that it was not Cat's birthday, nor anywhere near. Jerry simply had a strong urge to make a gesture of affection: once more, a normal symptom of temporary field fatigue. He cabled Craw to stay close to him but the initiative was with Jerry and Jerry made no further contact till the night of day five, when he demanded – and got – a crash meeting within the hour. This took place at their standing after-dark emergency rendezvous, an all-night roadside café in the New Territories, under the guise of a casual encounter between old colleagues. Craw's letter marked 'personal to Smiley only', was a follow-up to his telegram. It arrived at the Circus by hand of the Cousins' courier two days after the episode it describes, on day seven therefore. Writing on the assumption that the Cousins would contrive to read the text despite seals and other devices, Craw crammed it with evasions, worknames and cryptonyms, which are here restored to their real meaning:

Westerby was very angry. He demanded to know what the hell Sam Collins was doing in Hong Kong and in what way Collins was involved in the Ko case. I have not seen him so disturbed before. I asked him what made him think Collins was around. He replied that he had seen him that very night – eleven fifteen exactly – sitting in a parked car in the Midlevels, on a terrace just below Star Heights, under a streetlamp, reading a newspaper. The position Collins had taken up, said Westerby, gave him a clear view to Lizzie Worthington's windows on the eighth floor, and it was Westerby's assumption that he was engaged in some sort of surveillance. Westerby, who was on foot at the time, insists that he 'damn nearly went up to Sam and asked him outright'. But Sarratt discipline held firm, and he kept going down the hill, on his own side of the road. But he does claim that as soon as Collins saw him, he started the car and drove up the hill at speed. Westerby has the licence number, and of course it is the correct one. Collins confirms the rest.

In accordance with our agreed position in this contingency (your Signal of Feb 15th) I gave Westerby the following answers:

1 Even if it was Collins, the Circus had no control over his movements. Collins had left the Circus under a cloud, before the fall, he was a known gambler, drifter, wheeler-dealer etc, and the East was his natural stomping ground. I told Westerby he was being a fat-headed idiot to assume that Collins was still on the payroll or, worse, had any part in the Ko case.

2 Collins is facially a type, *I said: regular-featured, moustached, etc, looked like half the pimps in London. I doubted whether, from across a road at eleven fifteen at night, Westerby could be certain of his identification. Westerby retorted that he had A1 vision and that Sam had his newspaper open at the racing page. 3 Anyway, what was Westerby himself doing, I enquired, mooning round Star Heights at eleven fifteen at night? Answer, returning from a drink with the UPI mob and hoping for a cab. At this I pretended to explode, and said that nobody who had been on a UPI thrash could see an elephant at five yards, let alone Sam Collins at twenty-five, in a car, at dead of night. Over and out – I hope.*

That Smiley was seriously concerned about this incident goes without saying. Only four people knew of the Collins ploy: Smiley, Connie Sachs, Craw and Sam himself. That Jerry should have stumbled on him provided an added anxiety in an operation already loaded with imponderables. But Craw was deft, and Craw believed he had talked Jerry down, and Craw was the man on the spot. Just possibly, in a perfect world, Craw might have made it his business to find out whether there had really been a UPI party in the Midlevels that night – and on learning that there had not, he might have challenged Jerry again to explain his presence in the region of Star Heights, and in that case Jerry would probably have thrown a tantrum and produced some other story that was not checkable: that he had been with a woman, for instance, and Craw could mind his bloody business. Of which the net result would have been needless bad blood and the same take-it-or-leave-it situation as before.

It is also tempting, but unreasonable, to expect of Smiley that with so many other pressures upon him – the continued and unabating quest for Nelson, daily sessions with the Cousins, rearguard actions round the Whitehall corridors – he should have drawn the inference closest to his own lonely experience: namely that Jerry, having no taste for sleep or company that evening, had wandered the night pavements till he found himself standing outside the building where Lizzie lived, and hung about, as Smiley did, on his own nocturnal wanderings, without exactly knowing what he wanted, beyond the off-chance of a sight of her.

The rush of events which carried Smiley along was far too powerful to permit of such fanciful abstractions. Not only did the eighth day, when it came, put the Circus effectively on a war footing: it is also the pardonable vanity of lonely people everywhere to assume they have no counterparts.

Chapter 14

THE EIGHTH DAY

The jolly mood of the fifth floor was a great relief after the depression of the previous gathering. A burrowers' honeymoon Guillam called it, and tonight was its highest point, its attenuated starburst of a consummation, and it came exactly eight days, in the chronology which historians afterwards impose on things, after Jerry and Lizzie and Tiu had had their full and frank exchange of views on the subject of Tiny Ricardo and the Russian goldseam – to the great delight of the Circus planners. Guillam had wangled Molly along specially. They had run in all directions, these shady night animals, down old paths and new paths and old paths grown over till they were rediscovered; and now at last, behind their twin leaders Connie Sachs alias Mother Russia, and the misted di Salis alias the Doc, they crammed themselves, all twelve of them, into the very throne-room itself, under Karla's portrait, in an obedient half circle round their chief, *bolshies* and *yellow perils* together. A plenary session then, and for people unused to such drama, a monument of history indeed. And Molly primly at Guillam's side, her hair brushed long to hide the bite marks on her neck.

Di Salis does most of the talking. The other ranks feel this to be appropriate. After all, Nelson Ko is the Doc's patch entirely: Chinese to the sleeve-ends of his tunic. Reining himself right in – his spiky, wet hair, his knees, feet and fussing fingers all but still for once, he keeps things in a low and almost deprecating key of which the inexorable climax is accordingly more thrilling. And the climax even has a name. It is Ko Sheng-hsiu, alias Ko, Nelson, later known also as Yao Kai-sheng, under which name he was later disgraced in the Cultural Revolution.

'But within these walls, gentlemen,' pipes the Doc, whose awareness of the female sex is inconsistent, 'we shall continue to call him Nelson.'

Born 1928 of humble proletarian stock, in Swatow – to quote the official sources, says the Doc – and soon afterwards removed to Shanghai. No mention, in either official or unofficial handouts, of Mr Hibbert's Lord's Life Mission school, but a sad reference to 'exploitation at the hands of western imperialists in childhood', who poisoned him with religion. When the Japanese reached Shanghai, Nelson joined the refugee trail to Chungking, all as Mr Hibbert has described. From an early age, once more according to official records, the Doc continues, Nelson secretly devoted himself to seminal revolutionary reading and took an active part in clandestine Communist groups, despite the oppression of the loathsome Chiang Kai-shek rabble. On the refugee trail he also attempted 'on many occasions to escape to Mao but his extreme youth held him back. Returning to Shanghai he became, already as a student, a leading cadre member of the outlawed Communist movement and undertook special assignments in and around the Kiangnan shipyards to subvert the pernicious influence of KMT Fascist elements. At the University of Communications he appealed publicly for a united front of students and peasants. Graduated with conspicuous excellence in 1951 . . .'

Di Salis interrupts himself, and in a sharp release of tension throws up one arm, and clenches the hair at the back of his head.

'The usual unctuous portrait, Chief, of a student hero who sees the light before his time,' he sings.

'What about Leningrad?' Smiley asks, from his desk, while he jots the occasional note.

'Nineteen fifty-three to six.'

'Yes, Connie?'

Connie is in her wheelchair again. She blames the freezing month, and that toad Karla jointly.

'We have a Brother Bretlev, darling. Bretlev, Ivan Ivanovitch, Academician, Leningrad faculty of shipbuilding, old-time China hand, devilled in Shanghai for Centre's China hounds. Revolutionary warhorse, latter-day Karla-trained talent-spotter trawling the overseas students for likely lads and lasses.'

For the burrowers on the Chinese side – the yellow perils – this intelligence is new and thrilling, and produces an excited crackle of chairs and papers, till on Smiley's nod, di Salis lets go his head and takes up his narrative once more.

'Nineteen fifty-seven returned to Shanghai and was put in charge of a railway workshop – '

Smiley again: 'But his dates at Leningrad were fifty-three to fifty-six?'

'Correct,' says di Salis.

'Then there seems to be a missing year.'

Now no papers crackle and no chairs either.

'A tour of Soviet shipyards is the official explanation,' says di Salis with a smirk at Connie and a mysterious, knowing writhe of the neck.

'Thank you,' says Smiley and makes another note. 'Fifty-seven,' he repeats. 'Was that before or after the Sino-Soviet split, Doc?'

'Before. The split started in earnest in fifty-nine.'

Smiley asks here whether Nelson's brother receives a mention anywhere: or is Drake as much disowned in Nelson's China as Nelson is in Drake's?

'In one of the earliest official biographies Drake is referred to, but not by name. In the later ones, a brother is said to have died during the Communist takeover of forty-nine.'

Smiley makes a rare joke, which is followed by dense, relieved laughter. 'This case is littered with people pretending to be dead,' he complains. 'It will be a positive relief to me to find a real corpse somewhere.' Only hours later, this *mot* was remembered with a shudder.

'We also have a note that Nelson was a model student at Leningrad,' di Salis goes on. 'At least in Russian eyes. They sent him back with the highest references.'

Connie from her iron chair allows herself another interjection. She has brought Trot, her mangy brown mongrel, with her. He lies misshapenly across her vast lap, stinking and occasionally sighing, but not even Guillam, who is a dog-hater, has the nerve to banish him.

'Oh and so they would, dear, wouldn't they?' she cries. 'The Russians would praise Nelson's talents to the skies, course they would, specially if Brother Bretlev Ivan Ivanovitch has snapped him up at University, and Karla's lovelies have spirited him off to training school and all! Bright little mole like Nelson, give him a decent start in life for when he gets home to China! Didn't do him much good later though, did it, Doc? Not when the Great Beastly Cultural Revolution got him in the neck! The generous admiration of Soviet imperialist running dogs wasn't at all the thing to be wearing in your cap *then*, was it?'

Of Nelson's fall, few details are available, the Doc proclaims, speaking louder in response to Connie's outburst. 'One must assume that it was violent, and as Connie has pointed out, those who were highest in Russian favour fell the hardest.' He glances at the sheet of paper which he holds crookedly before his blotched face. 'I won't give you all his appointments at the time of his disgrace, Chief, because he lost them anyway. But there is no doubt that he did indeed have effective management of most of the shipbuilding, in Kiangnan and consequently of a large part of China's naval tonnage.'

'I see,' says Smiley quietly. Jotting, he purses his lips as if in disapproval, while his eyebrows lift very high.

'His post at Kiangnan also procured him a string of seats on the naval planning committees and in the field of communications and strategic policy. By sixty-three his name is beginning to pop up regularly in the Cousins' Peking watch reports.'

'Well done, Karla,' Guillam says quietly from his place

at Smiley's side, and Smiley, still writing, actually echoes this sentiment with a 'Yes'.

'The only one, Peter dear!' Connie yells, suddenly unable to contain herself. 'The only one of all those toads to see it coming! A voice in the wilderness, wasn't he, Trot? "Look out for the yellow peril," he told 'em. "One day they're going to turn round and bite the hand that's feeding 'em, sure as eggs. And when that happens you'll have eight hundred million new enemies banging on your own back door. *And* your guns will all be pointing the wrong way. Mark my words." Told em,' she repeats, hauling at the mongrel's ear in her emotion. 'Put it all in a paper, "Threat of deviation by emerging Socialist partner". Circulated every little brute in Moscow Centre's Collegium. Drafted it word for word in his clever little mind while he was doing a spot of bird in Siberia for Uncle Joe Stalin, bless him. "Spy on your friends today, they're certain to be your enemies tomorrow," he told them. Oldest dictum in the trade, Karla's favourite. When he was given his job back he practically nailed it up on the door in Dzerzhinsky Square. No one paid a blind bit of notice. Not a scrap. Fell on barren ground, my dear. Five years later, he was proved right, and the Collegium didn't thank him for that either, *I* can tell you! He's been right a sight too often for their liking, the boobies, hasn't he, Trot! *You* know, don't you darling, *you* know what the old fool-woman's on about!' At which she lifts the dog a few inches in the air by its forepaws and lets it flop back on to her lap again.

Connie can't bear old Doc hogging the limelight, they secretly agree. She sees the logic of it, but the woman in her can't abide the reality.

'Very well, he was purged, Doc,' Smiley says quietly, restoring calm. 'Let's go back to sixty-seven, shall we?' And puts his chin back in his hand.

In the gloom, Karla's portrait peers stodgily down as di Salis resumes. 'Well, the usual grim story, one supposes, Chief,' he chants. 'The dunce's cap no doubt. Spat on in the street. Wife and children kicked and beaten up. Indoctrination camps, labour education "on a scale commensurate with the crime". Urged to reconsider the peasant virtues. One report has him sent to a rural commune to test himself. And when he came crawling back to Shanghai they'd have made him start at the bottom again, driving bolts into a railway line, or whatever. As far as the *Russians* were concerned – if that's what we're talking about' – he hurries on before Connie can interrupt yet again – 'he was a washout. No access, no influence, no friends.'

'How long did it take him to climb back?' Smiley enquires, with a characteristic lowering of the eyelids.

'About three years ago he started to be functional again. In the long run he has what Peking needs most: brains, technical knowhow, experience. But his *formal* rehabilitation didn't really occur till the beginning of seventy-three.'

While di Salis goes on to describe the stages of Nelson's ritual reinstatement, Smiley quietly draws a folder to him and refers to certain other dates which for reasons as yet unexplained are suddenly acutely relevant to him.

'The payments to Drake have their beginnings in mid-seventy-two,' he murmurs. 'They rise steeply in mid-seventy-three.'

'With Nelson's *access*, darling,' Connie whispers after him, like a prompter from the wings. 'The more he knows, the more he tells, and the more he tells the more he gets. Karla only pays for goodies, and even then it hurts like blazes.'

By seventy-three – says di Salis – having made all the proper confessions, Nelson has been embraced into the Shanghai municipal revolutionary committee, and appointed responsible person in a naval unit of the People's Liberation Army. Six months later –

'Date?' Smiley interrupts.

'July seventy-three.'

'Then Nelson was formally rehabilitated when?'

'The process began in January seventy-three.'

'Thank you.'

Six months later, di Salis continues, Nelson is seen to be acting in an unknown capacity with the Central Committee of the Chinese Communist Party.

'Holy *smoke*,' says Guillam softly, and Molly Meakin gives his hand a hidden squeeze.

'And a report from the Cousins,' says di Salis, 'undated as usual but well attested, has Nelson down as an informal adviser to the Munitions and Ordnance Committee of the Ministry of Defence.'

Rather than orchestrate this revelation with his customary range of mannerisms, di Salis again contrives to keep rock still, to great effect.

'In terms of *eligibility*, Chief,' he goes on quietly, 'from an *operational* standpoint, we on the China side of your house would regard this as one of the key positions in the whole of the Chinese administration. If we could pick ourselves one slot for an agent inside the Mainland, Nelson's might well be the one.'

'Reasons?' Smiley enquires, still alternating between his jottings and the open folder before him.

'The Chinese Navy is still in the stone age. We do have a formal interest in Chinese technical intelligence, naturally, but our real priorities, like those of Moscow no doubt, are strategic and political. Beyond that, Nelson could supply us with the total capacity of all Chinese shipyards. Beyond that again, he could tell us the Chinese submarine potential, which has been frightening the daylights out of the Cousins for years. And of ourselves too, I may add, off and on.'

'So think what it's doing for Moscow,' an old burrower murmurs out of turn.

'The Chinese are supposedly developing their own version of the Russian G-2 class submarine,' di Salis explains. 'No one knows a lot about it. Have they their own design? Have they two or four tubes? Are they armed with sea-to-air missiles or sea-to-sea? What is the financial appropriation for them? There's talk of a Han class. We had word they laid one down in seventy-one. We've never had confirmation. In Dairen in sixty-four they allegedly built a G class armed with ballistic missiles, but it still hasn't been officially sighted. And so forth and so on,' says di Salis deprecatingly, for like most of the Circus he has a rooted dislike of military matters and would prefer the more artistic targets. 'For hard and fast detail on those subjects the Cousins would pay a fortune. In a couple of years Langley could spend hundreds of millions in research, overflights, satellites, listening devices and God knows what – and still not come up with an answer half as good as one photograph. So if Nelson – ' He lets the sentence hang, which is somehow a lot more effective than making it finite. Connie whispers 'Well *done*, Doc,' but still for a while nobody else speaks. They are held back by Smiley's jotting, and his continued examination of the folder.

'Good as Haydon,' Guillam mutters. 'Better. China's the last frontier. Toughest nut in the trade.'

Smiley sits back, his calculations apparently finished.

'Ricardo made his trip a few months after Nelson's formal rehabilitation,' he says.

Nobody sees fit to question this.

'Tiu travels to Shanghai and six weeks later Ricardo – '

In the far background, Guillam hears the bark of the Cousins' telephone switched through to his room, and it is a thing he afterwards avers most strongly – whether in truth or with hindsight – that the unlovable image of Sam Collins was at this point conjured out of his subconscious memory like a djini out of a lamp, and that he wondered yet again how he could ever have been so unthinking as to let Sam Collins deliver that vital letter to Martello.

'Nelson has one more string to his bow, Chief,' di Salis continues, just as everyone is assuming he is done. 'I hesitate to offer it with any confidence, but in the circumstances I dare not omit it altogether. A barter report from the West Germans, dated a few weeks ago. According to *their* sources, Nelson is lately a member of what we have for want of information dubbed The Peking Tea Club, an embryonic body which we believe has been set up to co-ordinate the Chinese intelligence effort. He came in first as an adviser on electronic surveillance, and was then co-opted as a full member. It functions, so far as we can fathom, somewhat as our own Steering Group. But I must emphasise that this is a shot in the dark. We know absolutely nothing about the Chinese services, and nor do the Cousins.'

For once at a loss for words, Smiley stares at di Salis, opens his mouth, closes it, then pulls off his glasses and polishes them.

'And Nelson's *motive*?' he asks, still oblivious to the steady bark of the Cousins' bell. 'A shot in the dark, Doc? How would you see that?'

Di Salis gives an enormous shrug, so that his tallow hair bucks like a floor mop. 'Oh, anybody's guess,' he says waspishly. 'Who believes in *motive* these days? It would have been perfectly natural for him to respond to recruitment overtures in Leningrad, of course, provided they were made in the right way. Not a disloyal thing at all. Not doctrinally, anyway. Russia was China's big elder brother. Nelson needed merely to be told he had been chosen as one of a special vanguard of vigilantes. I see no great art to that.'

Outside the room, the green phone just goes on ringing, which is remarkable. Martello is not usually so persistent. Only Guillam and Smiley are allowed to pick it up. But Smiley has not heard it, and Guillam is damned if he will budge while di Salis is extemporising on Nelson's possible reasons for becoming Karla's mole.

'When the Cultural Revolution came, many people in Nelson's position believed that Mao had gone mad,' di Salis explains, still reluctant to theorise. 'Even some of his own generals thought so. The humiliations Nelson suffered made him conform outwardly, but inwardly, perhaps, he remained bitter – who knows? – vengeful.'

'The alimony payments to Drake started at a time when Nelson's rehabilitation was barely complete,' Smiley objects mildly. 'What is the presumption there, Doc?'

All this is just too much for Connie and once again she brims over.

'Oh George, how can you be so naïve? *You* can find the line, dear, *course* you can! Those poor Chinese can't afford to hang a top technician in the cupboard half his life and not use him! Karla saw the drift, didn't he, Doc? He read the wind and went with it. He kept his poor little Nelson on a string and as soon as he started to come out of the wilderness again he had his legmen get alongside him: "It's *us*, remember? Your friends! *We* don't let you down! *We* don't spit on you in the street! Let's get back to business!" You'd play it just the same way yourself, you know you would!'

'And the money?' Smiley asks. 'The half million?'

'Stick and carrot! Blackmail implicit, rewards enormous. Nelson's hooked both ways.'

But it is di Salis, Connie's outburst notwithstanding, who has the last word:

'He's Chinese. He's pragmatic. He's Drake's brother. He can't get out of China – '

'Not yet,' says Smiley softly, glancing at the folder again.

' – and he knows very well his market value to the Russian service. "You can't eat politics, you can't sleep with them," Drake liked to say, so you might as well make money out of them – '

'Against the day when you can leave China and spend it,' Smiley concludes, and – as Guillam tiptoes from the room – closes the folder and takes up his sheet of jottings. 'Drake tried to get him out once and failed, so Nelson took the Russians' money till . . . till what? Till Drake has better luck perhaps.'

In the background, the insistent snarling of the green telephone has finally ceased.

'Nelson is Karla's mole,' Smiley remarks at last, once more almost himself. 'He's sitting on a priceless crock of Chinese intelligence. That alone we could do with. He's acting on Karla's orders. The orders themselves are of inestimable value to us. They would show us precisely how much the Russians know about their Chinese enemy, and even what they intend toward him. We could take backbearings galore. Yes, Peter?'

In the breaking of tragic news there is no transition. One minute a concept stands; the next it lies smashed, and for those affected the world has altered irrevocably. As a cushion, however, Guillam had used official Circus stationery and the written word. By writing his message to Smiley in signal form, he hoped that the sight of it would prepare him in advance. Walking quietly to the desk, the form in his hand, he laid it on the glass sheet and waited.

'*Charlie Marshall*, the other pilot, by the way,' Smiley asked of the gathering, still oblivious. 'Have the Cousins run him to earth yet, Molly?'

'His story is much the same as Ricardo's,' Molly Meakin replied, glancing queerly at Guillam. Still at Smiley's side, he looked suddenly grey and middle-aged and ill. 'Like Ricardo, he flew for the Cousins in the Laos war, Mr Smiley. They were contemporaries at Langley's secret aviation school in Oklahoma. They dumped him when Laos ended and have no further word on him. Enforcement says he has ferried opium, but they say that of all of the Cousins' pilots.'

'I think you should read that,' Guillam said, pointing firmly at the message.

'Marshall must be Westerby's next step. We have to maintain the pressure,' Smiley said.

Picking up the signal form at last, Smiley held it critically to his left side, where the reading light was brightest. He read with his eyebrows raised and his lids lowered. As always, he read twice. His expression did not change, but those nearest him said the movement went out of his face.

'Thank you, Peter,' he said quietly, laying the paper down again. 'And thank you everyone else. Connie and the Doc, perhaps you'd stay behind. I trust the rest of you will get a good night's sleep.'

Among the younger sparks this hope was greeted with cheerful laughter, for it was well past midnight already.

* * *

The girl from upstairs slept, a neat brown doll along the length of one of Jerry's legs, plump and immaculate by the orange night-light of the rain-soaked Hong Kong sky. She was snoring her head off and Jerry was staring through the window thinking of Lizzie Worthington. He thought of the twin claw marks on her chin and wondered again who had put them there. He thought of Tiu, imagining him as her jailer, and he rehearsed the name *horse-writer* until it really annoyed him. He wondered how much more waiting there was, and whether at the end of it he might have a chance with her, which was all he asked: a chance. The girl stirred, but only to scratch her rump. From next door, Jerry heard a ritual clicking as the habitual mah-jong party washed the pieces before disturbing them.

The girl had not been unduly responsive to Jerry's courtship at first – a gush of impassioned notes, jammed through her letter box at all hours of the previous few days – but she did need to pay her gas bill. Officially, she was the property of a businessman, but recently his visits had become fewer and most recently had ceased altogether, with the result that she could afford neither the fortune-teller nor mah-jong, nor the stylish clothes she had set her heart on for the day she broke into Kung Fu films. So she succumbed, but on a clear financial understanding. Her main fear was of being known to consort with the hideous *kwailo* and for this reason she had put on her entire out-door equipment to descend the one floor; a brown raincoat with transatlantic brass buckles on the epaulettes, plastic yellow boots and a plastic umbrella with red roses. Now this equipment lay around the parquet floor like armour after the battle, and she slept with the same noble exhaustion. So that when the phone rang her only response was a drowsy Cantonese oath.

Lifting the receiver Jerry nursed the idiotic hope it might be Lizzie, but it wasn't.

'Get your ass down here fast,' Luke promised, 'and Stubbsie will *love* you. *Move* it. I'm doing you the favour of our career.'

'Where's here?' Jerry asked.

'Downstairs, you ape.'
He rolled the girl off him but she still didn't wake.

The roads glittered with the unexpected rain and a thick halo ringed the moon. Luke drove as if they were in a jeep, in high gear with hammer changes on the corners. Fumes of whisky filled the car.
'What have you got, for Christ's sake?' Jerry demanded. 'What's going on?'
'Great meat. Now shut up.'
'I don't want meat. I'm suited.'
'You'll want this one. *Man*, you'll want this one.'
They were heading for the harbour tunnel. A flock of cyclists without lights lurched out of a side turning and Luke had to mount the central reservation to avoid them. Look for a damn great building site, Luke said. A patrol car overtook them, all lights flashing. Thinking he was going to be stopped, Luke lowered his window.
'We're *press*, you idiots,' he screamed. 'We're *stars*, hear me?'
Inside the patrol car as it passed they had a glimpse of a Chinese sergeant and his driver, and an august-looking European perched in the back like a judge. Ahead of them, to the right of the carriageway, the promised building site sprang into view, a cage of yellow girders and bamboo scaffolding alive with sweating coolies. Cranes, glistening in the wet, dangled over them like whips. The floodlighting came from the ground and poured wastefully into the mist.
'Look for a low place, just near,' Luke ordered, slowing down to sixty. 'White. Look for a white place.'
Jerry pointed to it, a two-storey complex of weeping stucco, neither new nor old, with a twenty-foot bamboo-stand by the entrance, and an ambulance. The ambulance stood open and the three drivers lounged in it, smoking, watching the police who milled around the forecourt as if it were a riot they were handling.
'He's giving us an hour's start over the field.'
'Who?'

'Rocker. Rocker is. Who do you think?'
'Why?'
'Because he hit me, I guess. He loves me. He loves you too. He said to bring you specially.'
'Why?'
The rain fell steadily.
'*Why? Why? Why?*' Luke echoed, furious. 'Just hurry!'
The bamboos were out of scale, higher than the wall. A couple of orange-clad priests were sheltering against them, clapping cymbals. A third held an umbrella. There were flower stalls, mainly marigolds, and hearses, and from somewhere out of sight the sounds of leisurely incantation. The entrance lobby was a jungle swamp reeking of formaldehyde.
'Big Moo's special envoy,' said Luke.
'Press,' said Jerry.
The police nodded them through, not looking at their cards.
'Where's the Superintendent?' said Luke.
The smell of formaldehyde was awful. A young sergeant led them. They pushed through a glass door to a room where old men and women, maybe thirty of them, mostly in pyjama suits, waited phlegmatically as if for a late train, under shadowless neon lights and an electric fan. One old man was clearing out his throat, snorting on to the green tiled floor. Only the plaster wept. Seeing the giant *kwailos* they stared in polite amazement. The pathologist's office was yellow. Yellow walls, yellow blinds, closed. An airconditioner that wasn't working. The same green tiles, easily washed down.
'Great *smell*,' said Luke.
'Like home,' Jerry agreed.
Jerry wished it was battle. Battle was easier. The sergeant told them to wait while he went ahead. They heard the squeak of trolleys, low voices, the clamp of a freezer door, the low hiss of rubber soles. A volume of *Gray's Anatomy* lay next to the telephone. Jerry turned the pages, staring at the illustrations. Luke perched on a chair. An assistant in short rubber boots and overalls brought tea.

White cups, green rims, and the Hong Kong monogram with a crown.

'Can you tell the sergeant to hurry, please?' said Luke. 'You'll have the whole damn town here in a minute.'

'Why us?' said Jerry again.

Luke poured some tea on to the tiled floor and while it ran into the gutter he topped up the cup from his whisky flask. The sergeant returned, beckoning quickly with his slender hand. They followed him back through the waiting room. This way there was no door, just a corridor, and a turn like a public lavatory, and they were there. The first thing Jerry saw was the trolley chipped to hell. There's nothing older or more derelict than worn-out hospital equipment, he thought. The walls were covered in green mould, green stalactites hung from the ceiling, a battered spittoon was filled with used tissues. They clean out the noses, he remembered, before they pull down the sheet to show you. It's a courtesy so that you aren't shocked. The fumes of formaldehyde made his eyes run. A Chinese pathologist was sitting at the window, making notes on a pad. A couple of attendants were hovering, and more police. There seemed to be a general sense of apology around. Jerry couldn't make it out. The Rocker was ignoring them. He was in a corner, murmuring to the august-looking gentleman from the back of the patrol car, but the corner wasn't far away and Jerry heard 'slur on our reputation' spoken twice in an indignant, nervous tone. A white sheet covered the body, with a blue cross on it made in two equal lengths. So that they can use it either way round, Jerry thought. It was the only trolley in the room. The only sheet. The rest of the exhibition was inside the two big freezers with the wooden doors, walk-in size, big as a butcher's shop. Luke was going out of his mind with impatience.

'Jesus, Rocker!' he called across the room. 'How much longer you going to keep the lid on this? We got work to do.'

No one bothered with him. Tired of waiting, Luke yanked back the sheet. Jerry looked and looked away. The autopsy room was next door, and he could hear the sound of sawing, like the snarling of a dog.

No wonder they're all so apologetic, Jerry thought stupidly. *Bringing a roundeye corpse to a place like this.*

'Jesus *Christ*,' Luke was saying. 'Holy *Christ*. Who did it to him? How do you *make* those marks? That's a Triad thing. *Jesus*.'

The dampened window gave on to the courtyard. Jerry could see the bamboo rocking in the rain and the liquid shadows of an ambulance delivering another customer, but he doubted whether any of them looked like this. A police photographer had appeared and there were flashes. A telephone extension hung on the wall. The Rocker was talking into it. He still hadn't looked at Luke, or at Jerry.

'I want him out of here,' the august gentleman said.

'Soon as you like,' said the Rocker. He returned to the telephone. 'In the Walled City, sir . . . Yes, sir . . . In an alley, sir. Stripped. Lot of alcohol . . . The forensic pathologist recognised him immediately, sir. Yes sir, the bank's here already, sir.' He rang off. 'Yes sir, no sir, three bags full, sir,' he growled. He dialled a number.

Luke was making notes. 'Jesus,' he kept saying in awe. 'Jesus. They must have taken *weeks* to kill him. Months.'

In actual fact, they had killed him twice, Jerry decided. Once to make him talk and once to shut him up. The things they had done to him first were all over his body, in big and small patches, the way fire hits a carpet, eats holes, then suddenly gives up. Then there was the thing round his neck, a different, faster death altogether. They had done that last, when they didn't want him any more.

Luke called to the pathologist. 'Turn him over, will you? Would you mind please turning him over, *sir*?'

The Superintendent had put down the phone.

'What's the story?' said Jerry, straight at him. 'Who is he?'

'Name of Frost,' the Rocker said, staring back with his dropped eye. 'Senior official of the South Asian and China. Trustee Department.'

'Who killed him?' Jerry asked.

'Yeah, who did it? That's the point,' said Luke, writing hard.
'Mice,' said the Rocker.
'Hong Kong has no Triads, no Communists, and no Kuomintang. Right, Rocker?'
'And no whores,' the Rocker growled.
The august gentleman spared the Rocker further reply.
'A vicious case of mugging,' he declared, over the policeman's shoulder. 'A filthy, vicious mugging exemplifying the need for public vigilance at all times. He was a loyal servant of the bank.'
'That's not a mugging,' said Luke, looking at Frost again. 'That's a *party*.'
'He certainly had some damned odd friends,' the Rocker said, still staring at Jerry.
'What's that supposed to mean?' said Jerry.
'What's the story so far?' said Luke.
'He was on the town till midnight. Celebrating in the company of a couple of Chinese males. One cathouse after another. Then we lose him. Till tonight.'
'The bank's offering a reward of fifty thousand dollars,' said the august man.
'Hong Kong or US?' said Luke, writing.
The august man said 'Hong Kong' very tartly.
'Now you boys go easy,' the Rocker warned. 'There's a sick wife in Stanley Hospital, and there's kids – '
'And there's the reputation of the bank,' said the august man.
'That will be our first concern,' said Luke.
They left half an hour later, still ahead of the field.
'Thanks,' said Luke to the Superintendent.
'For nothing,' said the Rocker. His dropped eyelid, Jerry noticed, leaked when he was tired.
We've shaken the tree, thought Jerry, as they drove away. Boy oh boy, have we shaken the tree.

They sat in the same attitudes, Smiley at his desk, Connie in her wheelchair, di Salis glaring into the languid smoke-coil of his pipe. Guillam stood at Smiley's side, the grate of Martello's voice still in his ears. Smiley, with a slight circular movement of his thumb, was polishing his spectacles with the end of his tie.

Di Salis the Jesuit spoke first. Perhaps he had the most to disown. 'There is nothing in logic to link us with this incident. Frost was a libertine. He kept Chinese women. He was manifestly corrupt. He took our bribe without demur. Heaven knows what bribes he has not taken in the past. I will not have it laid at my door.'

'Oh *stuff*,' Connie muttered. She sat expressionless and the dog lay sleeping on her lap. Her crippled hands lay over his brown back for warmth. In the background dark Fawn was pouring tea.

Smiley spoke to the signal form. Nobody had seen his face since he had first looked down to read it.

'Connie, I want the arithmetic,' he said.

'Yes, dear.'

'Outside these four walls, who is conscious that we leaned on Frost?'

'Craw. Westerby. Craw's policeman. And if they've any *nous* the Cousins will have guessed.'

'Not Lacon, not Whitehall.'

'And *not* Karla, dear,' Connie declared, with a sharp look at the murky portrait.

'No. Not Karla. I believe that,' From his voice, they could feel the intensity of the conflict as his intellect forced its will upon his emotions. 'For Karla, it would be a most exaggerated response. If a bank account is blown, all he need do is open another one elsewhere. He doesn't need *this*.' With the tips of his fingers, he precisely moved the signal form an inch up the glass. 'The ploy went as planned. The response was simply – ' He began again. 'The response was more than we expected. Operationally, nothing is amiss. Operationally, we have advanced the case.'

'We've *drawn* them, dear,' Connie said firmly.

Di Salis blew up completely. 'I insist you do not speak as if we were all of us accomplices here. There is no proven link and I consider it invidious that you should suggest there is.'

Smiley remained remote in his response.

'I would consider it invidious if I suggested anything else. I ordered this initiative. I refuse not to look at the consequences merely because they are ugly. Put it on my shoulders. But don't let's deceive ourselves.'

'Poor devil didn't know enough, did he?' Connie mused, seemingly to herself. At first nobody took her up. Then Guillam did: what did she mean by that?

'Frost had nothing to betray, darling,' she explained. 'That's the worst that can happen to anyone. What could he give them? One zealous journalist, name of Westerby. They had that already, little dears. So of course they went on. And on.' She turned in Smiley's direction. He was the only one who shared so much history with her. 'We used to make it a *rule*, remember George, when the boys and girls went in? We always gave them something they could confess, bless them.'

With loving care Fawn set down a paper cup of tea on Smiley's desk, a slice of lemon floating on the tea. His skull-like grin moved Guillam to repressed fury.

'When you've handed that round, get out,' he snapped in his ear. Still smirking, Fawn left.

'Where is Ko in his mind at this moment?' Smiley asked, still talking to the signal form. He had locked his fingers under his chin and might have been praying.

'Funk and fuzzie-headedness,' Connie declared with confidence. 'Fleet Street on the prowl, Frost dead and he's still no further forward.'

'Yes. Yes, he'll dither. "Can he hold the dam? Can he plug the leaks? Where *are* the leaks anyway?" . . . That's what we wanted. We've got it.' He made the smallest movement of his bowed head, and it pointed toward Guillam. 'Peter, you will please ask the Cousins to step up their surveillance on Tiu. Static posts only, tell them. No street work, no frightening the game, no nonsense of that kind. Telephone, mail, the easy things only. Doc, when did Tiu last visit the Mainland?'

Di Salis grudgingly gave a date.

'Find out the route he travelled and where he bought his ticket. In case he does it again.'

'It's on record already,' di Salis retorted sulkily, and made a most unpleasing sneer, looking to heaven and writhing with his lips and shoulders.

'Then kindly be so good as to make me a separate note of it,' Smiley replied, with unshakable forbearance. 'Westerby,' he went on in the same flat voice, and for a second Guillam had the sickening feeling that Smiley was suffering from some kind of hallucination and thought that Jerry was in the room with him, to receive his orders like the rest of them. 'I pull him out – I can do that. His paper recalls him, why shouldn't it? Then what? Ko waits. He listens. He hears nothing. And he relaxes.'

'And enter the narcotics heroes,' Guillam said, glancing at the calendar. 'Sol Eckland rides again.'

'Or, I pull him out and I replace him, and another field-man takes up the trail. Is he any less at risk than Westerby is now?'

'It never works,' Connie muttered. 'Changing horses. Never. You know that. Briefing, training, re-gearing, new relationships. Never.'

'I don't see that he *is* at risk!' di Salis asserted shrilly.

Swinging angrily round, Guillam started to slap him down, but Smiley spoke ahead of him.

'Why not, Doc?'

'Accepting your hypothesis – which I don't – Ko is not a man of violence. He's a successful businessman and his maxims are face, and expediency, and merit, and hard work. I won't have him spoken of as if he were some kind of thug. I grant you, he has people, and perhaps his people are less nice than he when it comes to method. Much as we are Whitehall's people. That doesn't make blackguards of Whitehall, I trust.'

For Christ's sake, out with it, thought Guillam.

'Westerby is not a Frost,' di Salis persisted in the same didactic, nasal whine. 'Westerby is not a dishonest servant. Westerby has not betrayed Ko's confidence, or Ko's money, or Ko's brother. In Ko's eyes Westerby represents a large newspaper. And Westerby has let it be known – both to Frost and to Tiu, I understand – that this paper possesses a greater degree of knowledge in the matter than he himself. Ko understands the world. By removing one journalist, he will not remove the risk. To the contrary, he will bring out the whole pack.'

'Then what is in his mind?' said Smiley.

'Uncertainty. Much as Connie said. He cannot gauge the threat. The Chinese have little place for abstracts, less still for abstract situations. He would like the threat to blow over, and if nothing concrete occurs, he will assume it has done so. That is not a habit confined to the Occident. I am extending your hypothesis.' He stood up. 'I am not endorsing it. I refuse to. I dissociate myself from it absolutely.'

He stalked out. On Smiley's nod, Guillam followed him. Only Connie stayed behind.

Smiley closed his eyes and his brow was drawn into a rigid knot above the bridge of his nose. For a long while Connie said nothing at all. Trot lay as dead across her lap, and she gazed down at him, fondling his belly.

'Karla wouldn't give two pins, would he, dearie?' she murmured. 'Not for one dead Frost, nor for ten. That's the difference, really. We can't write it much larger than that, can we, not these days? Who was it who used to say "we're fighting for the survival of Reasonable Man"? Steed-Asprey? Or was it Control? I loved that. It covered it all. Hitler. The new thing. That's who we are: reasonable. Aren't we, Trot? We're not just English. We're reasonable.' Her voice fell a little. 'Darling, what about Sam? Have you had *Thoughts*?'

It was still a long while before Smiley spoke, and when he did so, his voice was harsh, like a voice to keep her at arm's length.

'He's to stand by. Do nothing till he has the green light. He knows that. He's to wait till the green light.' He drew in a deep breath and let it out again. 'He may not even be needed. We may quite well manage without him. It all depends how Ko jumps.'

'George darling, *dear* George.'

In silent ritual she pushed herself to the grate, took up the poker and with a huge effort stirred the coals, clinging to the dog with her free hand.

Jerry stood at the kitchen window, watching the yellow dawn cut up the harbour mist. Last night there had been a storm, he remembered. Must have hit an hour before Luke telephoned. He had followed it from the mattress while the girl lay snoring along his leg. First the smell of vegetation, then the wind rustling guiltily in the palm trees, dry hands rubbed together. Then the hiss of rain like tons of molten shot being shaken into the sea. Finally the sheet lightning rocking the harbour in the long slow breaths while salvos of thunder cracked over the dancing rooftops. I killed him, he thought. Give or take a little, it was me who gave him the shove. 'It's not just the generals, it's every man who carries a gun.' Quote source and context.

The phone was ringing. Let it ring, he thought. Probably Craw, wetting his pants. He picked up the receiver. Luke, sounding even more than usually American:

'Hey, man! Big drama! Stubbsie just came through on the wire. Personal for Westerby. Eat before reading. Want to hear it?'

'No.'

'A swing through the war zones. Cambodia's airlines and the siege economy. Our man amid shot and shell! You're in luck, sailor! They want you to get your ass shot off!'

And leave Lizzie to Tiu, he thought, ringing off.

And for all I know, to that bastard Collins too, lurking in her shadow like a white slaver. Jerry had worked to Sam a couple of times while Sam was plain Mr Mellon of Vientiane, an uncannily successful trader, headman of the local roundeye crooks. He reckoned him one of the most unappetising operators he had come across.

He returned to his place at the window thinking of Lizzie again, up there on her giddy rooftop. Thinking of little Frost, and of his fondness for being alive. Thinking of the smell that had greeted him when he returned here, to his flat.

It was everywhere. It overrode the reek of the girl's deodorant, the stale cigarette smoke and the smell of gas and the smell of cooking oil from the mah-jong players next door. Catching it, Jerry had actually charted in his imagination the route Tiu had taken as he foraged: where he had lingered, and where he had skimped on his journey through Jerry's clothes, Jerry's pantry and Jerry's few possessions. A smell of rosewater and almonds mixed, favoured by an early wife.

Chapter 15

SIEGE TOWN

When you leave Hong Kong it ceases to exist. When you have passed the last Chinese policeman in British ammunition boots and puttees, and held your breath as you race sixty foot above the grey slum rooftops, when the out-islands have dwindled into the blue mist, you know that the curtain has been rung down, the props cleared away, and the life you lived there was all illusion. But this time, for once, Jerry couldn't rise to that feeling. He carried the memory of the dead Frost and the live girl with him, and they were still beside him as he reached Bangkok. As usual it took him all day to find what he was looking for; as usual, he was about to give up. In Bangkok, in Jerry's view, that happened to everyone: a tourist looking for a *wat*, a journalist for a story – or Jerry for Ricardo's friend and partner Charlie Marshall – your prize sits down the far end of some damned alley, jammed between a silted *klong* and a pile of concrete trash, and it costs you five dollars US more than you expected. Also, though this was theoretically Bangkok's dry season, Jerry could not remember ever being here except in rain, which cascaded in unheralded bursts from the polluted sky. Afterwards, people always told him he got the one wet day.

He started at the airport because he was already there and because he reasoned that in the South-east no one can fly for long without flying through Bangkok. Charlie wasn't around any more, they said. Someone assured him Charlie had given up flying after Ric died. Someone else said he was in jail. Someone else again that he was most likely in 'one of the dens'. A ravishing Air Vietnam hostess said with a giggle that he was making freight-hops to Saigon. She only ever saw him in Saigon.

'Out of where?' Jerry asked.

'Maybe Phnom Penh, maybe Vientiane,' she said – but Charlie's destination, she insisted, was always Saigon and he never hit Bangkok. Jerry checked the telephone directory and there was no Indocharter listed. On an off-chance he looked up Marshall too, discovered one – even a Marshall, C – called him, but found himself talking not to the son of a Kuomintang warlord who had christened himself with high military rank, but to a puzzled Scottish trader who kept saying 'listen, but *do* come round'. He went to the jail where the *farangs* are locked up when they can't pay or have been rude to a general, and checked the record. He walked along the balconies and peered through the cage doors and spoke to a couple of crazed hippies. But while they had a good deal to say about being locked up, they hadn't seen Charlie Marshall and they hadn't heard of him, and to put it delicately they didn't care about him either. In a black mood he drove to the so-called sanatorium where addicts enjoy their cold turkey, and there was great excitement because a man in a strait-jacket had succeeded in putting his own eyes out with his fingers, but it wasn't Charlie Marshall, and no, they had no pilots, no Corsicans, no Corsican Chinese and *certainly* no son of a Kuomintang general.

So Jerry started on the hotels where pilots might hang out in transit. He didn't like the work because it was deadening and more particularly he knew that Ko had a big outfit here. He had no serious doubt that Frost had blown him; he knew that most rich overseas Chinese legitimately run several passports and the Swatownese more than several; he knew that Ko had a Thai passport in his pocket and probably a couple of Thai generals as well. And he knew that when they were cross the Thais killed a great deal sooner and more thoroughly than almost everyone else, even though, when they condemned a man to the firing squad, they shot him through a stretched bed sheet in order not to offend the laws of the Lord Buddha. For that reason, among a good few others, Jerry felt less than comfortable shouting Charlie Marshall's name all over the big hotels.

He tried the Erawan, the Hyatt, the Miramar and the Oriental and about thirty others, and at the Erawan he trod specially lightly, remembering that China Airsea had a suite there, and Craw said Ko used it often. He formed a picture of Lizzie with her blonde hair playing hostess for him or stretched out at the poolside sunning her long body while the tycoons sipped their Scotches and wondered how much would buy an hour of her time. While he drove round, a sudden rainstorm pelted fat drops so foul with smuts that they blackened the gold of the street temples. The taxi-driver aqua-planed on the flooded roads, missing the water-buffaloes by inches; the garish buses jingled and charged at them; blood-stained Kung Fu posters screamed at them, but Marshall – Charlie Marshall – *Captain* Marshall – was not a name to anyone, though Jerry dispensed coffee-money liberally. He's got a girl, thought Jerry. He's got a girl, and uses her place, just as I would. At the Oriental he tipped the porter and arranged to collect messages and use the telephone and best of all, he obtained a receipt for two nights' lodging with which to taunt Stubbs. But his trail round the hotels had scared him, he felt exposed and at risk, so to sleep, for a dollar a night, he took a prepaid room in a nameless backstreet dosshouse, where the formalities of registration were dispensed with: a place like a row of beach huts, with all the room doors opening straight on to the pavement in order to make fornication easier, and open garages with plastic curtains that screened the number of your car. By the evening he was reduced to stomping the air-freight agencies, asking about a firm called Indocharter, though he wasn't too keen to do that either, and he was seriously wondering whether to believe the Air Vietnam hostess and take up the trail in Saigon, when a Chinese girl in one of the agencies said:

'Indocharter? That's Captain Marshall's line.'

She directed him to a bookshop where Charlie Marshall bought his literature and collected his mail whenever he was in town. The shop was also run by Chinese, and when Jerry mentioned Marshall the old proprietor burst out laughing and said Charlie hadn't been in for months. The old man was very small with false teeth that grimaced.

'He owe you money? Charlie Marshall owe you money, clash a plane for you?' He once more hooted with laughter and Jerry joined in.

'Super. Great. Listen, what do you do with all the mail when he doesn't come here? Do you send it on?'

Charlie Marshall, he didn't get no mail, the old man said.

'Ah, but, sport, if a letter comes tomorrow, where will you send it?'

To Phnom Penh, the old man said, pocketing his five dollars, and fished a scrap of paper from his desk so that Jerry could copy down the address.

'Maybe I should buy him a book,' said Jerry looking round. 'What does he like?'

'Flench,' the old man said automatically, and taking Jerry upstairs, showed him his sanctum for roundeye culture. For the English, pornography printed in Brussels. For the French, row after row of tattered classics: Voltaire, Montesquieu, Hugo. Jerry bought a copy of *Candide* and slipped it into his pocket. Visitors to this room were *ex officio* celebrities apparently, for the old man produced a visitors' book and Jerry signed it *J. Westerby, newshound.* The comments column was played for laughs, so he wrote 'a most distinguished emporium'. Then he looked back through the pages and asked:

'Charlie Marshall sign here too, sport?'

The old man showed him Charlie Marshall's signature a couple of times – 'address: here', he had written.

'How about his friend?'

'Flend?'

'Captain Ricardo.'

At this the old man grew very solemn and gently took away the book.

* * *

He went round to the Foreign Correspondents' Club at the Oriental and it was empty except for a troop of Japanese who had just returned from Cambodia. They told him the state of play there as of yesterday and he got a little drunk. And as he was leaving, to his momentary horror, the dwarf appeared, in town for consultation with the local bureau. He had a Thai boy in tow, which made him particularly pert: 'Why *Westerby*! But *how's* the Secret Service today?' He played this joke on pretty well everyone, but it didn't improve Jerry's peace of mind. At the dosshouse he drank a lot more Scotch but the exertions of his fellow guests kept him awake. Finally, in self-defence, he went out and found himself a girl, a soft little creature from a bar up the road, but when he lay alone again his thoughts once more homed on Lizzie. Like it or not, she was his bed companion. How much was she consciously involved with them? he wondered. Did she know what she was playing with when she set Jerry up for Tiu? Did she know what Drake's boys had done to Frost? Did she know they might do it to Jerry? It even entered his mind that she might have been there while they did it, and that thought appalled him. No question: Frost's body was still very fresh in his memory. It was one of the worst.

By two in the morning he decided he was going to have a bout of fever, he was sweating and turning so much. Once he heard sounds of soft footsteps inside the room, and flung himself into a corner, clutching a teak table lamp ripped from its socket. At four he was woken by that amazing Asian hubbub: pig-like hawking sounds, bells, cries of old men *in extremis*, the crowing of a thousand roosters echoing in the tile and concrete corridors. He fought with the broken plumbing and began the laborious business of getting clean from a thin trickle of cold water. At five the radio was turned on full blast to get him out of bed and a whine of Asian music announced that the day had begun in earnest. By then he had shaved as if it were his wedding day and at eight he cabled his plans to the comic for the Circus to intercept. At eleven he caught the plane to Phnom Penh. As he climbed aboard the Air

Cambodge Caravelle the ground hostess turned her lovely face to him and, in her best lilting English, melodiously wished him a *nice fright*.

'Thanks. Yes. Super,' he said, and chose the seat over the wing where you stood the best chance. As they slowly took off, he saw a group of fat Thais playing lousy golf on perfect links just beside the runway.

There were eight names on the flight manifest when Jerry read it at the check-in, but only one other passenger boarded the plane, a black-clad American boy with a briefcase. The rest was cargo, stacked aft in brown gunny bags and rush boxes. A siege plane, Jerry thought automatically. You fly in with the goods, you fly out with the lucky. The stewardess offered him an old *Jours de France* and a barley sugar. He read the *Jours de France* to put some French back into his mind, then remembered *Candide* and read that. He had brought Conrad because in Phnom Penh he always read Conrad, it tickled him to remind himself he was sitting in the last of the true Conrad river ports.

To land they flew in high, then pancaked through the cloud in a tight uneasy spiral to avoid random small arms fire from the jungle. There was no ground control but Jerry hadn't expected any. The stewardess didn't know how close the Khmer Rouge were to the town but the Japanese had said fifteen kilometres on all fronts and where there were no roads, less. The Japanese had said the airport was under fire but only from rockets and sporadically. No 105s – not yet, but there's always a beginning, thought Jerry. The cloud continued and Jerry hoped to heaven the altimeter was accurate. Then olive earth leapt at them and Jerry saw bomb craters spattered like egg-spots, and the yellow lines from the tyre tracks of the convoys. As they landed featherlight on the pitted runway, the inevitable naked brown children splashed contentedly in a mud-filled crater.

Sun had broken through the cloud and, despite the roar of aircraft, Jerry had the illusion of stepping into a quiet summer's day. In Phnom Penh, like nowhere else Jerry had ever been, war took place in an atmosphere of peace. He remembered the last time he was here, before the bombing halt. A group of Air France passengers bound for Tokyo had been dawdling curiously on the apron, not realising they had landed in a battle. No one told them to take cover, no one was with them. F4s and one-elevens were screaming over the airfield, there was shooting from the perimeter, Air America choppers were landing the dead in nets like frightful catches from some red sea, and the Boeing 707, in order to take off, had to crawl across the entire airfield running the gauntlet in slow motion. Spellbound, Jerry watched her lollop out of range of the ground fire, and all the way he waited for the thump that would tell him she had been hit in the tail. But she kept going as if the innocent were immune, and disappeared sweetly into the untroubled horizon.

Now, ironically, with the end so close, he noticed that the accent was on the cargo of survival. On the further side of the airfield, huge chartered all-Silver American transport planes, 707s and four-engined turbo-prop c130s marked *Transworld, Bird Airways*, or not marked at all, were landing and taking off in a clumsy, dangerous shuttle as they brought in the ammunition and rice from Thailand and Saigon, and the oil and ammunition from Thailand. On his hasty walk to the terminal Jerry saw two landings, and each time held his breath waiting for the late back-charge of the jets as they fought and shivered to a halt inside the *revêtement* of earth-filled ammunition boxes at the soft end of the landing strip. Even before they stopped, flight handlers in flak-jackets and helmets had converged like unarmed platoons to wrest their precious sacks from the holds.

Yet even these bad omens could not destroy his pleasure at being back.

'*Vous restez combien de temps, monsieur*?' the immigration officer enquired.

'*Toujours*, sport,' said Jerry. 'Long as you'll have me. Longer.' He thought of asking after Charlie Marshall then and there, but the airport was stiff with police and spooks of every sort and as long as he didn't know what he was up against it seemed wise not to advertise his interest. There was a colourful array of old aircraft with new insignia but he couldn't see any belonging to Indocharter, whose registered markings, Craw had told him at the valedictory briefing just before he left Hong Kong, were believed to be Ko's racing colours: grey and pale blue.

He took a taxi and rode in front, gently declining the driver's courteous offers of girls, shows, clubs, boys. The *flamboyants* made a luscious arcade of orange against the slate monsoon sky. He stopped at a haberdasher to change money *au cours flexible*, a term he loved. The money-changers used to be Chinese, Jerry remembered. This one was Indian. The Chinese get out early, but the Indians stay to pick the carcass. Shanty towns lay left and right of the road. Refugees crouched everywhere, cooking, dozing in silent groups. A ring of small children sat passing round a cigarette.

'*Nous sommes un village avec une population des millions,*' said the driver in his schoolroom French.

An army convoy drove at them, headlights on, sticking to the centre of the road. The taxi-driver obediently pulled in to the dirt. An ambulance brought up the rear, both doors open. The bodies were stacked feet outward, legs like pigs' trotters, marbled and bruised. Dead or alive, it scarcely mattered. They passed a cluster of stilt houses smashed by rockets, and entered a provincial French square: a restaurant, an épicerie, a charcuterie, advertisements for Byrrh and Coca-Cola. On the kerb, children squatted, watching over litre wine-bottles filled with stolen petrol. Jerry remembered that too: that was what had happened in the shellings. The shells touched off the petrol and the result was a blood-bath. It would happen again this time. Nobody learned anything, nothing changed, the offal was cleared away by morning.

'Stop!' said Jerry and on the spur of the moment handed the driver the piece of paper on which he had written down the Bangkok bookshop's address for Charlie Marshall. He had imagined he should creep up on the place at dead of night, but in the sunlight, there seemed no point any more.

'*Yaller*?' the driver asked, turning to look at him in surprise.

'That's it, sport.'

'*Vous connaissez cette maison*?'

'Chum of mine.'

'*A vous? Un ami à vous*?'

'Press,' said Jerry, which explains any lunacy.

The driver shrugged and pointed the car down a long boulevard, past the French cathedral, into a mud road lined with courtyard villas which became quickly dingier as they approached the edge of town. Twice Jerry asked the driver what was special about the address, but the driver had lost his charm and shrugged away the questions. When they stopped, he insisted on being paid off, and drove away racing the gear changes in rebuke. It was just another villa, the lower half hidden behind a wall pierced with a wrought-iron gate. He pushed the bell and heard nothing. When he tried to force the gate it wouldn't move. He heard a window slam and thought, as he looked quickly up, that he saw a brown face slip away behind the mosquito wire. Then the gate buzzed and yielded and he walked up a few steps to a tiled verandah and another door, this one of solid teak with a tiny shaded grille for looking out but not in. He waited, then hammered heavily on the knocker, and heard the echoes bounding all over the house. The door was double, with a join at the centre. Pressing his face to the gap, he found himself looking on to a strip of tiled floor and two steps, presumably the last two steps of a staircase. On the lower of these stood two smooth brown feet, naked, and two bare shins, but he saw no further than the knees.

'Hullo!' he yelled, still at the gap. '*Bonjour*! Hullo!' And when the legs still did not move: '*Je suis un ami de Charlie Marshall! Madame, Monsieur, je suis un ami anglais de Charlie Marshall! Je veux lui parler.*'

He took out a five-dollar bill and shoved it through the gap but nothing bit, so he took it back and instead tore a piece of paper from his notebook. He headed his message 'to Captain C. Marshall' and introduced himself by name as 'a British journalist with a proposal to our mutual interest', and gave the address of his hotel. Threading this note also through the gap, he looked for the brown legs again but they had vanished, so he walked till he found a *cyclo*, then rode in the *cyclo* till he found a cab: and no thank you, no thank you, he didn't want a girl – except that, as usual, he did.

The hotel used to be the *Royal*. Now it was the *Phnom*. A flag was flying from the mast-head, but its grandeur looked already desperate. Signing himself in, he saw living flesh basking round the courtyard pool and once more thought of Lizzie. For the girls, this was the hard school, and if she'd carried little packets for Ricardo then ten to one she'd been through it. The prettiest belonged to the richest and the richest were Phnom Penh's Rotarian crooks: the gold and rubber smugglers, the police chiefs, the big-fisted Corsicans who made neat deals with the Khmer Rouge in mid-battle. There was a letter waiting for him, the flap not sealed. The receptionist, having read it himself, politely watched Jerry do the same. A gilt-edged invitation card with an Embassy crest invited him to dinner. His host was someone he had never heard of. Mystified he turned the card over. A scrawl on the back read 'Knew your friend George of the *Guardian*', and guardian was the word that introduced. Dinner and dead-letter boxes, he thought: what Sarratt scathingly called the great Foreign Office disconnection.

'*Téléphone*?' Jerry enquired.

'*Il est foutu, monsieur.*'

'*Electricité?*'

'*Aussi foutue, monsieur, mais nous avons beaucoup de l'eau.*'

'Keller?' said Jerry with a grin.

'*Dans la cour, monsieur,*'

He walked into the gardens. Among the flesh sat a bunch of warries from the Fleet Street heavies, drinking Scotch and exchanging hard stories. They looked like boy-pilots in the Battle of Britain fighting a borrowed war, and they watched him in collective contempt for his upper-class origins. One wore a white kerchief, and lank hair bravely tossed back.

'Christ, it's the Duke,' he said. 'How'd you get here? Walk on the Mekong?'

But Jerry didn't want them, he wanted Keller. Keller was permanent. He was a wireman and he was American and Jerry knew him from other wars. More particularly no *uitlander* newsman came to town without putting his cause at Keller's feet and if Jerry was to have credibility, then Keller's chop would supply it and credibility was increasingly dear to him. He found Keller in the carpark. Broad shoulders, grey-headed, one sleeve rolled down. He was standing with his sleeved arm stuffed into his pocket, watching a driver hose out the inside of a Mercedes.

'Max. Super.'

'*Ripping*,' said Keller, after glancing at him, then went back to his watching. Beside him stood a pair of slim Khmer boys looking like fashion photographers in high-heeled boots and bell-bottoms and cameras dangling over their glittering, un-buttoned shirts. As Jerry looked on, the driver stopped hosing and began scrubbing the upholstery with an army pack of lint which turned brown the more he rubbed. Another American joined the group and Jerry guessed he was Keller's newest stringer. Keller went through stringers fairly fast.

'What happened?' said Jerry, as the driver began hosing again.

'Two-dollar hero caught a very expensive bullet,' said the stringer. 'That's what happened.' He was a pale Southerner with an air of being amused and Jerry was prepared to dislike him.

'Right, Keller?' Jerry said.

'Photographer,' Keller said.

Keller's wire service ran a stable of them. All the big services did: Cambodian boys, like the couple standing here. They paid them two US to go to the front and twenty for every photo printed. Jerry had heard that Keller was losing them at the rate of one a week.

'Took it clean through the shoulder while he was running and stooping,' said the stringer. 'Lost it through the lower back. Went through him like grass through a goose.' He seemed impressed.

'Where is he?' said Jerry for something to say, while the driver continued to mop and hose and scrub.

'Dying right up the road there. What happened, see, couple of weeks back those bastards in the New York bureau dug their toes in about medication. We used to ship them to Bangkok. Not now. Man, not now. Know something? Up the road they lie on the floor and have to bribe the nurses to take them water. Right, boys?'

The two Cambodians smiled politely.

'Want something, Westerby?' Keller asked.

Keller's face was grey and pitted. Jerry knew him best from the Sixties in the Congo where Keller burned his hand pulling a kid out of a lorry. Now the fingers were welded like a webbed claw, but otherwise he looked the same. Jerry remembered that incident best because he had been holding the other end of the kid.

'Comic wants me to take a look round,' Jerry said.

'Can you still do that?'

Jerry laughed and Keller laughed and they drank Scotch in the bar till the car was ready, chatting about old times. At the main entrance they picked up a girl who had been waiting all day, just for Keller, a tall Californian with too much camera and long, restless legs. As the phones weren't working Jerry insisted on stopping off at the British Embassy so that he could reply to his invitation. Keller wasn't very polite.

'You some kinda spook or something these days, Westerby, slanting your stories, ass-licking for deep background and a pension on the side or something?' There were people who said that was roughly Keller's position, but there are always people.

'Sure,' said Jerry amiably. 'Been at it for years.'

The sandbags at the entrance were new and new anti-grenade wires glistened in the teeming sunlight. In the lobby, with the spine-breaking irrelevance which only diplomats can quite achieve, a big partitioned poster recommended 'British High Performance Cars' to a city parched of fuel, and supplied cheerful photographs of several unavailable models.

'I will tell the Counsellor you have accepted,' said the receptionist solemnly.

The Mercedes smelt a little warm still from the blood but the driver had turned up the airconditioning.

'What do they do in there, Westerby?' Keller asked. 'Knit or something?'

'Or something,' Jerry smiled, mainly to the Californian girl.

Jerry sat in the front, Keller and the girl in the back.

'Okay. So hear this,' said Keller.

'Sure' said Jerry.

Jerry had his notebook open and scribbled while Keller talked. The girl wore a short skirt and Jerry and the driver could see her thighs in the mirror. Keller had his good hand on her knee. Her name of all things was Lorraine and like Jerry she was formally taking a swing through the war zones for her group of mid-West dailies. Soon they were the only car. Soon even the *cyclos* stopped, leaving them peasants, and bicycles, and buffaloes, and the flowered bushes of the approaching countryside.

'Heavy fighting on all the main highways,' Keller intoned, at near dictation speed. 'Rocket attacks at night, *plastics* during the day, Lon Nol still thinks he's God and the US Embassy has hot flushes supporting him then trying to throw him out.' He gave statistics, ordnance, casualties, the scale of US aid. He named generals known to be selling American arms to the Khmer Rouge, and generals who ran phantom armies in order to claim the troops' pay, and generals who did both. 'The usual snafu. Bad guys are too weak to take the towns, good guys are too crapped out to take the countryside and nobody wants to fight except the Coms. Students ready to set fire to the place soon as they're no longer exempt from the war, food riots any day now, corruption like there was no tomorrow, no one can live on his salary, fortunes being made and the place bleeding to death. Palace is unreal and the Embassy is a nut-house, more spooks than straight guys and all pretending they've got a secret. Want more?'

'How long do you give it?'

'A week. Ten years.'

'How about the airlines?'

'Airlines is all we have. Mekong's good as dead, so's the roads. Airlines have the whole ballpark. We did a story on that. You see it? They ripped it to pieces. Jesus,' he said to the girl. 'Why do I have to give a re-run for the Poms?'

'More,' said Jerry, writing.

'Six months ago this town had five registered airlines. Last three months we got thirty-four new licences issued and there's like another dozen in the pipeline. Going rate is three million riels to the Minister personally and two million spread around his people. Less if you pay gold, less still if you pay abroad. We're working route thirteen,' he said to the girl. 'Thought you'd like to take a look.'

'Great,' said the girl, and pressed her knees together, entrapping Keller's one good hand.

They passed a statue with its arm shot off and after that the road followed the river bend.

'That's if Westerby here can handle it,' Keller added as an afterthought.

'Oh, I think I'm in pretty good shape,' said Jerry and the girl laughed, changing sides a moment.

'KR got themselves a new position out on the far bank there, hun,' Keller explained, talking to the girl in preference. Across the brown, fast water, Jerry saw a couple of T28s, poking around looking for something to bomb. There was a fire, quite a big one, and the smoke column rose straight into the sky like a virtuous offering.

'Where do the overseas Chinese come in?' Jerry asked. 'In Hong Kong no one's heard of this place.'

'Chinese control eighty per cent of our commerce and that includes airlines. Old or new. Cambodian's lazy, see, hun? Your Cambodian's content to take his profit out of American aid. Your Chinese aren't like that. Oh no, siree. Chinese like to work, Chinese like to turn their cash over. They fixed our money market, our transport monopoly, our rate of inflation, our siege economy. War's getting to be a wholly-owned Hong Kong subsidiary. Hey Westerby, you still got that wife you told me about, the cute one with the eyes?'

'Took the other road,' Jerry said.

'Too bad, she sounded real great. He had this great wife,' said Keller.

'How about you?' asked Jerry.

Keller shook his head and smiled at the girl. 'Care if I smoke, hun?' he asked confidingly.

There was a gap in Keller's welded claw which could have been drilled specially to hold a cigarette, and the rim of it was brown with nicotine. Keller put his good hand back on her thigh. The road turned to track and deep ruts appeared where the convoys had passed. They entered a short tunnel of trees and as they did so, a thunder of shellfire opened to their right, and the trees arched like trees in a typhoon.

'*Wow*,' the girl yelled. 'Can we slow down a little?' And she began hauling at the straps of her camera.

'Be my guest. Medium artillery,' said Keller. 'Ours,' he added as a joke. The girl lowered the window and shot off some film. The barrage continued, the trees danced, but the peasants in the paddy didn't even lift their heads. When it died, the bells of the water-buffaloes went on ringing like an echo. They drove on. On the near river bank, two kids had an old bike and were swapping rides. In the water, a shoal of them were diving in and out of an inner tube, brown bodies glistening. The girl photographed them too.

'You still speak French, Westerby? Me and Westerby did a thing together in the Congo a while back,' he explained to the girl.

'I heard,' she said knowingly.

'Poms get education, hun,' Keller explained. Jerry

hadn't remembered him so talkative. 'They get *raised*. That right, Westerby? Specially lords, right? Westerby's some kind of lord.'

'That's us, sport. Scholars to a man. Not like your hayseeds.'

'Well you speak to the driver, right? We got instructions for him, you do the saying. He hasn't had time to learn English yet. Go left.'

'*A gauche*,' said Jerry.

The driver was a boy, but he already had the guide's boredom.

In the mirror, Jerry noticed that Keller's burnt hand was shaking as he drew on the cigarette. He wondered if it always did. They passed through a couple of villages. It was very quiet. He thought of Lizzie and the claw marks on her chin. He longed to do something plain with her, like taking a walk over English fields. Craw said she was a suburban drag-up. It touched him that she had a fantasy about horses.

'Westerby.'

'Yes, sport?'

'That thing you have with your fingers. Drumming them. Mind not doing that? Bugs me. It's repressive somehow.' He turned to the girl. 'They been pounding this place for years, hun,' he said expansively. 'Years.' He blew out a gust of cigarette smoke.

'About the airline thing,' Jerry suggested, pencil ready to write again. 'What's the arithmetic?'

'Most of the companies take drywing leases out of Vientiane. That includes maintenance, pilot, depreciation but not fuel. Maybe you knew that. Best is own your own plane. That way you have the two things. You milk the siege and you get your ass out when the end comes. Watch for the kids, hun,' he told the girl, as he drew again on his cigarette. 'While there's kids around there won't be trouble. When the kid's disappear it's bad news. Means they've hidden them. Always watch for kids.'

The girl Lorraine was fiddling with her camera again. They had reached a rudimentary checkpoint. A couple of sentries peered in as they passed but the driver didn't even slow down. They approached a fork and the driver stopped.

'The river,' Keller ordered. 'Tell him to stay on the river bank.'

Jerry told him. The boy seemed surprised: seemed even about to object, then changed his mind.

'Kids in the villages,' Keller was saying, 'kids at the front. No difference. Either way, kids are a weathervane. Khmer soldiers take their families with them to war as a matter of course. If the father dies, there'll be nothing for the family anyway, so they might as well come along with the military where there's food. Another thing, hun, another thing is, the widows must be right on hand to claim evidence of the father's death, right? That's a human interest thing for you, right, Westerby? If they don't claim, the commanding officer will deny it and steal the man's pay for himself. Be my guest,' he said, as she wrote. 'But don't think anyone will print it. This war's over. Right, Westerby?'

'*Finito*,' Jerry agreed.

She would be funny, he decided. If Lizzie were here, she would definitely see a funny side and laugh at it. Somewhere among all her imitations, he reckoned, there was a lost original, and he definitely intended to find it. The driver drew up beside an old woman and asked her something in Khmer, but she put her face in her hands and turned her head away.

'Why'd she do *that* for God's sakes?' the girl cried angrily. 'We didn't want anything bad. Jesus!'

'Shy,' said Keller, in a flattening voice.

Behind them, the artillery barrage fired another salvo and it was like a door slamming, barring the way back. They passed a *wat* and entered a market square made of wooden houses. Saffron-clad monks stared at them, but the girls tending the stalls ignored them and the babies went on playing with the bantams.

'So what was the checkpoint for?' the girl asked, as she photographed. 'Are we somewhere dangerous now?'

'Getting there, hun, getting there. Now shut up.'

Ahead of them, Jerry could hear the sound of automatic fire, M16's and AK47s mixed. A jeep raced at them out of the trees, and at the last second veered, banging and tripping over the ruts. At the same moment the sunshine went out. Till now they had accepted it as their right, a liquid, vivid light washed clean by the rainstorms. This was March and the dry season; this was Cambodia, where war, like cricket, was played in decent weather. But now black clouds collected, the trees closed round them like winter and the wooden houses pulled into the dark.

'What do the Khmer Rouge dress like?' the girl asked in a quieter voice. 'Do they have *uniforms*?'

'Feathers and a G-string,' Keller roared. 'Some are even bottomless.' As he laughed, Jerry heard the taut strain in his voice, and glimpsed the trembling claw as he drew on his cigarette. 'Hell, hun, they dress like farmers for Christ's sake. They just have these black pyjamas.'

'Is it always so empty?'

'Varies,' said Keller.

'And Ho Chi-minh sandals,' Jerry put in distractedly.

A pair of green water birds lifted across the track. The sound of firing was no louder.

'Didn't you have a daughter or something? What happened there?' Keller said.

'She's fine. Great.'

'Called what?'

'Catherine,' said Jerry.

'Sounds like we're going away from it,' Lorraine said, disappointed. They passed an old corpse with no arms. The flies had settled on the face-wounds in a black lava.

'Do they always do that?' the girl asked, curious.

'Do what, hun?'

'Take off the boots?'

'Sometimes they take the boots off, sometimes they're the wrong damn size,' said Keller, in another queer snap of anger. 'Some cows got horns, some cows don't, and some cows is horses. Now shut up will you? Where you from?'

'Santa Barbara,' said the girl. Abruptly the trees ended. They turned a bend and were in the open again, with the brown river right beside them. Unbidden, the driver stopped, then gently backed into the trees.

'Where's he going?' the girl asked. 'Who told him to do that?'

'I think he's worried about his tyres, sport,' said Jerry, making a joke of it.

'At thirty bucks a day?' said Keller, also as a joke.

They had found a little battle. Ahead of them, dominating the river bend, stood a smashed village on high waste ground without a living tree near it. The ruined walls were white and the torn edges yellow. With so little vegetation the place looked like the remnants of a Foreign Legion fort and perhaps it was just that. Inside the walls brown lorries clustered, like lorries at a building site. They heard a few shots, a light rattle. It could have been huntsmen shooting at the evening flight. Tracer flashed, a trio of mortar bombs struck, the ground shook, the car vibrated, and the driver quietly unwound his window while Jerry did the same. But the girl had opened her door and was getting out, one classic leg after the other. Rummaging in a black airbag, she produced a telefoto lens, screwed it into her camera and studied the enlarged image.

'That's all there is?' she asked doubtfully. 'Shouldn't we see the enemy as well? I don't see anything but our guys and a lot of dirty smoke.'

'Oh they're out the other side there, hun,' Keller began.

'Can't we see?' There was a small silence while the two men conferred without speaking.

'Look,' said Keller. 'This was just a tour, okay, hun? The detail of the thing gets very varied. Okay?'

'I just think it would be great to see the enemy. I want confrontation, Max. I really do. I like it.'

They started walking.

Sometimes you do it to save face, thought Jerry, other times you just do it because you haven't done your job unless you've scared yourself to death. Other times again, you go in order to remind yourself that survival is a fluke.

But mostly you go because the others go; for *machismo*; and because in order to belong you must share. In the old days, perhaps, Jerry had gone for more select reasons. In order to know himself: the Hemingway game. In order to raise his threshold of fear. Because in battle, as in love, desire escalates. When you have been machine-gunned, single rounds seem trivial. When you've been shelled to pieces, the machine-gunning's child's play, if only because the impact of plain shot leaves your brain in place, where the clump of a shell blows it through your ears. And there is a peace: he remembered that too. At bad times in his life – money, children, women all adrift – there had been a sense of peace that came from realising that staying alive was his only responsibility. But this time – he thought – this time it's the most damn fool reason of all, and that's because I'm looking for a drugged-out pilot who knows a man who used to have Lizzie Worthington for his mistress. They were walking slowly because the girl in her short skirt had difficulty picking her way over the slippery ruts.

'Great chick,' Keller murmured.

'Made for it,' Jerry agreed dutifully.

With embarrassment Jerry remembered how in the Congo they used to be confidants, confessing their loves and weaknesses. To steady herself on the rutted ground, the girl was swinging her arms about.

Don't point, thought Jerry, *for Christ's sake don't point. That's how photographers get theirs.*

'Keep walking, hun,' Keller said shrilly. 'Don't think of anything. Walk. Want to go back, Westerby?'

They stepped round a little boy playing privately with stones in the dust. Jerry wondered whether he was gun-deaf. He glanced back. The Mercedes was still parked in the trees. Ahead, he could pick out men in low firing positions among the rubble, more men than he had realised. The noise rose suddenly. On the far bank, a couple of bombs exploded in the middle of the fire. The T28s were trying to spread the flames. A ricochet tore into the bank below them, flinging up wet mud and dust. A peasant rode past them on his bicycle, serenely. He rode into the village, through it, and out again, slowly past the ruins and into the trees beyond. No one shot at him, no one challenged him. He could be theirs or ours, thought Jerry. He came into town last night, tossed a *plastic* into a cinema, and now he's returning to his kind.

'Jesus,' cried the girl with a laugh, 'why didn't *we* think of bicycles?'

With a clutter of bricks falling, a volley of machine-gun bullets slapped all round them. Below them in the river bank, by the grace of God, ran a line of empty leopard spots, shallow firing positions dug into the mud. Jerry had picked them out already. Grabbing the girl, he threw her down. Keller was already flat. Lying beside her, Jerry discerned a deep lack of interest. Better a bullet or two here than getting what Frostie got. The bullets threw up screens of mud and whined off the road. They lay low, waiting for the firing to tire. The girl was looking excitedly across the river, smiling. She was blue-eyed and flaxen and Aryan. A mortar bomb landed behind them on the verge and for the second time Jerry shoved her flat. The blast swept over them and when it was past, feathers of earth drifted down like a propitiation. But she came up still smiling. When the Pentagon thinks of civilisation, thought Jerry, it thinks of you. In the fort the battle had suddenly thickened. The lorries had disappeared, a dense pall had gathered, the flash and din of mortar was incessant, light machine-gun fire challenged and answered itself with increasing swiftness. Keller's pocked face appeared white as death over the edge of his leopard spot.

'KR's got them by the balls,' he yelled. 'Across the river, ahead, and now from the other flank. We should have taken the other lane!'

Christ, Jerry thought, as the rest of the memories came back to him, Keller and I once fought over a girl, too. He tried to remember who she was, and who had won.

They waited, the firing died. They walked back to the car and gained the fork in time to meet the retreating convoy. Dead and wounded were littered along the roadside, and women crouched among them, fanning the stunned faces with palm leaves. They got out of the car again. Refugees trundled buffaloes and handcarts and one another, while they screamed at their pigs and children. One old woman screamed at the girl's camera, thinking the lens was a gun barrel. There were sounds Jerry couldn't place, like the ringing of bicycle bells and wailing, and sounds he could, like the drenched sobs of the dying and the clump of approaching mortar fire. Keller was running beside a lorry, trying to find an English-speaking officer; Jerry loped beside him yelling the same questions in French.

'Ah to hell,' said Keller, suddenly bored. 'Let's go home.' His English lordling's voice: 'The *people* and the *noise*,' he explained. They returned to the Mercedes.

For a while they were stuck in the column, with the lorries cutting them into the side and the refugees politely tapping at the window asking for a ride. Once Jerry thought he saw Deathwish the Hun riding pillion on an army motorbike. At the next fork Keller ordered the driver to turn left.

'More private,' he said, and put his good hand back on the girl's knee. But Jerry was thinking of Frost in the mortuary, and the whiteness of his screaming jaw.

'My old mother *always* told me,' Keller declared, in a folksy drawl. 'Son, don't never go back through the jungle the same way as you came. Hun?'

'Yes?'

'Hun, you just lost your cherry. My humble congratulations.' The hand slipped a little higher.

From all round them came the sound of pouring water like so many burst pipes as a sudden torrent of rain fell. They passed a settlement full of chickens running in a flurry. A barber's chair stood empty in the rain. Jerry turned to Keller.

'This siege economy thing,' he resumed, as they settled to one another again. 'Market forces and so forth. You reckon that story will go?'

'Could do,' said Keller airily. 'It's been done a few times. But it travels.'

'Who are the main operators?'

Keller named a few.

'Indocharter?'

'Indocharter's one,' said Keller.

Jerry took a long shot. 'There's a clown called Charlie Marshall flies for them, half Chinese. Somebody said he'd talk. Met him?'

'Nope.'

He reckoned that was far enough. 'What do most of them use for machines?'

'Whatever they can get. DC4s, you name it. One's not enough. You need two at least, fly one, cannibalise the second for parts. Cheaper to ground a plane and strip it than bribe the customs to release the spares.'

'What's the profit?'

'Unprintable.'

'Much opium around?'

'There's a whole damn refinery out on the Bassac, for Christ's sakes. Looks like something out of Prohibition times. I can arrange a tour, if that's what you're after.'

The girl Lorraine was at the window, staring at the rain.

'I don't see any kids, Max,' she announced. 'You said to look out for no kids, that's all. Well I've been watching and they've disappeared.' The driver stopped the car. 'It's raining and I read somewhere that when it rains Asian kids like to come out and play. So, you know, where's the kids?' she said. But Jerry wasn't listening to what she'd read. Ducking and peering through the windscreen all at once, he saw what the driver saw, and it made his throat dry.

'You're the boss, sport,' he said to Keller quietly. 'Your car, your war and your girl.'

In the mirror, to his pain, Jerry watched Keller's pumice-stone face torn between experience and incapacity.

'Drive at them slowly,' Jerry said, when he could wait no longer. '*Lentement.*'

'That's right,' Keller said. 'Do that.'

Fifty yards ahead of them, shrouded by the teeming rain, a grey lorry had pulled broadside across the track, blocking it. In the mirror, a second had pulled out behind them, blocking their retreat.

'Better show our hands,' said Keller in a hoarse rush. With his good one he wound down his window. The girl and Jerry did the same. Jerry wiped the windscreen clear of mist and put his hands on the console. The driver held the wheel at the top.

'Don't smile at them, don't speak to them,' Jerry ordered.

'Jesus Christ,' said Keller. 'Holy God.'

All over Asia, thought Jerry, pressmen had their favourite stories of what the Khmer Rouge did to you, and most of them were true. Even Frost at this moment would have been grateful for his relatively peaceful end. He knew newsmen who carried poison, even a concealed gun, to save themselves from just this moment. If you're caught, the first night is the only night to get out, he remembered: before they take your shoes, and your health, and God knows what other parts of you. The first night is your only chance, said the folklore. He wondered whether he should repeat it for the girl but he didn't want to hurt Keller's feelings. They were ploughing forward in first gear, engine whining. The rain was flying all over the car, thundering on the roof, smacking the bonnet and darting through the open windows. If we bog down we're finished, he thought. Still the lorry ahead had not moved and it was no more than fifteen yards away, a glistening monster in the downpour. In the dark of the lorry's cab they saw thin faces watching them. At the last minute, it lurched backward into the foliage, leaving just enough room to pass. The Mercedes tilted. Jerry had to hold the door pillar to stop himself rolling on to the driver. The two offside wheels skidded and whined, the bonnet swung and all but lurched on to the fender of the lorry.

'No licence plates,' Keller breathed. 'Holy Christ.'

'Don't hurry,' Jerry warned the driver. '*Toujours lentement*. Don't put on your lights.' He was watching in the mirror.

'And those were the black pyjamas?' the girl said excitedly. 'And you wouldn't even let me take a picture?'

No one spoke.

'What did they want? Who are they trying to ambush?' she insisted.

'Somebody else,' said Jerry. 'Not us.'

'Some bum following us,' said Keller. 'Who cares?'

'Shouldn't we warn someone?'

'There isn't the apparatus,' said Keller.

They heard shooting behind them but they kept going.

'Fucking rain,' Keller breathed, half to himself. 'Why the hell do we get rain suddenly?'

It had all but stopped.

'But Christ, Max,' the girl protested, 'if they've got us pinned out on the floor like this why don't they just finish us off?'

Before Keller could reply, the driver did it for him in French, softly and politely, though only Jerry understood.

'When they want to come, they will come,' he said, smiling at her in the mirror. 'In the bad weather. While the Americans are adding another five metres of concrete to their Embassy roof, and the soliders are crouching in capes under their trees and the journalists are drinking whisky, and the generals are at the *fumerie*, the Khmer Rouge will come out of the jungle and cut our throats.'

'What did he say?' Keller demanded. 'Translate that, Westerby.'

'Yeah, what *was* all that?' said the girl. 'It sounded really great. Like a proposition or something.'

'Didn't quite get it actually, sport. Sort of out-gunned me.'

They all broke out laughing, too loud, the driver as well.

And all through it, Jerry realised, he had thought of nobody but Lizzie. Not to the exclusion of danger – quite the contrary. Like the new glorious sunshine which now engulfed them, she was the prize of his survival.

* * *

At the Phnom, the same sun was beating gaily on the poolside. There had been no rain in the town, but a bad rocket near the girls' school had killed eight or nine children. The Southern stringer had that moment returned from counting them.

'So how did Maxie make out at the bang-bangs?' he asked Jerry as they met in the hall. 'Seems to me like his nerve is creaking at the joints a little these days.'

'Take your grinning little face out of my sight,' Jerry advised. 'Otherwise actually I'll smack it,' Still grinning, the Southerner departed.

'We could meet tomorrow,' the girl said to Jerry. 'Tomorrow's free all day.'

Behind her, Keller was making his way slowly up the stairs, a hunched figure in a one-sleeved shirt, pulling himself by the banister rail.

'We could even meet tonight if you wanted,' Lorraine said.

For a while, Jerry sat alone in his room writing post-cards for Cat. Then he set course for Max's bureau. He had a few more questions about Charlie Marshall. Besides, he had a notion old Max would appreciate his company. His duty done, he took a cyclo and rode up to Charlie Marshall's house again, but though he pummelled on the door and yelled, all he could see was the same bare brown legs motionless at the bottom of the stairs, this time by candlelight. But the page torn from his notebook had disappeared. He returned to the town and, still with an hour to kill, settled at a pavement café, in one of a hundred empty chairs, and drank a long Pernod, remembering how once the girls of the town had ticked past him here on their little wicker carriages, whispering clichés of love in sing-song French. Tonight, the darkness trembled to nothing more lovely than the occasional thud of gunfire, while the town huddled, waiting for the blow.

Yet it was not the shelling but the silence that held the greatest fear. Like the jungle itself this silence, not gunfire, was the natural element of the approaching enemy.

* * *

When a diplomat wants to talk, the first thing he thinks of is food, and in diplomatic circles one dined early because of the curfew. Not that diplomats were subject to such rigours, but it is a charming arrogance of diplomats the world over to suppose they set an example – to whom, or of what, the devil himself will never know. The Counsellor's house was in a flat, leafy enclave bordering Lon Nol's palace. In the driveway, as Jerry arrived, an official limousine was emptying its occupants, watched over by a jeep stiff with militia. It's either royalty or religion, Jerry thought as he got out; but it was nothing more than an American diplomat and his wife arriving for a meal.

'Ah. You must be Mr Westerby,' said his hostess.

She was tall and Harrods and amused by the idea of a *journalist*, as she was amused by anyone who was not a diplomat, and of counsellor rank at that. 'John has been *dying* to meet you,' she declared brightly, and Jerry supposed she was putting him at his ease. He followed the trail upstairs. His host stood at the top, a wiry man with a moustache and a stoop and a boyishness which Jerry more usually associated with the clergy.

'Oh well done! Smashing. You're the cricketer. Well done. Mutual friends, right? We're not allowed to use the balcony tonight, I'm afraid,' he said with a naughty glance toward the American corner. 'Good men are too scarce, apparently. Got to stay under cover. Seen where you are?' He stabbed a commanding finger at a leather-framed *placement* chart showing the seating arrangement. 'Come and meet some people. Just a minute.' He drew him slightly aside, but only slightly. 'It all goes through me, right? I've made that absolutely clear. Don't let them get you into a corner, right? Quite a little *squall* running, if you follow me. Local thing, Not your problem.'

The senior American appeared at first sight small, being dark and tidy, but when he stood to shake Jerry's hand, he was nearly Jerry's height. He wore a tartan jacket of raw silk and in his other hand he held a walkie-talkie radio in a black plastic case. His brown eyes were intelligent but over-respectful, and as they shook hands, a voice inside Jerry said 'Cousin'.

'Glad to know you, Mr Westerby. I understand you're from Hong Kong. Your Governor there is a very good friend of mine. Beckie, this is Mr Westerby, a friend of the Governor of Hong Kong, and a good friend of John, our host.'

He indicated a large woman bridled in dull, handbeaten silver from the market. Her bright clothes flowed in an Asian medley.

'Oh, Mr *Westerby*,' she said. 'From Hong Kong. *Hullo*.'

The remaining guests were a mixed bag of local traders. Their womenfolk were Eurasian, French and Corsican. A houseboy hit a silver gong. The dining-room ceiling was concrete, but as they trooped in Jerry saw several eyes lift to make sure. A silver cardholder told him he was 'The Honourable G. Westerby', a silver menu holder promised him *le roast beef à l'anglaise*, silver candlesticks held long candles of a devotional kind, Cambodian boys flitted and backed at the half-crouch with trays of food cooked this morning while the electricity was on. A much travelled French beauty sat to Jerry's right with a lace handkerchief between her breasts. She held another in her hand, and each time she ate or drank she dusted her little mouth. Her name card called her Countess Sylvia.

'*Je suis très, très diplomée,*' she whispered to Jerry, as she pecked and dabbed. '*J'ai fait la science politique, mécanique et l'éléctricité générale*. In January I have a bad heart. Now I recover.'

'Ah well, now me, I'm not qualified at *anything*,' Jerry insisted, making far too much of a joke of it. 'Jack of all trades, master of none, that's us.' To put this into French took him quite some while and he was still labouring at it when from somewhere fairly close, a burst of machine-gun fire sounded, far too long for the health of the gun. There were no answering shots. The conversation hung.

'Some bloody idiot shooting at the geckos I should think,' said the Counsellor, and his wife laughed at him fondly down the table, as if the war were a little sideshow they had laid on between them for their guests. The silence returned, deeper and more pregnant than before. The little Countess put her fork on her plate and it clanged like a tram in the night.

'*Dieu*,' she said.

At once, everyone started talking. The American wife asked Jerry where he was *raised* and when they had been through that she asked him where his *home* was, so Jerry gave Thurloe Square, old Pet's place, because he didn't feel like talking about Tuscany.

'We own land in Vermont,' she said firmly. 'But we haven't built on it yet.'

Two rockets fell at the same time. Jerry reckoned they were east about half a mile. Glancing round to see whether the windows were closed, Jerry caught the brown gaze of the American husband fixed on him with mysterious urgency.

'You have plans for tomorrow, Mr Westerby?'

'Not particularly.'

'If there's anything we can do, let me know.'

'Thanks,' said Jerry, but he had the feeling that wasn't the point of the question.

A Swiss trader with a wise face had a funny story. He used Jerry's presence to repeat it.

'Not long ago the whole town was alight with shooting, Mr Westerby,' he said. 'We were all going to die. Oh, *definitely*. Tonight we die! Everything: shells, tracer, poured into the sky, one million dollars' worth of ammunition, we heard afterwards. Hours on end. Some of my friends went round shaking hands with one another.' An army of ants emerged from under the table and began marching in single column across the perfectly laundered damask cloth, making a careful detour round the silver candlesticks and the flower bowl brimming with hibiscus. 'The Americans radioed around, hopped up and down, we all considered very carefully our position on the evacuation list, but a funny thing, you know: the telephones were working and we even had electricity. What did the target turn out to be?'

– they were already laughing hysterically – 'Frogs! Some very greedy *frogs*!'

'Toads,' somebody corrected him, but it didn't stop the laughter.

The American diplomat, a model of courteous self-criticism, supplied the amusing epilogue.

'The Cambodians have an old superstition, Mr Westerby. When there's an eclipse of the moon, you must make a lot of noise. You must shoot off fireworks, you must bang tin cans, or best still, fire off a million dollars' worth of ordnance. Because if you don't, why the frogs will gobble up the moon. We *should* have known, but we *didn't* know, and in consequence we were made to look very, very silly indeed,' he said proudly.

'Yes, I'm afraid you boobed there, old boy,' the Counsellor said with satisfaction.

But though the American's smile remained frank and open, his eyes continued to impart something far more pressing – such as a message between professionals.

Someone talked about servants, and their amazing fatalism. An isolated detonation, loud and seemingly quite near, ended the performance. As the Countess Sylvia reached for Jerry's hand, their hostess smiled interrogatively at her husband down the table.

'John, darling,' she asked in her most hospitable voice, 'was that incoming or outgoing?'

'Outgoing,' he replied with a laugh. 'Oh, outgoing, definitely. Ask your journalist friend if you don't believe me. He's been through a few wars, haven't you, Westerby?'

At which the silence, yet again, joined them like a forbidden topic. The American lady clung to that piece of land in Vermont. Perhaps, after all, they *should* build on it. Perhaps, after all, it was time.

'Maybe we should just *write* to that architect,' she said.

'Maybe we should at that,' her husband agreed – at which moment, they were flung into a pitched battle. From very close, a prolonged burst of pompoms lit the washing in the courtyard and a cluster of machine guns, as many as twenty, crackled in a sustained and desperate fire. By the flashes they saw the servants scurry into the house, and over the firing they heard orders given and replied to, scream for scream, and the crazy ringing of handgongs. Inside the room, nobody moved except the American diplomat, who lifted his walkie-talkie to his lips, drew out an aerial and murmured something before putting it to his ear. Jerry glanced downward and saw the Countess's hand battened trustingly on to his own. Her cheek brushed his shoulder. The firing faltered. He heard the clump of a small bomb close. No vibration, but the flames of the candles tilted in salute and on the mantelshelf a couple of heavy invitation cards flopped over with a slap, and lay still, the only recognisable casualties. Then as a last and separate sound, they heard the grizzle of a departing single-engined plane like the distant grousing of a child. It was capped by the Counsellor's easy laughter as he addressed his wife.

'Ah, well now, that *wasn't* the eclipse, I'm afraid, was it, Hills? That was the advantage of having Lon Nol as our neighbour. One of his pilots gets fed up with not being paid now and then so he takes up a plane and has a potshot at the palace. Darling, are you going to take the gels off to powder their noses and do whatever you all do?'

It's anger, Jerry decided, catching the senior American's eye again. He's like a man with a mission to the poor who has to waste his time with the rich.

Downstairs, Jerry, the Counsellor and the American stood silent in the ground floor study. The Counsellor had acquired a wolfish shyness.

'Yes, well,' he said. 'Now I've put you both on the map perhaps I should leave you to it. Whisky in the decanter, right, Westerby?'

'Right, John,' said the American, but the Counsellor didn't seem to hear.

'Just remember, Westerby, the mandate's *ours*, right? We're keeping the bed warm. Right?' With a knowing wag of the finger, he disappeared.

The study was candlelit, a small masculine room with no mirrors or pictures, just a ribbed teak ceiling and a green metal desk, and the feeling of deathlike quiet again in the blackness outside, though the geckos and the bullfrogs would have baffled the most sophisticated microphone.

'Hey let me get that,' said the American, arresting Jerry's progress to the sideboard, and made a show of getting the mix just right for him: 'Water or soda, don't let me drown it.'

'Seems kind of a long way round to bring two friends together,' the American said, in a taut, chatty tone, from the sideboard as he poured.

'Does rather.'

'John's a great guy but he's kind of a stickler for protocol. Your people have no resources here right now, but they have certain rights, so John likes to make sure that the ball doesn't slip out of his court for good. I can understand his point of view. Just that things take a little longer sometimes.'

He handed Jerry a long brown envelope from inside the tartan jacket, and with the same pregnant intensity as before watched while he broke the seal. The paper had a smeared and photographic quality.

Somewhere a child moaned, and was silenced. The garage, he thought: the servants have filled the garage with refugees and the Counsellor is not to know.

ENFORCEMENT SAIGON *reports Charlie* MARSHALL *rpt MARSHALL scheduled hit Battambang ETA 1930 tomorrow via Pailin . . . converted* DC*4 Carvair, Indocharter markings manifest quotes miscellaneous cargo . . . scheduled continue Phnom Penh.*

Then he read the time and date of transmission and anger hit him like a windstorm. He remembered yesterday's foot-slogging in Bangkok and today's harebrained taxi ride with Keller and the girl, and with a 'Jesus *Christ*' he slammed the message back on the table between them.

'How long have you been sitting on this? That's not tomorrow. That's tonight!'

'Unfortunately our host could not arrange the wedding any earlier. He has an extremely crowded social programme. Good luck.'

Just as angry as Jerry, he quietly took back the signal, slipped it into the pocket of his jacket and disappeared upstairs to his wife, who was busy admiring her hostess's indifferent collection of pilfered Buddhas.

He stood alone. A rocket fell, and this time it was close. The candles went out and the night sky seemed finally to be splitting with the strain of this illusory, Gilbertian war. Mindlessly the machine guns joined the clatter. The little bare room with its tiled floor rattled and sang like a sound machine.

Only as suddenly to stop again, leaving the town in silence.

'Something wrong, old boy?' the Counsellor enquired genially from the doorway. 'Yank rub you up the wrong way, did he? They seem to want to run the world single-handed these days.'

'I'll need six hour options,' Jerry said. The Counsellor didn't quite follow. Having explained to him how they worked, Jerry stepped quickly into the night.

'Got transport, have you, old boy? That's the way. They'll shoot you otherwise. Mind how you go.'

He strode quickly, driven by his irritation and disgust. It was long after curfew. There were no street lamps, no stars. The moon had vanished, and the squeak of his crêpe soles ran with him like an unwanted, unseen companion. The only light came from the perimeter of the palace across the road but none spilled on to Jerry's side of the street. High walls blocked off the inner building, high wires crowned the walls, the barrels of the light anti-aircraft guns gleamed bronze against the black and soundless sky. Young soldiers dozed in groups and as Jerry stomped past them a fresh roll of gong-beats sounded: the master of the guard was keeping the sentries awake. There was no traffic, but between the sentry posts the refugees had made up their own night villages in a long column down the pavement. Some had draped themselves with strips of brown tarpaulin, some had plank bunks and some were cooking by tiny flames, though God alone knew what they had found to eat. Some sat in neat social groups, facing in upon each other. On an ox-cart, a girl lay with a boy, children Cat's age when he last had seen her in the flesh. But from the hundreds of them not one sound came, and after he had gone a distance he actually turned and peered to make sure they were there. If they were, the darkness and the silence hid them. He thought of the dinner party. It had taken place in another land, another universe entirely. He was irrelevant here, yet somehow he had contributed to the disaster.

Just remember the mandate's ours, right? We're keeping the bed warm.

For no reason that he knew of, the sweat began running off him and the night air made no cooling impact. The dark was as hot as the day. Ahead of him in the town a stray rocket struck carelessly, then two more. They creep into the paddies until they're within range, he thought. They lie up, hugging their bits of drainpipe and their little bomb, then fire and run like hell for the jungle. The palace was behind him. A battery fired a salvo and for a few seconds he was able to see his way by the flashes. The road was broad, a boulevard, and as best he could he kept to the crown. Occasionally he made out the gaps of the side streets passing him in geometric regularity. If he stooped he could even see the treetops retreating into the paler sky. Once a cyclo pattered by, toppling nervously out of the turning, hitting the kerb, then steadying. He thought of shouting to it but he preferred to keep on striding. A male voice greeted him doubtfully out of the darkness – a whisper, nothing indiscreet.

'*Bon soir? Monsieur? Bon soir?*'

The sentries stood every hundred metres in ones or twos, holding their carbines in both hands. Their murmurs came to him like invitations, but Jerry was always careful and kept his hands wide of his pockets where they could watch them. Some, seeing the enormous sweating round-eye, laughed and waved him on. Others stopped him at pistol point and gazed up at him earnestly by the light of bicycle lamps while they asked him questions in order to practise their French. Some requested cigarettes, and these he gave. He tugged off his drenched jacket and ripped his shirt open to the waist, but still the air wouldn't cool him and he wondered again whether he had a fever, and whether, like last night in Bangkok, he would wake up in his bedroom crouching in the darkness waiting to brain someone with a table lamp.

The moon appeared, lapped by the foam of the rain-clouds. By its light his hotel resembled a locked fortress. He reached the garden wall and followed it leftward along the trees until it turned again. He threw his jacket over the wall and with difficulty climbed after it. He crossed the lawn to the steps, pushed open the door to the lobby and stepped back with a sick cry of disgust. The lobby was in pitch blackness except for a single moonbeam, which shone like a spotlight on to a huge luminous chrysalis spun around the naked brown larva of a human body.

'*Vous désirez, monsieur*?' a voice asked softly.

It was the night watchman in his hammock, asleep under a mosquito net.

The boy handed him a key and a note and silently accepted his tip. Jerry struck his lighter and read the note. '*Darling, I'm in room twenty-eight and lonely. Come and see me. L.*'

What the hell? he thought: maybe it'll put the bits back together again. He climbed the stairs to the second floor, forgetting her terrible banality, thinking only of her long legs and her tilting rump as she negotiated the ruts along the river bank; her cornflower eyes and her regular all-American gravity as she lay in the leopard spot; thinking only of his own yearning for human touch. Who gives a damn about Keller? he thought. To hold someone is to exist. Perhaps she's frightened too. He knocked on the door, waited, gave it a shove.

'Lorraine? It's me. Westerby.'

Nothing happened. He lurched toward the bed, conscious of the absence of any female smell, even face powder or deodorant. On his way there he saw by the same moonlight the dreadfully familiar sight of blue jeans, heavy beanboots and a tattered Olivetti portable not unlike his own.

'Come one step nearer and it's statutory rape,' said Luke, uncorking the bottle on his bedside table.

Chapter 16

Friends Of Charlie Marshall

He crept out before light, having slept on Luke's floor. He took his typewriter and shoulder bag though he expected to use neither. He left a note for Keller asking him to wire Stubbs that he was following the siege story out to the provinces. His back ached from the floor and his head from the bottle.

Luke had come for the bang-bangs, he said: bureau was giving him a rest from Big Moo. Also Jake Chiu, his irate landlord, had finally thrown him out of his apartment.

'I'm destitute, Westerby!' he had cried, and began wailing round the room, '*destitute*', till Jerry, to buy himself some sleep and stop the neighbours' banging, slipped his spare-key off its ring and flung it at him.

'Until I get back,' he warned. 'Then *out*. Understood?'

Jerry asked about the Frost thing. Luke had forgotten all about it and had to be reminded. Ah *him*, he said. *Him*. Yeah, well there were stories he'd been cheeky to the Triads and maybe in a hundred years they would all come true, but meanwhile who gave a damn?

But sleep hadn't come so easy, even then. They discussed today's arrangements. Luke had proposed to do whatever Jerry was doing. Dying alone was a bore, he had insisted. Better they got drunk and found some whores. Jerry had replied that Luke would have to wait a while before the two of them went into the sunset together, because he was going fishing for the day, and he was going alone.

'Fishing for what, for hell's sakes? If there's a story,

share it. Who gave you Frost for free? Where can you go that is not more beautiful for Brother Lukie's presence?'

Pretty well anywhere, Jerry had said unkindly, and managed to leave without waking him.

He made first for the market and sipped a *soupe chinoise*, studying the stalls and shop fronts. He selected a young Indian who was offering nothing but plastic buckets, water bottles and brooms, yet looking very prosperous on the profits.

'What else do you sell, sport?'

'Sir, I sell all things to all gentlemen.'

They foxed around. No, said Jerry, it was nothing to smoke that he wanted, and nothing to swallow, nothing to sniff and nothing for the wrists either. And no, thank you, with all respect to the many beautiful sisters, cousins and young men of his circle, Jerry's other needs were also taken care of.

'Then, oh gladness, sir, you are a most happy man.'

'I was *really* looking for something for a friend,' said Jerry.

The Indian boy looked sharply up and down the street and he wasn't foxing any more.

'A *friendly* friend, sir?'

'Not very.'

They shared a cyclo. The Indian had an uncle who sold Buddhas in the silver market, and the uncle had a back room, with locks and bolts on the door. For thirty American dollars Jerry bought a neat brown Walther automatic with twenty rounds of ammunition. The Sarratt bearleaders, he reckoned as he climbed back into the cyclo, would have fallen into a deep swoon. First, for what they called improper dressing, a crime of crimes. Second because they preached the hardy nonsense that small guns gave more trouble than use. But they'd have had a bigger fit still if he'd carted his Hong Kong Webley through customs to Bangkok and thence to Phnom Penh, so in Jerry's view they could count themselves lucky, because he wasn't walking into this one naked whatever their doctrine of the week. At the airport there was no plane to Battambang, but there was never a plane to anywhere. There were the all-silver rice jets howling on and off the landing strip, and there were new *revêtements* being built after a fresh fall of rockets in the night. Jerry watched the earth arriving in lorryloads, and the coolies filling ammunition boxes frantically. In another life, he decided, I'll go into the sand business and flog it to besieged cities.

In the waiting room, Jerry found a group of stewardesses drinking coffee and laughing, and in his breezy way he joined them. A tall girl who spoke English made a doubtful face and disappeared with his passport and five dollars.

'*C'est impossible*,' they all assured him, while they waited for her. '*C'est tout occupé*.'

The girl returned smiling. 'The pilot is *very* susceptible,' she said. 'If he don't like you, he don't take you. But I show him your photograph and he has agreed to *surcharger*. He is allowed to take only thirty-one *personnes* but he take you, he don't care, he do it for friendship if you give him one thousand five hundred riels.'

The plane was two-thirds empty, and the bullet holes in the wings wept dew like undressed wounds.

At that time, Battambang was the safest town left in Lon Nol's dwindling archipelago, and Phnom Penh's last farm. For an hour, they lumbered over supposedly Khmer Rouge-infested territory without a soul in sight. As they circled, someone shot lazily from the paddies and the pilot pulled a couple of token turns to avoid being hit, but Jerry was more concerned to mark the ground layout before they touched down: the parkbays; which runways were civil and which were military; the wired-off enclave which contained the freight huts. They landed in an air of pastoral affluence. Flowers grew round the gun emplacements, fat brown chickens scurried in the shell holes, water and electricity abounded, though a telegram to Phnom Penh already took a week.

Jerry trod very carefully now. His instinct for cover was stronger than ever. *The Honourable Gerald Westerby, the distinguished hack, reports on the siege economy*. When you're my size, sport, you have to have a hell of a good reason for whatever you're doing. So he put out smoke, as the jargon goes. At the enquiry desk, watched by several quiet men, he asked for the names of the best hotels in town and wrote down a couple while he continued to study the groupings of planes and buildings. Meandering from one office to another he asked what facilities existed to air-freight news copy to Phnom Penh and no one had the least idea. Continuing his discreet reconnaissance he waved his cablecard around and enquired how to get to the governor's palace, implying that he might have business with the great man personally. By now he was the most distinguished reporter who had ever been to Battambang. Meanwhile, he noted the doors marked 'crew' and the doors marked 'private', and the position of the men's rooms, so that later, when he was clear, he could make himself a sketch plan of the entire concourse, with emphasis on the exits to the wired-off part of the airfield. Finally he asked who was in town just now among the pilots. He was friendly with several, he said, so his simplest plan – should it become necessary – was probably to ask one of them to take his copy in his flightbag. A stewardess gave names from a list and while she did this Jerry gently turned the list round and read off the rest. The Indocharter flight was listed but no pilot was mentioned.

'Captain Andreas still flying for Indocharter?' he enquired.

'Le Capitaine *qui*, monsieur?'

'Andreas. We used to call him André. Little fellow, always wore dark glasses. Did the Kampong Cham run.'

She shook her head. Only Captain Marshall and Captain Ricardo, she said, flew for Indocharter, but le Capitaine *Ric* had immolated himself in an accident. Jerry affected no interest, but established in passing that Captain Marshall's Carvair was due to take off in the afternoon, as forecast in last night's signal, but there was no freight space available, everything was taken, Indocharter was always fully contracted.

'Know where I can reach him?'

'Captain Marshall never flies in the mornings, monsieur.'

He took a cab into town. The best hotel was a flea-bitten dugout in the main street. The street itself was narrow, stinking and deafening, an Asian boomtown in the making, pounded by the din of Hondas and crammed with the frustrated Mercedes of the quick rich. Keeping his cover going, he took a room and paid for it in advance, to include 'special service' which meant nothing more exotic than clean sheets as opposed to those which still bore the marks of other bodies. He told his driver to return in an hour. By force of habit he secured an inflated receipt. He showered, changed and listened courteously while the houseboy showed him where to climb in after curfew, then he went out to find breakfast because it was still only nine in the morning.

He carried his typewriter and shoulder bag with him. He saw no other roundeyes. He saw basket-makers, skin-sellers and fruit-sellers, and once again the inevitable bottles of stolen petrol laid along the pavement waiting for an attack to touch them off. In a mirror hung in a tree, he watched a dentist extract teeth from a patient tied in a high chair, and the red-tipped tooth being solemnly added to the thread which displayed the day's catch. All of these things Jerry ostentatiously recorded in his notebook, as became a zealous reporter of the social scene. And from a pavement café, as he consumed cold beer and fresh fish, he watched the dingy half-glazed offices marked 'Indo-charter' across the road, and waited for someone to come and unlock the door. No one did. *Captain Marshall never flies in the mornings, monsieur.* At a chemist's shop which specialised in children's bicycles he bought a roll of sticking plaster and back in his room taped the Walther to his ribs rather than have it waving around in his waistband. Thus equipped, the intrepid journalist set forth to live some more cover – which sometimes, in the psychology of a fieldman, is no more than a gratuitous act of self-legitimisation as the heat begins to gather.

The governor lived on the edge of town, behind a verandah and French colonial portals, and a secretariat seventy strong. The vast concrete hall led to a waiting room never finished, and to much smaller offices behind, and in one of these, after a fifty-minute wait, Jerry was admitted to the diminutive presence of a tiny, very senior black-suited Cambodian sent by Phnom Penh to handle noisome correspondents. Word said he was the son of a general and managed the Battambang end of the family opium business. His desk was much too big for him. Several attendants lounged about and they all looked very severe. One wore uniform with a lot of medal ribbons. Jerry asked for deep background and made a list of several charming dreams: that the Communist enemy was all but beaten; that there was serious discussion about reopening the entire national road system; that tourism was the growth industry of the province. The general's son spoke slow and beautiful French and it clearly gave him great pleasure to hear himself, for he kept his eyes half closed and smiled as he spoke, as if listening to beloved music.

'I may conclude, monsieur, with a word of warning to your country. You are American?'

'English.'

'It is the same. Tell your government, sir. If you do not help us to continue the fight against the Communists, we shall go to the Russians and ask them to replace you in our struggle.'

Oh, mother, thought Jerry. Oh boy. Oh God.

'I will give them that message,' he promised, and made to go.

'*Un instant, monsieur,*' said the senior official sharply, and there was a stirring among his dozing courtiers. He opened a drawer and pulled out an imposing folder. Frost's will, Jerry thought. My death warrant. Stamps for Cat.

'You are a writer?'

'Yes.'

Ko's putting the arm on me. The pen tonight, and wake up with my throat cut tomorrow.

'You were at the Sorbonne, monsieur?' the official enquired.

'Oxford.'

'Oxford in London?'

'Yes.'

'Then you have read the great French poets, monsieur?'

'With intense pleasure,' Jerry replied fervently. The courtiers were looking extremely grave.

'Then perhaps *monsieur* will favour me with his opinion of the following few verses.' In his dignified French, the little official began to read aloud, slowly conducting with his palm.

'*Deux amants assis sur la terre*
Regardaient la mer,'
he began, and continued for perhaps twenty excruciating lines while Jerry listened in mystification.

'*Voilà*,' said the official finally, and put the file aside. '*Vous l'aimez*?' he enquired, severely fixing his eye upon a neutral part of the room.

'*Superbe*,' said Jerry with a gush of enthusiasm. '*Merveilleux*. The sensitivity.'

'They are by whom would you think?'

Jerry grabbed a name at random. 'By Lamartine?'

The senior official shook his head. The courtiers were observing Jerry even more closely.

'Victor Hugo?' Jerry ventured.

'They are by me,' said the official and with a sigh returned his poems to the drawer. The courtiers relaxed. 'See that this literary person has every facility,' he ordered.

Jerry returned to the airport to find it a milling, dangerous chaos. Mercedes raced up and down the approach as if someone had invaded their nest, the forecourt was a turmoil of beacons, motorcycles and sirens; and the hall, when he argued his way through the cordon, was jammed with scared people fighting to read noticeboards, yell at each other and hear the blaring loudspeakers all at the same time. Forcing a path to the information desk, Jerry found it closed. He leapt on the counter and saw the airfield through a hole in the anti-blast board. A squad of armed soldiers was jog-trotting down the empty runway toward a group of white poles where the national flags drooped in the windless air. They lowered two of the flags to half mast, and inside the hall the loudspeakers interrupted themselves to blare a few bars of the national anthem. Over the seething heads, Jerry searched for someone he might talk to. He selected a lank missionary with cropped yellow hair and glasses and a six-inch silver cross pinned to the pocket of his brown shirt. A pair of Cambodians in dog-collars stood miserably beside him.

'*Vous parlez français*?'

'Yes, but I also speak English!'

A lilting, corrective tone. Jerry guessed he was a Dane.

'I'm press. What's the fuss?' He was shouting at the top of his voice.

'Phnom Penh is closed,' the missionary bellowed in reply. 'No planes may leave or land.'

'Why?'

'Khmer Rouge have hit the ammunition dump in the airport. The town is closed till morning at the least.'

The loudspeaker began chattering again. The two priests listened. The missionary stooped nearly double to catch their murmured translation.

'They have made a great damage and devastated half a dozen planes already. Oh yes! They have laid them waste entirely. The authority is also suspecting sabotage. Maybe she also takes some prisoners. Listen, why are they putting an ammunition house inside the airport in the first case? That was most dangerous. What is the reason here?'

'Good question,' Jerry agreed.

He ploughed across the hall. His master plan was already dead, as his master plans usually were. The 'crew only' door was guarded by a pair of very serious crushers and in the tension he saw no chance of brazening his way through. The thrust of the crowd was toward the passenger exit, where harassed ground staff were refusing to accept boarding tickets, and harassed police were being besieged with letters of *laissez passer* designed to put the prominent outside their reach. He let it carry him. At the edges, a team of French traders was screaming for a refund, and the elderly were preparing to settle for the night. But the centre pushed and peered and exchanged fresh rumours, and the momentum carried him steadily to the front. Reaching it, Jerry discreetly took out his cable card and climbed over the improvised barrier. The senior policeman was sleek and well-covered and he watched Jerry disdainfully while his subordinates toiled. Jerry strode straight up to him, his shoulder bag dangling from his hand, and pressed the cable card under his nose.

'*Securité americaine*,' he roared in awful French, and with a snarl at the two men on the swing doors, barged his way on to the tarmac and kept going, while his back waited all the time for a challenge or a warning shot or, in the trigger-happy atmosphere, a shot that was not even a warning. He walked angrily, with rough authority, swinging his shoulder bag, Sarratt-style, to distract. Ahead of him – sixty yards, soon fifty – stood a row of single-engined military trainers without insignia. Beyond lay the caged enclosure, and the freight huts, numbered nine to eighteen, and beyond the freight huts Jerry saw a cluster of hangars and park bays, marked prohibited in just about every language except Chinese. Reaching the trainers, Jerry strode imperiously along the line of them as if he were carrying out an inspection. They were anchored with bricks on wires. Pausing but not stopping, he stabbed irritably at a brick with his buckskin boot, yanked at an aileron and shook his head. From their sandbagged emplacement, to his left, an anti-aircraft guncrew watched him indolently.

'*Qu'est-ce que vous faîtes*?'

Half turning, Jerry cupped his hands to his mouth. 'Watch the damn sky for Christ's sakes,' he yelled in good American, pointing angrily to heaven, and kept going till he reached the high cage. It was open and the huts lay ahead of him. Once past them he would be out of sight of both the terminal and the control tower. He was walking on smashed concrete with couch-grass in the cracks. There was nobody in sight. The huts were weather-board, thirty feet long, ten high, with palm roofs. He reached the first. The boarding on the windows read 'Bomb Cluster Fragmentation Without Fuses'. A trodden dust-path led to the hangars on the other side. Through the gap Jerry glimpsed the parrot colours of parked cargo planes.

'Got you,' Jerry muttered aloud, as he emerged on the safe side of the huts, because there ahead of him, clear as day, like a first sight of the enemy after months of lonely marching, a battered blue-grey DC4 Carvair, fat as a frog, squatted on the crumbling tarmac with her nose cone open. Diesel oil was dripping in a fast black rain from both her starboard engines and a spindly Chinese in a sailing cap laden with military insignia stood smoking under the loading bay while he marked an inventory. Two coolies scurried back and forth with sacks, and a third worked the ancient loading lift. At his feet, chickens scrabbled petulantly. And on the fuselage, in flaming crimson against Drake Ko's faded racing colours, ran the letters OCHART. The others had been lost in a repair job.

Oh, Charlie's indestructible, completely *immortal! Charlie* Marshall, *Mr Tiu, a fantastic half Chinese, all skin and bones and opium and a completely brilliant pilot . . .*

He'd bloody well better be, sport, thought Jerry with a shudder, as the coolies loaded sack after sack through the open nose and into the battered belly of the plane.

The Reverend Ricardo's lifelong Sancho Panza, your Grace, Craw had said, in extension of Lizzie's description. *Half Chow, as the good lady advised us, and the proud veteran of many futile wars.*

Jerry remained standing, making no attempt to conceal himself, dangling the bag from his fist and wearing the apologetic grin of an English stray. Coolies now seemed to be converging on the plane from several points at once: there were many more than two. Turning his back on them, Jerry repeated his routine of strolling along the line of huts, much as he had walked along the line of trainers, or along the corridor toward Frost's room, peering through cracks in the weatherboard and seeing nothing but the occasional broken packing case. *The concession to operate out of Battambang costs half a million US renewable,* Keller had said. At that price, who pays for redecoration? The line of huts broke and he came on four army lorries loaded high with fruit, vegetables and unmarked gunny bags. Their tailboards faced the plane and they sported artillery insignia. Two soldiers stood in each lorry, handing the gunny bags down to the coolies. The sensible thing would have been to drive the lorries on to the tarmac, but a mood of discretion prevailed. *The army likes to be in on things,* Keller had said. *The navy can make millions out of one convoy down the Mekong, the air force is sitting pretty: bombers fly fruit and the choppers can airlift the rich Chinese instead of the wounded out of the siege towns. Fighter boys go a little hungry because they have to land where they take off. But the army really has to scratch around to make a living.*

Jerry was closer to the plane now and could hear the squawking as Charlie Marshall fired commands at the coolies.

The huts began again. Number eighteen had double doors and the name *Indocharter* daubed in green down the woodwork, so that from any distance the letters looked like Chinese characters. In the gloomy interior, a Chinese peasant couple squatted on the dust floor. A tethered pig lay with its head on the old man's slippered foot. Their other possession was a long rush parcel meticulously bound with string. It could have been a corpse. A water jar stood in one corner with two rice bowls at its base. There was nothing else in the hut. 'Welcome to the Indocharter transit lounge,' Jerry thought. With the sweat running down his ribs, he tagged himself to the line of coolies till he drew alongside Charlie Marshall, who went on squawking in Khmer at the top of his voice while his shaking pen checked each load on the inventory.

He wore an oily white short-sleeved shirt with enough gold stripes on the epaulettes to make a full general in anybody's air force. Two American combat patches were stitched to his shirt front, amid an amazing collection of medal ribbons and Communist red stars. One patch read 'Kill a Commie for Christ', and the other 'Christ was a Capitalist at Heart'. His head was turned down and his face was in the shadow of his huge sailing cap, which slopped freely over his ears. Jerry waited for him to look up. The coolies were already yelling for Jerry to move on, but Charlie Marshall kept his head turned stubbornly down while he added and wrote on the inventory and squawked furiously back at them.

'Captain Marshall, I'm doing a story on Ricardo for a London newspaper,' said Jerry quietly. 'I want to ride with you as far as Phnom Penh and ask you some questions.'

As he spoke, he gently laid the volume of *Candide* on top of the inventory, with three one-hundred dollar bills poking outward in a discreet fan. When you want a man to look one way, says the Sarratt school of illusionists, always point him in the other.

'They tell me you like Voltaire,' he said.

'I don't like anybody,' Charlie Marshall retorted in a scratchy falsetto at the inventory, while the cap slipped still lower over his face. 'I hate the whole human race, hear me?' His vituperation, despite its Chinese cadence, was unmistakably French-American. 'Jesus Christ, I hate mankind so damn much that if it don't hurry and blow itself to pieces I'm personally going to buy some bombs and go out there *myself*!'

He had lost his audience. Jerry was halfway up the steel ladder before Charlie Marshall had completed his thesis.

'Voltaire didn't know a damn bloody thing!' he screamed at the next coolie. 'He fought the wrong damn war, hear me? Put it over there you lazy coon and grab another handful! *Dépêche-toi, crétin, oui*?'

But all the same he jammed Voltaire into the back pocket of his baggy trousers.

The inside of the plane was dark and roomy and cool as a cathedral. The seats had been removed, and perforated green shelves like Meccano had been fitted to the walls.

Carcasses of pig and guinea fowl hung from the roof. The rest of the cargo was stowed in the gangway, starting from the tail end, which gave Jerry no good feeling about taking off, and consisted of fruit and vegetables and the gunny bags which Jerry had spotted in the army trucks, marked 'grain', 'rice', 'flour', in letters large enough for the most illiterate narcotics agent to read. But the sticky smell of yeast and molasses which already filled the hold required no labels at all. Some of the bags had been arranged in a ring, to make a sitting area for Jerry's fellow passengers. Chief of these were two austere Chinese men, dressed very poorly in grey, and from their sameness and their demure superiority Jerry at once inferred an expertise of some kind. He remembered explosives-wallahs and pianists he had occasionally ferried thanklessly in and out of badland. Next to them, but respectfully apart, four hillsmen armed to the teeth sat smoking, and cropping from their rice bowls. Jerry guessed Meo or one of the Shan tribes from the northern borders where Charlie Marshall's father had his army, and he guessed from their ease that they were part of the permanent help. In a separate class altogether sat the quality: the colonel of artillery himself, who had thoughtfully supplied the transport and the troop escort, and his companion a senior officer of customs, without whom nothing could have been achieved. They reclined regally in the gangway, on chairs specially provided, watching proudly while the loading continued, and they wore their best uniforms as the ceremony demanded

There was one other member of the party and he lurked alone on top of the cases in the tail, head almost against the roof, and it was not possible to make him out in any detail. He sat with a bottle of whisky to himself, and even a glass to himself. He wore a Fidel Castro hat and a full beard. Gold links glittered on his dark arms, known in those days (to all but those who wore them) as CIA bracelets, on the happy assumption that a man ditched in hostile country could buy his way to safety by doling out a link at a time. But his eyes, as they watched Jerry along the well-oiled barrel of an AK47 automatic rifle, had a fixed brightness. 'He was covering me through the nose cone,' thought Jerry. 'He had a bead on me from the moment I left the hut.'

The two Chinese were cooks, he decided in a moment of inspiration: *cooks* being the underworld nickname for chemists. Keller had said that the Air Opium lines had taken to bringing in the raw base and refining it in Phnom Penh, but were having hell's own job persuading the cooks to come and work in siege conditions.

'Hey you! Voltaire!'

Jerry hurried forward to the edge of the hold. Looking down he saw the old peasant couple standing at the bottom of the ladder and Charlie Marshall trying to wrench the pig from them while he shoved the old woman up the steel ladder.

'When she come up you gotta reach out and grab her, hear me?' he called, holding the pig in his arms. 'She fall down and break her ass we gotta whole lot more trouble with the coons. You some crazy narcotics hero, Voltaire?'

'No.'

'Well, you grab hold of her completely, hear me?'

She started up the ladder. When she had gone a few rungs she began croaking and Charlie Marshall contrived to get the pig under his arm while he gave her a sharp crack on the rump and screamed at her in Chinese. The husband scurried up after her and Jerry hauled them both to safety. Finally Charlie Marshall's own clown's head appeared through the cone, and though it was swamped by the hat, Jerry had his first glimpse of the face beneath: skeletal and brown, with sleepy Chinese eyes and a big French mouth which twisted all ways when he squawked. He shoved the pig through, Jerry grabbed it and carted it, screaming and wriggling, to the old peasants. Then Charlie hauled his own fleshless frame aboard, like a spider climbing out of a drain. At once, the officer of customs and the colonel of artillery stood up, brushed the seats of their uniforms, and progressed swiftly along the gangway to the shadowed man in the Castro hat squatting on the packing cases. Reaching him, they waited respectfully, like sidesmen taking the offertory to the altar.

The linked bracelets flashed, an arm reached down, once, twice, and a devout silence descended while the two men carefully counted a lot of bank notes and everybody watched. In rough unison they returned to the top of the ladder where Charlie Marshall waited with the manifest. The officer of customs signed it, the colonel of artillery looked on approvingly, then they both saluted and disappeared down the ladder. The nose cone juddered to an almost-closed position, Charlie Marshall gave it a kick, flung some matting across the gap, and clambered quickly over the packing cases to an inside stairway leading to the cabin. Jerry clambered after him, and having settled himself into the co-pilot's seat, he silently totted up his blessings.

'We're about five hundred tons overweight. We're leaking oil. We're carrying an armed bodyguard. We're forbidden to take off. We're forbidden to land, Phnom Penh airport's probably got a hole the size of Buckinghamshire. We have an hour and a half of Khmer Rouge between us and salvation, and if anybody turns sour on us the other end, ace operator Westerby is caught with his knickers round his ankles and about two hundred gunny bags of opium base in his arms.'

'You know how to fly this thing?' Charlie Marshall yelled, as he struck at a row of mildewed switches. 'You some kinda great flying hero, Voltaire?'

'I hate it all.'

'Me too.'

Seizing a swat, Charlie Marshall flung himself upon a huge bottle-fly that was buzzing round the windscreen, then started the engines one by one, until the whole dreadful plane was heaving and rattling like a London bus on its last journey home up Clapham Hill. The radio crackled and Charlie Marshall took time off to give an obscene instruction to the control tower, first in Khmer and afterwards, in the best aviation tradition, in English. Heading for the far end of the runway, they passed a couple of gun emplacements and for a moment Jerry expected an overzealous crew to loose off at the fuselage, till in gratitude he remembered the army colonel and his lorries and his pay-off. Another bottle-fly appeared and this time Jerry took possession of the fly swat. The plane seemed to be gathering no speed at all, but half the instruments read zero so he couldn't be sure. The din of the wheels on the runway seemed louder than the engines. Jerry remembered old Sambo's chauffeur driving him back to school: the slow, inevitable progress down the Western by-pass toward Slough and finally Eton.

A couple of the hillsmen had come forward to see the fun and were laughing their heads off. A clump of palm trees came hopping toward them but the plane kept its feet firmly on the ground. Charlie Marshall absently pulled back the stick and retracted the landing gear. Uncertain whether the nose had really lifted, Jerry thought of school again, and competing in the long jump, and recalled the same sensation of not rising, yet ceasing to be on the earth. He felt the jolt and heard the swish of leaves as the under-belly cropped the trees. Charlie Marshall was screaming at the plane to pull itself into the damn air, and for an age they made no height at all, but hung and wheezed a few feet above a winding road which climbed inexorably into a ridge of hills. Charlie Marshall was lighting a cigarette so Jerry held the wheel in front of him and felt the live kick of the rudder. Taking back the controls, Charlie Marshall pointed the plane into a slow bank at the lowest point of the range. He held the turn, crested the range and went on to make a complete circle. As they looked down on the brown rooftops and the river and the airport, Jerry reckoned they had an altitude of a thousand feet. As far as Charlie Marshall was concerned, that was a comfortable cruising height, for now at last he took his hat off and, with the air of a man who had done a good job well, treated himself to a large glass of Scotch from the bottle at his feet. Below them dusk was gathering, and the brown earth was fading softly into mauve.

'Thanks,' said Jerry, accepting the bottle. 'Yes, I think I might.'

Jerry kicked off with a little small-talk – if it is possible to talk small while you are shouting at the top of your voice.

'Khmer Rouge just blew up the airport ammunition dump!' he bellowed. 'It is closed for landing and take-off.'

'They did?' For the first time since Jerry had met him, Charlie Marshall seemed both pleased and impressed.

'They say you and Ricardo were great buddies.'

'We bomb everything. We killed half the human race already. We see more dead people than live people. Plain of Jars, Da Nang, we're such big damn heroes that when we die Jesus Christ going to come down personally with a chopper and fish us out the jungle.'

'They tell me Ric was a great guy for business!'

'Sure! He the greatest! Know how many offshore companies we got, me and Ricardo? Six. We got foundations in Liechtenstein, corporations in Geneva, we got a bank manager in the Dutch Antilles, lawyers, Jesus. Know how much money I got?' He slapped his back pocket. 'Three hundred US exactly. Charlie Marshall and Ricardo killed half the whole damn human race together. Nobody give us no money. My father killed the other half and he got plenty *plenty* money. Ricardo, he always got these crazy schemes always. Shell cases. Jesus. We're going to pay the coons to collect up all the shell cases in Asia, sell 'em for the next war!' The nose dropped and he hauled it up again with a foul French oath. 'Latex! We gotta steal all the latex out of Kampong Cham! We fly to Kampong Cham, we got big choppers, red crosses. So what do we do? We bring out the damn wounded. Hold still, you crazy bastard, hear me?' He was talking to the plane again. In the nose cone, Jerry noticed a long line of bullet holes which had not been very well patched. *Tear here*, he thought absurdly. 'Human hair. We were gonna be millionaires out of hair. All the coon-girls in the villages got to grow long hair and we're going to cut it off and fly it to Bangkok for wigs.'

'Who was it paid Ricardo's debts so that he could fly for Indocharter?'

'Nobody!'

'Somebody told me it was Drake Ko.'

'I never heard of Drake Ko. On my deathbed I tell my mother, my father: bastard Charlie, the General's boy, he never heard of Drake Ko in his life.'

'What did Ricardo do for Ko that was so special that Ko paid all his debts?'

Charlie Marshall drank some whisky straight from the bottle, then handed it to Jerry. His fleshless hands shook wildly whenever he took them off the stick, and his nose ran all the while. Jerry wondered how many pipes a day he was up to. He had once known a *pied-noir* Corsican hotelier in Luang Prabang who needed sixty to do a good day's work. *Captain Marshall never flies in the mornings*, he thought.

'Americans always in a hurry,' Charlie Marshall complained, shaking his head. 'Know why we gotta take this stuff to Phnom Penh now? Everybody impatient. Everybody want quickshot these days. Nobody got time to smoke. Everybody got to turn on quick. You wanta kill the human race, you gotta take time, hear me?'

Jerry tried again. One of the four engines had given up, but another had developed a howl as if from a broken silencer, so that he had to yell even louder than before.

'What did Ricardo do for all that money?' he repeated.

'Listen, Voltaire, okay? I don't like politics, I'm just a simple opium smuggler, okay? You like politics you go back below and talk to those crazy Shans. "You can't eat politics. You can't screw politics. You can't smoke politics." He tell my father.'

'Who did?'

'Drake Ko tell my father, my father tell me and me I tell the whole damn human race! Drake Ko some philosopher, hear me?'

For its own reasons the plane had begun falling steadily

till it was a couple of hundred feet above the paddies. They saw a village and cooking fires burning and figures running wildly toward the trees, and Jerry wondered seriously whether Charlie Marshall had noticed. But at the last minute, like a patient jockey, he hauled and leaned and finally got the horse's head up and they both had some more Scotch.

'You know him well?'

'Who?'

'Ko.'

'I never met him in my life, Voltaire. You wanna talk about Drake Ko, you go ask my father. He cut your throat.'

'How about Tiu? – Tell me, who's the couple with the pig?' Jerry yelled, to keep the conversation going while Charlie took back the bottle for another pull.

'Haw people, down from Chiang Mai. They worried about their lousy son in Phnom Penh. They think he too damn hungry so they take him a pig.'

'So how about Tiu?'

'I never heard of Mr Tiu, hear me?'

'Ricardo was seen up in Chiang Mai three months ago,' Jerry yelled.

'Yeah, well Ric's a damn fool,' said Charlie Marshall with feeling. 'Ric's gotta keep his ass out of Chiang Mai or somebody shoot it right off. Anybody lying dead they gotta keep their damn mouth shut, hear me? I say to him: "Ric, you my partner. Keep your damn mouth shut and your ass out of sight or certain people get personally pretty mad with you."'

The plane entered a raincloud and at once began losing height fast. Rain raced over the iron deck and down the insides of the windows. Charlie Marshall flicked some switches up and down, there was a bleeping from the controls panel and a couple of pinlights came on, which no amount of swearing could put out. To Jerry's amazement they began climbing again, though in the racing cloud he doubted his judgment of the angle. Glancing behind him in order to check, he was in time to glimpse the bearded figure of the dark-skinned paymaster in the Fidel Castro cap retreating down the cabin ladder, holding his AK47 by the barrel. They continued climbing, the rain ended and the night surrounded them like another country. The stars broke suddenly above them, they jolted over the moonlit crevasses of the cloud tops, they lifted again, the cloud vanished for good, and Charlie Marshall put on his hat and announced that both starboard engines had now ceased to play any part in the festivities. In this moment of respite, Jerry asked his maddest question.

'So where's Ricardo now, sport? Got to find him, see. Promised my paper I'd have a word with him. Can't disappoint them, can we?'

Charlie Marshall's sleepy eyes had all but closed. He was sitting in a half-trance, with his head against the seat and the brim of his hat over his nose.

'What that, Voltaire? You speak at all?'

'Where is Ricardo now?'

'Ric?' Charlie Marshall repeated, glancing at Jerry in a sort of wonder. 'Where Ricardo is, Voltaire?'

'That's it, sport. Where is he? I'd like to have an exchange of views with him. That's what the three hundred bucks were about. There's another five hundred if you could find the time to arrange an introduction.'

Springing suddenly to life, Charlie Marshall delved for the *Candide* and slammed it into Jerry's lap while he delivered himself of a furious outburst.

'I don't know where Ricardo is *ever*, hear me? I never don't want a friend in my life. If I see that crazy Ricardo I shoot his balls right off in the street, hear me? He dead. So he can stay dead till he dies. He tell everyone he got killed. So maybe for once in my life I'm going to believe that bastard!'

Pointing the plane angrily into the cloud, he let it fall toward the slow flashes of Phnom Penh's artillery batteries to make a perfect three point landing in what to Jerry was pitch darkness. He waited for the burst of machine-gun fire from the ground defences, he waited for the sickening free-fall as they nose-dived into a mammoth crater, but all he saw, quite suddenly, was a newly assembled *revêtement* of the familiar mud-filled ammunition boxes, arms open and palely lit, waiting to receive them. As they taxied toward it a brown jeep pulled in front of them with a green light winking on the back, like a flashlight being turned on and off by hand. The plane was humping over grass. Hard beside the *revêtement* Jerry could see a pair of green lorries, and a tight knot of waiting figures, looking anxiously toward them, and behind them the dark shadow of a twin-engined sports plane. They parked, and Jerry heard at once from the hold beneath their penthouse the creak of the nose cone opening, followed by the clatter of feet on the iron ladder and the quick call and answer of voices. The speed of their departure took him by surprise. But he heard something else that turned his blood cold, and made him charge down the steps to the belly of the plane.

'Ricardo!' he yelled. 'Stop! Ricardo!'

But the only passengers left were the old couple clutching their pig and their parcel. Seizing the steel ladder, he let himself fall, jolting his spine as he hit the tarmac. The jeep had already left with the Chinese cooks and their Shan bodyguard. As he ran forward, Jerry could see the jeep racing for an open gateway at the perimeter of the airfield. It passed through, two sentries slammed the gates and took up their position as before. Behind him, the helmeted flight-handlers were already swarming toward the Carvair. A couple of lorryloads of police looked on and for a moment the western fool in Jerry was seduced into thinking they might be playing some restraining rôle, till he realised they were Phnom Penh's guard-of-honour for a three-ton load of opium. But his main eye was for one figure only, and that was the tall bearded man with the Fidel Castro hat and the AK47 and the heavy limp that sounded like a hard-soft drumbeat as the rubber-soled flying boots hobbled down the steel ladder. Jerry saw him just. The door of the little Beechcraft waited open for him, and there were two ground-crew poised to help him in. As he reached them they held out their hands for the rifle but Ricardo waved them aside. He had turned and was looking for Jerry. For a second they saw each other. Jerry was falling and Ricardo was lifting the gun, and for twenty seconds Jerry reviewed his life from birth till now while a few more bullets ripped and whined round the battle-torn airfield. By the time Jerry looked up again the firing had stopped, Ricardo was inside the plane and his helpers were pulling away the chocks. As the little plane lifted into the flashes, Jerry ran like the devil for the darkest part of the perimeter before anybody else decided that his presence was obstructive to good trading.

Just a lovers' tiff, he told himself, sitting in the cab, as he held his hands over his head and tried to damp down the wild shaking of his chest. That's what you get for trying to play footsy-footsy with an old flame of Lizzie Worthington.

Somewhere a rocket fell and he didn't give a damn.

He allowed Charlie Marshall two hours, though he reckoned one was generous. It was past curfew but the day's crisis had not ended with the dark, there were traffic checks all the way to le Phnom and the sentries held their machine pistols at the ready. In the square, two men were screaming at each other by torchlight before a gathering crowd. Further down the boulevard, troops had surrounded a floodlit house and were leaning against the wall of it, fingering their guns. The driver said the secret police had made an arrest there. A colonel and his people were still inside with a suspected agitator. In the hotel forecourt, tanks were parked, and in his bedroom he found Luke lying on the bed drinking contentedly.

'Any water?' Jerry asked.

'Yip.'

He turned on the bath and started to undress until he remembered the Walther.

'Filed?' he asked.

'Yip,' said Luke again. 'And so have you.'

'Ha ha.'

'I had Keller cable Stubbsie under your byline.'

'The airport story?'

Luke handed him a tearsheet. 'Added some true Westerby colour. How the buds are bursting in the cemeteries. Stubbsie loves you.'

'Well thanks.'

In the bathroom Jerry unstuck the Walther from the plaster and slipped it in the pocket of his jacket where he would be able to get at it.

'Where we going tonight?' Luke called, through the closed door.

'Nowhere.'

'Hell's that mean?'

'I've got a date.'

'A woman?'

'Yes.'

'Take Lukie. Three in a bed.'

Jerry sank gratefully into the tepid water. 'No.'

'Call her. Tell her to whip in a whore for Lukie. Listen, there's that hooker from Santa Barbara downstairs. I'm not proud. I'll bring her.'

'No.'

'For Christ's sakes,' Luke shouted, now serious. 'Why the hell not?' He had come right to the locked door to make his protest.

'Sport, you've got to get off my back,' Jerry advised. 'Honest. I love you but you're not everything to me, right? So stay off.'

'Thorn in your breeches, huh?' Long silence. 'Well don't get your ass shot off, pardner, it's a stormy night out there.'

When Jerry returned to the bedroom, Luke lay on the bed in the foetal position staring at the wall and drinking methodically.

'You know you're worse than a bloody woman,' Jerry told him, pausing at the door to look back at him.

The whole childish exchange would not have caused another moment's thought, had it not been for the way things turned out afterwards.

* * *

This time Jerry didn't bother with the bell on the gate, but climbed the wall and grazed his hands on the broken glass that ran along the top of it. He didn't make for the front door either, or go through the formality of watching the brown legs standing on the bottom stair. Instead, he stood in the garden waiting for the clump of his heavy landing to fade and for his eyes and ears to catch a sign of habitation from the big villa which loomed darkly above him with the moon behind it.

A car drew up without lights and two figures got out, by their size and quietness Cambodian. They pressed the gate bell, and at the front door murmured the magic password through the crack, and were instantly, silently admitted. Jerry tried to fathom the layout. It puzzled him that no telltale smell escaped either from the front of the house or into the garden where he stood. There was no wind. He knew that for a large *divan* secrecy was vital, not because the law was punitive, but because the bribes were. The villa possessed a chimney and a courtyard and two floors: a place to live comfortably as a French *colon*, with a little family of concubines and half-caste children. The kitchen , he guessed, would be given over to preparation. The safest place to smoke would undoubtedly be upstairs, in rooms which looked on to the courtyard. And since there was no smell from the front door, Jerry reckoned that they were using the rear of the courtyard rather than the wings or the front.

He trod soundlessly till he came to the paling which marked the rear boundary. It was lush with flowers and creeper. A barred window gave a first foothold to his buckskin boot, an overflow pipe a second, a high extractor fan a third, and as he climbed past it to the upper balcony he caught the smell he expected: warm and sweet and beckoning. On the balcony there was still no light, though the two Cambodian girls who squatted there were easily visible in the moonlight, and he could see their scared eyes fixing him as he appeared out of the sky. Beckoning them to their feet, he walked them ahead of him, led by the smell. The shelling had stopped, leaving the night to the geckos. Jerry remembered that Cambodians liked to gamble on the number of times they cheeped: tomorrow will be a lucky day; tomorrow won't; tomorrow I will take a bride; no, the day after. The girls were very young and they must have been waiting for the customers to send for them. At the rush door they hesitated and stared unhappily back at him. Jerry signalled and they began pulling aside layers of matting until a pale light gleamed on to the balcony, no stronger than a candle. He stepped inside, keeping the girls ahead of him.

The room must once have been the master bedroom, with a second, smaller room connecting. He had his hand on the shoulder of one girl. The other followed submissively. Twelve customers lay in the first room, all men. A few girls lay between them, whispering. Barefooted coolies ministered, moving with great deliberation from one recumbent body to the next, threading a pellet on to the needle, lighting it and holding it across the bowl of the pipe while the customer took a long steady draught and the pellet burned itself out. The conversation was slow and murmured and intimate, broken by soft ripples of grateful laughter. Jerry recognised the wise Swiss from the Counsellor's dinner party. He was chatting to a fat Cambodian. No one was interested in Jerry. Like the orchids at Lizzie Worthington's apartment block, the girls authenticated him.

'Charlie Marshall,' Jerry said quietly. A coolie pointed to the next room. Jerry dismissed the two girls and they slipped away. The second room was smaller and Marshall lay in the corner, while a Chinese girl in an elaborate *cheongsam* crouched over him preparing his pipe. Jerry supposed she was the daughter of the house, and that Charlie Marshall was getting the grand treatment because he was both an habitué and a supplier. He knelt the other side of him. An old man was watching from the doorway. The girl watched also, the pipe still in her hands.

'What you want, Voltaire? Why don't you leave me be?'

'Just a little stroll, sport. Then you can come back.'

Taking his arm, Jerry lifted him gently to his feet, while the girl helped.

'How many has he had?' he asked the girl. She held up three fingers.

'And how many does he like?' he asked.

She lowered her head, smiling. A whole lot more, she was saying.

Charlie Marshall walked shakily at first, but by the time they reached the balcony he was prepared to argue, so Jerry lifted him up and carried him across his body like a fire victim, down the wooden steps and across the courtyard. The old man bowed them obligingly through the front door, a grinning coolie held the gate on to the street, and both were clearly very thankful to Jerry for showing so much tact. They had gone perhaps fifty yards when a pair of Chinese boys came rushing down the road at them, yelling and waving sticks like small paddles. Setting Charlie Marshall upright but holding him firmly with his left hand, Jerry let the first boy strike, deflected the paddle then hit him at half strength with a two-knuckle punch just below the eye. The boy ran away, his friend after him. Still clutching Charlie Marshall, Jerry walked him till they came to the river, and a heavy patch of darkness, then he sat him down on the bank like a puppet in the sloped, dry grass.

'You gonna blow my brains out, Voltaire?'

'We're going to have to leave that to the opium, sport,' said Jerry.

Jerry liked Charlie Marshall and in a perfect world he would have been glad to spend an evening with him at the *fumerie* and hear the story of his wretched but extraordinary life. But now his fist grasped Charlie Marshall's tiny arm remorselessly lest he took it into his hollow head to bolt; for he had a feeling Charlie could run very fast when he became desperate. He half-lay, therefore, much as he had lounged among the magic mountain of possessions in old Pet's place, on his left haunch and his left elbow, holding Charlie Marshall's wrist into the mud, while Charlie Marshall lay flat on his back. From the river thirty feet below them came the murmured chant of the sampans as they drifted like long leaves across the golden moon-path. From the sky – now in front, now behind them – came the occasional ragged flashes of outgoing gunfire as some bored battery commander decided to justify his existence. Now and then, from much nearer, came the lighter, sharper snap as the Khmer Rouge replied, but once more these were only tiny interludes between the racket of the geckos, and the greater silence beyond. By the moonlight Jerry looked at his watch, then at the crazed face, trying to calculate the strength of Charlie Marshall's cravings. Like a baby's feed, he thought. If Charlie was a night smoker and slept in the mornings, then his needs must come on fast. The wet on his face was already unearthly. It flowed from the heavy pores, and from the stretched eyes, and from the sniffing, weeping nose. It channelled itself meticulously along the engraved creases, making neat reservoirs in the caverns.

'Jesus, Voltaire. Ricardo's my friend. He got a lot of philosophy, that guy. You want to hear him talk, Voltaire. You wanna hear his ideas.'

'Yes,' Jerry agreed. 'I do.'

Charlie Marshall grabbed hold of Jerry's hand.

'Voltaire, these are good guys, hear me? Mr Tiu . . . Drake Ko. They don't want to hurt nobody. They wanna do business. They got something to sell, they got people buying it! It's a service! Nobody gets his ricebowl broken. Why you want to screw that up? You're a nice guy, yourself. I saw. You carry the old boy's pig, okay? Whoever saw a roundeye carry a slanteye pig before? But Jesus, Voltaire, you screw it out of me, they will kill you very completely because that Mr Tiu, he's a businesslike and very philosophical gentleman, hear me? They kill *me*, they kill *Ricardo*, they kill *you*, they kill the whole damn human race!'

The artillery fired a barrage, and this time the jungle replied with a small salvo of missiles, perhaps six, which hissed over their heads like whirring boulders from a catapult. Moments later they heard the detonations somewhere in the centre of the town. After them, nothing. Not the wail of a fire engine, not the siren of an ambulance.

'Why would they kill *Ricardo*?' Jerry asked. 'What's *Ricardo* done wrong?'

'Voltaire! Ricardo's my friend! Drake Ko my father's friend! Those old men big brothers, they fight some lousy war together in Shanghai about two hundred and fifty years ago, okay? I go see my father. I tell him: "Father, you gotta love me once. You gotta quit calling me your spider-bastard, and you gotta tell your good friend Drake Ko to take the heat off Ricardo. You gotta say, 'Drake Ko, that Ricardo and my Charlie, they are like you and me. They brothers, same as us. They learn to fly together in Oklahoma, they kill the human race together. And they some pretty good friends. And that's a fact.'" My father hate me very bad, okay?'

'Okay.'

'But he send Drake Ko a damn long personal message all the same.'

Charlie Marshall breathed in, on and on, as if his little breast could scarcely hold enough air to feed him. 'That Lizzie. She some woman. Lizzie, she go personally to Drake Ko herself. Also on a very private basis. And she say to him: "Mr Ko, you gotta take the heat off Ric." That's a very delicate situation there, Voltaire. We all got to hold on to each other tight or we fall off the crazy mountain top, hear me? Voltaire, let me go. I beg! I completely beg for Christ's sake, *je m'abîme*, hear me? That's all I know!'

Watching him, listening to his racked outburst, how he collapsed and rallied and broke again and rallied less, Jerry felt he was witnessing the last martyred writhing of a friend. His instinct was to lead Charlie slowly and let him ramble. His dilemma was that he didn't know how much time he had before whatever happens to an addict happened. He asked questions but often Charlie didn't seem to hear them. At other times he appeared to answer questions Jerry hadn't put. And sometimes a delayed action mechanism threw out an answer to a question which Jerry had long abandoned. At Sarratt, the inquisitors said, a broken man was dangerous because he paid you money he didn't have in order to buy your love. But for whole precious minutes Charlie could pay nothing at all.

'Drake Ko never went to Vientiane in his life!' Charlie yelled suddenly. 'You crazy, Voltaire! A big guy like Ko bothering with a dirty little Asian town? Drake Ko some philosopher, Voltaire! You wanna watch that guy pretty careful!' Everyone, it seemed, was some philosopher – or everyone but Charlie Marshall. 'In Vientiane nobody even heard Ko's name! Hear me, Voltaire?'

At another point, Charlie Marshall wept and seized Jerry's hands and enquired between sobs whether Jerry also had had a father.

'Yes, sport, I did,' said Jerry patiently. 'And in his way, he was a general too.'

Over the river two white flares shed an amazing daylight, inspiring Charlie to reminisce on the hardships of their early days together in Vientiane. Sitting bolt upright, he drew a house in diagram in the mud. That's where Lizzie and Ric and Charlie Marshall lived, he said proudly: in a stinking flea-hut on the edge of town, a place so lousy even the geckos got sick from it. Ric and Lizzie had the royal suite, which was the only room this flea-hut contained, and Charlie's job was to keep out of the way and pay the rent and fetch the booze. But the memory of their dreadful economic plight moved Charlie suddenly to a fresh storm of tears.

'So what did you live on, sport?' Jerry asked, expecting nothing from the question. 'Come on. It's over now. What did you live on?'

More tears while Charlie confessed to a monthly allowance from his father, whom he loved and revered.

'That crazy Lizzie' – said Charlie through his grief – 'that crazy Lizzie she make trips to Hong Kong for Mellon.'

Somehow Jerry contrived to keep himself steady in order not to shake Charlie from his course.

'*Mellon.* Who's this Mellon?' he asked. But the soft tone made Charlie sleepy, and he started playing with the mud-house, adding a chimney and smoke.

'Come on damn you! *Mellon. Mellon*!' Jerry shouted straight into Charlie's face, trying to shock him into replying. '*Mellon*, you hashed-out wreck! Trips to Hong Kong!' Lifting Charlie to his feet he shook him like a rag doll, but it took a lot more shaking to produce the answer, and in the course of it Charlie Marshall implored Jerry to understand what it was like to love, really to love, a crazy roundeye hooker and know you could never have her, even for a night.

Mellon was a creepy English trader, nobody knew what he did. A little of this, a little of that, Charlie said. People were scared of him. Mellon said he could get Lizzie into the bigtime heroin trail. 'With your passport and your body,' Mellon had told her, 'you can go in and out of Hong Kong like a princess.'

Exhausted, Charlie sank to the ground and crouched before his mud-house. Squatting beside him, Jerry fastened his fist to the back of Charlie's collar, careful not to hurt him.

'So she did that for him did she, Charlie? Lizzie carried for Mellon.' With his palm, he gently tipped Charlie's head round till his lost eyes were staring straight at him.

'Lizzie don't carry for *Mellon*, Voltaire,' Charlie corrected him. 'Lizzie carry for *Ricardo*. Lizzie don't love Mellon. She love *Ric* and me.'

Staring glumly at the mud-house, Charlie burst suddenly into raucous dirty laughter, which then petered out with no explanation.

'You louse it up, Lizzie!' Charlie called teasingly, poking a finger into the mud door. 'You louse it up as usual, honey! You talk too much. Why you tell everyone you Queen of England? Why you tell everyone you some great spook-lady? Mellon get very very mad with you, Lizzie. Mellon throw you out, right out on your ass. Ric got pretty mad too, remember? Ric smash you up real bad and Charlie have to take you to the doctor in the middle of the damn night, remember? You got one hell of a big mouth, Lizzie, hear me? You my sister, but you got the biggest damn mouth *ever*!'

Till Ricardo closed it for her, Jerry thought, remembering the grooves on her chin. Because she spoiled the deal with Mellon.

Still crouching at Charlie's side and clutching him by the scruff, Jerry watched the world around him vanish and in place of it he saw Sam Collins sitting in his car below Star Heights, with a clear view of the eighth floor, while he studied the racing page of the newspaper at eleven o'clock at night. Not even the clump of a rocket falling quite close could distract him from that freezing vision. Also he heard Craw's voice above the mortar fire, intoning on the subject of Lizzie's criminality. When funds were low, Craw had said, Ricardo made her carry little parcels across frontiers for him.

And how did London-town learn *that*, your Grace – he would have liked to ask old Craw – if not from Sam Collins alias Mellon himself?

A three-second rainstorm had washed away Charlie's mud-house and he was furious about it. He was splashing around on all fours looking for it, weeping and cursing frantically. The fit passed, and he started talking about his father again, and how the old man had found employment for his natural son with a certain distinguished Vientiane airline – though Charlie till then had been quite keen to get out of flying for good on account of losing his nerve.

One day, it seemed, the General just lost patience with Charlie. He called together his bodyguard and came down from his hilltop in the Shans to a little opium town called Fang not far inside the Thai border. There, after the fashion of patriarchs the world over, the General rebuked Charlie for his spendthrift ways.

Charlie had a special squawk for his father, and a special

way of puffing out his wasted cheeks in military disapproval:

"'So you better do some proper damn work for a change, hear me, you *kwailo* spider-bastard? You better stay away from horse gambling, hear me, and strong liquor, and opium. And you better take those Commie stars off your tits and sack that stink-friend Ricardo of yours. And you better cease financing his woman, hear me? Because I don't gonna keep you one day more, not one *hour*, you spider-bastard, and I hate you so much one day I kill you because you remind me of that Corsican whore your mother!"'

Then the job itself, and Charlie's father the General still speaking:

"'Certain very fine Chiu Chow gentlemen who are pretty good friends of pretty good friends of mine, hear me, happen to have a controlling interest in a certain aviation company. Also I got certain shares in that company. Also this company happens to bear the distinguished title of Indocharter Aviation. Why you laugh, you *kwailo* ape! Don't laugh at me! So these good friends, they do me a favour to assist me in my disgrace for my three-legged spider-bastard son and I pray sincerely you may fall out of the sky and break your *kwailo* neck."'

So Charlie flew his father's opium for Indocharter: one, two flights a week at first, but regular, honest work and he liked it. His nerve came back, he steadied down, and he felt real gratitude toward his old man. He tried, of course, to get the Chiu Chow boys to take Ricardo too but they wouldn't. After a few months they did agree to pay Lizzie twenty bucks a week to sit in the front office and sweetmouth the clients. These were the golden days, Charlie implied. Charlie and Lizzie earned the money, Ricardo wasted it on ever crazier enterprises, everybody was happy, everybody was employed. Till one evening, like a Nemesis, Tiu appeared and screwed the whole thing up. He appeared just as they were locking up the company's offices, straight off the pavement without an appointment, asking for Charlie Marshall by name and describing himself as part of the company's Bangkok management. The Chiu Chow boys came out of the back office, took one look at Tiu, vouched for his good faith, and made themselves scarce.

Charlie broke off in order to weep on Jerry's shoulder.

'Now listen to me carefully, sport,' Jerry urged. 'Listen. This is the bit I like, okay? You tell me this bit carefully, and I'll take you home. Promise. *Please.*'

But Jerry had it wrong. It was no longer a matter of making Charlie talk. Jerry was now the drug on which Charlie Marshall depended. It was no longer a matter of holding him down, either. Charlie Marshall clutched Jerry's breast as if it were the last raft on his lonely sea, and their conversation had become a desperate monologue from which Jerry stole his facts while Charlie Marshall cringed and begged and howled for his tormentor's attention, making jokes and laughing at them through his tears. Downriver one of Lon Nol's machine guns which had not yet been sold to the Khmer Rouge was firing tracer into the jungle by the light of another flare. Long golden bolts flowed in streams above and below the water, and lit a small cave where they disappeared into the trees.

Charlie's sweat-soaked hair was pricking Jerry's chin and Charlie was gabbling and dribbling all at the same time.

'Mr Tiu don't wanna talk in no office, Voltaire. Oh no! Mr Tiu don't dress too good, either. Tiu very Chiu Chow person, he use Thai passport like Drake Ko, he use crazy name and keep a very very low appearance when he come to Vientiane. "Captain Marshall," he say to me, "how you like earn a lot of extra cash by performing certain interesting and varied work outside the Company's hours, tell me? How you like fly a certain unconventional journey for me once? They tell me you some pretty damn fine pilot these days, very steady. How you like earn yourself not less than maybe four to five thousand bucks for one day's work, not even a whole day? How would that personally attract you, Captain Marshall?" "Mr Tiu," I tell him' – Charlie is shouting hysterically now – '"without in any way prejudicing my negotiating position, Mr Tiu, for five thousand bucks US in my present serene mood I go down to hell for you and I bring you the devil's balls back." Mr Tiu say he come back one day and I gotta keep my damn mouth shut.'

Suddenly Charlie had changed to his father's voice and he was calling himself a spider-bastard and the son of a Corsican whore: till gradually it dawned on Jerry that Charlie was describing the next episode in the story.

Amazingly, it turned out, Charlie had kept to himself the secret of Tiu's offer until he next saw his father, this time in Chiang Mai for a celebration of the Chinese New Year. He had not told Ric, and he had not even told Lizzie, maybe because at this point they weren't getting on too well any more, and Ric was having himself a lot of women on the side.

The General's counsel was not encouraging.

'"Don't you touch that horse! That Tiu got some pretty highly big connections, and they all a bit too special for a crazy little spider-bastard like you, hear me! Jesus Christ, who ever heard of a Swatownese give five thousand dollars to a lousy half-*kwailo* to improve his mind with travel?"'

'So you passed the deal to Ric, right?' said Jerry quickly. 'Right, Charlie? You told Tiu "sorry but try Ricardo". Is that how it went?'

But Charlie Marshall was missing believed dead. He had fallen straight off Jerry's chest and lay flat in the mud with his eyes closed and only his occasional gulps for breath – greedy, rasping draughts of it – and the crazy beating of his pulse where Jerry held his wrist, testified to the life inside the frame.

'Voltaire,' Charlie whispered. 'On the Bible, Voltaire. You're a good man. Take me home. Jesus, take me home, Voltaire.'

Stunned, Jerry stared at the prone and broken figure and knew that he had to ask one more question, even if it was the last in both their lives. Reaching down, he dragged Charlie to his feet for the last time. And there, for an hour in the black road, struggling on his arm, while more aimless barrages stabbed the darkness, Charlie Marshall screamed, and begged, and swore he would love Jerry always if only he didn't have to reveal what arrangements his friend Ricardo had made for his survival. But Jerry explained that without that, the mystery was not even half revealed. And perhaps Charlie Marshall, in his ruin and despair, as he sobbed out the forbidden secrets, understood Jerry's reasoning: that in a city about to be given back to the jungle, there was no destruction unless it was complete.

As gently as he could, Jerry carried Charlie Marshall down the road, back to the villa and up the steps, where the same silent faces gratefully received him. I should have got more, he thought. I should have told him more as well: I didn't tend the two-way traffic in the way they ordered. I stayed too long with the business of Lizzie and Sam Collins. I did it upside-down, I foozled my shopping list, I loused it up like Lizzie. He tried to feel sorry about that but he couldn't, and the things he remembered best were the things that weren't on the list at all, and they were the same things that stood up in his mind like monuments while he typed his message to dear old George.

He typed with the door locked and the gun in his belt. There was no sign of Luke, so Jerry assumed he had gone off to a whorehouse still in his drunken sulk. It was a long signal, the longest of his career: 'Know this much in case you don't hear from me again.' He reported his contact with the Counsellor, he gave his next port of call, and gave Ricardo's address, and a portrait of Charlie Marshall, and of the three-sided household in the flea-hut, but only in the most formal terms, and he left out entirely his newfound knowledge regarding the rôle played by the unsavoury Sam Collins. After all, if they knew it already, what was the point of telling it to them again? He left out the place names and the proper names and made a separate key of them, then spent another hour putting the two messages into a first-base code which wouldn't fool a cryptographer for five minutes, but was beyond the ken of ordinary mortals, and of mortals like his host the British

Counsellor. He ended with a reminder to housekeepers to check whether Blatt and Rodney had made that latest money-draft to Cat. He burned the *en clair* texts, rolled the encoded versions into a newspaper, then lay on the newspaper and dozed, the gun awkwardly at his side. At six he shaved, transferred his signals to a paperback novel which he felt able to part with, and took himself for a walk in the morning quiet. In the *place*, the Counsellor's car was parked conspicuously. The Counsellor himself was parked equally conspicuously on the terrace of a pretty bistro, wearing a Riviera straw hat reminiscent of Craw, and treating himself to hot croissants and *café au lait*. Seeing Jerry, he gave an elaborate wave. Jerry wandered over to him.

'Morning,' said Jerry.

'Ah, you've got it! Good man!' the Counsellor cried, bounding to his feet. 'Been *longing* to read it ever since it came out!'

Parting with the signal, conscious only of its omissions, Jerry had a feeling of end-of-term. He might come back, he might not, but things would never be quite the same again.

The exact circumstances of Jerry's departure from Phnom Penh are relevant because of Luke, later.

For the first part of the morning that remained, Jerry pursued his obsessional search for cover, which was the natural antidote, perhaps, to his increasing sense of nakedness. Diligently he went on the stomp for refugee and orphan stories which he filed through Keller at midday, together with a quite decent atmosphere piece on his visit to Battambang, which though never used has at least a place in his dossier. There were two refugee camps at that time, both blossoming, one in an enormous hotel on the Bassac, Sihanouk's personal and unfinished dream of paradise; one in the marshalling yards near the airport, two or three families packed in each carriage. He visited both and they were the same: young Australian heroes struggling with the impossible, the only water filthy, a rice handout twice a week and the children chirruping 'hi' and 'bye bye' after him, while he trailed his Cambodian interpreter up and down their lines, besieging everyone with questions, acting large and looking for that extra something that would melt Stubbsie's heart.

At a travel office he noisily booked a passage to Bangkok in a feeble attempt to brush over his tracks. Making for the airport, he had a sudden sense of *déjà vu*. Last time I was here, I went water-skiing, he thought. The roundeye traders kept houseboats moored along the Mekong. And for a moment he saw himself – and the city – in the days when the Cambodian war still had a certain ghastly innocence: ace operator Westerby, risking mono for the first time, bouncing boyishly over the brown water of the Mekong, towed by a jolly Dutchman in a speed launch which burned enough petrol to feed a family for a week. The greatest hazard was the two-foot wave, he remembered, which rolled down the river every time the guards on the bridge let off a depth charge to prevent Khmer Rouge divers from blowing it up. But now the river was theirs, so was the jungle. And so, tomorrow or the next day, was the town.

At the airport, he ditched the Walther in a rubbish bin and at the last minute bribed his way aboard a plane to Saigon which was his destination. Taking off, he wondered who had the longer expectation of survival: himself or the city.

Luke, on the other hand, with the key to Jerry's Hong Kong flat nestling in his pocket presumably – or more properly to Deathwish the Hun's flat – flew to Bangkok, and as luck had it he flew unwittingly under Jerry's name, since Jerry was on the flight list, and Luke was not, and the remaining places were all taken. In Bangkok he attended a hasty bureau conference at which the magazine's local manpower was carved up between various bits of the crumbling Vietnam front. Luke got Hue and Da Nang, and accordingly left for Saigon next day, and thence north by connecting midday plane.

Contrary to later rumour, the two men did not meet in Saigon.

Nor did they meet in the course of the Northern rollback.

The last they saw of each other, in any mutual sense, was on that final evening in Phnom Penh, when Jerry had bawled Luke out and Luke had sulked, and that is a fact – a commodity which was afterwards notoriously hard to come by.

Chapter 17

RICARDO

At no time in the entire case did George Smiley hold the ring with such tenacity as now. In the Circus, nerves were stretched to snapping point. The bloody inertia and the bouts of frenzy which Sarratt habitually warned against became one and the same. Each day that brought no hard news from Hong Kong was another day of disaster. Jerry's long signal was put under the microscope and held to be ambiguous, then neurotic. Why had he not pressed Marshall harder? Why had he not raised the Russian spectre again? He should have grilled Charlie about the goldseam, he should have carried on where he left off with Tiu. Had he forgotten that his main job was to sow alarm and only afterwards to obtain information? As to his obsession with that wretched daughter of his – God Almighty, doesn't the fellow *know* what signals cost? (They seemed to forget it was the Cousins who were footing the bill.) And what was all this about having no more to do with British Embassy officials standing proxy for the absent Circus resident? All right, there had been a delay in the pipeline in getting the signal across from the Cousins' side of the house. Jerry had still run Charlie Marshall to earth, hadn't he? It was absolutely no part of a fieldman's job to dictate the do's and don'ts to London. Housekeeping Section, who had arranged the contract, wanted him rebuked by return.

Pressure from outside the Circus was even fiercer. Colonial Wilbraham's faction had not been idle, and the Steering Group, in a startling about-turn, decided that the

Governor of Hong Kong should after all be informed of the case, and soon. There was high talk of calling him back to London on a pretext. The panic had arisen because Ko had once more been received at Government House, this time at one of the Governor's talk-in suppers, at which influential Chinese were invited to air their opinions off the record.

By contrast, Saul Enderby and his fellow hardliners pulled the opposite way: 'To hell with the Governor. What we want is full partnership with the Cousins immediately!' George should go to Martello *today*, said Enderby, and make a clean breast of the whole case, and invite them to take over the last stage of development. He should stop playing hide-and-seek about Nelson, he should admit that he had no resources, he should let the Cousins compute the possible intelligence dividend for themselves, and if they brought the job off, so much the better: let them claim the credit on Capitol Hill, to the confusion of their enemies. The result of this generous and timely gesture, Enderby argued – coming bang in the middle of the Vietnam fiasco – would be an indissoluble intelligence partnership for years to come, a view which, in his shifty way, Lacon seemed to support. Caught in the crossfire, Smiley suddenly found himself saddled with a double reputation. The Wilbraham set branded him as anti-colonial and pro-American, while Enderby's men accused him of ultra-conservatism in the handling of the special relationship. Much more serious, however, was Smiley's impression that some hint of the row had reached Martello by other routes, and that he would be able to exploit it. For example, Molly Meakin's sources spoke of a burgeoning relationship between Enderby and Martello at the personal level, and not just because their children were all being educated at the Lycée in South Kensington. It seemed that the two men had taken to fishing together in Scotland at weekends, where Enderby had a bit of water. Martello supplied the plane, said the joke later, and Enderby supplied the fish. Smiley also learned around this time, in his unworldly way, what everyone else had known from the beginning and assumed he knew too. Enderby's third and newest wife was American, and rich. Before their marriage she had been a considerable hostess of the Washington establishment, a rôle she was now repeating with some success in London.

But the underlying cause of everybody's agitation was finally the same. On the Ko front, nothing ultimately was happening. Worse still, there was an agonising shortage of operational intelligence. Every day now, at ten o'clock, Smiley and Guillam presented themselves at the Annexe, and every day came away less satisfied. Tiu's domestic telephone line was tapped, so was Lizzie Worthington's. The tapes were locally monitored, then flown back to London for detailed processing. Jerry had sweated Charlie Marshall on a Wednesday. On the Friday, Charlie was sufficiently recovered from his ordeal to ring Tiu from Bangkok and pour out his heart to him. But after listening for less than thirty seconds Tiu cut him short with an instruction to 'get in touch with Harry right away' which left everybody mystified: nobody had a Harry anywhere. On the Saturday there was drama because the watch on Ko's home number had him cancelling his regular Sunday morning golf date with Mr Arpego. Ko pleaded a pressing business engagement. This was it! This was the breakthrough! Next day, with Smiley's consent, the Hong Kong Cousins locked a surveillance van, two cars and a Honda on to Ko's Rolls-Royce as it entered town. What secret mission, at five thirty on a Sunday morning, was so important to Ko that he would abandon his weekly golf? The answer turned out to be his fortune-teller, a venerable old Swatownese who operated from a seedy spirit temple in a side street off the Hollywood Road. Ko spent more than an hour with him before returning home, and though some zealous child inside one of the Cousins' vans trained a concealed directional microphone on the temple window for the entire session, the only sounds he recorded apart from the traffic turned out to be cluckings from the old man's henhouse. Back at the Circus, di Salis was called in.

What on earth would anyone be going to the fortune-teller at six in the morning for, least of all a millionaire?

Greatly amused by their perplexity, di Salis twirled his hair in delight. A man of Ko's standing would insist on being the first client in a fortune-teller's day, he said, while the great man's mind was still clear to receive the intimations of the spirits.

Then nothing happened for five weeks. Nothing. The mail and phone checks spewed out wads of indigestible raw material, which when refined produced not a single intelligence lead. Meanwhile, the artificial deadline imposed by the Enforcement Agency drew steadily nearer, on which day Ko should become open game for whoever could pin something on him soonest.

Yet Smiley kept his head. He resisted all recriminations, both of his own handling of the case, and of Jerry's. The tree had been shaken, he maintained, Ko was running scared, time would show they were right. He refused to be hustled into some dramatic gesture to Martello, and he held resolutely to the terms of the deal which he had outlined in his letter, and of which a copy now lodged with Lacon. He also refused, as his charter allowed him, to enter into any discussion of operational detail, either God or the forces of logic or, better, the forces of Ko's except where issues of protocol or local mandate were concerned. To give way on this, he knew very well, would only have meant providing the doubters with fresh ammunition with which to shoot him down.

He held this line for five weeks and on the thirty-sixth day, either God or the forces of logic, or, better, the forces of Ko's human chemistry, delivered to Smiley a substantial, if mysterious, consolation. Ko took to the water. Accompanied by Tiu and an unknown Chinese later identified as the lead captain of Ko's junk fleet, he spent the better part of three days touring the Hong Kong outislands, returning each evening at dusk. Where they went, there was as yet no telling. Martello proposed a series of helicopter over-flights to observe their course but Smiley turned down the suggestion flat. Static surveillance from the quayside confirmed that they apparently left and returned by a different route each day, and that was all. And on the last day, the fourth, the boat did not return at all.

Panic. Where had it gone? Martello's masters in Langley, Virginia, flew into a complete spin and decided that Ko and the *Admiral Nelson* had deliberately strayed into China waters. Even that they had been abducted. Ko would never be seen again, and Enderby, going downhill fast, actually telephoned Smiley and told him it would be 'your damn fault if Ko pops up in Peking yelling the odds about secret service persecution'. Even Smiley, for one agonising day, secretly wondered whether, against all reason, Ko had indeed gone to join his brother.

Then, of course, next morning early, the launch calmly sailed back into the main harbour looking as if it had just returned from a regatta, and Ko gaily disembarked, following his beautiful Liese down the gangway, her gold hair trailing in the sunlight like a soap commercial.

It was this intelligence which, after very long thought and a renewed and detailed reading of Ko's file – not to mention much tense debate with Connie and di Salis – determined Smiley to take two decisions at once, or in gambler's terms, to play the only two cards that were left to him.

One: Jerry should advance to the 'last stage', by which Smiley meant Ricardo. He hoped by this step to maintain the pressure on Ko, and provide Ko, if he needed it, with the final proof that he must act.

Two: Sam Collins should 'go in'.

This second decision was reached in consultation with Connie Sachs alone. It finds no mention on Jerry's main dossier, but only in a secret appendix later released, with deletions, for wider scrutiny.

The fragmenting effect upon Jerry of these delays and hesitations was something not the greatest intelligence chief on earth could have included in his calculations. To be aware of it was one thing – and Smiley undoubtedly was, and even took one or two steps to forestall it. To be guided by it, to set it on the same plane as the factors of high policy which he was having daily fired at him, would have been downright irresponsible. A general is nothing without priorities.

The fact remains that Saigon was the worst place on earth for Jerry to be kicking his heels. Periodically, as the delays dragged on, there was talk at the Circus of sending him somewhere more salubrious, for instance to Singapore or Kuala Lumpur, but the arguments of expediency and cover always kept him where he was: besides, tomorrow everything might change. There was also the matter of his personal safety. Hong Kong was not to be considered, and in both Singapore and Bangkok Ko's influence was sure to be strong. Then cover again: with the collapse approaching, where more natural than Saigon? Yet it was a half life Jerry lived, and in a half town. For forty years, give or take, war had been Saigon's staple industry, but the American pullout of seventy-three had produced a slump from which, to the end, the city never properly recovered, so that even this long-awaited final act, with its cast of millions, was playing to quite poor audiences. Even when he took his obligatory rides to the sharp end of the fighting, Jerry had a sense of watching a rained-off cricket match where the contestants wanted only to go back to the pavilion. The Circus forbade him to leave Saigon on the grounds that he might be needed elsewhere at any moment, but the injunction, literally observed, would have made him look ridiculous, and he ignored it. Xuan Loc was a boring French rubber town fifty miles out, on what was now the city's tactical perimeter. For this was a different war entirely from Phnom Penh's, more technical and more European in inspiration. Where the Khmer Rouge had no armour, the North Vietnamese had Russian tanks and 130 millimetre artillery which they drew up on the classic Russian pattern wheel to wheel, as if they were about to storm Berlin under Marshal Zhukov, and nothing would move till the last gun was laid and primed. He found the town half deserted, and the Catholic church empty except for one French priest.

'*C'est terminé,*' the priest explained to him simply. The South Vietnamese would do what they always did, he said. They would stop the advance, then turn and run.

They drank wine together staring at the empty square.

Jerry filed the story saying the rot this time was irreversible and Stubbsie shoved it on the spike with a laconic, 'Prefer people to prophecies Stubbs.'

Back in Saigon, on the steps of the Hotel Caravelle, begging children peddled useless garlands of flowers. Jerry gave them money and took their flowers to save them face, then dumped them in the wastepaper basket in his room. When he sat downstairs they tapped on the window and sold him *Stars and Stripes*. In the empty bars where he drank, the girls collected round him desperately as if he was their last chance before the end. Only the police were in their element. They stood at every corner in white helmets and fresh white gloves, as if already waiting to direct the victorious enemy traffic when it arrived. In white jeeps, they rode like monarchs past the refugees in their birdcoops on the pavement. He returned to his hotel room and Hercule rang, Jerry's favourite Vietnamese, whom he had been avoiding for all he was worth. Hercule, as he called himself, was anti-establishment and anti-Thieu and had made a quiet living supplying British journalists with information on the Vietcong, on the questionable grounds that the British were not involved in the war. 'The British are my friends!' he begged into the phone. 'Get me out! I need papers. I need money!'

Jerry said 'Try the Americans' and rang off hopelessly.

The Reuters office, when Jerry filed his stillborn copy, was a monument to forgotten heroes and the romance of failure. Under the glass desktops lay the photographed heads of tousled boys, on the walls famous rejection slips and samples of editorial fury; in the air, a stink of old newsprint, and the Somewhere-in-England sense of makeshift habitation which enshrines the secret nostalgia of every exiled correspondent. There was a travel agent just round the corner, and later it turned out that Jerry had twice in that period booked himself passages to Hong Kong, then not appeared at the airport. He was serviced by an earnest young Cousin named Pike who had Information cover and occasionally came to the hotel with signals in yellow envelopes marked RUSH PRESS for authenticity. But the message inside was the same: no decision, stand by, no decision. He read Ford Madox Ford and a truly terrible novel about old Hong Kong. He read Greene and Conrad and T. E. Lawrence, and still no word came. The shellings sounded worst at night, and the panic was everywhere, like a spreading plague.

In search of Stubbsie's people not prophecies, he went down to the American Embassy where ten thousand-odd Vietnamese were beating at the doors in an effort to prove their American citizenship. As he watched, a South Vietnamese officer rode up in a jeep, leapt out and began yelling at the women, calling them whores and traitors – picking, as it happened, a group of *bona fide* US wives to bear the brunt.

Again Jerry filed, and again Stubbs threw his story out, which no doubt added to his depression.

A few days later the Circus planners lost their nerve. As the rout continued, and worsened, they signalled Jerry to fly at once to Vientiane and keep his head down till ordered otherwise by a Cousins' postman. So he went, and took a room at the Constellation, where Lizzie had liked to hang out, and he drank at the bar where Lizzie had liked to drink, and he occasionally chatted to Maurice the proprietor, and he waited. The bar was of concrete, two foot deep, so that if need arose it could do duty as a bomb shelter or firing position. Each night, in the mournful dining room attached to it, one old *colon* ate and drank fastidiously, a napkin tucked into his collar. Jerry sat reading at another table. They were the only diners, ever, and they never spoke. In the streets, the Pathet Lao – not long down from the hills – walked righteously in pairs, wearing Maoist caps and tunics, and avoiding the glances of the girls. They had commandeered the corner villas, and the villas along the road to the airport. They had camped in immaculate tents which peeked over the walls of overgrown gardens.

'Will the coalition hold?' Jerry asked Maurice once.

Maurice was not a political man.

'It's the way it is,' he replied in a stage French accent, and in silence handed Jerry a ballpoint pen as a consolation. It had *Lowenbräu* written on it: Maurice owned the concession for the whole of Laos, selling – it was said – several bottles a year. Jerry avoided absolutely the street which housed the Indocharter offices, just as he restrained himself from taking a look, out of curiosity, at the flea-hut on the edge of town which, on Charlie Marshall's testimony, had housed their *ménage à trois*. When asked, Maurice said there were very few Chinese left in town these days. 'Chinese do not like,' he said with another smile, tilting his head at the Pathet Lao on the pavement outside.

There remains the mystery of the telephone transcripts. Did Jerry ring Lizzie from the Constellation, or not? And if he did ring her, did he mean to talk to her, or only to listen to her voice? And if he intended to talk to her, then what did he propose to say? Or was the very act of making the phone call – like the act of booking airline passages in Saigon – in itself sufficient catharsis to hold him back from the reality?

What is certain is that nobody, neither Smiley nor Connie nor anyone else who read the crucial transcripts, can be seriously accused of failing in their duty, for the entry was at best ambivalent:

'0055 hrs HK time. Incoming overseas call, personal for subject. Operator on the line. Subject accepts call, says "hullo" *several times.*

Operator: Speak up please, caller!

Subject: Hullo? Hullo?

Operator: Can you hear me, caller? Speak up, please!

Subject: Hullo? Liese Worth here. Who's calling, please?

Call disconnected from caller's end.'

The transcript nowhere mentions Vientiane as the place

of origin and it is even doubtful whether Smiley saw it, since his cryptonym does not appear in the signing panel.

Anyway, whether it was Jerry who made the call or someone else, the next day a pair of Cousins, not one, brought him his marching orders, and at long, long last the welcome relief of action. The bloody inertia, however many interminable weeks of it, had ended finally – and as it happened for good.

He spent the afternoon fixing himself visas and transport, and next morning at dawn he crossed the Mekong into North East Thailand, carrying his shoulder bag and his typewriter. The long wooden ferryboat was crammed with peasants and shrieking pigs. At the shack which controlled the crossing point he pledged himself to return to Laos by the same route. Documentation would otherwise be impossible, the officials warned him severely. If I return at all, he thought. Looking back to the receding shores of Laos, he saw an American car parked on the towpath, and beside it two slender stationary figures watching. The Cousins we have always with us.

On the Thai bank, everything was immediately impossible. Jerry's visa was not enough, his photographs bore no likeness, the whole area was forbidden to *farangs*. Ten dollars secured a revised opinion. After the visa, the car. Jerry had insisted on an English-speaking driver and the rate had been fixed accordingly, but the old man who waited for him spoke nothing but Thai and little of that. By bawling English phrases into the nearby rice shop, Jerry finally hooked a fat supine boy who had some English and said he could drive. A laborious contract was drawn up. The old man's insurance did not cover another driver and anyway it was out of date. An exhausted travel clerk issued a new policy while the boy went home to make his arrangements. The car was a clapped-out red Ford with bald tyres. Of all the ways Jerry didn't intend to die in the next day or two, this was one of them. They haggled, Jerry put up another twenty dollars. At a garage full of chickens he watched every move of the mechanics till the new tyres were in place.

Having thus wasted an hour they set out at a breakneck speed south-eastward over flat farm country. The boy played 'The lights are always out in Massachusetts' five times before Jerry asked for silence.

The road was tarmac but deserted. Occasionally a yellow bus came sidewinding down the hill toward them and at once the driver accelerated and stayed on the crown till the bus had yielded a foot and thundered past. Once, while he was dozing, Jerry was startled by the crunch of bamboo fencing and woke in time to see a fountain of splinters lift into the sunlight just ahead of him, and a pick-up truck rolling into the ditch in slow motion. He saw the door float upward like a leaf and the flailing driver follow it through the fence and into the high grass. The boy hadn't even slowed down, though his laughter made them swerve all over the road. Jerry shouted 'Stop!' but the boy would have none of it.

'You want to get blood on your suit? You leave that to the doctors,' he advised sternly. 'I look after you, okay? This very bad country here. Lot of Commies.'

'What's your name?' said Jerry resignedly.

It was unpronounceable, so they settled on Mickey.

It was two more hours before they hit the first barrier. Jerry dozed again, rehearsing his lines. There's always one more door you have to put your foot in, he thought. He wondered whether a day would come – for the Circus – for the comic – when the old entertainer would not be able to pull the gags any more, when just the sheer energy of bare-arsing his way over the threshold would defeat him, and he would stand there flaccid, sporting his friendly salesman's grin, while the words died in his throat. Not this time, he thought hastily. Dear God, not this time, please.

They stopped, and a young monk scurried out of the trees carrying a *wat* bowl and Jerry dropped a few *baht* into it. Mickey opened the boot. A police sentry peered inside, then ordered Jerry out and led him over to a captain who sat in a shaded hut all his own. The captain took a long while to notice Jerry at all.

'He ask you American?' said Mickey.

Jerry produced his papers.

On the other side of the barrier, the perfect tarmac road ran straight as a pencil over the flat scrubland.

'He says what you want here?' Mickey said.

'Business with the colonel.'

Driving on, they passed a village and a cinema. Even the latest films up here are silents, Jerry recalled. He had once done a story about them. Local actors made the voices, and invented whatever plots came into their heads. He remembered John Wayne with a squeaky Thai voice, and the audience ecstatic, and the interpreter explaining to him that they were hearing an imitation of the local mayor who was a famous queen. They were passing forest but the shoulders of the road had been cleared fifty yards on either side to cut the risk of ambush. Occasionally, they came on sharp white lines which had nothing to do with earthbound traffic. The road had been laid by the Americans with an eye to auxiliary landing strips.

'You know this colonel guy?' Mickey asked.

'No,' said Jerry.

Mickey laughed in delight. 'Why you want?'

Jerry didn't bother to answer.

The second roadblock came twenty miles later, in the centre of a small village given over to police. A cluster of grey trucks stood in the courtyard of the *wat*, four jeeps were parked beside the roadblock. The village lay at a junction. At right-angles to their road, a yellow dust-path crossed the plain and snaked into the hills to either side. This time Jerry took the initiative, leaping from the car immediately with a merry cry of 'Take me to your leader!' Their leader turned out to be a nervous young captain with the anxious frown of a man trying to keep abreast of matters beyond his learning. He sat in the police station with his pistol on the desk. The police station was temporary, Jerry noticed. Out of the window, he saw the bombed ruins of what he took to be the last one.

'My colonel is a busy man,' the captain said, through Mickey the driver.

'He is also a very brave man,' Jerry said.

There was dumb show till they had established 'brave'.

'He has shot many Communists,' Jerry said. 'My paper wishes to write about this brave Thai colonel.'

The captain spoke for quite a while and suddenly Mickey began hooting with laughter.

'The captain say we don't got no Commies! We only got Bangkok! Poor people up here don't know nothing, because Bangkok don't give them no schools so the Commies come talk to them in the night and the Commies tell them all their sons all go Moscow, learn be big doctors, so they blow up the police station.'

'Where can I find the colonel?'

'Captain say we stay here.'

'Will he ask the colonel to come to us?'

'Colonel very busy man.'

'Where is the colonel?'

'He next village.'

'What is the name of the next village?'

The driver once more collapsed with laughter.

'It don't got no name. That village all dead.'

'What was the village called before it died?'

Mickey said a name.

'Is the road open as far as this dead village?'

'Captain say military secret. That mean he don't know.'

'Will the captain let us through to take a look?'

A long exchange followed.

'Sure,' said Mickey finally. 'He say we go.'

'Will the captain radio the colonel and tell him we are coming?'

'Colonel very busy man.'

'Will he radio him?'

'Sure,' said the driver, as if only a hideous *farang* could have made a meal of such a patently obvious detail.

They climbed back into the car. The boom lifted and they continued along the perfect tarmac road with its cleared shoulders and occasional landing marks. For twenty minutes they drove without seeing another living thing but Jerry wasn't consoled by the emptiness. He had heard that for every Communist guerrilla fighting with a gun in the hills, it took five in the plains to produce the rice, the ammunition and the infra-structure, and these were the plains. They came to a dust-path on their right, and the dust of it was smeared across the tarmac from recent use. Mickey swung down it, following the heavy tyre tracks, playing 'The lights are always out in Massachusetts' very loud, Jerry notwithstanding.

'This way the Commies think we plenty people,' he explained amid more laughter, thus making it impossible for him to object. To Jerry's surprise he also produced a huge, long-barrelled .45 target pistol from the bag beneath his seat. Jerry ordered him sharply to shove it back where it came from. Minutes later, they smelt burning, then they drove through wood-smoke, then they reached what was left of the village: clusters of cowed people, a couple of acres of burnt teak trees like a petrified forest, three jeeps, twenty-odd police, and a stocky lieutenant-colonel at their centre. Villagers and police alike were gazing at a patch of smouldering ash sixty yards across, in which a few charred beams sketched the outline of the burned houses. The colonel watched them park and he watched them walk over. He was a fighting man. Jerry saw it immediately. He was squat and strong and he neither smiled nor scowled. He was swarthy and greying and he could have been Malay, except that he was thicker in the trunk. He wore parachute wings and flying wings and a couple of rows of medal ribbons. He wore battle drill and a regulation automatic in a leather holster on his right thigh, and the restraining straps hung open.

'You the newsman?' he asked Jerry, in flat, military American.

'That's right.'

The colonel's eye turned to the driver. He said something, and Mickey walked hastily back to his car, got into it and stayed there.

'What do you want?'

'Anybody die here?'

'Three people. I just shot them. We got thirty-eight million.' His functional American-English, all but perfect, came as a growing surprise.

'Why did you shoot them?'

'At night the CTs held classes here. People come from all around to hear the CTs.'

Communist Terrorists, thought Jerry. He had an inkling it was originally a British phrase. A string of lorries was nosing down the dust-path. Seeing them, the villagers began picking up their bedrolls and children. The colonel gave an order and his men formed them into a rough file while the lorries turned round.

'We find them a better place,' the colonel said. 'They start again.'

'Who did you shoot?'

'Last week two of my men got bombed. The CTs operated from this village.' He picked out a sullen woman at that moment clambering on the lorry and called her back so that Jerry could take a look at her. She stood with her head bowed.

'They stay in her house,' he said. 'This time I shoot her husband. Next time I shoot her.'

'And the other two?' Jerry asked.

He asked because to keep asking is to stay punching, but it was Jerry, not the colonel, who was under interrogation. The colonel's brown eyes were hard and appraising and held a lot in reserve. They looked at Jerry enquiringly but without anxiety.

'One of the CTs sleep with a girl here,' he said simply. 'We're not only the police. We're the judge and courts as well. There's no one else. Bangkok don't care for a lot of public trials up here.'

The villagers had boarded the lorries. They drove away without looking back. Only the children waved over the tailboards. The jeeps followed, leaving the three of them, and the two cars, and a boy, perhaps fifteen.

'Who's he?' said Jerry.

'He comes with us. Next year, year after maybe, I shoot him too.'

Jerry rode in the jeep beside the colonel, who drove. The boy sat impassively in the back murmuring yes and no while the colonel lectured him in a firm, mechanical tone. Mickey followed in the taxi. On the floor of the jeep, between the seat and the pedals, the colonel kept four grenades in a cardboard carton. A small machine gun lay along the rear seat, and the colonel didn't bother to move it for the boy. Above the driving mirror beside the votive pictures hung a postcard portrait of John Kennedy with the legend 'Ask not what your country can do for you. Ask rather what you can do for your country.' Jerry had taken his notebook out. The lecture to the boy continued.

'What are you saying to him?'

'I am explaining the principles of democracy.'

'What are they?'

'No Communism and no generals,' he replied and laughed.

At the main road they turned right, further into the interior, Mickey following in the red Ford.

'Dealing with Bangkok is like climbing that big tree,' the colonel said to Jerry, interrupting himself to point at the forest. 'You climb one branch, go up a bit, change branches, the branch breaks, you go up again. Maybe one day, you get to the top general. Maybe never.'

Two small kids flagged them down and the colonel stopped to let them squeeze in beside the boy.

'I don't do that too often,' he said with another sudden smile. 'I do that to show you I'm a nice guy. The CTs get to know you stop for kids, they put out kids to stop you. You got to vary yourself. That way you stay alive.'

He had turned into the forest again. They drove a few miles and let the small children out, but not the sullen boy. The trees stopped and gave way to desolate scrub-land. The sky grew white, with the shadows of the hills just breaking through the mist.

'What's he done?' Jerry asked.

'Him? He's a CT,' the colonel said. 'We catch him.' In the forest Jerry saw a flash of gold, but it was only a *wat*. 'Last week one of my police turns informer to CT. I send him on patrol, shoot him, make him a big hero. I fix the wife a pension, I buy a big flag for the body, I make a great funeral and the village gets a bit richer. That guy's not an informer any more. He's a folk hero. You got to win the hearts and minds of the people.'

'No question,' Jerry agreed.

They had reached a wide dry paddy field, with two women hoeing at the centre, and otherwise nothing in sight but a far hedge, and rocky duneland fading into the white sky. Leaving Mickey in the Ford, Jerry and the colonel began walking across the field, the sullen boy trailing behind them.

'You British?'

'Yes.'

'I was at Washington International Police Academy,' said the colonel. 'Very nice place. I read law enforcement at Michigan State. They showed us a good time. You want to keep clear of me a little?' he asked politely, as they trod meticulously over a plough. 'They shoot me, not you. They shoot a *farang*, they get too much trouble here. They don't want that. Nobody shoots a *farang* in my territory.'

They had reached the women. The colonel spoke to them, walked a distance, stopped, looked back at the sullen boy and returned to the women and spoke to them a second time.

'What's that about?' said Jerry.

'I ask them if there's any CTs around. They tell me no. Then I think: maybe the CTs want this boy back. So I go back and tell them: "If anything goes wrong, we shoot you women first."' They had reached the hedge. The dunes lay ahead of them, overgrown with high bushes and palms like sword blades. The colonel cupped his hands and yelled until an answering call came.

'I learn that in the jungle,' he explained with another smile. 'When you're in the jungle, always call first.'

'What jungle was that?' said Jerry.

'Stand near to me now please. Smile when you speak to me. They like to see you very clear.'

They had reached a small river. Around it, a hundred or more men and boys picked indifferently at the rocks with picks and spades, or humped bags of cement from one vast pile to another. A handful of armed police looked negligently on. The colonel called up the boy and spoke to him, and the boy bowed his head and the colonel boxed him sharply on the ears. The boy muttered something and the colonel hit him again, then patted him on the shoulder, whereupon like a freed but crippled bird he scuffled away to join the labour force.

'You write about CTs, you write about my dam too,' the colonel ordered, as they started their return walk. 'We're going to make this fine pasture here. They will name it after me.'

'What jungle did you fight in?' Jerry repeated, as they started back.

'Laos. Very hard fighting.'

'You volunteered?'

'Sure. I got kids, need the money. I join PARU. Heard of PARU? The Americans ran it. They got it made. I write a letter resigning from the Thai police. They put it in a drawer. If I get killed, they pull out the letter to prove I resigned before I joined PARU.'

'That where you met Ricardo?'

'Sure. Ricardo my friend. We fought together, shoot a lot of badguys.'

'I want to see him,' said Jerry. 'I met a girl of his in Saigon. She told me he had a place up here. I want to make him a business proposition.'

They passed the women again. The colonel waved at them but they ignored him. Jerry was watching his face but he could as soon have watched a boulder back on the dunes. The colonel climbed into the jeep. Jerry jumped in after him.

'I thought maybe you could take me to him. I could even make him rich for a few days.'

'This for your paper?'
'It's private.'
'A private business proposition?' the colonel asked.
'That's right.'
As they drove back to the road, two yellow cement-mixer lorries came toward them and the colonel had to back to let them pass. Automatically, Jerry noticed the name painted on the yellow sides. As he did so, he caught the colonel's eye watching him. They continued toward the interior, driving as fast as the jeep would go, in order to beat anybody's bad intentions along the way. Faithfully, Mickey followed behind.
'Ricardo is my friend and this is my territory,' the colonel repeated in his excellent American. The statement, though familiar, was this time an entirely explicit warning. 'He lives here under my protection, according to an arrangement we have. Everybody here know that. The villagers know it, CT knows it. Nobody hurts Ricardo or I'll shoot every CT on the dam.'
As they turned off the main road into the dust-path, Jerry saw the light skidmarks of a small plane written on the tarmac.
'This where he lands?'
'Only in the rainy season.' The colonel continued outlining his ethical position in the matter. 'If Ricardo kills you, that's his business. One *farang* shoots another on my territory, that's natural.' He could have been explaining basic arithmetic to a child. 'Ricardo is my friend,' he repeated without embarrassment. 'My comrade.'
'He expecting me?'
'Please pay attention to him. Captain Ricardo is sometimes a sick man.'

Tiu make a special place for him, Charlie Marshall had said, *a place where only crazy people go. Tiu say to him, 'you stay alive, you keep the plane, you ride shotgun for Charlie Marshall any time you like, carry money for him, watch his back for him, if that's the way Charlie wants it. That's the deal and Drake Ko don't never break a deal,' he say. But if Ric make trouble, or if Ric louses up, or if Ric shoot his big mouth off about certain matters, Tiu and his people kill that crazy bastard so completely he don't never know who he is.*

'Why doesn't Ric just take the plane and run for it?' Jerry had asked.

Tiu got Ric's passport, Voltaire. Tiu buy Ric's debts and his business enterprises and his police record. Tiu pinned about fifty tons of opium on him and Tiu got the proof all ready for the narcs for if ever he need it. Ric, he's free to walk out any damn time he wants. They got prisons waiting for him all over the damn world.

The house stood on stilts at the centre of a wide dust-path with a balcony all round it and a small stream beside it and a couple of Thai girls under it, and one of them was feeding her baby while the other stirred a cookpot. Behind the house lay a flat brown field with a shed at one end big enough to house a small plane – say a Beechcraft – and there was a silvered track of pressed grass down the field where one might recently have landed. There were no trees near the house, and it stood on a small rise. It had all-round vision and broad windows not very high, which Jerry guessed had been altered to provide a wide angle of fire from inside. Short of the house, the colonel told Jerry to get out, and walked back with him to Mickey's car. He spoke to Mickey and Mickey leapt out and unlocked the boot. The colonel reached under the car-seat and pulled out the target pistol and tossed it contemptuously into the jeep. He frisked Jerry, then Mickey, then he searched the car for himself. Then he told them both to wait, and he climbed the steps to the first floor. The girls ignored him.

'He fine colonel,' said Mickey.

They waited.

'England rich country,' said Mickey.

'England a very *poor* country,' Jerry retorted as they continued to watch the house.

'Poor country, rich people,' said Mickey. He was still shaking with laughter at his own good joke as the colonel came out of the house, climbed into the jeep, and drove away.

'Wait here,' said Jerry. He walked slowly to the foot of the steps, cupped his hands to his mouth and called upwards.

'My name's Westerby. You may remember shooting at me in Phnom Penh a few weeks ago. I'm a poor journalist with expensive ideas.'

'What do you want, Voltaire? Somebody told me you were dead already.'

A Latin American voice, deep and feathered, from the darkness above.

'I want to blackmail Drake Ko, I reckon that between us we could sting him for a couple of million bucks and you could buy your freedom.'

In the darkness of the trap above him, Jerry saw a single gun barrel, like a cyclopic eye, wink, then settle its gaze on him again.

'*Each*,' Jerry called. 'Two for you, two for me. I've got it all worked out. With my brains and your information and Lizzie Worthington's figure, I reckon it's a dead cert.'

He started walking slowly up the steps. *Voltaire*, he thought. When it came to spreading the word, Charlie Marshall didn't hang around. As to being dead already – give it a little time, he thought.

As Jerry climbed through the trap, he moved from the dark into the light, and the Latin American voice said, 'Stay right there.' Doing as he was told, Jerry was able to look round the room, which was a mix between a small armaments museum and an American PX. On the centre table on a tripod stood an AK47 similar to the one Ricardo had already fired at him, and as Jerry had suspected it covered all four approaches through the windows. But in case it didn't, there were a couple of spares, and beside each gun a decent pile of ammunition clips. Grenades lay about like fruit, in clusters of three and four, and on the hideous walnut cocktail cabinet, under a plastic effigy of the Madonna, lay a selection of pistols and automatics for all occasions. There was only one room but it was large, with a low bed with japanned and lacquered ends, and Jerry had a silly moment wondering how the devil Ricardo had ever got it into his Beechcraft. There were two refrigerators and an icemaker, and there were painfully-worked oil paintings of nude Thai girls, drawn with the sort of erotic inaccuracy that usually comes with too little access to the subject. There was a filing cabinet with a Luger on it and there was a bookshelf with works on company law, international taxation, and sexual technique. On the walls hung several locally carved icons of saints, the Virgin, and the Christ child. On the floor lay a steel scaffold of a rowing boat, with a sliding seat for improving the figure.

At the centre of all this, in much the same pose in which Jerry had first set eyes on him, sat Ricardo in a senior executive's swivel chair, wearing his CIA bracelets and a sarong and a gold cross on his handsome bare chest. His beard was a lot less full than when Jerry had seen it last and he guessed the girls had clipped it for him. He wore no cap, and his crinkly black hair was threaded into a small gold ring at the back of his neck. He was broad-shouldered and muscular and his skin was tanned and oily and his chest was matted.

He also had a bottle of Scotch at his elbow, and a jug of water, but no ice because there was no electricity for the refrigerators.

'Take off your jacket, please, Voltaire,' Ricardo ordered, so Jerry did, and with a sigh Ricardo stood up, and picked an automatic from the table, and walked slowly round Jerry studying his body while he gently probed it for weapons.

'You play tennis?' he enquired from behind him, running one hand very lightly down Jerry's back. 'Charlie said you got muscles like a gorilla.' But Ricardo did not really ask questions of anyone but himself. 'I like very much tennis. I am an extremely good player. I win always. Here, unfortunately, I have little opportunity.' He sat down again. 'Sometimes you got to hide with the enemy to get away from your friends. I ride horses, box, shoot. I got degrees, I fly an aeroplane, I know a lot of things about life, I'm very intelligent, but owing to unforeseen circumstances I live in the jungle like a monkey.' The automatic lay casually in his left hand. 'That what you call a paranoid, Voltaire? Somebody who think everybody his enemy?'

'I rather think it is.'

To produce the well-trodden witticism, Ricardo laid a finger to his bronzed and oiled breast.

'Well this paranoid got real enemies,' he said.

'With two million bucks,' said Jerry, still standing where Ricardo had left him, 'I'm sure most of them could be eliminated.'

'Voltaire, I must tell you honestly that I regard your business proposition as crap.'

Ricardo laughed. That was to say, he made a fine display of his white teeth against the newly clipped beard, and flexed his stomach muscles a little, and kept his eyes fixed dead level on Jerry's face while he sipped his glass of whisky. He's got a brief, thought Jerry, same as I have.

If he shows up, you hear him out, Tiu had no doubt said to him. And when Ricardo had heard him out – then what?

'I definitely understood you had had an accident, Voltaire,' said Ricardo sadly, and shook his head as if complaining about the poor quality of his information. 'You want a drink?'

'I'll pour it for myself,' said Jerry. The glasses were in a cabinet, all different colours and sizes. Deliberately, Jerry walked over to it and helped himself to a long pink tumbler with a dressed girl outside and a naked girl inside. He poured a couple of fingers of Scotch into it, added a little water, and sat down opposite Ricardo at the table while Ricardo studied him with interest.

'You do exercises, weight-lifting, something?' he enquired confidingly.

'Just the odd bottle,' said Jerry.

Ricardo laughed inordinately, still examining him very closely with his flickering bedroom eyes.

'That was a very bad thing you did to little Charlie, you know that? I don't like you to sit on my friend's head in the darkness while he catch cold turkey. Charlie going to take a long while to recover. That's no way to make friends with Charlie's friends, Voltaire. They say you even been rude to Mr Ko. Took my little Lizzie out to dinner. That true?'

'I took her out to dinner.'

'You screw her?'

Jerry didn't answer. Ricardo gave another burst of laughter, which stopped as suddenly as it had started. He took a long draught of whisky and sighed.

'Well, I hope she's grateful, that's all.' He was at once a much misunderstood man. 'I forgive her. Okay? You see Lizzie again: tell her I, Ricardo, forgive her. I train her. I put her on the right road. I tell her a lot of things, art, culture, politics, business, religion, I teach her how to make love, and I send her into the world. Where would she be without my connections? Where? Living in the jungle with Ricardo like a monkey. She owes me everything. *Pygmalion*: know that movie? Well, I'm the professor. I tell her some things – know what I mean? – I tell her things no man can tell her but Ricardo. Seven years in Vietnam. Two years in Laos. Four thousand dollars a month from CIA and me a Catholic. You think I can't tell her some things, a girl like that from nowhere, an English scrubber? She got a kid, you know that? Little boy in London. She walk out on him, imagine. Such a mother huh? Worse than a whore.'

Jerry found nothing useful to say. He was looking at the two large rings side by side on the middle fingers of Ricardo's heavy right hand, and in his memory measuring them against the twin scars on Lizzie's chin. It was a downward blow, he decided, a right cross while she was below him. It seemed strange he hadn't broken her jaw. Perhaps he had, and she'd had a lucky mend.

'You gone deaf, Voltaire? I said outline to me your business proposition. Without prejudice, you understand. Except I don't believe a word of it.'

Jerry helped himself to some more whisky. 'I thought maybe if you told me what it was Drake Ko wanted you to do that time you flew for him, and if Lizzie could get me alongside Ko, and we all kept our hands on the table, we'd have a good chance of taking him to the cleaners.'

Now he said it, it sounded even lamer than when he had rehearsed it, but he didn't particularly care.

'You crazy, Voltaire. Crazy. You're making pictures in the air.'

'Not if Ko was asking you to fly into the China Mainland for him, I'm not. Ko can own the whole of Hong Kong for all I care, but if the Governor ever got to hear of that little adventure, I reckon he and Ko would stop kissing overnight. That's for openers. There's more.'

'What are you talking about, Voltaire? China? What nonsense is this you are telling me? The China *Mainland*?' He shrugged his glistening shoulders and drank, smirking into his glass. 'I do not read you, Voltaire. You talk through your ass. What makes you think I fly to China for Ko? Ridiculous. Laughable.'

As a liar, Jerry reckoned, Ricardo was about three leagues lower down the chart than Lizzie, which was saying quite a lot.

'My editor makes me think it, sport. My editor is a very sharp fellow. Lot of influential and knowledgeable friends. They tell him things. Now for instance, my editor has a very good hunch that not long after you died so tragically in that aircrash of yours you sold a damn great load of raw opium to a friendly American purchaser engaged in the suppression of dangerous drugs. Another hunch of his tells him it was Ko's opium, not yours to sell at all, and that it was addressed to the China Mainland. Only, you decided to play the angles instead.' He went straight on, while Ricardo's eyes watched him over the top of his whisky glass. 'Now if that were so, and Ko's ambition were, let us say, to reintroduce the opium habit to the Mainland – slowly, but gradually creating new markets, you follow me – well, I reckon he would go a very long distance to prevent that information making the front pages of the world's press. That's not all, either. There's another aspect altogether, even more lucrative.'

'What's that, Voltaire?' Ricardo asked, and continued watching him as fixedly as if he had him in the sights of his rifle. 'What are these other aspects you refer to? Kindly tell me, please.'

'Well I think I'll hold back on that one,' said Jerry with a frank smile. 'I think I'll keep it warm while you give me a little something in return.'

A girl came silently up the stairs carrying bowls of rice and lemon grass and boiled chicken. She was trim and entirely beautiful. They could hear voices from underneath the house, including Mickey's, and the sound of the baby laughing.

'Who you got down there, Voltaire?' Ricardo asked vaguely, half waking from his reverie. 'You got some damn bodyguard or something?'

'Just the driver.'

'He got guns?'

Receiving no reply, Ricardo shook his head in wonder. 'You're some crazy fellow,' he remarked, as he waved at the girl to get out. 'You're some really crazy fellow.' He handed Jerry a bowl and chopsticks. 'Holy Maria. That Tiu, he's a pretty rough guy. I'm a pretty rough guy myself. But those Chinese can be very hard people, Voltaire. You mess with a guy like Tiu, you get pretty big trouble.'

'We'll beat them at their own game,' said Jerry. 'We'll use English lawyers. We'll stack it so high a board of bishops couldn't knock it down. We'll collect witnesses. You, Charlie Marshall, whoever else knows. Give dates and times of what he said and did. We'll show him a copy and we'll bank the others and we'll make a contract with him. Signed, sealed, and delivered. Legal as hell. That's what he likes. Ko's a very legal-minded man. I've been into his business affairs. I've seen his bank statements, his assets. The story's pretty good as it stands. But with the other aspects I'm talking about, I reckon it's cheap at five million. Two for you. Two for me. One for Lizzie.'

'For her, nothing.'

Ricardo was stooping over the filing cabinet. Pulling open a drawer, he began picking through the contents, studying brochures and correspondence.

'You ever been to Bali, Voltaire?'

Solemnly pulling on a pair of reading glasses, Ricardo sat at the table again and began studying the file. 'I bought some land there a few years back. A deal I made. I make many deals. Walk, ride, I got a Honda seven fifty there, a girl. In Laos we kill everybody, in Vietnam we burn the whole damn countryside, so I buy this land in Bali, bit of land we don't burn for once and a girl we don't kill, know what I mean? Fifty acres of scrub. Here, come here.'

Peering over his shoulder, Jerry saw a planner's mimeographed diagram of an isthmus broken into numbered building plots, and in the bottom left corner the words 'Ricardo and Worthington Ltd, Dutch Antilles.'

'You come into business with me, Voltaire. We develop this thing together, okay? Build fifty houses, have one each, nice people, put Charlie Marshall out there as manager, get some girls, make a colony maybe, artists, concerts sometimes: you like music, Voltaire?'

'I need hard facts,' Jerry insisted firmly. 'Dates, times, places, witnesses' statements. When you've told me, I'll trade you. I'll explain those other aspects to you – the lucrative ones. I'll explain the whole deal.'

'Sure,' said Ricardo distractedly, still studying the map. 'We screw him. Sure we do.'

This is how they lived together, Jerry thought: with one foot in fairyland and the other in jail, bolstering each other's fantasies, a beggars' opera with a cast of three.

For a while now, Ricardo fell in love with his sins and there was nothing Jerry could do to stop him. In Ricardo's simple world, to talk about himself was to get to know the other person better. So he talked about his big soul, about his great sexual potency and his concern for its continuation, but most of all he talked about the horrors of war, a subject on which he considered himself uniquely well informed. 'In Vietnam, I fall in love with a girl,

Voltaire. I, Ricardo, I fall in love. This is very rare and holy to me. Black hair, straight back, face like a Madonna, little tits. Each morning I stop the jeep as she walks to school, each morning she says "no". "Listen," I tell her, "Ricardo is not American. He is Mexican." She never even heard of Mexico. I go crazy, Voltaire. For weeks I, Ricardo, live like a monk. The other girls, I don't touch them any more. Every morning. Then one day I'm in first gear already and she throws up her hand – stop! She gets in beside me. She leaves school, goes out to live in a kampong, I tell you one day the name. The B52s go in and flatten the village. Some hero doesn't read the map too good. Little villages, they're like stones on the beach, each one the same. I'm in the chopper behind. Nothing's stopping me. Charlie Marshall's beside me and he's screaming me I'm crazy. I don't care. I go down, land, I find her. The whole village dead. I find her. She's dead too, but I find her. I get back to base, the military police beat me up, I get seven weeks in solitary, lose my service stripes. Me. Ricardo.'

'You poor thing,' said Jerry, who had played these games before and hated them – disbelieved or believed them, but always hated them.

'You are right,' said Ricardo, acknowledging Jerry's homage with a bow. 'Poor is the correct word. They treat us like peasants. Me and Charlie, we fly everything. We were never properly rewarded. Wounded, dead, bits of bodies, dope. For nothing. Jesus, that was shooting, that war. Twice I fly into Yunnan province. I am fearless. Totally. Even my good looks do not make me afraid for myself.'

'Counting Drake Ko's trip,' Jerry reminded him. 'You would have been there three times, wouldn't you?'

'I train pilots for the Cambodian air force. For nothing. The Cambodian air force, Voltaire! Eighteen generals, fifty-four planes – and Ricardo. End of your time, you get the life insurance, that's the deal. A hundred thousand US. Only you. Ricardo die, his next of kin get nothing, that's the deal. Ricardo make it, he get it all. I talk to some friends from the French Foreign Legion once, they know the racket, they warn me. "Take care, Ricardo. Soon they send you to bad spots you can't get out of. That way they don't have to pay you." Cambodians want me to fly on half fuel. I got wing-tanks and refuse. Another time they fix my hydraulics. I engineer the plane myself. That way they don't kill me. Listen, I snap my fingers, Lizzie come back to me. Okay?'

Lunch was over.

'So how did it go with Tiu and Drake?' said Jerry. With confession, they say at Sarratt, all you have to do is tilt the stream a little.

For the first time, it seemed to Jerry, Ricardo stared at him with the full intensity of his animal stupidity.

'You confuse me, Voltaire. If I tell you too much, I have to shoot you. I'm a very talkative person, you follow me? I get lonely up here, it is my disposition always to be lonely. I like a guy, I talk to him, then I regret myself. I remember my business commitments, follow me?'

An inner stillness came over Jerry now, as Sarratt man became Sarratt recording angel, with no part to play but to receive and to remember. Operationally, he knew, he stood close to journey's end: even if the journey back was, at best, imponderable. Operationally, by any precedents he understood, muted bells of triumph should have been sounding in his awe-struck ear. But that didn't happen. And the fact that it didn't was an early warning to him, even then, that his quest was no longer, in every respect, on all fours with that of the Sarratt bearleaders.

At first – with allowances for Ricardo's vaulting ego – the story went much as Charlie Marshall had said it went. Tiu came to Vientiane dressed like a coolie and smelling of cat-scent and asked around for the finest pilot in town and naturally he was at once referred to Ricardo, who as it happened was resting between business commitments and available for certain specialised and highly rewarded work in the aviation field.

Unlike Charlie Marshall, Ricardo told his story with a

studious directness, as if he expected to be dealing with intellects inferior to his own. Tiu introduced himself as a person with wide contacts in the aviation industry, mentioned his undefined link with Indocharter, and went over the ground he had already covered with Charlie Marshall. Finally he came to the project in hand – which is to say that, in fine Sarratt style, he fed Ricardo the cover story. A certain major Bangkok trading company with which Tiu was proud to be associated, he said, was in the throes of an extremely legitimate deal with certain officials in a neighbouring friendly foreign country.

'I ask him Voltaire, very seriously. "Mr Tiu, maybe you just discovered the moon. I never heard yet an Asian country with a friendly foreign neighbour." Tiu laughed at my joke. He naturally considered it a witty contribution,' said Ricardo very seriously, in one of his strange outbreaks of business-school English.

Before consummating their profitable and legitimate deal, however – Tiu explained, in Ricardo's language – his business associates were faced with the problem of paying off certain officials and other parties inside that friendly foreign country who had cleared away tiresome bureaucratic obstacles.

'Why was this a problem?' Ricardo had asked, not unnaturally.

Suppose, said Tiu, the country was Burma. Just suppose. In modern Burma, officials were not allowed to enrich themselves, nor could they easily bank money. In such a case, some other means of payment would have to be found.

Ricardo suggested gold. Tiu, said Ricardo, regretted himself: in the country he had in mind, even gold was difficult to negotiate. The currency selected in this case was therefore to be opium, he said: four hundred kilos of it. The distance was not great, the inside of a day would see Ricardo there and back; the fee was five thousand dollars, and the remaining details would be vouchsafed to him just before departure in order to avoid 'a needless erosion of the memory', as Ricardo put it, in another of those bizarre linguistic flourishes which must have formed a major part of Lizzie's education at his hands. Upon Ricardo's return from what Tiu was certain would be a painless and instructive flight, five thousand US dollars in convenient denominations would at once be his – subject of course to Ricardo producing, in whatever form should prove convenient, confirmation that the consignment had reached its destination. A receipt, for example.

Ricardo, as he described his own footwork, now showed a crude cunning in his dealings with Tiu. He told him he would think about this offer. He spoke of other pressing commitments and his ambitions to open his own airline. Then he set to work to find out who the hell Tiu was. He discovered at once that, following their interview, Tiu had returned not to Bangkok but to Hong Kong on the direct flight. He made Lizzie pump the Chiu Chow boys at Indocharter, and one of them let slip that Tiu was a big cat in China Airsea, because when he was in Bangkok he stayed in the China Airsea suite at the Erawan Hotel. By the time Tiu returned to Vientiane to hear Ricardo's answer, Ricardo therefore knew a lot more about him – even, though he made little of it, that Tiu was right-hand man to Drake Ko.

Five thousand US dollars for a one-day trip, he now told Tiu at this second interview, was either too little or too much. If the job was as soft as Tiu insisted, it was too much. If it was as totally crazy as Ricardo suspected, it was too little. Ricardo suggested a different arrangement: 'a business compromise', he said. He was suffering, he explained – in a phrase he had no doubt used often – from 'a temporary problem of liquidity'. In other words (Jerry interpreting) he was broke as usual, and the creditors were at his throat. What he required immediately was a regular income, and this was best obtained by Tiu arranging for him to be taken on by Indocharter as a pilot-consultant for a year at an agreed salary of twenty-five thousand US dollars.

Tiu did not seem too shocked by the idea, said Ricardo. Upstairs in the stilt-house, the room grew very quiet.

Secondly, instead of being paid five thousand dollars on delivery of the consignment, Ricardo wanted an advance of twenty thousand US dollars now to settle his outstanding commitments. Ten thousand would be considered earned as soon as he had delivered the opium, and the other ten thousand would be deductible 'at source' – another Ricardo *nom de guerre* – from his Indocharter salary over the remaining months of his employment. If Tiu and his associates couldn't manage this, Ricardo explained, then unfortunately he would have to leave town before he could make the opium delivery.

Next day, with variations, Tiu agreed to the terms. Rather than advance Ricardo twenty thousand dollars, Tiu and his associates proposed to buy Ricardo's debts directly from his creditors. That way, he explained, they would feel more comfortable. The same day, the arrangement was 'sanctified' – Ricardo's religious convictions were never far away – by a formidable contract, drawn up in English and signed by both parties. Ricardo – Jerry silently recorded – had just sold his soul.

'What did Lizzie think of the deal?' Jerry asked.

He shrugged his glistening shoulders. 'Women,' Ricardo said.

'Sure,' said Jerry, returning his knowing smile.

Ricardo's future thus secured, he resumed a 'suitable professional life-style', as he called it. A scheme to float an all-Asian football pool claimed his attention, so did a fourteen-year-old girl in Bangkok named Rosie whom, on the strength of his Indocharter salary, he periodically visited for the purpose of training her for life's great stage. Occasionally, but not often, he flew the odd run for Indocharter, but nothing demanding:

'Chaing Mai couple of times. Saigon. Couple of times into the Shans visit Charlie Marshall's old man, collect a little mud maybe, take him a few guns, rice, gold. Battambang, maybe.'

'Where's Lizzie meanwhile?' Jerry asked, in the same easy man-to-man tone as before.

The same contemptuous shrug. 'Sitting in Vientiane.

Does her knitting. Scrubs a little at the Constellation. That's an old woman already, Voltaire. I need youth. Optimism. Energy. People who respect me. It is my nature to give. How can I give to an old woman?'

'Until?' Jerry asked.

'Huh?'

'So when did the kissing stop?'

Misunderstanding the phrase, Ricardo looked suddenly very dangerous, and his voice dropped to a low warning. 'What the hell you mean?'

Jerry soothed him with the friendliest of smiles.

'How long did you draw your pay and kick around before Tiu collected on the contract?'

Six weeks, said Ricardo, recovering his composure. Maybe eight. Twice the trip was on, then cancelled. Once, it seemed, he was ordered to Chiang Mai and loafed for a couple of days till Tiu called to say the people at the other end weren't ready. Increasingly Ricardo had the feeling he was mixed up in something deep, he said, but history, he implied, had always cast him for the great rôles of life and at least the creditors were off his back.

Ricardo broke off, and once more studied Jerry closely, scratching his beard in contemplation. Finally he sighed, and pouring them both a whisky, pushed a glass across the table. Below them, the perfect day was preparing its own slow death. The green trees had grown heavy. The wood-smoke from the girls' cookpot smelt damp.

'Where you go from here, Voltaire?'

'Home,' said Jerry.

Ricardo let out a fresh burst of laughter.

'You stay the night, I send you one of my girls.'

'I'll make my own damn way, actually, sport,' Jerry said. Like fighting animals, the two men surveyed each other, and for a moment the spark of battle was very close indeed.

'You some crazy fellow, Voltaire,' Ricardo muttered.

But Sarratt man prevailed. 'Then one day the trip was on, right?' Jerry said. 'And nobody cancelled. Then what? Come on, sport, let's have the story.'

'Sure,' said Ricardo. 'Sure, Voltaire,' and drank, still watching him. 'How it happened,' he said. 'Listen, I tell you how it happened, Voltaire.'

And then I'll kill you, said his eyes.

Ricardo was in Bangkok. Rosie was being demanding. Tiu had insisted Ricardo should always be within reach and one morning early, maybe five o'clock, a messenger arrived at their love-nest summoning him to the Erawan immediately. Ricardo was impressed by the suite. He would have wished it for himself.

'Ever seen Versailles, Voltaire? A desk so big as a B52. This Tiu is a very different human individual to the cat-scent coolie who came to Vientiane, okay? This is a very influential person. "Ricardo," he tell me, "this time is for certain. This time we deliver."'

His orders were simple. In a few hours there was a commercial flight to Chiang Mai. Ricardo should take it. Rooms had been booked for him at the Hotel Rincome. He should stay the night there. Alone. No drink, no women, no society.

'"You better take plenty to read, Mr Ricardo," he tell me. "Mr Tiu," I tell him. "You tell me where to fly. You don't tell me where to read. Okay?" This guy is very arrogant behind his big desk, understand me, Voltaire? I am obliged to teach him manners.'

Next morning, someone would call for Ricardo at six o'clock at his hotel announcing himself as a friend of Mr Johnny. Ricardo should go with him.

Things went as planned. Ricardo flew to Chiang Mai, spent an abstemious night at the Rincome, and at six o'clock two Chinese, not one, called for him and drove him north for some hours till they came to a Hakka village. Leaving the car, they walked for half an hour till they reached an empty field with a hut at one end of it. Inside the hut stood 'a dandy little Beechcraft', brand new, and inside the Beechcraft sat Tiu with a lot of maps and documents on his lap, in the seat beside the pilot's. The rear seats had been removed to make space for the gunny bags. A couple of Chinese crushers stood off watching, and the overall mood, Ricardo implied, was not all he would have liked.

'First I got to empty my pockets. My pockets are very personal to me, Voltaire. They are like a lady's handbag. Mementos. Letters. Photographs. My Madonna. They retain everything. My passport, my pilot's licence, my money . . . even my bracelets,' he said, and lifted his brown arms so that the gold links jingled.

After that, he said with a frown of disapproval, there were yet more documents to sign. Such as a power of attorney, signing over whatever bits of Ricardo's life were left to him after his Indocharter contract. Such as various confessions to 'previous technically illegal undertakings', several of them – Ricardo asserted in considerable outrage – performed on behalf of Indocharter. One of the Chinese crushers even turned out to be a lawyer. Ricardo considered this particularly unsporting.

Only then did Tiu unveil the maps, and the instructions, which Ricardo now reproduced in a blend of his own style and Tiu's: '"You head north, Mr Ricardo, and you keep heading north. Maybe you clip the edge off Laos, maybe you stay over the Shans, I don't give a damn. Flying is your business, not mine. Fifty miles inside the China border, you pick up the Mekong and follow it. Then you keep going north till you find a little hill town called Tienpao, stuck on a tributary of that very famous river. Head due east twenty miles, you find a landing strip, one white flare, one green, you do me a favour please. You land there. A man will be waiting for you. He speaks very lousy English, but he speaks it. Here is half one dollar bill. This man will have the other half. Unload the opium. This man will give you a package, and certain particular instructions. The package is your receipt, Mr Ricardo. When you return, bring it with you and obey all instructions most absolutely, including especially your place of landing. Do you understand me entirely, Mr Ricardo?"'

'What kind of package?' Jerry asked.

'He don't say and I don't care. "You do that," he tell

me, "and keep your big mouth shut, Mr Ricardo, and my associates will look after you all your life like you are their son. Your children, they look after, your girls. Your girl in Bali. All your life they will be grateful men. But you screw them, or you go big-mouthing round town, they definitely kill you, Mr Ricardo, believe me. Not tomorrow, maybe, not the next day, but they definitely kill you. We got a contract, Mr Ricardo. My associates don't never break a contract. They are very legal men." I got sweat on me, Voltaire. I am in perfect condition, a fine athlete, but I sweat. "Don't you worry, Mr Tiu," I tell him. "Mr Tiu, sir, any time you want to fly opium into Red China, Ricardo's your man." Voltaire, believe me, I was very concerned.'

Ricardo squeezed his nose as if it were smarting with sea water.

'Hear this, Voltaire. Listen most attentively. When I was young and crazy, I flew twice into Yunnan province for the Americans. To be a hero, one must do certain crazy things, and if you crash, maybe one day they get you out. But each time I flew, I look down at the lousy brown earth and I see Ricardo in a wood cage. No women, extremely lousy food, no place to sit, no place to stand or sleep, chains on my arms, no status or position assured to me. "See the imperialist spy and running dog." Voltaire, I do not like this vision. To be locked all my life in China for pushing opium? I am not enthusiastic. "Sure, Mr Tiu! Bye-bye! See you this afternoon!" I have to consider most seriously.'

The brown haze of the sinking sun suddenly filled the room. On Ricardo's chest, despite the perfection of his condition, the same sweat had gathered. It lay in beads over the matted black hair and on his oiled shoulders.

'Where was Lizzie in all this?' Jerry asked again.

Ricardo's answer was nervous and already angry.

'In Vientiane! On the moon! In bed with Charlie! What the hell do I care?'

'Did she know of the deal with Tiu?'

Ricardo gave only a scowl of contempt.

Time to go, Jerry thought. Time to light the last fuse and run. Below, Mickey was making a great hit with Ricardo's women. Jerry could hear his sing-song chattering, broken by their high-pitched laughter, like the laughter of a whole class at a girls' school.

'So away you flew,' he said. He waited, but Ricardo remained lost in thought.

'You took off and headed north,' Jerry said.

Lifting his eyes a little, Ricardo held Jerry in a bullish, furious stare, till the invitation to describe his own heroic feat finally got the better of him.

'I never flew so good in my life. Never. I was magnificent. That little black Beechcraft. North a hundred miles because I don't trust nobody. Maybe those clowns have got me locked on a radar screen somewhere? I don't take no chances. Then east, but very slowly, very low over the mountains, Voltaire. I fly between the cow's legs, okay? In the war we have little landing strips up there, crazy listening places in the middle of badland. I flew those places, Voltaire. I know them. I find one right at the top of a mountain, you can reach it only from the air. I take a look, I see the fuel dump, I land, I refuel, I take a sleep, it's crazy. But Jesus, Voltaire, it's not Yunnan province, okay? It's not China, and Ricardo, the American war criminal and opium smuggler, is not going to spend the rest of his life hanging from a hen-hook in Peking, okay? Listen, I brought that plane back south again. I know places, I know places I could lose a whole air force, believe me.'

Ricardo became suddenly very vague about the next few months of his life. He had heard of the Flying Dutchman, and he said that was what he became. He flew, hid again, flew, resprayed the Beechcraft, changed the registration once a month, sold the opium in small lots in order not to be conspicuous, a kilo here, fifty there, bought a Spanish passport from an Indian but had no faith in it, kept away from everyone he knew, including Rosie in Bangkok, and even Charlie Marshall. It was also the time, Jerry remembered from his briefing by old Craw, when Ricardo sold Ko's opium to the Enforcement heroes, but got the cold shoulder on his story. On Tiu's orders, said Ricardo, the Indocharter boys had been quick to post him dead, and changed his flight-route southward to distract attention. Ricardo heard of this and did not object to being dead.

'What did you do about Lizzie?' Jerry asked.

Again, Ricardo flared. '*Lizzie, Lizzie!* You got some fixation about that scrubber, Voltaire, that you throw *Lizzie* in my face all the time? I never knew a woman so irrelevant. Listen, I give her to Drake Ko, okay? I make her fortune.' Seizing his whisky glass, he drank from it, glowering.

She was lobbying for him, Jerry thought. She and Charlie Marshall. Plodding the pavements trying to buy Ricardo's neck for him.

'You referred boastingly to other lucrative aspects of the case,' Ricardo said, in a peremptory resumption of his business-school English. 'Kindly advise me what they are, Voltaire.'

Sarratt man had this part off pat.

'Number one: Ko was being paid large sums by the Russian Embassy in Vientiane. The money was siphoned through Indocharter and ended up in a slush account in Hong Kong. We've got the proof. We've got photostats of the bank statements.'

Ricardo pulled a face as if his whisky didn't taste right, then went on drinking.

'Whether the money was for reviving the opium habit in Red China or for some other service, we don't yet know,' said Jerry. 'But we will. Point two. Do you want to hear it or am I keeping you awake?'

Ricardo had yawned.

'Point two,' Jerry continued. 'Ko has a younger brother in Red China. Used to be called Nelson. Ko pretends he's dead, but he's now a big beef with the Peking administration. Ko's been trying to get him out for years. Your job was to take in opium and bring back out a package. The package was brother Nelson. That's why Ko was going to love you like his own son if you brought him out. And that's why he was going to kill you if you didn't. If that's not a five million dollar touch what is?'

Nothing much happened to Ricardo as Jerry watched him in the failing light, except that the slumbering animal in him visibly woke. To set down his glass, he leaned forward slowly, but he couldn't conceal the tautness of his shoulders or the knotting of the muscles of his stomach. To flash a smile of exceptional goodwill at Jerry, he turned quite languidly, but his eyes had a brightness that was like a signal to attack; so that when he reached forward and patted Jerry's cheek affectionately with his right hand, Jerry was quite ready to fall straight back with it, if necessary, on the off-chance he would manage to throw Ricardo across the room.

'Five million bucks, Voltaire!' Ricardo exclaimed with steely-bright excitement. 'Five million! Listen – we got to do something for poor old Charlie Marshall, okay? For love. Charlie's always broke. Maybe we put him in charge of the football pool once. Wait a minute. I get some more Scotch, we celebrate.' He stood up, his head tilted to one side, he held out his naked arms. 'Voltaire,' he said softly. '*Voltaire!*' Affectionately, he took Jerry by the cheeks and kissed him. 'Listen, that's some research you guys did! That's some pretty smart editor you work for. You be my business partner. Like you say. Okay? I need an Englishman in my life. I got to be like Lizzie once, marry a schoolmaster. You do that for Ricardo, Voltaire? You hold me down a little?'

'No problem,' said Jerry, smiling back.

'You play with the guns a minute, okay?'

'Sure.'

'I got to tell those girls some little thing.'

'Sure.'

'Personal family thing.'

'I'll be here.'

From the top of the trap Jerry looked urgently down after him. Mickey the driver was dandling the baby on his arm, chucking it under the ear. In a mad world you keep the fiction going, he thought. Stick to it till the bitter end and leave the first bite to him. Returning to the desk, Jerry took Ricardo's pencil and his pad of paper and wrote out a non-existent address in Hong Kong where he could be reached at any time. Ricardo had still not returned, but when Jerry stood he saw him coming out of the trees behind the car. He likes contracts, he thought. Give him something to sign. He took a fresh sheet of paper: *I Jerry Westerby do solemnly swear to share with my friend Captain Tiny Ricardo all proceeds relating to our joint exploitation of his life story*, he wrote, and signed his name. Ricardo was coming up the steps. Jerry thought of helping himself from the private armoury but he guessed Ricardo was waiting for him to do just that. While Ricardo poured more whisky, Jerry handed him the two sheets of paper.

'I'll draft a legal deposition,' he said, looking straight into Ricardo's burning eyes. 'I have an English lawyer in Bangkok whom I trust entirely. I'll have him check it over and bring it back to you to sign. After that we'll plan the march-route and I'll talk to Lizzie. Okay?'

'Sure. Listen, it's dark out there. They got a lot of badguys in that forest. You stay the night. I talk to the girls. They like you. They say you very strong man. Not so strong as me, but strong.'

Jerry said something about not wasting time. He'd like to make Bangkok by tomorrow, he said. To himself, he sounded as lame as a three-legged mule, good enough to get in, maybe, but never to get out. But Ricardo seemed content to the point of serenity. Maybe it's the ambush deal, thought Jerry, something the colonel is arranging.

'Go well, horse-writer. Go well, my friend.'

Ricardo put both hands on the back of Jerry's neck and let his thumbpoints settle into Jerry's jaw, then drew Jerry's head forward for another kiss and Jerry let it happen. Though his heart thumped and his wet spine felt sore against his shirt, Jerry let it happen. Outside it was half dark. Ricardo did not see them to the car but watched them indulgently from under the stilts, the girls sitting at his feet, while he waved with both naked arms. From the car Jerry turned and waved back. The last sun lay dying in the teak trees. My last ever he thought.

'Don't start the engine,' he told Mickey quietly. 'I want to check the oil.'

Perhaps it's just me who's mad. Perhaps I really got myself a deal, he thought.

Sitting in the driver's seat, Mickey released the catch and Jerry pulled up the bonnet but there was no little *plastic*, no leaving present from his new friend and partner. He pulled up the dipstick and pretended to read it.

'You want oil, horse-writer?' Ricardo yelled down the dustpath.

'No, we're all right. So long!'

'So long.'

He had no torch, but when he crouched and groped under the chassis in the gloom, he again found nothing.

'You lost something, horse-writer?' Ricardo called again, cupping his hands to his mouth.

'Start the engine,' Jerry said and got into the car.

'Lights on, Mister?'

'Yes, Mickey. Lights on.'

'Why he call you horse-writer?'

'Mutual friends.'

If Ricardo has tipped off the CTs, thought Jerry, it won't make any damn difference either way. Mickey put on the lights, and inside the car the American dashboard lit up like a small city.

'Let's go,' said Jerry.

'Quick-quick?'

'Yes, quick-quick.'

They drove five miles, seven, nine. Jerry was watching them on the indicator, reckoning twenty to the first checkpoint and forty-five to the second. Mickey had hit seventy and Jerry was in no mood to complain. They were on the crown of the road and the road was straight and beyond the ambush strips the tall teaks slid past them like orange ghosts.

'Fine man,' Mickey said. 'He plenty fine lover. Those girls say he some pretty fine lover.'

'Watch for wires,' Jerry said.

On the right the trees broke and a red dust-track disappeared into the cleft.

'He get pretty good time in there,' said Mickey. 'Girls, he get kids, he get whisky, PX. He get real good time.'

'Pull in, Mickey. Stop the car. Here in the middle of the road where it's level. Just do it, Mickey.'

Mickey began laughing.

'Girls get good time too,' Mickey said. 'Girls get candy, little baby get candy, everybody get candy!'

'Stop the damn car!'

Taking his own good time, Mickey brought the car to a halt, still giggling about the girls.

'Is that thing accurate?' Jerry asked, his finger pressed to the petrol gauge.

'Accurate?' Mickey echoed, puzzled by the English.

'Petrol. Gas. Full? Or half full? Or three-quarters? Has it been reading right on the journey?'

'Sure. He right.'

'When we arrived at the burnt village, Mickey, you had half-full gas. You still have half-full gas.'

'Sure.'

'You put any in? From a can? You fill car?'

'No.'

'Get out.'

Mickey began protesting but Jerry leaned across him, opened his door, shoved Mickey straight through it on to the tarmac and followed him. Seizing Mickey's arm, he jammed it into his back and frogmarched him at a gallop, straight across the road to the edge of the wide soft shoulder, and twenty yards into it, then threw him into the scrub and fell half beside him, half on to him, so that the wind went out of Mickey's stomach in a single astonished hiccup, and it took him all of half a minute before he was able to give vent to an indignant 'Why for?' But Jerry by that time was pushing his face back into the earth to keep it out of the blast. The old Ford seemed to burn first and explode afterwards, finally lifting into the air in one last assertion of life, before collapsing dead and flaming on its side. While Mickey gasped in admiration, Jerry looked at his watch. Eighteen minutes since they had left the stilt-house. Maybe twenty. Should have happened sooner, he thought. Not surprising Ricardo was keen for us to go. At Sarratt they wouldn't even have seen it coming. This was an eastern treat, and Sarratt's natural soul was with Europe and the good old days of the cold war: Czecho, Berlin and the old fronts. Jerry wondered which brand of grenade it was. The Vietcong preferred the American type. They loved its double action. All you needed, they said, was a wide throat to the petrol tank. You took out the pin, you put an elastic band over the spring, you slipped the grenade into the petrol tank, and you waited patiently for the petrol to eat its way through the rubber. The result was one of those western inventions it took the Vietcong to discover. Ricardo must have used fat elastic bands, he decided.

They made the first checkpoint in four hours, walking on the road. Mickey was extremely happy about the insurance situation, assuming that since Jerry had paid the premium, the money was automatically theirs to squander. Jerry could not deter him from this view. But Mickey was also scared: first of CTs, then of ghosts, then of the colonel. So Jerry explained to him that neither the ghosts nor the CTs would venture near the road after that little episode. As for the colonel, though Jerry didn't mention this to Mickey – well, he was a father and a soldier and he had a dam to build: not for nothing was he building it with Drake Ko's cement and China Airsea's transport.

At the checkpoint, they eventually found a truck to take Mickey home. Riding with him a distance, Jerry promised the comic's support in any insurance haggle but Mickey in his euphoria was deaf to doubts. Amid much laughter, they exchanged addresses, and many hearty handshakes, then Jerry dropped off at a roadside café to wait half a day for the bus that would carry him eastward toward a fresh field of war.

* * *

Need Jerry have ever gone to Ricardo in the first place? Would the outcome, for himself, have been different if he had not? Or did Jerry, as Smiley's defenders to this day insist, by his pass at Ricardo, supply the last crucial heave which shook the tree and caused the coveted fruit to fall? For the Smiley Supporters' Club there is no question: the visit to Ricardo was the final straw and Ko's back broke under it. Without it, he might have gone on dithering until the open season started, by which time Ko himself, and the intelligence on him, would be up for grabs. End of argument. And on the face of it, the facts demonstrate a wonderful causality. For this is what happened. A mere six hours after Jerry and his driver Mickey had picked themselves out of the dust of that roadside in north-east Thailand, the whole of the Circus fifth floor exploded into a blaze of ecstatic jubilation which would have out-shone the pyre of Mickey's borrowed Ford car any night. In the rumpus room, where Smiley announced the news, Doc di Salis actually danced a stiff little jig, and Connie would unquestionably have joined him if her arthritis had not held her to that wretched chair. Trot howled, Guillam and Molly embraced, and only Smiley, amid so much revelry, preserved his usual slightly startled air, though Molly swore she saw him redden as he blinked around the company.

He had just had word, he said. A flash communication from the Cousins. At seven this morning, Hong Kong time, Tiu had telephoned Ko at Star Heights, where he had been spending the night relaxing with Lizzie Worth. Lizzie herself took the call in the first instance, but Ko came in on the extension and sharply ordered Lizzie to ring off, which she did. Tiu had proposed breakfast in town at once: 'At George's place,' said Tiu, to the great entertainment of the transcribers. Three hours later, Tiu was on the phone to his travel agent making hasty plans for a business trip to Mainland China. His first stop would be Canton, where China Airsea kept a representative, but his ultimate destination was Shanghai.

So how did Ricardo get through to Tiu so fast without

the telephone? The most likely theory is the colonel's police link to Bangkok. And from Bangkok? Heaven knows. Trade telex, the exchange-rate network, anything is possible. The Chinese have their own ways of doing these things.

On the other hand, it may just be that Ko's patience chose this moment to snap of its own accord – and that the breakfast 'at George's place' was about something entirely different. Either way, it was the breakthrough they had all been dreaming of, the triumphant vindication of Smiley's footwork. By lunchtime, Lacon had called in person to offer his congratulations and by early evening Saul Enderby had made a gesture nobody from the wrong side of Trafalgar Square had ever made before. He had sent round a crate of champagne from Berry Brothers and Rudd, a vintage Krug, a real beauty. Attached to it was a note to George saying 'to the first day of summer'. And indeed, though late April, it seemed to be just that. Through the thick net curtains of the lower floors, the plane trees were already in leaf. Higher up, a cluster of hyacinths had blossomed in Connie's window box. 'Red,' she said, as she drank Saul Enderby's health. 'Karla's favourite colour, bless him.'

Chapter 18

THE RIVER BEND

The airbase was neither beautiful nor victorious. Technically it was under Thai command, and in practice the Thais were allowed to collect the garbage and occupy the stockade close to the perimeter. The checkpoint was a separate town. Amid smells of charcoal, urine, pickled fish and calor gas, chains of collapsing tin hovels plied the historic trades of military occupation. The brothels were manned by crippled pimps, the tailor shops offered wedding tuxedos, the bookshops offered pornography and travel, the bars were called Sunset Strip, Hawaii and Lucky Time. At the MP hut Jerry asked for Captain Urquhart of public relations and the black sergeant squared to throw him out when he said he was press. On the base telephone, Jerry heard a lot of clicking and popping before a slow Southern voice said, 'Urquhart isn't around just now. My name is Masters. Who's this again?'

'We met last summer at General Crosse's briefing,' Jerry said.

'Well now, so we did, man,' said the same amazingly slow voice, reminding him of Deathwish. 'Pay off your cab. Be right down. Blue jeep. Wait for the whites of its eyes.'

A long silence followed, presumably while the codewords Urquhart and Crosse were hunted down in the contingency book.

A flow of airforce personnel was passing in and out of the camp, blacks and whites, in scowling segregated groups. A white officer passed. The blacks gave him the black power salute. The officer warily returned it. The enlisted men wore Charlie-Marshall-style patches on their uniforms, mostly in praise of drugs. The mood was sullen, defeated and innately violent. The Thai troops greeted nobody. Nobody greeted the Thais.

A blue jeep with lights flashing and siren wailing pulled up with a ferocious skid the other side of the boom. The sergeant waved Jerry through. A moment later he was careering over the runway at breakneck speed toward a long string of low white huts at the centre of the airfield. His driver was a lanky boy with all the signs of a probationer.

'You Masters?' Jerry asked.

'No, sir. Sir, I just carry the major's bags,' he said.

They passed a ragged baseball game, siren wailing all the time, lights still flashing.

'Great cover,' said Jerry.

'What's that, sir?' the boy yelled above the din.

'Forget it.'

It was not the biggest base. Jerry had seen larger. They passed lines of Phantoms and helicopters and as they approached the white huts he realised they comprised a separate spook encampment with their own compound and aerial masts, and their own cluster of little black-painted small planes – weirdos, they used to be called – which before the pullout had dropped and collected God knew whom in God knew where.

They entered by a side door which the boy unlocked. The short corridor was empty and soundless. A door stood ajar at the end of it, made of traditional fake rosewood. Masters wore a short-sleeved airforce uniform with few insignia. He had medals and the rank of major and Jerry guessed he was the para-military type of Cousin, maybe not even career. He was sallow and wiry with resentful tight lips and hollow cheeks. He stood before a faked fireplace, under an Andrew Wyeth reproduction, and there was something strangely still about him, and disconnected. He was like a man being deliberately slow because everyone else was in a hurry. The boy made the introductions and hesitated. Masters stared at him until he left, then turned his colourless gaze to the rosewood table where the coffee was.

'Look like you need breakfast,' Masters said.

He poured coffee and proffered a plate of doughnuts, all in slow motion.

'Facilities,' he said.

'Facilities,' Jerry agreed.

An electric typewriter lay on the desk, and plain paper beside it. Masters walked stiffly to a chair and perched on the arm. Taking up a copy of *Stars and Stripes*, he read it ostentatiously while Jerry settled at the desk.

'Hear you're going to win it all back for us single-handed,' said Masters to his *Stars and Stripes*. 'Well now.'

Setting up his portable in preference to the electric, Jerry stabbed out his report in a series of quick smacks which to his own ear grew louder as he laboured. Perhaps to Masters's ear also, for he looked up frequently, though only as far as Jerry's hands, and the toy-town portable.

Jerry handed him his copy.

'Your orders are to remain here,' Masters said, articulating each word with great deliberation. 'Your orders are to remain here while we des-patch your signal. Man, will we despatch that signal. Your orders are to stand by for confirmation and further instructions. That figure? Does that figure, *sir*?'

'Sure,' said Jerry.

'Heard the glad news by any chance?' Masters enquired. They were facing each other. Not three feet lay between them. Masters was staring at Jerry's signal but his eyes did not appear to be scanning the lines.

'What news is that, sport?'

'We just lost the war, Mr Westerby. Yes, sir. Last of the brave just had themselves scraped off the roof of the Saigon Embassy by chopper like a bunch of rookies caught with their pants down in a whorehouse. Maybe that doesn't affect you. Ambassador's dog survived, you'll be relieved to hear. Newsman took it out on his damn lap. Maybe that doesn't affect you either. Maybe you're not a dog-lover. Maybe you feel about dogs same way I personally feel about newsmen, Mr Westerby, sir.'

Jerry had by now caught the smell of brandy on Masters's breath which no amount of coffee could conceal, and he guessed he had been drinking for a long time without succeeding in getting drunk.

'Mr Westerby, sir?'

'Yes, old boy.'

Masters held out his hand.

'*Old boy*, I want you to shake me by the hand.'

The hand stuck between them, thumb upward.

'What for?' said Jerry.

'I want you to extend the hand of welcome, sir. The United States of America has just applied to join the club of second class powers, of which I understand your own fine nation to be chairman, president and oldest member. *Shake it!*'

'Proud to have you aboard,' said Jerry and obligingly shook the major's hand.

He was at once rewarded by a brilliant smile of false gratitude.

'Why sir, I call that *real* handsome of you, Mr Westerby. Anything we can do to make your stay with us more comfortable, I invite you to let me know. If you want to rent the place, no reasonable offer refused, we say.'

'You could shove a little Scotch through the bars,' Jerry said, pulling a dead grin.

'Mah pleasure,' said Masters, in a drawl so long it was like a slow punch. 'Man after my own heart. Yes, sir.'

Masters left him with a half bottle of J & B, from the cupboard, and some back-numbers of *Playboy*.

'We keep these handy for English gentlemen who didn't see fit to lift a damn finger to help us,' he explained confidingly.

'Very thoughtful of you,' said Jerry.

'I'll go send your letter home to Mummy. How *is* the Queen, by the way?'

Masters didn't turn a key but when Jerry tested the door handle it was locked. The windows overlooking the airfield were smoked and double glazed. On the runway, aircraft landed and took off without making a sound. This is how they tried to win, Jerry thought: from inside soundproof rooms, through smoked glass, using machines at arm's length. This is how they lost. He drank, feeling nothing. So it's over, he thought, and that was all. So what was his next stop? Charlie Marshall's old man? Little swing through the Shans, heart to heart chat with the General's bodyguard? He waited, his thoughts crowding formlessly. He sat down, then lay on the sofa and for a while slept, he never knew how long. He woke abruptly to the sound of canned music occasionally interrupted by an announcement of homely-wise assurance. Would Captain somebody do so and so? Once the speaker offered higher education. Once cut-price washing machines. Once, prayer. Jerry prowled the room, made nervous by the crematorium quiet and the music.

He crossed to the other window, and in his mind Lizzie's face bobbed along at his shoulder, the way once the orphan's had, but no more. He drank more whisky. I should have slept in the truck, he thought. Altogether I should sleep more. So they've lost the war at last. The sleep had done him no good. It seemed a long time since he'd slept the way he'd like to. Old Frostie had rather put an end to that. His hand was shaking: Christ, look at that. He thought of Luke. Time we went on a bend together. He must be back by now, if he hasn't had his arse shot off. Got to stop the old brain a bit, he thought. But sometimes the old brain hunted on its own these days. Bit too much, actually. Got to tie it down, he told himself sternly. *Man.* He thought of Ricardo's grenades. Hurry up, he thought. Come on, let's have a decision. *Where* next? *Who* now? No whys. His face was dry and hot, and his hands moist. He had a headache just above the eyes. Bloody music, he thought. Bloody, bloody end-of-world music. He was casting round urgently for somewhere to switch it off when he saw Masters standing in the doorway, an envelope in his hand and nothing in his eyes. Jerry read the signal. Masters settled on the chair arm again.

'"Son, come home,"' Masters intoned, mocking his own Southern drawl. '"Come directly home. Do not pass *go*. Do not collect two hundred dollars." The Cousins will fly you to Bangkok. From Bangkok you will pro-ceed immediately to London, England, *not* repeat not London, Ontario, by a flight of *your* choosing. You will on no account return to Hong Kong. You will not! No *sir*! Mission accomplished, *son*. Thank you and well done. Her Majesty is *so thrilled*. So hurry home to dinner, we got hominy grits and turkey, and *blue*-berry pie. Sounds like a bunch of fairies you're working for, *man*.'

Jerry re-read the signal.

'Plane leaves for Bangkok one one hundred,' Masters said. He wore his watch on the inside of his wrist, so that its information was private to himself. 'Hear me?'

Jerry grinned. 'Sorry, sport. Slow reader. Thanks. Too many big words. Lot to get the old mind round. Look, left my things at the hotel.'

'My houseboys are at your royal command.'

'Thanks, but if you don't mind, I'd prefer to avoid the official connection.'

'Please yourself, sir, please yourself.'

'I'll find a cab at the gates. There and back in an hour. Thanks,' he repeated.

'Thank *you*.'

Sarratt man provided a smart piece of tradecraft for the kiss-off. 'Mind if I leave that there?' he asked, nodding to his scruffy portable, where it lay beside Masters's golf-ball IBM.

'Sir, it shall be our most treasured possession.'

If Masters had bothered to look at him at that moment, he might have hesitated when he saw the purposeful brightness in Jerry's eye. If he had known Jerry's voice better perhaps, or noticed its particularly friendly huskiness, he might also have hesitated. If he had seen the way Jerry clawed at his forelock, forearm across his body in an attitude of instinctive self-concealment, or responded to Jerry's sheepish grin of thanks as the probationer returned to drive him to the gates in the blue jeep: well, again he might have had his doubts. But Major Masters was not only an embittered professional with a lot of disillusionment to his credit. He was a Southern gentleman suffering the stab of defeat at the hands of unintelligible savages; and he hadn't too much time just then for the contortions of a bone-weary overdue Brit who used his expiring spookhouse as a post office.

A mood of festivity attended the leavetaking of the Circus's Hong Kong operations party, and it was only enriched by the secrecy of the arrangements. The news of Jerry's reappearance triggered it. The content of his signal intensified it, and coincided with word from the Cousins that Drake Ko had cancelled all his social and business engagements and withdrawn to the seclusion of his house, Seven Gates in Headland Road. A photograph of Ko, taken in longshot from the Cousins' surveillance van, showed him in quarter profile, standing in his own large garden, at the end of an arbour of rose trees, staring out to sea. The concrete junk was not visible but he was wearing his floppy beret.

'Like a latter-day Jay Gatsby, my dear!' Connie Sachs cried in delight, as they all pored over it. 'Mooning at the blasted light at the end of the pier or whatever the ninny did!'

When the van returned that way two hours later, Ko was in the identical pose so they didn't bother to re-shoot. More significant was the fact that Ko had ceased to use the telephone altogether – or, at the very least, those lines on which the Cousins ran a tap.

Sam Collins also sent a report, the third in a stream, but by far his longest to date. As usual, it arrived in a special cover addressed to Smiley personally, and as usual he discussed its contents with nobody but Connie Sachs. And at the very moment when the party was leaving for London Airport, a last-minute message from Martello advised them that Tiu had returned from China, and was at present closeted with Ko in Headland Road.

But the most important ceremony, then and later, in

Guillam's recollection, and the most disturbing, was a small war-party held in Martello's rooms in the Annexe, which exceptionally was attended not only by the usual quintet of Martello, his two quiet men, Smiley and Guillam, but by Lacon and Saul Enderby as well, who significantly arrived in the same official car. The purpose of the ceremony – called by Smiley – was the formal handing over of the keys. Martello was now to receive a complete portrait of the Dolphin case, including the all-important link with Nelson. He was to be indoctrinated, with certain minor omissions, which only showed up later, as a full partner in the enterprise. How Lacon and Enderby muscled in on the occasion Guillam never quite knew and Smiley was afterwards understandably reticent about it. Enderby declared flatly that he had come along in the 'interest of good order and military discipline'. Lacon looked more than usually wan and disdainful. Guillam had the strongest impression they were up to something, and this was strengthened by his observation of the inter-play between Enderby and Martello: in short, these new-found buddies cut each other so dead they put Guillam in mind of two secret lovers meeting at communal breakfast in a country house, a situation in which he often found himself.

It was the *scale* of the thing, Enderby explained at one point. Case was blowing up so big he really thought there ought to be a few official flies on the wall. It was the Colonial lobby, he explained at another. Wilbraham was raising a stink with Treasury.

'All right, so we've heard the dirt,' said Enderby, when Smiley had finished his lengthy summary, and Martello's praises had all but brought the roof down. 'Now whose finger's on the trigger, George, point one?' he demanded to know, and after that the meeting became very much Enderby's show, as meetings with Enderby usually did. 'Who calls the shots when it gets hot? You, George? Still? I mean you've done a good planning job, I grant you, but it's old Marty here who's providing the artillery, isn't it?'

At which Martello had another bout of deafness, while

he beamed upon all the great and lovely British people he was privileged to be associated with, and let Enderby go on doing his hatchet-work for him.

'Marty, how do *you* see this one?' Enderby pressed, as if he really had no idea; as if he never went fishing with Martello, or gave lavish dinners for him, or discussed top secret matters out of school.

A strange insight came to Guillam at this moment, though he kicked himself afterwards for making too little of it. *Martello knew*. The revelations about Nelson, which Martello had affected to be dazzled by, were not revelations at all, but restatements of information which he and his quiet men already possessed. Guillam read it in their pale, wooden faces and their watchful eyes. He read it in Martello's fulsomeness. *Martello knew*.

'Ah technically this is George's show, Saul,' Martello reminded Enderby loyally, in answer to his question, but with just enough spin on the *technically* to put the rest in doubt. 'George is on the bridge, Saul. We're just there to stoke the engines.'

Enderby staged an unhappy frown and shoved a match between his teeth.

'George, how does that grab *you*? You content to let that happen, are you? Let Marty chuck in the cover, the accommodation out there, communications, all the cloak and dagger stuff, surveillance, charging round Hong Kong and whatnot? While you call the shots? Crikey. Bit like wearing someone else's dinner jacket, I'd have thought.'

Smiley was firm enough but, to Guillam's eye, a deal too concerned with the question, and not nearly concerned enough with the thinly-veiled collusion.

'Not at all,' said Smiley. 'Martello and I have a clear understanding. The spearhead of the operation will be handled by ourselves. If supportive action is required, Martello will supply it. The product is then shared. If one is thinking in terms of a dividend for the American investment, it comes with the partition of the product. The responsibility for obtaining it remains ours.' He ended strongly. 'The letter of agreement setting all this out has of course long been on file.'

Enderby glanced at Lacon. 'Oliver, you said you'd send me that. Where is it?'

Lacon put his long head on one side and pulled a dreary smile at nothing in particular. 'Kicking around your Third Room I should think, Saul.'

Enderby tried another tack. 'And you two guys can see the deal holding up in all contingencies, can you? I mean, who's handling the safe houses, all that? Burying the body, sort of thing?'

Smiley again. 'Housekeeping Section has already rented a cottage in the country, and is preparing it for occupation,' he said stolidly.

Enderby took the wet matchstick from his mouth and broke it into the ashtray. 'Could have had my place if you'd asked,' he muttered absently. 'Bags of room. Nobody ever there. Staff. Everything.' But he went on worrying at his theme. 'Look here. Answer me this one. Your man panics. He cuts and runs through the back streets of Hong Kong. Who plays cops and robbers to get him back?'

Don't answer it! Guillam prayed. He has absolutely no business to plumb around like this! Tell him to get lost!

Smiley's answer, though effective, lacked the fire Guillam longed for.

'Oh I suppose one can always invent a *hypothesis*,' he objected mildly. 'I think the best one can say is that Martello and I would at that stage pool our thoughts and act for the best.'

'George and I have a fine working relationship, Saul,' Martello declared handsomely. 'Just fine.'

'Much *tidier*, you see, George,' Enderby resumed, through a fresh matchstick. 'Much *safer* if it's an all-Yank do. Marty's people make a balls and all they do is apologise to the Governor, post a couple of blokes to Walla-Walla and promise not to do it again. That's it. What everyone expects of 'em anyway. Advantage of a disgraceful reputation, right, Marty? Nobody's surprised if you screw the housemaid.'

'Why, *Saul*,' said Martello and laughed richly at the great British sense of humour.

'Much more tricky if *we're* the naughty boys,' Enderby went on. 'Or *you* are, rather. Governor could blow you down with one puff, the way it's set up at the moment. Wilbraham's crying all over his desk already.'

Against Smiley's distracted obduracy, there was however no progress to be made, so, for the while, Enderby bowed out and they resumed their discussion of the 'meat-and-potatoes', which was Martello's amusing phrase for modalities. But before they finished Enderby had one last shot at dislodging Smiley from his primacy, choosing again the issue of the efficient handling and aftercare of the catch.

'George, who's going to manage all the grilling and stuff? You using that funny little Jesuit of yours, the one with the smart name?'

'Di Salis will be responsible for the Chinese aspects of the debriefing and our Soviet Research Section for the Russian side.'

'That the crippled don-woman, is it, George? The one bloody Bill Haydon shoved out to grass for drinking?'

'It is they, between them, who have brought the case this far,' said Smiley.

Inevitably, Martello sprang into the breach.

'Ah now George, I won't have that! Sir, I will not! Saul, Oliver, I wish you to know that I regard the Dolphin case, in all its aspects, Saul, as a personal triumph for George here, and for George *alone*!'

With a big hand all round for dear old George, they made their way back to Cambridge Circus.

'Gunpowder, treason and plot!' Guillam expostulated. 'Why's Enderby selling you down the river? What's all that tripe about losing the letter?'

'Yes,' said Smiley at last, but from far away. 'Yes, that's very careless of them. I thought I'd send them a copy actually. Blind, by hand, for information only. Enderby seemed so *woolly*, didn't he. Will you attend to that, Peter, ask the mothers?'

The mention of the letter of agreement – *heads* of agreement as Lacon called it – revived Guillam's worst misgivings. He remembered how he had foolishly allowed Sam Collins to be the bearer of it, and how, according to Fawn, he had spent more than an hour cloistered with Martello under the pretext of delivering it. He remembered Sam Collins also as he had glimpsed him in Lacon's anteroom, the mysterious confidant of Lacon and Enderby, lazing around Whitehall like a blasted Cheshire cat. He remembered Enderby's taste for backgammon, which he played for very high stakes, and it even passed through his head, as he tried to sniff out the conspiracy, that Enderby might be a client of Sam Collins's club. From that notion he soon pulled back, discounting it as too absurd. But ironically it later turned out to be true. And he remembered his fleeting conviction – based on little but the physiognomy of the three Americans, and therefore soon also to be dismissed – that they knew already what Smiley had come to tell them.

But Guillam did not pull back from the notion of Sam Collins as the ghost at that morning's feast, and as he boarded the plane at London Airport, exhausted by his long and energetic farewell from Molly, the same ghost grinned at him through the smoke of Sam's infernal brown cigarette.

The flight was uneventful, except in one respect. They were three strong, and in the seating arrangements Guillam had won a small battle in his running war with Fawn. Over Housekeeping Section's dead body, Guillam and Smiley flew first class, while Fawn the babysitter took an aisle seat at the front of the tourist compartment, cheek by jowl with the airline security guards, who slept innocently for most of the journey while Fawn sulked. There had never been any suggestion, fortunately, that Martello and his quiet men would fly with them, for Smiley was determined that that should not on any account happen. As it was, Martello flew west, staging in Langley for instructions, and continuing through Honolulu and Tokyo in order to be on hand in Hong Kong for their arrival.

As an unconsciously ironic footnote to their departure, Smiley left a long handwritten note to Jerry, to be presented to him on his arrival at the Circus, congratulating him on his first-rate performance. The carbon copy is still in Jerry's dossier. Nobody has thought to remove it. Smiley speaks of Jerry's 'unswerving loyalty', and of 'setting the crown on more than thirty years of service'. He includes an apocryphal message from Ann 'who joins me in wishing you an equally distinguished career as a novelist'. And he winds up rather awkwardly with the sentiment that 'one of the privileges of our work is that it provides us with such wonderful colleagues. I must tell you that we all think of you in those terms.'

Certain people do still ask why no anxious word about Jerry's whereabouts had reached the Circus before take-off. He was after all several days overdue. Once more they look for ways of blaming Smiley, but there is no evidence of a lapse on the Circus's side. For the transmission of Jerry's report from the airbase in North East Thailand – his last – the Cousins had cleared a line through Bangkok direct to the Annexe in London. But the arrangement was valid for one signal and one answer-back only, and a follow-up was not envisaged. Accordingly the grizzle, when it came, was routed first to Bangkok on the military network, thence to the Cousins in Hong Kong on *their* network – since Hong Kong was held to have a total lien on all Dolphin-starred material – and only then, marked 'routine', repeated by Hong Kong to London, where it kicked around in several laminated rosewood in-trays before anybody noted its significance. And it must be admitted that the languid Major Masters had attached very little significance to the no-show, as he later called it, of some travelling English fairy. 'ASSUME EXPLANATION YOUR END' his message ends. Major Masters now lives in Norman, Oklahoma, where he runs a small automobile repair business.

Nor did Housekeeping Section have any reason to panic – or so they still plead. Jerry's instructions, on reaching

Bangkok, were to find himself a plane, any plane, using his air-travel card, and get himself to London. No date was mentioned, and no airline. The whole purpose was to leave things fluid. Most likely he had stopped over somewhere for a bit of relaxation. Many homing fieldmen do, and Jerry was on record as sexually voracious. So they kept their usual watch on flight lists and made a provisional booking at Sarratt for the two weeks' drying-out and recycling ceremony, then returned their attention to the far more urgent business of setting up the Dolphin safe house. This was a charming millhouse, quite remote, though situated in the commuter town of Maresfield in Sussex, and on most days they found a reason for going down there. As well as di Salis and a sizeable part of his Chinese archive, a small army of interpreters and transcribers had to be accommodated, not to mention technicians, babysitters and a Chinese-speaking doctor. In no time at all, the residents were complaining noisily to the police about the influx of Japanese. The local paper carried a story that they were a visiting dance troupe. Housekeeping Section had inspired the leak.

Jerry had nothing to collect at the hotel, and as it happened no hotel, but he reckoned he had an hour to get clear, perhaps two. He had no doubt the Americans had the whole town wired, and he knew there would be nothing easier, if London asked for it, than for Major Masters to have Jerry's name and description broadcast as an American deserter travelling on a false-flag passport. Once his taxi was clear of the gates, therefore, he took it to the southern edge of town, waited, then took a second taxi and pointed it due north. A wet haze lay over the paddies and the straight road ran into it endlessly. The radio pumped out female Thai voices like an endless slow motion nursery rhyme. They passed an American electronics base, a circular grid a quarter of a mile wide floating in the haze and known locally as the Elephant Cage. Giant bodkins marked the perimeter, and at the middle, surrounded by webs of strung wire, burned a single infernal light, like the promise of a future war. He had heard there were twelve hundred language students inside the place, but not one soul was to be seen.

He needed time, and in the event he helped himself to more than one week. Even now, he needed that long to bring himself to the point, because Jerry at heart was a soldier and voted with his feet. *In the beginning was the deed*, Smiley liked to say to him, in his failed-priest mood, quoting from one of his German poets. For Jerry, that simple maxim had become a pillar of his uncomplicated philosophy. What a man thinks is his own business. What matters is what he does.

Reaching the Mekong by early evening, he selected a village and strolled idly for a couple of days up and down the river bank, trailing his shoulder bag and kicking at an empty Coca-Cola tin with the toe of his buckskin boot. Across the river, behind the brown ant-hill mountains, lay the Ho Chi-minh trail. He had once watched a B52 strike from this very point, three miles away in Central Laos. He remembered how the ground shook under his feet and the sky emptied and burned, and he had known, he had really for a moment known, what it was like to be in the middle of it.

The same night, to use his own jolly phrase, Jerry Westerby blew the walls out, much along the lines the housekeepers expected of him, if not in quite the circumstances. In a riverside bar where they played old tunes on a nickelodeon, he drank black market PX Scotch and night after night drove himself into oblivion, leading one laughing girl after another up the unlit staircase to a tattered bedroom, till finally he stayed there sleeping, and didn't come down. Waking with a jolt, clear-headed at dawn, to the screaming of roosters, and the clatter of the river traffic, Jerry forced himself to think long and generously of his chum and mentor, George Smiley. It was an act of will that made him do this, almost an act of obedience. He wished, quite simply, to rehearse the articles of his Creed, and his Creed till now had been old George. At Sarratt, they have a very worldly and relaxed attitude to the motives of a fieldman, and no patience at all for the fiery-eyed zealot who grinds his teeth and says 'I hate Communism'. If he dates it that much, they argue, he's most likely in love with it already. What they really like – and what Jerry possessed, what he *was*, in effect – was the fellow who hadn't a lot of time for flannel but loved the service and knew – though God forbid he should make a fuss of it – that *we* were right. *We* being a necessarily flexible notion, but to Jerry it meant George and that was that.

Old George. Super. Good morning.

He saw him as he liked to remember him best, the first time they met, at Sarratt, soon after the war. Jerry was still an army subaltern, his time nearly up and Oxford looming, and he was bored stiff. The course was for London Occasionals: people who, having done the odd bit of skulduggery without going formally on to the Circus payroll, were being groomed as an auxiliary reserve. Jerry had already volunteered for full-time employment, but Circus personnel had turned him down, which scarcely helped his mood. So when Smiley waddled into the paraffin-heated lecture hut in his heavy overcoat and spectacles, Jerry inwardly groaned and prepared himself for another creaking fifty minutes of boredom – on good places to look for dead letter boxes, most likely – followed by a sort of clandestine nature ramble through Rickmansworth trying to spot hollow trees in graveyards. There was comedy while the Directing Staff fought to crank the lectern lower so that George could see over the top. In the end, he stood himself a little fussily at the side of it and declared that his subject this afternoon was 'problems of maintaining courier lines inside enemy territory'. Slowly it dawned on Jerry that he was talking not from the textbook but from experience: that this owlish little pedant with the diffident voice and the blinking, apologetic manner had sweated out three years in some benighted German town, holding the threads of a very respectable network, while he waited for the boot through the door panel or the pistol butt across the face that would introduce him to the pleasures of interrogation.

When the meeting was over, Smiley asked to see him. They met in a corner of an empty bar, under the antlers where the darts board hung.

'I'm so sorry we couldn't have you,' he said. 'I think our feeling was, you needed a little more time *outside* first.' Which was their way of saying he was immature. Too late, Jerry remembered Smiley as one of the non-speaking members of the Selection Board which had failed him. 'Perhaps if you could get your degree, and make your way a little in a different walk of life, they would change their way of thinking. Don't lose touch, will you?'

After which, somehow, old George had always been there. Never surprised, never out of patience, old George had gently but firmly re-jigged Jerry's life till it was Circus property. His father's empire collapsed: George was waiting with his hands out to catch him. His marriages collapsed: George would sit all night for him, hold his head.

'I've always been grateful to this service that it gave me a chance to pay,' Smiley had said. 'I'm sure one should feel that. I don't think we should be afraid of . . . devoting ourselves. Is that old-fashioned of me?'

'You point me, I'll march,' Jerry had replied. 'Tell me the shots and I'll play them.'

There was still time. He knew that. Train to Bangkok, hop on a plane home, and the worst he would get was a flea in his ear for jumping ship for a few days. *Home*, he repeated to himself. Bit of a problem. Home to Tuscany, and the yawning emptiness of the hilltop without the orphan? Home to old Pet, sorry about the bust teacup? Home to dear old Stubbsie, key appointment as desk jockey with special responsibility for the spike? Or home to the Circus: 'We think you'd be happiest in Banking Section.' Even – great thought – home to Sarratt, training job, winning the hearts and minds of new entrants while he commuted dangerously from a maisonette in Watford.

On the third or fourth morning he woke very early. Dawn was just rising over the river, turning it first red, then orange, now brown. A family of water-buffaloes wallowed in the mud, their bells jingling. In midstream, three sampans were linked in a long and complicated trawl. He heard a hiss and saw a net curl, then fall like hail on the water.

Yet it's not for want of a future that I'm here, he thought. It's for want of a present.

Home's where you go when you run out of homes, he thought. Which brings me to Lizzie. Vexed issue. Shove it on the back burner. Spot of breakfast.

Sitting on the teak balcony munching eggs and rice Jerry remembered George breaking the news to him about Haydon. El Vino's bar, Fleet Street, a rainy midday. Jerry had never found it possible to hate anyone for very long, and after the initial shock there had really not been much more to say.

'Well, no point in crying in the old booze, is there, sport? Can't leave the ship to the rats. Soldier on, that's the thing.'

To which Smiley agreed: yes, that was the thing, to soldier on, grateful for the chance to pay. Jerry had even found a sort of rum comfort in the fact that Bill was one of the clan. He had never seriously doubted, in his vague way, that his country was in a state of irreversible decline, nor that his own class was to blame for the mess. 'We *made* Bill,' ran his argument, 'so it's right we should carry the brunt of his betrayal.' Pay in fact. Pay. What old George was on about.

Pottering beside the river again, breathing the free warm air, Jerry chucked flat stones to make them bounce.

Lizzie, he thought. Lizzie Worthington, suburban bolter. Ricardo's pupil and punchball. Charlie Marshall's big sister and earth mother and unattainable whore. Drake Ko's cagebird. My dinner companion for all of four hours. And to Sam Collins – to repeat the question – what had she been to him? For Mr Mellon, Charlie's 'creepy British trader' of eighteen months ago, she was a courier working the Hong Kong heroin trail. But she was more than that. Somewhere along the line Sam had shown her a bit of ankle and told her she was working for Queen and country. Which glad news Lizzie had promptly shared with her admiring circle of friends. To Sam's fury, and he dropped her like a hot brick. So Sam had set her up as a patsy of some kind. A coat-trailer on probation. In one way this thought amused Jerry very much, for Sam had a reputation as an ace operator, whereas Lizzie Worthington might well star at Sarratt as the archetypal Woman Never to Be Recruited as Long as She Can Speak or Breathe.

Less funny was the question of what she meant to Sam *now*. What kept him skulking in her shadow like a patient murderer, smiling his grim iron smile? That question worried Jerry very much. Not to put too fine a point on it, he was obsessed by it. He definitely did not wish to see Lizzie taking another of her dives. If she went anywhere from Ko's bed, it was going to be into Jerry's. For some while, off and on – ever since he had met her, in fact – he had been thinking how much Lizzie would benefit from the bracing Tuscan air. And while he didn't know the hows and whys of Sam Collins's presence in Hong Kong, nor even what the Circus at large intended for Drake Ko, he had the strongest possible impression – and here was the nub of the thing – that by pushing off to London at this moment, far from carting Lizzie away on his white charger, Jerry was leaving her sitting on a very large bomb.

Which struck him as unacceptable. In other times, he might have been prepared to leave that problem to the owls, as he had left so many other problems in his day. But these were not other times. This time, as he now realised, it was the Cousins who were paying the piper, and while Jerry had no particular quarrel with the Cousins, their presence made it a much rougher ball-game. So that whatever vague notions he had about George's humanity did not apply.

Also, he cared about Lizzie. Urgently. There was nothing imprecise in his feelings at all. He ached for her, warts and all. She was his kind of loser, and he loved her. He had worked it out and drawn the line, and that, after several days of counting on beads, was his net, unalterable solution. He was a little awed, but very pleased by it.

Gerald Westerby, he told himself. You were present at your birth. You were present at your several marriages and at some of your divorces and you will certainly be present at your funeral. High time, in our considered view, that you were present at certain other crucial moments in your history.

Taking a bus up-river a few miles, he walked again, rode on cyclos, sat in bars, made love to the girls, thinking only of Lizzie. The inn where he stayed was full of children and one morning he woke to find two of them sitting on his bed, marvelling at the enormous length of the *farang*'s legs and giggling at the way his bare feet hung over the end. Maybe I'll just stay here, he thought. But by then he was fooling, because he knew that he had to go back and ask her; even if the answer was a custard pie. From the balcony he launched paper aeroplanes for the children, and they clapped and danced, watching them float away.

He found a boatman and when evening came he crossed the river to Vientiane, avoiding the formalities of immigration. Next morning, also without formality, he wangled himself aboard an unscheduled Royal Air Lao DC8, and by afternoon he was airborne, and in possession of a delicious warm whisky and chatting merrily to a couple of friendly opium dealers. As they landed, black rain was falling and the windows of the airport bus were foul with dust. Jerry didn't mind at all. For the first time in his life, returning to Hong Kong was quite like coming home after all.

Inside the reception area, nevertheless, Jerry played a cautious hand. No trumpets, he told himself: definitely. The few days' rest had done wonders for his presence of mind. Having taken a good look round he made for the men's room instead of the immigration desks and lay up there till a big load of Japanese tourists arrived, then barged over to them and asked who spoke English. Having cut out four of them, he showed them his Hong

Kong press card and while they stood in line waiting for their passport check he besieged them with questions about why they were here and what they proposed to do, and with whom, and wrote wildly on his pad before choosing four more, and repeating the process. Meanwhile he waited for the police on duty to change watch. At four o'clock they did and he at once made for a door signed 'No Entry' which he had marked earlier. He banged on it till it was opened, and started to walk through to the other side.

'Where the hell are you going?' asked an outraged Scottish police inspector.

'Home to a comic, sport. Got to file the dirt on our friendly Japanese visitors.'

He showed his press card.

'Well go through the damn gates like everyone else.'

'Don't be bloody silly. I haven't got my passport. That's why your distinguished colleague brought me through this way in the first place.'

Bulk, a ranking voice, a patently British appearance, an affecting grin, won him a space in a city-bound bus five minutes later. Outside his apartment block, he dawdled but saw no one suspicious, but this was China and who could tell? The lift as usual emptied for him. Riding in it he hummed Deathwish the Hun's one record in anticipation of a hot bath and change of clothes. At his front door, he had a moment's anxiety when he noticed the tiny wedges he had left in place lying on the floor, till he belatedly remembered Luke, and smiled at the prospect of their reunion. He unlocked the burglar door and as he did so he heard the sound of humming from inside, a droning monotone, which could have been an airconditioner, but not Deathwish's, it was too useless and inefficient. Bloody idiot Luke has left the gramophone on, he thought, and it's about to blow up. Then he thought: I'm doing him an injustice, it's that fridge. Then he opened the door and saw Luke's dead body strewn across the floor with half his head shot to pieces, and half the flies in Hong Kong swarming over it and round it; and all he could think to do, as he quickly closed the door behind him, and jammed his handkerchief over his mouth, was run into the kitchen in case there was still someone there. Returning to the living room, he pushed Luke's feet aside and dug up the parquet brick where he cached his forbidden side-arm and his escape kit, and put them in his pocket before he vomited.

Of course, he thought. That's why Ricardo was so certain the horse-writer was dead.

Join the club, he thought, as he stood out in the street again, with the rage and grief pounding in his ears and eyes. Nelson Ko's dead but he's running China. Ricardo's dead, but Drake Ko says he can stay alive as long as he sticks to the shady side of the street. Jerry Westerby the horse-writer is also completely dead, except that Ko's stupid pagan vicious bastard of a henchman, Mr bloody Tiu, was so thick he shot the wrong roundeye.

Chapter 19

GOLDEN THREAD

The inside of the American Consulate in Hong Kong could have been the inside of the Annexe, right down to the ever-present fake rosewood and bland courtesy and the airport chairs and the heartening portrait of the President, even if this time it was Ford. Welcome to your Howard Johnson spookhouse, Guillam thought. The section they worked in was called the isolation ward and had its own doorway to the street, guarded by two marines. They had passes in false names – Guillam's was Gordon – and for the duration of their stay there, except on the telephone, they never spoke to a soul inside the building except one another. 'We're not just deniable, gentlemen,' Martello had told them proudly in the briefing, 'we're also invisible as well.' That was how it was going to be played, he said. The US Consul General could put his hand on the Bible and swear to the Governor they weren't there and his staff were not involved, said Martello. 'Blindeye right down the line.' After that, he handed over to George because: 'George this is your show from soup to nuts.'

Downhill they had five minutes' walk to the Hilton, where Martello had booked them rooms. Uphill, though it would have been hard going, they had ten minutes' walk to Lizzie Worth's apartment block. They had been here five days and now it was evening, but they had no way of telling because there were no windows in the operations room. There were maps and sea-charts instead, and a couple of telephones manned by Martello's quiet men, Murphy and his friend. Martello and Smiley had a big desk each. Guillam, Murphy and his friend shared the table with the telephones and Fawn sat moodily at the centre of an empty row of cinema chairs along the back wall, like a bored critic at a preview, sometimes picking his teeth and sometimes yawning but refusing to take himself off, as Guillam repeatedly advised him. Craw had been spoken to and ordered to keep clear of everything: a total duckdive. Smiley was frightened for him since Frost's death, and would have preferred him evacuated, but the old boy wouldn't leave.

It was also, for once, the hour of the quiet men: 'our final detailed briefing', Martello had called it. 'Ah, that's if it's okay by *you*, George.' Pale Murphy, wearing a white shirt and blue trousers, was standing on the raised podium before a wall chart soliloquising from pages of notes. The rest of them, including Smiley and Martello, sat at his feet and listened mainly in silence. Murphy could have been describing a vacuum cleaner, and to Guillam that made his monologue the more hypnotic. The chart showed largely sea, but at the top and to the left hung a lace-fringe of the South China coast. Behind Hong Kong, the spattered outskirts of Canton were just visible below the batten which held the chart in place, and due south of Hong Kong at the very mid-point of the chart stretched the green outline of what looked to be a cloud divided into four sections marked A, B, C and D respectively. These, said Murphy reverently, were the fishing beds and the cross at the centre was Centre Point, sir. Murphy spoke only to Martello, whether it was George's show from soup to nuts or not.

'Sir, basing on the last occasion Drake exited Red China, sir, and updating our assessment to the situation as of now, we and navy int. between us, sir – '

'Murphy, Murphy,' put in Martello quite kindly, 'ease off a little, will you, friend? This isn't training school any more, okay? Loosen your girdle, will you, son?'

'Sir. One. Weather,' Murphy said, quite untouched by this appeal. 'April and May are the transitional months, sir, between the north-east monsoons and the beginning of the south-west monsoons. Forecasts day-to-day are unpredictable, sir, but no extreme conditions are foreseen for the trip.' He was using the pointer to show the line from Swatow southward to the fishing beds, then from the fishing beds north-west past Hong Kong up the Pearl River to Canton.

'Fog?' Martello said.

'Fog is traditional for the season and cloud is anticipated at six to seven oktas,.sir.'

'What the hell's an *okta*, Murphy?'

'One okta is one eighth of sky area covered, sir. Oktas have replaced the former tenths. No typhoons have been recorded in April for over fifty years and navy int. call typhoons unlikely. Wind is easterly, nine to ten knots but any fleet that runs with it must count on periods of calm, also contrary winds too, sir. Humidity around eighty per cent, temperature fifteen to twenty-four centigrade. Sea conditions calm with a small swell. Currents around Swatow tend to run north-east through the Taiwan Strait, at around three sea miles per day. But further westward – on *this* side, sir – '

'That's one thing I *do* know, Murphy,' Martello put in sharply. 'I know where west is, dammit.' Then he grinned at Smiley as if to say 'these young whipper-snappers'.

Murphy was again unmoved. 'We have to be prepared to calculate the speed factor and consequently the progress of the fleet at any one point in its journey, sir.'

'Sure, sure.'

'Moon, sir,' Murphy continued. 'Assuming the fleet to have exited Swatow on the night of Friday April twenty-fifth, the moon would be three days off of full – '

'Why do we assume that, Murphy?'

'Because that's when the fleet exited Swatow, sir. We had confirmation from navy int. one hour ago. Column of junks sighted at the eastern end of fishing bed C and easing westward with the wind, sir. Positive identification of the lead junk confirmed.'

There was a prickly pause. Martello coloured.

'You're a clever boy, Murphy,' Martello said, in a

warning tone. 'But you should have given me that information a little earlier.'

'Yes, sir. Assuming also that the intention of the junk containing Nelson Ko is to hit Hong Kong waters on the night of May four, the moon will be in its last quarter, sir. If we follow precedents right down the line – '

'We do,' said Smiley firmly. 'The escape is to be an exact repetition of Drake's own journey in fifty-one.'

Once more, no one doubted him, Guillam noticed. Why not? It was utterly bewildering.

' – then our junk should hit the southernmost out-island of Po Toi at twenty hundred hours tomorrow, and rejoin the fleet up along the Pearl River in time to make Canton harbour between zero ten thirty and twelve hundred hours following day, May five, sir.'

While Murphy droned on, Guillam covertly kept his eye on Smiley, thinking, as he often thought, that he knew him no better today than when he first met him back in the dark days of the cold war in Europe. Where did he slip away to at all odd hours? Mooning about Ann? About Karla? What company did he keep that brought him back to the hotel at four in the morning? Don't tell me George is having a second spring, he thought. Last night at eleven there had been a scream from London, so Guillam had trailed up here to unbutton it. Westerby adrift, they said. They were terrified Ko had had him murdered or, worse, abducted and tortured, and that the operation would abort in consequence. Guillam thought it more likely Jerry was holed up with a couple of air-hostesses somewhere en route to London but with that priority on the signal he had no option but to wake Smiley and tell him. He rang his room and got no answer so he dressed and banged on Smiley's door and finally he was reduced to picking the lock, for now it was Guillam's turn to panic: he thought Smiley might be ill.

But Smiley's room was empty and his bed unslept in, and when Guillam went through his things he was fascinated to see that the old fieldman had gone to the length of sewing false name tapes in his shirts. That was all he discovered, however. So he settled in Smiley's chair and dozed and didn't wake till four when he heard a tiny flutter and opened his eyes to see Smiley stooped and peering at him about six inches away. How he got into the room so silently, God alone knew.

'Gordon?' he asked softly. 'What can I do for you?' – for they were on an operational footing, of course, and lived with the assumption the rooms were bugged. For the same reason Guillam did not speak, but handed Smiley the envelope containing Connie's message, which he read and re-read, then burned. Guillam was impressed how seriously he took the news. Even at that hour, he insisted on going straight up to the Consulate to attend to it, so Guillam went along to carry his bags.

'Instructive evening?' he asked lightly, as they plodded the short way up the hill.

'I? Oh, to a point, thank you, to a point.' Smiley replied, doing his disappearing act, and that was all Guillam or anyone could get out of him about his nocturnal or other ambles. Meanwhile, without the smallest explanation of his source, George was bringing in hard operational data in a manner which brooked no enquiry from anyone.

'Ah George, we can count on that, can we?' Martello asked in bewilderment, on the first occasion that this happened.

'What? Oh yes, yes, indeed you may.'

'Great. Great footwork, George. I admire you,' said Martello heartily, after a further puzzled silence, and from then on they had gone along with it, they had no choice. For nobody, not even Martello, quite dared to challenge his authority.

'How many days' fishing is that, Murphy?' Martello was asking.

'Fleet will have had seven days' fishing and hopefully make Canton with full holds, sir.'

'That figure, George?'

'Yes, oh yes, nothing to add, thank you.'

Martello asked what time the fleet would have to leave the fishing beds in order for Nelson's junk to make tomorrow evening's rendezvous on time.

'I have put it at eleven tomorrow morning,' Smiley said, without looking up from his notes.

'Me too,' said Murphy.

'This rogue junk, Murphy,' Martello said, with another deferential glance at Smiley.

'Yes, sir,' said Murphy.

'Can it break away from the pack that easy? What would be its cover for entering Hong Kong waters, Murphy?'

'Happens all the time, sir. Red Chinese junk fleets operate a collective catch system without profit motivation, sir. Consequence of that, you get the single junks that break away at night time and come in without lights and sell their fish to the out-islanders for money.'

'*Literally* moonlighting!' Martello exclaimed, much amused by the felicity of the expression.

Smiley had turned to the map of Po Toi island on the other wall and was tilting his head in order to intensify the magnification of his spectacles.

'What size of junk are we talking of?' Martello asked.

'Twenty-eight man long-liners, sir, baited for shark, golden thread and conger.'

'Did Drake use that type also?'

'Yes,' said Smiley, still watching the map. 'Yes, he did.'

'And she can come that close in, can she? Provided the weather allows?'

Again it was Smiley who answered. Till today, Guillam had not heard him so much as speak of a boat in his life.

'The draw of a long-liner is less than five fathoms,' he remarked. 'She can come in as close as she wishes, provided always that the sea is not too rough.'

From the back bench, Fawn gave an immoderate laugh. Wheeling round in his chair Guillam shot him a foul look. Fawn leered and shook his head, marvelling at his masters' omniscience.

'How many junks make up a fleet?' Martello asked.

'Twenty to thirty,' said Smiley.
'Check,' said Murphy meekly.
'So what does Nelson do, George? Kind of get out to the edge of the pack there, and stray a little?'
'He'll hang back,' said Smiley. 'The fleets like to move in column astern. Nelson will tell his skipper to take the rear position.'
'Will he, by God,' Martello muttered under his breath. 'Murphy, what identifications are traditional?'
'Very little known in that area, sir. Boat people are notoriously evasive. They have no respect for marine regulations. Out to sea they show no lights at all, mostly for fear of pirates.'
Smiley was lost to them again. He had sunk into a wooden immobility, and though his eyes stayed fixed on the big sea chart, his mind, Guillam knew, was anywhere but with Murphy's dreary recitation of statistics. Not so Martello.
'How much coastal trade do we have overall, Murphy?'
'Sir, there are no controls and no data.'
'Any quarantine checks as the junks enter Hong Kong waters, Murphy?' Martello asked.
'Theoretically all vessels should stop and have themselves checked, sir.'
'And in practice, Murphy?'
'Junks are a law to themselves, sir. Technically Chinese junks are forbidden to sail between Victoria Island and Kowloon Point, sir, but the last thing the Brits want is a hassle with the Mainland over rights of way. Sorry, sir.'
'Not at all,' said Smiley politely, still gazing at the chart. 'Brits we are and Brits we shall remain.'
It's his Karla expression, Guillam decided: the one that comes over him when he looks at the photograph. He catches sight of it, it surprises him and for a while he seems to study it, its contours, its blurred and sightless gaze. Then the light slowly goes out of his eyes, and somehow the hope as well, and you feel he's looking inward, in alarm.
'Murphy, did I hear you mention navigation lights?'

Smiley enquired, turning his head, but still staring toward the chart.

'Yes, sir.'

'I expect Nelson's junk to carry three,' said Smiley. 'Two green lights vertically on the stern mast and one red light to starboard.'

'Yes, sir.'

Martello tried to catch Guillam's eye but Guillam wouldn't play.

'But it may not,' Smiley warned as an afterthought. 'It may carry none at all, and simply signal from close in.'

Murphy resumed. A new heading. Communications.

'Sir, in the communications area, sir, few junks have their own transmitters but most all have receivers. Once in a while you get a skipper who buys a cheap walkie-talkie with range about one mile to facilitate the trawl, but they've been doing it so long they don't have much call to speak to each other, I guess. Then as to finding their way, well navy int. says that's near enough a mystery. We have reliable information that many long-liners operate on a primitive compass, a hand lead-and-line, or even just a rusty alarm clock for finding true north.'

'Murphy, how the *hell* do they work *that*, for God's sakes?' Martello cried.

'Line with a lead plumb and wax stuck to it, sir. They sound the bed, and know where they are from what sticks to the wax.'

'Well they *really* do it the hard way,' Martello declared.

A phone rang. Martello's other quiet man took the call, listened, then put his hand over the mouthpiece.

'Quarry Worth's just gotten back, sir,' he said to Smiley. 'Party drove around for an hour, now she's checked in her car back at the block. Mac says sounds like she's running a bath so maybe she plans going out again later.'

'And she's alone,' Smiley said impassively. It was a question.

'She alone there, Mac?' He gave a hard laugh. 'I'll bet you would, you dirty bastard. Yes, *sir*, the lady's all alone taking a bath, and Mac there says when will we ever get to use video as well. Is the lady *singing* in the bath, Mac?' He rang off. 'She's not singing.'

'Murphy, get on with the war,' Martello snapped.

Smiley would like the interception plans rehearsed once more, he said.

'Why George! Please! It's your show, remember?'

'Perhaps we could look again at the big map of Po Toi island, could we? And then Murphy could break it down for us, would you mind?'

'*Mind*, George, *mind*!' Martello cried, so Murphy began again, this time using a pointer. Navy int. observation posts *here*, sir . . . constant two-way communication with base, sir . . . no presence at all within two sea-miles of the landing zone . . . Navy int. to advise base the moment the Ko launch starts back for Hong Kong, sir . . . interception will take place by regular British police vessel as the Ko launch enters harbour . . . US to supply op. int. and stand off only, for unforeseen supportive situation . . .

Smiley monitored every detail with a prim nod of his head.

'After all, Marty,' he put in, at one point, 'once Ko has Nelson aboard, there's nowhere else he *can* go is there? Po Toi is right at the edge of China waters. It's us or nothing.'

One day thought Guillam, as he continued listening, one of two things will happen to George. He'll cease to care, or the paradox will kill him. If he ceases to care, he'll be half the operator he is. If he doesn't, that little chest will blow up from the struggle of trying to find the explanation for what we do. Smiley himself, in a disastrous off-the-record chat to senior officers, had put the names to his dilemma, and Guillam, with some embarrassment, recalled them to this day. To be *inhuman in defence of our humanity*, he had said, *harsh in defence of compassion*. To be *single-minded in defence of our disparity*. They had filed out in a veritable ferment of protest. Why didn't George just do the job and shut up instead of taking his faith out and polishing it in public till the flaws showed? Connie had even murmured a Russian aphorism in Guillam's ear which she insisted on attributing to Karla.

'There'll be no war, will there, Peter darling?' she had said reassuringly, squeezing his hand as he led her along the corridor. 'But in the struggle for peace not a single stone will be left standing, bless the old fox. I'll bet they didn't thank him for *that* one in the Collegium either.'

A thud made Guillam swing round. Fawn was changing cinema seats again. Seeing Guillam, he flared his nostrils in an insolent sneer.

'He's off his head,' thought Guillam with a shiver.

Fawn too, for different reasons, was now causing Guillam serious anxiety. Two days ago, in Guillam's company, he had been the author of a disgusting incident. Smiley as usual had gone out alone. To kill time, Guillam had hired a car and driven Fawn up to the China border, where he had sniggered and puffed at the mysterious hills. Returning, they were waiting at some country traffic lights when a Chinese boy drew alongside on a Honda. Guillam was driving. Fawn had the passenger seat. Fawn's window was lowered, he had taken his jacket off and was resting his left arm on the door where he could admire a new gilt watch he had bought himself in the Hilton shopping concourse. As they pulled away, the Chinese boy ill-advisedly made a dive for the watch, but Fawn was much too quick for him. Catching hold of the boy's wrist instead, he held on to it, towing him beside the car while the boy struggled vainly to break free. Guillam had driven fifty yards or so before he realised what had happened and he at once stopped the car, which was what Fawn was waiting for. He jumped out before Guillam could stop him, lifted the boy straight off his Honda, led him to the side of the road and broke both his arms for him, then returned smiling to the car. Terrified of a scandal, Guillam drove rapidly from the scene, leaving the boy screaming and staring at his dangling arms. He reached Hong Kong determined to report Fawn to George immediately, but luckily for Fawn it was eight hours before Smiley surfaced, and by then Guillam reckoned George had enough on his plate already.

Another phone was ringing, the red. Martello took the call himself. He listened a moment then burst into a loud laugh.

'They found him,' he told Smiley, holding the phone to him.

'Found whom?'

The phone hovered between them.

'Your *man*, George. Your Weatherby – '

'Westerby,' Murphy corrected him, and Martello shot him a venomous look.

'They got him,' said Martello.

'Where is he?'

'Where *was* he, you mean! George, he just had himself the time of his life in two cathouses up along the Mekong. If our people are not exaggerating, he's the hottest thing since Barnum's baby elephant left town in forty-nine!'

'And where is he now, please?'

Martello handed him the phone. 'Why don't you just have 'em read you the signal, okay? They have some story that he crossed the river.' He turned to Guillam, and winked. 'They tell me there's a couple of places in Vientiane where he might find himself a little action too,' he said, and went on laughing richly while Smiley sat patiently with the telephone to his ear.

Jerry chose a cab with two wing-mirrors and sat in the front. In Kowloon he hired a car from the biggest outfit he could find, using the escape passport and driving licence because marginally he thought the false name was safer, if only by an hour. As he headed up the Midlevels it was dusk and still raining and huge haloes hung from the neon lights that lit the hillside. He passed the American Consulate and drove past Star Heights twice, half expecting to see Sam Collins, and on the second occasion he knew for sure he had found her flat and that her light was burning: an arty Italian affair by the look of it, that hung across the picture window in a gracious droop, three hundred dollars' worth of pretension. Also the frosted glass of a bathroom was lit. The third time he passed he saw her pulling a wrap over her shoulders and instinct or something about the formality of her gesture told him she was once more preparing to go out for the evening, but that this time she was dressed to kill.

Every time he allowed himself to remember Luke, a darkness covered his eyes and he imagined himself doing the noble, useless things like telephoning Luke's family in California, or the dwarf at the bureau, or even for whatever purpose the Rocker. Later, he thought. Later, he promised himself, he would mourn Luke in fitting style.

He coasted slowly into the driveway which led to the entrance till he came to the sliproad to the carpark. The park was three tiers deep and he idled round it till he found her red Jaguar stowed in a safe corner behind a chain to discourage careless neighbours from approaching its peerless paintwork. She had put a mock leopardskin cover on the steering wheel. She just couldn't do enough for the damn car. Get pregnant, he thought in a burst of fury. Buy a dog. Keep mice. For two pins he'd have smashed the front in, but those two pins had held Jerry back more times than he liked to count. If she's not using it, then he's sending a limousine for her, he thought. Maybe with Tiu riding shotgun, even. Or maybe he'll come himself. Or maybe she's just getting herself dolled up for the evening sacrifice and not going out at all. He wished it was Sunday. He remembered Craw saying that Drake Ko spent Sundays with his family, and that on Sundays Lizzie had to make her own running. But it wasn't Sunday and neither did he have dear old Craw at his elbow telling him, on what evidence Jerry could only guess, that Ko was away in Bangkok or Timbuctoo conducting his business.

Grateful that the rain was turning to fog, he headed back up the slipway to the drive and at the junction found a narrow piece of shoulder where, if he parked hard against the barrier, the other traffic could complain but squeeze past. He grazed the barrier and didn't care. From where he now sat he could watch the pedestrians coming in and out under the striped awning to the block, and the cars joining or leaving the main road. He felt no sense of caution at all. He lit a cigarette and the limousines crackled past him both ways but none belonged to Ko. Occasionally, as a car edged by him, the driver paused to hoot or shout a complaint and Jerry ignored him. Every few seconds his eyes took in the mirrors and once when a plump figure not unlike Tiu padded guiltily up behind him he actually dropped the safety catch of the pistol in his jacket pocket before admitting to himself that the man lacked Tiu's brawn. Probably been collecting gambling debts from the *pak-pai* drivers, he thought, as the figure went by him.

He remembered being with Luke at Happy Valley. He remembered being with Luke.

He was still looking in the mirror when the red Jaguar hissed up the slipway behind him, just the driver and the roof closed, no passenger, and the one thing he hadn't thought of was that she might take the lift down to the carpark and collect the car herself rather than have the porter bring it to the door for her as he did before. Pulling out after her, he glanced up and saw the lights still burning in her window. Had she left somebody behind? Or did she propose to come back shortly? Then he thought, don't be so damn clever, she's just careless about lights.

The last time I spoke to Luke, it was to tell him to get out of my hair, he thought, and the last time he spoke to me was to tell me he'd covered my back with Stubbsie.

She had turned down the hill toward the town. He headed down after her and for a space nothing followed him, which seemed unnatural, but these were unnatural hours, and Sarratt man was dying in him faster than he could handle. She was heading for the brightest part of town. He supposed he still loved her, though just now he was prepared to suspect anybody of anything. He kept close behind her remembering that she used her mirror seldom. In this dusky fog she would only see his headlights anyway. The fog hung in patches and the harbour looked as if it was on fire, with the shafts of crane-light playing like waterhoses on the crawling smoke. In Central she ducked into another basement garage, and he drove straight in after her and parked six bays away, but she didn't notice him. Remaining in the car, she paused to repair her make-up and he actually saw her working on her chin, powdering the scars. Then she got out and went through the ritual of locking, though a kid with a razor blade could have cut through the soft-top in one easy movement. She was dressed in a silk cape of some kind and a long silk dress, and as she walked toward the stone spiral stair she raised both her hands and carefully lifted her hair, which was gathered at the neck, and laid the pony tail down the outside of the cape. Getting out after her he followed her as far as the hotel lobby, and turned aside in time to avoid being photographed by a bi-sexual drove of chattering fashion journalists in satins and bows.

Hanging back in the comparative safety of the corridor, Jerry pieced the scene together. It was a large private party and Lizzie had joined it from the blind side. The other guests were arriving at the front entrance, where the Rolls-Royces were so thick on the ground that nobody was special. A woman with blue-grey hair presided, swaying about and speaking gin-sodden French. A prim Chinese public relations girl with a couple of assistants made up the receiving line, and as the guests filed in, the girl and her cohorts came forward frightfully cordially and asked for names and sometimes invitation cards before consulting a list and saying 'Oh yes, of *course*.' The blue-grey woman smiled and growled. The cohorts handed out lapel-pins for the men and orchids for the women, then lighted on the next arrivals.

Lizzie Worthington went through this screening woodenly. Jerry gave her a minute to clear, watched her through the double doors marked *soirée* with a Cupid's arrow, then attached himself to the queue. The public relations girl was bothered by his buckskin boots. His suit was disgusting enough but it was the boots that bothered her. On her course of training, he decided while she stared at them, she had been taught to place a lot of value on shoes.

Millionaires may be tramps from the socks up but a pair of two hundred dollar Guccis is a passport not to be missed. She frowned at his presscard, then at her guest list, then at his presscard again, and once more at his boots and she threw a lost glance at the blue-grey lush, who kept on smiling and growling. Jerry guessed she was drugged clean out of her mind. Finally the girl put up her own special smile for the marginal consumer and handed him a disc the size of a coffee saucer painted fluorescent pink with PRESS an inch high in white.

'Tonight we are making *everybody* beautiful, Mr Westerby,' she said.

'Have a job with me, sport.'

'You like my *parfum*, Mr Westerby?'

'Sensational,' said Jerry.

'It is called *juice of the vine,* Mr Westerby, one hundred Hong Kong for a little bottle but tonight Maison Flaubert gives free samples to all our guests. Madame Montifiori . . . oh, of *course*, welcome to House of Flaubert. You like my *parfum*, Madame Montifiori?'

A Eurasian girl in a *cheongsam* held out a tray and whispered 'Flaubert wishes you an exotic night.'

'For Christ's sake,' Jerry said.

Inside the double doors a second receiving line was manned by three pretty boys flown in from Paris for their charm, and a posse of security men that would have done credit to a President. For a moment he thought they might frisk him and he knew that if they tried he was going to pull down the temple with him. They eyed Jerry without friendliness, counting him part of the help, but he was light-haired and they let him go.

'The press is in the third row back from the catwalk,' said a hermaphrodite blond in a cowboy leather suit, handing him a presskit. 'You have no camera, monsieur?'

'I just do the captions,' Jerry said, jamming a thumb over his shoulder, 'Spike here does the pictures,' and walked into the reception room peering round him, grinning extravagantly, waving at whoever caught his eye.

The pyramid of champagne glasses was six feet tall with

black satin steps so that the waiters could take them from the top. In the sunken ice-coffins lay magnums awaiting burial. There was a wheelbarrow full of cooked lobsters and a wedding cake of *paté de foie gras* with *Maison Flaubert* done in aspic on the top. Space music was playing and there was even conversation under it, if only the bored drone of the extremely rich. The catwalk stretched from the foot of the long window to the centre of the room. The window faced the harbour, but the fog broke the view into patches. The airconditioning was turned up so that the women could wear their mink without sweating. Most of the men wore dinner jackets but the young Chinese playboys sported New-York-style slacks and black shirts and gold chains. The British *taipans* stood in one sodden circle with their womenfolk, like bored officers at a garrison get-together.

Feeling a hand on his shoulder Jerry swung fast, but all he found in front of him was a little Chinese queer called Graham who worked for one of the local gossip rags. Jerry had once helped him out with a story he was trying to sell to the comic. Rows of armchairs faced the catwalk in a rough horseshoe, and Lizzie was sitting in the front between Mr Arpego and his wife or paramour. Jerry recognised them from Happy Valley. They looked as though they were chaperoning Lizzie for the evening. The Arpegos talked to her but she seemed barely to hear them. She sat straight and beautiful and she had taken off her cape and from where Jerry sat she could have been stark naked except for her pearl collar and her pearl earrings. At least she's still intact, he thought. She hasn't rotted or got cholera or had her head shot off. He remembered the line of gold hairs running down her spine as he stood over her that first evening in the lift. Queer Graham sat next to Jerry, and Phoebe Wayfarer sat two along. He knew her only vaguely but gave her a fat wave.

'Gosh. Super. Pheeb. You look terrific. Should be up there on the catwalk, sport, showing a bit of leg.'

He thought she was a bit tight, and perhaps she thought he was, though he'd drunk nothing since the plane. He took out a pad and wrote on it, playing the professional, trying to rein himself in. Easy as you go. Don't frighten the game. When he read what he had written, he saw the words 'Lizzie Worthington' and nothing else. Chinese Graham read it too and laughed.

'My new byline,' said Jerry, and they laughed together, too loud, so that people in front turned their heads as the lights began to dim. But not Lizzie, though he thought she might have recognised his voice.

Behind them, the doors were being closed and as the lights went lower Jerry had a mind to fall asleep in this soft and kindly chair. The space music gave way to a jungle beat brushed out on a cymbal, till only a single chandelier flickered over the black catwalk, answering the churned and patchy lights of the harbour in the window behind. The drumbeat rose in a slow crescendo from amplifiers everywhere. It went on a long time, just drums, very well played, very insistent, till gradually grotesque human shadows became visible against the harbour window. The drumbeats stopped. In a racked silence two black girls strode flank against flank down the catwalk, wearing nothing but jewels. Their skulls were shaven and they wore round ivory earrings and diamond collars like the iron rings of slave girls. Their oiled limbs shone with clustered diamonds, pearls and rubies. They were tall, and beautiful, and lithe, and utterly unexpected, and for a moment they cast over the whole audience the spell of absolute sexuality. The drums recovered and soared, spotlights raced over jewels and limbs. They writhed out of the steaming harbour and advanced on the spectators with the anger of sensuous enslavement. They turned and walked slowly away, challenging and disdaining with their haunches. Lights came on, there was a crash of nervous applause followed by laughter and drinks. Everyone was talking at once and Jerry was talking loudest: to Miss Lizzie Worthington the well known aristocratic society beauty whose mother couldn't even boil an egg, and to the Arpegos who owned Manila and one or two of the out-islands, as Captain Grant of the Jockey Club had once assured him. Jerry was holding his notebook like a headwaiter.

'Lizzie Worthington, *gosh*, all Hong Kong at your feet, ma'am, if I may say so. My paper is doing an exclusive on this event, Miss Worth or Worthington, and we're hoping to feature you, your dresses, your fascinating life-style and your even more fascinating friends. My photographers are bringing up the rear.' He bowed to the Arpegos. 'Good evening, madame. Sir. Proud to have you with us I'm sure. This your first visit to Hong Kong?'

He was doing his big-puppy number, the boyish soul of the party. A waiter brought champagne and he insisted on transferring the glasses to their hands rather than let them help themselves. The Arpegos were much amused by this performance. Craw said they were crooks. Lizzie was staring at him and there was something in her eyes he couldn't make out, something real and appalled, as if she, not Jerry, had just opened the door on Luke.

'Mr Westerby has already done one story on me, I understand,' she said. 'I don't think it was ever printed, was it, Mr Westerby?'

'Who you write for?' Mr Arpego demanded suddenly. He wasn't smiling any more. He looked dangerous and ugly, and she had clearly reminded him of something he had heard about and didn't like. Something Tiu had warned him of, for instance.

Jerry told him.

'Then go write for them. Leave this lady alone. She don't give interviews. You got work to do, you work somewhere else. You didn't come here to play. Earn your money.'

'Couple of questions for *you*, then Mr Arpego. Just before I go. How can I write you down, sir? As a rude Filipino millionaire? Or only half a millionaire?'

'For God's sake,' Lizzie breathed, and by a mercy the lights went out again, the drumbeat began, everyone went back to his corner and a woman's voice with a French accent began a soft commentary on the loudspeaker. At the back of the catwalk the two black girls were performing long insinuating shadow dances. As the first model appeared, Jerry saw Lizzie stand up ahead of him in the darkness, pull her cape over her shoulders, and walk fast and softly up the aisle past him and toward the doors, head bowed. Jerry went after her. In the lobby she half turned as if to look at him and it crossed his mind she was expecting him. Her expression was the same and it reflected his own mood. She looked haunted and tired and utterly confused.

'Lizzie!' he called, as if he had just sighted an old friend, and ran quickly to her side before she could reach the powder room door. 'Lizzie! My God! It's been years! A lifetime! Super!'

A couple of security guards looked on meekly as he flung his arms round her for the kiss of long friendship. He had slipped his left hand under her cape and as he bent his laughing face to hers, he laid the small revolver against the bare flesh of her back, the barrel just below her nape, and in that way, linked to her with bonds of old affection, led her straight into the street, chatting gaily all the way, and hailed a cab. He hadn't wanted to produce the gun, but he couldn't risk having to manhandle her. That's the way it goes, he thought. You come back to tell her you love her, and end up by marching her off at gun point. She was shivering and furious but he didn't think she was afraid, and he didn't even think she was sorry to be leaving that awful gathering.

'That's all I need,' she said, as they wound up the hill again, through the fog. 'Perfect. Bloody perfect.'

She wore a scent that was strange to him, but he thought it smelt a deal better than juice of the vine.

Guillam was not bored exactly, but neither was his capacity for concentration infinite, as George's appeared to be. When he wasn't wondering what the devil Jerry Westerby was up to, he found himself basking in the erotic deprival of Molly Meakin or else remembering the Chinese boy with his arms inside out, whining like a half-shot hare after the disappearing car. Murphy's theme was now the island of Po Toi and he was dilating on it remorselessly.

Volcanic, sir, he said.

Hardest rock substance of the whole Hong Kong group, sir, he said.

And the most southerly of the islands, he said, and right there on the edge of China waters.

Seven hundred and ninety feet high, sir, fishermen use it as a navigation point from far out to sea, *sir*, he said.

Technically not one island but a group of six islands, the other five being barren and treeless and uninhabited.

Fine temple, sir. Great antiquity. Fine wood carvings but little natural water.

'Jesus Christ, Murphy, we're not *buying* the damn place, are we?' Martello expostulated. With action close, and London far away, Martello had lost a lot of his gloss, Guillam noticed, and all his Englishness. His tropical suits were honest-to-cornball American, and he needed to talk to people, preferably his own. Guillam suspected that even London was an adventure for him, and Hong Kong was already enemy territory. Whereas under stress Smiley went quite the other way: he became private, and rigidly polite.

'Po Toi itself has a shrinking population of one hundred and eight farmers and fishermen, most Communist, three living villages and three dead ones, sir,' said Murphy. He droned on. Smiley continued to listen intently but Martello impatiently doodled on his pad.

'And *tomorrow*, sir,' said Murphy, '*tomorrow* is the night of Po Toi's annual festival intended to pay homage to Tin Hau, the goddess of the sea, sir.'

Martello stopped doodling. 'These people really believe that crap?'

'Everybody has a right to his religion, sir.'

'They teach you that at training college too, Murphy?' Martello returned to his doodling.

There was an uncomfortable silence before Murphy valiantly took up his pointer and laid the tip on the southern edge of the island's coastline.

'This festival of Tin Hau, sir, is concentrated in the one main harbour, sir, right here on the south-west point where the ancient temple is situated. Mr Smiley's informed prediction, sir, has the Ko landing operation taking place *here*, away from the main bay, in a small cove on the east side of the island. By landing on that side of the island which has *no* habitation, *no* natural access to the sea, at a point in time when the diversion of the island festival in the *main* bay – '

Guillam never heard the ring. He just heard the voice of Martello's other quiet man answering the call: '*Yes, Mac,*' then the squeak of his airline chair as he sat bolt upright, staring at Smiley. 'Right, *Mac.* Sure, Mac. Right now. Yes. Hold it. Right beside me. Hold everything.'

Smiley was already standing over him, his hand held out for the phone. Martello was watching Smiley. On the podium, Murphy had his back turned while he pointed out further intriguing features of Po Toi, not quite registering the interruption.

'This island is also known to seamen as Ghost Rock, sir,' he explained in the same dreary voice. 'But nobody seems to know why.'

Smiley listened briefly then put down the telephone.

'Thank you, Murphy,' he said courteously. 'That was very interesting.'

He stood dead still a moment, his fingers to his upper lip, in a Pickwickian posture of deliberation. 'Yes,' he repeated. 'Yes, very.'

He walked as far as the door, then paused again.

'Marty, forgive me, I shall have to leave you for a while. Not above an hour or two, I trust. I shall telephone you in any event.'

He reached for the door handle, then turned to Guillam.

'Peter, I think you had better come along too, would you mind? We may need a car and you seem admirably unmoved by the Hong Kong traffic. Did I see Fawn somewhere? Ah, there are you are.'

* * *

On Headland Road the flowers had a hairy brilliance, like ferns sprayed for Christmas. The pavement was narrow and seldom used, except by amahs to exercise the children, which they did without talking to them, as if they were walking dogs. The Cousins' surveillance van was a deliberately forgettable brown Mercedes lorry, battered looking, with clay dust on the wings and the letters H. K. DEVp and BLDg SURVEY Ltd sprayed on one side. An old aerial with Chinese streamers trailing from it drooped over the cab, and as the lorry nosed its lugubrious way past the Ko residence – for the second, or was it the fourth time that morning? – nobody gave it a thought. In Headland Road, as everywhere in Hong Kong, somebody is always building.

Stretched inside the lorry, on rexine-covered bunks fitted for the purpose, the two men watched intently from among a forest of lenses, cameras and radio telephone appliances. For them also, their progress past Seven Gates was becoming something of a routine.

'No change?' said the first.

'No change,' the second confirmed.

'No change,' the first repeated, into the radio telephone, and heard the assuring voice of Murphy the other end, acknowledging the message.

'Maybe they're waxworks,' said the first, still watching. 'Maybe we should go give them a prod and see if they holler.'

'Maybe we should at that,' said the second.

In all their professional lives, they were agreed, they had never followed anything that kept so still. Ko stood where he always stood, at the end of the rose-arbour, his back to them as he stared out to sea. His little wife sat apart from him, dressed as usual in black, on a white garden chair, and she seemed to be staring at her husband. Only Tiu made any movement. He also was sitting, but to Ko's other side, and he was munching what looked like a doughnut.

Reaching the main road, the lorry lumbered toward Stanley, pursuing for cover reasons its fictional reconnaissance of the region.

Chapter 20

LIESE'S LOVER

Her flat was big and unreconciled: a mix of airport lounge, executive suite and tart's boudoir. The drawing-room ceiling was raked to a lopsided point, like the nave of a subsiding church. The floor changed levels restlessly, the carpet was as thick as grass and left shiny footprints where they walked. The enormous windows gave limitless but lonely views, and when she closed the blinds and drew the curtains, the two of them were suddenly in a suburban bungalow with no garden. The amah had gone to her room behind the kitchen and when she appeared Lizzie sent her back there. She crept out scowling and hissing. Wait till I tell the master, she was saying.

He put the chain across the front door and after that he took her with him, steering her from room to room, making her walk a little ahead of him on his left side, open the doors for him and even the cupboards. The bedroom was a television stage-set for a *femme fatale*, with a round, quilted bed and a sunken round bath behind Spanish screens. He looked through the bedside lockers for a small-arm because though Hong Kong is not particularly gun-ridden, people who have lived in Indo China usually have something. Her dressing room looked as though she'd emptied one of the smart Scandinavian décor shops in Central by telephone. The dining room was done in smoked glass, polished chrome and leather, with fake Gainsborough ancestors staring soggily at the empty chairs: all the mummies who couldn't boil eggs, he thought. Black tigerskin steps led to Ko's den and here Jerry lingered, staring round, fascinated despite himself, seeing the man in everything, and his kinship with old Sambo. The king-sized desk with the *bombé* legs and ball-and-claw feet, the presidential cutlery. The inkwells, the sheathed paper-knife and scissors, the untouched works of legal reference, the very ones old Sambo trailed around with him: Simons on Tax, Charlesworth on Company Law. The framed testimonials on the wall. The citation for his Order of the British Empire beginning 'Elizabeth the Second by the Grace of God . . .' The medal itself, embalmed in satin, like the arms of a dead knight. Group photographs of Chinese elders on the steps of a spirit temple. Victorious racehorses. Lizzie laughing to him. Lizzie in a swimsuit, looking stunning. Lizzie in Paris. Gently, he pulled open the desk drawers and discovered the embossed stationery of a dozen different companies. In the cupboards, empty files, an IBM electric typewriter with no plug on it, an address book with no addresses entered. Lizzie naked from the waist up, glancing round at him over her long back. Lizzie, God help her, in a wedding dress, clutching a posy of gardenias. Ko must have sent her to a bridal parlour for the photograph.

There were no photographs of gunny bags of opium.

The executive sanctuary, Jerry thought, standing there. Old Sambo had several: girls who had flats from him, one even a house, yet saw him only a few times a year. But always this one secret, special room, with the desk and the unused telephones and the instant-mementos, a physical corner carved off someone else's life, a shelter from his other shelters.

'Where is he?' Jerry asked, remembering Luke again.

'Drake?'

'No, Father Christmas.'

'You tell me.'

He followed her to the bedroom.

'Do you often not know?' he asked.

She was pulling off her earrings, dropping them in a jewellery box. Then her clasp, her necklace and bracelets.

'He rings me wherever he is, night or day, we never care. This is the first time he's cut himself off.'

'Can you ring him?'

'*Any* bloody time,' she retorted with savage sarcasm. 'Course I can. Number One Wife and me get on just *great*. Didn't you know?'

'What about at the office?'

'He's not going to the office.'

'What about Tiu?'

'Sod Tiu.'

'Why?'

'Because he's a pig,' she snapped pulling open a cupboard.

'He could pass on messages for you.'

'If he felt like it, which he doesn't.'

'Why not?'

'How the hell should I know?' She hauled out a pullover and some jeans and chucked them on the bed. 'Because he resents me. Because he doesn't trust me. Because he doesn't like roundeyes horning in on Big Sir. Now get out while I change.'

So he wandered into the dressing room again, keeping his back to her, hearing the rustle of silk and skin.

'I saw Ricardo,' he said. 'We had a full and frank exchange of views.'

He needed very much to hear whether they had told her. He needed to absolve her from Luke. He listened, then went on:

'Charlie Marshall gave me his address, so I popped up and had a chat with him.'

'Great,' she said. 'So now you're family.'

'They told me about Mellon. Said you carried dope for him.'

She didn't speak so he turned to look at her and she was sitting on the bed with her head in her hands. In the jeans and pullover she looked about fifteen years old, and half a foot shorter.

'What the hell do you want?' she whispered at last, so

quietly she might have been putting the question to herself.

'You,' he said. 'For keeps.'

He didn't know whether she heard, because all she did was let out a long breath and whisper 'Oh Jesus' at the end of it.

'Mellon a friend of yours?' she asked finally.

'No.'

'Pity. He needs a friend like you.'

'Does Arpego know where Ko is?'

She shrugged.

'So when did you last hear from him?'

'A week.'

'What did he say?'

'He had things to arrange.'

'What things?'

'For Christ's sake stop asking questions! The whole sodding world is asking questions, so just don't join the queue, right?'

He stared at her and her eyes were alight with anger and despair. He opened the balcony door and stepped outside.

I need a brief, he thought bitterly. Sarratt bearleaders, where are you now I need you? It hadn't dawned on him till now that when he cut the cable, he was also dropping the pilot.

The balcony ran along three sides. The fog had temporarily cleared. Behind him hung the Peak, its shoulders festooned in gold lights. Banks of running cloud made changing caverns round the moon. The harbour had dug out all its finery. At its centre an American aircraft carrier, floodlit and dressed overall, basked like a pampered woman amid a cluster of attendant launches. On her deck, a line of helicopters and small fighters reminded him of the airbase in Thailand. A column of ocean-going junks drifted past her, headed for Canton.

'Jerry?'

She was standing in the open doorway, watching him down a line of tub trees.

'Come on in. I'm hungry,' she said.

It was a kitchen where nobody cooked or ate, but it had a Bavarian corner with pine settles, alpine pictures and ashtrays saying *Carlsberg*. She gave him coffee from an ever-ready percolator, and he noticed how, when she was on guard, she kept her shoulders forward and her forearms across her body, the way the orphan used to. She was shivering. He thought she had been shivering ever since he laid the gun on her and he wished he hadn't done that, because it was beginning to dawn on him that she was in as bad a state as he was, and perhaps a damn sight worse, and that the mood between them was like two people after a disaster, each in a separate hell. He fixed her a brandy and soda and the same for himself and sat her in the drawing room where it was warmer, and he watched her while she hugged herself and drank the brandy, staring at the carpet.

'Music?' he asked.

She shook her head.

'I represent myself,' he said. 'No connection with any other firm.'

She might not have heard.

'I'm free and willing,' he said. 'It's just that a friend of mine died.'

He saw her nod, but only in sympathy. He was sure it rang no bell with her at all.

'The Ko thing is getting very grubby,' he said. 'It's not going to work out well. They're very rough boys you're mixed up with. Ko included. Looked at cold, he's a grade A public enemy. I thought maybe you'd like a leg out of it all. That's why I came back. My Galahad act. It's just I don't quite know what's gathering around you. Mellon, all that. Maybe we should unbutton it together and see what's there.'

After which not very articulate explanation, the telephone rang. It had one of those throttled croaks which are designed to spare the nerves.

The telephone was across the room on a gilded trolley. A pinlight winked on it with each dull note and the rippled glass shelves picked up the reflection. She glanced at it, then at Jerry and her face was at once alert with hope. Jumping to his feet he pushed the trolley over to her and its wheels stammered in the deep pile. The flex uncoiled behind him as he walked, till it was like a child's scribble across the room. She lifted the receiver quickly and said 'Worth' in the slightly rude tone which women learn when they live alone. He thought of telling her the line was bugged but he didn't know what he was warning her against: he had no position any more, this side or that side. He didn't know what the sides were, but his head was suddenly full of Luke again and the hunter in him was wide awake.

She had the telephone to her ear but she hadn't spoken again. Once she said 'yes', as if she were acknowedging instructions, and once she said 'no' strongly. Her expression had turned blank, her voice told him nothing. But he sensed obedience, and he sensed concealment, and as he did so, the anger lit in him completely and nothing else mattered.

'No,' she said to the phone, 'I left the party early.'

He knelt beside her, trying to listen, but she kept the receiver pressed hard against her.

Why didn't she ask him where he was? Why didn't she ask when she would see him? Whether he was all right? Why he hadn't phoned? Why did she look at Jerry like this, show no relief?

His hand on her cheek, he forced her head round and whispered to the other ear.

'Tell him you *must* see him! You'll come to him. *Anywhere.*'

'Yes,' she said again into the phone. 'All right. Yes.'

'Tell him! Tell him you must see him!'

'I must see you,' she said finally. 'I'll come to you wherever you are.'

The receiver was still in her hand. She made a shrug, asking for instruction and her eyes were still turned to Jerry – not as her Sir Galahad, but as just another part of a hostile world that encircled her.

'*I love you!*' he whispered. 'Say what you say!'

'I love you,' she said shortly, with her eyes closed, and rang off before he could stop her.

'He's coming here,' she said. 'And damn you.'

Jerry was still kneeling beside her. She stood up in order to get clear of him.

'Does he know?' Jerry asked.

'Know what?'

'That I'm here?'

'Perhaps.' She lit a cigarette.

'Where is he now?'

'I don't know.'

'When will he be here?'

'He said soon.'

'Is he alone?'

'He didn't say.'

'Does he carry a gun?'

She was across the room from him. Her strained grey eyes still held him in their furious, frightened glare. But Jerry was indifferent to her mood. A feverish urge for action had overcome all other feelings.

'Drake Ko. The nice man who set you up here. Does he carry a gun? Is he going to shoot me? Is Tiu with him? Just questions that's all.'

'He doesn't wear it in bed, if that's what you mean.'

'Where are you going?'

'I thought you two men would prefer to be left alone.'

Leading her back to the sofa, he sat her facing the double doors at the far end of the room. They were panelled with frosted glass and on the other side of them lay the hall and the front entrance. He opened them, clearing her line of view to anybody coming in.

'Do you have rules about letting people in, you two?' She didn't follow his question. 'There's a peephole here. Does he insist you check every time before you open?'

'He'll ring on the house phone from downstairs. Then he'll use his door key.'

The front door was laminated hardboard, not solid but solid enough. Sarratt folklore said, if you are taking a lone intruder unawares, don't get behind the door or you'll never get out again. For once Jerry was inclined to agree. Yet to keep to the open side was to be a sitting duck for anyone aggressively inclined, and Jerry was by no means sure that Ko was either unaware, or alone. He considered going behind the sofa but if there was to be shooting he didn't want the girl to be in the line of it, he definitely didn't. Her new-found passivity, her lethargic stare, did nothing to reassure him. His brandy glass was beside hers on the table and he put it quietly out of sight behind a vase of plastic orchids. He emptied the ashtray, and set an open copy of *Vogue* in front of her on the table.

'You play music when you're alone?'

'Sometimes.'

He chose Ellington.

'Too loud?'

'Louder,' she said. Suspicious, he turned down the sound, watching her. As he did so the house phone whistled twice from the hall.

'Take care,' he warned, and gun in hand moved to the open side of the front door, the sitting-duck position, three feet from the arc, close enough to spring forward, far enough to shoot and throw himself, which was what he had in mind as he dropped into the half crouch. He held the gun in his left hand and nothing in his right because at that distance he couldn't miss with either hand, whereas if he had to strike he wanted his right hand free. He remembered the way Tiu carried his hands curled, and he warned himself not to get in close. Whatever he did, to do it from a distance. A groin kick but don't follow it in. Stay outside those hands.

'You say "come on up",' he told her.

'Come on up,' Lizzie repeated into the phone. She rang off and unhooked the chain.

'When he comes in, smile for the camera. Don't shout.'

'Go to hell.'

From the lift-well, to his sharpened ear, came the clump of a lift arriving and the monotonous 'ping' of the bell. He heard footsteps approaching the door, one pair only, steady, and remembered Drake Ko's comic, slightly ape-like gait at Happy Valley, how the knees tipped through the grey flannels. A key slid into the lock, one hand came round the door, and the rest with no apparent forethought followed. By then, Jerry had sprung with all his weight, flattening the unresisting body against the wall. A picture of Venice fell, the glass smashed, he slammed the door, all in the same moment as he found a throat and jammed the barrel of the pistol straight into the deep flesh. Then the door was unlocked a second time from outside, very fast, the wind went out of his body, his feet flew upward, a crippling shock of pain spread from his kidneys and felled him on the thick carpet, a second blow caught him in the groin and made him gasp as he jerked his knees to his chin. Through his streaming eyes he saw the little, furious figure of Fawn the babysitter standing over him, shaping for a third strike, and the rigid grin of Sam Collins as he peered calmly over Fawn's shoulder to see what the damage was. And still in the doorway, wearing an expression of grave apprehension as he straightened his collar after Jerry's unprovoked assault on him, the flustered figure of his one-time guide and mentor Mr George Smiley, breathlessly calling his leashdogs to order.

Jerry was able to sit, but only if he leaned forward. He held both hands in front of him, his elbows jammed into his lap. The pain was all over his body, like poison spreading from a central source. The girl watched from the hall doorway. Fawn was lurking, hoping for another excuse to hit him. Sam Collins was at the other end of the room, sitting in a winged armchair with his legs crossed. Smiley had poured Jerry a neat brandy, and was stooping over him, poking the glass into his hand.

'What are you doing here, Jerry?' Smiley said. 'I don't understand.'

'Courting,' said Jerry, and closed his eyes as a wave of black pain swept over him. 'Developed an unscheduled affection for our hostess there. Sorry about that.'

'That was a very dangerous thing to do, Jerry,' Smiley

objected. 'You could have wrecked the entire operation. Suppose I had been Ko. The consequences would have been disastrous.'

'I'll say they would.' He drank some brandy. 'Luke's dead. Lying in my flat with his head shot off.'

'Who's Luke?' Smiley asked, forgetting their meeting at Craw's house.

'No one. Just a friend.' He drank again. 'American journalist. A drunk. No loss to anyone.'

Smiley glanced at Sam Collins but Sam shrugged.

'Nobody *we* know,' he said.

'Ring them all the same,' said Smiley.

Sam picked up the mobile telephone and walked out of the room with it because he knew the layout.

'Put the burn on her have you?' Jerry said, with a nod of his head toward Lizzie. 'About the only thing left in the book that hasn't been done to her, I should think.' He called over to her. 'How are you doing there, sport? Sorry about the tussle. Didn't break anything, did we?'

'No,' she said.

'Put the bite on you about your wicked past, did they? Stick and carrot? Promised to wipe the slate clean? Silly girl, Lizzie. Not allowed a past in this game. Can't have a future either. *Verboten*.'

He turned back to Smiley:

'That's all it was, George. No philosophy to it. Old Lizzie just got under my skin.'

Tilting back his head, he studied Smiley's face through half closed eyes. And with the clarity which pain sometimes brings, he observed that by his action he had put Smiley's own existence under threat.

'Don't worry,' he said gently. 'Won't happen to *you*, that's for sure.'

'Jerry,' said Smiley.

'Yessir,' said Jerry and made a show of sitting to attention.

'Jerry, you don't understand what's going on. How much you could upset things. Billions of dollars and thousands of men could not obtain a part of what we stand to gain from this one operation. A war general would laugh himself silly at the thought of such a tiny sacrifice for such an enormous dividend.'

'Don't ask *me* to get you off the hook, old boy,' Jerry said, looking up into the face again. 'You're the owl, remember? Not me.'

Sam Collins returned. Smiley glanced at him in question.

'He's not one of theirs either,' said Sam.

'They were aiming for me,' said Jerry. 'They got Lukie instead. He's a big bloke. Or was.'

'And he's in your flat?' Smiley asked. 'Dead. Shot. And in your flat?'

'Been there some while.'

Smiley to Collins: 'We shall have to brush over the traces, Sam. We can't risk a scandal.'

'I'll get back to them now,' Collins said.

'And find out about planes,' Smiley called after him. 'Two, first class.'

Collins nodded.

'Don't like that fellow one bit,' Jerry confessed. 'Never did. Must be his moustache.' He shoved a thumb toward Lizzie. 'What's she got that's so hot for you all, anyway, George? Ko doesn't whisper his inmost secrets to her. She's a roundeye.' He turned to Lizzie. 'Does he?'

She shook her head.

'If he did, she wouldn't remember,' he went on. 'She's thick as hell about those things. She's probably never even heard of Nelson.' He called to her again. 'You. Who's Nelson? Come on, who is he? Ko's little dead son, isn't he? That's right. Named his boat after him, didn't he? And his gee-gee.' He turned back to Smiley. 'See? Thick. Leave her out of it, that's my advice.'

Collins had returned with a note of flight times. Smiley read it, frowning through his spectacles. 'We shall have to send you home at once, Jerry,' he said. 'Guillam's waiting downstairs with a car. Fawn will go along as well.'

'I'd just like to be sick again, if you don't mind.'

Reaching upward, Jerry took hold of Smiley's arm for

support and at once Fawn sprang forward, but Jerry shot out a warning finger at him, as Smiley ordered him back.

'You keep your distance, you poisonous little leprechaun,' Jerry advised. 'You're allowed one bite and that's all. The next one won't be so easy.'

He moved in a crouch, trailing his feet slowly, hands clutched over his groin. Reaching the girl he stopped in front of her.

'Did they have pow-wows up here, Ko and his lovelies, sport? Ko bring his boy friends up here for a natter, did he?'

'Sometimes.'

'And you helped with the mikes did you, like the good little housewife? Let the sound boys in, tended the lamp? Course you did.'

She nodded.

'Still not enough,' he objected, as he hobbled to the bathroom. 'Still doesn't answer my question. Must be more to it than that. *Far* more.'

In the bathroom he held his face under cold water, drank some, and immediately vomited. On the way back, he looked for the girl again. She was in the drawing room and in the way that people under stress look for trivial things to do, she was sorting the gramophone records, putting each in its proper sleeve. In a distant corner Smiley and Collins were quietly conferring. Closer at hand, Fawn was waiting at the door.

'Bye, sport,' he said to her. Putting his hand on her shoulder he drew her round till her grey eyes looked straight at him.

'Goodbye,' she said, and kissed him, not in passion exactly, but at least with more deliberation than the waiters got.

'I was a sort of accessory before the fact,' he explained. 'I'm sorry about that. I'm not sorry about anything else. You'd better look after that sod Ko, too. Because if they don't manage to kill him, I may.'

He touched the lines on her chin, then shuffled toward the door where Fawn stood, and turned round to take his leave of Smiley, who was alone again. Collins had been sent off to telephone. Smiley stood as Jerry remembered him best, his short arms slightly lifted from his sides, his head back a little, his expression at once apologetic and enquiring, as if he'd just left his umbrella on the underground. The girl had turned away from both of them, and was still sorting the records.

'Love to Ann then,' Jerry said.

'Thank you.'

'You're wrong, sport. Don't know how, don't know why, but you're wrong. Still, too late for that I suppose.' He felt sick again and his head was shrieking from the pains in his body. 'You come any nearer than that,' he said to Fawn, 'and I will definitely break your bloody neck, you understand?' He turned back to Smiley who stood in the same posture and gave no sign of having heard.

'Season of the year to you then,' said Jerry.

With a last nod but none to the girl Jerry limped into the corridor, Fawn following. Waiting for the lift he saw the elegant American standing at his open doorway, watching his departure.

'Ah yeah I forgot about you,' he called very loudly. 'You're running the bug on her flat, aren't you? The Brits blackmail her and the Cousins bug her, lucky girl gets it all ways.'

The American vanished, closing the door quickly after him. The lift came and Fawn shoved him in.

'Don't do that,' Jerry warned him. 'This gentleman's name is Fawn,' he told the other occupants of the lift, in a very loud voice. They mostly wore dinner jackets and sequined dresses. 'He's a member of the British Secret Service and he's just kicked me in the balls. The Russians are coming,' he added, to their doughy, indifferent faces. 'They're going to take away all your bloody money.'

'Drunk,' said Fawn in disgust.

In the lobby Lawrence the porter watched with keen interest. In the forecourt, a Peugeot saloon waited, blue. Peter Guillam was sitting in the driving seat.

'Get in,' he snapped.

The passenger door was locked. Jerry climbed into the back, Fawn after him.

'What the hell do you think you're up to?' Guillam demanded through clenched teeth. 'Since when did half-arsed London Occasionals cut anchor in mid-operation?'

'Keep clear,' Jerry warned Fawn. 'Just the hint of a frown from you right now is enough to get me going. I mean that. I warn you. Official.'

The ground mist had returned, rolling over the bonnet. The passing city offered itself like the framed glimpses of a junk yard: a painted sign, a shop window, strands of cable strung across a neon, a clump of suffocated foliage; the inevitable building site, floodlit. In the mirror, Jerry saw a black Mercedes following, male passenger, male driver.

'Cousins bringing up the tail,' he announced.

A spasm of pain in the abdomen almost blacked him out, and for a moment he actually thought Fawn had hit him again, but it was only an after-thought of the first time. In Central, he made Guillam pull up and was sick in the gutter in full public view, leaning his head through the window while Fawn crouched tensely over him. Behind them, the Mercedes stopped too.

'Nothing like a spot of pain,' he exclaimed, settling in the car again, 'for getting the old brain out of mothballs once in a while. Eh Peter?'

In his black anger Guillam made an obscene answer.

You don't understand what's going on, Smiley had said. *How much you could upset things. Billions of dollars and thousands of men could not obtain a part of what we stand to gain . . .*

How? he kept asking himself. Gain *what*? His knowledge of Nelson's position inside Chinese affairs was sketchy. Craw had told him only the minimum he needed to know. *Nelson has access to the Crown jewels of Peking, your Grace. Whoever gets his hooks on Nelson has earned a lifetime's merit for himself and his noble house.*

They were skirting the harbour, heading for the tunnel.

From sea level the American aircraft carrier looked strangely small against the merry backdrop of Kowloon.

'How's Drake getting him out by the way?' he asked Guillam chattily. 'Not trying to fly him again, *that's* for sure. Ricardo put the lid on that one for good, didn't he?'

'Suction,' Guillam snapped – which was very silly of him, thought Jerry jubilantly, he should have kept his mouth shut.

'Swimming?' Jerry asked. 'Nelson on the Mirs Bay ticket. *That's* not Drake's way is it? Nelson's too old for that one anyway. Freeze to death, even if the sharks didn't get his whatnots. How about the pig-train, come out with the grunters? Sorry you've got to miss the big moment, sport, all on acount of me.'

'So am I, as a matter of fact. I'd like to kick your teeth in.'

Inside Jerry's brain, the sweet music of rejoicing sounded. *It's true!* he told himself. *That's what's happening! Drake's bringing Nelson out and they're all queuing up for his finish!*

Behind Guillam's lapse – just one word, but in Sarratt terms totally unforgivable, indivisibly wrong – there lay nevertheless a revelation as dazzling as anything which Jerry was presently enduring, and in some respects vastly more bitter. If anything mitigates the crime of indiscretion – and in Sarratt terms nothing does – then Guillam's experiences of the last hour – half of it spent driving Smiley frantically through rush-hour traffic, and half of it waiting, in desperate indecision, in the car outside Star Heights – would surely qualify. Everything he had feared in London, the most Gothic of his apprehensions regarding the Enderby-Martello connection, and the supporting rôles of Lacon and Sam Collins, had in these sixty minutes been proven to him beyond all reasonable doubt as right, and true, and justified, and if anything somewhat understated.

They had driven first to Bowen Road in the Midlevels, to an apartment block so blank and featureless and large that even those who lived there must have had to look twice at the number before they were sure they were entering the right one. Smiley pressed a bell marked *Mellon* and, idiot that he was, Guillam asked 'Who's Mellon?' at exactly the same time as he remembered that it was Sam Collins's workname. Then he did a double take and asked himself – but not Smiley, they were in the lift by now – what maniac, after Haydon's ravages, could conceivably award himself the same workname which he had used before the fall? Then Collins opened the door to them, wearing his Thai silk dressing gown, a brown cigarette jammed into a holder, and his washable non-iron smile, and the next thing was, they were grouped in a parquet drawing room with bamboo chairs and Sam had switched two transistor radios to different programmes, one voice, the other music, to provide rudimentary anti-bug security while they talked. Sam listened, ignoring Guillam entirely, then promptly phoned Martello direct – Sam had a *direct line* to him, please note, no dialling, nothing, a straight landline apparently – to ask in veiled language 'how things stood with chummy'. Chummy – Guillam learned later – being gambling slang for a mug. Martello replied that the surveillance van had just reported in. Chummy and Tiu were presently sitting in Causeway Bay aboard the *Admiral Nelson*, said the watchers, and the directional mikes (as usual) were picking up so much bounce from the water that the transcribers would need days if not weeks to clean off the extraneous sound and find out whether the two men had ever said anything interesting. Meanwhile they had dropped one man at the quayside as a static post, with orders to advise Martello immediately should the boat weigh anchor or either of the two quarries disembark.

'Then we must go there at once,' said Smiley, so they piled back into the car, and while Guillam drove the short distance to Star Heights, seething and listening impotently to their terse conversation, he became with every moment more convinced that he was looking at a spider's web, and that only George Smiley, obsessed by the promise of the case and the image of Karla, was myopic enough, and trusting enough, and in his own paradoxical way innocent enough, to bumble straight into the middle of it.

George's age, thought Guillam. Enderby's political ambitions, his fondness for the hawkish, pro-American stance – not to mention the crate of champagne and his outrageous courtship of the fifth floor. Lacon's tepid support of Smiley, while he secretly cast around for a successor. Martello's stopover in Langley. Enderby's attempt, *only days ago*, to prise Smiley away from the case and hand it to Martello on a plate. And now, most eloquent and ominous of all, the reappearance of Sam Collins as the joker in the pack with a private line to Martello! And Martello, Heaven help us, acting dumb about where George got his information from – the direct line notwithstanding.

To Guillam all these threads added up to one thing only, and he could not wait to take Smiley aside and by any means at his command deflect him sufficiently from the operation, just for one moment, for him to see where he was heading. To tell him about the letter. About Sam's visit to Lacon and Enderby in Whitehall.

Instead of which? He was to return to England. Why was he to return to England? Because a genial thick-skulled hack named Westerby had had the gall to slip the leash.

Even without his crying awareness of impending disaster, the disappointment to Guillam would have been scarcely supportable. He had endured a great deal for this moment. Disgrace and exile to Brixton under Haydon, poodling for old George instead of getting back to the field, putting up with George's obsessive secretiveness, which Guillam privately considered both humiliating and self-defeating – but at least it had been a journey with a destination, till bloody Westerby, of all people, had robbed him even of that. But to return to London knowing that for the next twenty-two hours at least, he was leaving Smiley and the Circus to a bunch of wolves, without even the chance to warn him – to Guillam it was the crowning cruelty of a frustrated career, and if blaming Jerry helped, then damn him, he would blame Jerry or anybody else.

'Send Fawn!'

'Fawn's not a gentleman,' Smiley would have replied – or words that meant the same.

You can say *that* again too, thought Guillam, remembering the broken arms.

Jerry was equally conscious of abandoning someone to the wolves, even if it was Lizzie Worthington rather than George Smiley. As he gazed through the rear window of the car, it seemed to him that the very world that he was moving through had been abandoned also. The street markets were deserted, the pavements, even the doorways. Above them, the Peak loomed fitfully, its crocodile spine daubed by a ragged moon. It's the Colony's last day, he decided. Peking has made its proverbial telephone call. 'Get out, party over.' The last hotel was closing, he saw the empty Rolls-Royces lying like scrap around the harbour, and the last blue-rinse roundeye matron, laden with her tax-free furs and jewellery, tottering up the gangway of the last cruise-ship, the last China-watcher frantically feeding his last miscalculations into the shredder, the looted shops, the empty city waiting like a carcass for the hordes. For a moment it was all one vanishing world – here, Phnom Penh, Saigon, London, a world on loan, with the creditors standing at the door, and Jerry himself, in some unfathomable way, a part of the debt that was owed.

I've always been grateful to this service that it gave me a chance to pay. Is that how you *feel? Now? As a survivor, so to speak?*

Yes, George, he thought. Put the words into my mouth, old boy. That's how I feel. But perhaps not quite in the sense *you* mean it, sport. He saw Frost's cheerful, fond little face as they drank and fooled. He saw it the second time, locked in that awful scream. He felt Luke's friendly hand upon his shoulder, and saw the same hand lying on the floor, flung back over his head to catch a ball that would never come, and he thought: trouble is, sport, the paying is actually done by the other poor sods.

Like Lizzie for instance.

He'd mention that to George one day, if they ever, over a glass, should get back to that sticky little matter of just why we climb the mountain. He'd make a point there – nothing aggressive, not rocking the boat you understand, sport – about the selfless and devoted way in which we sacrifice other people, such as Luke and Frost and Lizzie. George would have a perfectly good answer, of course. Reasonable. Measured. Apologetic. George saw the bigger picture. Understood the imperatives. Of course he did. He was an owl.

The harbour tunnel was approaching and he was thinking of her shivering last kiss, and remembering the drive to the mortuary all at the same time, because the scaffold of a new building rose ahead of them out of the fog, and like the scaffold on the way to the mortuary it was floodlit, and glistening coolies were swarming over it in yellow helmets.

Tiu doesn't like her either, he thought. Doesn't like roundeyes who spill the beans on Big Sir.

Forcing his mind in other directions he tried to imagine what they would do with Nelson: stateless, homeless, a fish to be devoured or thrown back into the sea at will. Jerry had seen a few of those fish before: he had been present for their capture; at their swift interrogation; he had led more than one of them back across the border they had so recently crossed, for hasty *recycling*, as the Sarratt jargon had it so charmingly – 'quick before they notice he has left home'. And if they didn't put him back? If they kept him, this great prize they all so coveted? Then after the years of his debriefing – two, three even – he had heard some ran for five – Nelson would become one more Wandering Jew of the spy trade, to be hidden, and moved again, and hidden, to be loved not even by those to whom he had betrayed his trust.

And what will Drake do with Lizzie – he wondered –

while that little drama unfolds? Which particular scrapheap is she headed for this time?

They were at the mouth of the tunnel and they had slowed almost to a halt. The Mercedes lay right behind them. Jerry let his head fall forward. He put both hands over his groin while he rocked himself and grunted in pain. From an improvised police box, like a sentry post, a Chinese constable watched curiously.

'If he comes over to us, tell him we've got a drunk on our hands,' Guillam snapped. 'Show him the sick on the floor.'

They crawled into the tunnel. Two lanes of northbound traffic were bunched nose to bumper by the bad weather. Guillam had taken the right-hand stream. The Mercedes drew up beside them on their left. In the mirror, through half-closed eyes, Jerry saw a brown lorry grind down the hill after them.

'Give me some change,' Guillam said. 'I'll need change as I come out.'

Fawn delved in his pockets, but using one hand only.

The tunnel pounded to the roar of engines. A hooting match started. Others began joining in. To the encroaching fog was added the stench of exhaust fumes. Fawn closed his window. The din rose and echoed till the car trembled to it. Jerry put his hands to his ears.

'Sorry, sport. Going to bring up again I'm afraid.'

But this time he leaned toward Fawn, who with a muttered 'Filthy bastard' started hastily to wind his window down again, until Jerry's head crashed into the lower part of his face, and Jerry's elbow hacked down into his groin. For Guillam, caught between driving and defending himself, Jerry had one pounding chop on the point where the shoulder socket meets the collarbone. He started the strike with the arm quite relaxed, converting the speed into power at the last possible moment. The impact made Guillam scream 'Christ!' and lifted him straight out of his seat as the car veered to the right. Fawn had an arm round Jerry's neck and with his other hand he was trying to press Jerry's head over it, which would definitely have killed him. But there is a blow they teach at Sarratt for cramped spaces which is called a tiger's claw, and is delivered by driving the heel of the hand upward into the opponent's windpipe, keeping the arm crooked and the fingers pressed back for tension. Jerry did that now, and Fawn's head hit the back window so hard that the safety glass starred. In the Mercedes, the two Americans went on looking ahead of them, as if they were driving to a state funeral. He thought of squeezing Fawn's windpipe with his finger and thumb but it didn't seem necessary. Recovering his gun from Fawn's waistband, Jerry opened the right-hand door. Guillam made one desperate dive for him, ripping the sleeve of his faithful but very old blue suit to the elbow. Jerry swung the gun on to his arm and saw his face contort with pain. Fawn got a leg out but Jerry slammed the door on it and heard him shout 'Bastard!' again and after that he just kept running back toward town, against the stream. Bounding and weaving between the land-locked cars, he pelted out of the tunnel and up the hill until he reached the little sentry hut. He thought he heard Guillam yelling. He thought he heard a shot but it could have been a car backfiring. His groin was hurting amazingly, but he seemed to run faster under the impetus of the pain. A policeman on the kerb shouted at him, another held out his arms, but Jerry brushed them aside, and they gave him the final indulgence of the roundeye. He ran until he found a cab. The driver spoke no English so he had to point the way. 'That's it, sport. Up there. Left, you bloody idiot. That's it,' – until they reached her block.

He didn't know whether Smiley and Collins were still there, or whether Ko had turned up, perhaps with Tiu, but there was very little time to play games finding out. He didn't ring the bell because he knew the mikes would pick it up. Instead he fished a card from his wallet, scribbled on it, shoved it through the letterbox and waited in a crouch, shivering and sweating and panting like a dray-horse while he listened for her tread and nursed his groin. He waited an age and finally the door opened and she stood there staring at him while he tried to get upright.

'Christ, it's Galahad,' she muttered. She wore no make-up and Ricardo's claw marks were deep and red. She wasn't crying; he didn't think she did that, but her face looked older than the rest of her. To talk, he drew her into the corridor and she didn't resist. He showed her the door leading to the fire-steps.

'Meet me the other side of it in five seconds flat, hear me? *Don't* telephone anybody, *don't* make a clatter leaving, and *don't* ask any bloody silly questions. Bring some warm clothes. Now do it, sport. Don't dither. *Please.*'

She looked at him, at his torn sleeve, and sweat-stained jacket; and his mop of forelock hanging over his eye.

'It's me or nothing,' he said. 'And believe me, it's a big nothing.'

She walked back to her flat alone, leaving the door ajar. But she came out much faster and for safety's sake she didn't even close the door. On the fire-stairs he led the way. She carried a shoulder bag and wore a leather coat. She had brought a cardigan for him to replace the torn jacket, he supposed Drake's because it was miles too small, but he managed to squeeze into it. He emptied his jacket pockets into her handbag and chucked the jacket down the rubbish chute. She was so quiet following him that he twice looked back to make sure she was still there. Reaching the ground floor, he peered through the glass mesh window and drew back in time to see the Rocker in person, accompanied by a heavy subordinate, approach the porter in his kiosk and show him his police pass. They followed the stair as far as the car park and she said, 'Let's take the red canoe.'

'Don't be bloody stupid, we left it in town.'

Shaking his head, he led her past the cars into a squalid open-air compound full of refuse and building junk, like the backyard at the Circus. From here, between walls of weeping concrete, a giddy stairway fell toward the town, overhung by black branches and cut into sections by the winding road. The jarring of the downward steps hurt his groin a lot. The first time they reached the road, Jerry took her straight across it. The second time, alerted by the blood-red flash of an alarm light in the distance, he hauled her into the trees to avoid the beam of a police car whining down the hill at speed. At the underpass they found a *pak-pai* and Jerry gave the address.

'Where the hell's that?' she said.

'Somewhere you don't have to register,' said Jerry. 'Just shut up and let me be masterful, will you. How much money have you got with you?'

She opened her bag and counted from a fat wallet.

'I won it off Tiu at mah-jong,' she said and for some reason he sensed she was romancing.

The driver dropped them at the end of the alley and they walked the short distance to the low gateway. The house had no lights, but as they approached the front door it opened and another couple flitted past them out of the darkness. They entered the hall and the door closed behind them and they followed a handborne pinlight through a short maze of brick walls until they reached a smart interior lobby in which piped music played. On the serpentine sofa in the centre sat a trim Chinese lady with a pencil and a notebook on her lap, to all the world a model châtelaine. She saw Jerry and smiled, she saw Lizzie and her smile broadened.

'For the whole night,' Jerry said.

'Of course,' she replied.

They followed her upstairs to a small corridor. The open doors gave glimpses of silk counterpanes, low lights, mirrors. Jerry chose the least suggestive, declined the offer of a second girl to make up the numbers, gave her money and ordered a bottle of Rémy Martin. Lizzie followed him in, chucked her shoulder bag on the bed and while the door was still open broke into a taut laugh of relief.

'Lizzie Worthington,' she announced, 'this is where they said you'd end up, you brazen bitch, and blow me if they weren't right!'

There was a chaise-longue and Jerry lay on it, staring at the ceiling, feet crossed, the brandy glass in his hand.

Lizzie took the bed and for a time neither spoke. The place was very still. Occasionally, from the floor above, they heard a cry of pleasure or muffled laughter, once of protest. She went to the window and peered out.

'What's out there?' he asked.

'Bloody brick wall, about thirty cats, stack of empties.'

'Foggy?'

'Vile.'

She sauntered to the bathroom, poked around, came out again.

'Sport,' said Jerry quietly.

She paused, suddenly wary.

'Are you sober and of sound judgment?'

'Why?'

'I want you to tell me everything you told them. When you've done that, I want you to tell me everything they asked you, whether you could answer it or not. And when you've done that, we'll try to take a little thing called a backbearing and work out where those bastards all are in the scheme of the universe.'

'It's a replay,' she said finally.

'What of?'

'I don't know. It's all to be exactly the way it happened before.'

'So what happened before?'

'Whatever it was,' she said wearily, 'it's going to happen again.'

Chapter 21

NELSON

It was one in the morning. She had bathed. She came out of the bathroom wearing a white wrap and no shoes and her hair in a towel, so that the proportions of her were all suddenly different.

'They've even got those bits of paper stretched across the loo,' she said. 'And toothmugs in cellophane bags.'

She dozed on the bed and he on the sofa, and once she said. 'I'd like to but it doesn't work,' and he replied that after being kicked where Fawn had kicked him the libido tended to be a bit quiescent anyway. She told him about her schoolmaster – Mr Bloody Worthington, she called him – and 'her one shot at going straight', and about the child she had borne him out of politeness. She talked about her terrible parents, and about Ricardo and what a sod he was, and how she had loved him, and how a girl in the Constellation Bar had advised her to poison him with laburnum, so one day after he had beaten her half to death she put a 'damn great dose in his coffee'. But perhaps she hadn't got the right stuff, she said, because all that happned was that he was sick for days and 'the one thing worse than Ricardo healthy was Ricardo at death's door'. How another time she actually got a knife into him while he was in the bath but all he did was stick a bit of plaster over it and swipe her again.

How when Ricardo did his disappearing act she and Charlie Marshall refused to accept that he was dead, and mounted a Ricardo Lives! campaign, as they called it, and how Charlie went and badgered his old man, all just as he had described to Jerry. How Lizzie packed up her rucksack and went down to Bangkok, where she barged straight into the China Airsea suite at the Erawan, intending to beard Tiu, and found herself face to face with Ko instead, having met him only once before very briefly, at a bunfight in Hong Kong given by one Sally Cale, a blue-rinse bull-dyke in the antique trade who pushed heroin on the side. And how that was quite a scene she played, beginning with Ko's sharp instruction to get out, and ending with 'Nature taking her course' as she put it cheerfully: 'Another step on Lizzie Worthington's unswerving road to perdition.' So that slowly and deviously, with Charlie Marshall's old man pulling, 'and Lizzie pushing, as you might say', they put together a very Chinese contract, to which the main signatories were Ko and Charlie's old man, and the commodities to be transacted were, one, Ricardo and, two, his recently retired life partner, Lizzie.

In which said contract, Jerry learned with no particular surprise, both she and Ricardo gratefully acquiesced.

'You should have let him rot,' said Jerry, remembering the twin rings on his right hand, and the Ford car blown to bits.

But Lizzie hadn't seen it that way at all, and she didn't now.

'He was one of us,' she said. 'Although he was a sod.'

But having bought his life, she felt free of him.

'Chinese arrange marriages every day. So why shouldn't Drake and Liese?'

What was all the *Liese* stuff? Jerry asked. Why *Liese* instead of *Lizzie*?

She didn't know. Something Drake didn't talk about, she said. There had once been a Liese in his life, he told her, and his fortune-teller had promised him that one day he would get another, and he reckoned Lizzie was near enough, so they gave it a shove and called it Liese and while she was about it she pared her surname to plain Worth.

'Blonde bird,' she said absently.

The name-change had a practical purpose too, she said. Having chosen a new name for her, Ko took the trouble to have the local police record of her old one destroyed.

'Till that sod Mellon marches in and says he'll get them to rewrite it, with a special mention about me carrying his bloody heroin,' she said.

Which brought them back to where they were now. And why.

To Jerry, their sleepy wanderings occasionally had the calm of after-love. He lay on the divan, wide awake, but Lizzie talked between dozes, taking up her story dreamily where she had left it when she fell asleep, and he knew that near enough she was telling him the truth because it made nothing of her that he did not already know, and understand. He realised also that, with time, Ko had become an anchor for her. He gave her the authority from which to survey her Odyssey, somewhat as the schoolmaster had.

'Drake never broke a promise in his life,' she said once, as she rolled over and sank back into a fitful sleep. He remembered the orphan: just never lie to me.

Hours, lifetimes later, she was woken by a squawk of ecstasy next door.

'Christ,' she declared appreciatively. 'She *really* hit the moon.' The squawk repeated itself. 'Uha! Faking it.' Silence.

'You awake?' she asked.

'Yes.'

'What are you going to do?'

'Tomorrow?'

'Yes.'

'I don't know,' he said.

'Join the club,' she whispered, and seemed to fall asleep again.

I need the Sarratt brief again, he thought. Very badly I need it. Put in a limbo call to Craw, he thought. Ask dear old George for a spot of that philosophical advice he's taken to doling out these days. He must be around. Somewhere.

* * *

Smiley was around but at that moment he could not have given Jerry any help at all. He would have traded all his knowledge for a little understanding. The isolation ward had no night-time and they lay or lounged under the punctured daylight of the ceiling, the three Cousins and Sam one side of the room, Smiley and Guillam the other, and Fawn striding up and down the line of the cinema seats, looking caged and furious and squeezing what appeared to be a squash-ball in each tiny fist. His lips were black and swollen and one eye was shut. A clot of blood under his nose refused to go away. Guillam had his right arm strapped to his shoulder and his eyes were on Smiley all the while. But so were the eyes of everyone, or everyone but Fawn. A phone rang but it was the communications room upstairs saying Bangkok had reported Jerry traced for certain as far as Vientiane.

'Tell them the trail's cold, Murphy,' Martello ordered, his eyes still on Smiley. 'Tell them any damn thing. Just get them off our backs. Right, George?'

Smiley nodded.

'Right,' said Guillam firmly, speaking for him.

'The trail's cold, honey,' Murphy echoed into the phone. The *honey* came as a surprise. Murphy had not till now shown such signs of human tenderness. 'You want to make a signal or do I have to do it for you? We're not interested, right? Kill it.'

He rang off.

'Rockhurst has found her car,' Guillam said for the second time, while Smiley still stared ahead of him. 'In an underground carpark in Central. There is a hire car down there too. Westerby rented it. Today. In his workname. George?'

Smiley gave a nod so slight it might have been no more than an attack of sleepiness which he had staved away.

'At least he's doing something, George,' said Martello pointedly, down the room from his own small caucus of Collins and the quiet men. 'Some people would say, when you have a rogue elephant, best thing to do is go out there and shoot him.'

'You have to find him first,' snapped Guillam, whose nerves were at breaking point.

'I'm not even sure George wants to do that, Peter,' Martello said in a reprise of his avuncular style. 'I think George may be lifting his eye from the ball a little on this, to the grave peril of our common enterprise.'

'What do you want George to do?' Guillam rejoined tartly. 'Walk the streets till he finds him? Have Rockhurst circulate his name and description so that every journalist in town knows there's a manhunt for him?'

At Guillam's side, Smiley remained hunched and inert, like an old man.

'Westerby's a professional,' Guillam insisted. 'He's not a natural but he's good. He can lie up for months in a town like this and Rockhurst wouldn't get a scent of him.'

'Not even with the girl in tow?' said Murphy.

His strapped arm notwithstanding Guillam stooped to Smiley.

'It's your operation,' he whispered urgently. 'If you say we've got to wait, we'll wait. Just give the order. All these people want is an excuse to take over. Anything but a vacuum. Anything.'

Prowling the line of the cinema chairs, Fawn gave vent to a sarcastic murmur.

'Talk, talk, talk. That's all they can do.'

Martello tried again.

'George. Is this island British or is it not? You guys can shake this town out any time.' He pointed to a windowless wall. 'We have a man out there – your man – who seems bent on running amok. Nelson Ko is the biggest catch you or I are ever likely to land. The biggest of my career, and I will stake my wife, my grandmother and the deeds of my plantation, the biggest even of yours.'

'No takers,' said Sam Collins the gambler, through his grin.

Martello stuck to his guns.

'Are we going to let him rob us of the prize, George, while we sit here passively asking one another how it came about that Jesus Christ was born on Christmas Day and not on December twenty-six or seven?'

Smiley peered at Martello at last, then up at Guillam who stood stiffly at his side, tipping back his shoulders to support the sling, and finally he looked downward at his own, locked, conflicting hands and for a period quite meaningless in time he studied himself in his mind, and reviewed his quest for Karla, whom Ann called *his black Grail*. He thought of Ann and her repeated betrayals of him in the name of her own Grail, which she called love. He recalled how, against his better judgment, he had tried to share her faith, and like a true believer, renew it each day, despite her anarchic interpretations of its meaning. He thought of Haydon, steered at Ann by Karla. He thought of Jerry and the girl, and he thought of Peter Worthington her husband, and the doglike look of kinship which Worthington had bestowed on him, when he called to interview him in the terrace house in Islington: 'You and I are the ones they leave behind,' ran the message.

He thought of Jerry's other tentative loves along his untidy trail, the half-paid bills the Circus had picked up for him, and it would have been handy to lump Lizzie in with them as just one more, but he couldn't do that. He was not Sam Collins, and he had not the smallest doubt that at this moment Jerry's feeling for the girl was a cause which Ann would warmly have espoused. But he was not Ann either. For a cruel moment, nevertheless, as he sat, still locked in indecision, he did honestly wonder whether Ann was right, and his striving had become nothing other than a private journey among the beasts and villains of his own insufficiency, in which he ruthlessly involved simplistic minds like Jerry's.

You're wrong, sport. Don't know how, don't know why, but you're wrong.

The fact that I am wrong, he had once replied to Ann, in the midstream of one of their endless arguments, *does not make you right.*

He heard Martello again, speaking in present time.

'George, we have people waiting with *open arms* for what we can give them. What Nelson can.'

A phone was ringing. Murphy took the call and relayed the message to the silent room: 'Landline from the aircraft carrier, sir. Navy int. has the junks dead on schedule, sir. South wind favourable and good fishing along the way. Sir, I don't even think Nelson's riding with them. I don't see why he should.'

The focus shifted abruptly to Murphy, who had never before been heard to express an opinion.

'What the hell's *that*, Murphy?' Martello demanded, quite astonished. 'You been to the fortune-teller too, son?'

'Sir, I was down on the ship this morning and those people have a lot of data. They can't figure why anybody who lives in Shanghai would ever want to exit out of Swatow. They would do it all different, sir. They would fly or train to Canton, then take the bus maybe to Waichow. They say that's a lot safer, sir.'

'These are Nelson's people,' Smiley said, as the heads swung sharply back on him. 'They're his clan. He would rather be at sea with them, even if he's at risk. He trusts them.' He turned to Guillam. 'We'll do this,' he said. 'Tell Rockhurst to distribute a description of Westerby and the girl together. You say he hired the car under his work-name? Used his escape papers?'

'Yes.'

'Worrell?'

'Yes.'

'The police are looking for a Mr and Mrs Worrell then, British. No photographs, and make sure the descriptions are vague enough not to arouse suspicion. Marty.'

Martello was all attentiveness.

'Is Ko still on his boat?' Smiley asked.

'Nestled right in there with Tiu, George.'

'It is just possible Westerby may try to reach him. You have a static post at the quayside. Put more men down there. Tell them to keep eyes in the back of their heads.'

'What are they looking for?'

'Trouble. The same goes for surveillance on his house.

Tell me – ' he sank into his thoughts a moment, but Guillam need not have worried. 'Tell me – can you simulate a fault on Ko's home telephone line?'

Martello glanced at Murphy.

'Sir, we don't have the apparatus handy,' Murphy said, 'but I guess we could . . .'

'Then cut it,' Smiley said simply. 'Cut the whole cable if necessary. Try and do it near some roadworks.'

Having dispensed his orders, Martello came lightly across the room, and sat himself at Smiley's side.

'Ah George, about tomorrow, now. Do you think we might, ah, put a little hardware on standby, as well?' From the desk where he was telephoning Rockhurst, Guillam watched the dialogue most intently. From across the room, so did Sam Collins. 'Just seems there's no telling what your man Westerby might do, George. We have to be prepared for all emergencies, right?'

'By all means stand anything by. But for the time being, if you don't mind, we'll leave the interception plans as they are. And the competence with me.'

'Sure, George. Sure,' said Martello fulsomely, and with the same church-like reverence tiptoed back to his own camp.

'What did he want?' Guillam demanded in a low voice, crouching at Smiley's side. 'What's he trying to get you to agree to?'

'I will not have it, Peter,' Smiley warned, also under his breath. He was suddenly very angry. 'I shall not hear you again. I shall not tolerate your Byzantine notions of a palace plot. These people are our hosts and our allies. We have a written agreement with them. We have quite enough to worry about already without grotesque, and, I may tell you honestly, paranoid fancies. Now please – '

'I tell *you*!' Guillam began, but Smiley closed him down.

'I want you to get hold of Craw. Call on him if necessary. Perhaps the journey would do you good. Tell him Westerby's on the rampage. He's to let us know at once if he has word of him. He'll know what to do.'

Still walking the line of seats, Fawn watched Guillam

leave, while his fists continued restlessly kneading whatever was inside them.

In Jerry's world it was also three in the morning, and the madame had found him a razor, but no fresh shirt. He had shaved and cleaned himself up as best he could, but his body still ached from head to toe. He stood over Lizzie where she lay on the bed and promised to be back in a couple of hours but he doubted whether she even heard him. *More papers print girls instead of news*, he remembered, *and the world be a damn sight better place, Mr Westerby*.

He took *pak-pais*, knowing they were less under the thumb of the police. Otherwise he walked, and the walking helped his body and his mystical process of decision taking, because back there on the divan it had suddenly become impossible. He needed to move in order to find direction. He was heading for Deep Water Bay, and he knew he was entering badland. Now that he was on the loose they would be on to that launch like leeches. He wondered who they had, what they were using. If it was the Cousins he would look for too much hardware, and overmanning. Rain was coming on and he feared it would clear the fog. Above him, the moon was already partly free and as he padded silently down the hill he could make out by its pale light the nearest stockbroker junks groaning and tugging at their moorings. A south-east wind, he noticed, and rising. If it's a static observation post, they'll go for height, he thought, and sure enough, there on the promontory to his right, he saw a battered-looking Mercedes van tucked between the trees, and the aerial with its Chinese streamers. He waited, watching the fog roll, till a car came down the hill with its lights full on, and as soon as it was past him he darted across the road, knowing that not all the hardware in the world would enable them to see him behind the advancing headlights. At the water's level the visibility was down to zero, and he had to grope in order to pick out the rickety wooden causeway he remembered from his previous reconnaissance. Then he found what he was looking for.

The same toothless old woman sat in her sampan grinning up at him through the fog.

'Ko,' he whispered. '*Admiral Nelson. Ko*?'

The echo of her cackle bounded away across the water.

'Po Toi!' she screamed. 'Tin Hau! Po Toi!'

'Today?'

'Today!'

'Tomorrow?'

'Tomollow!'

He tossed her a couple of dollars and her laughter followed him as he crept away.

I'm right, Lizzie's right, *we're* right, he thought. He's going to the festival. He hoped to God Lizzie was staying put. If she woke up, he wouldn't put it past her to wander.

He walked, trying to stamp away the aching in his groin and back. Take it stage by stage, he thought. Nothing big. Just play it as it comes. The fog was like a corridor leading to different rooms. Once he met an invalid car crawling along the kerb, as its owner exercised his Alsation dog. Once, two old men in undervests performing their morning exercises. In a public garden small children stared at him from a rhododendron bush which they seemed to have made their home, for their clothes were draped over the branches and they were naked as the refugee kids in Phnom Penh.

She was sitting up waiting for him when he returned and she looked terrible.

'Don't do that again,' she warned, and shoved her arm through his as they set out to find some breakfast and a boat. 'Don't ever bloody walk out on me without warning.'

Hong Kong at first possessed no boats at all that day. Jerry would not contemplate the big out-island ferries which took the trippers. He knew the Rocker would have them sewn up. He refused to go down to the bays and make conspicuous enquiries. When he telephoned the listed water-taxi firms whatever they had was either rented or too small for the voyage. Then he remembered Luigi Tan the fixer, who was a myth at the Foreign Correspondents' club: Luigi could get you anything from a Korean dance troupe to a cut-price air-ticket faster than any fixer in town. They took a taxi to the other side of Wanchai, where Luigi had his lair, then walked. It was eight in the morning but the hot fog had not lifted. The unlit signs sprawled over the narrow lanes like spent lovers: Happy Boy, Lucky Place, Americana. The crowded food stalls added their warm smells to the reek of petrol fumes and smuts. Through splits in the wall they sometimes glimpsed a canal. 'Anyone tell you where to find me,' Luigi Tan liked to say. 'Ask for the big guy with one leg.'

They found him behind the counter of his shop, just tall enough to look over it, a tiny, darting half-Portuguese who had once earned a living Chinese boxing in the grimy booths of Macao. The front of the shop was six foot wide. His wares were new motorbikes and relics of the old China Service, which he called antiques; daguerreotypes of hatted ladies in tortoiseshell frames, a battered travelling box, an opium clipper's log. Luigi knew Jerry already but he liked Lizzie much better, and insisted that she go ahead so that he could study her hind quarters while he ushered them under a washing line, to an outhouse marked *private*, with three chairs and a telephone on the floor. Crouching till he was rolled into a neat ball, Luigi talked Chinese to the telephone and English to Lizzie. He was a grandfather, he said, but virile, and had four sons, all good. Even number four son was off his hands. All good drivers, good workers and good husbands. Also, he said to Lizzie, he had a Mercedes complete with stereo.

'Maybe I take you ride in it one day,' he said.

Jerry wondered whether she realised that he was proposing marriage, or perhaps something slightly less.

And yes, Luigi thought he had a boat as well.

After two phone calls he knew he had a boat, which he only ever lent to friends, at a nominal cost. He gave Lizzie his credit card case to count the number of cards, then his wallet to admire the family snaps, one of which showed a lobster caught by number four son on the day of his recent wedding, though the son was not visible.

'Po Toi bad place,' said Luigi Tan to Lizzie, still on the telephone. 'Very dirty place. Rough sea, lousy festival, bad food. Why you want to go there?'

For Tin Hau of course, Jerry said patiently, answering for her. For the famous temple and the festival.

Luigi Tan preferred to speak to Lizzie.

'You go Lantau,' he advised. 'Lantau good island. Nice food, good fish, nice people. I tell them you go Lantau, eat at Charlie's, Charlie my friend.'

'Po Toi,' said Jerry firmly

'Po Toi hell of a lot of cash.'

'We've got a hell of a lot of cash,' said Lizzie with a lovely smile, and Luigi looked at her again, contemplatively, the long up and down look.

'Maybe I come with you,' he said to her.

'No,' said Jerry.

Luigi drove them to Causeway Bay and rode with them on the sampan. The boat was a fourteen-foot power boat, common as driftwood, but Jerry reckoned she was sound and Luigi said she had a deep keel. A boy lounged on the stern, trailing one foot in the water.

'My nephew,' said Luigi, ruffling the boy's hair proudly. 'He got mother in Lantau. He take you Lantau, eat Charlie's place, give you good time. You pay me later.'

'Old boy,' said Jerry patiently. 'Sport. We don't want Lantau. We want Po Toi. Only Po Toi. Po Toi or nothing. Drop us there and go.

'Po Toi bad weather, bad festival. Bad place. Too near China water. Lot of Commies.'

'Po Toi or nothing,' Jerry said.

'Boat too small,' said Luigi, with a frightful loss of face, and it took all of Lizzie's charm to build him up again.

For another hour the boys primed the boat and all Jerry and Lizzie could do was sit in the half cabin keeping out of sight and sip judicious shots of Rémy Martin. Periodically one or other of them sank into a private reverie. When Lizzie did this, she hugged herself and rocked slowly on her haunches, head down. Whereas Jerry yanked at his forelock, and once he yanked so hard she touched his arm to stop him, and he laughed.

Almost carelessly they pulled away from the harbour.

'Stay out of sight,' Jerry ordered, and for safety's sake put his arm round her to keep her in the meagre shelter of the open cabin.

The American aircraft carrier had stripped off her ornamental garb and lay grey and menacing, like an unsheathed knife above the water. At first, they had nothing but the same sticky calm. On the shore, shelves of mist pressed on to the grey highrises, and brown smoke columns slid into a white expressionless sky. On the flat water their boat felt high as a balloon. But as they slipped the shelter and headed east, the waves slapped her sides hard enough to wind her, the bow pitched and cracked, and they had to brace themselves to keep upright. With the little bow lifting and tugging like a bad horse, they tumbled past cranes and godowns and factories and the stumps of quarried hillsides. They were running straight into the wind and spray was flying on all sides. The coxswain at the wheel was laughing and crowing to his mate, and Jerry supposed it was the mad roundeyes they were laughing at, who chose to do their courting in a pitching tub. A giant tanker passed them, not seeming to move, brown junks running in her wake. From the dockyards, where a freighter was laid-to, the white flashes of the welders' lamps signalled to them across the water. The boys' laughter eased and they began to talk sensibly because they were at sea. Looking back between the swaying walls of transport ships Jerry saw the Island drawing slowly away from him, cut like a table mountain by the cloud. Once more, Hong Kong was ceasing to exist.

They passed another headland. As the sea roughened, the pitching steadied and the cloud above them dropped until its base was only a few feet above their mast, and for a while they stayed in this lower, unreal world, advancing under cover of its protective blanket. The fog ended suddenly and left them in dancing sunlight. Southward, on hills of violent lushness, an orange navigation lamp winked at them through the clear air.

'What do we do now?' she asked softly, looking through the porthole.

'Smile and pray,' said Jerry.

'I'll smile, you pray,' she said.

A pilot's launch was pulling alongside and for a moment he definitely expected to see the hideous face of the Rocker glowering down on him, but the crew ignored them entirely.

'Who are they?' she whispered. 'What do they think?'

'It's routine,' said Jerry. 'It's meaningless.'

The launch veered away. That's it, thought Jerry, with no particular feeling, they've spotted us.

'You sure it was just routine?' she asked.

'Hundreds of boats go to the festival,' he said.

The boat bucked violently, and kept bucking. Great seaworthiness, he thought, hanging on to Lizzie. Great keel. If this goes on, we won't have anything to decide. The sea will do it for us. It was one of those trips where if you made it nobody noticed, and if you didn't they'd say you threw your life away. The east wind could swirl right round on itself at any moment, he thought. In the season between west monsoons, nothing was ever sure. He listened anxiously to the erratic galloping of the engine. If it gives up we'll finish on the rocks.

Suddenly his nightmares multiplied unreasonably. *The butane*, he thought. *Christ, the butane!* While the boys were preparing the boat, he had glimpsed two cylinders stowed in the front hold beside the water-tanks, presumably for cooking Luigi's lobsters. Fool that he was, he had made nothing of them till now. He worked it out. Butane is heavier than air. All cylinders leak. It's just a question of degree. With this sea pounding the bows they leak faster, and the escaped gas will now be lying in the bilge about two feet from the spark of the engine, with a nice blend of oxygen to assist combustion. Lizzie had slipped from his grasp and stood astern. The sea was suddenly crowded. Out of nowhere, a fleet of fishing junks had gathered, and she was gazing at them earnestly. Grabbing her arm he hauled her back to the cover of the cabin.

'Where do you think you are?' he shouted. 'Bloody Cowes?'

She studied him a moment, then gently kissed him, then kissed him again.

'You calm down,' she warned. She kissed him a third time, muttered 'Yes,' as if her expectations had been fulfilled, then sat quiet for a while, looking at the deck but keeping hold of his hand.

Jerry reckoned they were making five knots into the wind. A small plane zoomed overhead. Holding her out of sight he looked up sharply, but was too late to read the markings.

'And good morning to *you*,' he thought.

They were rounding the last point, tossing and groaning in the spray. Once, the propellers lifted clean out of the water with a roar. As they hit the sea again, the engine faltered, choked, but decided to stay alive. Touching Lizzie's shoulder Jerry pointed ahead of them to where the bare, steep island of Po Toi loomed like a cutout against the cloud-torn sky: two peaks, sheer from the water, the larger to the south, and a saddle between. The sea had turned iron blue and the wind ripped over it, slapping the breath from their mouths and hurling spray at them like hail. On the port bow lay Beaufort Island: a lighthouse, a jetty, no inhabitants. The wind dropped as though it had never been. Not a breeze greeted them as they entered the unruffled water of the island's lee. The sun's heat was direct and harsh. Ahead of them, perhaps a mile, lay the mouth of Po Toi's main bay, and behind it, the low brown ghosts of China's islands. Soon they could make out a whole untidy fleet of junks and cruise boats jamming the bay, as the first jingle of drums and cymbals and unco-ordinated chanting floated to them across the water. On the hill behind lay the shanty village, its tin roofs twink-ling, and on its own small headland stood one solid building, the temple of Tin Hau, with a bamboo scaffold lashed round it in a rudimentary grandstand, and a large crowd with a pall of smoke hanging over it and dabs of gold between.

'Which side was it?' he asked her.

'I don't know. We climbed to a house and walked from there.'

Each time he spoke to her he looked at her, but now she avoided his gaze. Tapping the coxswain on the shoulder he pointed the course he wanted him to take. The boy at once began protesting. Squaring to him, Jerry showed him a bunch of money, pretty well all he had left. With an ill grace, the boy swung across the mouth of the harbour, weaving between the boats toward a small granite headland where a tumbledown jetty offered a risky landing. The din of the festival was much louder. They could smell charcoal and suckling pig, and hear concerted bursts of laughter, but for the time being the crowd was out of sight to them, as they were to the crowd.

'Here!' he yelled. 'Put in here. Now! *Now*!'

The jetty leaned drunkenly as they clambered on to it. They had not even reached land before their boat had turned for home. Nobody said goodbye. They climbed up the rock, hand in hand, and walked straight into a money game that was being watched by a large and laughing crowd. At the centre stood a clownish old man with a bag of coins and he was throwing them down the rock one by one while barefooted boys hurled themselves after them, pushing each other almost to the cliff-edge in their zeal.

'They took a boat,' Guillam said. 'Rockhurst has interviewed the proprietor. The proprietor is a friend of Westerby, and yes it was Westerby and a beautiful girl, and they wanted to go to Po Toi for Tin Hau.'

'And how did Rockhurst play that?' Smiley asked.

'Said in that case it wasn't the couple he was looking for. Bowed out. Disappointed. The harbour police have also belatedly reported sighting it on a course for the festival.'

'Want us to put up a spotter plane, George?' Martello asked nervously. 'Navy int. have all sorts standing by.'

Murphy had a bright suggestion. 'Why don't we just go right in with choppers and scoop Nelson off that end junk?' he demanded.

'Murphy, shut up,' Martello said.

'They're making for the island,' Smiley said firmly. 'We know they are. I don't think we need aircover to prove it.'

Martello was not satisfied. 'Then maybe we should send a couple of people out to that island, George. Maybe we ought to do a little interfering finally.'

Fawn was standing stock still. Even his fists had stopped working.

'No,' said Smiley.

At Martello's side Sam Collins's grin grew a little thinner.

'Any reason?' Martello asked.

'Right up to the last minute, Ko has one sanction. He can signal his brother not to come ashore,' Smiley said. 'The merest hint of a disturbance on the island could persuade him to do that.'

Martello gave a nervous, angry sigh. He had put aside the pipe he sometimes smoked and was drawing heavily on Sam's supply of brown cigarettes, which seemed to be endless.

'George, what does this man *want*?' he demanded in exasperation. 'Is this a blackmail thing now, a disruption? I don't see a category here.' A dreadful thought struck him. His voice dropped and he pointed with the full length of his arm across the room. 'Now just don't tell me we got one of these *new ones* on our hands, for Christ's sakes! Don't tell me he's one of those cold-war converts with a middle-aged mission to wash his soul in public. Because if he is, and we are going to read this guy's frank life story in *The Washington Post* next week, George, I personally am going to put the whole Fifth Fleet on that island, if that's what it takes to hold him down.' He turned to Murphy. 'I have contingencies, right?'

'Right.'

'George, I want a landing party on standby. You guys can come aboard or stay home. Please yourselves.'

Smiley stared at Martello, then at Guillam with his strapped and useless arm, then at Fawn, who was poised like a diver at the end of a springboard, eyes half closed and heels together, while he lifted himself slowly up and down on his toes.

'Fawn and Collins,' Smiley said at last.

'You two boys take them down to the aircraft carrier and hand them right over to the people there. Murphy comes back.'

A smoke-cloud marked the place where Collins had been sitting. Where Fawn had stood, two squash balls slowly rolled a distance before coming to a halt.

'God help us all,' somebody murmured fervently. It was Guillam, but Smiley ignored him.

The lion was three-men long and the crowd was laughing because it nipped at them and because self-appointed picadors were prodding it with sticks while it lolloped in dance-steps down the narrow path, to the clatter of the drums and cymbals. Reaching the headland, the procession slowly turned itself and started to retrace its steps, and at this point Jerry drew Lizzie quickly into the middle of it, bending low in order to make less of his height. The track was mud and full of puddles. Soon the dance was leading them past the temple and down concrete steps toward a sand beach where the suckling pigs were being roasted.

'Which way?' he asked her.

She guided him quickly left, out of the dance, along the back of a shanty village and over a wooden bridge across an inlet. They climbed along a fringe of cypress trees, Lizzie leading, until they were alone again, standing over the perfect horsehoe bay, looking down on Ko's *Admiral Nelson* where she lay at the very centre, like a grand lady among the hundreds of pleasure boats and junks around her. There was nobody visible on deck, not even crew. A clutch of grey police boats, five or six of them, was anchored further out to sea.

And why not, thought Jerry, since this was a festival?

She had let go his hand and, when he turned to her, she

was still staring at Ko's launch and he saw the shadow of confusion in her face.

'Is this really the way he brought you?' he asked.

It was the way, she said, and turned to him to look, to confirm or weigh things in her mind. Then with her forefinger she gravely traced his lips, at the centre of them where she had kissed them. 'Jesus,' she said, and as gravely shook her head.

They started climbing again. Glancing up, Jerry saw the brown island peak deceptively near, and on the hillside, groups of rice terraces gone to ruin. They entered a small village populated by nothing but surly dogs, and the bay vanished from sight. The school house was open and empty. Through the doorway, they saw charts of fighting aircraft. Washing jars stood on the step. Cupping her hands, Lizzie rinsed her face. The huts were slung with wire and brick to anchor them against typhoons. The path turned to sand and the going grew harder.

'Still right?' he asked.

'It's just *up*,' she said, as if she were sick of telling him. 'It's just *up*, and then the *house*, and bingo. I mean, Christ, what do you think I am, a bloody nitwit?'

'I won't say a thing,' said Jerry. He put his arm round her and she pressed in to him, giving herself exactly as she had done on the dancing floor.

They heard a blare of music from the temple as somebody tested the loudspeakers, and after it the wail of a slow tune. The bay was in view again. A crowd had gathered on the shore. Jerry saw more puffs of smoke and, in the windless heat of this side of the island, caught a whiff of joss. The water was blue and clear and calm. Round it, white lights burned on poles. The Ko launch had not stirred, nor had the police.

'See him?' he asked.

She was studying the crowd. She shook her head.

'Probably having a kip after lunch,' she said carelessly.

The beating of the sun was ferocious. When they entered the shadow of the hillside it was like a sudden dusk, and when they reached the sunlight it stung their faces like the heat of a close fire. The air was alive with dragonflies, the hillside strewn with big boulders, but where bushes grew they wound and straggled everywhere, producing rich trumpets, red and white and yellow. Old picnic cans lay in profusion.

'And that's the house you meant?'

'I told you,' she said.

It was a ruin: a broken brown-plastered villa with gaping walls and a view. It had been built with some grandeur above a dried-up stream and was reached by a concrete footbridge. The mud stank and hummed with insects. Between palms and bracken the remains of a verandah gave a vast prospect of the sea and of the bay. As they crossed the footbridge he took her arm.

'So let's play it from here,' he said. 'No interrogations. Just tell.'

'We walked up here, like I said. Me, Drake, and bloody Tiu. The boys brought a basket and the booze. I said "where are we going?" and he said "picnic". Tiu didn't want me but Drake said I could come. "You *hate* walking," I said. "I've never even seen you cross a *road* before!" "Today we walk," he says, doing his Captain of Industry Act. So I tag along and shut up.'

A thick cloud was already obscuring the peak above them and rolling slowly down the hill. The sun had vanished. In moments the cloud reached them, and they were alone at the world's end, unable to see even their feet. They groped their way into the house. She sat apart from him, on a bust roof beam. Chinese slogans were daubed in red paint down the door pillars. The floor was littered with picnic refuse and long twists of lining paper.

'He tells the boys to hop it so they hop it; him and Tiu have a long earnest natter in whatever they're speaking this week, and halfway through lunch he breaks into English and tells me Po Toi's *his* island. It's where he first landed when he left China. The boat people dumped him here. "My people," he calls them. That's why he comes to the festival every year and that's why he gives money to the temple, and that's why we've sweated up the bloody hill for a picnic. They then go back into Chinese, and I get the feeling Tiu is tearing him off a strip for talking too much, but Drake's all excited and little-boy and won't listen. Then they go on up.'

'*Up*?'

'Up to the top. "Old ways are the best," he says to me. "We shall stick to what is proven" – then his Baptist bit – "hold fast to that which is good, Liese. That is what God likes."'

Jerry glanced into the fog-bank above him, and he could have sworn he heard the crackle of a small plane, but at that moment he didn't mind too much whether it was there or not, because he had the two things he most badly needed. He had the girl with him, and he had the information: for now he finally understood exactly what she had been worth to Smiley and Sam Collins, and how she had unconsciously betrayed to them the vital clue to Ko's intentions.

'So they went on to the top. Did you go with them?'

'No.'

'Did you see where they went?'

'To the top. I told you.'

'Then what?'

'They looked down the other side. Talked. Pointed. More talk, more pointing, then down they come again and Drake's even more excited, the way he gets when he's brought off a big deal and Number One's not there to disapprove. Tiu looks dead solemn, and that is the way he gets when Drake acts fond of me. Drake wants to stay and have a couple of brandies so Tiu goes back to Hong Kong in a huff. Drake gets amorous and decides we'll spend the night on the boat and go home in the morning, so that's what we do.'

'Where does he moor the boat? Here? In the bay?'

'No.'

'Where?'

'Off Lantau.'

'You went straight there, did you?'

She shook her head.

'We did a round of the island.'

'*This* island?'

'There was a place he wanted to look at in the dark. A bit of coast round the other side. The boys had to shine the lamps on it. "That's where I land in fifty-one," he said. "The boat people were frightened to put into the main harbour. They were frightened of police and ghosts and pirates and customs men. They say the islanders will cut their throats."'

'And in the night?' said Jerry softly. 'While you were moored off Lantau?'

'He told me he had a brother and loved him.'

'That was the first time he told you?'

She nodded.

'He tell you where the brother was?'

'No.'

'But you knew?'

This time she didn't even nod.

From below, the clatter of the festival rose criss-cross through the cloud. He lifted her gently to her feet.

'Bloody questions,' she muttered.

'They're nearly over,' he promised. He kissed her and she let him, but did not otherwise take part.

'Let's go up and take a look,' he said.

Ten minutes more and the sunlight returned and blue sky opened above them. With Lizzie leading, they scrambled quickly over several false peaks toward the saddle. The sounds from the bay stopped and the colder air filled with screaming, wheeling gulls. They approached the crest, the path widened, they walked side by side. A few steps more and the wind had hit them with a force that made them gasp and reel back. They were at the knife-edge, looking down into an abyss. At their very feet the cliff fell vertical to a boiling sea, and the foam smothered the headlands. Dumpling clouds were blowing from the east and behind them the sky was black. Perhaps two hundred metres down lay an inlet which the breakers did not cover. Fifty yards out from it, a brown shoal of rock checked the sea's force, and the spume washed it in white rings.

'That it?' he yelled above the wind. 'He landed there? That bit of coast?'

'Yes.'

'Shone the lights on it?'

'Yes.'

Leaving her where she stood, he moved slowly up the knife-edge, crouching almost double while the wind rushed over his ears and covered his face in a sticky salt sweat and his stomach screamed in pain from what he supposed was a punctured gut or internal bleeding or both. At the inmost point before the cliff cut back into the sea, he once more looked down and now he thought he could just make out a skimpy path, sometimes no more than a seam of rock, or a ridge of rough grass, eking its way cautiously toward the inlet. There was no sand in the inlet but some of the rocks looked dry. Returning to her, he led her away from the knife-edge. The wind dropped, and they heard the din of the festival again much louder than before. The snap of firecrackers made a toy war.

'It's his brother Nelson,' he explained. 'In case you hadn't gathered, Ko's bringing him out of China. Tonight's the night. Trouble is, he's a much sought-after character. Lot of people would like a chat with him. That's where Mellon came in.' He took a breath. 'My view is that you should get the hell out of here. How do you see that? Drake's not going to want you around, that's for sure.'

'Is he going to want you?' she asked.

'I think, what you should do, you should go back to the harbour,' he said. 'Are you listening?'

She managed, 'Of course I am.'

'You look for a nice friendly-looking roundeye family. Choose the woman for once and not the bloke. Tell her you've had a row with your boyfriend and can they take you home in their boat? If they'll have you, stay the night with them, otherwise go to a hotel. Spin them one of your stories. Christ, *that's* no problem, is it?'

A police helicopter pattered overhead in a long curve, presumably to observe the festival. Instinctively he grabbed her shoulders and drew her into the rock.

'Remember the second place we went – the big band sound – the bar?' He was still holding her.

She said, 'Yes.'

'I'll pick you up there tomorrow night.'

'I don't know,' she said.

'Be there anyway at seven. At seven, got it?'

She pushed him gently away from her, as if she were determined to stand alone.

'Tell him I kept faith,' she said. 'It's what he cares about most. I stuck to the deal. If you see him, tell him, "Liese stuck to the deal."'

'Sure.'

'Not *sure*. *Yes*. Tell him. He did everything he promised. He said he'd look after me. He did. He said he'd let Ric go. He did that too. He always stuck to a deal.'

He lifted her head, holding it with both his hands, but she insisted on going on.

'And tell him – and tell him – tell him they made it impossible. They fenced me in.'

'Be there from seven on,' he said. 'Even if I'm a bit late. Now come on, that's not too difficult, is it? You don't need a university degree to hoist that aboard.' He was gentling her, battling for a smile, striving for a last complicity before they separated.

She nodded.

She wanted to say something else but it didn't work. She took a few steps, turned and looked back at him and he waved – one big flap of the arm. She took a few more and kept going till she was below the line of the hill, but he did hear her shout 'Seven then', or thought he did. Having watched her out of sight, Jerry returned to the knife-edge, where he sat down for a bit of a breather before the Tarzan stuff. A snatch of John Donne came back to him, one of the few things he had picked up at school, though somehow he never got quotations completely right, or thought he didn't:

On a huge hill
Cragged and steep, Truth stands, and he that will
Reach her, about must, and about must go.

Or something. For an hour, deep in thought, two hours, he lay in the lee of the rock and watched the daylight turn to dusk over the Chinese islands a few miles into the sea. Then he pulled off his buckskin boots, and re-threaded the laces in a herringbone, the way he used to thread them for his cricket boots. Then he put them on again and tied them as tight as they would go. It could be Tuscany again, he thought, and the five hills which he used to gawp at from the hornet field. Except that this time he wasn't proposing to walk out on anyone. Not the girl. Not Luke. Not even himself. Even if it took a lot of footwork.

'Navy int. has the junk fleet making around six knots and slap on course,' Murphy announced. 'Quit the beds right on one one hundred, just like they were following our projection.'

From somewhere he had scrounged a set of bakelite toy boats which he could fix to the chart. Standing, he pointed them proudly in a single column at Po Toi island.

Murphy had returned, but his colleague had stayed with Sam Collins and Fawn, so they were four.

'And Rockhurst has found the girl,' said Guillam quietly, putting down the other phone. His shoulder was playing up, and he was extremely pale.

'Where?' said Smiley.

Still at the chart, Murphy turned. At his desk, where he was keeping a log of events, Martello put down his pen.

'Picked her up at Aberdeen harbour as she landed,' Guillam went on. 'She'd cadged a lift back from Po Toi with a clerk and his wife from the Hong Kong and Shanghai Bank.'

'So what's the story?' Martello demanded before Smiley could speak. 'Where's Westerby?'

'She doesn't know,' said Guillam.

'Ah come on!' Martello protested.

'She says they had a row and left in different boats. Rockhurst says give him another hour with her.'

Smiley spoke. 'And Ko?' he asked. 'Where's he?'

'His launch is still in Po Toi harbour,' Guillam replied. 'Most of the other boats have already left. But Ko's is where it was this morning. Sitting pretty, Rockhurst says, and everyone below.'

Smiley peered at the sea chart, then at Guillam, then at the map of Po Toi.

'If she told Westerby what she told Collins,' he said, 'then he's stayed on the island.'

'With what in mind?' Martello demanded, very loud. 'George, for what purpose is *that* man remaining on *that* island?'

An age went by for all of them.

'He's waiting,' Smiley said.

'For *what*, may I enquire?' Martello persisted in the same determined tone.

Nobody saw Smiley's face. It had found its own bit of shadow. They saw his shoulders hunch, they saw his hand rise to his spectacles as if to remove them, they saw it fall back empty in defeat, on to the rosewood table.

'Whatever we do, we must let Nelson land,' he said firmly.

'And whatever *do* we do?' Martello demanded, getting up and coming round the table. 'Weatherby's not *here*, George. He never entered the Colony. He can leave by the same damn route!'

'Please don't shout at me,' Smiley said.

Martello ignored him. 'Which is it going to be, that's all? The conspiracy or the fuck-up?'

Guillam was standing his height, barring the way, and for an extraordinary moment it seemed possible that, broken shoulder notwithstanding, he proposed physically to restrain Martello from coming any closer to where Smiley sat.

'Peter,' Smiley said quietly. 'I see there's a telephone behind you. Perhaps you'd be good enough to pass it to me.'

* * *

With the full moon, the wind had dropped and the sea settled. Jerry had not descended all the way to the inlet but made a last camp thirty feet above it, in the cover of a shrub, where he had protection. His hands and knees were cut to ribbons and a branch had grazed his cheek, but he felt good: hungry and alert. In the sweat and danger of the scramble he had forgotten his pain. The inlet was larger than he imagined when he had looked down on it from higher up, and the granite cliffs at sea level were pierced with caves. He was trying to guess Drake's plan – for since Lizzie, he now thought of him as Drake. He had been trying all day. What Drake had to do, he would do from the sea because he was not capable of the nightmarish climb down the cliff. Jerry had wondered at first whether Drake might try to intercept Nelson before he landed, but could see no safe way for Nelson to slip the fleet and make a sea-meeting with his brother.

The sky darkened, the stars came, and the moon-path grew brighter. And Westerby? he thought: what does *A* do now? *A* was one hell of a long way from the syndicate solutions of Sarratt, *that* was for sure.

Drake would also be a fool to attempt to bring his launch to this side of the island, he decided. She was unwieldy and drew too much water to come inshore on a windward coast. A small boat was better and a sampan or a rubber dinghy best. Clambering down the cliff till his boots hit pebbles, Jerry huddled against the rock, watching the breakers thump and the sparks of phosphorus riding with the spume.

'She'll be back by now,' he thought. With any luck she's talked her way into someone's house and is charming the kids and wrapping herself round a cup of Bovril. *Tell him I kept faith*, she said.

The moon lifted, and still Jerry waited, training his eyes on the darkest spots in an effort to improve his vision. Then over the clatter of the sea he could have sworn he heard the awkward slap of water on a wooden hull and the short grumble of an engine switched on and off again. He saw no light. Edging his way along the shadowed rock he crept as close to the water's edge as he dared and once more crouched, waiting. As the wave of surf soaked him to his thighs, he saw what he was waiting for: against the path of the moon, not twenty yards from him, the arched cabin and curled prow of a single sampan rocking on its anchor. He heard a splash and a muffled order, and as he sank as low as the slope allowed, he picked out against the star-strewn sky the unmistakable shape of Drake Ko in his Anglo-French beret wading cautiously ashore, followed by Tiu carrying an M16 machine gun across both arms. So there you are, thought Jerry, addressing himself, rather than Drake Ko. End of the long trail. Luke's killer, Frostie's killer – whether by proxy or in the flesh is immaterial – Lizzie's lover, Nelson's father, Nelson's brother. Welcome to the man who never broke a deal in his life.

Drake also had a burden but it was less ferocious, and Jerry knew long before he made it out that it was a lamp and a power pack, pretty much like the ones he had used in the Circus water-games on the Helford Estuary, except that the Circus favoured ultra-violet, and shoddy wire-framed spectacles which were useless in rain or spray.

Reaching the beach, the two men made their way grunting over the shingle until they reached the highest point, then like himself they merged against the black rock. He reckoned they were sixty feet from him. He heard a grunt, and saw the flame of a cigarette lighter, then the red glow of two cigarettes followed by the murmur of Chinese voices. Wouldn't mind one myself, thought Jerry. Stooping, he spread out one large hand and began loading it with pebbles until it was full, then padded as stealthily as he could manage along the base of the rock toward the two red embers. By his calculation he was eight paces from them. He had the pistol in his left hand and the pebbles in his right, and he was listening to the clump of the waves, how they gathered, tottered and fell, and he was thinking that it was going to be a lot easier to have a chat with Drake once Tiu was out of the way.

Very slowly, in the classic posture of the outfielder, he

leaned back, raised his left elbow in front of him and crooked his right arm behind him, prepared for a throw at full stretch. A wave fell, he heard the shuffle of the undertow, the grumble as another gathered. Still he waited, right arm back, palm sweating as he clasped the pebbles. Then as the wave reached its height he hurled them high up the cliff using all his strength, before ducking to a crouch, gaze fixed upon the embers of the two cigarettes. He waited, then heard the pebbles patter against the rock above him, and the hailstorm gather as they tumbled down. In the next instant he heard Tiu's short curse and saw one red ember fly into the air as he leapt to his feet, machine gun in hand, barrel lifted to the cliff and his back to Jerry. Drake was scrambling for cover.

First Jerry hit Tiu very hard with the pistol, taking care to keep his fingers inside the guard. Then he hit him again with his closed right hand, a two-knuckle strike at full force, with the fist turned down and turning, as they say at Sarratt, and a lot of follow-through at the end. As Tiu went down, Jerry caught his cheekbone with the whole weight of his swinging right boot, and heard the snap of his closing jaw. And as he stooped to pick up the M16 he smashed the butt of it into Tiu's kidneys, thinking very angrily of both Luke and Frost, but also of that cheap crack he had made about Lizzie not rating more than the journey from Kowloonside to Hong Kongside. Greetings from the horse-writer, he thought.

Then he looked toward Drake, who, having stepped forward, was still no more than a black shape against the sea: a crooked silhouette with piecrust ears sticking out below the line of his odd beret. A strong wind had risen again, or perhaps Jerry was only now aware of it. It rattled in the rocks behind them, and made Drake's broad trousers billow.

'That Mr Westerby, the English newsman?' he enquired, in precisely the deep, harsh tones he had used at Happy Valley.

'The same,' said Jerry.

'You're a very political man, Mr Westerby. What the hell do you want here?'

Jerry was recovering his breath and for a moment he didn't feel quite ready to answer.

'Mr Ricardo tell my people it is your aim to blackmail me. Is money your aim, Mr Westerby?'

'Message from your girl,' Jerry said, feeling he should discharge that promise first. 'She says she keeps faith. She's on your side.'

'I don't have a side, Mr Westerby. I'm an army of one. What do you want? Mr Marshall tells my people you are some kind of hero. Heroes are very political persons, Mr Westerby. I don't care for heroes.'

'I came to warn you. They want Nelson. You mustn't take him back to Hong Kong. They've got him all sewn up. They've got plans that will last him the rest of his life. And you as well. They're queuing up for both of you.'

'What do you *want*, Mr Westerby?'

'A deal.'

'Nobody wants a deal. They want a commodity. The deal obtains for them the commodity. What do you want?' Drake repeated, raising his voice in command. 'Tell me please.'

'You bought yourself the girl with Ricardo's life,' said Jerry. 'I thought I might buy her back with Nelson's. I'll speak to them for you. I know what they want. They'll settle.'

That's the last foot in the last door for me, he thought.

'A *political* settlement, Mr Westerby? With *your* people? I made many political settlements with them. They told me God loved children. Did you ever notice God love an Asian child, Mr Westerby? They told me God was a *kwailo* and his mother had yellow hair. They told me God was a peaceful man, but I read once that there have never been so many civil wars as in the Kingdom of Christ. They told me – '

'Your brother's right behind you, Mr Ko.'

Drake swung round. On their left, heading from the east, a dozen or more junks in full sail trembled southward across the moon-path in ragged column, lights prickling in the water. Dropping to his knees, Drake began frantically groping for the lamp. Jerry found the tripod, wrenched it open, Drake stood the lamp on it but his hands were shaking wildly and Jerry had to help him. Jerry seized the flexes, struck a match and clipped the cables to the terminals. They were staring out to sea, side by side. Drake flashed the lamp once, then again, first red, then green.

'Wait,' Jerry said softly. 'You're too soon. Go easy or you'll muck it all up.'

Moving him gently aside, Jerry bent to the eyepiece and scanned the busy line of boats.

'Which one?' Jerry asked.

'The last,' said Ko.

Holding the last junk in view, though it was still only a shadow, Jerry signalled again, one red, one green, and a moment later heard Drake let out a cry of joy as an answering flicker darted back across the water.

'Can he fix on that?' said Jerry.

'Sure,' said Ko, still looking out to sea. 'Sure. He will fix on that.'

'Then leave it alone. Don't do any more.'

Ko turned to him, and Jerry saw the excitement in his face, and felt his dependence.

'Mr Westerby. I am advising you sincerely. If you have played a trick on me for my brother Nelson, your Christian Baptist hell will be a very comfortable place by comparison with what my people do to you. But if you help me I give you everything. That is my contract and I never broke a contract in my life. My brother also made certain contracts.' He looked out to sea.

The forward junks were out of sight. Only the tail-enders remained. From far away Jerry fancied he heard the uneven rumble of an engine, but he knew his mind was all over the place and it could have been the tumble of the waves. The moon passed behind the peak and the shadow of the mountain fell like a black knife-point on to the sea, leaving the far fields silver. Stooped to the lamp, Drake gave another cry of pleasure.

'Here! Here! Take a look, Mr Westerby.'

Through the eyepiece, Jerry made out a single phantom junk, unlit except for three pale lamps, two green ones on the mast, red to starboard, making its way toward them. It passed from the silver into the blackness and he lost it. From behind him, he heard a groan from Tiu. Ignoring it, Drake remained stooped to the eyepiece, one arm held wide like a Victorian photographer while he began calling softly in Chinese. Running up the shingle Jerry pulled the pistol from Tiu's belt, picked up the M16 and, taking both to the sea's edge, chucked them in. Drake was preparing to repeat the signal again but mercifully he couldn't find the button and Jerry was in time to stop him. Once more Jerry thought he heard the rumble, not of one engine but of two. Running out on to the headland, he peered anxiously north and south in search of a patrol boat, but again he saw nothing, and again he blamed the surf and his strained imagination. The junk was nearer, beating in toward the island, her brown batwing sail suddenly tall and terribly conspicuous against the sky. Drake had run to the water's edge and was waving and yelling across the sea.

'Keep your voice down!' Jerry hissed from beside him.

But Jerry had become an irrelevance. Drake's whole life was for Nelson. From the shelter of the near headland, Drake's sampan tottered alongside the rocking junk. The moon came out of hiding and for a moment Jerry forgot his anxiety as a little grey-clad figure, small and sturdy, in stature Drake's antithesis, in a kapok coat and bulging proletarian cap, lowered himself over the side and leapt for the waiting arms of the sampan's crew. Drake gave another cry, the junk filled its sails and slid behind the headland till only the green lights on its masthead remained visible above the rocks, and then vanished. The sampan was making for the beach and Jerry could see Nelson's stocky frame as he stood on the bow waving with both hands and Drake Ko in his beret wild on the beach, dancing like a madman, waving back.

The throb of engines grew steadily louder, but still Jerry couldn't place them. The sea was empty, and when he looked upward he saw only the hammerhead cliff and its peak black against the stars. The brothers met, and embraced, and stayed locked in each other's arms, not moving. Seizing hold of both of them, pummelling them, Jerry cried out for all his life.

'Get back in the boat! Hurry!'

They saw no one but each other. Running back to the water's edge Jerry grabbed the sampan's prow and held it, still calling to them as he saw the sky behind the peak turn yellow, then quickly brighten as the throb of engines swelled to a roar and three blinding searchlights burst on them from blackened helicopters. The rocks danced to the whirl of landing lights, the sea furrowed and the pebbles bounced and flew around in storms. For a fraction of a second Jerry saw Drake's face turn to him beseeching help: as if, too late, he had recognised where help lay. He mouthed something, but the din drowned it. Jerry hurled himself foward. Not for Nelson's sake, still less for Drake's; but for what linked them, and what linked him to Lizzie. But long before he reached them, a dark swarm closed on the two men, tore them apart and bundled the baggy shape of Nelson into the helicopter's hold. In the mayhem Jerry had drawn his gun and held it in his hand. He was screaming, though he could not hear himself above the hurricanes of war. The helicopter was lifting. A single figure remained in the open doorway, looking down, and perhaps it was Fawn, for he looked dark and mad. Then an orange flash broke from the doorway, then a second and a third and after that Jerry wasn't counting any more. In fury he threw up his hands, his open mouth still calling, his face still silently imploring. Then he fell, and lay there, till there was once more no sound but the surf flopping on the beach and Drake Ko's hopeless, choking grief against the victorious armadas of the West, which had stolen his brother and left their hard-pressed soldier dead at his feet.

Chapter 22

BORN AGAIN

In the Circus a mood of wild triumph broke out when the grand news came through from the Cousins. Nelson landed, Nelson bagged! Not a hair of his head injured! For two days there was speculation about medals, knighthoods and promotions. They must do *something* for George, at last, they *must*! Not so, said Connie shrewdly from the touchline. They would never forgive him for taking up Bill Haydon.

The euphoria was followed by certain perplexing rumours. Connie and Doc di Salis, for instance, who were eagerly ensconced in the Maresfield safe house, now dubbed the *Dolphinarium*, waited a full week for their body to arrive and waited in vain. So did the interpreters, transcribers, inquisitors, babysitters and allied trades who made up the rest of the reception and interrogation unit there.

The match was rained off, said the housekeepers. Another date would be fixed. Stand by, they said. But quite soon a source at the local estate agent in the neighbouring town of Uckfield revealed that the housekeepers were trying to renege on the lease. Sure enough, after another week the team was stood down 'pending policy decisions'. It was never reassembled.

Next, word filtered out that Enderby and Martello jointly – the combination even then seemed odd – were chairing an Anglo-American processing committee. It would meet alternately in Washington and London and have responsibility for simultaneous distribution of the

Dolphin product, codename CAVIAR, on either side of the Atlantic.

Quite incidentally, it emerged that Nelson was somewhere in the United States, in an armed compound already prepared for him in Philadelphia. The explanation was even slower in coming. It was *felt* – presumably *by* somebody, but feelings are hard to trace among so many corridors – that Nelson would be safer there. Physically safer. Think of the Russians. Think of the Chinese. Also, the housekeepers insisted, the Cousins' processing and evaluation units were more of a scale to handle the unprecedented take which was expected. Also, they said, the Cousins could afford the cost.

Also –

'Also gammon and spinach!' Connie stormed, when she heard the news.

She and di Salis waited moodily to be invited to join the Cousins' team. Connie even got herself the injections to be ready, but no call came.

More explanations. The Cousins had a new man at Harvard, the housekeepers said, when Connie sailed in on them in her wheelchair.

'Who?' she demanded in fury.

A professor somebody, young, a Moscow-gazer. He had made a *life speciality* of the dark side of Moscow Centre, they said, and had recently published a paper for private distribution only, but based on Company archives, in which he had referred to the *mole principle* and even in veiled terms to Karla's private army.

'Of course he did, the maggot!' she blurted at them, through her bitter tears of frustration. 'And he hogged it all from Connie's blasted reports, didn't he? Culpepper, that's his name, and he knows as much about Karla as my left toe!'

The housekeepers were unmoved, however, by thoughts of Connie's toe. It was Culpepper, not Sachs, who had the new committee's vote.

'Wait till George gets back!' Connie warned them in a

voice of thunder. The threat left them strangely unaffected.

Di Salis fared no better. China-watchers were two a penny in Langley, he was told. A glut on the market, old boy. Sorry, but Enderby's orders, said housekeepers.

Enderby's? di Salis echoed.

The committee's, they said vaguely. It was a joint decision.

So di Salis took his cause to Lacon, who liked to think of himself as a poor man's ombudsman in such matters, and Lacon in turn took di Salis to luncheon, at which they split the bill down the middle because Lacon did not hold with civil servants treating one another at the taxpayers' expense.

'How do you all *feel* about Enderby by the by?' he asked, at some point in the meal, interrupting di Salis's plaintive monologue about his familiarity with the Chiu Chow and Hakka dialects. *Feeling* was playing a large part just at the moment. 'Does he go down well over there? I'd have thought you liked his way of seeing things. Isn't he rather sound, wouldn't you say?'

Sound in the Whitehall vocabulary in those days meant hawkish.

Rushing back to the Circus, di Salis duly reported this amazing question to Connie Sachs – as Lacon, of course, wished him to – and Connie was thereafter seen little. She spent her time quietly 'packing her trunk' as she called it: that is to say, preparing her Moscow Centre archive for posterity. There was a new young burrower she favoured, a goatish but obliging youth called Doolittle. She made this Doolittle sit at her feet while she gave him of her wisdom.

'The old order's hoofing it,' she warned whoever would listen. 'That twerp Enderby is oiling through the back door. It's a pogrom.'

They treated her at first with much the same derision as Noah had to put up with when he started building his ark. No slouch at tradecraft still, Connie meanwhile secretly took Molly Meakin aside and persuaded her to put in a letter of resignation. 'Tell the housekeepers you're looking for something more fulfilling, dear,' she advised, with much winking and pinching. 'They'll give you a rise at the very least.'

Molly had fears of being taken at her word, but Connie knew the game too well. So she wrote her letter, and was at once ordered to stay behind after hours. Certain changes were in the air, the housekeepers told her in great confidence. There was a move to create a younger and more vigorous service with closer links to Whitehall. Molly solemnly promised to reconsider her decision, and Connie Sachs resumed her packing with fresh determination.

Then where *was* George Smiley all this while? In the Far East? No, in Washington! Nonsense! He was back home and skulking down in the country somewhere – Cornwall was his favourite – taking a well-earned rest and mending his fences with Ann!

Then one of the housekeepers let slip that George might be *suffering from a spot of strain*, and this phrase struck a chill everywhere, for even the dimmest little gnome in Banking Section knew that strain, like old age, was a disease for which there was only one known remedy, and it did not entail recovery.

Guillam came back eventually, but only to sweep Molly off on leave, and he refused to say anything at all. Those who saw him on his swift passage through the fifth floor said he looked shot-about, and obviously in need of a break. Also he seemed to have had an accident to his collar bone: his right shoulder was all strapped up. From housekeepers it became known that he had spent a couple of days in the care of the Circus leech at his private clinic in Manchester Square. But still there was no Smiley, and the housekeepers showed only a steely bonhomie when asked when he would return. The housekeepers in these cases become the Star Chamber, feared but needed. Unobtrusively, Karla's portrait disappeared, the wits ironically said for cleaning.

What was odd, and in a way rather terrible, was that none of them thought to drop in on the little house in

Bywater Street and simply ring the door bell. If they had done so, they would have found Smiley there, most likely in his dressing gown, either clearing up plates or preparing food he didn't eat. Sometimes, usually at dusk, he took himself for a solitary walk in the park and peered at people as if he half recognised them, so that they peered in return, and then looked down. Or he would go and sit himself in one of the cheaper cafés in the King's Road, taking a book for company, and sweet tea for refreshment – for he had abandoned his good intentions about sticking to saccharine for his waistline. They would have noticed that he spent a deal of time looking at his hands, and polishing his spectacles on his tie, or re-reading the letter Ann had left for him, which was very long, but only because of repetitions.

Lacon called on him, and so did Enderby, and once Martello came along with them, dressed in his London character again, for everyone agreed, and none with greater sincerity than Smiley, that in the interests of the service the handover should be as smooth and painless as possible. Smiley made certain requests regarding staff, and these were carefully noted by Lacon, who let him understand that toward the Circus – if toward no one else – Treasury was at present in a spending mood. In the secret world at least, sterling was on the up. It was not merely the success of the Dolphin affair which accounted for this change of heart, Lacon said. The American enthusiasm for Enderby's appointment had been overwhelming. It had been *felt* even at the highest diplomatic levels. *Spontaneous applause* was how Lacon described it.

'Saul really knows how to talk to them,' he said.

'Oh, does he? Ah, good. Well, good,' Smiley said, and bucked his head in approval, as the deaf do.

Even when Enderby confided to Smiley that he proposed to appoint Sam Collins as his head of operations, Smiley showed nothing but courtesy toward the suggestion. Sam was a *hustler*, Enderby explained, and *hustlers* were what Langley liked these days. The silk shirt crowd had taken a real nosedive, he said.

'No doubt,' said Smiley.

The two men agreed that Roddy Martindale, though he had bags of entertainment value, was *not* cut out for the game. Old Roddy real was *too* queer, said Enderby, and the Minister was scared stiff of him. Nor did he exactly go down swimmingly with the Americans, even those who happened to be that way themselves. Also, Enderby was a bit chary of taking in any more Etonians. Gave the wrong impression.

A week later, the housekeepers re-opened Sam's old room on the fifth floor and removed the furniture. Collins's ghost laid for good, said certain unwise voices with relish. Then on the Monday an ornate desk arrived, with a red leather top, and several fake hunting prints from the walls of Sam's club, which was in the process of being taken over by one of the larger gambling syndicates, to the satisfaction of all parties.

Little Fawn was not seen again. Not even when several of the more muscular London out-stations were revived, including the Brixton scalp-hunters to whom he had formerly belonged, and the Acton lamplighters under Toby Esterhase. But he was not missed either. Like Sam Collins, somehow, he had stalked the story without ever quite belonging to it. But unlike Sam, he stayed in the thickets when it ended, and never reappeared.

To Sam Collins, also, on his first day back in harness, fell the task of breaking the sad news of Jerry's death. He did it in the rumpus room, just a small, unaffected speech, and everyone agreed he did it well. They had not thought he had it in him.

'For fifth floor ears only,' he told them. His audience was appalled, then proud. Connie wept, and tried to claim him as another of Karla's victims, but she was held back in this for want of information about who or what had killed him. It was operational, went the word, and it was noble.

Back in Hong Kong, the Foreign Correspondents' Club showed much initial concern for its missing children Luke and Westerby. Thanks to heavy lobbying by its members, a full-scale confidential enquiry was set up, under the chairmanship of the vigilant Superintendent Rockhurst, to solve the double riddle of their disappearance. The authorities promised full publication of all findings and the United States Consul General offered five thousand dollars of his own money to anyone coming forward with helpful information. As a gesture to local feeling, he included Jerry Westerby's name in the offer. The two became known as The Missing Newsmen, and suggestions of a disgraceful attachment between them were rampant. Luke's bureau matched the five-thousand-dollar figure, and the dwarf, though he was inconsolable, entered a strong bid to have the moneys paid to him. It was he, after all, working on both fronts at once, who had learned from Deathwish that the Cloudview Road apartment, which Luke had last used, had been redecorated from floor to ceiling before the Rocker's sharp-eyed investigators got round to visiting it. Who ordered this? Who paid? Nobody knew. It was the dwarf, also, who collected first hand reports that Jerry had been seen at Kai Tak airport interviewing Japanese package tourists. But the Rocker's committee of enquiry was obliged to reject them. The Japanese concerned were *willing but unreliable witnesses*, they said, when it came to identifying a roundeye who sprang at them after a long journey. As to Luke: well, the way he had been going, they said, he was heading for some kind of breakdown anyway. The knowing spoke of amnesia, brought on by alcohol and fast living. After a while, even the best stories grow cold. Rumours went out that the two men had been seen hunting together during the Hue collapse – or was it Da Nang? – and drinking together in Saigon. Another had them sitting side by side on the waterfront at Manila.

'Holding hands?' the dwarf asked.

'Worse,' was the reply.

The Rocker's name was also in wide circulation, thanks to his success in a recent spectacular narcotics trial mounted with the help of the American Drug Enforcement Administration. Several Chinese and a glamorous English adventuress, a heroin carrier, were featured and though as usual the Mr Big was never brought to justice, it was said the Rocker came within an ace of nailing him. 'Our tough but honest troubleshooter,' wrote the *South China Morning Post* in an editorial praising his astuteness. 'Hong Kong could do with more like him.'

For other distractions, the Club could turn to the dramatic reopening of High Haven, behind a twenty-foot floodlit wire perimeter patrolled by guard dogs. But there were no free lunches any more and the joke soon faded.

As to old Craw, for months he was not seen and not spoken of. Till one night he appeared looking much aged and soberly dressed, and sat in his former corner gazing into space. A few were still left who recognised him. The Canadian cowboy suggested a rubber of Shanghai bowling, but he declined. Then a strange thing happened. An argument broke out concerning a silly point of Club protocol. Nothing serious at all: whether some item of tradition about signing chits was still useful to the Club's running. As trifling as that. But for some reason it made the old fellow absolutely furious. Rising to his feet, he stomped towards the lifts, tears pouring down his face while he hurled one insult after another at them.

'Don't change anything,' he advised them, shaking his stick in fury. 'The old order changeth *not*, let it all run on. You won't stop the wheel, not together, not divided, you snivelling, arselicking novices! You're a bunch of suicidal tits to try!'

Past it, they agreed, as the doors closed on him. Poor fellow. Embarrassing.

Was there really a conspiracy against Smiley, of the scale that Guillam supposed? And if so, how was it affected by Westerby's own maverick intervention? No information is available, and even those who trust each other well are not disposed to discuss the question. Certainly there was a secret understanding between Enderby and Martello that the Cousins should have first bite of Nelson – as well as joint credit for procuring him – against their championship of Enderby for chief. Certainly Lacon and Collins, in their vastly different spheres, were party to it. But at what point they proposed to seize Nelson for themselves and by what means – for instance the more conventional recourse of a concerted *démarche* at ministerial level in London – will probably never be known. But there can be no doubt, as it turned out, that Westerby was a blessing in disguise. He gave them the excuse they were looking for.

And did Smiley *know* of the conspiracy, deep down? Was he aware of it, and did he secretly even welcome the solution? Peter Guillam, who has since had three good years in exile in Brixton to consider his opinion, insists that the answer to both questions is a firm *yes.* There is a letter George wrote to Ann Smiley – he says – in the heat of the crisis, presumably in one of the long waiting periods in the isolation ward. Guillam leans heavily on it for his theory. Ann showed it to him when he called on her in Wiltshire in the hope of bringing about a reconciliation, and though the mission failed, she produced it from her handbag in the course of their talk. Guillam memorised a part, he claims, and wrote it down as soon as he got back to the car. Certainly the style flies a lot higher than anything Guillam would aspire to for himself.

I honestly do wonder, without wishing to be morbid, how I reached this present pass. So far as I can ever remember of my youth, I chose the secret road because it seemed to lead straightest and furthest toward my country's goal. The enemy in those days was someone we could point at and read about in the papers. Today, all I know is that I have learned to interpret the whole of life in terms of conspiracy. That is the sword I have lived by, and as I look round me now I see it is the sword I shall die by as well. These people terrify me but I am one of them. If they stab me in the back, then at least that is the judgment of my peers.

As Guillam points out, the letter was essentially from Smiley's blue period.

These days, he says, the old boy is much more himself. Occasionally he and Ann have lunches, and Guillam personally is convinced that they will simply get together one day and that will be that. But George never mentions Westerby. And nor does Guillam, for George's sake.

JOHN LE CARRÉ

A PERFECT SPY

Magnus Pym, counsellor at the British Embassy in Vienna, has suddenly vanished, believed defected. The chase is on: for a missing husband, a devoted father, and a lifetime secret agent. Pym's life, it is revealed, is entirely made up of secrets. Dominated by a father of mythic dimensions, a confidence trickster on an epic scale, Pym has from the age of seventeen been controlled by two agents who have been his lifelong mentors. It is these two men, betrayed by his disappearance, who are orchestrating the search, racing each other and time itself, desperate for clues to find the perfect spy . . .

'Magnificent . . . a masterpiece . . . a knockout of a novel . . . a deeply personal mystery from a real magician'
David Hughes in The Mail on Sunday

HODDER AND STOUGHTON PAPERBACKS

JOHN LE CARRÉ

THE SPY WHO CAME IN FROM THE COLD

With this superb novel of suspense, le Carré changed the rules of the game. His story is one last breathlessly perilous assignment for the agent who wants desperately to end his career of espionage and 'come in from the cold'.

'Superbly constructed, with an atmosphere of chilly hell'

J. B. Priestley

'Complex and fearful'

The Sunday Times

JOHN LE CARRÉ

TINKER TAILOR SOLDIER SPY

Le Carré has created a remarkable challenge to Smiley and his people: a mole – a Soviet double agent – who's burrowed his way up to the highest level of British Intelligence. His treachery has already blown some of their vital secret operations and their best networks. The mole is one of their own kind. But which one?

'A thoroughly enjoyable spy novel about the discovery of a double agent at the highest level of the British Intelligence bureaucracy . . . the plot is as tangled and suspenseful as any action fan could require . . . keeps one guessing right to the end'

The New York Times

HODDER AND STOUGHTON PAPERBACKS